Evan Harrington

Evan Harrington

George Meredith

MINT EDITIONS

Evan Harrington was first published in 1861.

This edition published by Mint Editions 2021.

ISBN 9781513278452 | E-ISBN 9781513278919

Published by Mint Editions®

minteditionbooks.com

Publishing Director: Jennifer Newens
Design & Production: Rachel Lopez Metzger
Project Manager: Micaela Clark
Typesetting: Westchester Publishing Services

Contents

Book III

Book IV

Book V

BOOK I

I

Above Buttons

Long after the hours when tradesmen are in the habit of commencing business, the shutters of a certain shop in the town of Lymport-on-the-Sea remained significantly closed, and it became known that death had taken Mr. Melchisedec Harrington, and struck one off the list of living tailors. The demise of a respectable member of this class does not ordinarily create a profound sensation. He dies, and his equals debate who is to be his successor: while the rest of them who have come in contact with him, very probably hear nothing of his great launch and final adieu till the winding up of cash-accounts; on which occasions we may augur that he is not often blessed by one or other of the two great parties who subdivide this universe. In the case of Mr. Melchisedec it was otherwise. This had been a grand man, despite his calling, and in the teeth of opprobrious epithets against his craft. To be both generally blamed, and generally liked, evinces a peculiar construction of mortal. Mr. Melchisedec, whom people in private called the great Mel, had been at once the sad dog of Lymport, and the pride of the town. He was a tailor, and he kept horses; he was a tailor, and he had gallant adventures; he was a tailor, and he shook hands with his customers. Finally, he was a tradesman, and he never was known to have sent in a bill. Such a personage comes but once in a generation, and, when he goes, men miss the man as well as their money.

That he was dead, there could be no doubt. Kilne, the publican opposite, had seen Sally, one of the domestic servants, come out of the house in the early morning and rush up the street to the doctor's, tossing her hands; and she, not disinclined to dilute her grief, had, on her return, related that her master was then at his last gasp, and had refused, in so many words, to swallow the doctor.

"'I won't swallow the doctor!' he says, 'I won't swallow the doctor!'" Sally moaned. "'I never touched him,' he says, 'and I never will.'"

Kilne angrily declared, that in his opinion, a man who rejected medicine in extremity, ought to have it forced down his throat: and considering that the invalid was pretty deeply in Kilne's debt, it naturally assumed the form of a dishonest act on his part; but Sally scornfully dared any one to lay hand on her master, even for his own good. "For," said she, "he's got his eyes awake, though he do lie so helpless. He marks ye!"

"Ah! ah!" Kilne sniffed the air. Sally then rushed back to her duties.

"Now, there's a man!" Kilne stuck his hands in his pockets and began his meditation: which, however, was cut short by the approach of his neighbour Barnes, the butcher, to whom he confided what he had heard, and who exclaimed professionally, "Obstinate as a pig!" As they stood together they beheld Sally, a figure of telegraph, at one of the windows, implying that all was just over.

"Amen!" said Barnes, as to a matter-of-fact affair.

Some minutes after, the two were joined by Grossby, the confectioner, who listened to the news, and observed:

"Just like him! I'd have sworn he'd never take doctor's stuff"; and, nodding at Kilne, "liked his medicine best, eh?"

"Had a-hem!—good lot of it," muttered Kilne, with a suddenly serious brow.

"How does he stand on your books?" asked Barnes.

Kilne shouldered round, crying: "Who the deuce is to know?"

"I don't," Grossby sighed. "In he comes with his 'Good morning, Grossby, fine day for the hunt, Grossby,' and a ten-pound note. 'Have the kindness to put that down in my favour, Grossby.' And just as I am going to say, 'Look here,—this won't do,' he has me by the collar, and there's one of the regiments going to give a supper party, which he's to order; or the Admiral's wife wants the receipt for that pie; or in comes my wife, and there's no talking of business then, though she may have been bothering about his account all the night beforehand. Something or other! and so we run on."

"What I want to know," said Barnes, the butcher, "is where he got his tenners from?"

Kilne shook a sagacious head: "No knowing!"

"I suppose we shall get something out of the fire?" Barnes suggested.

"That depends!" answered the emphatic Kilne.

"But, you know, if the widow carries on the business," said Grossby, "there's no reason why we shouldn't get it all, eh?"

"There ain't two that can make clothes for nothing, and make a profit out of it," said Kilne.

"That young chap in Portugal," added Barnes, "he won't take to tailoring when he comes home. D' ye think he will?"

Kilne muttered: "Can't say!" and Grossby, a kindly creature in his way, albeit a creditor, reverting to the first subject of their discourse, exclaimed, "But what a one he was!—eh?"

"Fine!—to look on," Kilne assented.

"Well, he was like a Marquis," said Barnes.

Here the three regarded each other, and laughed, though not loudly. They instantly checked that unseemliness, and Kilne, as one who rises from the depths of a calculation with the sum in his head, spoke quite in a different voice:

"Well, what do you say, gentlemen? shall we adjourn? No use standing here."

By the invitation to adjourn, it was well understood by the committee Kilne addressed, that they were invited to pass his threshold, and partake of a morning draught. Barnes, the butcher, had no objection whatever, and if Grossby, a man of milder make, entertained any, the occasion and common interests to be discussed, advised him to waive them. In single file these mourners entered the publican's house, where Kilne, after summoning them from behind the bar, on the important question, what it should be? and receiving, first, perfect acquiescence in his views as to what it should be, and then feeble suggestions of the drink best befitting that early hour and the speaker's particular constitution, poured out a toothful to each, and one to himself.

"Here's to him, poor fellow!" said Kilne; and was deliberately echoed twice.

"Now, it wasn't that," Kilne pursued, pointing to the bottle in the midst of a smacking of lips, "that wasn't what got him into difficulties. It was expensive luckshries. It was being above his condition. Horses! What's a tradesman got to do with horses? Unless he's retired! Then he's a gentleman, and can do as he likes. It's no use trying to be a gentleman if you can't pay for it. It always ends bad. Why, there was he, consorting with gentlefolks—gay as a lark! Who has to pay for it?"

Kilne's fellow-victims maintained a rather doleful tributary silence.

"I'm not saying anything against him now," the publican further observed. "It's too late. And there! I'm sorry he's gone, for one. He was as kind a hearted a man as ever breathed. And there! perhaps it was just as much my fault; I couldn't say 'No' to him,—dash me, if I could!"

Lymport was a prosperous town, and in prosperity the much-despised British tradesman is not a harsh, he is really a well-disposed, easy soul, and requires but management, manner, occasional instalments—just to freshen the account—and a surety that he who debits is on the spot, to be a right royal king of credit. Only the account must never drivel. "Stare aut crescere" appears to be his feeling on that point, and the departed Mr. Melchisedec undoubtedly understood him there; for the running on of the account looked deplorable and extraordinary now that Mr. Melchisedec was no longer in a position to run on with it, and it was precisely his doing so which had prevented it from being brought to a summary close long before. Both Barnes, the butcher; and Grossby, the confectioner, confessed that they, too, found it hard ever to say "No" to him, and, speaking broadly, never could.

"Except once," said Barnes, "when he wanted me to let him have a ox to roast whole out on the common, for the Battle of Waterloo. I stood out against him on that. 'No, no,' says I, 'I'll joint him for ye, Mr. Harrington. You shall have him in joints, and eat him at home';-ha! ha!"

"Just like him!" said Grossby, with true enjoyment of the princely disposition that had dictated the patriotic order.

"Oh!—there!" Kilne emphasized, pushing out his arm across the bar, as much as to say, that in anything of such a kind, the great Mel never had a rival.

"That 'Marquis' affair changed him a bit," said Barnes.

"Perhaps it did, for a time," said Kilne. "What's in the grain, you know. He couldn't change. He would be a gentleman, and nothing 'd stop him."

"And I shouldn't wonder but what that young chap out in Portugal 'll want to be one, too; though he didn't bid fair to be so fine a man as his father."

"More of a scholar," remarked Kilne. "That I call his worst fault—shilly-shallying about that young chap. I mean his." Kilne stretched a finger toward the dead man's house. "First, the young chap's to be sent into the Navy; then it's the Army; then he's to be a judge, and sit on criminals; then he goes out to his sister in Portugal; and now there's nothing but a tailor open to him, as I see, if we're to get our money."

"Ah! and he hasn't got too much spirit to work to pay his father's debts," added Barnes. "There's a business there to make any man's fortune-properly directed, I say. But, I suppose, like father like son, he'll becoming the Marquis, too. He went to a gentleman's school, and he's had foreign training. I don't know what to think about it. His sisters over there—they were fine women."

"Oh! a fine family, every one of 'em! and married well!" exclaimed the publican.

"I never had the exact rights of that 'Marquis' affair," said Grossby; and, remembering that he had previously laughed knowingly when it was alluded to, pursued: "Of course I heard of it at the time, but how did he behave when he was blown upon?"

Barnes undertook to explain; but Kilne, who relished the narrative quite as well, and was readier, said: "Look here! I'll tell you. I had it from his own mouth one night when he wasn't—not quite himself. He was coming down King William Street, where he stabled his horse, you know, and I met him. He'd been dining out-somewhere out over Fallow field, I think it was; and he sings out to me, 'Ah! Kilne, my good fellow!' and I, wishing to be equal with him, says, 'A fine night, my lord!' and he draws himself up—he smelt of good company—says he, 'Kilne! I'm not a lord, as you know, and you have no excuse for mistaking me for one, sir!' So I pretended I had mistaken him, and then he tucked his arm under mine, and said, 'You're no worse than your betters, Kilne. They took me for one at Squire Uplift's to-night, but a man who wishes to pass off for more than he is, Kilne, and impose upon people,' he says, 'he's contemptible, Kilne! contemptible!' So that, you know, set me thinking about 'Bath' and the 'Marquis,' and I couldn't help smiling to myself, and just let slip a question whether he had enlightened them a bit. 'Kilne,' said he, 'you're an honest man, and a neighbour, and I'll tell you what happened. The Squire,' he says, 'likes my company, and I like his table. Now the Squire 'd never do a dirty action, but the Squire's nephew, Mr. George Uplift, he can't forget that I earn my money, and once or twice I have had to correct him.' And I'll wager Mel did it, too! Well, he goes on: 'There was Admiral Sir Jackson Racial and his lady, at dinner, Squire Falco of Bursted, Lady Barrington, Admiral Combleman—our admiral, that was; "Mr. This and That", I forget their names—and other ladies and gentlemen whose acquaintance I was not honoured with.' You know his way of talking. 'And there was a goose on the table,' he says; and, looking stern at me, 'Don't laugh yet!' says he, like thunder. 'Well, he goes on: Mr. George caught my eye across the table, and said, so as not to be heard by his uncle, "If that bird was rampant, you would see your own arms, Marquis."' And Mel replied, quietly for him to hear, 'And as that bird is couchant, Mr. George, you had better look to your sauce.' Couchant means squatting, you know. That's heraldry! Well, that wasn't bad sparring of Mel's. But, bless you!

he was never taken aback, and the gentlefolks was glad enough to get him to sit down amongst 'em. So, says Mr. George, 'I know you're a fire-eater, Marquis,' and his dander was up, for he began marquising Mel, and doing the mock polite at such a rate, that, by-and-by, one of the ladies who didn't know Mel called him 'my lord' and 'his lordship.' 'And,' says Mel, 'I merely bowed to her, and took no notice.' So that passed off: and there sits Mel telling his anecdotes, as grand as a king. And, by and-by, young Mr. George, who hadn't forgiven Mel, and had been pulling at the bottle pretty well, he sings out, 'It's Michaelmas! the death of the goose! and I should like to drink the Marquis's health!' and he drank it solemn. But, as far as I can make out, the women part of the company was a little in the dark. So Mel waited till there was a sort of a pause, and then speaks rather loud to the Admiral, 'By the way, Sir Jackson, may I ask you, has the title of Marquis anything to do with tailoring?' Now Mel was a great favourite with the Admiral, and with his lady, too, they say—and the Admiral played into his hands, you see, and, says he, 'I'm not aware that it has, Mr. Harrington.' And he begged for to know why he asked the question—called him, 'Mister,' you understand. So Mel said, and I can see him now, right out from his chest he spoke, with his head up 'When I was a younger man, I had the good taste to be fond of good society, and the bad taste to wish to appear different from what I was in it': that's Mel speaking; everybody was listening; so he goes on: 'I was in the habit of going to Bath in the season, and consorting with the gentlemen I met there on terms of equality; and for some reason that I am quite guiltless of,' says Mel, 'the hotel people gave out that I was a Marquis in disguise; and, upon my honour, ladies and gentlemen—I was young then, and a fool—I could not help imagining I looked the thing. At all events, I took upon myself to act the part, and with some success, and considerable gratification; for, in my opinion,' says Mel, 'no real Marquis ever enjoyed his title so much as I did. One day I was in my shop—No. 193, Main Street, Lymport—and a gentleman came in to order his outfit.' I received his directions, when suddenly he started back, stared at me, and exclaimed:

"My dear Marquis! I trust you will pardon me for having addressed you with so much familiarity." I recognized in him one of my Bath acquaintances. That circumstance, ladies and gentlemen, has been a lesson to me. Since that time I have never allowed a false impression with regard to my position to exist. 'I desire,' says Mel, smiling, 'to have my exact measure taken everywhere; and if the Michaelmas bird is to be associated with me, I am sure I have no objection; all I can say is, that I cannot justify it by letters patent of nobility.' That's how Mel put it. Do you think they thought worse of him? I warrant you he came out of it in flying colours. Gentlefolks like straight-forwardness in their inferiors—that's what they do. Ah!" said Kilne, meditatively, "I see him now, walking across the street in the moonlight, after he'd told me that. A fine figure of a man! and there ain't many Marquises to match him."

To this Barnes and Grossby, not insensible to the merits of the recital they had just given ear to, agreed. And with a common voice of praise in the mouths of his creditors, the dead man's requiem was sounded.

II

The Heritage of the Son

Toward evening, a carriage drove up to the door of the muted house, and the card of Lady Racial, bearing a hurried line in pencil, was handed to the widow.

It was when you looked upon her that you began to comprehend how great was the personal splendour of the husband who could eclipse such a woman. Mrs. Harrington was a tall and a stately dame. Dressed in the high waists of the matrons of that period, with a light shawl drawn close over her shoulders and bosom, she carried her head well; and her pale firm features, with the cast of immediate affliction on them, had much dignity: dignity of an unrelenting physical order, which need not express any remarkable pride of spirit. The family gossips who, on both sides, were vain of this rare couple, and would always descant on their beauty, even when they had occasion to slander their characters, said, to distinguish them, that Henrietta Maria had a Port, and Melchisedec a Presence: and that the union of a Port and a Presence, and such a Port and such a Presence, was so uncommon, that you might search England through and you would not find another, not even in the highest ranks of society. There lies some subtle distinction here; due to the minute perceptions which compel the gossips of a family to coin phrases that shall express the nicest shades of a domestic difference. By a Port, one may understand them to indicate something unsympathetically impressive; whereas a Presence would seem to be a thing that directs the most affable appeal to our poor human weaknesses. His Majesty King George IV, for instance, possessed a Port: Beau Brummel wielded a Presence. Many, it is true, take a Presence to mean no more than a shirt-frill, and interpret a Port as the art of walking erect. But this is to look upon language too narrowly.

On a more intimate acquaintance with the couple, you acknowledge the aptness of the fine distinction. By birth Mrs. Harrington had claims to rank as a gentlewoman. That is, her father was a lawyer of Lymport. The lawyer, however, since we must descend the genealogical tree, was known to have married his cook, who was the lady's mother. Now Mr. Melchisedec was mysterious concerning his origin; and, in his cups, talked largely and wisely of a great Welsh family, issuing from a line of princes; and it is certain that he knew enough of their history to have instructed them on particular points of it. He never could think that his wife had done him any honour in espousing him; nor was she the woman to tell him so. She had married him for love, rejecting various suitors, Squire Uplift among them, in his favour. Subsequently she had committed the profound connubial error of transferring her affections, or her thoughts, from him to his business, which, indeed, was much in want of a mate; and while he squandered the guineas, she patiently picked up the pence. They had not lived unhappily. He was constantly courteous to her. But to see the Port at that sordid work considerably ruffled the Presence—put, as it were, the peculiar division between them; and to behave toward her as the same woman who had attracted his youthful ardours was a task for his magnificent mind, and may have ranked with him as an indemnity for his general conduct, if his reflections ever stretched so far. The townspeople of Lymport were correct in saying that his wife, and his wife alone, had, as they termed it, kept him together. Nevertheless, now that he was dead, and could no longer be kept together, they entirely forgot their respect for her, in the outburst of their secret admiration for the popular man. Such is the constitution of the inhabitants of this dear Island of Britain, so falsely accused by the Great Napoleon of being a nation of shopkeepers. Here let any one proclaim himself Above Buttons, and act on the assumption, his fellows with one accord hoist him on their heads, and bear him aloft, sweating, and groaning, and cursing, but proud of him! And if he can contrive, or has any good wife at home to help him, to die without going to the dogs, they are, one may say, unanimous in crying out the same eulogistic funeral oration as that commenced by Kilne, the publican, when he was interrupted by Barnes, the butcher, "Now, there's a man!—"

Mrs. Harrington was sitting in her parlour with one of her married nieces, Mrs. Fiske, and on reading Lady Racial's card she gave word for her to be shown up into the drawing-room. It was customary among Mrs. Harrington's female relatives, who one and all abused and adored the great Mel, to attribute his shortcomings pointedly to the ladies; which was as much as if their jealous generous hearts had said that he was sinful, but that it was not his fault. Mrs. Fiske caught the card from her aunt, read the superscription, and exclaimed: "The idea! At least she might have had the decency! She never set her foot in the house before—and right enough too! What can she want now? I decidedly would refuse to see her, aunt!"

The widow's reply was simply, "Don't be a fool, Ann!"

Rising, she said: "Here, take poor Jacko, and comfort him till I come back."

Jacko was a middle-sized South American monkey, and had been a pet of her husband's. He was supposed to be mourning now with the rest of the family. Mrs. Fiske received him on a shrinking lap, and had found time to correct one of his indiscretions before she could sigh and say, in the rear of her aunt's retreating figure, "I certainly never would let myself, down so"; but Mrs. Harrington took her own counsel, and Jacko was of her persuasion, for he quickly released himself from Mrs. Fiske's dispassionate embrace, and was slinging his body up the balusters after his mistress.

"Mrs. Harrington," said Lady Racial, very sweetly swimming to meet her as she entered the room, "I have intruded upon you, I fear, in venturing to call upon you at such a time?"

The widow bowed to her, and begged her to be seated.

Lady Racial was an exquisitely silken dame, in whose face a winning smile was cut, and she was still sufficiently youthful not to be accused of wearing a flower too artificial.

"It was so sudden! so sad!" she continued. "We esteemed him so much. I thought you might be in need of sympathy, and hoped I might—Dear Mrs. Harrington! can you bear to speak of it?"

"I can tell you anything you wish to hear, my lady," the widow replied. Lady Racial had expected to meet a woman much more like what she conceived a tradesman's wife would be: and the grave reception of her proffer of sympathy slightly confused her. She said:

"I should not have come, at least not so early, but Sir Jackson, my husband, thought, and indeed I imagined—You have a son, Mrs. Harrington? I think his name is—"

"Evan, my lady."

"Evan. It was of him we have been speaking. I imagined that is, we thought, Sir Jackson might—you will be writing to him, and will let him know we will use our best efforts to assist him in obtaining some position worthy of his—superior to—something that will secure him from the harassing embarrassments of an uncongenial employment."

The widow listened to this tender allusion to the shears without a smile of gratitude. She replied: "I hope my son will return in time to bury his father, and he will thank you himself, my lady."

"He has no taste for—a—for anything in the shape of trade, has he, Mrs. Harrington?"

"I am afraid not, my lady."

"Any position—a situation—that of a clerk even—would be so much better for him!"

The widow remained impassive.

"And many young gentlemen I know, who are clerks, and are enabled to live comfortably, and make a modest appearance in society; and your son, Mrs. Harrington, he would find it surely an improvement upon—many would think it a step for him."

"I am bound to thank you for the interest you take in my son, my lady."

"Does it not quite suit your views, Mrs. Harrington?" Lady Racial was surprised at the widow's manner.

"If my son had only to think of himself, my lady."

"Oh! but of course,"—the lady understood her now—"of course! You cannot suppose, Mrs. Harrington, but that I should anticipate he would have you to live with him, and behave to you in every way as a dutiful son, surely?"

"A clerk's income is not very large, my lady."

"No; but enough, as I have said, and with the management you would bring, Mrs. Harrington, to produce a modest, respectable maintenance. My respect for your husband, Mrs. Harrington, makes me anxious to press my services upon you." Lady Racial could not avoid feeling hurt at the widow's want of common gratitude.

"A clerk's income would not be more than L100 a year, my lady."

"To begin with—no; certainly not more." The lady was growing brief.

"If my son puts by the half of that yearly, he can hardly support himself and his mother, my lady."

"Half of that yearly, Mrs. Harrington?"

"He would have to do so, and be saddled till he dies, my lady."

"I really cannot see why."

Lady Racial had a notion of some excessive niggardly thrift in the widow, which was arousing symptoms of disgust.

Mrs. Harrington quietly said: "There are his father's debts to pay, my lady."

"His father's debts!"

"Under L5000, but above L4000, my lady."

"Five thousand pounds! Mrs. Harrington!" The lady's delicately gloved hand gently rose and fell. "And this poor young man—" she pursued.

"My son will have to pay it, my lady."

For a moment the lady had not a word to instance. Presently she remarked: "But, Mrs. Harrington, he is surely under no legal obligation?"

"He is only under the obligation not to cast disrespect on his father's memory, my lady; and to be honest, while he can."

"But, Mrs. Harrington! surely! what can the poor young man do?"

"He will pay it, my lady."

"But how, Mrs. Harrington?"

"There is his father's business, my lady."

His father's business! Then must the young man become a tradesman in order to show respect for his father? Preposterous! That was the lady's natural inward exclamation. She said, rather shrewdly, for one who knew nothing of such things: "But a business which produces debts so enormous, Mrs. Harrington!"

The widow replied: "My son will have to conduct it in a different way. It would be a very good business, conducted properly, my lady."

"But if he has no taste for it, Mrs. Harrington? If he is altogether superior to it?"

For the first time during the interview, the widow's inflexible countenance was mildly moved, though not to any mild expression.

"My son will have not to consult his tastes," she observed: and seeing the lady, after a short silence, quit her seat, she rose likewise, and touched the fingers of the hand held forth to her, bowing.

"You will pardon the interest I take in your son," said Lady Racial. "I hope, indeed, that his relatives and friends will procure him the means of satisfying the demands made upon him."

"He would still have to pay them, my lady," was the widow's answer.

"Poor young man! indeed I pity him!" sighed her visitor. "You have hitherto used no efforts to persuade him to take such a step,—Mrs. Harrington?"

"I have written to Mr. Goren, who was my husband's fellow-apprentice in London, my lady; and he is willing to instruct him in cutting, and measuring, and keeping accounts."

Certain words in this speech were obnoxious to the fine ear of Lady Racial, and she relinquished the subject.

"Your husband, Mrs. Harrington—I should so much have wished!—he did not pass away in—in pain!"

"He died very calmly, my lady."

"It is so terrible, so disfiguring, sometimes. One dreads to see!—one can hardly distinguish! I have known cases where death was dreadful! But a peaceful death is very beautiful! There is nothing shocking to the mind. It suggests heaven! It seems a fulfilment of our prayers!"

"Would your ladyship like to look upon him?" said the widow.

Lady Racial betrayed a sudden gleam at having her desire thus intuitively fathomed.

"For one moment, Mrs. Harrington! We esteemed him so much! May I?"

The widow responded by opening the door, and leading her into the chamber where the dead man lay.

At that period, when threats of invasion had formerly stirred up the military fire of us Islanders, the great Mel, as if to show the great Napoleon what character of being a British shopkeeper really was, had, by remarkable favour, obtained a lieutenancy of militia dragoons: in the uniform of which he had revelled, and perhaps, for the only time in his life, felt that circumstances had suited him with a perfect fit. However that may be, his solemn final commands to his wife, Henrietta Maria, on whom he could count for absolute obedience in such matters, had been, that as soon as the breath had left his body, he should be taken from his bed, washed, perfumed, powdered, and in that uniform dressed and laid out; with directions that he should be so buried at the expiration of three days, that havoc in his features might be hidden from men. In this array Lady Racial beheld him. The curtains of the bed were drawn aside. The beams of evening fell soft through the blinds of the room, and cast a subdued light on the figure of the vanquished warrior. The Presence, dumb now for evermore, was sadly illumined for its last exhibition. But one who looked closely might have seen that Time had somewhat spoiled that perfect fit which had aforetime been his pride; and now that the lofty spirit had departed, there had been extreme difficulty in persuading the sullen excess of clay to conform to the dimensions of those garments. The upper part of the chest alone would bear its buttons, and across one portion of the lower limbs an ancient seam had started; recalling an incident to them who had known him in his brief hour of glory. For one night, as he was riding home from Fallow field, and just entering the gates of the town, a mounted trooper spurred furiously past, and slashing out at him, gashed his thigh. Mrs. Melchisedec found him lying at his door in a not unwonted way; carried him up-stairs in her arms, as she had done many a time before, and did not perceive his condition till she saw the blood on her gown. The cowardly assailant was never discovered; but Mel was both gallant and had, in his military career, the reputation of being a martinet. Hence, divers causes were suspected. The wound failed not to mend, the trousers were repaired: Peace about the same time was made, and the affair passed over.

Looking on the fine head and face, Lady Racial saw nothing of this. She had not looked long before she found covert employment for her handkerchief. The widow standing beside her did not weep, or reply to her whispered excuses at emotion; gazing down on his mortal length with a sort of benignant friendliness; aloof, as one whose duties to that form of flesh were well-nigh done. At the feet of his master, Jacko, the monkey, had jumped up, and was there squatted, with his legs crossed, very like a tailor! The imitative wretch had got a towel, and as often as Lady Racial's handkerchief travelled to her eyes, Jacko's peery face was hidden, and you saw his lithe skinny body doing grief's convulsions till, tired of this amusement, he obtained possession of the warrior's helmet, from a small round table on one side of the bed; a calque of the barbarous military-Georgian form, with a huge knob of horse-hair projecting over the peak; and under this, trying to adapt it to his rogue's head, the tricksy image of Death extinguished himself.

All was very silent in the room. Then the widow quietly disengaged Jacko, and taking him up, went to the door, and deposited him outside. During her momentary absence, Lady Racial had time to touch the dead man's forehead with her lips, unseen.

III

The Daughters of the Shears

Three daughters and a son were left to the world by Mr. Melchisedec. Love, well endowed, had already claimed to provide for the daughters: first in the shape of a lean Marine subaltern, whose days of obscuration had now passed, and who had come to be a major of that corps: secondly, presenting his addresses as a brewer of distinction: thirdly, and for a climax, as a Portuguese Count: no other than the Senor Silva Diaz, Conde de Saldar: and this match did seem a far more resplendent one than that of the two elder sisters with Major Strike and Mr. Andrew Cogglesby. But the rays of neither fell visibly on Lymport. These escaped Eurydices never reappeared, after being once fairly caught away from the gloomy realms of Dis, otherwise Trade. All three persons of singular beauty, a certain refinement, some Port, and some Presence, hereditarily combined, they feared the clutch of that fell king, and performed the widest possible circles around him. Not one of them ever approached the house of her parents. They were dutiful and loving children, and wrote frequently; but of course they had to consider their new position, and their husbands, and their husbands' families, and the world, and what it would say, if to it the dreaded rumour should penetrate! Lymport gossips, as numerous as in other parts, declared that the foreign nobleman would rave in an extraordinary manner, and do things after the outlandish fashion of his country: for from him, there was no doubt, the shop had been most successfully veiled, and he knew not of Pluto's close relationship to his lovely spouse.

The marriages had happened in this way. Balls are given in country towns, where the graces of tradesmen's daughters may be witnessed and admired at leisure by other than tradesmen: by occasional country gentlemen of the neighbourhood, with light minds: and also by small officers: subalterns wishing to do tender execution upon man's fair enemy, and to find a distraction for their legs. The classes of our social fabric have, here and there, slight connecting links, and provincial public balls are one of these. They are dangerous, for Cupid is no respecter of class-prejudice; and if you are the son of a retired tea-merchant, or of a village doctor, or of a half-pay captain, or of anything superior, and visit one of them, you are as likely to receive his shot as any shopboy. Even masquerading lords at such places, have been known to be slain outright; and although Society allows to its highest and dearest to save the honour of their families, and heal their anguish, by indecorous compromise, you, if you are a trifle below that mark, must not expect it. You must absolutely give yourself for what you hope to get. Dreadful as it sounds to philosophic ears, you must marry. This, having danced with Caroline Harrington, the gallant Lieutenant Strike determined to do. Nor, when he became aware of her father's occupation, did he shrink from his resolve. After a month's hard courtship, he married her straight out of her father's house. That he may have all the credit due to him, it must be admitted that he did not once compare, or possibly permit himself to reflect on, the dissimilarity in their respective ranks, and the step he had taken downward, till they were man and wife: and then not in any great degree, before Fortune had given him his majority; an advance the good soldier frankly told his wife he did not owe to her. If we may be permitted to suppose the colonel of a regiment on friendly terms with one of his corporals, we have an estimate of the domestic life of Major and Mrs. Strike. Among the garrison males, his comrades, he passed for a disgustingly jealous brute.

The ladies, in their pretty language, signalized him as a "finick."

Now, having achieved so capital a marriage, Caroline, worthy creature, was anxious that her sisters should not be less happy, and would have them to visit her, in spite of her husband's protests.

"There can be no danger," she said, for she was in fresh quarters, far from the nest of contagion. The lieutenant himself ungrudgingly declared that, looking on the ladies, no one for an instant could suspect; and he saw many young fellows ready to be as great fools as he had been another voluntary confession he made to his wife; for the candour of which she thanked him, and pointed out that it seemed to run in the family; inasmuch as Mr. Andrew Cogglesby, his rich relative, had seen and had proposed for Harriet. The lieutenant flatly said he would never allow it. In fact he had hitherto concealed the non-presentable portion of his folly very satisfactorily from all save the mess-room, and Mr. Andrew's passion was a severe dilemma to him. It need scarcely be told that his wife, fortified by the fervid brewer, defeated him utterly. What was more, she induced him to be an accomplice in deception. For though the lieutenant protested that he washed his hands of it, and that it was a fraud and a snare, he certainly did not avow the condition of his wife's parents to Mr. Andrew, but alluded to them in passing as "the country people." He supposed "the country people" must be asked, he said. The brewer offered to go down to them. But the lieutenant drew an unpleasant picture of the country people, and his wife became so grave at the proposal, that Mr. Andrew said he wanted to marry the lady and not the "country people," and if she would have him, there he was. There he was, behaving with a particular and sagacious kindness to the raw lieutenant since Harriet's arrival. If the lieutenant sent her away, Mr. Andrew would infallibly pursue her, and light on a discovery. Twice cursed by Love, twice the victim of tailordom, our excellent Marine gave away Harriet Harrington in marriage to Mr. Andrew Cogglesby.

Thus Joy clapped hands a second time, and Horror deepened its shadows.

From higher ground it was natural that the remaining sister should take a bolder flight. Of the loves of the fair Louisa Harrington and the foreign Count, and how she first encountered him in the brewer's saloons, and how she, being a humorous person, laughed at his "loaf" for her, and wore the colours that pleased him, and kindled and soothed his jealousy, little is known beyond the fact that she espoused the Count, under the auspices of the affluent brewer, and engaged that her children should be brought up in the faith of the Catholic Church: which Lymport gossips called, paying the Devil for her pride.

The three sisters, gloriously rescued by their own charms, had now to think of their one young brother. How to make him a gentleman! That was their problem.

Preserve him from tailordom—from all contact with trade—they must; otherwise they would be perpetually linked to the horrid thing they hoped to outlive and bury. A cousin of Mr. Melchisedec's had risen to be an Admiral and a knight for valiant action in the old war, when men could rise. Him they besought to take charge of the youth, and make a distinguished seaman of him. He courteously declined. They then attacked the married Marine—Navy or Army being quite indifferent to them as long as they could win for their brother the badge of one Service, "When he is a gentleman at once!" they said, like those who see the end of their labours. Strike basely pretended to second them. It would have been delightful to him, of course, to have the tailor's son messing at the same table, and claiming him when he pleased with a familiar "Ah, brother!" and prating of their relationship everywhere. Strike had been a fool: in revenge for it he laid out for himself a masterly career of consequent wisdom. The brewer—uxorious Andrew Cogglesby—might and would have bought the commission. Strike laughed at the idea of giving money for what could be got for nothing. He told them to wait.

In the meantime Evan, a lad of seventeen, spent the hours not devoted to his positive profession—that of gentleman—in the offices of the brewery, toying with big books and balances, which he despised with the combined zeal of the sucking soldier and emancipated tailor.

Two years passed in attendance on the astute brother-in-law, to whom Fortune now beckoned to come to her and gather his laurels from the pig-tails. About the same time the Countess sailed over from Lisbon on a visit to her sister Harriet (in reality, it was whispered in the Cogglesby saloons, on a diplomatic mission from the Court of Lisbon; but that could not be made ostensible). The Countess narrowly examined Evan, whose steady advance in his profession both her sisters praised.

"Yes," said the Countess, in a languid alien accent. "He has something of his father's carriage—something. Something of his delivery—his readiness."

It was a remarkable thing that these ladies thought no man on earth like their father, and always cited him as the example of a perfect gentleman, and yet they buried him with one mind, and each mounted guard over his sepulchre, to secure his ghost from an airing.

"He can walk, my dears, certainly, and talk—a little. Tete-a-tete, I do not say. I should think there he would be—a stick! All you English are. But what sort of a bow has he got, I ask you? How does he enter a room? And, then his smile! his laugh! He laughs like a horse—absolutely! There's no music in his smile. Oh! you should see a Portuguese nobleman smile. O mio Deus! honeyed, my dears! But Evan has it not. None of you English have. You go so."

The Countess pressed a thumb and finger to the sides of her mouth, and set her sisters laughing.

"I assure you, no better! not a bit! I faint in your society. I ask myself—Where am I? Among what boors have I fallen? But Evan is no worse than the rest of you; I acknowledge that. If he knew how to dress his shoulders properly, and to direct his eyes—Oh! the eyes! you should see how a Portuguese nobleman can use his eyes! Soul! my dears, soul! Can any of you look the unutterable without being absurd! You look so."

And the Countess hung her jaw under heavily vacuous orbits, something as a sheep might yawn.

"But I acknowledge that Evan is no worse than the rest of you," she repeated. "If he understood at all the management of his eyes and mouth! But that's what he cannot possibly learn in England—not possibly! As for your poor husband, Harriet! one really has to remember his excellent qualities to forgive him, poor man! And that stiff bandbox of a man of yours, Caroline!" addressing the wife of the Marine, "he looks as if he were all angles and sections, and were taken to pieces every night and put together in the morning. He may be a good soldier—good anything you will—but, Diacho! to be married to that! He is not civilized. None of you English are. You have no place in the drawing-room. You are like so many intrusive oxen—absolutely! One of your men trod on my toe the other night, and what do you think the creature did? Jerks back, then the half of him forward—I thought he was going to break in two—then grins, and grunts, 'Oh! 'm sure, beg pardon, 'm sure!' I don't know whether he didn't say, MARM!"

The Countess lifted her hands, and fell away in laughing horror. When her humour, or her feelings generally, were a little excited, she spoke her vernacular as her sisters did, but immediately subsided into the deliberate delicately-syllabled drawl.

"Now that happened to me once at one of our great Balls," she pursued. "I had on one side of me the Duchesse Eugenia de Formosa de Fontandigua; on the other sat the Countess de Pel, a widow. And we were talking of the ices that evening. Eugenia, you must know, my dears, was in love with the Count Belmarana. I was her sole confidante. The Countess de Pel—a horrible creature! Oh! she was the Duchess's determined enemy-would have stabbed her for Belmarana, one of the most beautiful men! Adored by every woman! So we talked ices, Eugenic and myself, quite comfortably, and that horrible De Pel had no idea in life! Eugenia had just said, 'This ice sickens me! I do not taste the flavour of the vanille.' I answered, 'It is here! It must—it cannot but be here! You love the flavour of the vanille?' With her exquisite smile, I see her now saying, 'Too well! it is necessary to me! I live on it!'—when up he came. In his eagerness, his foot just effleured my robe. Oh! I never shall forget! In an instant he was down on one knee it was so momentary that none saw it but we three, and done with ineffable grace. 'Pardon!' he said, in his sweet Portuguese; 'Pardon!' looking up—the handsomest man I ever beheld; and when I think of that odious wretch the other night, with his 'Oh! 'm sure, beg pardon, 'm sure! 'pon my honour!' I could have kicked him—I could, indeed!"

Here the Countess laughed out, but relapsed into:

"Alas! that Belmarana should have betrayed that beautiful trusting creature to De Pel. Such scandal! a duel!—the Duke was wounded. For a whole year Eugenia did not dare to appear at Court, but had to remain immured in her country-house, where she heard that Belmarana had married De Pel! It was for her money, of course. Rich as Croesus, and as wicked as the black man below! as dear papa used to say. By the way, weren't we talking of Evan? Ah,—yes!"

And so forth. The Countess was immensely admired, and though her sisters said that she was "foreignized" overmuch, they clung to her desperately. She seemed so entirely to have eclipsed tailordom, or "Demogorgon," as the Countess was pleased to call it. Who could suppose this grand-mannered lady, with her coroneted anecdotes and delicious breeding, the daughter of that thing? It was not possible to suppose it. It seemed to defy the fact itself.

They congratulated her on her complete escape from Demogorgon. The Countess smiled on them with a lovely sorrow.

"Safe from the whisper, my dears; the ceaseless dread? If you knew what I have to endure! I sometimes envy you. 'Pon my honour, I sometimes wish I had married a fishmonger! Silva, indeed, is a most excellent husband. Polished! such polish as you know not of in England. He has a way—a wriggle with his shoulders in company—I cannot describe it to you; so slight! so elegant! and he is all that a woman could desire. But who could be safe in any part of the earth, my dears, while papa will go about so, and behave so extraordinarily? I was at dinner at your English embassy a month ago, and there was Admiral Combleman, then on the station off Lisbon, Sir Jackson Racial's friend, who was the Admiral at Lymport formerly. I knew him at once, and thought, oh! what shall I do! My heart was like a lump of lead. I would have given worlds that we might one of us have smothered the other! I had to sit beside him—it always happens! Thank heaven! he did not identify me. And then he told an anecdote of Papa. It was the dreadful old 'Bath' story. I thought I should have died. I could not but fancy the Admiral suspected. Was it not natural? And what do you think I had the audacity to do? I asked him coolly, whether the Mr. Harrington he mentioned was not the son of Sir Abraham Harrington, of Torquay,—the gentleman who lost his yacht in the Lisbon waters last year? I brought it on myself.

'Gentleman, ma'am,—MA'AM!' says the horrid old creature, laughing, 'gentleman! he's a — I cannot speak it: I choke!' And then he began praising Papa. Diacho! what I suffered. But, you know, I can keep my countenance, if I perish. I am a Harrington as much as any of us!"

And the Countess looked superb in the pride with which she said she was what she would have given her hand not to be. But few feelings are single on this globe, and junction of sentiments need not imply unity in our yeasty compositions.

"After it was over—my supplice," continued the Countess, "I was questioned by all the ladies—I mean our ladies—not your English. They wanted to know how I could be so civil to that intolerable man. I gained a deal of credit, my dears. I laid it all on—Diplomacy." The Countess laughed bitterly. "Diplomacy bears the burden of it all. I pretended that Combleman could be useful to Silva! Oh! what hypocrites we all are, mio Deus!"

The ladies listening could not gainsay this favourite claim of universal brotherhood among the select who wear masks instead of faces.

With regard to Evan, the Countess had far outstripped her sisters in her views. A gentleman she had discovered must have one of two things—a title or money. He might have all the breeding in the world; he might be as good as an angel; but without a title or money he was under eclipse almost total. On a gentleman the sun must shine. Now, Evan had no title, no money. The clouds were thick above the youth. To gain a title he would have to scale aged mountains. There was one break in his firmament through which the radiant luminary might be assisted to cast its beams on him still young. That divine portal was matrimony. If he could but make a rich marriage he would blaze transfigured; all would be well! And why should not Evan marry an heiress, as well as another?

"I know a young creature who would exactly suit him," said the Countess. "She is related to the embassy, and is in Lisbon now. A charming child—just sixteen! Dios! how the men rave about her! and she isn't a beauty,—there's the wonder; and she is a little too gauche too English in her habits and ways of thinking; likes to be admired, of course, but doesn't know yet how to set about getting it. She rather scandalizes our ladies, but when you know her!—She will have, they say, a hundred thousand pounds in her own right! Rose Jocelyn, the daughter of Sir Franks, and that eccentric Lady Jocelyn. She is with her uncle, Melville, the celebrated diplomate though, to tell you the truth, we turn him round our fingers, and spin him as the boys used to do the cockchafers. I cannot forget our old Fallow field school-life, you see, my dears. Well, Rose Jocelyn would just suit Evan. She is just of an age to receive an impression. And I would take care she did. Instance me a case where I have failed?"

"Or there is the Portuguese widow, the Rostral. She's thirty, certainly; but she possesses millions! Estates all over the kingdom, and the sweetest creature. But, no. Evan would be out of the way there, certainly. But—our women are very nice: they have the dearest, sweetest ways: but I would rather Evan did not marry one of them. And then there's the religion!"

This was a sore of the Countess's own, and she dropped a tear in coming across it.

"No, my dears, it shall be Rose Jocelyn!" she concluded: "I will take Evan over with me, and see that he has opportunities. It shall be Rose, and then I can call her mine; for in verity I love the child."

It is not my part to dispute the Countess's love for Miss Jocelyn; and I have only to add that Evan, unaware of the soft training he was to undergo, and the brilliant chance in store for him, offered no impediment to the proposition that he should journey to Portugal with his sister (whose subtlest flattery was to tell him that she should not be ashamed to own him there); and ultimately, furnished with cash for the trip by the remonstrating brewer, went.

So these Parcae, daughters of the shears, arranged and settled the young man's fate. His task was to learn the management of his mouth, how to dress his shoulders properly, and to direct his eyes—rare qualities in man or woman, I assure you; the management of the mouth being especially admirable, and correspondingly difficult. These achieved, he was to place his battery in position, and win the heart and hand of an heiress.

Our comedy opens with his return from Portugal, in company with Miss Rose, the heiress; the Honourable Melville Jocelyn, the diplomate; and the Count and Countess de Saldar, refugees out of that explosive little kingdom.

IV

On Board the Jocasta

From the Tagus to the Thames the Government sloop-of-war, Jocasta, had made a prosperous voyage, bearing that precious freight, a removed diplomatist and his family; for whose uses let a sufficient vindication be found in the exercise he affords our crews in the science of seamanship. She entered our noble river somewhat early on a fine July morning. Early as it was, two young people, who had nothing to do with the trimming or guiding of the vessel, stood on deck, and watched the double-shore, beginning to embrace them more and more closely as they sailed onward. One, a young lady, very young in manner, wore a black felt hat with a floating scarlet feather, and was clad about the shoulders in a mantle of foreign style and pattern. The other you might have taken for a wandering Don, were such an object ever known; so simply he assumed the dusky sombrero and dangling cloak, of which one fold was flung across his breast and drooped behind him. The line of an adolescent dark moustache ran along his lip, and only at intervals could you see that his eyes were blue and of the land he was nearing. For the youth was meditative, and held his head much down. The young lady, on the contrary, permitted an open inspection of her countenance, and seemed, for the moment at least, to be neither caring nor thinking of what kind of judgement would be passed on her. Her pretty nose was up, sniffing the still salt breeze with vivacious delight.

"Oh!" she cried, clapping her hands, "there goes a dear old English gull! How I have wished to see him! I haven't seen one for two years and seven months. When I'm at home, I'll leave my window open all night, just to hear the rooks, when they wake in the morning. There goes another!"

She tossed up her nose again, exclaiming:

"I'm sure I smell England nearer and nearer! I smell the fields, and the cows in them. I'd have given anything to be a dairy-maid for half an hour! I used to lie and pant in that stifling air among those stupid people, and wonder why anybody ever left England. Aren't you glad to come back?"

This time the fair speaker lent her eyes to the question, and shut her lips; sweet, cold, chaste lips she had: a mouth that had not yet dreamed of kisses, and most honest eyes.

The young man felt that they were not to be satisfied by his own, and after seeking to fill them with a doleful look, which was immediately succeeded by one of superhuman indifference, he answered:

"Yes! We shall soon have to part!" and commenced tapping with his foot the cheerful martyr's march.

Speech that has to be hauled from the depths usually betrays the effort. Listening an instant to catch the import of this cavernous gasp upon the brink of sound, the girl said:

"Part? what do you mean?"

Apparently it required a yet vaster effort to pronounce an explanation. The doleful look, the superhuman indifference, were repeated in due order: sound, a little more distinct, uttered the words:

"We cannot be as we have been, in England!" and then the cheerful martyr took a few steps farther.

"Why, you don't mean to say you're going to give me up, and not be friends with me, because we've come back to England?" cried the girl in a rapid breath, eyeing him seriously.

Most conscientiously he did not mean it! but he replied with the quietest negative.

"No?" she mimicked him. "Why do you say 'No' like that? Why are you so mysterious, Evan? Won't you promise me to come and stop with us for weeks? Haven't you said we would ride, and hunt, and fish together, and read books, and do all sorts of things?"

He replied with the quietest affirmative.

"Yes? What does 'Yes!' mean?" She lifted her chest to shake out the dead-alive monosyllable, as he had done. "Why are you so singular this morning, Evan? Have I offended you? You are so touchy!"

The slur on his reputation for sensitiveness induced the young man to attempt being more explicit.

"I mean," he said, hesitating; "why, we must part. We shall not see each other every day. Nothing more than that." And away went the cheerful martyr in sublimest mood.

"Oh! and that makes you, sorry?" A shade of archness was in her voice.

The girl waited as if to collect something in her mind, and was now a patronizing woman.

"Why, you dear sentimental boy! You don't suppose we could see each other every day for ever?"

It was perhaps the cruelest question that could have been addressed to the sentimental boy from her mouth. But he was a cheerful martyr!

"You dear Don Doloroso!" she resumed. "I declare if you are not just like those young Portugals this morning; and over there you were such a dear English fellow; and that's why I liked you so much! Do change! Do, please, be lively, and yourself again. Or mind; I'll call you Don Doloroso, and that shall be your name in England. See there!—that's—that's? what's the name of that place? Hoy! Mr. Skerne!" She hailed the boatswain, passing, "Do tell me the name of that place."

Mr. Skerne righted about to satisfy her minutely, and then coming up to Evan, he touched his hat, and said:

"I mayn't have another opportunity—we shall be busy up there—of thankin' you again, sir, for what you did for my poor drunken brother Bill, and you may take my word I won't forget it, sir, if he does; and I suppose he'll be drowning his memory just as he was near drowning himself."

Evan muttered something, grimaced civilly, and turned away. The girl's observant brows were moved to a faintly critical frown, and nodding intelligently to the boatswain's remark, that the young gentleman did not seem quite himself, now that he was nearing home, she went up to Evan, and said:

"I'm going to give you a lesson in manners, to be quits with you. Listen, sir. Why did you turn away so ungraciously from Mr. Skerne, while he was thanking you for having saved his brother's life? Now there's where you're too English. Can't you bear to be thanked?"

"I don't want to be thanked because I can swim," said Evan.

"But it is not that. Oh, how you trifle!" she cried. "There's nothing vexes me so much as that way you have. Wouldn't my eyes have sparkled if anybody had come up to me to thank me for such a thing? I would let them know how glad I was to have done such a thing! Doesn't it make them happier, dear Evan?"

"My dear Miss Jocelyn!"

"What?"

The honest grey eyes fixed on him, narrowed their enlarged lids. She gazed before her on the deck, saying:

"I'm sure I can't understand you. I suppose it's because I'm a girl, and I never shall till I'm a woman. Heigho!"

A youth who is engaged in the occupation of eating his heart, cannot shine to advantage, and is as much a burden to himself as he is an enigma to others. Evan felt this; but he could do nothing and say nothing; so he retired deeper into the folds of the Don, and remained picturesque and scarcely pleasant.

They were relieved by a summons to breakfast from below.

She brightened and laughed. "Now, what will you wager me, Evan, that the Countess doesn't begin:

'Sweet child! how does she this morning? blooming?' when she kisses me?"

Her capital imitation of his sister's manner constrained him to join in her laugh, and he said:

"I'll back against that, I get three fingers from your uncle, and 'Morrow, young sir!'"

Down they ran together, laughing; and, sure enough, the identical words of the respective greetings were employed, which they had to enjoy with all the discretion they could muster.

Rose went round the table to her little cousin Alec, aged seven, kissed his reluctant cheek, and sat beside him, announcing a sea appetite and great capabilities, while Evan silently broke bread. The Count de Saldar, a diminutive tawny man, just a head and neck above the tablecloth, sat sipping chocolate and fingering dry toast, which he would now and then dip in jelly, and suck with placidity, in the intervals of a curt exchange of French with the wife of the Hon. Melville, a ringleted English lady, or of Portuguese with the Countess; who likewise sipped chocolate and fingered dry toast, and was mournfully melodious. The Hon. Melville, as became a tall islander, carved beef, and ate of it, like a ruler of men. Beautiful to see was the compassionate sympathy of the Countess's face when Rose offered her plate for a portion of the world-subjugating viand, as who should say: "Sweet child! thou knowest not yet of sorrows, thou canst ballast thy stomach with beef!" In any other than an heiress, she would probably have thought: "This is indeed a disgusting little animal, and most unfeminine conduct!"

Rose, unconscious of praise or blame, rivalled her uncle in enjoyment of the fare, and talked of her delight in seeing England again, and anything that belonged to her native land. Mrs. Melville perceived that it pained the refugee Countess, and gave her the glance intelligible; but the Countess never missed glances, or failed to interpret them. She said:

"Let her. I love to hear the sweet child's prattle."

"It was fortunate" (she addressed the diplomatist) "that we touched at Southampton and procured fresh provision!"

"Very lucky for Us!" said he, glaring shrewdly between a mouthful.

The Count heard the word "Southampton," and wished to know how it was comprised. A passage of Portuguese ensued, and then the Countess said:

"Silva, you know, desired to relinquish the vessel at Southampton. He does not comprehend the word 'expense,' but" (she shook a dumb Alas!) "I must think of that for him now!"

"Oh! always avoid expense," said the Hon. Melville, accustomed to be paid for by his country.

"At what time shall we arrive, may I ask, do you think?" the Countess gently inquired.

The watch of a man who had his eye on Time was pulled out, and she was told it might be two hours before dark. Another reckoning, keenly balanced, informed the company that the day's papers could be expected on board somewhere about three o'clock in the afternoon.

"And then," said the Hon. Melville, nodding general gratulation, "we shall know how the world wags."

How it had been wagging the Countess's straining eyes under closed eyelids were eloquent of.

"Too late, I fear me, to wait upon Lord Livelyston to-night?" she suggested.

"To-night?" The Hon. Melville gazed blank astonishment at the notion. "Oh! certainly, too late tonight. A-hum! I think, madam, you had better not be in too great a hurry to see him. Repose a little. Recover your fatigue."

"Oh!" exclaimed the Countess, with a beam of utter confidence in him, "I shall be too happy to place myself in your hands—believe me."

This was scarcely more to the taste of the diplomatist. He put up his mouth, and said, blandly:

"I fear—you know, madam, I must warn you beforehand—I, personally, am but an insignificant unit over here, you know; I, personally, can't guarantee much assistance to you—not positive. What I can do—of course, very happy!" And he fell to again upon the beef.

"Not so very insignificant!" said the Countess, smiling, as at a softly radiant conception of him.

"Have to bob and bow like the rest of them over here," he added, proof against the flattery.

"But that you will not forsake Silva, I am convinced," said the Countess; and, paying little heed to his brief "Oh! what I can do," continued: "For over here, in England, we are almost friendless. My relations—such as are left of them—are not in high place." She turned to Mrs. Melville, and renewed the confession with a proud humility. "Truly, I have not a distant cousin in the Cabinet!"

Mrs. Melville met her sad smile, and returned it, as one who understood its entire import.

"My brother-in-law-my sister, I think, you know—married a—a brewer! He is rich; but, well! such was her taste! My brother-in-law is indeed in Parliament, and he—"

"Very little use, seeing he votes with the opposite party," the diplomatist interrupted her.

"Ah! but he will not," said the Countess, serenely. "I can trust with confidence that, if it is for Silva's interest, he will assuredly so dispose of his influence as to suit the desiderations of his family, and not in any way oppose his opinions to the powers that would willingly stoop to serve us!"

It was impossible for the Hon. Melville to withhold a slight grimace at his beef, when he heard this extremely alienized idea of the nature of a member of the Parliament of Great Britain. He allowed her to enjoy her delusion, as she pursued:

"No. So much we could offer in repayment. It is little! But this, in verity, is a case. Silva's wrongs have only to be known in England, and I am most assured that the English people will not permit it. In the days of his prosperity, Silva was a friend to England, and England should not—should not—forget it now. Had we money! But of that arm our enemies have deprived us: and, I fear, without it we cannot hope to have the justice of our cause pleaded in the English papers. Mr. Redner, you know, the correspondent in Lisbon, is a sworn foe to Silva. And why but because I would not procure him an invitation to Court! The man was so horridly vulgar; his gloves were never clean; I had to hold a bouquet to my nose when I talked to him. That, you say, was my fault! Truly so. But what woman can be civil to a low-bred, pretentious, offensive man?"

Mrs. Melville, again appealed to, smiled perfect sympathy, and said, to account for his character:

"Yes. He is the son of a small shopkeeper of some kind, in Southampton, I hear."

"A very good fellow in his way," said her husband.

"Oh! I can't bear that class of people," Rose exclaimed. "I always keep out of their way. You can always tell them."

The Countess smiled considerate approbation of her exclusiveness and discernment. So sweet a smile!

"You were on deck early, my dear?" she asked Evan, rather abruptly.

Master Alec answered for him: "Yes, he was, and so was Rose. They made an appointment, just as they used to do under the oranges."

"Children!" the Countess smiled to Mrs. Melville.

"They always whisper when I'm by," Alec appended.

"Children!" the Countess's sweetened visage entreated Mrs. Melville to re-echo; but that lady thought it best for the moment to direct Rose to look to her packing, now that she had done breakfast.

"And I will take a walk with my brother on deck," said the Countess. "Silva is too harassed for converse."

The parties were thus divided. The silent Count was left to meditate on his wrongs in the saloon; and the diplomatist, alone with his lady, thought fit to say to her, shortly: "Perhaps it would be as well to draw away from these people a little. We've done as much as we could for them, in bringing them over here. They may be trying to compromise us. That woman's absurd. She's ashamed of the brewer, and yet she wants to sell him—or wants us to buy him. Ha! I think she wants us to send a couple of frigates, and threaten bombardment of the capital, if they don't take her husband back, and receive him with honours."

"Perhaps it would be as well," said Mrs. Melville. "Rose's invitation to him goes for nothing."

"Rose? inviting the Count? down to Hampshire?" The diplomatist's brows were lifted.

"No, I mean the other," said the diplomatist's wife.

"Oh! the young fellow! very good young fellow. Gentlemanly. No harm in him."

"Perhaps not," said the diplomatist's wife.

"You don't suppose he expects us to keep him on, or provide for him over here—eh?"

The diplomatist's wife informed him that such was not her thought, that he did not understand, and that it did not matter; and as soon as the Hon. Melville saw that she was brooding something essentially feminine, and which had no relationship to the great game of public life, curiosity was extinguished in him.

On deck the Countess paced with Evan, and was for a time pleasantly diverted by the admiration she could, without looking, perceive that her sorrow-subdued graces had aroused in the breast of a susceptible naval lieutenant. At last she spoke:

"My dear! remember this. Your last word to Mr. Jocelyn will be: 'I will do myself the honour to call upon my benefactor early.' To Rose you will say: 'Be assured, Miss Jocelyn "Miss Jocelyn—" I shall not fail in hastening to pay my respects to your family in Hampshire.' You will remember to do it, in the exact form I speak it."

Evan laughed: "What! call him benefactor to his face? I couldn't do it."

"Ah! my child!"

"Besides, he isn't a benefactor at all. His private secretary died, and I stepped in to fill the post, because nobody else was handy."

"And tell me of her who pushed you forward, Evan?"

"My dear sister, I'm sure I'm not ungrateful."

"No; but headstrong: opinionated. Now these people will endeavour—Oh! I have seen it in a thousand little things—they wish to shake us off. Now, if you will but do as I indicate! Put your faith in an older head, Evan. It is your only chance of society in England. For your brother-in-law—I ask you, what sort of people will you meet at the Cogglesbys? Now and then a nobleman, very much out of his element. In short, you have fed upon a diet which will make you to distinguish, and painfully to know the difference! Indeed! Yes, you are looking about for Rose. It depends upon your behaviour now, whether you are to see her at all in England. Do you forget? You wished once to inform her of your origin. Think of her words at the breakfast this morning!"

The Countess imagined she had produced an impression. Evan said: "Yes, and I should have liked to have told her this morning that I'm myself nothing more than the son of a—"

"Stop!" cried his sister, glancing about in horror. The admiring lieutenant met her eye. Blandishingly she smiled on him: "Most beautiful weather for a welcome to dear England?" and passed with majesty.

"Boy!" she resumed, "are you mad?"

"I hate being such a hypocrite, madam."

"Then you do not love her, Evan?"

This may have been dubious logic, but it resulted from a clear sequence of ideas in the lady's head. Evan did not contest it.

"And assuredly you will lose her, Evan. Think of my troubles! I have to intrigue for Silva; I look to your future; I smile, Oh heaven! how do I not smile when things are spoken that pierce my heart! This morning at the breakfast!"

Evan took her hand, and patted it.

"What is your pity?" she sighed.

"If it had not been for you, my dear sister, I should never have held my tongue."

"You are not a Harrington! You are a Dawley!" she exclaimed, indignantly.

Evan received the accusation of possessing more of his mother's spirit than his father's in silence.

"You would not have held your tongue," she said, with fervid severity: "and you would have betrayed yourself! and you would have said you were that! and you in that costume! Why, goodness gracious! could you bear to appear so ridiculous?"

The poor young man involuntarily surveyed his person. The pains of an impostor seized him. The deplorable image of the Don making confession became present to his mind. It was a clever stroke of this female intriguer. She saw him redden grievously, and blink his eyes; and not wishing to probe him so that he would feel intolerable disgust at his imprisonment in the Don, she continued:

"But you have the sense to see your duties, Evan. You have an excellent sense, in the main. No one would dream—to see you. You did not, I must say, you did not make enough of your gallantry. A Portuguese who had saved a man's life, Evan, would he have been so boorish? You behaved as if it was a matter of course that you should go overboard after anybody, in your clothes, on a dark night. So, then, the Jocelyns took it. I barely heard one compliment to you. And Rose—what an effect it should have had on her! But, owing to your manner, I do believe the girl thinks it nothing but your ordinary business to go overboard after anybody, in your clothes, on a dark night. 'Pon my honour, I believe she expects to see you always dripping!" The Countess uttered a burst of hysterical humour. "So you miss your credit. That inebriated sailor should really have been gold to you. Be not so young and thoughtless."

The Countess then proceeded to tell him how foolishly he had let slip his great opportunity. A Portuguese would have fixed the young lady long before. By tender moonlight, in captivating language, beneath the umbrageous orange-groves, a Portuguese would have accurately calculated the effect of the perfume of the blossom on her sensitive nostrils, and know the exact moment when to kneel, and declare his passion sonorously.

"Yes," said Evan, "one of them did. She told me."

"She told you? And you—what did you do?"

"Laughed at him with her, to be sure."

"Laughed at him! She told you, and you helped her to laugh at love! Have you no perceptions? Why did she tell you?"

"Because she thought him such a fool, I suppose."

"You never will know a woman," said the Countess, with contempt.

Much of his worldly sister at a time was more than Evan could bear. Accustomed to the symptoms of restiveness, she finished her discourse, enjoyed a quiet parade up and down under the gaze of the lieutenant, and could find leisure to note whether she at all struck the inferior seamen, even while her mind was absorbed by the multiform troubles and anxieties for which she took such innocent indemnification.

The appearance of the Hon. Melville Jocelyn on deck, and without his wife, recalled her to business. It is a peculiarity of female diplomatists that they fear none save their own sex. Men they regard as their natural prey: in women they see rival hunters using their own weapons. The Countess smiled a slowly-kindling smile up to him, set her brother adrift, and delicately linked herself to Evan's benefactor.

"I have been thinking," she said, "knowing your kind and most considerate attentions, that we may compromise you in England."

He at once assured her he hoped not, he thought not at all.

"The idea is due to my brother," she went on; "for I—women know so little!—and most guiltlessly should we have done so. My brother perhaps does not think of us foremost; but his argument I can distinguish. I can see, that were you openly to plead Silva's cause, you might bring yourself into odium, Mr. Jocelyn; and heaven knows I would not that! May I then ask, that in England we may be simply upon the same footing of private friendship?"

The diplomatist looked into her uplifted visage, that had all the sugary sparkles of a crystallized preserved fruit of the Portugal clime, and observed, confidentially, that, with every willingness in the world to serve her, he did think it would possibly be better, for a time, to be upon that footing, apart from political considerations.

"I was very sure my brother would apprehend your views," said the Countess. "He, poor boy! his career is closed. He must sink into a different sphere. He will greatly miss the intercourse with you and your sweet family."

Further relieved, the diplomatist delivered a high opinion of the young gentleman, his abilities, and his conduct, and trusted he should see him frequently.

By an apparent sacrifice, the lady thus obtained what she wanted.

Near the hour speculated on by the diplomatist, the papers came on board, and he, unaware how he had been manoeuvred for lack of a wife at his elbow, was quickly engaged in appeasing the great British hunger for news; second only to that for beef, it seems, and equally acceptable salted when it cannot be had fresh.

Leaving the devotee of statecraft with his legs crossed, and his face wearing the cognizant air of one whose head is above the waters of events, to enjoy the mighty meal of fresh and salted at discretion, the Countess dived below.

Meantime the Jocasta, as smoothly as before she was ignorant of how the world wagged, slipped up the river with the tide; and the sun hung red behind the forest of masts, burnishing a broad length of the serpentine haven of the nations of the earth. A young Englishman returning home can hardly look on this scene without some pride of kinship. Evan stood at the fore part of the vessel. Rose, in quiet English attire, had escaped from her aunt to join him, singing in his ears, to spur his senses: "Isn't it beautiful? Isn't it beautiful? Dear old England!"

"What do you find so beautiful?" he asked.

"Oh, you dull fellow! Why the ships, and the houses, and the smoke, to be sure."

"The ships? Why, I thought you despised trade, mademoiselle?"

"And so I do. That is, not trade, but tradesmen. Of course, I mean shopkeepers."

"It's they who send the ships to and fro, and make the picture that pleases you, nevertheless."

"Do they?" said she, indifferently, and then with a sort of fervour, "Why do you always grow so cold to me whenever we get on this subject?"

"I cold?" Evan responded. The incessant fears of his diplomatic sister had succeeded in making him painfully jealous of this subject. He turned it off. "Why, our feelings are just the same. Do you know what I was thinking when you came up? I was thinking that I hoped I might never disgrace the name of an Englishman."

"Now, that's noble!" cried the girl. "And I'm sure you never will. Of an English gentleman, Evan. I like that better."

"Would your rather be called a true English lady than a true English woman, Rose?"

"Don't think I would, my dear," she answered, pertly; "but 'gentleman' always means more than 'man' to me."

"And what's a gentleman, mademoiselle?"

"Can't tell you, Don Doloroso. Something you are, sir," she added, surveying him.

Evan sucked the bitter and the sweet of her explanation. His sister in her anxiety to put him on his guard, had not beguiled him to forget his real state.

His sister, the diplomatist and his lady, the refugee Count, with ladies' maids, servants, and luggage, were now on the main-deck, and Master Alec, who was as good as a newspaper correspondent for private conversations, put an end to the colloquy of the young people. They were all assembled in a circle when the vessel came to her moorings. The diplomatist glutted with news, and thirsting for confirmations; the Count dumb, courteous, and quick-eyed; the honourable lady complacent in the consciousness of boxes well packed; the Countess breathing mellifluous long-drawn adieux that should provoke invitations. Evan and Rose regarded each other.

The boat to convey them on shore was being lowered, and they were preparing to move forward. Just then the vessel was boarded by a stranger.

"Is that one of the creatures of your Customs? I did imagine we were safe from them," exclaimed the Countess.

The diplomatist laughingly requested her to save herself anxiety on that score, while under his wing. But she had drawn attention to the intruder, who was seen addressing one of the midshipmen. He was a man in a long brown coat and loose white neckcloth, spectacles on nose, which he wore considerably below the bridge and peered over, as if their main use were to sight his eye; a beaver hat, with broadish brim, on his head. A man of no station, it was evident to the ladies at once, and they would have taken no further notice of him had he not been seen stepping toward them in the rear of the young midshipman.

The latter came to Evan, and said: "A fellow of the name of Goren wants you. Says there's something the matter at home."

Evan advanced, and bowed stiffly.

Mr. Goren held out his hand. "You don't remember me, young man?

I cut out your first suit for you when you were breeched, though! Yes-ah! Your poor father wouldn't put his hand to it. Goren!"

Embarrassed, and not quite alive to the chapter of facts this name should have opened to him, Evan bowed again.

"Goren!" continued the possessor of the name. He had a cracked voice, that when he spoke a word of two syllables, commenced with a lugubrious crow, and ended in what one might have taken for a curious question.

"It is a bad business brings me, young man. I'm not the best messenger for such tidings. It's a black suit, young man! It's your father!"

The diplomatist and his lady gradually edged back but Rose remained beside the Countess, who breathed quick, and seemed to have lost her self-command.

Thinking he was apprehended, Mr. Goren said: "I'm going down to-night to take care of the shop. He's to be buried in his old uniform. You had better come with me by the night-coach, if you would see the last of him, young man."

Breaking an odd pause that had fallen, the Countess cried aloud, suddenly:

"In his uniform!"

Mr. Goren felt his arm seized and his legs hurrying him some paces into isolation. "Thanks! thanks!" was murmured in his ear. "Not a word more. Evan cannot bear it. Oh! you are good to have come, and we are grateful. My father! my father!"

She had to tighten her hand and wrist against her bosom to keep herself up. She had to reckon in a glance how much Rose had heard, or divined. She had to mark whether the Count had understood a syllable. She had to whisper to Evan to hasten away with the horrible man.

She had to enliven his stunned senses, and calm her own. And with mournful images of her father in her brain, the female Spartan had to turn to Rose, and speculate on the girl's reflective brows, while she said, as over a distant relative, sadly, but without distraction: "A death in the family!" and preserved herself from weeping her heart out, that none might guess the thing who did not positively know it. Evan touched the hand of Rose without meeting her eyes. He was soon cast off in Mr. Goren's boat. Then the Countess murmured final adieux; twilight under her lids, but yet a smile, stately, affectionate, almost genial. Rose, her sweet Rose, she must kiss. She could have slapped Rose for appearing so reserved and cold. She hugged Rose, as to hug oblivion of the last few minutes into her. The girl leant her cheek, and bore the embrace, looking on her with a kind of wonder.

Only when alone with the Count, in the brewer's carriage awaiting her on shore, did the lady give a natural course to her grief; well knowing that her Silva would attribute it to the darkness of their common exile. She wept: but in the excess of her misery, two words of strangely opposite signification, pronounced by Mr. Goren; two words that were at once poison and antidote, sang in her brain; two words that painted her dead father from head to foot, his nature and his fortune: these were the Shop, and the Uniform.

Oh! what would she not have given to have-seen and bestowed on her beloved father one last kiss! Oh! how she hoped that her inspired echo of Uniform, on board the Jocasta, had drowned the memory, eclipsed the meaning, of that fatal utterance of Shop!

V

The Family and the Funeral

It was the evening of the second day since the arrival of the black letter in London from Lymport, and the wife of the brewer and the wife of the Major sat dropping tears into one another's laps, in expectation of their sister the Countess. Mr. Andrew Cogglesby had not yet returned from his office. The gallant Major had gone forth to dine with General Sir George Frebuter, the head of the Marines of his time. It would have been difficult for the Major, he informed his wife, to send in an excuse to the General for non-attendance, without entering into particulars; and that he should tell the General he could not dine with him, because of the sudden decease of a tailor, was, as he let his wife understand, and requested her to perceive, quite out of the question. So he dressed himself carefully, and though peremptory with his wife concerning his linen, and requiring natural services from her in the button department, and a casual expression of contentment as to his ultimate make-up, he left her that day without any final injunctions to occupy her mind, and she was at liberty to weep if she pleased, a privilege she did not enjoy undisturbed when he was present; for the warrior hated that weakness, and did not care to hide his contempt for it.

Of the three sisters, the wife of the Major was, oddly enough, the one who was least inveterately solicitous of concealing the fact of her parentage. Reticence, of course, she had to study with the rest; the Major was a walking book of reticence and the observances; he professed, also, in company with herself alone, to have had much trouble in drilling her to mark and properly preserve them. She had no desire to speak of her birthplace. But, for some reason or other, she did not share her hero's rather petulant anxiety to keep the curtain nailed down on that part of her life which preceded her entry into the ranks of the Royal Marines. Some might have thought that those fair large blue eyes of hers wandered now and then in pleasant unambitious walks behind the curtain, and toyed with little flowers of palest memory. Utterly tasteless, totally wanting in discernment, not to say gratitude, the Major could not presume her to be; and yet his wits perceived that her answers and the conduct she shaped in accordance with his repeated protests and long-reaching apprehensions of what he called danger, betrayed acquiescent obedience more than the connubial sympathy due to him. Danger on the field the Major knew not of; he did not scruple to name the word in relation to his wife. For, as he told her, should he, some day, as in the chapter of accidents might occur, sally into the street a Knight Companion of the Bath and become known to men as Sir Maxwell Strike, it would be decidedly disagreeable for him to be blown upon by a wind from Lymport. Moreover she was the mother of a son. The Major pointed out to her the duty she owed her offspring. Certainly the protecting aegis of his rank and title would be over the lad, but she might depend upon it any indiscretion of hers would damage him in his future career, the Major assured her. Young Maxwell must be considered.

For all this, the mother and wife, when the black letter found them in the morning at breakfast, had burst into a fit of grief, and faltered that she wept for a father. Mrs. Andrew, to whom the letter was addressed, had simply held the letter to her in a trembling hand. The Major compared their behaviour, with marked encomiums of Mrs. Andrew. Now this lady and her husband were in obverse relative positions. The brewer had no will but his Harriet's. His esteem for her combined the constitutional feelings of an insignificantly-built little man for a majestic woman, and those of a worthy soul for the wife of his bosom. Possessing, or possessed by her, the good brewer was perfectly happy. She, it might be thought, under these circumstances, would not have minded much his hearing what he might hear. It happened, however, that she was as jealous of the winds of Lymport as the Major himself; as vigilant in debarring them from access to the brewery as now the Countess could have been. We are not dissecting human nature suffice it, therefore, from a mere glance at the surface, to say, that just as moneyed men are careful of their coin, women who have all the advantages in a conjunction, are miserly in keeping them, and shudder to think that one thing remains hidden, which the world they move in might put down pityingly in favour of their spouse, even though to the little man 'twere naught. She assumed that a revelation would diminish her moral stature; and certainly it would not increase that of her husband. So no good could come of it. Besides, Andrew knew, his whole conduct was a tacit admission, that she had condescended in giving him her hand. The features of their union might not be changed altogether by a revelation, but it would be a shock to her.

Consequently, Harriet tenderly rebuked Caroline, for her outcry at the breakfast-table; and Caroline, the elder sister, who had not since marriage grown in so free an air, excused herself humbly, and the two were weeping when the Countess joined them and related what she had just undergone.

Hearing of Caroline's misdemeanour, however, Louisa's eyes rolled aloft in a paroxysm of tribulation. It was nothing to Caroline; it was comparatively nothing to Harriet; but the Count knew not Louisa had a father: believed that her parents had long ago been wiped out. And the Count was by nature inquisitive: and if he once cherished a suspicion he was restless; he was pointed in his inquiries: he was pertinacious in following out a clue: there never would be peace with him! And then, as they were secure in their privacy, Louisa cried aloud for her father, her beloved father! Harriet wept silently. Caroline alone expressed regret that she had not set eyes on him from the day she became a wife.

"How could we, dear?" the Countess pathetically asked, under drowning lids.

"Papa did not wish it," sobbed Mrs. Andrew.

"I never shall forgive myself!" said the wife of the Major, drying her cheeks. Perhaps it was not herself whom she felt she never could forgive.

Ah! the man their father was! Incomparable Melchisedec! he might well be called. So generous! so lordly! When the rain of tears would subside for a moment, one would relate an anecdote or childish reminiscence of him, and provoke a more violent outburst.

"Never, among the nobles of any land, never have I seen one like him!" exclaimed the Countess, and immediately requested Harriet to tell her how it would be possible to stop Andrew's tongue in Silva's presence.

"At present, you know, my dear, they may talk as much as they like—they can't understand one another one bit."

Mrs. Cogglesby comforted her by the assurance that Andrew had received an intimation of her wish for silence everywhere and toward everybody; and that he might be reckoned upon to respect it, without demanding a reason for the restriction. In other days Caroline and Louisa had a little looked down on Harriet's alliance with a dumpy man—a brewer—and had always kind Christian compassion for him if his name were mentioned. They seemed now, by their silence, to have a happier estimate of Andrew's qualities.

While the three sisters sat mingling their sorrows and alarms, their young brother was making his way to the house. As he knocked at the door he heard his name pronounced behind him, and had no difficulty in recognizing the worthy brewer.

"What, Van, my boy! how are you? Quite a foreigner! By George, what a hat!"

Mr. Andrew bounced back two or three steps to regard the dusky sombrero.

"How do you do, sir?" said Evan.

"Sir to you!" Mr. Andrew briskly replied. "Don't they teach you to give your fist in Portugal, eh? I'll 'sir' you. Wait till I'm Sir Andrew, and then 'sir' away. You do speak English still, Van, eh? Quite jolly, my boy?"

Mr. Andrew rubbed his hands to express that state in himself. Suddenly he stopped, blinked queerly at Evan, grew pensive, and said, "Bless my soul! I forgot."

The door opened, Mr. Andrew took Evan's arm, murmured a "hush!" and trod gently along the passage to his library.

"We're safe here," he said. "There—there's something the matter up-stairs. The women are upset about something. Harriet—" Mr. Andrew hesitated, and branched off: "You've heard we've got a new baby?"

Evan congratulated him; but another inquiry was in Mr. Andrew's aspect, and Evan's calm, sad manner answered it.

"Yes,"—Mr. Andrew shook his head dolefully—"a splendid little chap! a rare little chap! a we can't help these things, Van! They will happen. Sit down, my boy."

Mr. Andrew again interrogated Evan with his eyes.

"My father is dead," said Evan.

"Yes!" Mr. Andrew nodded, and glanced quickly at the ceiling, as if to make sure that none listened overhead. "My parliamentary duties will soon be over for the season," he added, aloud; pursuing, in an under-breath:

"Going down to-night, Van?"

"He is to be buried to-morrow," said Evan.

"Then, of course, you go. Yes: quite right. Love your father and mother! always love your father and mother! Old Tom and I never knew ours. Tom's quite well-same as ever. I'll," he rang the bell, "have my chop in here with you. You must try and eat a bit, Van. Here we are, and there we go. Old Tom's wandering for one of his weeks. You'll see him some day. He ain't like me. No dinner to-day, I suppose, Charles?"

This was addressed to the footman. He announced:

"Dinner to-day at half-past six, as usual, sir," bowed, and retired.

Mr. Andrew pored on the floor, and rubbed his hair back on his head. "An odd world!" was his remark.

Evan lifted up his face to sigh: "I'm almost sick of it!"

"Damn appearances!" cried Mr. Andrew, jumping on his legs.

The action cooled him.

"I'm sorry I swore," he said. "Bad habit! The Major's here—you know that?" and he assumed the Major's voice, and strutted in imitation of the stalwart marine. "Major—a—Strike! of the Royal Marines! returned from China! covered with glory!—a hero, Van! We can't expect him to be much of a mourner. And we shan't have him to dine with us today—that's something." He sank his voice: "I hope the widow'll bear it."

"I hope to God my mother is well!" Evan groaned.

"That'll do," said Mr. Andrew. "Don't say any more."

As he spoke, he clapped Evan kindly on the back.

A message was brought from the ladies, requiring Evan to wait on them. He returned after some minutes.

"How do you think Harriet's looking?" asked Mr. Andrew. And, not waiting for an answer, whispered,

"Are they going down to the funeral, my boy?"

Evan's brow was dark, as he replied: "They are not decided."

"Won't Harriet go?"

"She is not going—she thinks not."

"And the Countess—Louisa's upstairs, eh?—will she go?"

"She cannot leave the Count—she thinks not."

"Won't Caroline go? Caroline can go. She—he—I mean—Caroline can go?"

"The Major objects. She wishes to."

Mr. Andrew struck out his arm, and uttered, "the Major!"—a compromise for a loud anathema. But the compromise was vain, for he sinned again in an explosion against appearances.

"I'm a brewer, Van. Do you think I'm ashamed of it? Not while I brew good beer, my boy!—not while I brew good beer! They don't think worse of me in the House for it. It isn't ungentlemanly to brew good beer, Van. But what's the use of talking?"

Mr. Andrew sat down, and murmured, "Poor girl! poor girl!"

The allusion was to his wife; for presently he said: "I can't see why Harriet can't go. What's to prevent her?"

Evan gazed at him steadily. Death's levelling influence was in Evan's mind. He was ready to say why, and fully.

Mr. Andrew arrested him with a sharp "Never mind! Harriet does as she likes. I'm accustomed to—hem! what she does is best, after all. She doesn't interfere with my business, nor I with hers. Man and wife."

Pausing a moment or so, Mr. Andrew intimated that they had better be dressing for dinner. With his hand on the door, which he kept closed, he said, in a businesslike way, "You know, Van, as for me, I should be very willing—only too happy—to go down and pay all the respect I could." He became confused, and shot his head from side to side, looking anywhere but at Evan. "Happy now and to-morrow, to do anything in my power, if Harriet—follow the funeral—one of the family—anything I could do: but—a—we'd better be dressing for dinner." And out the enigmatic little man went.

Evan partly divined him then. But at dinner his behaviour was perplexing. He was too cheerful. He pledged the Count. He would have the Portuguese for this and that, and make Anglican efforts to repeat it, and laugh at his failures. He would not see that there was a father dead. At a table of actors, Mr. Andrew overdid his part, and was the worst. His wife could not help thinking him a heartless little man.

The poor show had its term. The ladies fled to the boudoir sacred to grief. Evan was whispered that he was to join them when he might, without seeming mysterious to the Count. Before he reached them, they had talked tearfully over the clothes he should wear at Lymport, agreeing that his present foreign apparel, being black, would be suitable, and would serve almost as disguise, to the inhabitants at large; and as Evan had no English wear, and there was no time to procure any for him, that was well. They arranged exactly how long he should stay at Lymport, whom he should visit, the manner he should adopt toward the different inhabitants. By all means he was to avoid the approach of the gentry. For hours Evan, in a trance, half stupefied, had to listen to the Countess's directions how he was to comport himself in Lymport.

"Show that you have descended among them, dear Van, but are not of them. Our beautiful noble English poet expresses it so. You have come to pay the last mortal duties, which they will respect, if they are not brutes, and attempt no familiarities. Allow none: gently, but firmly. Imitate Silva. You remember, at Dona Risbonda's ball? When he met the Comte de Dartigues, and knew he was to be in disgrace with his

Court on the morrow? Oh! the exquisite shade of difference in Silva's behaviour towards the Comte. So finely, delicately perceptible to the Comte, and not a soul saw it but that wretched Frenchman! He came to me: 'Madame,' he said, 'is a question permitted?' I replied, 'As-many as you please, M. le Comte, but no answers promised.' He said: 'May I ask if the Courier has yet come in?'—'Nay, M. le Comte,' I replied, 'this is diplomacy. Inquire of me, or better, give me an opinion on the new glace silk from Paris.'—'Madame,' said he, bowing, 'I hope Paris may send me aught so good, or that I shall grace half so well.' I smiled, 'You shall not be single in your hopes, M. le Comte. The gift would be base that you did not embellish.' He lifted his hands, French-fashion: 'Madame, it is that I have received the gift.'—'Indeed! M. le Comte.'—'Even now from the Count de Saldar, your husband.' I looked most innocently, 'From my husband, M. le Comte?'—'From him, Madame. A portrait. An Ambassador without his coat! The portrait was a finished performance.' I said: 'And may one beg the permission to inspect it?'—'Mais,' said he, laughing: 'were it you alone, it would be a privilege to me.' I had to check him. 'Believe me, M. le Comte, that when I look upon it, my praise of the artist will be extinguished by my pity for the subject.' He should have stopped there; but you cannot have the last word with a Frenchman—not even a woman. Fortunately the Queen just then made her entry into the saloon, and his mot on the charity of our sex was lost. We bowed mutually, and were separated." (The Countess employed her handkerchief.) "Yes, dear Van! that is how you should behave. Imply things. With dearest Mama, of course, you are the dutiful son. Alas! you must stand for son and daughters. Mama has so much sense! She will understand how sadly we are placed. But in a week I will come to her for a day, and bring you back."

So much his sister Louisa. His sister Harriet offered him her house for a home in London, thence to project his new career. His sister Caroline sought a word with him in private, but only to weep bitterly in his arms, and utter a faint moan of regret at marriages in general. He loved this beautiful creature the best of his three sisters (partly, it may be, because he despised her superior officer), and tried with a few smothered words to induce her to accompany him: but she only shook her fair locks and moaned afresh. Mr. Andrew, in the farewell squeeze of the hand at the street-door, asked him if he wanted anything. He negatived the requirement of anything whatever, with an air of careless decision, though he was aware that his purse barely contained more than would take him the distance, but the instincts of this amateur gentleman were very fine and sensitive on questions of money. His family had never known him beg for a shilling, or admit his necessity for a penny: nor could he be made to accept money unless it was thrust into his pocket. Somehow his sisters had forgotten this peculiarity of his. Harriet only remembered it when too late.

"But I dare say Andrew has supplied him," she said.

Andrew being interrogated, informed her what had passed between them.

"And you think a Harrington would confess he wanted money!" was her scornful exclamation. "Evan would walk—he would die rather. It was treating him like a mendicant."

Andrew had to shrink in his brewer's skin.

By some fatality all who were doomed to sit and listen to the Countess de Saldar, were sure to be behindhand in an appointment.

When the young man arrived at the coach-office, he was politely informed that the vehicle, in which a seat had been secured for him, was in close alliance with time and tide, and being under the same rigid laws, could not possibly have waited for him, albeit it had stretched a point to the extent of a pair of minutes, at the urgent solicitation of a passenger.

"A gentleman who speaks so, sir," said a volunteer mimic of the office, crowing and questioning from his throat in Goren's manner. "Yok! yok! That was how he spoke, sir."

Evan reddened, for it brought the scene on board the Jocasta vividly to his mind. The heavier business obliterated it. He took counsel with the clerks of the office, and eventually the volunteer mimic conducted him to certain livery stables, where Evan, like one accustomed to command, ordered a chariot to pursue the coach, received a touch of the hat for a lordly fee, and was soon rolling out of London.

VI

My Gentleman on the Road

The postillion had every reason to believe that he carried a real gentleman behind him; in other words, a purse long and liberal. He judged by all the points he knew of: a firm voice, a brief commanding style, an apparent indifference to expense, and the inexplicable minor characteristics, such as polished boots, and a striking wristband, and so forth, which will show a creature accustomed to step over the heads of men. He had, therefore, no particular anxiety to part company, and jogged easily on the white highway, beneath a moon that walked high and small over marble clouds.

Evan reclined in the chariot, revolving his sensations. In another mood he would have called, them thoughts, perhaps, and marvelled at their immensity. The theme was Love and Death. One might have supposed, from his occasional mutterings at the pace regulated by the postillion, that he was burning with anxiety to catch the flying coach. He had forgotten it: forgotten that he was giving chase to anything. A pair of wondering feminine eyes pursued him, and made him fret for the miles to throw a thicker veil between him and them. The serious level brows of Rose haunted the poor youth; and reflecting whither he was tending, and to what sight, he had shadowy touches of the holiness there is in death, from which came a conflict between the imaged phantoms of his father and of Rose, and he sided against his love with some bitterness. His sisters, weeping for their father and holding aloof from his ashes, Evan swept from his mind. He called up the man his father was: the kindliness, the readiness, the gallant gaiety of the great Mel. Youths are fascinated by the barbarian virtues; and to Evan, under present influences, his father was a pattern of manhood. He asked himself: Was it infamous to earn one's bread? and answered it very strongly in his father's favour. The great Mel's creditors were not by to show him another feature of the case.

Hitherto, in passive obedience to the indoctrination of the Countess, Evan had looked on tailors as the proscribed race of modern society. He had pitied his father as a man superior to his fate; but despite the fitfully honest promptings with Rose (tempting to him because of the wondrous chivalry they argued, and at bottom false probably as the hypocrisy they affected to combat), he had been by no means sorry that the world saw not the spot on himself. Other sensations beset him now. Since such a man was banned by the world, which was to be despised?

The clear result of Evan's solitary musing was to cast a sort of halo over Tailordom. Death stood over the pale dead man, his father, and dared the world to sneer at him. By a singular caprice of fancy, Evan had no sooner grasped this image, than it was suggested that he might as well inspect his purse, and see how much money he was master of.

Are you impatient with this young man? He has little character for the moment. Most youths are like Pope's women; they have no character at all. And indeed a character that does not wait for circumstances to shape it, is of small worth in the race that must be run. To be set too early, is to take the work out of the hands of the Sculptor who fashions men. Happily a youth is always at school, and if he was shut up and without mark two or three hours ago, he will have something to show you now: as I have seen blooming seaflowers and other graduated organisms, when left undisturbed to their own action. Where the Fates have designed that he shall present his figure in a story, this is sure to happen.

To the postillion Evan was indebted for one of his first lessons.

About an hour after midnight pastoral stillness and the moon begat in the postillion desire for a pipe. Daylight prohibits the dream of it to mounted postillions. At night the question is more human, and allows appeal. The moon smiles assentingly, and smokers know that she really lends herself to the enjoyment of tobacco.

The postillion could remember gentlemen who did not object: who had even given him cigars. Turning round to see if haply the present inmate of the chariot might be smoking, he observed a head extended from the window.

"How far are we?" was inquired.

The postillion numbered the milestones passed.

"Do you see anything of the coach?"

"Can't say as I do, sir."

He was commanded to stop. Evan jumped out.

"I don't think I'll take you any farther," he said.

The postillion laughed to scorn the notion of his caring how far he went. With a pipe in his mouth, he insinuatingly remarked, he could jog on all night, and throw sleep to the dogs. Fresh horses at Hillford;

fresh at Fallow field: and the gentleman himself would reach Lymport fresh in the morning.

"No, no; I won't take you any farther," Evan repeated.

"But what do it matter, sir?" urged the postillion.

"I'd rather go on as I am. I—a—made no arrangement to take you the whole way."

"Oh!" cried the postillion, "don't you go troublin' yourself about that, sir. Master knows it's touch-and-go about catchin' the coach. I'm all right."

So infatuated was the fellow in the belief that he was dealing with a perfect gentleman—an easy pocket!

Now you would not suppose that one who presumes he has sufficient, would find a difficulty in asking how much he has to pay. With an effort, indifferently masked, Evan blurted:

"By the way, tell me—how much—what is the charge for the distance we've come?"

There are gentlemen-screws: there are conscientious gentlemen. They calculate, and remonstrating or not, they pay. The postillion would rather have had to do with the gentleman royal, who is above base computation; but he knew the humanity in the class he served, and with his conception of Evan only partially dimmed, he remarked:

"Oh-h-h! that won't hurt you, sir. Jump along in,—settle that by-and-by."

But when my gentleman stood fast, and renewed the demand to know the exact charge for the distance already traversed, the postillion dismounted, glanced him over, and speculated with his fingers tipping up his hat. Meantime Evan drew out his purse, a long one, certainly, but limp. Out of this drowned-looking wretch the last spark of life was taken by the sum the postillion ventured to name; and if paying your utmost farthing without examination of the charge, and cheerfully stepping out to walk fifty miles, penniless, constituted a postillion's gentleman, Evan would have passed the test. The sight of poverty, however, provokes familiar feelings in poor men, if you have not had occasion to show them you possess particular qualities. The postillion's eye was more on the purse than on the sum it surrendered.

"There," said Evan, "I shall walk. Good night." And he flung his cloak to step forward.

"Stop a bit, sir!" arrested him.

The postillion rallied up sideways, with an assumption of genial respect. "I didn't calc'late myself in that there amount."

Were these words, think you, of a character to strike a young man hard on the breast, send the blood to his head, and set up in his heart a derisive chorus? My gentleman could pay his money, and keep his footing gallantly; but to be asked for a penny beyond what he possessed; to be seen beggared, and to be claimed a debtor-aleck! Pride was the one developed faculty of Evan's nature. The Fates who mould us, always work from the main-spring. I will not say that the postillion stripped off the mask for him, at that instant completely; but he gave him the first true glimpse of his condition. From the vague sense of being an impostor, Evan awoke to the clear fact that he was likewise a fool.

It was impossible for him to deny the man's claim, and he would not have done it, if he could. Acceding tacitly, he squeezed the ends of his purse in his pocket, and with a "Let me see," tried his waistcoat. Not too impetuously; for he was careful of betraying the horrid emptiness till he was certain that the powers who wait on gentlemen had utterly forsaken him. They had not. He discovered a small coin, under ordinary circumstances not contemptible; but he did not stay to reflect, and was guilty of the error of offering it to the postillion.

The latter peered at it in the centre of his palm; gazed queerly in the gentleman's face, and then lifting the spit of silver for the disdain of his mistress, the moon, he drew a long breath of regret at the original mistake he had committed, and said:

"That's what you're goin' to give me for my night's work?"

The powers who wait on gentlemen had only helped the pretending youth to try him. A rejection of the demand would have been infinitely wiser and better than this paltry compromise. The postillion would have fought it: he would not have despised his fare.

How much it cost the poor pretender to reply, "It's the last farthing I have, my man," the postillion could not know.

"A scabby sixpence?" The postillion continued his question.

"You heard what I said," Evan remarked.

The postillion drew another deep breath, and holding out the coin at arm's length:

"Well, sir!" he observed, as one whom mental conflict has brought to the philosophy of the case, "now, was we to change places, I couldn't a' done it! I couldn't a' done it!" he reiterated, pausing emphatically.

"Take it, sir!" he magnanimously resumed; "take it! You rides when you can, and you walks when you must. Lord forbid I should rob such a gentleman as you!"

One who feels a death, is for the hour lifted above the satire of postillions. A good genius prompted Evan to avoid the silly squabble that might have ensued and made him ridiculous. He took the money, quietly saying, "Thank you."

Not to lose his vantage, the postillion, though a little staggered by the move, rejoined: "Don't mention it."

Evan then said: "Good night, my man. I won't wish, for your sake, that we changed places. You would have to walk fifty miles to be in time for your father's funeral. Good night."

"You are it to look at!" was the postillion's comment, seeing my gentleman depart with great strides. He did not speak offensively; rather, it seemed, to appease his conscience for the original mistake he had committed, for subsequently came, "My oath on it, I don't get took in again by a squash hat in a hurry!"

Unaware of the ban he had, by a sixpenny stamp, put upon an unoffending class, Evan went ahead, hearing the wheels of the chariot still dragging the road in his rear. The postillion was in a dissatisfied state of mind. He had asked and received more than his due. But in the matter of his sweet self, he had been choused, as he termed it. And my gentleman had baffled him, he could not quite tell how; but he had been got the better of; his sarcasms had not stuck, and returned to rankle in the bosom of their author. As a Jew, therefore, may eye an erewhile bondsman who has paid the bill, but stands out against excess of interest on legal grounds, the postillion regarded Evan, of whom he was now abreast, eager for a controversy.

"Fine night," said the postillion, to begin, and was answered by a short assent. "Lateish for a poor man to be out—don't you think sir, eh?"

"I ought to think so," said Evan, mastering the shrewd unpleasantness he felt in the colloquy forced on him.

"Oh, you! you're a gentleman!" the postillion exclaimed.

"You see I have no money."

"Feel it, too, sir."

"I am sorry you should be the victim."

"Victim!" the postillion seized on an objectionable word. "I ain't no victim, unless you was up to a joke with me, sir, just now. Was that the game?"

Evan informed him that he never played jokes with money, or on men.

"Cause it looks like it, sir, to go to offer a poor chap sixpence." The postillion laughed hollow from the end of his lungs. "Sixpence for a night's work! It is a joke, if you don't mean it for one. Why, do you know, sir, I could go—there, I don't care where it is!—I could go before any magistrate livin', and he'd make ye pay. It's a charge, as custom is, and he'd make ye pay. Or p'rhaps you're a goin' on my generosity, and 'll say, he gev back that sixpence! Well! I shouldn't a' thought a gentleman'd make that his defence before a magistrate. But there, my man! if it makes ye happy, keep it. But you take my advice, sir. When you hires a chariot, see you've got the shiners. And don't you go never again offerin' a sixpence to a poor man for a night's work. They don't like it. It hurts their feelin's. Don't you forget that, sir. Lay that up in your mind."

Now the postillion having thus relieved himself, jeeringly asked permission to smoke a pipe. To which Evan said, "Pray, smoke, if it pleases you." And the postillion, hardly mollified, added, "The baccy's paid for," and smoked.

As will sometimes happen, the feelings of the man who had spoken out and behaved doubtfully, grew gentle and Christian, whereas those of the man whose bearing under the trial had been irreproachable were much the reverse. The postillion smoked—he was a lord on his horse; he beheld my gentleman trudging in the dust. Awhile he enjoyed the contrast, dividing his attention between the footfarer and moon. To have had the last word is always a great thing; and to have given my gentleman a lecture, because he shunned a dispute, also counts. And then there was the poor young fellow trudging to his father's funeral! The postillion chose to remember that now. In reality, he allowed, he had not very much to complain of, and my gentleman's courteous avoidance of provocation (the apparent fact that he, the postillion, had humbled him and got the better of him, equally, it may be), acted on his fine English spirit. I should not like to leave out the tobacco in this good change that was wrought in him. However, he presently astonished Evan by pulling up his horses, and crying that he was on his way to Hillford to bait, and saw no reason why he should not take a lift that part of the road, at all events. Evan thanked him briefly, but declined, and paced on with his head bent.

"It won't cost you nothing-not a sixpence!" the postillion sang out, pursuing him. "Come, sir! be a man! I ain't a hintin' at anything—jump in."

Evan again declined, and looked out for a side path to escape the fellow, whose bounty was worse to him than his abuse, and whose mention of the sixpence was unlucky.

"Dash it!" cried the postillion, "you're going down to a funeral—I think you said your father's, sir—you may as well try and get there respectable—as far as I go. It's one to me whether you're in or out; the horses won't feel it, and I do wish you'd take a lift and welcome. It's because you're too much of a gentleman to be beholden to a poor man, I suppose!"

Evan's young pride may have had a little of that base mixture in it, and certainly he would have preferred that the invitation had not been made to him; but he was capable of appreciating what the rejection of a piece of friendliness involved, and as he saw that the man was sincere, he did violence to himself, and said: "Very well; then I'll jump in."

The postillion was off his horse in a twinkling, and trotted his bandy legs to undo the door, as to a gentleman who paid. This act of service Evan valued.

"Suppose I were to ask you to take the sixpence now?" he said, turning round, with one foot on the step.

"Well, sir," the postillion sent his hat aside to answer. "I don't want it—I'd rather not have it; but there! I'll take it—dash the sixpence! and we'll cry quits."

Evan, surprised and pleased with him, dropped the bit of money in his hand, saying: "It will fill a pipe for you. While you're smoking it, think of me as in your debt. You're the only man I ever owed a penny to."

The postillion put it in a side pocket apart, and observed: "A sixpence kindly meant is worth any crown-piece that's grudged—that it is! In you jump, sir. It's a jolly night!"

Thus may one, not a conscious sage, play the right tune on this human nature of ours: by forbearance, put it in the wrong; and then, by not refusing the burden of an obligation, confer something better. The instrument is simpler than we are taught to fancy. But it was doubtless owing to a strong emotion in his soul, as well as to the stuff he was made of, that the youth behaved as he did. We are now and then above our own actions; seldom on a level with them. Evan, I dare say, was long in learning to draw any gratification from the fact that he had achieved without money the unparalleled conquest of a man. Perhaps he never knew what immediate influence on his fortune this episode effected.

At Hillford they went their different ways. The postillion wished him good speed, and Evan shook his hand. He did so rather abruptly, for the postillion was fumbling at his pocket, and evidently rounding about a proposal in his mind.

My gentleman has now the road to himself. Money is the clothing of a gentleman: he may wear it well or ill. Some, you will mark, carry great quantities of it gracefully: some, with a stinted supply, present a decent appearance: very few, I imagine, will bear inspection, who are absolutely stripped of it. All, save the shameless, are toiling to escape that trial. My gentleman, treading the white highway across the solitary heaths, that swell far and wide to the moon, is, by the postillion, who has seen him, pronounced no sham. Nor do I think the opinion of any man worthless, who has had the postillion's authority for speaking. But it is, I am told, a finer test to embellish much gentleman-apparel, than to walk with dignity totally unadorned. This simply tries the soundness of our faculties: that tempts them in erratic directions. It is the difference between active and passive excellence. As there is hardly any situation, however, so interesting to reflect upon as that of a man without a penny in his pocket, and a gizzard full of pride, we will leave Mr. Evan Harrington to what fresh adventures may befall him, walking toward the funeral plumes of the firs, under the soft midsummer flush, westward, where his father lies.

VII

Mother and Son

Rare as epic song is the man who is thorough in what he does. And happily so; for in life he subjugates us, and he makes us bondsmen to his ashes. It was in the order of things that the great Mel should be borne to his final resting-place by a troop of creditors. You have seen (since the occasion demands a pompous simile) clouds that all day cling about the sun, and, in seeking to obscure him, are compelled to blaze in his livery at fall of night they break from him illumined, hang mournfully above him, and wear his natural glories long after he is gone. Thus, then, these worthy fellows, faithful to him to the dust, fulfilled Mel's triumphant passage amongst them, and closed his career.

To regale them when they returned, Mrs. Mel, whose mind was not intent on greatness, was occupied in spreading meat and wine. Mrs. Fiske assisted her, as well as she could, seeing that one hand was entirely engaged by her handkerchief. She had already stumbled, and dropped a glass, which had brought on her sharp condemnation from her aunt, who bade her sit down, or go upstairs to have her cry out, and then return to be serviceable.

"Oh! I can't help it!" sobbed Mrs. Fiske. "That he should be carried away, and none of his children to see him the last time! I can understand Louisa—and Harriet, too, perhaps? But why could not Caroline? And that they should be too fine ladies to let their brother come and bury his father. Oh! it does seem—"

Mrs. Fiske fell into a chair, and surrendered to grief.

"Where is the cold tongue?" said Mrs. Mel to Sally, the maid, in a brief under-voice.

"Please mum, Jacko—!"

"He must be whipped. You are a careless slut."

"Please, I can't think of everybody and everything, and poor master—"

Sally plumped on a seat, and took sanctuary under her apron. Mrs. Mel glanced at the pair, continuing her labour.

"Oh, aunt, aunt!" cried Mrs. Fiske, "why didn't you put it off for another day, to give Evan a chance?"

"Master'd have kept another two days, he would!" whimpered Sally.

"Oh, aunt! to think!" cried Mrs. Fiske.

"And his coffin not bearin' of his spurs!" whimpered Sally.

Mrs. Mel interrupted them by commanding Sally to go to the drawing-room, and ask a lady there, of the name of Mrs. Wishaw, whether she would like to have some lunch sent up to her. Mrs. Fiske was requested to put towels in Evan's bedroom.

"Yes, aunt, if you're not infatuated!" said Mrs. Fiske, as she prepared to obey; while Sally, seeing that her public exhibition of sorrow and sympathy could be indulged but an instant longer, unwound herself for a violent paroxysm, blurting between stops:

"If he'd ony've gone to his last bed comfortable! . . . If he'd ony 've been that decent as not for to go to his last bed with his clothes on! . . . If he'd ony've had a comfortable sheet! . . . It makes a woman feel cold to think of him full dressed there, as if he was goin' to be a soldier on the Day o' Judgement!"

To let people speak was a maxim of Mrs. Mel's, and a wise one for any form of society when emotions are very much on the surface. She continued her arrangements quietly, and, having counted the number of plates and glasses, and told off the guests on her fingers, she, sat down to await them.

The first one who entered the room was her son.

"You have come," said Mrs. Mel, flushing slightly, but otherwise outwardly calm.

"You didn't suppose I should stay away from you, mother?"

Evan kissed her cheek.

"I knew you would not."

Mrs. Mel examined him with those eyes of hers that compassed objects in a single glance. She drew her finger on each side of her upper lip, and half smiled, saying:

"That won't do here."

"What?" asked Evan, and proceeded immediately to make inquiries about her health, which she satisfied with a nod.

"You saw him lowered, Van?"

"Yes, mother."

"Then go and wash yourself, for you are dirty, and then come and take your place at the head of the table."

"Must I sit here, mother?"

"Without a doubt—you must. You know your room. Quick!"

In this manner their first interview passed.

Mrs. Fiske rushed in to exclaim:

"So, you were right, aunt—he has come. I met him on the stairs. Oh! how like dear uncle Mel he looks, in the militia, with that moustache. I just remember him as a child; and, oh, what a gentleman he is!"

At the end of the sentence Mrs. Mel's face suddenly darkened: she said, in a deep voice:

"Don't dare to talk that nonsense before him, Ann."

Mrs. Fiske looked astonished.

"What have I done, aunt?"

"He shan't be ruined by a parcel of fools," said Mrs. Mel. "There, go! Women have no place here."

"How the wretches can force themselves to touch a morsel, after this morning!" Mrs. Fiske exclaimed, glancing at the table.

"Men must eat," said Mrs. Mel.

The mourners were heard gathering outside the door. Mrs. Fiske escaped into the kitchen. Mrs. Mel admitted them into the parlour, bowing much above the level of many of the heads that passed her.

Assembled were Messrs. Barnes, Kilne, and Grossby, whom we know; Mr. Doubleday, the ironmonger; Mr. Joyce, the grocer; Mr. Perkins, commonly called Lawyer Perkins; Mr. Welbeck, the pier-master of Lymport; Bartholomew Fiske; Mr. Coxwell, a Fallow field maltster, brewer, and farmer; creditors of various dimensions, all of them. Mr. Goren coming last, behind his spectacles.

"My son will be with you directly, to preside," said Mrs. Mel. "Accept my thanks for the respect you have shown my husband. I wish you good morning."

"Morning, ma'am," answered several voices, and Mrs. Mel retired.

The mourners then set to work to relieve their hats of the appendages of crape. An undertaker's man took possession of the long black cloaks. The gloves were generally pocketed.

"That's my second black pair this year," said Joyce.

"They'll last a time to come. I don't need to buy gloves while neighbours pop off."

"Undertakers' gloves seem to me as if they're made for mutton fists," remarked Welbeck; upon which Kilne nudged Barnes, the butcher, with a sharp "Aha!" and Barnes observed:

"Oh! I never wear 'em—they does for my boys on Sundays. I smoke a pipe at home."

The Fallow field farmer held his length of crape aloft and inquired: "What shall do with this?"

"Oh, you keep it," said one or two.

Coxwell rubbed his chin. "Don't like to rob the widder."

"What's left goes to the undertaker?" asked Grossby.

"To be sure," said Barnes; and Kilne added: "It's a job": Lawyer Perkins exclaiming confidently, "Perquisites of office, gentlemen; perquisites of office!" which settled the dispute and appeased every conscience.

A survey of the table ensued. The mourners felt hunger, or else thirst; but had not, it appeared, amalgamated the two appetites as yet. Thirst was the predominant declaration; and Grossby, after an examination of the decanters, unctuously deduced the fact, which he announced, that port and sherry were present.

"Try the port," said Kilne.

"Good?" Barnes inquired.

A very intelligent "I ought to know," with a reserve of regret at the extension of his intimacy with the particular vintage under that roof, was winked by Kilne.

Lawyer Perkins touched the arm of a mourner about to be experimental on Kilne's port—

"I think we had better wait till young Mr. Harrington takes the table, don't you see?"

"Yes,-ah!" croaked Goren. "The head of the family, as the saying goes!"

"I suppose we shan't go into business to-day?" Joyce carelessly observed.

Lawyer Perkins answered:

"No. You can't expect it. Mr. Harrington has led me to anticipate that he will appoint a day. Don't you see?"

"Oh! I see," returned Joyce. "I ain't in such a hurry. What's he doing?"

Doubleday, whose propensities were waggish, suggested "shaving," but half ashamed of it, since the joke missed, fell to as if he were soaping his face, and had some trouble to contract his jaw.

The delay in Evan's attendance on the guests of the house was caused by the fact that Mrs. Mel had lain in wait for him descending, to warn him that he must treat them with no supercilious civility, and to tell him partly the reason why. On hearing the potential relations in which they stood toward the estate of his father, Evan hastily and with the assurance of a son of fortune, said they should be paid.

"That's what they would like to hear," said Mrs. Mel. "You may just mention it when they're going to leave. Say you will fix a day to meet them."

"Every farthing!" pursued Evan, on whom the tidings were beginning to operate. "What! debts? my poor father!"

"And a thumping sum, Van. You will open your eyes wider."

"But it shall be paid, mother,—it shall be paid. Debts? I hate them. I'd slave night and day to pay them."

Mrs. Mel spoke in a more positive tense: "And so will I, Van. Now, go."

It mattered little to her what sort of effect on his demeanour her revelation produced, so long as the resolve she sought to bring him to was nailed in his mind; and she was a woman to knock and knock again, till it was firmly fixed there. With a strong purpose, and no plans, there were few who could resist what, in her circle, she willed; not even a youth who would gaily have marched to the scaffold rather than stand behind a counter. A purpose wedded to plans may easily suffer shipwreck; but an unfettered purpose that moulds circumstances as they arise, masters us, and is terrible. Character melts to it, like metal in the steady furnace. The projector of plots is but a miserable gambler and votary of chances. Of a far higher quality is the will that can subdue itself to wait, and lay no petty traps for opportunity. Poets may fable of such a will, that it makes the very heavens conform to it; or, I may add, what is almost equal thereto, one who would be a gentleman, to consent to be a tailor. The only person who ever held in his course against Mrs. Mel, was Mel,—her husband; but, with him, she was under the physical fascination of her youth, and it never left her. In her heart she barely blamed him. What he did, she took among other inevitable matters.

The door closed upon Evan, and waiting at the foot, of the stairs a minute to hear how he was received, Mrs. Mel went to the kitchen and called the name of Dandy, which brought out an ill-built, low-browed, small man, in a baggy suit of black, who hopped up to her with a surly salute. Dandy was a bird Mrs. Mel had herself brought down, and she had for him something of a sportsman's regard for his victim. Dandy was the cleaner of boots and runner of errands in the household of Melchisedec, having originally entered it on a dark night by the cellar. Mrs. Mel, on that occasion, was sleeping in her dressing-gown, to be ready to give the gallant night-hawk, her husband, the service he might require on his return to the nest. Hearing a suspicious noise below, she rose, and deliberately loaded a pair of horse-pistols, weapons Mel had worn in his holsters in the heroic days gone; and with these she stepped downstairs straight to the cellar, carrying a lantern at her girdle. She could not only load, but present and fire. Dandy was foremost in stating that she called him forth steadily, three times, before the pistol was discharged. He admitted that he was frightened, and incapable of speech, at the apparition of the tall, terrific woman. After the third time of asking he had the ball lodged in his leg and fell. Mrs. Mel was in the habit of bearing heavier weights than Dandy. She made no ado about lugging him to a chamber, where, with her own hands (for this woman had some slight knowledge of surgery, and was great in herbs and drugs) she dressed his wound, and put him to bed; crying contempt (ever present in Dandy's memory) at such a poor creature undertaking the work of housebreaker. Taught that he really was a poor creature for the work, Dandy, his nursing over, begged to be allowed to stop and wait on Mrs. Mel; and she who had, like many strong natures, a share of pity for the objects she despised, did not cast him out. A jerk in his gait, owing to the bit of lead Mrs. Mel had dropped into him, and a little, perhaps, to her self-satisfied essay in surgical science on his person, earned him the name he went by.

When her neighbours remonstrated with her for housing a reprobate, Mrs. Mel would say: "Dandy is well-fed and well-physicked: there's no harm in Dandy"; by which she may have meant that the food won his gratitude, and the physic reduced his humours. She had observed human nature. At any rate, Dandy was her creature; and the great Mel himself rallied her about her squire.

"When were you drunk last?" was Mrs. Mel's address to Dandy, as he stood waiting for orders.

He replied to it in an altogether injured way:

"There, now; you've been and called me away from my dinner to ask me that. Why, when I had the last chance, to be sure."

"And you were at dinner in your new black suit?"

"Well," growled Dandy, "I borrowed Sally's apron. Seems I can't please ye."

Mrs. Mel neither enjoined nor cared for outward forms of respect, where she was sure of complete subserviency. If Dandy went beyond the limits, she gave him an extra dose. Up to the limits he might talk as he pleased, in accordance with Mrs. Mel's maxim, that it was a necessary relief to all talking creatures.

"Now, take off your apron," she said, "and wash your hands, dirty pig, and go and wait at table in there"; she pointed to the parlour-door: "Come straight to me when everybody has left."

"Well, there I am with the bottles again," returned Dandy. "It's your fault this time, mind! I'll come as straight as I can."

Dandy turned away to perform her bidding, and Mrs. Mel ascended to the drawing-room to sit with Mrs. Wishaw, who was, as she told all who chose to hear, an old flame of Mel's, and was besides, what Mrs. Mel thought more of, the wife of Mel's principal creditor, a wholesale dealer in cloth, resident in London.

The conviviality of the mourners did not disturb the house. Still, men who are not accustomed to see the colour of wine every day, will sit and enjoy it, even upon solemn occasions, and the longer they sit the more they forget the matter that has brought them together. Pleading their wives and shops, however, they released Evan from his miserable office late in the afternoon.

His mother came down to him,—and saying, "I see how you did the journey—you walked it," told him to follow her.

"Yes, mother," Evan yawned, "I walked part of the way. I met a fellow in a gig about ten miles out of Fallow field, and he gave me a lift to Flatsham. I just reached Lymport in time, thank Heaven! I wouldn't have missed that! By the way, I've satisfied these men."

"Oh!" said Mrs. Mel.

"They wanted—one or two of them—what a penance it is to have to sit among those people an hour!—they wanted to ask me about the business, but I silenced them. I told them to meet me here this day week."

Mrs. Mel again said "Oh!" and, pushing into one of the upper rooms, "Here's your bedroom, Van, just as you left it."

"Ah, so it is," muttered Evan, eyeing a print. "The Douglas and the Percy: 'he took the dead man by the hand.' What an age it seems since I last saw that. There's Sir Hugh Montgomery on horseback—he hasn't moved. Don't you remember my father calling it the Battle of Tit-for-Tat? Gallant Percy! I know he wished he had lived in those days of knights and battles."

"It does not much signify whom one has to make clothes for," observed Mrs. Mel. Her son happily did not mark her.

"I think we neither of us were made for the days of pence and pounds," he continued. "Now, mother, sit down, and talk to me about him. Did he mention me? Did he give me his blessing? I hope he did not suffer. I'd have given anything to press his hand," and looking wistfully at the Percy lifting the hand of Douglas dead, Evan's eyes filled with big tears.

"He suffered very little," returned Mrs. Mel, "and his last words were about you."

"What were they?" Evan burst out.

"I will tell you another time. Now undress, and go to bed. When I talk to you, Van, I want a cool head to listen. You do nothing but yawn yard-measures."

The mouth of the weary youth instinctively snapped short the abhorred emblem.

"Here, I will help you, Van."

In spite of his remonstrances and petitions for talk, she took off his coat and waistcoat, contemptuously criticizing the cloth of foreign tailors and their absurd cut.

"Have you heard from Louisa?" asked Evan.

"Yes, yes—about your sisters by-and-by. Now, be good, and go to bed."

She still treated him like a boy, whom she was going to force to the resolution of a man.

Dandy's sleeping-room was on the same floor as Evan's. Thither, when she had quitted her son, she directed her steps. She had heard Dandy tumble up-stairs the moment his duties were over, and knew what to expect when the bottles had been in his way; for drink made Dandy savage, and a terror to himself. It was her command to him that, when he happened to come across liquor, he should immediately seek his bedroom and bolt the door, and Dandy had got the habit of obeying her. On this occasion he was vindictive against her, seeing that she had delivered him over to his enemy with malice prepense. A good deal of knocking, and summoning of Dandy by name, was required before she was admitted, and the sight of her did not delight him, as he testified.

"I'm drunk!" he bawled. "Will that do for ye?"

Mrs. Mel stood with her two hands crossed above her apron-string, noting his sullen lurking eye with the calm of a tamer of beasts.

"You go out of the room; I'm drunk!" Dandy repeated, and pitched forward on the bed-post, in the middle of an oath.

She understood that it was pure kindness on Dandy's part to bid her go and be out of his reach; and therefore, on his becoming so abusive as to be menacing, she, without a shade of anger, and in the most unruffled manner, administered to him the remedy she had reserved, in the shape of a smart box on the ear, which sent him flat to the floor. He rose, after two or three efforts, quite subdued.

"Now, Dandy, sit on the edge of the bed."

Dandy sat on the extreme edge, and Mrs. Mel pursued:

"Now, Dandy, tell me what your master said at the table."

"Talked at 'em like a lord, he did," said Dandy, stupidly consoling the boxed ear.

"What were his words?"

Dandy's peculiarity was, that he never remembered anything save when drunk, and Mrs. Mel's dose had rather sobered him. By degrees, scratching at his head haltingly, he gave the context.

"'Gentlemen, I hear for the first time, you've claims against my poor father. Nobody shall ever say he died, and any man was the worse for it. I'll meet you next week, and I'll bind myself by law. Here's Lawyer Perkins. No; Mr. Perkins. I'll pay off every penny. Gentlemen, look upon me as your debtor, and not my father.'"

Delivering this with tolerable steadiness, Dandy asked, "Will that do?"

"That will do," said Mrs. Mel. "I'll send you up some tea presently. Lie down, Dandy."

The house was dark and silent when Evan, refreshed by his rest, descended to seek his mother. She was sitting alone in the parlour. With a tenderness which Mrs. Mel permitted rather than encouraged, Evan put his arm round her neck, and kissed her many times. One of the symptoms of heavy sorrow, a longing for the signs of love, made Evan fondle his mother, and bend over her yearningly. Mrs. Mel said once: "Dear Van; good boy!" and quietly sat through his caresses.

"Sitting up for me, mother?" he whispered.

"Yes, Van; we may as well have our talk out."

"Ah!" he took a chair close by her side, "tell me my father's last words."

"He said he hoped you would never be a tailor."

Evan's forehead wrinkled up. "There's not much fear of that, then!"

His mother turned her face on him, and examined him with a rigorous placidity; all her features seeming to bear down on him. Evan did not like the look.

"You object to trade, Van?"

"Yes, decidedly, mother-hate it; but that's not what I want to talk to you about. Didn't my father speak of me much?"

"He desired that you should wear his militia sword, if you got a commission."

"I have rather given up hope of the Army," said Evan.

Mrs. Mel requested him to tell her what a colonel's full pay amounted to; and again, the number of years it required, on a rough calculation, to attain that grade. In reply to his statement she observed: "A tailor might realize twice the sum in a quarter of the time."

"What if he does-double, or treble?" cried Evan, impetuously; and to avoid the theme, and cast off the bad impression it produced on him, he rubbed his hands, and said: "I want to talk to you about my prospects, mother."

"What are they?" Mrs. Mel inquired.

The severity of her mien and sceptical coldness of her speech caused him to inspect them suddenly, as if she had lent him her eyes. He put them by, till the gold should recover its natural shine, saying: "By the way, mother, I've written the half of a History of Portugal."

"Have you?" said Mrs. Mel. "For Louisa?"

"No, mother, of course not: to sell it. Albuquerque! what a splendid fellow he was!"

Informing him that he knew she abominated foreign names, she said: "And your prospects are, writing Histories of Portugal?"

"No, mother. I was going to tell you, I expect a Government appointment. Mr. Jocelyn likes my work—I think he likes me. You know, I was his private secretary for ten months."

"You write a good hand," his mother interposed.

"And I'm certain I was born for diplomacy."

"For an easy chair, and an ink-dish before you, and lacqueys behind. What's to be your income, Van?"

Evan carelessly remarked that he must wait and see.

"A very proper thing to do," said Mrs. Mel; for now that she had fixed him to some explanation of his prospects, she could condescend in her stiff way to banter.

Slightly touched by it, Evan pursued, half laughing, as men do who wish to propitiate common sense on behalf of what seems tolerably absurd: "It's not the immediate income, you know, mother: one thinks of one's future. In the diplomatic service, as Louisa says, you come to be known to Ministers gradually, I mean. That is, they hear of you; and if you show you have some capacity—Louisa wants me to throw it up in time, and stand for Parliament. Andrew, she thinks, would be glad to help me to his seat. Once in Parliament, and known to Ministers, you—your career is open to you."

In justice to Mr. Evan Harrington, it must be said, he built up this extraordinary card-castle to dazzle his mother's mind: he had lost his right grasp of her character for the moment, because of an undefined suspicion of something she intended, and which sent him himself to take refuge in those flimsy structures; while the very altitude he reached beguiled his imagination, and made him hope to impress hers.

Mrs. Mel dealt it one fillip. "And in the meantime how are you to live, and pay the creditors?"

Though Evan answered cheerfully, "Oh, they will wait, and I can live on anything," he was nevertheless floundering on the ground amid the ruins of the superb edifice; and his mother, upright and rigid, continuing, "You can live on anything, and they will wait, and call your father a rogue," he started, grievously bitten by one of the serpents of earth.

"Good heaven, mother! what are you saying?"

"That they will call your father a rogue, and will have a right to," said the relentless woman.

"Not while I live!" Evan exclaimed.

"You may stop one mouth with your fist, but you won't stop a dozen, Van."

Evan jumped up and walked the room.

"What am I to do?" he cried. "I will pay everything. I will bind myself to pay every farthing. What more can I possibly do?"

"Make the money," said Mrs. Mel's deep voice.

Evan faced her: "My dear mother, you are very unjust and inconsiderate. I have been working and doing my best. I promise—what do the debts amount to?"

"Something like L5000 in all, Van."

"Very well." Youth is not alarmed by the sound of big sums. "Very well—I will pay it."

Evan looked as proud as if he had just clapped down the full amount on the table.

"Out of the History of Portugal, half written, and the prospect of a Government appointment?"

Mrs. Mel raised her eyelids to him.

"In time-in time, mother!"

"Mention your proposal to the creditors when you meet them this day week," she said.

Neither of them spoke for several minutes. Then Evan came close to her, saying:

"What is it you want of me, mother?"

"I want nothing, Van—I can support myself."

"But what would you have me do, mother?"

"Be honest; do your duty, and don't be a fool about it."

"I will try," he rejoined. "You tell me to make the money. Where and how can I make it? I am perfectly willing to work."

"In this house," said Mrs. Mel; and, as this was pretty clear speaking, she stood up to lend her figure to it.

"Here?" faltered Evan. "What! be a —"

"Tailor!" The word did not sting her tongue.

"I? Oh, that's quite impossible!" said Evan. And visions of leprosy, and Rose shrinking her skirts from contact with him, shadowed out and away in his mind.

"Understand your choice!" Mrs. Mel imperiously spoke. "What are brains given you for? To be played the fool with by idiots and women? You have L5000 to pay to save your father from being called a rogue. You can only make the money in one way, which is open to you. This business might produce a thousand pounds a-year and more. In seven or eight years you may clear your father's name, and live better all the time than many of your bankrupt gentlemen. You have told the creditors you will pay them. Do you think they're gaping fools, to be satisfied by a History of Portugal? If you refuse to take the business at once, they will sell me up, and quite right too. Understand your choice. There's Mr. Goren has promised to have you in London a couple of months, and teach you what he can. He is a kind friend. Would any of your gentlemen acquaintance do the like for you? Understand your choice. You will be a beggar—the son of a rogue—or an honest man who has cleared his father's name!"

During this strenuously uttered allocution, Mrs. Mel, though her chest heaved but faintly against her crossed hands, showed by the dilatation of her eyes, and the light in them, that she felt her words. There is that in the aspect of a fine frame breathing hard facts, which, to a youth who has been tumbled headlong from his card-castles and airy fabrics, is masterful, and like the pressure of a Fate. Evan drooped his head.

"Now," said Mrs. Mel, "you shall have some supper."

Evan told her he could not eat.

"I insist upon your eating," said Mrs. Mel; "empty stomachs are foul counsellors."

"Mother! do you want to drive me mad?" cried Evan.

She looked at him to see whether the string she held him by would bear the slight additional strain: decided not to press a small point.

"Then go to bed and sleep on it," she said—sure of him—and gave her cheek for his kiss, for she never performed the operation, but kept her mouth, as she remarked, for food and speech, and not for slobbering mummeries.

Evan returned to his solitary room. He sat on the bed and tried to think, oppressed by horrible sensations of self-contempt, that caused whatever he touched to sicken him.

There were the Douglas and the Percy on the wall. It was a happy and a glorious time, was it not, when men lent each other blows that killed outright; when to be brave and cherish noble feelings brought honour; when strength of arm and steadiness of heart won fortune; when the fair stars of earth—sweet women—wakened and warmed the love of squires of low degree. This legacy of the dead man's hand! Evan would have paid it with his blood; but to be in bondage all his days to it; through it to lose all that was dear to him; to wear the length of a loathed existence!—we should pardon a young man's wretchedness at the prospect, for it was in a time before our joyful era of universal equality. Yet he never cast a shade of blame upon his father.

The hours moved on, and he found himself staring at his small candle, which struggled more and more faintly with the morning light, like his own flickering ambition against the facts of life.

BOOK II

VIII

Introduces an Eccentric

At the Aurora—one of those rare antiquated taverns, smelling of comfortable time and solid English fare, that had sprung up in the great coffee days, when taverns were clubs, and had since subsisted on the attachment of steady bachelor Templars there had been dismay, and even sorrow, for a month. The most constant patron of the establishment—an old gentleman who had dined there for seven-and-twenty years, four days in the week, off dishes dedicated to the particular days, and had grown grey with the landlady, the cook, and the head-waiter—this old gentleman had abruptly withheld his presence. Though his name, his residence, his occupation, were things only to be speculated on at the Aurora, he was very well known there, and as men are best to be known: that is to say, by their habits. Some affection for him also was felt. The landlady looked on him as a part of the house. The cook and the waiter were accustomed to receive acceptable compliments from him monthly. His precise words, his regular ancient jokes, his pint of Madeira and after-pint of Port, his antique bow to the landlady, passing out and in, his method of spreading his table-napkin on his lap and looking up at the ceiling ere he fell to, and how he talked to himself during the repast, and indulged in short chuckles, and the one look of perfect felicity that played over his features when he had taken his first sip of Port—these were matters it pained them at the Aurora to have to remember.

For three weeks the resolution not to regard him as of the past was general. The Aurora was the old gentleman's home. Men do not play truant from home at sixty years of age. He must, therefore, be seriously indisposed. The kind heart of the landlady fretted to think he might have no soul to nurse and care for him; but she kept his corner near the fire-place vacant, and took care that his pint of Madeira was there. The belief was gaining ground that he had gone, and that nothing but his ghost would ever sit there again. Still the melancholy ceremony continued: for the landlady was not without a secret hope, that in spite of his reserve and the mystery surrounding him, he would have sent her a last word. The cook and head-waiter, interrogated as to their dealings with the old gentleman, testified solemnly to the fact of their having performed their duty by him. They would not go against their interests so much as to forget one of his ways, they said-taking oath, as it were, by their lower nature, in order to be credited: an instinct men have of one another. The landlady could not contradict them, for the old gentleman had made no complaint; but then she called to memory that fifteen years back, in such and such a year, Wednesday's, dish had been, by shameful oversight, furnished him for Tuesday's, and he had eaten it quietly, but refused his Port; which pathetic event had caused alarm and inquiry, when the error was discovered, and apologized for, the old gentleman merely saying, "Don't let it happen again." Next day he drank his Port, as usual, and the wheels of the Aurora went smoothly. The landlady was thus justified in averring that something had been done by somebody, albeit unable to point to anything specific. Women, who are almost as deeply bound to habit as old gentlemen, possess more of its spiritual element, and are warned by dreams, omens, creepings of the flesh, unwonted chills, suicide of china, and other shadowing signs, when a break is to be anticipated, or, has occurred. The landlady of the Aurora tavern was visited by none of these, and with that beautiful trust which habit gives, and which boastful love or vainer earthly qualities would fail in effecting, she ordered that the pint of Madeira should stand from six o'clock in the evening till seven—a small monument of confidence in him who was at one instant the "poor old dear"; at another, the "naughty old gad-about"; further, the "faithless old-good-for-nothing"; and again, the "blessed pet" of the landlady's parlour, alternately and indiscriminately apostrophized by herself, her sister, and daughter.

On the last day of the month a step was heard coming up the long alley which led from the riotous scrambling street to the plentiful cheerful heart of the Aurora. The landlady knew the step. She checked the natural flutterings of her ribbons, toned down the strong simper that was on her lips, rose, pushed aside her daughter, and, as the step approached, curtsied composedly. Old Habit lifted his hat, and passed. With the same touching confidence in the Aurora that the Aurora had in him, he went straight to his corner, expressed no surprise at his welcome by the Madeira, and thereby apparently indicated that his appearance should enjoy a similar immunity.

As of old, he called "Jonathan!" and was not to be disturbed till he did so. Seeing that Jonathan smirked and twiddled his napkin, the old gentleman added, "Thursday!"

But Jonathan, a man, had not his mistress's keen intuition of the deportment necessitated by the case, or was incapable of putting the screw upon weak excited nature, for he continued to smirk, and was remarking how glad he was, he was sure, and something he had dared to think and almost to fear, when the old gentleman called to him, as if he were at the other end of the room, "Will you order Thursday, or not, sir?" Whereat Jonathan flew, and two or three cosy diners glanced up from their plates, or the paper, smiled, and pursued their capital occupation.

"Glad to see me!" the old gentleman muttered, querulously. "Of course, glad to see a customer! Why do you tell me that? Talk! tattle! might as well have a woman to wait—just!"

He wiped his forehead largely with his handkerchief; as one whom Calamity hunted a little too hard in summer weather.

"No tumbling-room for the wine, too!"

That was his next grievance. He changed the pint of Madeira from his left side to his right, and went under his handkerchief again, feverishly. The world was severe with this old gentleman.

"Ah! clock wrong now!"

He leaned back like a man who can no longer carry his burdens, informing Jonathan, on his coming up to place the roll of bread and firm butter, that he was forty seconds too fast, as if it were a capital offence, and he deserved to step into Eternity for outstripping Time.

"But, I daresay, you don't understand the importance of a minute," said the old gentleman, bitterly. "Not you, or any of you. Better if we had run a little ahead of your minute, perhaps—and the rest of you! Do you think you can cancel the mischief that's done in the world in that minute, sir, by hurrying ahead like that? Tell me!"

Rather at a loss, Jonathan scanned the clock seriously, and observed that it was not quite a minute too fast.

The old gentleman pulled out his watch. He grunted that a lying clock was hateful to him; subsequently sinking into contemplation of his thumbs,—a sign known to Jonathan as indicative of the old gentleman's system having resolved, in spite of external outrages, to be fortified with calm to meet the repast.

It is not fair to go behind an eccentric; but the fact was, this old gentleman was slightly ashamed of his month's vagrancy and cruel conduct, and cloaked his behaviour toward the Aurora, in all the charges he could muster against it. He was very human, albeit an odd form of the race.

Happily for his digestion of Thursday, the cook, warned by Jonathan, kept the old gentleman's time, not the Aurora's: and the dinner was correct; the dinner was eaten in peace; he began to address his plate vigorously, poured out his Madeira, and chuckled, as the familiar ideas engendered by good wine were revived in him. Jonathan reported at the bar that the old gentleman was all right again.

One would like here to pause, while our worthy ancient feeds, and indulge in a short essay on Habit, to show what a sacred and admirable thing it is that makes flimsy Time substantial, and consolidates his triple life. It is proof that we have come to the end of dreams and Time's delusions, and are determined to sit down at Life's feast and carve for ourselves. Its day is the child of yesterday, and has a claim on to-morrow. Whereas those who have no such plan of existence and sum of their wisdom to show, the winds blow them as they list. Consider, then, mercifully the wrath of him on whom carelessness or forgetfulness has brought a snap in the links of Habit. You incline to scorn him because, his slippers misplaced, or asparagus not on his table the first day of a particular Spring month, he gazes blankly and sighs as one who saw the End. To you it may appear small. You call to him to be a man. He is: but he is also an immortal, and his confidence in unceasing orderly progression is rudely dashed.

But the old gentleman has finished his dinner and his Madeira, and says: "Now, Jonathan, 'thock' the Port!"—his joke when matters have gone well: meant to express the sound of the uncorking, probably. The habit of making good jokes is rare, as you know: old gentlemen have not yet attained to it: nevertheless Jonathan enjoys this one, which has seen a generation in and out, for he knows its purport to be, "My heart is open."

And now is a great time with this old gentleman. He sips, and in his eyes the world grows rosy, and he exchanges mute or monosyllable salutes here and there. His habit is to avoid converse; but he will let a light remark season meditation.

He says to Jonathan: "The bill for the month."

"Yes, sir," Jonathan replies. "Would you not prefer, sir, to have the items added on to the month ensuing?"

"I asked you for the bill of the month," said the old gentleman, with an irritated voice and a twinkle in his eye.

Jonathan bowed; but his aspect betrayed perplexity, and that perplexity was soon shared by the landlady for Jonathan said, he was convinced the old gentleman intended to pay for sixteen days, and the landlady could not bring her hand to charge him for more than two. Here was the dilemma foreseen by the old gentleman, and it added vastly to the flavour of the Port.

Pleasantly tickled, he sat gazing at his glass, and let the minutes fly. He knew the part he would act in his little farce. If charged for the whole month, he would peruse the bill deliberately, and perhaps cry out "Hulloa?" and then snap at Jonathan for the interposition of a remark. But if charged for two days, he would wish to be told whether they were demented, those people outside, and scornfully return the bill to Jonathan.

A slap on the shoulder, and a voice: "Found you at last, Tom!" violently shattered the excellent plot, and made the old gentleman start. He beheld Mr. Andrew Cogglesby.

"Drinking Port, Tom?" said Mr. Andrew. "I'll join you": and he sat down opposite to him, rubbing his hands and pushing back his hair.

Jonathan entering briskly with the bill, fell back a step, in alarm. The old gentleman, whose inviolacy was thus rudely assailed, sat staring at the intruder, his mouth compressed, and three fingers round his glass, which it was doubtful whether he was not going to hurl at him.

"Waiter!" Mr. Andrew carelessly hailed, "a pint of this Port, if you please."

Jonathan sought the countenance of the old gentleman.

"Do you hear, sir?" cried the latter, turning his wrath on him. "Another pint!" He added: "Take back the bill"; and away went Jonathan to relate fresh marvels to his mistress.

Mr. Andrew then addressed the old gentleman in the most audacious manner.

"Astonished to see me here, Tom? Dare say you are. I knew you came somewhere in this neighbourhood, and, as I wanted to speak to you very particularly, and you wouldn't be visible till Monday, why, I spied into two or three places, and here I am."

You might see they were brothers. They had the same bushy eyebrows, the same healthy colour in their cheeks, the same thick shoulders, and brisk way of speaking, and clear, sharp, though kindly, eyes; only Tom was cast in larger proportions than Andrew, and had gotten the grey furniture of Time for his natural wear. Perhaps, too, a cross in early life had a little twisted him, and set his mouth in a rueful bunch, out of which occasionally came biting things. Mr. Andrew carried his head up, and eyed every man living with the benevolence of a patriarch, dashed with the impudence of a London sparrow. Tom had a nagging air, and a trifle of acridity on his broad features. Still, any one at a glance could have sworn they were brothers, and Jonathan unhesitatingly proclaimed it at the Aurora bar.

Mr. Andrew's hands were working together, and at them, and at his face, the old gentleman continued to look with a firmly interrogating air.

"Want to know what brings me, Tom? I'll tell you presently. Hot,—isn't it?"

"What the deuce are you taking exercise for?" the old gentleman burst out, and having unlocked his mouth, he began to puff and alter his posture.

"There you are, thawed in a minute!" said Mr. Andrew. "What's an eccentric? a child grown grey. It isn't mine; I read it somewhere. Ah, here's the Port! good, I'll warrant."

Jonathan deferentially uncorked, excessive composure on his visage. He arranged the table-cloth to a nicety, fixed the bottle with exactness, and was only sent scudding by the old gentleman's muttering of: "Eavesdropping pie!" followed by a short, "Go!" and even then he must delay to sweep off a particular crumb.

"Good it is!" said Mr. Andrew, rolling the flavour on his lips, as he put down his glass. "I follow you in Port, Tom. Elder brother!"

The old gentleman also drank, and was mollified enough to reply: "Shan't follow you in Parliament."

"Haven't forgiven that yet, Tom?"

"No great harm done when you're silent."

"Capital Port!" said Mr. Andrew, replenishing the glasses. "I ought to have inquired where they kept the best Port. I might have known you'd stick by it. By the way, talking of Parliament, there's talk of a new election for Fallow field. You have a vote there. Will you give it to Jocelyn? There's talk of his standing.

"If he'll wear petticoats, I'll give him my vote."

"There you go, Tom!"

"I hate masquerades. You're penny trumpets of the women. That tattle comes from the bed-curtains. When a petticoat steps forward I give it my vote, or else I button it up in my pocket."

This was probably one of the longest speeches he had ever delivered at the Aurora. There was extra Port in it. Jonathan, who from his place of observation noted the length of time it occupied, though he was unable to gather the context, glanced at Mr. Andrew with a sly satisfaction. Mr. Andrew, laughing, signalled for another pint.

"So you've come here for my vote, have you?" said Mr. Tom.

"Why, no; not exactly that," Mr. Andrew answered, blinking and passing it by.

Jonathan brought the fresh pint, and Tom filled for himself, drank, and said emphatically, and with a confounding voice:

"Your women have been setting you on me, sir!"

Andrew protested that he was entirely mistaken.

"You're the puppet of your women!"

"Well, Tom, not in this instance. Here's to the bachelors, and brother Tom at their head!"

It seemed to be Andrew's object to help his companion to carry a certain quantity of Port, as if he knew a virtue it had to subdue him, and to have fixed on a particular measure that he should hold before he addressed him specially. Arrived at this, he said:

"Look here, Tom. I know your ways. I shouldn't have bothered you here; I never have before; but we couldn't very well talk it over in business hours; and besides you're never at the Brewery till Monday, and the matter's rather urgent."

"Why don't you speak like that in Parliament?" the old man interposed.

"Because Parliament isn't my brother," replied Mr. Andrew. "You know, Tom, you never quite took to my wife's family."

"I'm not a match for fine ladies, Nan."

"Well, Harriet would have taken to you, Tom, and will now, if you'll let her. Of course, it's a pity if she's ashamed of—hem! You found it out about the Lymport people, Tom, and, you've kept the secret and respected her feelings, and I thank you for it. Women are odd in those things, you know. She mustn't imagine I've heard a whisper. I believe it would kill her."

The old gentleman shook silently.

"Do you want me to travel over the kingdom, hawking her for the daughter of a marquis?"

"Now, don't joke, Tom. I'm serious. Are you not a Radical at heart? Why do you make such a set against the poor women? What do we spring from?"

"I take off my hat, Nan, when I see a cobbler's stall."

"And I, Tom, don't care a rush who knows it. Homo—something; but we never had much schooling. We've thriven, and should help those we can. We've got on in the world. . ."

"Wife come back from Lymport?" sneered Tom.

Andrew hurriedly, and with some confusion, explained that she had not been able to go, on account of the child.

"Account of the child!" his brother repeated, working his chin contemptuously. "Sisters gone?"

"They're stopping with us," said Andrew, reddening.

"So the tailor was left to the kites and the crows. Ah! hum!" and Tom chuckled.

"You're angry with me, Tom, for coming here," said Andrew. "I see what it is. Thought how it would be! You're offended, old Tom."

"Come where you like," returned Tom, "the place is open. It's a fool that hopes for peace anywhere. They sent a woman here to wait on me, this day month."

"That's a shame!" said Mr. Andrew, propitiatingly. "Well, never mind, Tom: the women are sometimes in the way.—Evan went down to bury his father. He's there now. You wouldn't see him when he was at the Brewery, Tom. He's—upon my honour! he's a good young fellow."

"A fine young gentleman, I've no doubt, Nan."

"A really good lad, Tom. No nonsense. I've come here to speak to you about him."

Mr. Andrew drew a letter from his pocket, pursuing: "Just throw aside your prejudices, and read this. It's a letter I had from him this morning. But first I must tell you how the case stands."

"Know more than you can tell me, Nan," said Tom, turning over the flavour of a gulp of his wine.

"Well, then, just let me repeat it. He has been capitally educated; he has always been used to good society: well, we mustn't sneer at it: good society's better than bad, you'll allow. He has refined tastes: well, you wouldn't like to live among crossing-sweepers, Tom. He's clever and accomplished, can speak and write in three languages: I wish I had his abilities. He has good manners: well, Tom, you know you like them as well as anybody. And now—but read for yourself."

"Yah!" went old Tom. "The women have been playing the fool with him since he was a baby. I read his rigmarole? No."

Mr. Andrew shrugged his shoulders, and opened the letter, saying: "Well, listen"; and then he coughed, and rapidly skimmed the introductory part. "Excuses himself for addressing me formally—poor boy! Circumstances have altered his position towards the world found his father's affairs in a bad state: only chance of paying off father's debts to undertake management of business, and bind himself to so much a year. But there, Tom, if you won't read it, you miss the poor young fellow's character. He says that he has forgotten his station: fancied he was superior to trade, but hates debt; and will not allow anybody to throw dirt at his father's name, while he can work to clear it; and will sacrifice his pride. Come, Tom, that's manly, isn't it? I call it touching, poor lad!"

Manly it may have been, but the touching part of it was a feature missed in Mr. Andrew's hands. At any rate, it did not appear favourably to impress Tom, whose chin had gathered its ominous puckers, as he inquired:

"What's the trade? he don't say."

Andrew added, with a wave of the hand: "Out of a sort of feeling for his sisters—I like him for it. Now what I want to ask you, Tom, is, whether we can't assist him in some way! Why couldn't we take him into our office, and fix him there, eh? If he works well—we're both getting old, and my brats are chicks—we might, by-and-by, give him a share."

"Make a brewer of him? Ha! there'd be another mighty sacrifice for his pride!"

"Come, come, Tom," said Andrew, "he's my wife's brother, and I'm yours; and—there, you know what women are. They like to preserve appearances: we ought to consider them."

"Preserve appearances!" echoed Tom: "ha! who'll do that for them better than a tailor?"

Andrew was an impatient little man, fitter for a kind action than to plead a cause. Jeering jarred on him; and from the moment his brother began it, he was of small service to Evan. He flung back against the partition of the compound, rattling it to the disturbance of many a quiet digestion.

"Tom," he cried, "I believe you're a screw!"

"Never said I wasn't," rejoined Tom, as he finished his glass. "I'm a bachelor, and a person—you're married, and an object. I won't have the tailor's family at my coat-tails."

Do you mean to say, Tom, you don't like the young fellow? The Countess says he's half engaged to an heiress; and he has a chance of appointments—of course, nothing may come of them. But do you mean to say, you don't like him for what he has done?"

Tom made his jaw disagreeably prominent. "'Fraid I'm guilty of that crime."

"And you that swear at people pretending to be above their station!" exclaimed Andrew. "I shall get in a passion. I can't stand this. Here, waiter! what have I to pay?"

"Go," cried the time-honoured guest of the Aurora to Jonathan advancing.

Andrew pressed the very roots of his hair back from his red forehead, and sat upright and resolute, glancing at Tom. And now ensued a curious scene of family blood. For no sooner did elderly Tom observe this bantam-like demeanour of his brother, than he ruffled his feathers likewise, and looked down on him, agitating his wig over a prodigious frown. Whereof came the following sharp colloquy; Andrew beginning:

"I'll pay off the debts out of my own pocket."

"You can make a greater fool of yourself, then?"

"He shan't be a tailor!"

"He shan't be a brewer!"

"I say he shall live like a gentleman!"

"I say he shall squat like a Turk!"

Bang went Andrew's hand on the table: "I've pledged my word, mind!"

Tom made a counter demonstration: "And I'll have my way!"

"Hang it! I can be as eccentric as you," said Andrew.

"And I as much a donkey as you, if I try hard," said Tom.

Something of the cobbler's stall followed this; till waxing furious, Tom sung out to Jonathan, hovering around them in watchful timidity, "More Port!" and the words immediately fell oily on the wrath of the brothers; both commenced wiping their heads with their handkerchiefs the faces of both emerged and met, with a half-laugh: and, severally determined to keep to what they had spoken, there was a tacit accord between them to drop the subject.

Like sunshine after smart rain, the Port shone on these brothers. Like a voice from the pastures after the bellowing of the thunder, Andrew's voice asked: "Got rid of that twinge of the gout, Tom? Did you rub in that ointment?" while Tom replied: "Ay. How about that rheumatism of yours? Have you tried that Indy oil?" receiving a like assurance.

The remainder of the Port ebbed in meditation and chance remarks. The bit of storm had done them both good; and Tom especially—the cynical, carping, grim old gentleman—was much improved by the nearer resemblance of his manner to Andrew's.

Behind this unaffected fraternal concord, however, the fact that they were pledged to a race in eccentricity, was present. They had been rivals before; and anterior to the date of his marriage, Andrew had done odd eclipsing things. But Andrew required prompting to it; he required to be put upon his mettle. Whereas, it was more nature with Tom: nature and the absence of a wife, gave him advantages over Andrew. Besides, he had his character to maintain. He had said the word: and the first vanity of your born eccentric is, that he shall be taken for infallible.

Presently Andrew ducked his head to mark the evening clouds flushing over the court-yard of the Aurora.

"Time to be off, Tom," he said: "wife at home."

"Ah!" Tom answered. "Well, I haven't got to go to bed so early."

"What an old rogue you are, Tom!" Andrew pushed his elbows forward on the table amiably. "'Gad, we haven't drunk wine together since—by George! we'll have another pint."

"Many as you like," said Tom.

Over the succeeding pint, Andrew, in whose veins the Port was merry, favoured his brother with an imitation of Major Strike, and indicated his dislike to that officer. Tom informed him that Major Strike was speculating.

"The ass eats at my table, and treats me with contempt."

"Just tell him that you're putting by the bones for him. He'll want 'em."

Then Andrew with another glance at the clouds, now violet on a grey sky, said he must really be off. Upon which Tom observed: "Don't come here again."

"You old rascal, Tom!" cried Andrew, swinging over the table: "it's quite jolly for us to be hob-a-nobbing together once more. "'Gad!—no, we won't though! I promised—Harriet. Eh? What say, Tom?"

"Nother pint, Nan?"

Tom shook his head in a roguishly-cosy, irresistible way. Andrew, from a shake of denial and resolve, fell into the same; and there sat the two brothers—a jolly picture.

The hour was ten, when Andrew Cogglesby, comforted by Tom's remark, that he, Tom, had a wig, and that he, Andrew, would have a wigging, left the Aurora; and he left it singing a song. Tom Cogglesby still sat at his table, holding before him Evan's letter, of which he had got possession; and knocking it round and round with a stroke of the forefinger, to the tune of, "Tinker, tailor, soldier, sailor, 'pothecary, ploughboy, thief"; each profession being sounded as a corner presented itself to the point of his nail. After indulging in this species of incantation for some length of time, Tom Cogglesby read the letter from beginning to end, and called peremptorily for pen, ink, and paper.

IX

The Countess in Low Society

By dint of stratagems worthy of a Court intrigue, the Countess de Saldar contrived to traverse the streets of Lymport, and enter the house where she was born, unsuspected and unseen, under cover of a profusion of lace and veil and mantilla, which only her heroic resolve to keep her beauties hidden from the profane townspeople could have rendered endurable beneath the fervid summer sun. Dress in a foreign style she must, as without it she lost that sense of superiority, which was the only comfort to her in her tribulations. The period of her arrival was ten days subsequent to the burial of her father. She had come in the coach, like any common mortal, and the coachman, upon her request, had put her down at the Governor's house, and the guard had knocked at the door, and the servant had informed her that General Hucklebridge was not the governor of Lymport, nor did Admiral Combleman then reside in the town; which tidings, the coach then being out of sight, it did not disconcert the Countess to hear; and she reached her mother, having, at least, cut off communication with the object of conveyance.

The Countess kissed her mother, kissed Mrs. Fiske, and asked sharply for Evan. Mrs. Fiske let her know that Evan was in the house.

"Where?" inquired the Countess. "I have news of the utmost importance for him. I must see him."

"Where is he, aunt?" said Mrs. Fiske. "In the shop, I think; I wonder he did not see you passing, Louisa."

The Countess went bolt down into a chair.

"Go to him, Jane," said Mrs. Mel. "Tell him Louisa is here, and don't return."

Mrs. Fiske departed, and the Countess smiled.

"Thank you, Mama! you know I never could bear that odious, vulgar little woman. Oh, the heat! You talk of Portugal! And, oh! poor dear Papa! what I have suffered!"

Flapping her laces for air, and wiping her eyes for sorrow, the Countess poured a flood of sympathy into her mother's ears and then said:

"But you have made a great mistake, Mama, in allowing Evan to put his foot into that place. He—beloved of an heiress! Why, if an enemy should hear of it, it would ruin him—positively blast him—for ever. And that she loves him I have proof positive. Yes; with all her frankness, the little thing cannot conceal that from me now. She loves him! And I desire you to guess, Mama, whether rivals will not abound? And what enemy so much to be dreaded as a rival? And what revelation so awful as that he has stood in a—in a—boutique?"

Mrs. Mel maintained her usual attitude for listening. It had occurred to her that it might do no good to tell the grand lady, her daughter; of Evan's resolution, so she simply said, "It is discipline for him," and left her to speak a private word with the youth.

Timidly the Countess inspected the furniture of the apartment, taking chills at the dingy articles she saw, in the midst of her heat. That she should have sprung from this! The thought was painful; still she could forgive Providence so much. But should it ever be known she had sprung from this! Alas! she felt she never could pardon such a dire betrayal. She had come in good spirits, but the mention of Evan's backsliding had troubled her extremely, and though she did not say to herself, What was the benefit resulting from her father's dying, if Evan would be so base-minded? she thought the thing indefinitely, and was forming the words on her mouth, One Harrington in a shop is equal to all! when Evan appeared alone.

"Why, goodness gracious! where's your moustache?" cried the Countess.

"Gone the way of hair!" said Evan, coldly stooping to her forehead.

"Such a distinction!" the Countess continued, reproachfully. "Why, mon Dieu! one could hardly tell you; as you look now, from the very commonest tradesman—if you were not rather handsome and something of a figure. It's a disguise, Evan—do you know that?"

"And I've parted with it—that's all," said Evan. "No more disguises for me!"

The Countess immediately took his arm, and walked with him to a window. His face was certainly changed. Murmuring that the air of Lymport was bad for him, and that he must leave it instantly, she bade him sit and attend to what she was about to say.

"While you have been here, degenerating, Evan, day by day—as you always do out of my sight—degenerating! no less a word!—I have been slaving in your interests. Yes; I have forced the Jocelyns socially to acknowledge us. I have not slept; I have eaten bare morsels. Do abstinence and vigils clear the wits? I know not! but indeed they have enabled me to do more in a week than would suffice for a lifetime.

Hark to me. I have discovered Rose's secret. Si! It is so! Rose loves you. You blush; you blush like a girl. She loves you, and you have let yourself be seen in a shop! Contrast me the two things. Oh! in verity, dreadful as it is, one could almost laugh. But the moment I lose sight of you, my instructions vanish as quickly as that hair on your superior lip, which took such time to perfect. Alas! you must grow it again immediately. Use any perfumer's contrivance. Rowland! I have great faith in Rowland. Without him, I believe, there would have been many bald women committing suicide! You remember the bottle I gave to the Count de Villa Flor? 'Countess,' he said to me, 'you have saved this egg-shell from a crack by helping to cover it'—for so he called his head—the top, you know, was beginning to shine like an egg. And I do fear me he would have done it. Ah! you do not conceive what the dread of baldness is! To a woman death—death is preferable to baldness! Baldness is death! And a wig—a wig! Oh, horror! total extinction is better than to rise again in a wig! But you are young, and play with hair. But I was saying, I went to see the Jocelyns. I was introduced to Sir Franks and his lady and the wealthy grandmother. And I have an invitation for you, Evan—you unmannered boy, that you do not bow! A gentle incline forward of the shoulders, and the eyes fixed softly, your upper lids drooping triflingly, as if you thanked with gentle sincerity, but were indifferent. Well, well, if you will not! An invitation for you to spend part of the autumn at Beckley Court, the ancestral domain, where there will be company the nobles of the land! Consider that. You say it was bold in me to face them after that horrible man committed us on board the vessel? A Harrington is anything but a coward. I did go and because I am devoted to your interests. That very morning, I saw announced in the paper, just beneath poor Andrew's hand, as he held it up at the breakfast-table, reading it, I saw among the deaths, Sir Abraham Harrington, of Torquay, Baronet, of quinsy! Twice that good man has come to my rescue! Oh! I welcomed him as a piece of Providence! I turned and said to Harriet, 'I see they have put poor Papa in the paper.' Harriet was staggered. I took the paper from Andrew, and pointed it to her. She has no readiness. She has had no foreign training. She could not comprehend, and Andrew stood on tiptoe, and peeped. He has a bad cough, and coughed himself black in the face. I attribute it to excessive bad manners and his cold feelings. He left the room. I reproached Harriet. But, oh! the singularity of the excellent fortune of such an event at such a time! It showed that our Harrington-luck had not forsaken us. I hurried to the Jocelyns instantly. Of course, it cleared away any suspicions aroused in them by that horrible man on board the vessel. And the tears I wept for Sir Abraham, Evan, in verity they were tears of deep and sincere gratitude! What is your mouth knitting the corners at? Are you laughing?"

Evan hastily composed his visage to the melancholy that was no counterfeit in him just then.

"Yes," continued the Countess, easily reassured, "I shall ever feel a debt to Sir Abraham Harrington, of Torquay. I dare say we are related to him. At least he has done us more service than many a rich and titled relative. No one supposes he would acknowledge poor Papa. I can forgive him that, Evan!" The Countess pointed out her finger with mournful and impressive majesty, "As we look down on that monkey, people of rank and consideration in society look on what poor dear Papa was."

This was partly true, for Jacko sat on a chair, in his favourite attitude, copied accurately from the workmen of the establishment at their labour with needle and thread. Growing cognizant of the infamy of his posture, the Countess begged Evan to drive him out of her sight, and took a sniff at her smelling-bottle.

She went on: "Now, dear Van, you would hear of your sweet Rose?"

"Not a word!" Evan hastily answered.

"Why, what does this indicate? Whims! Then you do love?"

"I tell you, Louisa, I don't want to hear a word of any of them," said Evan, with an angry gleam in his eyes. "They are nothing to me, nor I to them. I—my walk in life is not theirs."

"Faint heart! faint heart!" the Countess lifted a proverbial forefinger.

"Thank heaven, I shall have the consolation of not going about, and bowing and smirking like an impostor!" Evan exclaimed.

There was a wider intelligence in the Countess's arrested gaze than she chose to fashion into speech.

"I knew," she said, "I knew how the air of this horrible Lymport would act on you. But while I live, Evan, you shall not sink in the sludge. You, with all the pains I have lavished on you! and with your presence!—for you have a presence, so rare among young men in this England! You, who have been to a Court, and interchanged bows with duchesses, and I know not what besides—nay, I do not accuse you; but if you had not been a mere boy, and an English boy-poor Eugenia herself confessed to me that you had a look—a tender cleaving of the underlids—that made her catch her hand to her heart sometimes: it reminded her so acutely of false Belmarafa. Could you have had a greater compliment than that? You shall not stop here another day!"

"True," said Evan, "for I'm going to London to-night."

"Not to London," the Countess returned, with a conquering glance, "but to Beckley Court-and with me."

"To London, Louisa, with Mr. Goren."

Again the Countess eyed him largely; but took, as it were, a side-path from her broad thought, saying: "Yes, fortunes are made in London, if you would they should be rapid."

She meditated. At that moment Dandy knocked at the door, and called outside: "Please, master, Mr. Goren says there's a gentleman in the shop-wants to see you."

"Very well," replied Evan, moving. He was swung violently round.

The Countess had clutched him by the arm. A fearful expression was on her face.

"Whither do you go?" she said.

"To the shop, Louisa."

Too late to arrest the villanous word, she pulled at him. "Are you quite insane? Consent to be seen by a gentleman there? What has come to you? You must be lunatic! Are we all to be utterly ruined—disgraced?"

"Is my mother to starve?" said Evan.

"Absurd rejoinder! No! You should have sold everything here before this. She can live with Harriet—she—once out of this horrible element—she would not show it. But, Evan, you are getting away from me: you are not going?—speak!"

"I am going," said Evan.

The Countess clung to him, exclaiming: "Never, while I have the power to detain you!" but as he was firm and strong, she had recourse to her woman's aids, and burst into a storm of sobs on his shoulder—a scene of which Mrs. Mel was, for some seconds, a composed spectator.

"What's the matter now?" said Mrs. Mel.

Evan impatiently explained the case. Mrs. Mel desired her daughter to avoid being ridiculous, and making two fools in her family; and at the same time that she told Evan there was no occasion for him to go, contrived, with a look, to make the advice a command. He, in that state of mind when one takes bitter delight in doing an abhorred duty, was hardly willing to be submissive; but the despair of the Countess reduced him, and for her sake he consented to forego the sacrifice of his pride which was now his sad, sole pleasure. Feeling him linger, the Countess relaxed her grasp. Hers were tears that dried as soon as they had served their end; and, to give him the full benefit of his conduct, she said: "I knew Evan would be persuaded by me."

Evan pitifully pressed her hand, and sighed.

"Tea is on the table down-stairs," said Mrs. Mel. "I have cooked something for you, Louisa. Do you sleep here to-night?"

"Can I tell you, Mama?" murmured the Countess. "I am dependent on our Evan."

"Oh! well, we will eat first," said Mrs. Mel, and they went to the table below, the Countess begging her mother to drop titles in designating her to the servants, which caused Mrs. Mel to say:

"There is but one. I do the cooking"; and the Countess, ever disposed to flatter and be suave, even when stung by a fact or a phrase, added:

"And a beautiful cook you used to be, dear Mama!"

At the table, awaiting them, sat Mrs. Wishaw, Mrs. Fiske, and Mr. Goren, who soon found themselves enveloped in the Countess's graciousness. Mr. Goren would talk of trade, and compare Lymport business with London, and the Countess, loftily interested in his remarks, drew him out to disgust her brother. Mrs. Wishaw, in whom the Countess at once discovered a frivolous pretentious woman of the moneyed trading class, she treated as one who was alive to society, and surveyed matters from a station in the world, leading her to think that she tolerated Mr. Goren, as a lady-Christian of the highest rank should tolerate the insects that toil for us. Mrs. Fiske was not so tractable, for Mrs. Fiske was hostile and armed. Mrs. Fiske adored the great Mel, and she had never loved Louisa. Hence, she scorned Louisa on account of her late behaviour toward her dead parent. The Countess saw through her, and laboured to be friendly with her, while she rendered her disagreeable in the eyes of Mrs. Wishaw, and let Mrs. Wishaw perceive that sympathy was possible between them; manoeuvring a trifle too delicate, perhaps, for the people present, but sufficient to blind its keen-witted author to the something that was being concealed from herself, of which something, nevertheless, her senses apprehensively warned her: and they might have spoken to her wits, but that mortals cannot, unaided, guess, or will not, unless struck in the face by the fact, credit, what is to their minds the last horror.

"I came down in the coach, quite accidental, with this gentleman," said Mrs. Wishaw, fanning a cheek and nodding at Mr. Goren. "I'm an old flame of dear Mel's. I knew him when he was an apprentice in London. Now, wasn't it odd? Your mother—I suppose I must call you 'my lady'?"

The Countess breathed a tender "Spare me," with a smile that added, "among friends!"

Mrs. Wishaw resumed: "Your mother was an old flame of this gentleman's, I found out. So there were two old flames, and I couldn't help thinking! But I was so glad to have seen dear Mel once more:

"Ah!" sighed the Countess.

"He was always a martial-looking man, and laid out, he was quite imposing. I declare, I cried so, as it reminded me of when I couldn't have him, for he had nothing but his legs and arms—and I married Wishaw. But it's a comfort to think I have been of some service to dear, dear Mel! for Wishaw's a man of accounts and payments; and I knew Mel had cloth from him, and, the lady suggested bills delayed, with two or three nods, "you know! and I'll do my best for his son."

"You are kind," said the Countess, smiling internally at the vulgar creature's misconception of Evan's requirements.

"Did he ever talk much about Mary Fence?" asked Mrs. Wishaw. "'Polly Fence,' he used to say, 'sweet Polly Fence!'"

"Oh! I think so. Frequently," observed the Countess.

Mrs. Fiske primmed her mouth. She had never heard the great Mel allude to the name of Fence.

The Goren-croak was heard

"Painters have painted out 'Melchisedec' this afternoon. Yes,—ah! In and out-as the saying goes."

Here was an opportunity to mortify the Countess.

Mrs. Fiske placidly remarked: "Have we the other put up in its stead? It's shorter."

A twinge of weakness had made Evan request that the name of Evan Harrington should not decorate the shopfront till he had turned his back on it, for a time. Mrs. Mel crushed her venomous niece.

"What have you to do with such things? Shine in your own affairs first, Ann, before you meddle with others."

Relieved at hearing that "Melchisedec" was painted out, and unsuspicious of the announcement that should replace it, the Countess asked Mrs. Wishaw if she thought Evan like her dear Papa.

"So like," returned the lady, "that I would not be alone with him yet, for worlds. I should expect him to be making love to me: for, you know, my dear—I must be familiar—Mel never could be alone with you, without! It was his nature. I speak of him before marriage. But, if I can trust myself with him, I shall take charge of Mr. Evan, and show him some London society."

"That is indeed kind," said the Countess, glad of a thick veil for the utterance of her contempt. "Evan, though—I fear—will be rather engaged. His friends, the Jocelyns of Beckley Court, will—I fear—hardly dispense with him and Lady Splenders—you know her? the Marchioness of Splenders? No?—by repute, at least: a most beautiful and most fascinating woman; report of him alone has induced her to say that Evan must and shall form a part of her autumnal gathering at Splenders Castle. And how he is to get out of it, I cannot tell. But I am sure his multitudinous engagements will not prevent his paying due court to Mistress Wishaw."

As the Countess intended, Mistress Wishaw's vanity was reproved, and her ambition excited: a pretty doublestroke, only possible to dexterous players.

The lady rejoined that she hoped so, she was sure; and forthwith (because she suddenly seemed to possess him more than his son), launched upon Mel's incomparable personal attractions. This caused the Countess to enlarge upon Evan's vast personal prospects. They talked across each other a little, till the Countess remembered her breeding, allowed Mrs. Wishaw to run to an end in hollow exclamations, and put a finish to the undeclared controversy, by a traverse of speech, as if she were taking up the most important subject of their late colloquy. "But Evan is not in his own hands—he is in the hands of a lovely young woman, I must tell you. He belongs to her, and not to us. You have heard of Rose Jocelyn, the celebrated heiress?"

"Engaged?" Mrs. Wishaw whispered aloud.

The Countess, an adept in the lie implied—practised by her, that she might not subject herself to future punishment (in which she was so devout a believer, that she condemned whole hosts to it)—deeply smiled.

"Really!" said Mrs. Wishaw, and was about to inquire why Evan, with these brilliant expectations, could think of trade and tailoring, when the young man, whose forehead had been growing black, jumped up, and quitted them; thus breaking the harmony of the table; and as the Countess had said enough, she turned the conversation to the always welcome theme of low society. She broached death and corpses; and became extremely interesting, and very sympathetic: the only difference between the ghostly anecdotes she related, and those of the other ladies, being that her ghosts were all of them titled, and walked mostly under the burden of a coronet. For instance, there was the Portuguese Marquis de Col. He had married a Spanish wife, whose end was mysterious. Undressing, on the night of the anniversary of her death, and on the point of getting into bed, he beheld the dead woman lying on her back before him. All night long he had to sleep with this freezing phantom! Regularly, every fresh anniversary, he had to endure the same penance, no matter where he might be, or in what strange bed. On one occasion, when he took the live for the dead, a curious thing occurred, which the Countess scrupled less to relate than would men to hint at. Ghosts were the one childish enjoyment Mrs. Mel allowed herself, and she listened to her daughter intently, ready to cap any narrative; but Mrs. Fiske stopped the flood.

"You have improved on Peter Smithers, Louisa," she said.

The Countess turned to her mildly.

"You are certainly thinking of Peter Smithers," Mrs. Fiske continued, bracing her shoulders. "Surely, you remember poor Peter, Louisa? An old flame of your own! He was going to kill himself, but married a Devonshire woman, and they had disagreeables, and SHE died, and he was undressing, and saw her there in the bed, and wouldn't get into it, and had the mattress, and the curtains, and the counterpanes, and everything burnt. He told us it himself. You must remember it, Louisa?"

The Countess remembered nothing of the sort. No doubt could exist of its having been the Portuguese Marquis de Col, because he had confided to her the whole affair, and indeed come to her, as his habit was, to ask her what he could possibly do, under the circumstances. If Mrs. Fiske's friend, who married the Devonshire person, had seen the same thing, the coincidence was yet more extraordinary than the case. Mrs. Fiske said it assuredly was, and glanced at her aunt, who, as the Countess now rose, declaring she must speak to Evan, chid Mrs. Fiske, and wished her and Peter Smithers at the bottom of the sea.

"No, no, Mama," said the Countess, laughing, "that would hardly be proper," and before Mrs. Fiske could reply, escaped to complain to Evan of the vulgarity of those women.

She was not prepared for the burst of wrath with which Evan met her. "Louisa," said he, taking her wrist sternly, "you have done a thing I can't forgive. I find it hard to bear disgrace myself: I will not consent to bring it upon others. Why did you dare to couple Miss Jocelyn's name with mine?"

The Countess gave him out her arm's length. "Speak on, Van," she said, admiring him with a bright gaze.

"Answer me, Louisa; and don't take me for a fool any more," he pursued. "You have coupled Miss Jocelyn's name with mine, in company, and I insist now upon your giving me your promise to abstain from doing it anywhere, before anybody."

"If she saw you at this instant, Van," returned the incorrigible Countess, "would she desire it, think you? Oh! I must make you angry before her, I see that! You have your father's frown. You surpass him, for your delivery is more correct, and equally fluent. And if a woman is momentarily melted by softness in a man, she is for ever subdued by boldness and bravery of mien."

Evan dropped her hand. "Miss Jocelyn has done me the honour to call me her friend. That was in other days." His lip quivered. "I shall not see Miss Jocelyn again. Yes; I would lay down my life for her; but that's idle talk. No such chance will ever come to me. But I can save her from being spoken of in alliance with me, and what I am, and I tell you, Louisa, I will not have it." Saying which, and while he looked harshly at her, wounded pride bled through his eyes.

She was touched. "Sit down, dear; I must explain to you, and make you happy against your will," she said, in another voice, and an English accent. "The mischief is done, Van. If you do not want Rose Jocelyn to love you, you must undo it in your own way. I am not easily deceived. On the morning I went to her house in town, she took me aside, and spoke to me. Not a confession in words. The blood in her cheeks, when I mentioned you, did that for her. Everything about you she must know—how you bore your grief, and all. And not in her usual free manner, but timidly, as if she feared a surprise, or feared to be wakened to the secret in her bosom she half suspects—'Tell him!' she said, 'I hope he will not forget me.'"

The Countess was interrupted by a great sob; for the picture of frank Rose Jocelyn changed, and soft, and, as it were, shadowed under a veil of bashful regard for him, so filled the young man with sorrowful tenderness, that he trembled, and was as a child.

Marking the impression she had produced on him, and having worn off that which he had produced on her, the Countess resumed the art in her style of speech, easier to her than nature.

"So the sweetest of Roses may be yours, dear Van; and you have her in a gold setting, to wear on your heart. Are you not enviable? I will not—no, I will not tell you she is perfect. I must fashion the sweet young creature. Though I am very ready to admit that she is much improved by this—shall I call it, desired consummation?"

Evan could listen no more. Such a struggle was rising in his breast: the effort to quench what the Countess had so shrewdly kindled; passionate desire to look on Rose but for one lightning flash: desire to look on her, and muffled sense of shame twin-born with it: wild love and leaden misery mixed: dead hopelessness and vivid hope. Up to the neck in Purgatory, but his soul saturated with visions of Bliss! The fair orb of Love was all that was wanted to complete his planetary state, and aloft it sprang, showing many faint, fair tracts to him, and piling huge darknesses.

As if in search of something, he suddenly went from the room.

"I have intoxicated the poor boy," said the Countess, and consulted an attitude by the evening light in a mirror. Approving the result, she rang for her mother, and sat with her till dark; telling her she could not and would not leave her dear Mama that night. At the supper-table Evan did not appear, and Mr. Goren, after taking counsel of Mrs. Mel, dispersed the news that Evan was off to London. On the road again, with a purse just as ill-furnished, and in his breast the light that sometimes leads gentlemen, as well as ladies, astray.

X

My Gentleman on the Road Again

Near a milestone, under the moonlight, crouched the figure of a woman, huddled with her head against her knees, and careless hair falling to the summer's dust. Evan came upon this sight within a few miles of Fallowfield. At first he was rather startled, for he had inherited superstitious emotions from his mother, and the road was lone, the moon full. He went up to her and spoke a gentle word, which provoked no reply. He ventured to put his hand on her shoulder, continuing softly to address her. She was flesh and blood. Evan stooped his head to catch a whisper from her mouth, but nothing save a heavier fall of the breath she took, as of one painfully waking, was heard.

A misery beyond our own is a wholesome picture for youth, and though we may not for the moment compare the deep with the lower deep, we, if we have a heart for outer sorrows, can forget ourselves in it. Evan had just been accusing the heavens of conspiracy to disgrace him. Those patient heavens had listened, as is their wont. They had viewed and had not been disordered by his mental frenzies. It is certainly hard that they do not come down to us, and condescend to tell us what they mean, and be dumb-foundered by the perspicuity of our arguments the argument, for instance, that they have not fashioned us for the science of the shears, and do yet impel us to wield them. Nevertheless, they to whom mortal life has ceased to be a long matter perceive that our appeals for conviction are answered, now and then very closely upon the call. When we have cast off the scales of hope and fancy, and surrender our claims on mad chance, it is given us to see that some plan is working out: that the heavens, icy as they are to the pangs of our blood, have been throughout speaking to our souls; and, according to the strength there existing, we learn to comprehend them. But their language is an element of Time, whom primarily we have to know.

Evan Harrington was young. He wished not to clothe the generation. What was to the remainder of the exiled sons of Adam simply the brand of expulsion from Paradise, was to him hell. In his agony, anything less than an angel, soft-voiced in his path, would not have satisfied the poor boy, and here was this wretched outcast, and instead of being relieved, he was to act the reliever!

Striving to rouse the desolate creature, he shook her slightly. She now raised her head with a slow, gradual motion, like that of a wax-work, showing a white young face, tearless,-dreadfully drawn at the lips. After gazing at him, she turned her head mechanically to her shoulder, as to ask him why he touched her. He withdrew his hand, saying:

"Why are you here? Pardon me; I want, if possible, to help you."

A light sprang in her eyes. She jumped from the stone, and ran forward a step or two, with a gasp:

"Oh, my God! I want to go and drown myself."

Evan lingered behind her till he saw her body sway, and in a fit of trembling she half fell on his outstretched arm. He led her to the stone, not knowing what on earth to do with her. There was no sign of a house near; they were quite solitary; to all his questions she gave an unintelligible moan. He had not the heart to leave her, so, taking a sharp seat on a heap of flints, thus possibly furnishing future occupation for one of his craftsmen, he waited, and amused himself by marking out diagrams with his stick in the thick dust.

His thoughts were far away, when he heard, faintly uttered:

"Why do you stop here?"

"To help you."

"Please don't. Let me be. I can't be helped."

"My good creature," said Evan, "it's quite impossible that I should leave you in this state. Tell me where you were going when your illness seized you?"

"I was going," she commenced vacantly, "to the sea—the water," she added, with a shivering lip.

The foolish youth asked her if she could be cold on such a night.

"No, I'm not cold," she replied, drawing closer over her lap the ends of a shawl which would in that period have been thought rather gaudy for her station.

"You were going to Lymport?"

"Yes,—Lymport's nearest, I think."

"And why were you out travelling at this hour?"

She dropped her head, and began rocking to right and left.

While they talked the noise of waggon-wheels was heard approaching. Evan went into the middle of the road, and beheld a covered waggon, and a fellow whom he advanced to meet, plodding a little to the rear of the horses. He proved kindly. He was a farmer's man, he said, and was at that moment employed in removing the furniture of the farmer's son, who had failed as a corn-chandler in Lymport, to Hillford, which he expected to reach about morn. He answered Evan's request that he would afford the young woman conveyance as far as Fallowfield:

"Tak" her in? That I will.

"She won't hurt the harses," he pursued, pointing his whip at the vehicle: "there's my mate, Gearge Stoakes, he's in there, snorin' his turn. Can't you hear 'n asnorin' thraugh the wheels? I can; I've been laughin'! He do snore that loud-Gearge do!"

Proceeding to inform Evan how George Stokes had snored in that characteristic manner from boyhood, ever since he and George had slept in a hayloft together; and how he, kept wakeful and driven to distraction by George Stokes' nose, had been occasionally compelled, in sheer self-defence, madly to start up and hold that pertinacious alarum in tight compression between thumb and forefinger; and how George Stokes, thus severely handled, had burst his hold with a tremendous snort, as big as a bull, and had invariably uttered the exclamation, "Hulloa!—same to you, my lad!" and rolled over to snore as fresh as ever;—all this with singular rustic comparisons, racy of the soil, and in raw Hampshire dialect, the waggoner came to a halt opposite the stone, and, while Evan strode to assist the girl, addressed himself to the great task of arousing the sturdy sleeper and quieting his trumpet, heard by all ears now that the accompaniment of the wheels was at an end.

George, violently awakened, complained that it was before his time, to which he was true; and was for going off again with exalted contentment, though his heels had been tugged, and were dangling some length out of the machine; but his comrade, with a determined blow of the lungs, gave another valiant pull, and George Stokes was on his legs, marvelling at the world and man. Evan had less difficulty with the girl. She rose to meet him, put up her arms for him to clasp her waist, whispering sharply in an inward breath: "What are you going to do with me?" and indifferent to his verbal response, trustingly yielded her limbs to his guidance. He could see blood on her bitten underlip; as, with the help of the waggoner, he lifted her on the mattress, backed by a portly bundle, which the sagacity of Mr. Stokes had selected for his couch.

The waggoner cracked his whip, laughing at George Stokes, who yawned and settled into a composed ploughswing, without asking questions; apparently resolved to finish his nap on his legs.

"Warn't he like that Myzepper chap, I see at the circus, bound athert gray mare!" chuckled the waggoner. "So he'd 'a gone on, had ye 'a let 'n. No wulves waddn't wake Gearge till he'd slept it out. Then he'd say, 'marnin"!' to 'm. Are ye 'wake now, Gearge?"

The admirable sleeper preferred to be a quiet butt, and the waggoner leisurely exhausted the fun that was to be had out of him; returning to it with a persistency that evinced more concentration than variety in his mind. At last Evan said: "Your pace is rather slow. They'll be shut up in Fallowfield. I'll go on ahead. You'll find me at one of the inns-the Green Dragon."

In return for this speech, the waggoner favoured him with a stare, followed by the exclamation:

"Oh, no! dang that!"

"Why, what's the matter?" quoth Evan.

"You en't goin' to be off, for to leave me and Gearge in the lurch there, with that ther' young woman, in that ther' pickle!" returned the waggoner.

Evan made an appeal to his reason, but finding that impregnable, he pulled out his scanty purse to guarantee his sincerity with an offer of pledgemoney. The waggoner waved it aside. He wanted no money, he said.

"Look heer," he went on; "if you're for a start, I tells ye plain, I chucks that ther' young woman int' the road."

Evan bade him not to be a brute.

"Nark and crop!" the waggoner doggedly exclaimed.

Very much surprised that a fellow who appeared sound at heart, should threaten to behave so basely, Evan asked an explanation: upon which the waggoner demanded to know what he had eyes for: and as this query failed to enlighten the youth, he let him understand that he was a man of family experience, and that it was easy to tell at a glance that the complaint the young woman laboured under was one common to the daughters of Eve. He added that, should an emergency arise, he, though a family man, would be useless: that he always vacated the premises while those incidental scenes were being enacted at home; and that for him and George Stokes to be left alone with the young woman, why they would be of no more service to her than a couple of babies newborn themselves. He, for his part, he assured Evan, should take to his heels, and relinquish waggon, and horses, and all; while George probably would stand and gape; and the end of it would be, they would all be had up for murder. He diverged from the alarming prospect, by a renewal of the foregoing alternative to the gentleman who had constituted himself the young woman's protector. If he parted company with them, they would immediately part company with the young woman, whose condition was evident.

"Why, couldn't you tall that?" said the waggoner, as Evan, tingling at the ears, remained silent.

"I know nothing of such things," he answered, hastily, like one hurt.

I have to repeat the statement, that he was a youth, and a modest one. He felt unaccountably, unreasonably, but horridly, ashamed. The thought of his actual position swamped the sickening disgust at tailordom. Worse, then, might happen to us in this extraordinary world! There was something more abhorrent than sitting with one's legs crossed, publicly stitching, and scoffed at! He called vehemently to the waggoner to whip the horses, and hurry ahead into Fallowfield; but that worthy, whatever might be his dire alarms, had a regular pace, that was conscious of no spur: the reply of "All right!" satisfied him at least; and Evan's chaste sighs for the appearance of an assistant petticoat round a turn of the road, were offered up duly, to the measure of the waggoner's steps.

Suddenly the waggoner came to a halt, and said "Blest if that Gearge bain't a snorin' on his pins!"

Evan lingered by him with some curiosity, while the waggoner thumped his thigh to, "Yes he be! no he bain't!" several times, in eager hesitation.

"It's a fellow calling from the downs," said Evan.

"Ay, so!" responded the waggoner. "Dang'd if I didn't think 'twere that Gearge of our'n. Hark awhile."

At a repetition of the call, the waggoner stopped his team. After a few minutes, a man appeared panting on the bank above them, down which he ran precipitately, knocked against Evan, apologized with the little breath that remained to him, and then held his hand as to entreat a hearing. Evan thought him half-mad; the waggoner was about to imagine him the victim of a midnight assault. He undeceived them by requesting, in rather flowery terms, conveyance on the road and rest for his limbs. It being explained to him that the waggon was already occupied, he comforted himself aloud with the reflection that it was something to be on the road again for one who had been belated, lost, and wandering over the downs for the last six hours.

"Walcome to git in, when young woman gits out," said the waggoner. "I'll gi' ye my sleep on t' Hillford."

"Thanks, worthy friend," returned the new comer. "The state of the case is this—I'm happy to take from humankind whatsoever I can get. If this gentleman will accept of my company, and my legs hold out, all will yet be well."

Though he did not wear a petticoat, Evan was not sorry to have him. Next to the interposition of the Gods, we pray for human fellowship when we are in a mess. So he mumbled politely, dropped with him a little to the rear, and they all stepped out to the crack of the waggoner's whip.

"Rather a slow pace," said Evan, feeling bound to converse.

"Six hours on the downs makes it extremely suitable to me," rejoined the stranger.

"You lost your way?"

"I did, sir. Yes; one does not court those desolate regions wittingly. I am for life and society. The embraces of Diana do not agree with my constitution. If classics there be who differ from me, I beg them to take six hours on the downs alone with the moon, and the last prospect of bread and cheese, and a chaste bed, seemingly utterly extinguished. I am cured of my romance. Of course, when I say bread and cheese, I speak figuratively. Food is implied."

Evan stole a glance at his companion.

"Besides," the other continued, with an inflexion of grandeur, "for a man accustomed to his hunters, it is, you will confess, unpleasant—I speak' hypothetically—to be reduced to his legs to that extent that it strikes him shrewdly he will run them into stumps."

The stranger laughed.

The fair lady of the night illumined his face, like one who recognized a subject. Evan thought he knew the voice. A curious struggle therein between native facetiousness and an attempt at dignity, appeared to Evan not unfamiliar; and the egregious failure of ambition and triumph of the instinct, helped him to join, the stranger in his mirth.

"Jack Raikes?" he said: "surely?"

"The man!" it was answered to him. "But you? and near our old school—Viscount Harrington? These marvels occur, you see—we meet again by night."

Evan, with little gratification at the meeting, fell into their former comradeship; tickled by a recollection of his old schoolfellow's India-rubber mind.

Mr. Raikes stood about a head under him. He had extremely mobile features; thick, flexible eyebrows; a loose, voluble mouth; a ridiculous figure on a dandified foot. He represented to you one who was rehearsing a part he wished to act before the world, and was not aware that he took the world into his confidence.

How he had come there his elastic tongue explained in tropes and puns and lines of dramatic verse. His patrimony spent, he at once believed himself an actor, and he was hissed off the stage of a provincial theatre.

"Ruined, the last ignominy endured, I fled from the gay vistas of the Bench—for they live who would thither lead me! and determined, the day before the yesterday—what think'st thou? why to go boldly, and offer myself as Adlatus to blessed old Cudford! Yes! a little Latin is all that remains to me, and I resolved, like the man I am, to turn, hic, hac, hoc, into bread and cheese, and beer: Impute nought foreign to me, in the matter of pride."

"Usher in our old school—poor old Jack!" exclaimed Evan.

"Lieutenant in the Cudford Academy!" the latter rejoined. "I walked the distance from London. I had my interview with the respected principal. He gave me of mutton nearest the bone, which, they say, is sweetest; and on sweet things you should not regale in excess. Endymion watched the sheep that bred that mutton! He gave me the thin beer of our boyhood, that I might the more soberly state my mission. That beer, my friend, was brewed by one who wished to form a study for pantomimic masks. He listened with the gravity which is all his own to the recital of my career; he pleasantly compared me to Phaethon, congratulated the river Thames at my not setting it on fire in my rapid descent, and extended to me the three fingers of affectionate farewell. 'You an usher, a rearer of youth, Mr. Raikes? Oh, no! Oh, no!' That was all I could get out of him. "'Gad! he might have seen that I didn't joke with the mutton-bone. If I winced at the beer it was imperceptible. Now a man who can do that is what I call a man in earnest."

"You've just come from Cudford?" said Evan.

"Short is the tale, though long the way, friend Harrington. From Bodley is ten miles to Beckley. I walked them. From Beckley is fifteen miles to Fallowfield. Them I was traversing, when, lo! near sweet eventide a fair horsewoman riding with her groom at her horse's heels. 'Lady,' says I, addressing her, as much out of the style of the needy as possible, 'will you condescend to direct me to Fallowfield?'—'Are you going to the match?' says she. I answered boldly that I was. 'Beckley's in,' says she, 'and you'll be in time to see them out, if you cut across the downs there.' I lifted my hat—a desperate measure, for the brim won't bear much—but honour to women though we perish. She bowed: I cut across the downs. In fine, Harrington, old boy, I've been wandering among those downs for the last seven or eight hours. I was on the point of turning my back on the road for the twentieth time, I believe when I heard your welcome vehicular music, and hailed you; and I ask you, isn't it luck for a fellow who hasn't got a penny in his pocket, and is as hungry as five hundred hunters, to drop on an old friend like this?"

Evan answered with the question:

"Where was it you said you met the young lady?"

"In the first place, O Amadis! I never said she was young. You're on the scent, I see."

Nursing the fresh image of his darling in his heart's recesses, Evan, as they entered Fallowfield, laid the state of his purse before Jack, and earned anew the epithet of Amadis, when it came to be told that the occupant of the waggon was likewise one of its pensioners.

Sleep had long held its reign in Fallowfield. Nevertheless, Mr. Raikes, though blind windows alone looked on him, and nought foreign was to be imputed to him in the matter of pride, had become exceedingly solicitous concerning his presentation to the inhabitants of that quiet little country town; and while Evan and—the waggoner consulted the former with regard to the chances of procuring beds and supper, the latter as to his prospect of beer and a comfortable riddance of the feminine burden weighing on them all—Mr. Raikes was engaged in persuading his hat to assume something of the gentlemanly polish of its youth, and might have been observed now and then furtively catching up a leg to be dusted. Ere the wheels of the waggon stopped he had gained that ease of mind which the knowledge that you have done all a man may do and circumstances warrant, establishes. Capacities conscious of their limits may repose even proudly when they reach them; and, if Mr. Raikes had not quite the air of one come out of a bandbox, he at least proved to the discerning intelligence that he knew what sort of manner befitted that happy occasion, and was enabled by the pains he had taken to glance with a challenge at the sign of the hostelry, under which they were now ranked, and from which, though the hour was late, and Fallowfield a singularly somnolent little town, there issued signs of life approaching to festivity.

XI

Doings at an Inn

What every traveller sighs to find, was palatably furnished by the Green Dragon of Fallowfield—a famous inn, and a constellation for wandering coachmen. There pleasant smiles seasoned plenty, and the bill was gilded in a manner unknown to our days. Whoso drank of the ale of the Green Dragon kept in his memory a place apart for it. The secret, that to give a warm welcome is the breath of life to an inn, was one the Green Dragon boasted, even then, not to share with many Red Lions, or Cocks of the Morning, or Kings' Heads, or other fabulous monsters; and as if to show that when you are in the right track you are sure to be seconded, there was a friend of the Green Dragon, who, on a particular night of the year, caused its renown to enlarge to the dimensions of a miracle. But that, for the moment, is my secret.

Evan and Jack were met in the passage by a chambermaid. Before either of them could speak, she had turned and fled, with the words:

"More coming!" which, with the addition of "My goodness me!" were echoed by the hostess in her recess. Hurried directions seemed to be consequent, and then the hostess sallied out, and said, with a curtsey:

"Please to step in, gentlemen. This is the room, tonight."

Evan lifted his hat; and bowing, requested to know whether they could have a supper and beds.

"Beds, Sir!" cried the hostess. "What am I to do for beds! Yes, beds indeed you may have, but bed-rooms—if you ask for them, it really is more than I can supply you with. I have given up my own. I sleep with my maid Jane to-night."

"Anything will do for us, madam," replied Evan, renewing his foreign courtesy. "But there is a poor young woman outside."

"Another!" The hostess instantly smiled down her inhospitable outcry.

"She," said Evan, "must have a room to herself. She is ill."

"Must is must, sir," returned the gracious hostess. "But I really haven't the means."

"You have bed-rooms, madam?"

"Every one of them engaged, sir."

"By ladies, madam?"

"Lord forbid, Sir!" she exclaimed with the honest energy of a woman who knew her sex.

Evan bade Jack go and assist the waggoner to bring in the girl. Jack, who had been all the time pulling at his wristbands, and settling his coat-collar by the dim reflection of a window of the bar, departed, after, on his own authority, assuring the hostess that fever was not the young woman's malady, as she protested against admitting fever into her house, seeing that she had to consider her guests.

"We're open to all the world to-night, except fever," said the hostess. "Yes," she rejoined to Evan's order that the waggoner and his mate should be supplied with ale, "they shall have as much as they can drink," which is not a speech usual at inns, when one man gives an order for others, but Evan passed it by, and politely begged to be shown in to one of the gentlemen who had engaged bedrooms.

"Oh! if you can persuade any of them, sir, I'm sure I've nothing to say," observed the hostess. "Pray, don't ask me to stand by and back it, that's all."

Had Evan been familiar with the Green Dragon, he would have noticed that the landlady, its presiding genius, was stiffer than usual; the rosy smile was more constrained, as if a great host had to be embraced, and were trying it to the utmost stretch. There was, however, no asperity about her, and when she had led him to the door he was to enter to prefer his suit, and she had asked whether the young woman was quite common, and he had replied that he had picked her up on the road, and that she was certainly poor, the hostess said:

"I'm sure you're a very good gentleman, sir, and if I could spare your asking at all, I would."

With that she went back to encounter Mr. Raikes and his charge, and prime the waggoner and his mate.

A noise of laughter and talk was stilled gradually, as Evan made his bow into a spacious room, wherein, as the tops of pines are seen swimming on the morning mist, about a couple of dozen guests of divers conditions sat partially revealed through wavy clouds of tobacco-smoke. By their postures, which Evan's appearance by no means disconcerted, you read in a glance men who had been at ease for so many hours that they had no troubles in the world save the two ultimate perplexities of the British Sybarite, whose bed of roses is harassed by the pair of problems: first, what to do with his legs; secondly, how to imbibe liquor with the slightest possible derangement of those members subordinate to his upper structure. Of old the Sybarite complained. Not so our self-helpful islanders. Since they could not, now that work was done and jollity the game, take off their legs, they got away from them as far as they might, in fashions original or imitative: some by thrusting them out at full length; some by cramping them under their chairs: while some, taking refuge in a mental effort, forgot them, a process to be recommended if it did not involve occasional pangs of consciousness to the legs of their neighbours. We see in our cousins West of the great water, who are said to exaggerate our peculiarities, beings labouring under the same difficulty, and intent on its solution. As to the second problem: that of drinking without discomposure to the subservient limbs: the company present worked out this republican principle ingeniously, but in a manner beneath the attention of the Muse. Let Clio record that mugs and glasses, tobacco and pipes, were strewn upon the table. But if the guests had arrived at that stage when to reach the arm, or arrange the person, for a sip of good stuff, causes moral debates, and presents to the mind impediments equal to what would be raised in active men by the prospect of a great excursion, it is not to be wondered at that the presence of a stranger produced no immediate commotion. Two or three heads were half turned; such as faced him imperceptibly lifted their eyelids.

"Good evening, sir," said one who sat as chairman, with a decisive nod.

"Good night, ain't it?" a jolly-looking old fellow queried of the speaker, in an under-voice.

"'Gad, you don't expect me to be wishing the gentleman good-bye, do you?" retorted the former.

"Ha! ha! No, to be sure," answered the old boy; and the remark was variously uttered, that "Good night," by a caprice of our language, did sound like it.

"Good evening's 'How d' ye do?'—'How are ye?' Good night's 'Be off, and be blowed to you,'" observed an interpreter with a positive mind; and another, whose intelligence was not so clear, but whose perceptions had seized the point, exclaimed: "I never says it when I hails a chap; but, dash my buttons, if I mightn't 'a done, one day or another! Queer!"

The chairman, warmed by his joke, added, with a sharp wink: "Ay; it would be queer, if you hailed 'Good night' in the middle of the day!" and this among a company soaked in ripe ale, could not fail to run the electric circle, and persuaded several to change their positions; in the rumble of which, Evan's reply, if he had made any, was lost. Few, however, were there who could think of him, and ponder on that glimpse of fun, at the same time; and he would have been passed over, had not the chairman said: "Take a seat, sir; make yourself comfortable."

"Before I have that pleasure," replied Evan, "I—"

"I see where 'tis," burst out the old boy who had previously superinduced a diversion: "he's going to ax if he can't have a bed!"

A roar of laughter, and "Don't you remember this day last year?" followed the cunning guess. For awhile explication was impossible; and Evan coloured, and smiled, and waited for them.

"I was going to ask—"

"Said so!" shouted the old boy, gleefully.

"—one of the gentlemen who has engaged a bed-room to do me the extreme favour to step aside with me, and allow me a moment's speech with him."

Long faces were drawn, and odd stares were directed toward him, in reply.

"I see where 'tis"; the old boy thumped his knee. "Ain't it now? Speak up, sir! There's a lady in the case?"

"I may tell you thus much," answered Evan, "that it is an unfortunate young woman, very ill, who needs rest and quiet."

"Didn't I say so?" shouted the old boy.

But this time, though his jolly red jowl turned all round to demand a confirmation, it was not generally considered that he had divined so correctly. Between a lady and an unfortunate young woman, there seemed to be a strong distinction, in the minds of the company.

The chairman was the most affected by the communication. His bushy eyebrows frowned at Evan, and he began tugging at the brass buttons of his coat, like one preparing to arm for a conflict.

"Speak out, sir, if you please," he said. "Above board—no asides—no taking advantages. You want me to give up my bed-room for the use of your young woman, sir?"

Evan replied quietly: "She is a stranger to me; and if you could see her, sir, and know her situation, I think she would move your pity."

"I don't doubt it, sir—I don't doubt it," returned the chairman. "They all move our pity. That's how they get over us. She has diddled you, and she would diddle me, and diddle us all-diddle the devil, I dare say, when her time comes. I don't doubt it, sir."

To confront a vehement old gentleman, sitting as president in an assembly of satellites, requires command of countenance, and Evan was not browbeaten: he held him, and the whole room, from where he stood, under a serene and serious eye, for his feelings were too deeply stirred on behalf of the girl to let him think of himself. That question of hers, "What are you going to do with me?" implying such helplessness and trust, was still sharp on his nerves.

"Gentlemen," he said, "I humbly beg your pardon for disturbing you as I do."

But with a sudden idea that a general address on behalf of a particular demand must necessarily fail, he let his eyes rest on one there, whose face was neither stupid nor repellent, and who, though he did not look up, had an attentive, thoughtful cast about the mouth.

"May I entreat a word apart with you, sir?"

Evan was not mistaken in the index he had perused. The gentleman seemed to feel that he was selected from the company, and slightly raising his head, carelessly replied: "My bed is entirely at your disposal," resuming his contemplative pose.

On the point of thanking him, Evan advanced a step, when up started the irascible chairman.

"I don't permit it! I won't allow it!" And before Evan could ask his reasons, he had rung the bell, muttering: "They follow us to our inns, now, the baggages! They must harry us at our inns! We can't have peace and quiet at our inns!—"

In a state of combustion, he cried out to the waiter:

"Here, Mark, this gentleman has brought in a dirty wench: pack her up to my bed-room, and lock her in lock her in, and bring down the key."

Agreeably deceived in the old gentleman's intentions, Evan could not refrain from joining the murmured hilarity created by the conclusion of his order. The latter glared at him, and added: "Now, sir, you've done your worst. Sit down, and be merry."

Replying that he had a friend outside, and would not fail to accept the invitation, Evan retired. He was met by the hostess with the reproachful declaration on her lips, that she was a widow woman, wise in appearances, and that he had brought into her house that night work she did not expect, or bargain for. Rather (since I must speak truth of my gentleman) to silence her on the subject, and save his ears, than to propitiate her favour towards the girl, Evan drew out his constitutionally lean purse, and dropped it in her hand, praying her to put every expense incurred to his charge. She exclaimed:

"If Dr. Pillie has his full sleep this night, I shall be astonished"; and Evan hastily led Jack into the passage to impart to him, that the extent of his resources was reduced to the smallest of sums in shillings.

"I can beat my friend at that reckoning," said Mr. Raikes; and they entered the room.

Eyes were on him. This had ever the effect of causing him to swell to monstrous proportions in the histrionic line. Asking the waiter carelessly for some light supper dish, he suggested the various French, with "not that?" and the affable naming of another. "Nor that? Dear me, we shall have to sup on chops, I believe!"

Evan saw the chairman scrutinizing Raikes, much as he himself might have done, and he said: "Bread and cheese for me."

Raikes exclaimed: "Really? Well, my lord, you lead, and your taste is mine!"

A second waiter scudded past, and stopped before the chairman to say: "If you please, sir, the gentlemen upstairs send their compliments, and will be happy to accept."

"Ha!" was the answer. "Thought better of it, have they! Lay for three more, then. Five more, I guess." He glanced at the pair of intruders.

Among a portion of the guests there had been a return to common talk, and one had observed that he could not get that "Good Evening," and "Good Night," out of his head which had caused a friend to explain the meaning of these terms of salutation to him: while another, of a philosophic turn, pursued the theme: "You see, when we meets, we makes a night of it. So, when we parts, it's Good Night—natural! ain't it?" A proposition assented to, and considerably dilated on; but whether he was laughing at that, or what had aroused the fit, the chairman did not say.

Gentle chuckles had succeeded his laughter by the time the bread and cheese appeared.

In the rear of the provision came three young gentlemen, of whom the foremost lumped in, singing to one behind him, "And you shall have little Rosey!"

They were clad in cricketing costume, and exhibited the health and manners of youthful Englishmen of station. Frolicsome young bulls bursting on an assemblage of sheep, they might be compared to. The chairman welcomed them a trifle snubbingly. The colour mounted to the cheeks of Mr. Raikes as he made incision in the cheese, under their eyes, knitting his brows fearfully, as if at hard work.

The chairman entreated Evan to desist from the cheese; and, pulling out his watch, thundered: "Time!"

The company generally jumped on their legs; and, in the midst of a hum of talk and laughter, he informed Evan and Jack, that he invited them cordially to a supper up-stairs, and would be pleased if they would partake of it, and in a great rage if they would not.

Raikes was for condescending to accept.

Evan sprang up and cried: "Gladly, sir," and gladly would he have cast his cockney schoolmate to the winds, in the presence of these young cricketers; for he had a prognostication.

The door was open, and the company of jolly yeomen, tradesmen, farmers, and the like, had become intent on observing all the ceremonies of precedence: not one would broaden his back on the other; and there was bowing, and scraping, and grimacing, till Farmer Broadmead was hailed aloud, and the old boy stepped forth, and was summarily pushed through: the chairman calling from the rear, "Hulloa! no names to-night!" to which was answered lustily: "All right, Mr. Tom!" and the speaker was reproved with, "There you go! at it again!" and out and up they hustled.

The chairman said quietly to Evan, as they were ascending the stairs: "We don't have names to-night; may as well drop titles." Which presented no peculiar meaning to Evan's mind, and he smiled the usual smile.

To Raikes, at the door of the supper-room, the chairman repeated the same; and with extreme affability and alacrity of abnegation, the other rejoined, "Oh, certainly!"

No wonder that he rubbed his hands with more delight than aristocrats and people with gentlemanly connections are in the habit of betraying at the prospect of refection, for the release from bread and cheese was rendered overpoweringly glorious, in his eyes, by the bountiful contrast exhibited on the board before him.

XII

In which Ale is Shown to Have One Quality of Wine

To proclaim that yon ribs of beef and yonder ruddy Britons have met, is to furnish matter for an hour's comfortable meditation.

Digest the fact. Here the Fates have put their seal to something Nature clearly devised. It was intended; and it has come to pass. A thing has come to pass which we feel to be right! The machinery of the world, then, is not entirely dislocated: there is harmony, on one point, among the mysterious powers who have to do with us.

Apart from its eloquent and consoling philosophy, the picture is pleasant. You see two rows of shoulders resolutely set for action: heads in divers degrees of proximity to their plates: eyes variously twinkling, or hypocritically composed: chaps in vigorous exercise. Now leans a fellow right back with his whole face to the firmament: Ale is his adoration. He sighs not till he sees the end of the mug. Now from one a laugh is sprung; but, as if too early tapped, he turns off the cock, and primes himself anew. Occupied by their own requirements, these Britons allow that their neighbours have rights: no cursing at waste of time is heard when plates have to be passed: disagreeable, it is still duty. Field-Marshal Duty, the Briton's chief star, shines here. If one usurps more than his allowance of elbow-room, bring your charge against them that fashioned him: work away to arrive at some compass yourself.

Now the mustard ceases to travel, and the salt: the guests have leisure to contemplate their achievements. Laughs are more prolonged, and come from the depths.

Now Ale, which is to Beef what Eve was to Adam, threatens to take possession of the field. Happy they who, following Nature's direction, admitted not bright ale into their Paradise till their manhood was strengthened with beef. Some, impatient, had thirsted; had satisfied their thirst; and the ale, the light though lovely spirit, with nothing to hold it down, had mounted to their heads; just as Eve will do when Adam is not mature: just as she did—Alas!

Now, the ruins of the feast being removed, and a clear course left for the flow of ale, Farmer Broadmead, facing the chairman, rises. He stands in an attitude of midway. He speaks:

"Gentlemen! 'Taint fust time you and I be met here, to salbrate this here occasion. I say, not fust time, not by many a time, 'taint. Well, gentlemen, I ain't much of a speaker, gentlemen, as you know. Howsever, here I be. No denyin' that. I'm on my legs. This here's a strange enough world, and a man's a gentleman, I say, we ought for to be glad when we got 'm. You know: I'm coming to it shortly. I ain't much of a speaker, and if you wants somethin' new, you must ax elsewhere: but what I say is—Bang it! here's good health and long life to Mr. Tom, up there!"

"No names!" shouts the chairman, in the midst of a tremendous clatter.

Farmer Broadmead moderately disengages his breadth from the seat. He humbly axes pardon, which is accorded him with a blunt nod.

Ale (to Beef what Eve was to Adam) circulates beneath a dazzling foam, fair as the first woman.

Mr. Tom (for the breach of the rules in mentioning whose name on a night when identities are merged, we offer sincere apologies every other minute), Mr. Tom is toasted. His parents, who selected that day sixty years ago, for his bow to be made to the world, are alluded to with encomiums, and float down to posterity on floods of liquid amber.

But to see all the subtle merits that now begin to bud out from Mr. Tom, the chairman and giver of the feast; and also rightly to appreciate the speeches, we require to be enormously charged with Ale. Mr. Raikes did his best to keep his head above the surface of the rapid flood. He conceived the chairman in brilliant colours, and probably owing to the energy called for by his brain, the legs of the young man failed him twice, as he tried them. Attention was demanded. Mr. Raikes addressed the meeting.

The three young gentlemen-cricketers had hitherto behaved with a certain propriety. It did not offend Mr. Raikes to see them conduct themselves as if they were at a play, and the rest of the company paid actors. He had likewise taken a position, and had been the first to laugh aloud at a particular slip of grammar; while his shrugs at the aspirates transposed and the pronunciation prevalent, had almost established a free-masonry between him and one of the three young gentlemen-cricketers—a fair-haired youth, with a handsome, reckless face, who leaned on the table, humorously eyeing the several speakers, and exchanging by-words and laughs with his friends on each side of him.

But Mr. Raikes had the disadvantage of having come to the table empty in stomach—thirsty exceedingly; and, I repeat, that as, without experience, you are the victim of divinely given Eve, so, with no foundation to receive it upon, are you the victim of good sound Ale. He very soon lost his head. He would otherwise have seen that he must produce a wonderfully-telling speech if he was to keep the position he had taken, and had better not attempt one. The three young cricketers were hostile from the beginning. All of them leant forward, calling attention loudly laughing for the fun to come.

"Gentlemen!" he said: and said it twice. The gap was wide, and he said, "Gentlemen!" again.

This commencement of a speech proves that you have made the plunge, but not that you can swim. At a repetition of "Gentlemen!" expectancy resolved into cynicism.

"Gie'n a help," sang out a son of the plough to a neighbour of the orator.

"Hang it!" murmured another, "we ain't such gentlemen as that comes to."

Mr. Raikes was politely requested to "tune his pipe."

With a gloomy curiosity as to the results of Jack's adventurous undertaking, and a touch of anger at the three whose bearing throughout had displeased him, Evan regarded his friend. He, too, had drunk, and upon emptiness. Bright ale had mounted to his brain. A hero should be held as sacred as the Grand Llama: so let no more be said than that he drank still, nor marked the replenishing of his glass.

Raikes cleared his throat for a final assault: he had got an image, and was dashing off; but, unhappily, as if to make the start seem fair, he was guilty of his reiteration, "Gentlemen."

Everybody knew that it was a real start this time, and indeed he had made an advance, and had run straight through half a sentence. It was therefore manifestly unfair, inimical, contemptuous, overbearing, and base, for one of the three young cricketers at this period to fling back weariedly and exclaim: "By the Lord; too many gentlemen here!"

Evan heard him across the table. Lacking the key of the speaker's previous conduct, the words might have passed. As it was, they, to the ale-invaded head of a young hero, feeling himself the world's equal, and condemned nevertheless to bear through life the insignia of Tailordom, not unnaturally struck with peculiar offence. There was arrogance, too, in the young man who had interposed. He was long in the body, and, when he was not refreshing his sight by a careless contemplation of his finger-nails, looked down on his company at table, as one may do who comes from loftier studies. He had what is popularly known as the nose of our aristocracy: a nose that much culture of the external graces, and affectation of suavity, are required to soften. Thereto were joined thin lips and arched brows. Birth it was possible he could boast, hardly brains. He sat to the right of the fair-haired youth, who, with his remaining comrade, a quiet smiling fellow, appeared to be better liked by the guests, and had been hailed once or twice, under correction of the chairman, as Mr. Harry. The three had distinguished one there by a few friendly passages; and this was he who had offered his bed to Evan for the service of the girl. The recognition they extended to him did not affect him deeply. He was called Drummond, and had his place near the chairmen, whose humours he seemed to relish.

The ears of Mr. Raikes were less keen at the moment than Evan's, but his openness to ridicule was that of a man on his legs solus, amid a company sitting, and his sense of the same—when he saw himself the victim of it—acute. His face was rather comic, and, under the shadow of embarrassment, twitching and working for ideas—might excuse a want of steadiness and absolute gravity in the countenances of others.

The chairman's neighbour, Drummond, whispered him "Laxley will get up a row with that fellow."

"It's young Jocelyn egging him on," said the chairman.

"Um!" added Drummond: "it's the friend of that talkative rascal that's dangerous, if it comes to anything."

Mr. Raikes perceived that his host desired him to conclude. So, lifting his voice and swinging his arm, he ended: "Allow me to propose to you the Fly in Amber. In other words, our excellent host embalmed in brilliant ale! Drink him! and so let him live in our memories for ever!"

He sat down very well contented with himself, very little comprehended, and applauded loudly.

"The Flyin' Number!" echoed Farmer Broadmead, confidently and with clamour; adding to a friend, when both had drunk the toast to the dregs, "But what number that be, or how many 'tis of 'em, dishes me! But that's ne'ther here nor there."

The chairman and host of the evening stood up to reply, welcomed by thunders—"There ye be, Mr. Tom! glad I lives to see ye!" and "No names!" and "Long life to him!"

This having subsided, the chairman spoke, first nodding. "You don't want many words, and if you do, you won't get 'em from me."

Cries of "Got something better!" took up the blunt address.

"You've been true to it, most of you. I like men not to forget a custom."

"Good reason so to be," and "A jolly good custom," replied to both sentences.

"As to the beef, I hope you didn't find it tough: as to the ale—I know all about THAT!"

"Aha! good!" rang the verdict.

"All I can say is, that this day next year it will be on the table, and I hope that every one of you will meet Tom—will meet me here punctually. I'm not a Parliament man, so that'll do."

The chairman's breach of his own rules drowned the termination of his speech in an uproar.

Re-seating himself, he lifted his glass, and proposed: "The Antediluvians!"

Farmer Broadmead echoed: "The Antediloovians!" appending, as a private sentiment, "And dam rum chaps they were!"

The Antediluvians, undoubtedly the toast of the evening, were enthusiastically drunk, and in an ale of treble brew.

When they had quite gone down, Mr. Raikes ventured to ask for the reason of their receiving such honour from a posterity they had so little to do with. He put the question mildly, but was impetuously snapped at by the chairman.

"You respect men for their luck, sir, don't you? Don't be a hypocrite, and say you don't—you do. Very well: so do I. That's why I drink 'The Antediluvians'!"

"Our worthy host here" (Drummond, gravely smiling, undertook to elucidate the case) "has a theory that the constitutions of the Postdiluvians have been deranged, and their lives shortened, by the miasmas of the Deluge. I believe he carries it so far as to say that Noah, in the light of a progenitor, is inferior to Adam, owing to the shaking he had to endure in the ark, and which he conceives to have damaged the patriarch and the nervous systems of his sons. It's a theory, you know."

"They lived close on a thousand years, hale, hearty—and no water!" said the chairman.

"Well!" exclaimed one, some way down the table, a young farmer, red as a cock's comb: "no fools they, eh, master? Where there's ale, would you drink water, my hearty?" and back he leaned to enjoy the tribute to his wit; a wit not remarkable, but nevertheless sufficient in the noise it created to excite the envy of Mr. Raikes, who, inveterately silly when not engaged in a contest, now began to play on the names of the sons of Noah.

The chairman lanced a keen light at him from beneath his bushy eyebrows.

Before long he had again to call two parties to order. To Raikes, Laxley was a puppy: to Laxley, Mr. Raikes was a snob. The antagonism was natural: ale did but put the match to the magazine. But previous to an explosion, Laxley, who had observed Evan's disgust at Jack's exhibition of himself, and had been led to think, by his conduct and clothes in conjunction, that Evan was his own equal; a gentleman condescending to the society of a low-born acquaintance;—had sought with sundry propitiations, intelligent glances, light shrugs, and such like, to divide Evan from Jack. He did this, doubtless, because he partly sympathized with Evan, and to assure him that he took a separate view of him. Probably Evan was already offended, or he held to Jack, as a comrade should, or else it was that Tailordom and the pride of his accepted humiliation bellowed in his ears, every fresh minute: "Nothing assume!" I incline to think that the more ale he drank the fiercer rebel he grew against conventional ideas of rank, and those class-barriers which we scorn so vehemently when we find ourselves kicking at them. Whatsoever the reason that prompted him, he did not respond to Laxley's advances; and Laxley, disregarding him, dealt with Raikes alone.

In a tone plainly directed at him, he said: "Well, Harry, tired of this? The agriculturals are good fun, but I can't stand much of the small cockney. A blackguard who tries to make jokes out of the Scriptures ought to be kicked!"

Harry rejoined, with wet lips: "Wopping stuff, this ale! Who's that you want to kick?"

"Somebody who objects to his bray, I suppose," Mr. Raikes struck in, across the table, negligently thrusting out his elbow to support his head.

"Did you allude to me, sir?" Laxley inquired.

"I alluded to a donkey, sir." Raikes lifted his eyelids to the same level as Laxley's: "a passing remark on that interesting animal."

His friend Harry now came into the ring to try a fall.

"Are you an usher in a school?" he asked, meaning by his looks what men of science in fisticuffs call business.

Mr. Raikes started in amazement. He recovered as quickly.

"No, sir, not quite; but I have no doubt I should be able to instruct you upon a point or two."

"Good manners, for instance?" remarked the third young cricketer, without disturbing his habitual smile.

"Or what comes from not observing them," said Evan, unwilling to have Jack over-matched.

"Perhaps you'll give me a lesson now?" Harry indicated a readiness to rise for either of them.

At this juncture the chairman interposed.

"Harmony, my lads!—harmony to-night."

Farmer Broadmead, imagining it to be the signal for a song, returned:

"All right, Mr.— Mr. Chair! but we an't got pipes in yet. Pipes before harmony, you know, to-night."

The pipes were summoned forthwith. System appeared to regulate the proceedings of this particular night at the Green Dragon. The pipes charged, and those of the guests who smoked, well fixed behind them, celestial Harmony was invoked through the slowly curling clouds. In Britain the Goddess is coy. She demands pressure to appear, and great gulps of ale. Vastly does she swell the chests of her island children, but with the modesty of a maid at the commencement. Precedence again disturbed the minds of the company. At last the red-faced young farmer led off with "The Rose and the Thorn." In that day Chloe still lived; nor were the amorous transports of Strephon quenched. Mountainous inflation—mouse-like issue characterized the young farmer's first verse. Encouraged by manifest approbation he now told Chloe that he "by Heaven! never would plant in that bosom a thorn," with such a volume of sound as did indeed show how a lover's oath should be uttered in the ear of a British damsel to subdue her.

"Good!" cried Mr. Raikes, anxious to be convivial.

Subsiding into impertinence, he asked Laxley, "Could you tip us a Strephonade, sir? Rejoiced to listen to you, I'm sure! Promise you my applause beforehand."

Harry replied hotly: "Will you step out of the room with me a minute?"

"Have you a confession to make?" quoth Jack, unmoved. "Have you planted a thorn in the feminine flower-garden? Make a clean breast of it at the table. Confess openly and be absolved."

While Evan spoke a word of angry reproof to Raikes, Harry had to be restrained by his two friends. The rest of the company looked on with curiosity; the mouth of the chairman was bunched. Drummond had his eyes on Evan, who was gazing steadily at the three. Suddenly "The fellow isn't a gentleman!" struck the attention of Mr. Raikes with alarming force.

Raikes—and it may be because he knew he could do more than Evan in this respect—vociferated: "I'm the son of a gentleman!"

Drummond, from the head of the table, saw that a diversion was imperative. He leaned forward, and with a look of great interest said:

"Are you? Pray, never disgrace your origin, then."

"If the choice were offered me, I think I would rather have known his father," said the smiling fellow, yawning, and rocking on his chair.

"You would, possibly, have been exceedingly intimate—with his right foot," said Raikes.

The other merely remarked: "Oh! that is the language of the son of a gentleman."

The tumult of irony, abuse, and retort, went on despite the efforts of Drummond and the chairman. It was odd; for at Farmer Broadmead's end of the table, friendship had grown maudlin: two were seen in a drowsy embrace, with crossed pipes; and others were vowing deep amity, and offering to fight the man that might desire it.

"Are ye a friend? or are ye a foe?" was heard repeatedly, and consequences to the career of the respondent, on his choice of affirmatives to either of these two interrogations, emphatically detailed.

It was likewise asked, in reference to the row at the gentlemen's end: "Why doan' they stand up and have 't out?"

"They talks, they speechifies—why doan' they fight for 't, and then be friendly?"

"Where's the yarmony, Mr. Chair, I axes—so please ye?" sang out Farmer Broadmead.

"Ay, ay! Silence!" the chairman called.

Mr. Raikes begged permission to pronounce his excuses, but lapsed into a lamentation for the squandering of property bequeathed to him by his respected uncle, and for which—as far as he was intelligible—he persisted in calling the three offensive young cricketers opposite to account.

Before he could desist, Harmony, no longer coy, burst on the assembly from three different sources. "A Man who is given to Liquor," soared aloft with "The Maid of sweet Seventeen," who participated in the adventures of "Young Molly and the Kicking Cow"; while the guests selected the chorus of the song that first demanded it.

Evan probably thought that Harmony was herself only when she came single, or he was wearied of his fellows, and wished to gaze a moment on the skies whose arms were over and around his young beloved. He went to the window and threw it up, and feasted his sight on the moon standing on the downs. He could have wept at the bitter ignominy that severed him from Rose. And again he gathered his pride as a cloak, and defied the world, and gloried in the sacrifice that degraded him. The beauty of the night touched him, and mixed these feelings with mournfulness. He quite forgot the bellow and clatter behind. The beauty of the night, and heaven knows what treacherous hope in the depths of his soul, coloured existence warmly.

He was roused from his reverie by an altercation unmistakeably fierce.

Raikes had been touched on a tender point. In reply to a bantering remark of his, Laxley had hummed over bits of his oration, amid the chuckles of his comrades. Unfortunately at a loss for a biting retort, Raikes was reduced to that plain confession of a lack of wit; he offered combat.

"I'll tell you what," said Laxley, "I never soil my hands with a blackguard; and a fellow who tries to make fun of Scripture, in my opinion is one. A blackguard—do you hear? But, if you'll give me satisfactory proofs that you really are what I have some difficulty in believing the son of a gentleman—I'll meet you when and where you please."

"Fight him, anyhow," said Harry. "I'll take him myself after we finish the match to-morrow."

Laxley rejoined that Mr. Raikes must be left to him.

"Then I'll take the other," said Harry. "Where is he?"

Evan walked round to his place.

"I am here," he answered, "and at your service."

"Will you fight?" cried Harry.

There was a disdainful smile on Evan's mouth, as he replied: "I must first enlighten you. I have no pretensions to your blue blood, or yellow. If, sir, you will deign to challenge a man who is not the son of a gentleman, and consider the expression of his thorough contempt for your conduct sufficient to enable you to overlook that fact, you may dispose of me. My friend here has, it seems, reason to be proud of his connections. That you may not subsequently bring the charge against me of having led you to 'soil your hands'—as your friend there terms it—I, with all the willingness in the world to chastise you or him for your impertinence, must first give you a fair chance of escape, by telling you that my father was a tailor."

The countenance of Mr. Raikes at the conclusion of this speech was a painful picture. He knocked the table passionately, exclaiming:

"Who'd have thought it?"

Yet he had known it. But he could not have thought it possible for a man to own it publicly.

Indeed, Evan could not have mentioned it, but for hot fury and the ale. It was the ale in him expelling truth; and certainly, to look at him, none would have thought it.

"That will do," said Laxley, lacking the magnanimity to despise the advantage given him, "you have chosen the very best means of saving your skins."

"We'll come to you when our supply of clothes runs short," added Harry. "A snip!"

"Pardon me!" said Evan, with his eyes slightly widening, "but if you come to me, I shall no longer give you a choice of behaviour. I wish you good-night, gentlemen. I shall be in this house, and am to be found here, till ten o'clock to-morrow morning. Sir," he addressed the chairman, "I must apologize to you for this interruption to your kindness, for which I thank you very sincerely. It's 'good-night,' now, sir," he pursued, bowing, and holding out his hand, with a smile.

The chairman grasped it: "You're a hot-headed young fool, sir: you're an ill-tempered ferocious young ass. Can't you see another young donkey without joining company in kicks-eh? Sit down, and don't dare to spoil the fun any more. You a tailor! Who'll believe it? You're a nobleman in disguise. Didn't your friend say so?—ha! ha! Sit down." He pulled out his watch, and proclaiming that he was born into this world at the hour about to strike, called for a bumper all round.

While such of the company as had yet legs and eyes unvanquished by the potency of the ale, stood up to drink and cheer, Mark, the waiter, scurried into the room, and, to the immense stupefaction of the chairman, and amusement of his guests, spread the news of the immediate birth of a little stranger on the premises, who was declared by Dr. Pillie to be a lusty boy, and for whom the kindly landlady solicited good luck to be drunk.

XIII

The Match of Fallow Field Against Beckley

The dramatic proportions to which ale will exalt the sentiments within us, and our delivery of them, are apt to dwindle and shrink even below the natural elevation when we look back on them from the hither shore of the river of sleep—in other words, wake in the morning: and it was with no very self-satisfied emotions that Evan, dressing by the full light of day, reviewed his share in the events of the preceding night. Why, since he had accepted his fate, should he pretend to judge the conduct of people his superiors in rank? And where was the necessity for him to thrust the fact of his being that abhorred social pariah down the throats of an assembly of worthy good fellows? The answer was, that he had not accepted his fate: that he considered himself as good a gentleman as any man living, and was in absolute hostility with the prejudices of society. That was the state of the case: but the evaporation of ale in his brain caused him to view his actions from the humble extreme of that delightful liquor, of which the spirit had flown and the corpse remained.

Having revived his system with soda-water, and finding no sign of his antagonist below, Mr. Raikes, to disperse the sceptical dimples on his friend's face, alluded during breakfast to a determination he had formed to go forth and show on the cricket-field.

"For, you know," he observed, "they can't have any objection to fight one."

Evan, slightly colouring, answered: "Why, you said up-stairs, you thought fighting duels disgraceful folly."

"So it is, so it is; everybody knows that," returned Jack; "but what can a gentleman do?"

"Be a disgraceful fool, I suppose," said Evan: and Raikes went on with his breakfast, as if to be such occasionally was the distinguished fate of a gentleman, of which others, not so happy in their birth, might well be envious.

He could not help betraying that he bore in mind the main incidents of the festival over-night; for when he had inquired who it might be that had reduced his friend to wear mourning, and heard that it was his father (spoken by Evan with a quiet sigh), Mr. Raikes tapped an egg, and his flexible brows exhibited a whole Bar of contending arguments within. More than for the love of pleasure, he had spent his money to be taken for a gentleman. He naturally thought highly of the position, having bought it. But Raikes appreciated a capital fellow, and felt warmly to Evan, who, moreover, was feeding him.

If not born a gentleman, this Harrington had the look of one, and was pleasing in female eyes, as the landlady, now present, bore witness, wishing them good morning, and hoping they had slept well. She handed to Evan his purse, telling him she had taken it last night, thinking it safer for the time being in her pocket; and that the chairman of the feast paid for all in the Green Dragon up to twelve that day, he having been born between the hours, and liking to make certain: and that every year he did the same; and was a seemingly rough old gentleman, but as soft-hearted as a chicken. His name must positively not be inquired, she said; to be thankful to him was to depart, asking no questions.

"And with a dart in the bosom from those eyes—those eyes!" cried Jack, shaking his head at the landlady's resistless charms.

"I hope you was not one of the gentlemen who came and disturbed us last night, Sir?" she turned on him sharply.

Jack dallied with the imputation, but denied his guilt.

"No; it wasn't your voice," continued the landlady. "A parcel of young puppies calling themselves gentlemen! I know him. It's that young Mr. Laxley: and he the nephew of a Bishop, and one of the Honourables! and then the poor gals get the blame. I call it a shame, I do. There's that poor young creature up-stairs-somebody's victim she is: and nobody's to suffer but herself, the little fool!"

"Yes," said Raikes. "Ah! we regret these things in after life!" and he looked as if he had many gentlemanly burdens of the kind on his conscience.

"It's a wonder, to my mind," remarked the landlady, when she had placidly surveyed Mr. Raikes, "how young gals can let some of you men-folk mislead 'em."

She turned from him huffily, and addressed Evan:

"The old gentleman is gone, sir. He slept on a chair, breakfasted, and was off before eight. He left word, as the child was born on his birthright, he'd provide for it, and pay the mother's bill, unless you claimed the right. I'm afraid he suspected—what I never, never-no! but by what I've seen of you—never will believe. For you, I'd say, must be a gentleman, whatever your company. She asks one favour of you, sir:—for you to go and let her speak to you once before you go away for good. She's asleep now, and mustn't be disturbed. Will you do it, by-and-by? Please to comfort the poor creature, sir."

Evan consented. I am afraid also it was the landlady's flattering speech made him, without reckoning his means, add that the young mother and her child must be considered under his care, and their expenses charged to him. The landlady was obliged to think him a wealthy as well as a noble youth, and admiringly curtsied.

Mr. John Raikes and Mr. Evan Harrington then strolled into the air, and through a long courtyard, with brewhouse and dairy on each side, and a pleasant smell of baking bread, and dogs winking in the sun, cats at the corners of doors, satisfied with life, and turkeys parading, and fowls, strutting cocks, that overset the dignity of Mr. Raikes by awakening his imitative propensities. Certain white-capped women, who were washing in a tub, laughed, and one observed: "He's for all the world like the little bantam cock stickin' 'self up in a crow against the Spaniar'." And this, and the landlady's marked deference to Evan, induced Mr. Raikes contemptuously to glance at our national blindness to the true diamond, and worship of the mere plumes in which a person is dressed.

They passed a pretty flower-garden, and entering a smooth-shorn meadow, beheld the downs beautifully clear under sunlight and slowly-sailing images of cloud. At the foot of the downs, on a plain of grass, stood a white booth topped by a flag, which signalled that on that spot Fallow field and Beckley were contending.

"A singular old gentleman! A very singular old gentleman, that!" Raikes observed, following an idea that had been occupying him. "We did wrong to miss him. We ought to have waylaid him in the morning. Never miss a chance, Harrington."

"What chance?" Evan inquired.

"Those old gentlemen are very odd," Jack pursued, "very strange. He wouldn't have judged me by my attire. Admetus' flocks I guard, yet am a God! Dress is nothing to those old cocks. He's an eccentric. I know it; I can see it. He's a corrective of Cudford, who is abhorrent to my soul. To give you an instance, now, of what those old boys will do—I remember my father taking me, when I was quite a youngster, to a tavern he frequented, and we met one night just such an old fellow as this; and the waiter told us afterwards that he noticed me particularly. He thought me a very remarkable boy—predicted great things. For some reason or other my father never took me there again. I remember our having a Welsh rarebit there for supper, and when the waiter last night mentioned a rarebit, "gad he started up before me. I gave chase into my early youth. However, my father never took me to meet the old fellow again. I believe it lost me a fortune."

Evan's thoughts were leaping to the cricket-field, or he would have condoled with Mr. Raikes for a loss that evidently afflicted him still.

Now, it must be told that the lady's-maid of Mrs. Andrew Cogglesby, borrowed temporarily by the Countess de Saldar for service at Beckley Court, had slept in charge of the Countess's boxes at the Green Dragon: the Countess having told her, with the candour of high-born dames to their attendants, that it would save expense; and that, besides, Admiral Combleman, whom she was going to see, or Sir Perkins Ripley (her father's old friend), whom she should visit if Admiral Combleman was not at his mansion-both were likely to have full houses, and she could not take them by storm. An arrangement which left her upwards of twelve hours' liberty, seemed highly proper to Maria Conning, this lady's-maid, a very demure young person. She was at her bed-room window, as Evan passed up the courtyard of the inn, and recognized him immediately. "Can it be him they mean that's the low tradesman?" was Maria's mysterious exclamation. She examined the pair, and added: "Oh, no. It must be the tall one they mistook for the small one. But Mr. Harrington ought not to demean himself by keeping company with such, and my lady should know of it."

My lady, alighting from the Lymport coach, did know of it, within a few minutes after Evan had quitted the Green Dragon, and turned pale, as high-born dames naturally do when they hear of a relative's disregard of the company he keeps.

"A tailor, my lady!" said scornful Maria; and the Countess jumped and complained of a pin.

"How did you hear of this, Conning?" she presently asked with composure.

"Oh, my lady, he was tipsy last night, and kept swearing out loud he was a gentleman."

"Tipsy!" the Countess murmured in terror. She had heard of inaccessible truths brought to light by the magic wand of alcohol. Was Evan intoxicated, and his dreadful secret unlocked last night?

"And who may have told you of this, Conning?" she asked.

Maria plunged into one of the boxes, and was understood to say that nobody in particular had told her, but that among other flying matters it had come to her ears.

"My brother is Charity itself," sighed the Countess. "He welcomes high or low."

"Yes, but, my lady, a tailor!" Maria repeated, and the Countess, agreeing with her scorn as she did, could have killed her. At least she would have liked to run a bodkin into her, and make her scream. In her position she could not always be Charity itself: nor is this the required character for a high-born dame: so she rarely affected it.

"Order a fly: discover the direction Mr. Harrington has taken; spare me further remarks," she said; and Maria humbly flitted from her presence.

When she was gone, the Countess covered her face with her hands. "Even this creature would despise us!" she exclaimed.

The young lady encountered by Mr. Raikes on the road to Fallow field, was wrong in saying that Beckley would be seen out before the shades of evening caught up the ball. Not one, but two men of Beckley—the last two—carried out their bats, cheered handsomely by both parties. The wickets pitched in the morning, they carried them in again, and plaudits renewed proved that their fame had not slumbered. To stand before a field, thoroughly aware that every successful stroke you make is adding to the hoards of applause in store for you is a joy to your friends, an exasperation to your foes; I call this an exciting situation, and one as proud as a man may desire. Then, again, the two last men of an eleven are twins: they hold one life between them; so that he who dies extinguishes the other. Your faculties are stirred to their depths. You become engaged in the noblest of rivalries: in defending your own, you fight for your comrade's existence. You are assured that the dread of shame, if not emulation, is making him equally wary and alert.

Behold, then, the two bold men of Beckley fighting to preserve one life. Under the shadow of the downs they stand, beneath a glorious day, and before a gallant company. For there are ladies in carriages here, there are cavaliers; good county names may be pointed out. The sons of first-rate families are in the two elevens, mingled with the yeomen and whoever can best do the business. Fallow field and Beckley, without regard to rank, have drawn upon their muscle and science. One of the bold men of Beckley at the wickets is Nick Frim, son of the gamekeeper at Beckley Court; the other is young Tom Copping, son of Squire Copping, of Dox Hall, in the parish of Beckley. Last year, you must know, Fallow field beat. That is why Nick Frim, a renowned out-hitter, good to finish a score brilliantly with a pair of threes, has taken to blocking, and Mr. Tom cuts with caution, though he loves to steal his runs, and is usually dismissed by his remarkable cunning.

The field was ringing at a stroke of Nick Frim's, who had lashed out in his old familiar style at last, and the heavens heard of it, when Evan came into the circle of spectators. Nick and Tom were stretching from post to post, might and main. A splendid four was scored. The field took breath with the heroes; and presume not to doubt that heroes they are. It is good to win glory for your country; it is also good to win glory for your village. A Member of Parliament, Sir George Lowton, notes this emphatically, from the statesman's eminence, to a group of gentlemen on horseback round a carriage wherein a couple of fair ladies reclined.

"They didn't shout more at the news of the Battle of Waterloo. Now this is our peculiarity, this absence of extreme centralization. It must be encouraged. Local jealousies, local rivalries, local triumphs—these are the strength of the kingdom."

"If you mean to say that cricket's a —" the old squire speaking (Squire Uplift of Fallow field) remembered the saving presences, and coughed—"good thing, I'm one with ye, Sir George. Encouraged, egad! They don't want much of that here. Give some of your lean London straws a strip o' clean grass and a bit o' liberty, and you'll do 'em a service."

"What a beautiful hit!" exclaimed one of the ladies, languidly watching the ascent of the ball.

"Beautiful, d' ye call it?" muttered the squire.

The ball, indeed, was dropping straight into the hands of the long-hit-off. Instantly a thunder rolled. But it was Beckley that took the joyful treble—Fallow field the deeply—cursing bass. The long-hit-off, he who never was known to miss a catch-butter-fingered beast!—he has let the ball slip through his fingers.

Are there Gods in the air? Fred Linnington, the unfortunate of Fallow field, with a whole year of unhappy recollection haunting him in prospect, ere he can retrieve his character—Fred, if he does not accuse the powers of the sky, protests that he cannot understand it, which means the same.

Fallow field's defeat—should such be the result of the contest—he knows now will be laid at his door. Five men who have bowled at the indomitable Beckleyans think the same. Albeit they are Britons, it abashes them. They are not the men they were. Their bowling is as the bowling of babies; and see! Nick, who gave the catch, and pretends he did it out of commiseration for Fallow field, the ball has flown from his bat sheer over the booth. If they don't add six to the score, it will be the fault of their legs. But no: they rest content with a fiver and cherish their wind.

Yet more they mean to do, Success does not turn the heads of these Britons, as it would of your frivolous foreigners.

And now small boys (who represent the Press here) spread out from the marking-booth, announcing foremost, and in larger type, as it were, quite in Press style, their opinion—which is, that Fallow field will get a jolly good hiding; and vociferating that Beckley is seventy-nine ahead, and that Nick Frim, the favourite of the field, has scored fifty-one to his own cheek. The boys are boys of both villages: but they are British boys—they adore prowess. The Fallow field boys wish that Nick Frim would come and live on their side; the boys of Beckley rejoice in possessing him. Nick is the wicketkeeper of the Beckley eleven; long-limbed, wiry, keen of eye. His fault as a batsman is, that he will be a slashing hitter. He is too sensible of the joys of a grand spanking hit. A short life and a merry one, has hitherto been his motto.

But there were reasons for Nick's rare display of skill. That woman may have the credit due to her (and, as there never was a contest of which she did not sit at the springs, so is she the source of all superhuman efforts exhibited by men), be it told that Polly Wheedle is on the field; Polly, one of the upper housemaids of Beckley Court; Polly, eagerly courted by Fred Linnington, humbly desired by Nick Frim—a pert and blooming maiden—who, while her suitors combat hotly for an undivided smile, improves her holiday by instilling similar unselfish aspirations into the breasts of others.

Between his enjoyment of society and the melancholy it engendered in his mind by reflecting on him the age and decrepitude of his hat, Mr. John Raikes was doubtful of his happiness for some time. But as his taste for happiness was sharp, he, with a great instinct amounting almost to genius in its pursuit, resolved to extinguish his suspicion by acting the perfectly happy man. To do this, it was necessary that he should have listeners: Evan was not enough, and was besides unsympathetic;

he had not responded to Jack's cordial assurances of his friendship "in spite of anything," uttered before they came into the field.

Heat and lustre were now poured from the sky, on whose soft blue a fleet of clouds sailed heavily. Nick Frim was very wonderful, no doubt. He deserved that the Gods should recline on those gold-edged cushions above, and lean over to observe him. Nevertheless, the ladies were beginning to ask when Nick Frim would be out. The small boys alone preserved their enthusiasm for Nick. As usual, the men took a middle position. Theirs was the pleasure of critics, which, being founded on the judgement, lasts long, and is without disappointment at the close. It was sufficient that the ladies should lend the inspiration of their bonnets to this fine match. Their presence on the field is another beautiful instance of the generous yielding of the sex simply to grace our amusement, and their acute perception of the part they have to play.

Mr. Raikes was rather shy of them at first. But his acting rarely failing to deceive himself, he began to feel himself the perfectly happy man he impersonated, and where there were ladies he went, and talked of days when he had creditably handled a bat, and of a renown in the annals of Cricket cut short by mysterious calamity. The foolish fellow did not know that they care not a straw for cricketing fame. His gaiety presently forsook him as quickly as it had come. Instead of remonstrating at Evan's restlessness, it was he who now dragged Evan from spot to spot. He spoke low and nervously.

"We're watched!"

There was indeed a man lurking near and moving as they moved, with a speculative air. Writs were out against Raikes. He slipped from his friend, saying:

"Never mind me. That old amphitryon's birthday hangs on till the meridian; you understand. His table invites. He is not unlikely to enjoy my conversation. What mayn't that lead to? Seek me there."

Evan strolled on, relieved by the voluntary departure of the weariful funny friend he would not shake off, but could not well link with.

A long success is better when seen at a distance of time, and Nick Frim was beginning to suffer from the monotony of his luck. Fallow field could do nothing with him. He no longer blocked. He lashed out at every ball, and far flew every ball that was bowled. The critics saw, in this return to his old practices, promise of Nick's approaching extinction. The ladies were growing hot and weary. The little boys gasped on the grass, but like cunning circulators of excitement, spread a report to keep it up, that Nick, on going to his wickets the previous day, had sworn an oath that he would not lay down his bat till he had scored a hundred.

So they had still matter to agitate their youthful breasts, and Nick's gradual building up of tens, and prophecies and speculations as to his chances of completing the hundred, were still vehemently confided to the field, amid a general mopping of faces.

Evan did become aware that a man was following him. The man had not the look of a dreaded official. His countenance was sun-burnt and open, and he was dressed in a countryman's holiday suit. When Evan met his eyes, they showed perplexity. Evan felt he was being examined from head to heel, but by one unaccustomed to his part, and without the courage to decide what he ought consequently to do while a doubt remained, though his inspection was verging towards a certainty in his mind.

At last, somewhat annoyed that the man should continue to dog him wherever he moved, he turned on him and asked him what he wanted?

"Be you a Muster Eav'n Harrington, Esquire?" the man drawled out in the rustic music of inquiry.

"That is my name," said Evan.

"Ay," returned the man, "it's somebody lookin' like a lord, and has a small friend wi' shockin' old hat, and I see ye come out o' the Green Drag'n this mornin'—I don't reck'n there's e'er a mistaak, but I likes to make cock sure. Be you been to Poortigal, sir?"

"Yes," answered Evan, "I have been to Poortigal."

"What's the name o' the capital o' Portugal, sir?" The man looked immensely shrewd, and nodding his consent at the laughing reply, added:

"And there you was born, sir? You'll excuse my boldness, but I only does what's necessary."

Evan said he was not born there.

"No, not born there. That's good. Now, sir, did you happen to be born anywheres within smell o' salt water?"

"Yes," answered Evan, "I was born by the sea."

"Not far beyond fifty mile from Fall'field here, sir?"

"Something less."

"All right. Now I'm cock sure," said the man. "Now, if you'll have the kindness just to oblige me by—'he sped the words and the instrument jointly at Evan, takin' that there letter, I'll say good-bye, sir, and my work's done for the day."

Saying which, he left Evan with the letter in his hands. Evan turned it over curiously. It was addressed to "Evan Harrington, Esquire, T—— of Lymport."

A voice paralyzed his fingers: the clear ringing voice of a young horsewoman, accompanied by a little maid on a pony, who galloped up to the carriage upon which Squire Uplift, Sir George Lowton, Hamilton Jocelyn, and other cavaliers, were in attendance.

"Here I am at last, and Beckley's in still! How d' ye do, Lady Racial? How d' ye do, Sir George. How d' ye do, everybody. Your servant, Squire! We shall beat you. Harry says we shall soon be a hundred a-head of you. Fancy those boys! they would sleep at Fallow field last night. How I wish you had made a bet with me, Squire."

"Well, my lass, it's not too late," said the Squire, detaining her hand.

"Oh, but it wouldn't be fair now. And I'm not going to be kissed on the field, if you please, Squire. Here, Dorry will do instead. Dorry! come and be kissed by the Squire."

It was Rose, living and glowing; Rose, who was the brilliant young Amazon, smoothing the neck of a mettlesome gray cob. Evan's heart bounded up to her, but his limbs were motionless.

The Squire caught her smaller companion in his arms, and sounded a kiss upon both her cheeks; then settled her in the saddle, and she went to answer some questions of the ladies. She had the same lively eyes as Rose; quick saucy lips, red, and open for prattle. Rolls of auburn hair fell down her back, for being a child she was allowed privileges. To talk as her thoughts came, as well as to wear her hair as it grew, was a special privilege of this young person, on horseback or elsewhere.

"Now, I know what you want to ask me, Aunt Shorne. Isn't it about my Papa? He's not come, and he won't be able to come for a week.—Glad to be with Cousin Rosey? I should think I am! She's the nicest girl I ever could suppose. She isn't a bit spoiled by Portugal; only browned; and she doesn't care for that; no more do I. I rather like the sun when it doesn't freckle you. I can't bear freckles, and I don't believe in milk for them. People who have them are such a figure. Drummond Forth has them, but he's a man, and it doesn't matter for a man to have freckles. How's my uncle Mel? Oh, he's quite well. I mean he has the gout in one of his fingers, and it's swollen so, it's just like a great fat fir cone! He can't write a bit, and rests his hand on a table. He wants to have me made to write with my left hand as well as my right. As if I was ever going to have the gout in one of my fingers!"

Sir George Lowton observed to Hamilton Jocelyn, that Melville must take to his tongue now.

"I fancy he will," said Hamilton. "My father won't give up his nominee; so I fancy he'll try Fallow field. Of course, we go in for the agricultural interest; but there's a cantankerous old ruffian down here—a brewer, or something—he's got half the votes at his bidding. We shall see."

"Dorothy, my dear child, are you not tired?" said Lady Racial. "You are very hot."

"Yes, that's because Rose would tear along the road to get here in time, after we had left those tiresome Copping people, where she had to make a call. 'What a slow little beast your pony is, Dorry!'—she said that at least twenty times."

"Oh, you naughty puss!" cried Rose. "Wasn't it, 'Rosey, Rosey, I'm sure we shall be too late, and shan't see a thing: do come along as hard as you can'?"

"I'm sure it was not," Miss Dorothy retorted, with the large eyes of innocence. "You said you wanted to see Nick Frim keeping the wicket, and Ferdinand Laxley bowl. And, oh! you know something you said about Drummond Forth."

"Now, shall I tell upon you?" said Rose.

"No, don't!" hastily replied the little woman, blushing. And the cavaliers laughed out, and the ladies smiled, and Dorothy added: "It isn't much, after all."

"Then, come; let's have it, or I shall be jealous," said the Squire.

"Shall I tell?" Rose asked slily.

"It's unfair to betray one of your sex, Rose," remarked the sweetly-smiling lady.

"Yes, Lady Racial—mayn't a woman have secrets?" Dorothy put it with great natural earnestness, and they all laughed aloud. "But I know a secret of Rosey's," continued Miss Dorothy, "and if she tells upon me, I shall tell upon her."

"They're out!" cried Rose, pointing her whip at the wickets. "Good night to Beckley! Tom Copping 's run out."

Questions as to how it was done passed from mouth to mouth. Questions as to whether it was fair sprang from Tom's friends, and that a doubt existed was certain: the whole field was seen converging toward the two umpires.

Farmer Broadmead for Fallow field, Master Nat Hodges for Beckley.

"It really is a mercy there's some change in the game," said Mrs. Shorne, waving her parasol. "It's a charming game, but it wants variety a little. When do you return, Rose?"

"Not for some time," said Rose, primly. "I like variety very well, but I don't seek it by running away the moment I've come."

"No, but, my dear," Mrs. Shorne negligently fanned her face, "you will have to come with us, I fear, when we go. Your uncle accompanies us. I really think the Squire will, too; and Mr. Forth is no chaperon. Even you understand that."

"Oh, I can get an old man—don't be afraid," said Rose. "Or must I have and old woman, aunt?"

The lady raised her eyelids slowly on Rose, and thought: "If you were soundly whipped, my little madam, what a good thing it would be for you." And that good thing Mrs. Shorne was willing to do for Rose. She turned aside, and received the salute of an unmistakable curate on foot.

"Ah, Mr. Parsley, you lend your countenance to the game, then?"

The curate observed that sound Churchmen unanimously supported the game.

"Bravo!" cried Rose. "How I like to hear you talk like that, Mr. Parsley. I didn't think you had so much sense. You and I will have a game together—single wicket. We must play for something—what shall it be?"

"Oh—for nothing," the curate vacuously remarked.

"That's for love, you rogue!" exclaimed the Squire. "Come, come, none o' that, sir—ha! ha!"

"Oh, very well; we'll play for love," said Rose.

"And I'll hold the stakes, my dear—eh?"

"You dear old naughty Squire!—what do you mean?"

Rose laughed. But she had all the men surrounding her, and Mrs. Shorne talked of departing.

Why did not Evan bravely march away? Why, he asked himself, had he come on this cricket-field to be made thus miserable? What right had such as he to look on Rose? Consider, however, the young man's excuses. He could not possibly imagine that a damsel who rode one day to a match, would return on the following day to see it finished: or absolutely know that unseen damsel to be Rose Jocelyn. And if he waited, it was only to hear her sweet voice once again, and go for ever. As far as he could fathom his hopes, they were that Rose would not see him: but the hopes of youth are deep.

Just then a toddling small rustic stopped in front of Evan, and set up a howl for his "faythr." Evan lifted him high to look over people's heads, and discover his wandering parent. The urchin, when he had settled to his novel position, surveyed the field, and shouting, "Fayther, fayther! here I bes on top of a gentleman!" made lusty signs, which attracted not his father alone. Rose sang out, "Who can lend me a penny?" Instantly the curate and the squire had a race in their pockets. The curate was first, but Rose favoured the squire, took his money with a nod and a smile, and rode at the little lad, to whom she was saying: "Here, bonny boy, this will buy you—"

She stopped and coloured.

"Evan!"

The child descended rapidly to the ground.

A bow and a few murmured words replied to her.

"Isn't this just like you, my dear Evan? Shouldn't I know that whenever I met you, you would be doing something kind? How did you come here? You were on your way to Beckley!"

"To London," said Evan.

"To London! and not coming over to see me—us?"

Here the little fellow's father intervened to claim his offspring, and thank the lady and the gentleman: and, with his penny firmly grasped, he who had brought the lady and the gentleman together, was borne off a wealthy human creature.

Before much further could be said between them, the Countess de Saldar drove up.

"My dearest Rose!" and "My dear Countess!" and "Not Louisa, then?" and, "I am very glad to see you!" without attempting the endearing "Louisa"—passed.

The Countess de Saldar then admitted the presence of her brother.

"Think!" said Rose. "He talks of going on straight from here to London."

"That pretty pout will alone suffice to make him deviate, then," said the Countess, with her sweetest open slyness. "I am now on the point of accepting your most kind invitation. Our foreign habits allow us to visit thus early! He will come with me."

Evan tried to look firm, and speak as he was trying to look. Rose fell to entreaty, and from entreaty rose to command; and in both was utterly fascinating to the poor youth. Luxuriously—while he hesitated and dwelt on this and that faint objection—his spirit drank the delicious changes of her face. To have her face before him but one day seemed so rich a boon to deny himself, that he was beginning to wonder at his constancy in refusal; and now that she spoke to him so pressingly, devoting her guileless eyes to him alone, he forgot a certain envious feeling that had possessed him while she was rattling among the other males—a doubt whether she ever cast a thought on Mr. Evan Harrington.

"Yes; he will come," cried Rose; "and he shall ride home with me and my friend Drummond; and he shall have my groom's horse, if he doesn't mind. Bob can ride home in the cart with Polly, my maid; and he'll like that, because Polly's always good fun—when they're not in love with her. Then, of course, she torments them."

"Naturally," said the Countess.

Mr. Evan Harrington's final objection, based on his not having clothes, and so forth, was met by his foreseeing sister.

"I have your portmanteau packed, in with me, my dear brother; Conning has her feet on it. I divined that I should overtake you."

Evan felt he was in the toils. After a struggle or two he yielded; and, having yielded, did it with grace. In a moment, and with a power of self-compression equal to that of the adept Countess, he threw off his moodiness as easily as if it had been his Spanish mantle, and assumed a gaiety that made the Countess's eyes beam rapturously upon him, and was pleasing to Rose, apart from the lead in admiration the Countess had given her—not for the first time. We mortals, the best of us, may be silly sheep in our likes and dislikes: where there is no premeditated or instinctive antagonism, we can be led into warm acknowledgement of merits we have not sounded. This the Countess de Saldar knew right well.

Rose now intimated her wish to perform the ceremony of introduction between her aunt and uncle present, and the visitors to Beckley Court. The Countess smiled, and in the few paces that separated the two groups, whispered to her brother: "Miss Jocelyn, my dear."

The eye-glasses of the Beckley group were dropped with one accord. The ceremony was gone through. The softly-shadowed differences of a grand manner addressed to ladies, and to males, were exquisitely accomplished by the Countess de Saldar.

"Harrington? Harrington?" her quick ear caught on the mouth of Squire Uplift, scanning Evan.

Her accent was very foreign, as she said aloud: "We are entirely strangers to your game—your creecket. My brother and myself are scarcely English. Nothing save diplomacy are we adepts in!"

"You must be excessively dangerous, madam," said Sir George, hat in air.

"Even in that, I fear, we are babes and sucklings, and might take many a lesson from you. Will you instruct me in your creecket? What are they doing now? It seems very unintelligible—indistinct—is it not?"

Inasmuch as Farmer Broadmead and Master Nat Hodges were surrounded by a clamorous mob, shouting both sides of the case, as if the loudest and longest-winded were sure to wrest a favourable judgement from those two infallible authorities on the laws of cricket, the noble game was certainly in a state of indistinctness.

The squire came forward to explain, piteously entreated not to expect too much from a woman's inapprehensive wits, which he plainly promised (under eyes that had melted harder men) he would not. His forbearance and bucolic gallantry were needed, for he had the Countess's radiant full visage alone. Her senses were dancing in her right ear, which had heard the name of Lady Racial pronounced, and a voice respond to it from the carriage.

Into what a pit had she suddenly plunged! You ask why she did not drive away as fast as the horses would carry her, and fly the veiled head of Demogorgon obscuring valley and hill and the shining firmament, and threatening to glare destruction on her? You do not know an intriguer. She relinquishes the joys of life for the joys of intrigue. This is her element. The Countess did feel that the heavens were hard on her. She resolved none the less to fight her way to her object; for where so much had conspired to favour her—the decease of the generous Sir Abraham Harrington, of Torquay, and the invitation to Beckley Court—could she believe the heavens in league against her? Did she not nightly pray to them, in all humbleness of body, for the safe issue of her cherished schemes? And in this, how unlike she was to the rest of mankind! She thought so; she relied on her devout observances; they gave her sweet confidence, and the sense of being specially shielded even when specially menaced. Moreover, tell a woman to put back, when she is once clearly launched! Timid as she may be, her light bark bounds to meet the tempest. I speak of women who do launch: they are not numerous, but, to the wise, the minorities are the representatives.

"Indeed, it is an intricate game!" said the Countess, at the conclusion of the squire's explanation, and leaned over to Mrs. Shorne to ask her if she thoroughly understood it.

"Yes, I suppose I do," was the reply; "it—rather than the amusement they find in it." This lady had recovered Mr. Parsley from Rose, but had only succeeded in making the curate unhappy, without satisfying herself.

The Countess gave her the shrug of secret sympathy.

"We must not say so," she observed aloud—most artlessly, and fixed the squire with a bewitching smile, under which her heart beat thickly. As her eyes travelled from Mrs. Shorne to the squire, she had marked Lady Racial looking singularly at Evan, who was mounting the horse of Bob the groom.

"Fine young fellow, that," said the squire to Lady Racial, as Evan rode off with Rose.

"An extremely handsome, well-bred young man," she answered. Her eyes met the Countess's, and the Countess, after resting on their surface with an ephemeral pause, murmured: "I must not praise my brother," and smiled a smile which was meant to mean: "I think with you, and thank you, and love you for admiring him."

Had Lady Racial joined the smile and spoken with animation afterwards, the Countess would have shuddered and had chills of dread. As it was, she was passably content. Lady Racial slightly dimpled her cheek, for courtesy's sake, and then looked gravely on the ground. This was no promise; it was even an indication (as the Countess read her), of something beyond suspicion in the lady's mind; but it was a sign of delicacy, and a sign that her feelings had been touched, from which a truce might be reckoned on, and no betrayal feared.

She heard it said that the match was for honour and glory. A match of two days' duration under a broiling sun, all for honour and glory! Was it not enough to make her despise the games of men? For something better she played. Her game was for one hundred thousand pounds, the happiness of her brother, and the concealment of a horror. To win a game like that was worth the trouble. Whether she would have continued her efforts, had she known that the name of Evan Harrington was then blazing on a shop-front in Lymport, I cannot tell. The possessor of the name was in love, and did not reflect.

Smiling adieu to the ladies, bowing to the gentlemen, and apprehending all the homage they would pour out to her condescending beauty when she had left them, the Countess's graceful hand gave the signal for Beckley.

She stopped the coachman ere the wheels had rolled off the muffling turf, to enjoy one glimpse of Evan and Rose riding together, with the little maid on her pony in the rear. How suitable they seemed! how happy! She had brought them together after many difficulties—might it not be? It was surely a thing to be hoped for!

Rose, galloping freshly, was saying to Evan: "Why did you cut off your moustache?"

He, neck and neck with her, replied: "You complained of it in Portugal."

And she: "Portugal's old times now to me—and I always love old times. I'm sorry! And, oh, Evan! did you really do it for me?"

And really, just then, flying through the air, close to the darling of his heart, he had not the courage to spoil that delicious question, but dallying with the lie, he looked in her eyes lingeringly.

This picture the Countess contemplated. Close to her carriage two young gentlemen-cricketers were strolling, while Fallow field gained breath to decide which men to send in first to the wickets.

One of these stood suddenly on tiptoe, and pointing to the pair on horseback, cried, with the vivacity of astonishment:

"Look there! do you see that? What the deuce is little Rosey doing with the tailor-fellow?"

The Countess, though her cheeks were blanched, gazed calmly in Demogorgon's face, took a mental impression of the speaker, and again signalled for Beckley.

BOOK III

XIV

The Countess Describes the Field of Action

Now, to clear up a point or two: You may think the Comic Muse is straining human nature rather toughly in making the Countess de Saldar rush open-eyed into the jaws of Demogorgon, dreadful to her. She has seen her brother pointed out unmistakeably as the tailor-fellow. There is yet time to cast him off or fly with him. Is it her extraordinary heroism impelling her onward, or infatuated rashness? or is it her mere animal love of conflict?

The Countess de Saldar, like other adventurers, has her star. They who possess nothing on earth, have a right to claim a portion of the heavens. In resolute hands, much may be done with a star. As it has empires in its gift, so may it have heiresses. The Countess's star had not blinked balefully at her. That was one reason why she went straight on to Beckley.

Again: the Countess was a born general. With her star above, with certain advantages secured, with battalions of lies disciplined and zealous, and with one clear prize in view, besides other undeveloped benefits dimly shadowing forth, the Countess threw herself headlong into the enemy's country.

But, that you may not think too highly of this lady, I must add that the trivial reason was the exciting cause—as in many great enterprises. This was nothing more than the simple desire to be located, if but for a day or two, on the footing of her present rank, in the English country-house of an offshoot of our aristocracy. She who had moved in the first society of a foreign capital—who had married a Count, a minister of his sovereign, had enjoyed delicious high-bred badinage with refulgent ambassadors, could boast the friendship of duchesses, and had been the amiable receptacle of their pardonable follies; she who, moreover, heartily despised things English:—this lady experienced thrills of proud pleasure at the prospect of being welcomed at a third-rate English mansion. But then, that mansion was Beckley Court. We return to our first ambitions, as to our first loves not that they are dearer to us,—quit that delusion: our ripened loves and mature ambitions are probably closest to our hearts, as they deserve to be—but we return to them because our youth has a hold on us which it asserts whenever a disappointment knocks us down. Our old loves (with the bad natures I know in them) are always lurking to avenge themselves on the new by tempting us to a little retrograde infidelity. A schoolgirl in Fallow field, the tailor's daughter, had sighed for the bliss of Beckley Court. Beckley Court was her Elysium ere the ardent feminine brain conceived a loftier summit. Fallen from that attained eminence, she sighed anew for Beckley Court. Nor was this mere spiritual longing; it had its material side. At Beckley Court she could feel her foreign rank. Moving with our nobility as an equal, she could feel that the short dazzling glitter of her career was not illusory, and had left her something solid; not coin of the realm exactly, but yet gold. She could not feel this in the Cogglesby saloons, among pitiable bourgeoises—middle-class people daily soiled by the touch of tradesmen. They dragged her down. Their very homage was a mockery.

Let the Countess have due credit for still allowing Evan to visit Beckley Court to follow up his chance. If Demogorgon betrayed her there, the Count was her protector: a woman rises to her husband. But a man is what he is, and must stand upon that. She was positive Evan had committed himself in some manner. As it did not suit her to think so, she at once encouraged an imaginary conversation, in which she took the argument that it was quite impossible Evan could have been so mad, and others instanced his youth, his wrongheaded perversity, his ungenerous disregard for his devoted sister, and his known weakness: she replying, that undoubtedly they were right so far: but that he could not have said he himself was that horrible thing, because he was nothing of the sort: which faith in Evan's stedfast adherence to facts, ultimately silenced the phantom opposition, and gained the day.

With admiration let us behold the Countess de Saldar alighting on the gravel sweep of Beckley Court, the footman and butler of the enemy bowing obsequious welcome to the most potent visitor Beckley Court has ever yet embraced.

The despatches of a general being usually acknowledged to be the safest sources from which the historian of a campaign can draw, I proceed to set forth a letter of the Countess de Saldar, forwarded to her sister, Harriet Cogglesby, three mornings after her arrival at Beckley Court; and which, if it should prove false in a few particulars, does nevertheless let us into the state of the Countess's mind, and gives the result of that general's first inspection of the field of action. The Countess's epistolary English does small credit to her Fallow field education; but it is feminine, and flows more than her ordinary speech. Besides, leaders of men have always notoriously been above the honours of grammar. "My Dearest Harriet,

"Your note awaited me. No sooner my name announced, than servitors in yellow livery, with powder and buckles started before me, and bowing one presented it on a salver. A venerable butler—most impressive! led the way. In future, my dear, let it be de Saldar de Sancorvo. That is our title by rights, and it may as well be so in England. English Countess is certainly best. Always put the de. But let us be systematic, as my poor Silva says. He would be in the way here, and had better not come till I see something he can do. Silva has great reliance upon me. The farther he is from Lymport, my dear!—and imagine me, Harriet, driving through Fallow field to Beckley Court! I gave one peep at Dubbins's, as I passed. The school still goes on. I saw three little girls skipping, and the old swing-pole. Seminary For Young Ladies as bright as ever! I should have liked to have kissed the children and given them bonbons and a holiday.

"How sparing you English are of your crests and arms! I fully expected to see the Jocelyns' over my bed; but no—four posts totally without ornament! Sleep, indeed, must be the result of dire fatigue in such a bed. The Jocelyn crest is a hawk in jesses. The Elburne arms are, Or, three falcons on a field, vert. How heraldry reminds me of poor Papa! the evenings we used to spend with him, when he stayed at home, studying it so diligently under his directions! We never shall again! Sir Franks Jocelyn is the third son of Lord Elburne, made a Baronet for his patriotic support of the Ministry in a time of great trouble. The people are sometimes grateful, my dear. Lord Elburne is the fourteenth of his line—originally simple country squires. They talk of the Roses, but we need not go so very far back as that. I do not quite understand why a Lord's son should condescend to a Baronetcy. Precedence of some sort for his lady, I suppose. I have yet to learn whether she ranks by his birth, or his present title. If so, a young Baronetcy cannot possibly be a gain. One thing is certain. She cares very little about it. She is most eccentric. But remember what I have told you. It will be serviceable when you are speaking of the family.

"The dinner-hour, six. It would no doubt be full seven in Town. I am convinced you are half-an-hour too early. I had the post of honour to the right of Sir Franks. Evan to the right of Lady Jocelyn. Most fortunately he was in the best of spirits—quite brilliant. I saw the eyes of that sweet Rose glisten. On the other side of me sat my pet diplomatist, and I gave him one or two political secrets which astonished him. Of course, my dear, I was wheedled out of them. His contempt for our weak intellects is ineffable. But a woman must now and then ingratiate herself at the expense of her sex. This is perfectly legitimate. Tory policy at the table. The Opposition, as Andrew says, not represented. So to show that we were human beings, we differed among ourselves, and it soon became clear to me that Lady Jocelyn is the rankest of Radicals. My secret suspicion is, that she is a person of no birth whatever, wherever her money came from. A fine woman—yes; still to be admired, I suppose, by some kind of men; but totally wanting in the essentially feminine attractions.

"There was no party, so to say. I will describe the people present, beginning with the insignifacants.

"First, Mr. Parsley, the curate of Beckley. He eats everything at table, and agrees with everything. A most excellent orthodox young clergyman. Except that he was nearly choked by a fish-bone, and could not quite conceal his distress—and really Rose should have repressed her desire to laugh till the time for our retirement—he made no sensation. I saw her eyes watering, and she is not clever in turning it off. In that nobody ever equalled dear Papa. I attribute the attack almost entirely to the tightness of the white neck-cloths the young clergymen of the Established Church wear. But, my dear, I have lived too long away from them to wish for an instant the slightest change in anything they think, say, or do. The mere sight of this young man was most refreshing to my spirit. He may be the shepherd of a flock, this poor Mr. Parsley, but he is a sheep to one young person.

"Mr. Drummond Forth. A great favourite of Lady Jocelyn's; an old friend. He went with them to the East. Nothing improper. She is too cold for that. He is fair, with regular features, very self-possessed, and ready—your English notions of gentlemanly. But none of your men treat a woman as a woman. We are either angels, or good fellows, or heaven knows what that is bad. No exquisite delicacy, no insinuating softness, mixed with respect, none of that hovering over the border, as Papa used to say, none of that happy indefiniteness of manner which seems to declare 'I would love you if I might,' or 'I do, but I dare not tell,' even when engaged in the most trivial attentions—handing a footstool, remarking on the soup, etc. You none of you know how to meet a woman's smile, or to engage her eyes without boldness—to slide off them, as it were, gracefully. Evan alone can look between the eyelids of a woman. I have had to correct him, for to me he quite exposes the state of his heart towards dearest Rose. She listens to Mr. Forth with evident esteem. In Portugal we do not understand young ladies having male friends.

"Hamilton Jocelyn—all politics. The stiff Englishman. Not a shade of manners. He invited me to drink wine. Before I had finished my bow his glass was empty—the man was telling an anecdote of Lord Livelyston! You may be sure, my dear, I did not say I had seen his lordship.

"Seymour Jocelyn, Colonel of Hussars. He did nothing but sigh for the cold weather, and hunting. All I envied him was his moustache for Evan. Will you believe that the ridiculous boy has shaved!

"Then there is Melville, my dear diplomatist; and here is another instance of our Harrington luck. He has the gout in his right hand; he can only just hold knife and fork, and is interdicted Port-wine and penmanship. The dinner was not concluded before I had arranged that Evan should resume (gratuitously, you know) his post of secretary to him. So here is Evan fixed at Beckley Court as long as Melville stays. Talking of him, I am horrified suddenly. They call him the great Mel! "Sir Franks is most estimable, I am sure, as a man, and redolent of excellent qualities—a beautiful disposition, very handsome. He has just as much and no more of the English polish one ordinarily meets. When he has given me soup or fish, bowed to me over wine, and asked a conventional question, he has done with me. I should imagine his opinions to be extremely good, for they are not a multitude.

"Then his lady-but I have not grappled with her yet. Now for the women, for I quite class her with the opposite sex.

"You must know that before I retired for the night, I induced Conning to think she had a bad head-ache, and Rose lent me her lady's-maid—they call the creature Polly. A terrible talker. She would tell all about the family. Rose has been speaking of Evan. It would have looked better had she been quiet—but then she is so English!"

Here the Countess breaks off to say, that from where she is writing, she can see Rose and Evan walking out to the cypress avenue, and that no eyes are on them; great praise being given to the absence of suspicion in the Jocelyn nature.

The communication is resumed the night of the same day.

"Two days at Beckley Court are over, and that strange sensation I had of being an intruder escaped from Dubbins's, and expecting every instant the old schoolmistress to call for me, and expose me, and take me to the dark room, is quite vanished, and I feel quite at home, quite happy. Evan is behaving well. Quite the young nobleman. With the women I had no fear of him; he is really admirable with the men—easy, and talks of sport and politics, and makes the proper use of Portugal. He has quite won the heart of his sister. Heaven smiles on us, dearest Harriet!

"We must be favoured, my dear, for Evan is very troublesome—distressingly inconsiderate! I left him for a day-remaining to comfort poor Mama—and on the road he picked up an object he had known at school, and this creature, in shameful garments, is seen in the field where Rose and Evan are riding—in a dreadful hat—Rose might well laugh at it!—he is seen running away from an old apple woman, whose fruit he had consumed without means to liquidate; but, of course, he rushes bolt up to Evan before all his grand company, and claims acquaintance, and Evan was base enough to acknowledge him! He disengaged himself so far well by tossing his purse to the wretch, but if he knows not how to—cut, I assure him it will be his ruin. Resolutely he must cast the dust off his shoes, or he will be dragged down to their level. By the way, as to hands and feet, comparing him with the Jocelyn men, he has every mark of better blood. Not a question about it. As Papa would say—We have Nature's proof.

"Looking out on a beautiful lawn, and the moon, and all sorts of trees, I must now tell you about the ladies here.

"Conning undid me to-night. While Conning remains unattached, Conning is likely to be serviceable. If Evan, would only give her a crumb, she would be his most faithful dog. I fear he cannot be induced, and Conning will be snapped up by somebody else. You know how susceptible she is behind her primness—she will be of no use on earth, and I shall find excuse to send her back immediately. After all, her appearance here was all that was wanted.

"Mrs. Melville and her dreadful juvenile are here, as you may imagine—the complete Englishwoman. I smile on her, but I could laugh. To see the crow's-feet under her eyes on her white skin, and those ringlets, is really too ridiculous. Then there is a Miss Carrington, Lady Jocelyn's cousin, aged thirty-two—if she has not tampered with the register of her birth. I should think her equal to it. Between dark and fair. Always in love with some man, Conning tells me she hears. Rose's maid, Polly, hinted the same. She has a little money.

"But my sympathies have been excited by a little cripple—a niece of Lady Jocelyn's and the favourite grand-daughter of the rich old Mrs. Bonner—also here—Juliana Bonner. Her age must be twenty. You would take her for ten. In spite of her immense expectations, the Jocelyns hate her. They can hardly be civil to her. It is the poor child's temper. She has already begun to watch dear Evan—certainly the handsomest of the men here as yet, though I grant you, they are well-grown men, these Jocelyns, for an untravelled Englishwoman. I fear, dear Harriet, we have been dreadfully deceived about Rose. The poor child has not, in her own right, much more than a tenth part of what we supposed, I fear. It was that Mrs. Melville. I have had occasion to notice her quiet boasts here. She said this morning, 'when Mel is in the Ministry'—he is not yet in Parliament! I feel quite angry with the woman, and she is not so cordial as she might be. I have her profile very frequently while I am conversing with her.

"With Grandmama Bonner I am excellent good friends,—venerable silver hair, high caps, etc. More of this most interesting Juliana Bonner by-and-by. It is clear to me that Rose's fortune is calculated upon the dear invalid's death! Is not that harrowing? It shocks me to think of it.

"Then there is Mrs. Shorne. She is a Jocelyn—and such a history! She married a wealthy manufacturer—bartered her blood for his money, and he failed, and here she resides, a bankrupt widow, petitioning any man that may be willing for his love AND a decent home. AND—I say in charity.

"Mrs. Shorne comes here to-morrow. She is at present with—guess, my dear!—with Lady Racial. Do not be alarmed. I have met Lady Racial. She heard Evan's name, and by that and the likeness I saw she knew at once, and I saw a truce in her eyes. She gave me a tacit assurance of it—she was engaged to dine here yesterday, and put it off—probably to grant us time for composure. If she comes I do not fear her. Besides, has she not reasons? Providence may have designed her for a staunch ally—I will not say, confederate.

"Would that Providence had fixed this beautiful mansion five hundred miles from L——, though it were in a desolate region! And that reminds me of the Madre. She is in health. She always will be overbearingly robust till the day we are bereft of her. There was some secret in the house when I was there, which I did not trouble to penetrate. That little Jane F——was there—not improved.

"Pray, be firm about Torquay. Estates mortgaged, but hopes of saving a remnant of the property. Third son! Don't commit yourself there. We dare not baronetize him. You need not speak it—imply. More can be done that way.

"And remember, dear Harriet, that you must manage Andrew so that we may positively promise his vote to the Ministry on all questions when Parliament next assembles. I understood from Lord Livelyston, that Andrew's vote would be thought much of. A most amusing nobleman! He pledged himself to nothing! But we are above such a thing as a commercial transaction. He must countenance Silva. Women, my dear, have sent out armies—why not fleets? Do not spare me your utmost aid in my extremity, my dearest sister.

"As for Strike, I refuse to speak of him. He is insufferable and next to useless. How can one talk with any confidence of relationship with a Major of Marines? When I reflect on what he is, and his conduct to Caroline, I have inscrutable longings to slap his face. Tell dear Carry her husband's friend—the chairman or something of that wonderful company of Strike's—you know—the Duke of Belfield is coming here. He is a blood-relation of the Elburnes, therefore of the Jocelyns. It will not matter at all. Breweries, I find, are quite in esteem in your England. It was highly commendable in his Grace to visit you. Did he come to see the Major of Marines? Caroline is certainly the loveliest woman I ever beheld, and I forgive her now the pangs of jealousy she used to make me feel.

"Andrew, I hope, has received the most kind invitations of the Jocelyns. He must come. Melville must talk with him about the votes of his abominable brother in Fallow field. We must elect Melville and have the family indebted to us. But pray be careful that Andrew speaks not a word to his odious brother about our location here. It would set him dead against these hospitable Jocelyns. It will perhaps be as well, dear Harriet, if you do not accompany Andrew. You would not be able to account for him quite thoroughly. Do as you like—I do but advise, and you know I may be trusted—for our sakes, dear one! I am working for Carry to come with Andrew. Beautiful women always welcome. A prodigy!—if they wish to astonish the Duke. Adieu! Heaven bless your babes!"

The night passes, and the Countess pursues:

"Awakened by your fresh note from a dream of Evan on horseback, and a multitude hailing him Count Jocelyn for Fallow field! A morning dream. They might desire that he should change his name; but 'Count' is preposterous, though it may conceal something.

"You say Andrew will come, and talk of his bringing Caroline. Anything to give our poor darling a respite from her brute. You deserve great credit for your managing of that dear little good-natured piece of obstinate man. I will at once see to prepare dear Caroline's welcome, and trust her stay may be prolonged in the interest of common humanity. They have her story here already.

"Conning has come in, and says that young Mr. Harry Jocelyn will be here this morning from Fallow field, where he has been cricketing. The family have not spoken of him in my hearing. He is not, I think, in good odour at home—a scapegrace. Rose's maid, Polly, quite flew out when I happened to mention him, and broke one of my laces. These English maids are domesticated savage animals.

"My chocolate is sent up, exquisitely concocted, in plate of the purest quality—lovely little silver cups! I have already quite set the fashion for the ladies to have chocolate in bed. The men, I hear, complain that there is no lady at the breakfast-table. They have Miss Carrington to superintend. I read, in the subdued satisfaction of her eyes (completely without colour), how much she thanks me and the institution of chocolate in bed. Poor Miss Carrington is no match for her opportunities. One may give them to her without dread.

"It is ten on the Sabbath morn. The sweet churchbells are ringing. It seems like a dream. There is nothing but the religion attaches me to England; but that—is not that everything? How I used to sigh on Sundays to hear them in Portugal!

"I have an idea of instituting toilette-receptions. They will not please Miss Carrington so well.

"Now to the peaceful village church, and divine worship. Adieu, my dear. I kiss my fingers to Silva. Make no effort to amuse him. He is always occupied. Bread!—he asks no more. Adieu! Carry will be invited with your little man. . . You unhappily unable. . . She, the sister I pine to see, to show her worthy of my praises. Expectation and excitement! Adieu!"

Filled with pleasing emotions at the thought of the service in the quiet village church, and worshipping in the principal pew, under the blazonry of the Jocelyn arms, the Countess sealed her letter and addressed it, and then examined the name of Cogglesby; which plebeian name, it struck her, would not sound well to the menials of Beckley Court. While she was deliberating what to do to conceal it, she heard, through her open window, the voices of some young men laughing. She beheld her brother pass these young men, and bow to them. She beheld them stare at him without at all returning his salute, and then one of them—the same who had filled her ears with venom at Fallow field—turned to the others and laughed outrageously, crying—

"By Jove! this comes it strong. Fancy the snipocracy here—eh?"

What the others said the Countess did not wait to hear. She put on her bonnet hastily, tried the effect of a peculiar smile in the mirror, and lightly ran down-stairs.

XV

A Capture

The three youths were standing in the portico when the Countess appeared among them. She singled out him who was specially obnoxious to her, and sweetly inquired the direction to the village post. With the renowned gallantry of his nation, he offered to accompany her, but presently, with a different exhibition of the same, proposed that they should spare themselves the trouble by dropping the letter she held prominently, in the bag.

"Thanks," murmured the Countess, "I will go." Upon which his eager air subsided, and he fell into an awkward silent march at her side, looking so like the victim he was to be, that the Countess could have emulated his power of laughter.

"And you are Mr. Harry Jocelyn, the very famous cricketer?"

He answered, glancing back at his friends, that he was, but did not know about the "famous."

"Oh! but I saw you—I saw you hit the ball most beautifully, and dearly wished my brother had an equal ability. Brought up in the Court of Portugal, he is barely English. There they have no manly sports. You saw him pass you?"

"Him! Who?" asked Harry.

"My brother, on the lawn, this moment. Your sweet sister's friend. Your uncle Melville's secretary."

"What's his name?" said Harry, in blunt perplexity.

The Countess repeated his name, which in her pronunciation was "Hawington," adding, "That was my brother. I am his sister. Have you heard of the Countess de Saldar?"

"Countess!" muttered Harry. "Dash it! here's a mistake."

She continued, with elegant fan-like motion of her gloved fingers: "They say there is a likeness between us. The dear Queen of Portugal often remarked it, and in her it was a compliment to me, for she thought my brother a model! You I should have known from your extreme resemblance to your lovely young sister."

Coarse food, but then Harry was a youthful Englishman; and the Countess dieted the vanity according to the nationality. With good wine to wash it down, one can swallow anything. The Countess lent him her eyes for that purpose; eyes that had a liquid glow under the dove—like drooping lids. It was a principle of hers, pampering our poor sex with swinish solids or the lightest ambrosia, never to let the accompanying cordial be other than of the finest quality. She knew that clowns, even more than aristocrats, are flattered by the inebriation of delicate celestial liquors.

"Now," she said, after Harry had gulped as much of the dose as she chose to administer direct from the founts, "you must accord me the favour to tell me all about yourself, for I have heard much of you, Mr. Harry Jocelyn, and you have excited my woman's interest. Of me you know nothing."

"Haven't I?" cried Harry, speaking to the pitch of his new warmth. "My uncle Melville goes on about you tremendously—makes his wife as jealous as fire. How could I tell that was your brother?"

"Your uncle has deigned to allude to me?" said the Countess, meditatively. "But not of him—of you, Mr. Harry! What does he say?"

"Says you're so clever you ought to be a man."

"Ah! generous!" exclaimed the Countess. "The idea, I think, is novel to him. Is it not?"

"Well, I believe, from what I hear, he didn't back you for much over in Lisbon," said veracious Harry.

"I fear he is deceived in me now. I fear I am but a woman—I am not to be 'backed.' But you are not talking of yourself."

"Oh! never mind me," was Harry's modest answer.

"But I do. Try to imagine me as clever as a man, and talk to me of your doings. Indeed I will endeavour to comprehend you."

Thus humble, the Countess bade him give her his arm. He stuck it out with abrupt eagerness.

"Not against my cheek." She laughed forgivingly. "And you need not start back half-a-mile," she pursued with plain humour: "and please do not look irresolute and awkward—It is not necessary," she added. "There!"; and she settled her fingers on him, "I am glad I can find one or two things to instruct you in. Begin. You are a great cricketer. What else?"

Ay! what else? Harry might well say he had no wish to talk of himself. He did not know even how to give his arm to a lady! The first flattery and the subsequent chiding clashed in his elated soul, and caused him to deem himself one of the blest suddenly overhauled by an inspecting angel and found wanting: or, in his own more accurate style of reflection, "What a rattling fine woman this is, and what a deuce of a fool she must think me!"

The Countess leaned on his arm with dainty languor.

"You walk well," she said.

Harry's backbone straightened immediately.

"No, no; I do not want you to be a drill-sergeant. Can you not be told you are perfect without seeking to improve, vain boy? You can cricket, and you can walk, and will very soon learn how to give your arm to a lady. I have hopes of you. Of your friends, from whom I have ruthlessly dragged you, I have not much. Am I personally offensive to them, Mr. Harry? I saw them let my brother pass without returning his bow, and they in no way acknowledged my presence as I passed. Are they gentlemen?"

"Yes," said Harry, stupefied by the question. "One's Ferdinand Laxley, Lord Laxley's son, heir to the title; the other's William Harvey, son of the Chief Justice—both friends of mine."

"But not of your manners," interposed the Countess. "I have not so much compunction as I ought to have in divorcing you from your associates for a few minutes. I think I shall make a scholar of you in one or two essentials. You do want polish. Have I not a right to take you in hand? I have defended you already."

"Me?" cried Harry.

"None other than Mr. Harry Jocelyn. Will he vouchsafe to me his pardon? It has been whispered in my ears that his ambition is to be the Don Juan of a country district, and I have said for him, that however grovelling his undirected tastes, he is too truly noble to plume himself upon the reputation they have procured him. Why did I defend you? Women, you know, do not shrink from Don Juans—even provincial Don Juans—as they should, perhaps, for their own sakes! You are all of you dangerous, if a woman is not strictly on her guard. But you will respect your champion, will you not?"

Harry was about to reply with wonderful briskness. He stopped, and murmured boorishly that he was sure he was very much obliged.

Command of countenance the Countess possessed in common with her sex. Those faces on which we make them depend entirely, women can entirely control. Keenly sensible to humour as the Countess was, her face sidled up to his immovably sweet. Harry looked, and looked away, and looked again. The poor fellow was so profoundly aware of his foolishness that he even doubted whether he was admired.

The Countess trifled with his English nature; quietly watched him bob between tugging humility and airy conceit, and went on:

"Yes! I will trust you, and that is saying very much, for what protection is a brother? I am alone here—defenceless!"

Men, of course, grow virtuously zealous in an instant on behalf of the lovely dame who tells them bewitchingly, she is alone and defenceless, with pitiful dimples round the dewy mouth that entreats their guardianship and mercy!

The provincial Don Juan found words—a sign of clearer sensations within. He said:

"Upon my honour, I'd look after you better than fifty brothers!"

The Countess eyed him softly, and then allowed herself the luxury of a laugh.

"No, no! it is not the sheep, it is the wolf I fear."

And she went through a bit of the concluding portion of the drama of Little Red Riding Hood very prettily, and tickled him so that he became somewhat less afraid of her.

"Are you truly so bad as report would have you to be, Mr. Harry?" she asked, not at all in the voice of a censor.

"Pray don't think me—a—anything you wouldn't have me," the youth stumbled into an apt response.

"We shall see," said the Countess, and varied her admiration for the noble creature beside her with gentle exclamations on the beauty of the deer that ranged the park of Beckley Court, the grand old oaks and beeches, the clumps of flowering laurel, and the rich air swarming Summer.

She swept out her arm. "And this most magnificent estate will be yours? How happy will she be who is led hither to reside by you, Mr. Harry!"

"Mine? No; there's the bother," he answered, with unfeigned chagrin. "Beckley isn't Elburne property, you know. It belongs to old Mrs. Bonner, Rose's grandmama."

"Oh!" interjected the Countess, indifferently.

"I shall never get it—no chance," Harry pursued. "Lost my luck with the old lady long ago." He waxed excited on a subject that drew him from his shamefacedness. "It goes to Juley Bonner, or to Rosey; it's a toss-up which. If I'd stuck up to Juley, I might have had a pretty fair chance. They wanted me to, that's why I scout the premises. But fancy Juley Bonner!"

"You couldn't, upon your honour!" rhymed the Countess. (And Harry let loose a delighted "Ha! ha!" as at a fine stroke of wit.) "Are we enamoured of a beautiful maiden, Senor Harry?"

"Not a bit," he assured her eagerly. "I don't know any girl. I don't care for 'em. I don't, really."

The Countess impressively declared to him that he must be guided by her; and that she might the better act his monitress, she desired to hear the pedigree of the estate, and the exact relations in which it at present stood toward the Elburne family.

Glad of any theme he could speak on, Harry informed her that Beckley Court was bought by his grandfather Bonner from the proceeds of a successful oil speculation.

"So we ain't much on that side," he said.

"Oil!" was the Countess's weary exclamation. "I imagined Beckley Court to be your ancestral mansion. Oil!"

Harry deprecatingly remarked that oil was money.

"Yes," she replied; "but you are not one to mix oil with your Elburne blood. Let me see—oil! That, I conceive, is grocery. So, you are grocers on one side!"

"Oh, come! hang it!" cried Harry, turning red.

"Am I leaning on the grocer's side, or on the lord's?"

Harry felt dreadfully taken down. "One ranks with one's father," he said.

"Yes," observed the Countess; "but you should ever be careful not to expose the grocer. When I beheld my brother bow to you, and that your only return was to stare at him in that singular way, I was not aware of this, and could not account for it."

"I declare I'm very sorry," said Harry, with a nettled air. "Do just let me tell you how it happened. We were at an inn, where there was an odd old fellow gave a supper; and there was your brother, and another fellow—as thorough an upstart as I ever met, and infernally impudent. He got drinking, and wanted to fight us. Now I see it! Your brother, to save his friend's bones, said he was a tailor! Of course no gentleman could fight a tailor; and it blew over with my saying we'd order our clothes of him."

"Said he was a—!" exclaimed the Countess, gazing blankly.

"I don't wonder at your feeling annoyed," returned Harry. "I saw him with Rosey next day, and began to smell a rat then, but Laxley won't give up the tailor. He's as proud as Lucifer. He wanted to order a suit of your brother to-day; but I said—not while he's in the house, however he came here."

The Countess had partially recovered. They were now in the village street, and Harry pointed out the post-office.

"Your divination with regard to my brother's most eccentric behaviour was doubtless correct," she said. "He wished to succour his wretched companion. Anywhere—it matters not to him what!—he allies himself with miserable mortals. He is the modern Samaritan. You should thank him for saving you an encounter with some low creature."

Swaying the letter to and fro, she pursued archly: "I can read your thoughts. You are dying to know to whom this dear letter is addressed!"

Instantly Harry, whose eyes had previously been quite empty of expression, glanced at the letter wistfully.

"Shall I tell you?"

"Yes, do."

"It's to somebody I love."

"Are you in love then?" was his disconcerted rejoinder.

"Am I not married?"

"Yes; but every woman that's married isn't in love with her husband, you know."

"Oh! Don Juan of the provinces!" she cried, holding the seal of the letter before him in playful reproof. "Fie!"

"Come! who is it?" Harry burst out.

"I am not, surely, obliged to confess my correspondence to you? Remember!" she laughed lightly. "He already assumes the airs of a lord and master! You are rapid, Mr. Harry."

"Won't you really tell me?" he pleaded.

She put a corner of the letter in the box. "Must I?"

All was done with the archest elegance: the bewildering condescension of a Goddess to a boor.

"I don't say you must, you know: but I should like to see it," returned Harry.

"There!" She showed him a glimpse of "Mrs.," cleverly concealing plebeian "Cogglesby," and the letter slid into darkness. "Are you satisfied?"

"Yes," said Harry, wondering why he felt a relief at the sight of "Mrs." written on a letter by a lady he had only known half an hour.

"And now," said she, "I shall demand a boon of you, Mr. Harry. Will it be accorded?"

She was hurriedly told that she might count upon him for whatever she chose to ask; and after much trifling and many exaggerations of the boon in question, he heard that she had selected him as her cavalier for the day, and that he was to consent to accompany her to the village church.

"Is it so great a request, the desire that you should sit beside a solitary lady for so short a space?" she asked, noting his rueful visage.

Harry assured her he would be very happy, but hinted at the bother of having to sit and listen to that fool of a Parsley: again assuring her, and with real earnestness, which the lady now affected to doubt, that he would be extremely happy.

"You know, I haven't been there for ages," he explained.

"I hear it!" she sighed, aware of the credit his escort would bring her in Beckley, and especially with Harry's grandmama Bonner.

They went together to the village church. The Countess took care to be late, so that all eyes beheld her stately march up the aisle, with her captive beside her.

Nor was her captive less happy than he professed he would be. Charming comic side-play, at the expense of Mr. Parsley, she mingled with exceeding devoutness, and a serious attention to Mr. Parsley's discourse. In her heart this lady really thought her confessed daily sins forgiven her by the recovery of the lost sheep to Mr. Parsley's fold. The results of this small passage of arms were, that Evan's disclosure at Fallow field was annulled in the mind of Harry Jocelyn, and the latter gentleman became the happy slave of the Countess de Saldar.

XVI

Leads to a Small Skirmish Between Rose and Evan

Lady Jocelyn belonged properly to that order which the Sultans and the Roxalanas of earth combine to exclude from their little games, under the designation of blues, or strong-minded women: a kind, if genuine, the least dangerous and staunchest of the sex, as poor fellows learn when the flippant and the frail fair have made mummies of them. She had the frankness of her daughter, the same direct eyes and firm step: a face without shadows, though no longer bright with youth. It may be charged to her as one of the errors of her strong mind, that she believed friendship practicable between men and women, young or old. She knew the world pretty well, and was not amazed by extraordinary accidents; but as she herself continued to be an example of her faith: we must presume it natural that her delusion should cling to her. She welcomed Evan as her daughter's friend, walked half-way across the room to meet him on his introduction to her, and with the simple words, "I have heard of you," let him see that he stood upon his merits in her house. The young man's spirit caught something of hers even in their first interview, and at once mounted to that level. Unconsciously he felt that she took, and would take him, for what he was, and he rose to his worth in the society she presided over. A youth like Evan could not perceive, that in loving this lady's daughter, and accepting the place she offered him, he was guilty of a breach of confidence; or reflect, that her entire absence of suspicion imposed upon him a corresponding honesty toward her. He fell into a blindness. Without dreaming for a moment that she designed to encourage his passion for Rose, he yet beheld himself in the light she had cast on him; and, received as her daughter's friend, it seemed to him not so utterly monstrous that he might be her daughter's lover. A haughty, a grand, or a too familiar manner, would have kept his eyes clearer on his true condition. Lady Jocelyn spoke to his secret nature, and eclipsed in his mind the outward aspects with which it was warring. To her he was a gallant young man, a fit companion for Rose, and when she and Sir Franks said, and showed him, that they were glad to know him, his heart swam in a flood of happiness they little suspected.

This was another of the many forms of intoxication to which circumstances subjected the poor lover. In Fallow field, among impertinent young men, Evan's pride proclaimed him a tailor. At Beckley Court, acted on by one genuine soul, he forgot it, and felt elate in his manhood. The shades of Tailordom dispersed like fog before the full South-west breeze. When I say he forgot it, the fact was present enough to him, but it became an outward fact: he had ceased to feel it within him. It was not a portion of his being, hard as Mrs. Mel had struck to fix it. Consequently, though he was in a far worse plight than when he parted with Rose on board the Jocasta, he felt much less of an impostor now. This may have been partly because he had endured his struggle with the Demogorgon the Countess painted to him in such frightful colours, and found him human after all; but it was mainly owing to the hearty welcome Lady Jocelyn had extended to him as the friend of Rose.

Loving Rose, he nevertheless allowed his love no tender liberties. The eyes of a lover are not his own; but his hands and lips are, till such time as they are claimed. The sun must smile on us with peculiar warmth to woo us forth utterly-pluck our hearts out. Rose smiled on many. She smiled on Drummond Forth, Ferdinand Laxley, William Harvey, and her brother Harry; and she had the same eyes for all ages. Once, previous to the arrival of the latter three, there was a change in her look, or Evan fancied it. They were going to ride out together, and Evan, coming to his horse on the gravel walk, saw her talking with Drummond Forth. He mounted, awaiting her, and either from a slight twinge of jealousy, or to mark her dainty tread with her riding-habit drawn above her heels, he could not help turning his head occasionally. She listened to Drummond with attention, but presently broke from him, crying: "It's an absurdity. Speak to them yourself—I shall not."

On the ride that day, she began prattling of this and that with the careless glee that became her well, and then sank into a reverie. Betweenwhiles her eyes had raised tumults in Evan's breast by dropping on him in a sort of questioning way, as if she wished him to speak, or wished to fathom something she would rather have unspoken. Ere they had finished their ride, she tossed off what burden may have been on her mind as lightly as a stray lock from her shoulders. He thought that the singular look recurred. It charmed him too much for him to speculate on it.

The Countess's opportune ally, the gout, which had reduced the Hon. Melville Jocelyn's right hand to a state of uselessness, served her with her brother equally: for, having volunteered his services to the invalided diplomatist, it excused his stay at Beckley Court to himself, and was a mask to his intimacy with Rose, besides earning him the thanks of the family. Harry Jocelyn, released from the wing of the Countess, came straight to him, and in a rough kind of way begged Evan to overlook his rudeness.

"You took us all in at Fallow field, except Drummond," he said. "Drummond would have it you were joking. I see it now. And you're a confoundedly clever fellow into the bargain, or you wouldn't be quill-driving for Uncle Mel. Don't be uppish about it—will you?"

"You have nothing to fear on that point," said Evan. With which promise the peace was signed between them. Drummond and William Harvey were cordial, and just laughed over the incident. Laxley, however, held aloof. His retention of ideas once formed befitted his rank and station. Some trifling qualms attended Evan's labours with the diplomatist; but these were merely occasioned by the iteration of a particular phrase. Mr. Goren, an enthusiastic tailor, had now and then thrown out to Evan stirring hints of an invention he claimed: the discovery of a Balance in Breeches: apparently the philosopher's stone of the tailor craft, a secret that should ensure harmony of outline to the person and an indubitable accommodation to the most difficult legs.

Since Adam's expulsion, it seemed, the tailors of this wilderness had been in search of it. But like the doctors of this wilderness, their science knew no specific: like the Babylonian workmen smitten with confusion of tongues, they had but one word in common, and that word was "cut." Mr. Goren contended that to cut was not the key of the science: but to find a Balance was. An artistic admirer of the frame of man, Mr. Goren was not wanting in veneration for the individual who had arisen to do it justice. He spoke of his Balance with supreme self-appreciation. Nor less so the Honourable Melville, who professed to have discovered the Balance of Power, at home and abroad. It was a capital Balance, but inferior to Mr. Goren's. The latter gentleman guaranteed a Balance with motion: whereas one step not only upset the Honourable Melville's, but shattered the limbs of Europe. Let us admit, that it is easier to fit a man's legs than to compress expansive empires.

Evan enjoyed the doctoring of kingdoms quite as well as the diplomatist. It suited the latent grandeur of soul inherited by him from the great Mel. He liked to prop Austria and arrest the Czar, and keep a watchful eye on France; but the Honourable Melville's deep-mouthed phrase conjured up to him a pair of colossal legs imperiously demanding their Balance likewise. At first the image scared him. In time he was enabled to smile it into phantom vagueness. The diplomatist diplomatically informed him, it might happen that the labours he had undertaken might be neither more nor less than education for a profession he might have to follow. Out of this, an ardent imagination, with the Countess de Saldar for an interpreter, might construe a promise of some sort. Evan soon had high hopes. What though his name blazed on a shop-front? The sun might yet illumine him to honour!

Where a young man is getting into delicate relations with a young woman, the more of his sex the better—they serve as a blind; and the Countess hailed fresh arrivals warmly. There was Sir John Loring, Dorothy's father, who had married the eldest of the daughters of Lord Elburne. A widower, handsome, and a flirt, he capitulated to the Countess instantly, and was played off against the provincial Don Juan, who had reached that point with her when youths of his description make bashful confidences of their successes, and receive delicious chidings for their naughtiness—rebukes which give immeasurable rebounds. Then came Mr. Gordon Graine, with his daughter, Miss Jenny Graine, an early friend of Rose's, and numerous others. For the present, Miss Isabella Current need only be chronicled among the visitors—a sprightly maid fifty years old, without a wrinkle to show for it—the Aunt Bel of fifty houses where there were young women and little boys. Aunt Bel had quick wit and capital anecdotes, and tripped them out aptly on a sparkling tongue with exquisite instinct for climax and when to strike for a laugh. No sooner had she entered the hall than she announced the proximate arrival of the Duke of Belfield at her heels, and it was known that his Grace was as sure to follow as her little dog, who was far better paid for his devotion.

The dinners at Beckley Court had hitherto been rather languid to those who were not intriguing or mixing young love with the repast. Miss Current was an admirable neutral, sent, as the Countess fervently believed, by Providence. Till now the Countess had drawn upon her own resources to amuse the company, and she had been obliged to restrain herself from doing it with that unctuous feeling for rank which warmed her Portuguese sketches in low society and among her sisters. She retired before Miss Current and formed audience, glad of a relief to her inventive labour. While Miss Current and her ephemerals lightly skimmed the surface of human life, the Countess worked in the depths. Vanities, passions, prejudices beneath the surface, gave her full employment. How naturally poor Juliana Bonner was moved to mistake Evan's compassion for a stronger sentiment! The Countess eagerly assisted Providence to shuffle the company into their proper places. Harry Jocelyn was moodily happy, but good; greatly improved in the eyes of his grandmama Bonner, who attributed the change to the Countess, and partly forgave her the sinful consent to the conditions of her love-match with the foreign Count, which his penitent wife had privately confessed to that strict Churchwoman.

"Thank Heaven that you have no children," Mrs. Bonner had said; and the Countess humbly replied:

"It is indeed my remorseful consolation!"

"Who knows that it is not your punishment?" added Mrs. Bonner; the Countess weeping.

She went and attended morning prayers in Mrs. Bonner's apartments, alone with the old lady. "To make up for lost time in Catholic Portugal!" she explained it to the household.

On the morning after Miss Current had come to shape the party, most of the inmates of Beckley Court being at breakfast, Rose gave a lead to the conversation.

"Aunt Bel! I want to ask you something. We've been making bets about you. Now, answer honestly, we're all friends. Why did you refuse all your offers?"

"Quite simple, child," replied the unabashed ex-beauty.

"A matter of taste. I liked twenty shillings better than a sovereign."

Rose looked puzzled, but the men laughed, and Rose exclaimed:

"Now I see! How stupid I am! You mean, you may have friends when you are not married. Well, I think that's the wisest, after all. You don't lose them, do you? Pray, Mr. Evan, are you thinking Aunt Bel might still alter her mind for somebody, if she knew his value?"

"I was presuming to hope there might be a place vacant among the twenty," said Evan, slightly bowing to both. "Am I pardoned?"

"I like you!" returned Aunt Bel, nodding at him. "Where do you come from? A young man who'll let himself go for small coin's a jewel worth knowing."

"Where do I come from?" drawled Laxley, who had been tapping an egg with a dreary expression.

"Aunt Bel spoke to Mr. Harrington," said Rose, pettishly.

"Asked him where he came from," Laxley continued his drawl. "He didn't answer, so I thought it polite for another of the twenty to strike in."

"I must thank you expressly," said Evan, and achieved a cordial bow.

Rose gave Evan one of her bright looks, and then called the attention of Ferdinand Laxley to the fact that he had lost a particular bet made among them.

"What bet?" asked Laxley. "About the profession?"

A stream of colour shot over Rose's face. Her eyes flew nervously from Laxley to Evan, and then to Drummond. Laxley appeared pleased as a man who has made a witty sally: Evan was outwardly calm, while Drummond replied to the mute appeal of Rose, by saying:

"Yes; we've all lost. But who could hit it? The lady admits no sovereign in our sex."

"So you've been betting about me?" said Aunt Bel. "I'll settle the dispute. Let him who guessed 'Latin' pocket the stakes, and, if I guess him, let him hand them over to me."

"Excellent!" cried Rose. "One did guess 'Latin,' Aunt Bel! Now, tell us which one it was."

"Not you, my dear. You guessed 'temper.'"

"No! you dreadful Aunt Bel!"

"Let me see," said Aunt Bel, seriously. "A young man would not marry a woman with Latin, but would not guess it the impediment. Gentlemen moderately aged are mad enough to slip their heads under any yoke, but see the obstruction. It was a man of forty guessed 'Latin.' I request the Hon. Hamilton Everard Jocelyn to confirm it."

Amid laughter and exclamations Hamilton confessed himself the man who had guessed Latin to be the cause of Miss Current's remaining an old maid; Rose, crying:

"You really are too clever, Aunt Bel!"

A divergence to other themes ensued, and then Miss Jenny Graine said: "Isn't Juley learning Latin? I should like to join her while I'm here."

"And so should I," responded Rose. "My friend Evan is teaching her during the intervals of his arduous diplomatic labours. Will you take us into your class, Evan?"

"Don't be silly, girls," interposed Aunt Bel. "Do you want to graduate for my state with your eyes open?"

Evan objected his poor qualifications as a tutor, and Aunt Bel remarked, that if Juley learnt Latin at all, she should have regular instruction.

"I am quite satisfied," said Juley, quietly.

"Of course you are," Rose snubbed her cousin. "So would anybody be. But Mama really was talking of a tutor for Juley, if she could find one. There's a school at Bodley; but that's too far for one of the men to come over."

A school at Bodley! thought Evan, and his probationary years at the Cudford Establishment rose before him; and therewith, for the first time since his residence at Beckley, the figure of John Raikes.

"There's a friend of mine," he said, aloud, "I think if Lady Jocelyn does wish Miss Bonner to learn Latin thoroughly, he would do very well for the groundwork and would be glad of the employment. He is very poor."

"If he's poor, and a friend of yours, Evan, we'll have him," said Rose: "we'll ride and fetch him."

"Yes," added Miss Carrington, "that must be quite sufficient qualification."

Juliana was not gazing gratefully at Evan for his proposal.

Rose asked the name of Evan's friend. "His name is Raikes," answered Evan. "I don't know where he is now. He may be at Fallow field. If Lady Jocelyn pleases, I will ride over to-day and see."

"My dear Evan!" cried Rose, "you don't mean that absurd figure we saw on the cricket-field?" She burst out laughing. "Oh! what fun it will be! Let us have him here by all means."

"I shall not bring him to be laughed at," said Evan.

"I will remember he is your friend," Rose returned demurely; and again laughed, as she related to Jenny Graine the comic appearance Mr. Raikes had presented.

Laxley waited for a pause, and then said: "I have met this Mr. Raikes. As a friend of the family, I should protest against his admission here in any office whatever into the upper part of the house, at least. He is not a gentleman."

We don't want teachers to be gentlemen," observed Rose.

"This fellow is the reverse," Laxley pronounced, and desired Harry to confirm it; but Harry took a gulp of coffee.

"Oblige me by recollecting that I have called him a friend of mine," said Evan.

Rose murmured to him: "Pray forgive me! I forgot." Laxley hummed something about "taste." Aunt Bel led from the theme by a lively anecdote.

After breakfast the party broke into knots, and canvassed Laxley's behaviour to Evan, which was generally condemned. Rose met the young men strolling on the lawn; and, with her usual bluntness, accused Laxley of wishing to insult her friend.

"I speak to him—do I not?" said Laxley. "What would you have more? I admit the obligation of speaking to him when I meet him in your house. Out of it—that's another matter."

"But what is the cause for your conduct to him, Ferdinand?"

"By Jove!" cried Harry, "I wonder he puts up with it I wouldn't. I'd have a shot with you, my boy."

"Extremely honoured," said Laxley. "But neither you nor I care to fight tailors."

"Tailors!" exclaimed Rose. There was a sharp twitch in her body, as if she had been stung or struck.

"Look here, Rose," said Laxley; "I meet him, he insults me, and to get out of the consequences tells me he's the son of a tailor, and a tailor himself; knowing that it ties my hands. Very well, he puts himself hors de combat to save his bones. Let him unsay it, and choose whether he'll apologize or not, and I'll treat him accordingly. At present I'm not bound to do more than respect the house I find he has somehow got admission to."

"It's clear it was that other fellow," said Harry, casting a side-glance up at the Countess's window.

Rose looked straight at Laxley, and abruptly turned on her heel.

In the afternoon, Lady Jocelyn sent a message to Evan that she wished to see him. Rose was with her mother. Lady Jocelyn had only to say, that if he thought his friend a suitable tutor for Miss Bonner, they would be happy to give him the office at Beckley Court. Glad to befriend poor Jack, Evan gave the needful assurances, and was requested to go and fetch him forthwith. When he left the room, Rose marched out silently beside him.

"Will you ride over with me, Rose?" he said, though scarcely anxious that she should see Mr. Raikes immediately.

The singular sharpness of her refusal astonished him none the less.

"Thank you, no; I would rather not."

A lover is ever ready to suspect that water has been thrown on the fire that burns for him in the bosom of his darling. Sudden as the change was, it was very decided. His sensitive ears were pained by the absence of his Christian name, which her lips had lavishly made sweet to him. He stopped in his walk.

"You spoke of riding to Fallow field. Is it possible you don't want me to bring my friend here? There's time to prevent it."

Judged by the Countess de Saldar, the behaviour of this well-born English maid was anything but well-bred. She absolutely shrugged her shoulders and marched a-head of him into the conservatory, where she began smelling at flowers and plucking off sere leaves.

In such cases a young man always follows; as her womanly instinct must have told her, for she expressed no surprise when she heard his voice two minutes after.

"Rose! what have I done?"

"Nothing at all," she said, sweeping her eyes over his a moment, and resting them on the plants.

"I must have uttered something that has displeased you."

"No."

Brief negatives are not re-assuring to a lover's uneasy mind.

"I beg you—Be frank with me, Rose!"

A flame of the vanished fire shone in her face, but subsided, and she shook her head darkly.

"Have you any objection to my friend?"

Her fingers grew petulant with an orange leaf. Eyeing a spot on it, she said, hesitatingly:

"Any friend of yours I am sure I should like to help. But—but I wish you wouldn't associate with that—that kind of friend. It gives people all sorts of suspicions."

Evan drew a sharp breath.

The voices of Master Alec and Miss Dorothy were heard shouting on the lawn. Alec gave Dorothy the slip and approached the conservatory on tip-toe, holding his hand out behind him to enjoin silence and secrecy. The pair could witness the scene through the glass before Evan spoke.

"What suspicions?" he asked.

Rose looked up, as if the harshness of his tone pleased her.

"Do you like red roses best, or white?" was her answer, moving to a couple of trees in pots.

"Can't make up your mind?" she continued, and plucked both a white and red rose, saying: "There! choose your colour by-and-by, and ask Juley to sew the one you choose in your button-hole."

She laid the roses in his hand, and walked away. She must have known that there was a burden of speech on his tongue. She saw him move to follow her, but this time she did not linger, and it may be inferred that she wished to hear no more.

XVII

In which Evan Writes Himself Tailor

The only philosophic method of discovering what a young woman means, and what is in her mind, is that zigzag process of inquiry conducted by following her actions, for she can tell you nothing, and if she does not want to know a particular matter, it must be a strong beam from the central system of facts that shall penetrate her. Clearly there was a disturbance in the bosom of Rose Jocelyn, and one might fancy that amiable mirror as being wilfully ruffled to confuse a thing it was asked by the heavens to reflect: a good fight fought by all young people at a certain period, and now and then by an old fool or two. The young it seasons and strengthens; the old it happily kills off; and thus, what is, is made to work harmoniously with what we would have be.

After quitting Evan, Rose hied to her friend Jenny Graine, and in the midst of sweet millinery talk, darted the odd question, whether baronets or knights ever were tradesmen: to which Scottish Jenny, entirely putting aside the shades of beatified aldermen and the illustrious list of mayors that have welcomed royalty, replied that it was a thing quite impossible. Rose then wished to know if tailors were thought worse of than other tradesmen. Jenny, premising that she was no authority, stated she imagined she had heard that they were.

"Why?" said Rose, no doubt because she was desirous of seeing justice dealt to that class. But Jenny's bosom was a smooth reflector of facts alone.

Rose pondered, and said with compressed eagerness, "Jenny, do you think you could ever bring yourself to consent to care at all for anybody ever talked of as belonging to them? Tell me."

Now Jenny had come to Beckley Court to meet William Harvey: she was therefore sufficiently soft to think she could care for him whatever his origin were, and composed in the knowledge that no natal stigma was upon him to try the strength of her affection. Designing to generalize, as women do (and seem tempted to do most when they are secretly speaking from their own emotions), she said, shyly moving her shoulders, with a forefinger laying down the principle:

"You know, my dear, if one esteemed such a person very very much, and were quite sure, without any doubt, that he liked you in return—that is, completely liked you, and was quite devoted, and made no concealment—I mean, if he was very superior, and like other men—you know what I mean—and had none of the cringing ways some of them have—I mean; supposing him gay and handsome, taking—"

"Just like William," Rose cut her short; and we may guess her to have had some one in her head for her to conceive that Jenny must be speaking of any one in particular.

A young lady who can have male friends, as well as friends of her own sex, is not usually pressing and secret in her confidences, possibly because such a young lady is not always nursing baby-passions, and does not require her sex's coddling and posseting to keep them alive. With Rose love will be full grown when it is once avowed, and will know where to go to be nourished.

"Merely an idea I had," she said to Jenny, who betrayed her mental pre-occupation by putting the question for the questions last.

Her Uncle Melville next received a visit from the restless young woman. To him she spoke not a word of the inferior classes, but as a special favourite of the diplomatist's, begged a gift of him for her proximate birthday. Pushed to explain what it was, she said, "It's something I want you to do for a friend of mine, Uncle Mel."

The diplomatist instanced a few of the modest requests little maids prefer to people they presume to have power to grant.

"No, it's nothing nonsensical," said Rose; "I want you to get my friend Evan an appointment. You can if you like, you know, Uncle Mel, and it's a shame to make him lose his time when he's young and does his work so well—that you can't deny! Now, please, be positive, Uncle Mel. You know I hate—I have no faith in your 'nous verrons'. Say you will, and at once."

The diplomatist pretended to have his weather-eye awakened.

"You seem very anxious about feathering the young fellow's nest, Rosey?"

"There," cried Rose, with the maiden's mature experience of us, "isn't that just like men? They never can believe you can be entirely disinterested!"

"Hulloa!" the diplomatist sung out, "I didn't say anything, Rosey."

She reddened at her hastiness, but retrieved it by saying:

"No, but you listen to your wife; you know you do, Uncle Mel; and now there's Aunt Shorne and the other women, who make you think just what they like about me, because they hate Mama."

"Don't use strong words, my dear."

"But it's abominable!" cried Rose. "They asked Mama yesterday what Evan's being here meant? Why, of course, he's your secretary, and my friend, and Mama very properly stopped them, and so will I! As for me, I intend to stay at Beckley, I can tell you, dear old boy." Uncle Mel had a soft arm round his neck, and was being fondled. "And I'm not going to be bred up to go into a harem, you may be sure."

The diplomatist whistled, "You talk your mother with a vengeance, Rosey."

"And she's the only sensible woman I know," said Rose. "Now promise me—in earnest. Don't let them mislead you, for you know you're quite a child, out of your politics, and I shall take you in hand myself. Why, now, think, Uncle Mel! wouldn't any girl, as silly as they make me out, hold her tongue—not talk of him, as I do; and because I really do feel for him as a friend. See the difference between me and Juley!"

It was a sad sign if Rose was growing a bit of a hypocrite, but this instance of Juliana's different manner of showing her feelings toward Evan would have quieted suspicion in shrewder men, for Juliana watched Evan's shadow, and it was thought by two or three at Beckley Court, that Evan would be conferring a benefit on all by carrying off the romantically-inclined but little presentable young lady.

The diplomatist, with a placid "Well, well!" ultimately promised to do his best for Rose's friend, and then Rose said, "Now I leave you to the Countess," and went and sat with her mother and Drummond Forth. The latter was strange in his conduct to Evan. While blaming Laxley's unmannered behaviour, he seemed to think Laxley had grounds for it, and treated Evan with a sort of cynical deference that had, for the last couple of days, exasperated Rose.

"Mama, you must speak to Ferdinand," she burst upon the conversation, "Drummond is afraid to—he can stand by and see my friend insulted. Ferdinand is insufferable with his pride—he's jealous of everybody who has manners, and Drummond approves him, and I will not bear it."

Lady Jocelyn hated household worries, and quietly remarked that the young men must fight it out together.

"No, but it's your duty to interfere, Mama," said Rose; "and I know you will when I tell you that Ferdinand declares my friend Evan is a tradesman—beneath his notice. Why, it insults me!"

Lady Jocelyn looked out from a lofty window on such veritable squabbles of boys and girls as Rose revealed.

"Can't you help them to run on smoothly while they're here?" she said to Drummond, and he related the scene at the Green Dragon.

"I think I heard he was the son of Sir Something Harrington, Devonshire people," said Lady Jocelyn.

"Yes, he is," cried Rose, "or closely related. I'm sure I understood the Countess that it was so. She brought the paper with the death in it to us in London, and shed tears over it."

"She showed it in the paper, and shed tears over it?" said Drummond, repressing an inclination to laugh. "Was her father's title given in full?"

"Sir Abraham Harrington," replied Rose. "I think she said father, if the word wasn't too common-place for her."

"You can ask old Tom when he comes, if you are anxious to know," said Drummond to her ladyship. "His brother married one of the sisters. By the way, he's coming, too. He ought to clear up the mystery."

"Now you're sneering, Drummond," said Rose: "for you know there's no mystery to clear up."

Drummond and Lady Jocelyn began talking of old Tom Cogglesby, whom, it appeared, the former knew intimately, and the latter had known.

"The Cogglesbys are sons of a cobbler, Rose," said Lady Jocelyn. "You must try and be civil to them."

"Of course I shall, Mama," Rose answered seriously.

"And help the poor Countess to bear their presence as well as possible," said Drummond. "The Harringtons have had to mourn a dreadful mesalliance. Pity the Countess!"

"Oh! the Countess! the Countess!" exclaimed Rose to Drummond's pathetic shake of the head. She and Drummond were fully agreed about the Countess; Drummond mimicking the lady: "In verity, she is most mellifluous!" while Rose sugared her lips and leaned gracefully forward with "De Saldar, let me petition you—since we must endure our title—since it is not to be your Louisa?" and her eyes sought the ceiling, and her hand slowly melted into her drapery, as the Countess was wont to effect it.

Lady Jocelyn laughed, but said: "You're too hard upon the Countess. The female euphuist is not to be met with every day. It's a different kind from the Precieuse. She is not a Precieuse. She has made a capital selection of her vocabulary from Johnson, and does not work it badly, if we may judge by Harry and Melville. Euphuism—(affectation D.W.)—in 'woman' is the popular ideal of a Duchess. She has it by nature, or she has studied it: and if so, you must respect her abilities."

"Yes—Harry!" said Rose, who was angry at a loss of influence over her rough brother, "any one could manage Harry! and Uncle Mel 's a goose. You should see what a 'female euphuist' Dorry is getting. She says in the Countess's hearing: 'Rose! I should in verity wish to play, if it were pleasing to my sweet cousin?' I'm ready to die with laughing. I don't do it, Mama."

The Countess, thus being discussed, was closeted with old Mrs. Bonner: not idle. Like Hannibal in Italy, she had crossed her Alps in attaining Beckley Court, and here in the enemy's country the wary general found herself under the necessity of throwing up entrenchments to fly to in case of defeat. Sir Abraham Harrington of Torquay, who had helped her to cross the Alps, became a formidable barrier against her return.

Meantime Evan was riding over to Fallow field, and as he rode under black visions between the hedgeways crowned with their hop-garlands, a fragrance of roses saluted his nostril, and he called to mind the red and the white the peerless representative of the two had given him, and which he had thrust sullenly in his breast-pocket and he drew them out to look at them reproachfully and sigh farewell to all the roses of life, when in company with them he found in his hand the forgotten letter delivered to him on the cricket-field the day of the memorable match. He smelt at the roses, and turned the letter this way and that. His name was correctly worded on the outside. With an odd reluctance to open it, he kept trifling over the flowers, and then broke the broad seal, and these are the words that met his eyes:

> Mr. Evan Harrington
>
> "You have made up your mind to be a tailor, instead of a Tomnoddy. You're right. Not too many men in the world—plenty of nincompoops.
>
> "Don't be made a weathercock of by a parcel of women. I want to find a man worth something. If you go on with it, you shall end by riding in your carriage, and cutting it as fine as any of them. I'll take care your belly is not punished while you're about it.
>
> "From the time your name is over your shop, I give you L300 per annum.

"Or stop. There's nine of you. They shall have L40. per annum apiece, 9 times 40, eh? That's better than L300., if you know how to reckon. Don't you wish it was ninety-nine tailors to a man! I could do that too, and it would not break me; so don't be a proud young ass, or I'll throw my money to the geese. Lots of them in the world. How many geese to a tailor?

"Go on for five years, and I double it.

"Give it up, and I give you up.

"No question about me. The first tailor can be paid his L40 in advance, by applying at the offices of Messrs. Grist, Gray's Inn Square, Gray's Inn. Let him say he is tailor No. 1, and show this letter, signed Agreed, with your name in full at bottom. This will do—money will be paid—no questions one side or other. So on—the whole nine. The end of the year they can give a dinner to their acquaintance. Send in bill to Messrs. Grist.

"The advice to you to take the cash according to terms mentioned is advice of

A FRIEND

"P.S. You shall have your wine. Consult among yourselves, and carry it by majority what wine it's to be. Five carries it. Dozen and half per tailor, per annum—that's the limit."

It was certainly a very hot day. The pores of his skin were prickling, and his face was fiery; and yet he increased his pace, and broke into a wild gallop for a mile or so; then suddenly turned his horse's head back for Beckley. The secret of which evolution was, that he had caught the idea of a plotted insult of Laxley's in the letter, for when the blood is up we are drawn the way the tide sets strongest, and Evan was prepared to swear that Laxley had written the letter, because he was burning to chastise the man who had injured him with Rose.

Sure that he was about to confirm his suspicion, he read it again, gazed upon Beckley Court in the sultry light, and turned for Fallow field once more, devising to consult Mr. John Raikes on the subject.

The letter had a smack of crabbed age hardly counterfeit. The savour of an old eccentric's sour generosity was there. Evan fell into bitter laughter at the idea of Rose glancing over his shoulder and asking him what nine of him to a man meant. He heard her clear voice pursuing him. He could not get away from the mocking sound of Rose beseeching him to instruct her on that point. How if the letter were genuine? He began to abhor the sight and touch of the paper, for it struck division cold as death between him and his darling. He saw now the immeasurable hopes his residence at Beckley had lured him to. Rose had slightly awakened him: this letter was blank day to his soul. He saw the squalid shop, the good, stern, barren-spirited mother, the changeless drudgery, the existence which seemed indeed no better than what the ninth of a man was fit for. The influence of his mother came on him once more. Dared he reject the gift if true? No spark of gratitude could he feel, but chained, dragged at the heels of his fate, he submitted to think it true; resolving the next moment that it was a fabrication and a trap: but he flung away the roses.

As idle as a painted cavalier upon a painted drop-scene, the figure of Mr. John Raikes was to be observed leaning with crossed legs against a shady pillar of the Green Dragon; eyeing alternately, with an indifference he did not care to conceal, the assiduous pecking in the dust of some cocks and hens that had strayed from the yard of the inn, and the sleepy blinking in the sun of an old dog at his feet: nor did Evan's appearance discompose the sad sedateness of his demeanour.

"Yes; I am here still," he answered Evan's greeting, with a flaccid gesture. "Don't excite me too much. A little at a time. I can't bear it!"

"How now? What is it now, Jack?" said Evan.

Mr. Raikes pointed at the dog. "I've made a bet with myself he won't wag his tail within the next ten minutes. I beg of you, Harrington, to remain silent for both our sakes."

Evan was induced to look at the dog, and the dog looked at him, and gently moved his tail.

"I've lost!" cried Raikes, in languid anguish. "He's getting excited. He'll go mad. We're not accustomed to this in Fallow field."

Evan dismounted, and was going to tell him the news he had for him, when his attention was distracted by the sight of Rose's maid, Polly Wheedle, splendidly bonneted, who slipped past them into the inn, after repulsing Jack's careless attempt to caress her chin; which caused him to tell Evan that he could not get on without the society of intellectual women.

Evan called a boy to hold the horse.

"Have you seen her before, Jack?"

Jack replied: "Once. Your pensioner up-stairs she comes to visit. I do suspect there kinship is betwixt them. Ay! one might swear them sisters. She's a relief to the monotony of the petrified street—the old man with the brown-gaitered legs and the doubled-up old woman with the crutch. I heard the London horn this morning."

Evan thrust the letter in his hands, telling him to read and form an opinion on it, and went in the track of Miss Wheedle.

Mr. Raikes resumed his station against the pillar, and held the letter out on a level with his thigh. Acting (as it was his nature to do off the stage), he had not exaggerated his profound melancholy. Of a light soil and with a tropical temperament, he had exhausted all lively recollection of his brilliant career, and, in the short time since Evan had parted with him, sunk abjectly down into the belief that he was fixed in Fallow field for life. His spirit pitied for agitation and events. The horn of the London coach had sounded distant metropolitan glories in the ears of the exile in rustic parts.

Sighing heavily, Raikes opened the letter, in simple obedience to the wishes of his friend; for he would have preferred to stand contemplating his own state of hopeless stagnation. The sceptical expression he put on when he had read the letter through must not deceive us. John Raikes had dreamed of a beneficent eccentric old gentleman for many years: one against whom, haply, he had bumped in a crowded thoroughfare, and had with cordial politeness begged pardon of; had then picked up his walking-stick; restored it, venturing a witty remark; retired, accidentally dropping his card-case; subsequently, to his astonishment and gratification, receiving a pregnant missive from that old gentleman's lawyer. Or it so happened that Mr. Raikes met the old gentleman at a tavern, and, by the exercise of a signal dexterity, relieved him from a bone in his throat, and reluctantly imparted his address on issuing from the said tavern. Or perhaps it was a lonely highway where the old gentleman walked, and John Raikes had his name in the papers for a deed of heroism, nor was man ungrateful. Since he had eaten up his uncle, this old gentleman of his dreams walked in town and country-only, and alas! Mr. Raikes could never encounter him in the flesh. The muscles of his face, therefore, are no index to the real feelings of the youth when he had thoroughly mastered the contents of the letter, and reflected that the dream of his luck—his angelic old gentleman—had gone and wantonly bestowed himself upon Evan Harrington, instead of the expectant and far worthier John Raikes.

Worthier inasmuch as he gave him credence for existing long ere he knew of him and beheld him manifest.

Raikes retreated to the vacant parlour of the Green Dragon, and there Evan found him staring at the unfolded letter, his head between his cramped fists, with a contraction of his mouth. Evan was troubled by what he had seen up-stairs, and did not speak till Jack looked up and said, "Oh, there you are."

"Well, what do you think, Jack?"

"Yes—it's all right," Raikes rejoined in most matter-of-course tone, and then he stepped to the window, and puffed a very deep breath indeed, and glanced from the straight line of the street to the heavens, with whom, injured as he was, he felt more at home now that he knew them capable of miracles.

"Is it a bad joke played upon me?" said Evan.

Raikes upset a chair. "It's quite childish. You're made a gentleman for life, and you ask if it's a joke played upon you! It's maddening! There—there goes my hat!"

With a vehement kick, Mr. Raikes despatched his ancient head-gear to the other end of the room, saying that he must have some wine, and would; and disdainful was his look at Evan, when the latter attempted to reason him into economy. He ordered the wine; drank a glass, which coloured a new mood in him; and affecting a practical manner, said:

"I confess I have been a little hurt with you, Harrington. You left me stranded on the desert isle. I thought myself abandoned. I thought I should never see anything but the lengthening of an endless bill on my landlady's face—my sole planet. I was resigned till I heard my friend 'to-lool!' this morning. He kindled recollection. But, this is a tidy Port, and that was a delectable sort of young lady that you were riding with when we parted last! She laughs like the true metal. I suppose you know it's the identical damsel I met the day before, and owe it to for my run on the downs—I've a compliment ready made for her."

"You think that letter written in good faith?" said Evan.

"Look here." Mr. Raikes put on a calmness. "You got up the other night, and said you were a tailor—a devotee of the cabbage and the goose. Why the notion didn't strike me is extraordinary—I ought to have known my man. However, the old gentleman who gave the supper—he's evidently one of your beastly rich old ruffianly republicans—spent part of his time in America, I dare say. Put two and two together."

But as Harrington desired plain, prose, Mr. Raikes tamed his imagination to deliver it. He pointed distinctly at the old gentleman who gave the supper as the writer of the letter. Evan, in return, confided to him his history and present position, and Mr. Raikes, without cooling to his fortunate friend, became a trifle patronizing.

"You said your father—I think I remember at old Cudford's—was a cavalry officer, a bold dragoon?"

"I did," replied Evan. "I told a lie."

"We knew it; but we feared your prowess, Harrington."

Then they talked over the singular letter uninterruptedly, and Evan, weak among his perplexities of position and sentiment: wanting money for the girl up-stairs, for this distasteful comrade's bill at the Green Dragon, and for his own immediate requirements, and with the bee buzzing of Rose in his ears: "She despises you," consented in a desperation ultimately to sign his name to it, and despatch Jack forthwith to Messrs. Grist.

"You'll find it's an imposition," he said, beginning less to think it so, now that his name was put to the hated monstrous thing; which also now fell to pricking at curiosity. For he was in the early steps of his career, and if his lady, holding to pride, despised him—as, he was tortured into the hypocrisy of confessing, she justly might, why, then, unless he was the sport of a farceur, here seemed a gilding of the path of duty: he could be serviceable to friends. His claim on fair young Rose's love had grown in the short while so prodigiously asinine that it was a minor matter to constitute himself an old eccentric's puppet.

"No more an imposition than it's 50 of Virgil," quoth the rejected usher.

"It smells of a plot," said Evan.

"It's the best joke that will be made in my time," said Mr. Raikes, rubbing his hands.

"And now listen to your luck," said Evan; "I wish mine were like it!" and Jack heard of Lady Jocelyn's offer. He heard also that the young lady he was to instruct was an heiress, and immediately inspected his garments, and showed the sacred necessity there was for him to refit in London, under the hands of scientific tailors. Evan wrote him an introduction to Mr. Goren, counted out the contents of his purse (which Jack had reduced in his study of the pastoral game of skittles, he confessed), and calculated in a niggardly way, how far it would go to supply the fellow's wants; sighing, as he did it, to think of Jack installed at Beckley Court, while Jack, comparing his luck with Evan's, had discovered it to be dismally inferior.

"Oh, confound those bellows you keep blowing!" he exclaimed. "I wish to be decently polite, Harrington, but you annoy me. Excuse me, pray, but the most unexampled case of a lucky beggar that ever was known—and to hear him panting and ready to whimper!—it's outrageous. You've only to put up your name, and there you are—an independent gentleman! By Jove! this isn't such a dull world. John Raikes! thou livest in times. I feel warm in the sun of your prosperity, Harrington. Now listen to me. Propound thou no inquiries anywhere about the old fellow who gave the supper. Humour his whim—he won't have it. All Fallow field is paid to keep him secret; I know it for a fact. I plied my rustic friends every night. 'Eat you yer victuals, and drink yer beer, and none o' yer pryin's and peerin's among we!' That's my rebuff from Farmer Broadmead. And that old boy knows more than he will tell. I saw his cunning old eye on-cock. Be silent, Harrington. Let discretion be the seal of thy luck."

"You can reckon on my silence," said Evan. "I believe in no such folly. Men don't do these things."

"Ha!" went Mr. Raikes contemptuously.

Of the two he was the foolisher fellow; but quacks have cured incomprehensible maladies, and foolish fellows have an instinct for eccentric actions.

Telling Jack to finish the wine, Evan rose to go.

"Did you order the horse to be fed?"

"Did I order the feeding of the horse?" said Jack, rising and yawning. "No, I forgot him. Who can think of horses now?"

"Poor brute!" muttered Evan, and went out to see to him.

The ostler had required no instructions to give the horse a feed of corn. Evan mounted, and rode out of the yard to where Jack was standing, bare-headed, in his old posture against the pillar, of which the shade had rounded, and the evening sun shone full on him over a black cloud. He now looked calmly gay.

"I'm laughing at the agricultural Broadmead!" he said: "'None o' yer pryin's and peerin's!' He thought my powers of amusing prodigious. 'Dang 'un, he do maak a chap laugh!' Well, Harrington, that sort of homage isn't much, I admit."

Raikes pursued: "There's something in a pastoral life, after all."

"Pastoral!" muttered Evan. "I was speaking of you at Beckley, and hope when you're there you won't make me regret my introduction of you. Keep your mind on old Cudford's mutton-bone."

"I perfectly understood you," said Jack. "I'm Presumed to be in luck. Ingratitude is not my fault—I'm afraid ambition is!"

"Console yourself with it or what you can get till we meet—here or in London. But the Dragon shall be the address for both of us," Evan said, and nodded, trotting off.

XVIII

In which Evan Calls Himself Gentleman

The young cavalier perused that letter again in memory. Genuine, or a joke of the enemy, it spoke wakening facts to him. He leapt from the spell Rose had encircled him with. Strange that he should have rushed into his dream with eyes open! But he was fully awake now. He would speak his last farewell to her, and so end the earthly happiness he paid for in deep humiliation, and depart into that gray cold mist where his duty lay. It is thus that young men occasionally design to burst from the circle of the passions, and think that they have done it, when indeed they are but making the circle more swiftly. Here was Evan mouthing his farewell to Rose, using phrases so profoundly humble, that a listener would have taken them for bitter irony. He said adieu to her,—pronouncing it with a pathos to melt scornful princesses. He tried to be honest, and was as much so as his disease permitted.

The black cloud had swallowed the sun; and turning off to the short cut across the downs, Evan soon rode between the wind and the storm. He could see the heavy burden breasting the beacon-point, round which curled leaden arms, and a low internal growl saluted him advancing. The horse laid back his ears. A last gust from the opposing quarter shook the furzes and the clumps of long pale grass, and straight fell columns of rattling white rain, and in a minute he was closed in by a hissing ring. Men thus pelted abandon without protest the hope of retaining a dry particle of clothing on their persons. Completely drenched, the track lost, everything in dense gloom beyond the white enclosure that moved with him, Evan flung the reins to the horse, and curiously watched him footing on; for physical discomfort balanced his mental perturbation, and he who had just been chafing was now quite calm.

Was that a shepherd crouched under the thorn? The place betokened a shepherd, but it really looked like a bundle of the opposite sex; and it proved to be a woman gathered up with her gown over her head. Apparently, Mr. Evan Harrington was destined for these encounters. The thunder rolled as he stopped by her side and called out to her. She heard him, for she made a movement, but without sufficiently disengaging her head of its covering to show him a part of her face.

Bellowing against the thunder, Evan bade her throw back her garment, and stand and give him up her arms, that he might lift her on the horse behind him.

There came a muffled answer, on a big sob, as it seemed. And as if heaven paused to hear, the storm was mute.

Could he have heard correctly? The words he fancied he had heard sobbed were:

"Best bonnet."

The elements hereupon crashed deep and long from end to end, like a table of Titans passing a jest.

Rain-drops, hard as hail, were spattering a pool on her head. Evan stooped his shoulder, seized the soaked garment, and pulled it back, revealing the features of Polly Wheedle, and the splendid bonnet in ruins—all limp and stained.

Polly blinked at him penitentially.

"Oh, Mr. Harrington; oh, ain't I punished!" she whimpered.

In truth, the maid resembled a well-watered poppy.

Evan told her to stand up close to the horse, and Polly stood up close, looking like a creature that expected a whipping. She was suffering, poor thing, from that abject sense of the lack of a circumference, which takes the pride out of women more than anything. Note, that in all material fashions, as in all moral observances, women demand a circumference, and enlarge it more and more as civilization advances. Respect the mighty instinct, however mysterious it seem.

"Oh, Mr. Harrington, don't laugh at me," said Polly.

Evan assured her that he was seriously examining her bonnet.

"It's the bonnet of a draggletail," said Polly, giving up her arms, and biting her under-lip for the lift.

With some display of strength, Evan got the lean creature up behind him, and Polly settled there, and squeezed him tightly with her arms, excusing the liberty she took.

They mounted the beacon, and rode along the ridge whence the West became visible, and a washed edge of red over Beckley Church spire and the woods of Beckley Court.

"And what have you been doing to be punished? What brought you here?" said Evan.

"Somebody drove me to Fallow field to see my poor sister Susan," returned Polly, half crying.

"Well, did he bring you here and leave you?

"No: he wasn't true to his appointment the moment I wanted to go back; and I, to pay him out, I determined I'd walk it where he shouldn't overtake me, and on came the storm. . . And my gown spoilt, and such a bonnet!"

"Who was the somebody?"

"He's a Mr. Nicholas Frim, sir."

"Mr. Nicholas Frim will be very unhappy, I should think."

"Yes, that's one comfort," said Polly ruefully, drying her eyes.

Closely surrounding a young man as a young woman must be when both are on the same horse, they, as a rule, talk confidentially together in a very short time. His "Are you cold?" when Polly shivered, and her "Oh, no; not very," and a slight screwing of her body up to him, as she spoke, to assure him and herself of it, soon made them intimate.

"I think Mr. Nicholas Frim mustn't see us riding into Beckley," said Evan.

"Oh, my gracious! Ought I to get down, sir?" Polly made no move, however.

"Is he jealous?"

"Only when I make him, he is."

"That's very naughty of you."

"Yes, I know it is—all the Wheedles are. Mother says, we never go right till we've once got in a pickle."

"You ought to go right from this hour," said Evan.

"It's 'dizenzy—(?? D.W.)—does it," said Polly. "And then we're ashamed to show it. My poor Susan went to stay with her aunt at Bodley, and then at our cousin's at Hillford, and then she was off to Lymport to drown her poor self, I do believe, when you met her. And all because we can't bear to be seen when we're in any of our pickles. I wish you wouldn't look at me, Mr. Harrington."

"You look very pretty."

"It's quite impossible I can now," said Polly, with a wretched effort to spread open her collar. "I can see myself a fright, like my Miss Rose did, making a face in the looking-glass when I was undressing her last night. But, do you know, I would much rather Nicholas saw us than somebody!"

"Who's that?"

"Miss Bonner. She'd never forgive me."

"Is she so strict?"

"She only uses servants for spies," said Polly. "And since my Miss Rose come—though I'm up a step—I'm still a servant, and Miss Bonner 'd be in a fury to see my—though I'm sure we're quite respectable, Mr. Harrington—my having hold of you as I'm obliged to, and can't help myself. But she'd say I ought to tumble off rather than touch her engaged with a little finger."

"Her engaged?" cried Evan.

"Ain't you, sir?" quoth Polly. "I understand you were going to be, from my lady, the Countess. We all think so at Beckley. Why, look how Miss Bonner looks at you, and she's sure to have plenty of money."

This was Polly's innocent way of bringing out a word about her own young mistress.

Evan controlled any denial of his pretensions to the hand of Miss Bonner. He said: "Is it your mistress's habit to make faces in the looking-glass?"

"I'll tell you how it happened," said Polly. "But I'm afraid I'm in your way, sir. Shall I get off now?"

"Not by any means," said Evan. "Make your arm tighter."

"Will that do?" asked Polly.

Evan looked round and met her appealing face, over which the damp locks of hair straggled. The maid was fair: it was fortunate that he was thinking of the mistress.

"Speak on," said Evan, but Polly put the question whether her face did not want washing, and so earnestly that he had to regard it again, and compromised the case by saying that it wanted kissing by Nicholas Frim, which set Polly's lips in a pout.

"I'm sure it wants kissing by nobody," she said, adding with a spasm of passion: "Oh! I know the colours of my bonnet are all smeared over it, and I'm a dreadful fright."

Evan failed to adopt the proper measures to make Miss Wheedle's mind easy with regard to her appearance, and she commenced her story rather languidly.

"My Miss Rose—what was it I was going to tell? Oh!—my Miss Rose. You must know, Mr. Harrington, she's very fond of managing; I can see that, though I haven't known her long before she gave up short frocks; and she said to Mr. Laxley, who's going to marry her some day, 'She didn't like my lady, the Countess, taking Mr. Harry to herself like that.' I can't a-bear to speak his name, but I suppose he's not a bit more selfish than the rest of men. So Mr. Laxley said—just like the jealousy of men—they needn't talk of women! I'm sure nobody can tell what we have to put up with. We mustn't look out of this eye, or out of the other, but they're up and—oh, dear me! there's such a to-do as never was known—all for nothing!"

"My good girl!" said Evan, recalling her to the subject-matter with all the patience he could command.

"Where was I?" Polly travelled meditatively back. "I do feel a little cold."

"Come closer," said Evan. "Take this handkerchief—it's the only dry thing I have—cover your chest with it."

"The shoulders feel wettest," Polly replied, "and they can't be helped. I'll tie it round my neck, if you'll stop, sir. There, now I'm warmer."

To show how concisely women can narrate when they feel warmer, Polly started off:

"So, you know, Mr. Harrington, Mr. Laxley said—he said to Miss Rose, 'You have taken her brother, and she has taken yours.' And Miss Rose said, 'That was her own business, and nobody else's.' And Mr. Laxley said, 'He was glad she thought it a fair exchange.' I heard it all! And then Miss Rose said—for she can be in a passion about some things'—What do you mean, Ferdinand,' was her words, 'I insist upon your speaking out.' Miss Rose always will call gentlemen by their Christian names when she likes them; that's always a sign with her. And he wouldn't tell her. And Miss Rose got awful angry, and she's clever, is my Miss Rose, for what does she do, Mr. Harrington, but begins praising you up so that she knew it must make him mad, only because men can't abide praise of another man when it's a woman that says it—meaning, young lady; for my Miss Rose has my respect, however familiar she lets herself be to us that she likes. The others may go and drown themselves. Are you took ill, sir?"

"No," said Evan, "I was only breathing."

"The doctors say it's bad to take such long breaths," remarked artless Polly. "Perhaps my arms are pressing you?"

"It's the best thing they can do," murmured Evan, dejectedly.

"What, sir?"

"Go and drown themselves."

Polly screwed her lips, as if she had a pin between them, and continued: "Miss Rose was quite sensible when she praised you as her friend; she meant it—every word; and then sudden what does Mr. Laxley do, but say you was something else besides friend—worse or better; and she was silent, which made him savage, I could hear by his voice. And he said, Mr. Harrington, 'You meant it if she did not.' 'No,' says she, 'I know better; he's as honest as the day.' Out he flew and said such things: he said, Mr. Harrington, you wasn't fit to be Miss Rose's friend, even. Then she said, she heard he had told lies about you to her Mama, and her aunts; but her Mama, my lady, laughed at him, and she at her aunts. Then he said you—oh, abominable of him!"

"What did he say?" asked Evan, waking up.

"Why, if I were to tell my Miss Rose some things of him," Polly went on, "she'd never so much as speak to him another instant."

"What did he say?" Evan repeated.

"I hate him!" cried Polly. "It's Mr. Laxley that misleads Mr. Harry, who has got his good nature, and means no more harm than he can help. Oh, I didn't hear what he said of you, sir. Only I know it was abominable, because Miss Rose was so vexed, and you were her dearest friend."

"Well, and about the looking-glass?"

"That was at night, Mr. Harrington, when I was undressing of her. Miss Rose has a beautiful figure, and no need of lacing. But I'd better get down now."

"For heaven's sake, stay where you are."

"I tell her she stands as if she'd been drilled for a soldier," Polly quietly continued. "You're squeezing my arm with your elbow, Mr. Harrington. It didn't hurt me. So when I had her nearly undressed, we were talking about this and that, and you amongst 'em—and I, you know, rather like you, sir, if you'll not think me too bold—she started off by asking me what was the nickname people gave to tailors. It was one of her whims. I told her they were called snips—I'm off!"

Polly gave a shriek. The horse had reared as if violently stung.

"Go on," said Evan. "Hold hard, and go on."

"Snips—Oh! and I told her they were called snips. It is a word that seems to make you hate the idea. I shouldn't like to hear my intended called snip. Oh, he's going to gallop!"

And off in a gallop Polly was borne.

"Well," said Evan, "well?"

"I can't, Mr. Harrington; I have to press you so," cried Polly; "and I'm bounced so—I shall bite my tongue."

After a sharp stretch, the horse fell to a canter, and then trotted slowly, and allowed Polly to finish.

"So Miss Rose was standing sideways to the glass, and she turned her neck, and just as I'd said 'snip,' I saw her saying it in the glass; and you never saw anything so funny. It was enough to make anybody laugh; but Miss Rose, she seemed as if she couldn't forget how ugly it had made her look. She covered her face with her hands, and she shuddered! It is a word-snip! that makes you seem to despise yourself."

Beckley was now in sight from the edge of the downs, lying in its foliage dark under the grey sky backed by motionless mounds of vapour. Miss Wheedle to her great surprise was suddenly though safely dropped; and on her return to the ground the damsel instantly "knew her place," and curtseyed becoming gratitude for his kindness; but he was off in a fiery gallop, the gall of Demogorgon in his soul.

What's that the leaves of the proud old trees of Beckley Court hiss as he sweeps beneath them? What has suddenly cut him short? Is he diminished in stature? Are the lackeys sneering? The storm that has passed has marvellously chilled the air.

His sister, the Countess, once explained to him what Demogorgon was, in the sensation it entailed. "You are skinned alive!" said the Countess. Evan was skinned alive. Fly, wretched young man! Summon your pride, and fly! Fly, noble youth, for whom storms specially travel to tell you that your mistress makes faces in the looking-glass! Fly where human lips and noses are not scornfully distorted, and get thee a new skin, and grow and attain to thy natural height in a more genial sphere! You, ladies and gentlemen, who may have had a matter to conceal, and find that it is oozing out: you, whose skeleton is seen stalking beside you, you know what it is to be breathed upon: you, too, are skinned alive: but this miserable youth is not only flayed, he is doomed calmly to contemplate the hideous image of himself burning on the face of her he loves; making beauty ghastly. In vain—for he is two hours behind the dinner-bell—Mr. Burley, the butler, bows and offers him viands and wine. How can he eat, with the phantom of Rose there, covering her head, shuddering, loathing him? But he must appear in company: he has a coat, if he has not a skin. Let him button it, and march boldly. Our comedies are frequently youth's tragedies. We will smile reservedly as we mark Mr. Evan Harrington step into the midst of the fair society of the drawing-room. Rose is at the piano. Near her reclines the Countess de Saldar, fanning the languors from her cheeks, with a word for the diplomatist on one side, a whisper for Sir John Loring on the other, and a very quiet pair of eyes for everybody. Providence, she is sure, is keeping watch to shield her sensitive cuticle; and she is besides exquisitely happy, albeit outwardly composed: for, in the room sits his Grace the Duke of Belfield, newly arrived. He is talking to her sister, Mrs. Strike, masked by Miss Current. The wife of the Major has come this afternoon, and Andrew Cogglesby, who brought her, chats with Lady Jocelyn like an old acquaintance.

Evan shakes the hands of his relatives. Who shall turn over the leaves of the fair singer's music-book? The young men are in the billiard-room: Drummond is engaged in converse with a lovely person with Giorgione hair, which the Countess intensely admires, and asks the diplomatist whether he can see a soupcon of red in it. The diplomatist's taste is for dark beauties: the Countess is dark.

Evan must do duty by Rose. And now occurred a phenomenon in him. Instead of shunning her, as he had rejoiced in doing after the Jocasta scene, ere she had wounded him, he had a curious desire to compare her with the phantom that had dispossessed her in his fancy. Unconsciously when he saw her, he transferred the shame that devoured him, from him to her, and gazed coldly at the face that could twist to that despicable contortion.

He was in love, and subtle love will not be shamed and smothered. Love sits, we must remember, mostly in two hearts at the same time, and the one that is first stirred by any of the passions to wakefulness, may know more of the other than its owner. Why had Rose covered her head and shuddered? Would the girl feel that for a friend? If his pride suffered, love was not so downcast; but to avenge him for the cold she had cast on him, it could be critical, and Evan made his bearing to her a blank.

This somehow favoured him with Rose. Sheep's eyes are a dainty dish for little maids, and we know how largely they indulge in it; but when they are just a bit doubtful of the quality of the sheep, let the good animal shut his lids forthwith, for a time. Had she not been a little unkind to him in the morning? She had since tried to help him, and that had appeased her conscience, for in truth he was a good young man. Those very words she mentally pronounced, while he was thinking, "Would she feel it for a friend?" We dare but guess at the puzzle young women present now and then, but I should say that Evan was nearer the mark, and that the "good young man" was a sop she threw to that within her which wanted quieting, and was thereby passably quieted. Perhaps the good young man is offended? Let us assure him of our disinterested graciousness.

"Is your friend coming?" she asked, and to his reply said, "I'm glad"; and pitched upon a new song-one that, by hazard, did not demand his attentions, and he surveyed the company to find a vacant seat with a neighbour. Juley Bonner was curled up on the sofa, looking like a damsel who has lost the third volume of an exciting novel, and is divining the climax. He chose to avoid Miss Bonner. Drummond was leaving the side of the Giorgione lady. Evan passed leisurely, and Drummond said "You know Mrs. Evremonde? Let me introduce you."

He was soon in conversation with the glorious-haired dame.

"Excellently done, my brother!" thinks the Countess de Saldar.

Rose sees the matter coolly. What is it to her? But she had finished with song. Jenny takes her place at the piano; and, as Rose does not care for instrumental music, she naturally talks and laughs with Drummond, and Jenny does not altogether like it, even though she is not playing to the ear of William Harvey, for whom billiards have such attractions; but, at the close of the performance, Rose is quiet enough, and the Countess observes her sitting, alone, pulling the petals of a flower in her lap, on which her eyes are fixed. Is the doe wounded? The damsel of the disinterested graciousness is assuredly restless. She starts up and goes out upon the balcony to breathe the night-air, mayhap regard the moon, and no one follows her.

Had Rose been guiltless of offence, Evan might have left Beckley Court the next day, to cherish his outraged self-love. Love of woman is strongly distinguished from pure egoism when it has got a wound: for it will not go into a corner complaining, it will fight its duel on the field or die. Did the young lady know his origin, and scorn him? He resolved to stay and teach her that the presumption she had imputed to him was her own mistake. And from this Evan graduated naturally enough the finer stages of self-deception downward.

A lover must have his delusions, just as a man must have a skin. But here was another singular change in Evan. After his ale-prompted speech in Fallow field, he was nerved to face the truth in the eyes of all save Rose. Now that the truth had enmeshed his beloved, he turned to battle with it; he was prepared to deny it at any moment; his burnt flesh was as sensitive as the Countess's.

Let Rose accuse him, and he would say, "This is true, Miss Jocelyn—what then?" and behold Rose confused and dumb! Let not another dare suspect it. For the fire that had scorched him was in some sort healing, though horribly painful; but contact with the general air was not to be endured—was death! This, I believe, is common in cases of injury by fire. So it befell that Evan, meeting Rose the next morning was playfully asked by her what choice he had made between the white and the red; and he, dropping on her the shallow eyes of a conventional smile, replied, that unable to decide and form a choice, he had thrown both away; at which Miss Jocelyn gave him a look in the centre of his brows, let her head slightly droop, and walked off.

"She can look serious as well as grimace," was all that Evan allowed himself to think, and he strolled out on the lawn with the careless serenity of lovers when they fancy themselves heart-free.

Rose, whipping the piano in the drawing-room, could see him go to sit by Mrs. Evremonde, till they were joined by Drummond, when he left her and walked with Harry, and apparently shadowed the young gentleman's unreflective face; after which Harry was drawn away by the appearance of that dark star, the Countess de Saldar, whom Rose was beginning to detest. Jenny glided by William Harvey's side, far off. Rose, the young Queen of Friendship, was left deserted on her music-stool for a throne, and when she ceased to hammer the notes she was insulted by a voice that cried from below:

"Go on, Rose, it's nice in the sun to hear you," causing her to close her performances and the instrument vigorously.

Rose was much behind her age: she could not tell what was the matter with her. In these little torments young people have to pass through they gain a rapid maturity. Let a girl talk with her own heart an hour, and she is almost a woman. Rose came down-stairs dressed for riding. Laxley was doing her the service of smoking one of her rose-trees. Evan stood disengaged, prepared for her summons. She did not notice him, but beckoned to Laxley drooping over a bud, while the curled smoke floated from his lips.

"The very gracefullest of chimney-pots-is he not?" says the Countess to Harry, whose immense guffaw fails not to apprise Laxley that something has been said of him, for in his dim state of consciousness absence of the power of retort is the prominent feature, and when he has the suspicion of malicious tongues at their work, all he can do is silently to resent it. Probably this explains his conduct to Evan. Some youths have an acute memory for things that have shut their mouths.

The Countess observed to Harry that his dear friend Mr. Laxley appeared, by the cast of his face, to be biting a sour apple.

"Grapes, you mean?" laughed Harry. "Never mind! she'll bite at him when he comes in for the title."

"Anything crude will do," rejoined the Countess. "Why are you not courting Mrs. Evremonde, naughty Don?"

"Oh! she's occupied—castle's in possession. Besides—!" and Harry tried hard to look sly.

"Come and tell me about her," said the Countess.

Rose, Laxley, and Evan were standing close together.

"You really are going alone, Rose?" said Laxley.

"Didn't I say so?—unless you wish to join us?" She turned upon Evan.

"I am at your disposal," said Evan.

Rose nodded briefly.

"I think I'll smoke the trees," said Laxley, perceptibly huffing.

"You won't come, Ferdinand?"

"I only offered to fill up the gap. One does as well as another."

Rose flicked her whip, and then declared she would not ride at all, and, gathering up her skirts, hurried back to the house.

As Laxley turned away, Evan stood before him.

The unhappy fellow was precipitated by the devil of his false position.

"I think one of us two must quit the field; if I go I will wait for you," he said.

"Oh; I understand," said Laxley. "But if it's what I suppose you to mean, I must decline."

"I beg to know your grounds."

"You have tied my hands."

"You would escape under cover of superior station?"

"Escape! You have only to unsay—tell me you have a right to demand it."

The battle of the sophist victorious within him was done in a flash, as Evan measured his qualities beside this young man's, and without a sense of lying, said: "I have."

He spoke firmly. He looked the thing he called himself now. The Countess, too, was a dazzling shield to her brother. The beautiful Mrs. Strike was a completer vindicator of him; though he had queer associates, and talked oddly of his family that night in Fallow field.

"Very well, sir: I admit you manage to annoy me," said Laxley. "I can give you a lesson as well as another, if you want it."

Presently the two youths were seen bowing in the stiff curt style of those cavaliers who defer a passage of temper for an appointed settlement. Harry rushed off to them with a shout, and they separated; Laxley speaking a word to Drummond, Evan—most judiciously, the Countess thought—joining his fair sister Caroline, whom the Duke held in converse.

Drummond returned laughing to the side of Mrs. Evremonde, nearing whom, the Countess, while one ear was being filled by Harry's eulogy of her brother's recent handling of Laxley, and while her intense gratification at the success of her patient management of her most difficult subject made her smiles no mask, heard, "Is it not impossible to suppose such a thing?" A hush ensued—the Countess passed.

In the afternoon, the Jocelyns, William Harvey, and Drummond met together to consult about arranging the dispute; and deputations went to Laxley and to Evan. The former demanded an apology for certain expressions that day; and an equivalent to an admission that Mr. Harrington had said, in Fallow field, that he was not a gentleman, in order to escape the consequences. All the Jocelyns laughed at his tenacity, and "gentleman" began to be bandied about in ridicule of the arrogant lean-headed adolescent. Evan was placable enough, but dogged; he declined to make any admission, though within himself he admitted that his antagonist was not in the position of an impostor; which he for one honest word among them would be exposed as being, and which a simple exercise of resolution to fly the place would save him from being further.

Lady Jocelyn enjoyed the fun, and still more the serious way in which her relatives regarded it.

"This comes of Rose having friends, Emily," said Mrs. Shorne.

There would have been a dispute to arrange between Lady Jocelyn and Mrs. Shorne, had not her ladyship been so firmly established in her phlegmatic philosophy. She said: "Quelle enfantillage! I dare say Rose was at the bottom of it: she can settle it best. Defer the encounter between the boys until they see they are in the form of donkeys. They will; and then they'll run on together, as long as their goddess permits."

"Indeed, Emily," said Mrs. Shorne, "I desire you, by all possible means, to keep the occurrence secret from Rose. She ought not to hear of it."

"No; I dare say she ought not," returned Lady Jocelyn; "but I wager you she does. You can teach her to pretend not to, if you like. Ecce signum."

Her ladyship pointed through the library window at Rose, who was walking with Laxley, and showing him her pearly teeth in return for one of his jokes: an exchange so manifestly unfair, that Lady Jocelyn's womanhood, indifferent as she was, could not but feel that Rose had an object in view; which was true, for she was flattering Laxley into a consent to meet Evan half way.

The ladies murmured and hummed of these proceedings, and of Rose's familiarity with Mr. Harrington; and the Countess in trepidation took Evan to herself, and spoke to him seriously; a thing she had not done since her residence in Beckley. She let him see that he must be on a friendly footing with everybody in the house, or go which latter alternative Evan told her he had decided on. "Yes," said the Countess, "and then you give people full warrant to say it was jealousy drove you hence; and you do but extinguish yourself to implicate dear Rose. In love, Evan, when you run away, you don't live to fight another day."

She was commanded not to speak of love.

"Whatever it may be, my dear," said the Countess, "Mr. Laxley has used you ill. It may be that you put yourself at his feet"; and his sister looked at him, sighing a great sigh. She had, with violence, stayed her mouth concerning what she knew of the Fallow field business, dreading to alarm his sensitiveness; but she could not avoid giving him a little slap. It was only to make him remember by the smart that he must always suffer when he would not be guided by her.

Evan professed to the Jocelyns that he was willing to apologize to Laxley for certain expressions; determining to leave the house when he had done it. The Countess heard and nodded. The young men, sounded on both sides, were accordingly lured to the billiard-room, and pushed together: and when he had succeeded in thrusting the idea of Rose from the dispute, it did seem such folly to Evan's common sense, that he spoke with pleasant bonhommie about it. That done, he entered into his acted part, and towered in his conceit considerably above these aristocratic boors, who were speechless and graceless, but tigers for their privileges and advantages.

It will not be thought that the Countess intended to permit her brother's departure. To have toiled, and yet more, to have lied and fretted her conscience, for nothing, was as little her principle, as to quit the field of action till she is forcibly driven from it is that of any woman.

"Going, my dear," she said coolly. "To-morrow? Oh! very well. You are the judge. And this creature—the insolvent to the apple-woman, who is coming, whom you would push here—will expose us, without a soul to guide his conduct, for I shall not remain. And Carry will not remain. Carry—!" The Countess gave a semisob. "Carry must return to her brute—" meaning the gallant Marine, her possessor.

And the Countess, knowing that Evan loved his sister Caroline, incidentally related to him an episode in the domestic life of Major and Mrs. Strike.

"Greatly redounding to the credit of the noble martinet for the discipline he upholds," the Countess said, smiling at the stunned youth.

"I would advise you to give her time to recover from one bruise," she added. "You will do as it pleases you."

Evan was sent rushing from the Countess to Caroline, with whom the Countess was content to leave him.

The young man was daintily managed. Caroline asked him to stay, as she did not see him often, and (she brought it in at the close) her home was not very happy. She did not entreat him, but looking resigned, her lovely face conjured up the Major to Evan, and he thought, "Can I drive her back to her tyrant?" For so he juggled with himself to have but another day in the sunshine of Rose.

Andrew, too, threw out genial hints about the Brewery. Old Tom intended to retire, he said, and then they would see what they would see! He silenced every word about Lymport; called him a brewer already, and made absurd jokes, that were serviceable stuff nevertheless to the Countess, who deplored to this one and to that the chance existing that Evan might, by the urgent solicitations of his brother-in-law, give up diplomacy and its honours for a brewery and lucre!

Of course Evan knew that he was managed. The memoirs of a managed man have yet to be written; but if he be sincere he will tell you that he knew it all the time. He longed for the sugar-plum; he knew it was naughty to take it: he dared not for fear of the devil, and he shut his eyes while somebody else popped it into his mouth, and assumed his responsibility. Being man-driven or chicaned, is different from being managed. Being managed implies being led the way this other person thinks you should go: altogether for your own benefit, mind: you are to see with her eyes, that you may not disappoint your own appetites: which does not hurt the flesh, certainly; but does damage the conscience; and from the moment you have once succumbed, that function ceases to perform its office of moral strainer so well.

After all, was he not happier when he wrote himself tailor, than when he declared himself gentleman?

So he now imagined, till Rose, wishing him "Good night" on the balcony, and abandoning her hand with a steady sweet voice and gaze, said: "How generous of you to forgive my friend, dear Evan!" And the ravishing little glimpse of womanly softness in her, set his heart beating. If he thought at all, it was that he would have sacrificed body and soul for her.

BOOK IV

XIX

Second Despatch of the Countess

We do not advance very far in this second despatch, and it will be found chiefly serviceable for the indications it affords of our General's skill in mining, and addiction to that branch of military science. For the moment I must beg that a little indulgence be granted to her.

"Purely business. Great haste. Something has happened. An event? I know not; but events may flow from it.

"A lady is here who has run away from the conjugal abode, and Lady Jocelyn shelters her, and is hospitable to another, who is more concerned in this lady's sad fate than he should be. This may be morals, my dear: but please do not talk of Portugal now. A fineish woman with a great deal of hair worn as if her maid had given it one comb straight down and then rolled it up in a hurry round one finger. Malice would say carrots. It is called gold. Mr. Forth is in a glass house, and is wrong to cast his sneers at perfectly inoffensive people.

"Perfectly impossible we can remain at Beckley Court together—if not dangerous. Any means that Providence may designate, I would employ. It will be like exorcising a demon. Always excuseable. I only ask a little more time for stupid Evan. He might have little Bonner now. I should not object; but her family is not so good.

"Now, do attend. At once obtain a copy of Strike's Company people. You understand—prospectuses. Tell me instantly if the Captain Evremonde in it is Captain Lawson Evremonde. Pump Strike. Excuse vulgar words. Whether he is not Lord Laxley's half-brother. Strike shall be of use to us. Whether he is not mad. Captain E——'s address. Oh! when I think of Strike—brute! and poor beautiful uncomplaining Carry and her shoulder! But let us indeed most fervently hope that his Grace may be balm to it. We must not pray for vengeance. It is sinful. Providence will inflict that. Always know that Providence is quite sure to. It comforts exceedingly.

"Oh, that Strike were altogether in the past tense! No knowing what the Duke might do—a widower and completely subjugated. It makes my bosom bound. The man tempts me to the wickedest Frenchy ideas. There!

We progress with dear venerable Mrs. Bonner. Truly pious—interested in your Louisa. She dreads that my husband will try to convert me to his creed. I can but weep and say—never!

"I need not say I have my circle. To hear this ridiculous boy Harry Jocelyn grunt under my nose when he has led me unsuspectingly away from company—Harriet! dearest! He thinks it a sigh! But there is no time for laughing.

"My maxim in any house is—never to despise the good opinion of the nonentities. They are the majority. I think they all look up to me. But then of course you must fix that by seducing the stars. My diplomatist praises my abilities—Sir John Loring my style—the rest follow and I do not withhold my smiles, and they are happy, and I should be but that for ungrateful Evan's sake I sacrificed my peace by binding myself to a dreadful sort of half-story. I know I did not quite say it. It seems as if Sir A.'s ghost were going to haunt me. And then I have the most dreadful fears that what I have done has disturbed him in the other world. Can it be so? It is not money or estates we took at all, dearest! And these excellent young curates—I almost wish it was Protestant to speak a word behind a board to them and imbibe comfort. For after all it is nothing: and a word even from this poor thin mopy Mr. Parsley might be relief to a poor soul in trouble. Catholics tell you that what you do in a good cause is redeemable if not exactly right. And you know the Catholic is the oldest Religion of the two. I would listen to the Pope, staunch Protestant as I am, in preference to King Henry the Eighth. Though, as a woman, I bear him no rancour, for his wives were—fools, point blank. No man was ever so manageable. My diplomatist is getting liker and liker to him every day. Leaner, of course, and does not habitually straddle. Whiskers and morals, I mean. We must be silent before our prudish sister. Not a prude? We talk diplomacy, dearest. He complains of the exclusiveness of the port of Oporto, and would have strict alliance between Portugal and England, with mutual privileges. I wish the alliance, and think it better to maintain the exclusiveness. Very trifling; but what is life!

"Adieu. One word to leave you laughing. Imagine her situation! This stupid Miss Carrington has offended me. She has tried to pump Conning, who, I do not doubt, gave her as much truth as I chose she should have in her well. But the quandary of the wretched creature! She takes Conning into her confidence—a horrible malady just covered by high-neck dress! Skin! and impossible that she can tell her engaged—

who is—guess—Mr. George Up—! Her name is Louisa Carrington. There was a Louisa Harrington once. Similarity of names perhaps. Of course I could not let her come to the house; and of course Miss C. is in a state of wonderment and bad passions, I fear. I went straight to Lady Racial, my dear. There was nothing else for it but to go and speak. She is truly a noble woman—serves us in every way. As she should!—much affected by sight of Evan, and keeps aloof from Beckley Court. The finger of Providence is in all. Adieu! but do pray think of Miss Carrington! It was foolish of her to offend me. Drives and walks-the Duke attentive. Description of him when I embrace you. I give amiable Sir Franks Portuguese dishes. Ah, my dear, if we had none but men to contend against, and only women for our tools! But this is asking for the world, and nothing less.

"Open again," she pursues. "Dear Carry just come in. There are fairies, I think, where there are dukes! Where could it have come from? Could any human being have sent messengers post to London, ordered, and had it despatched here within this short time? You shall not be mystified! I do not think I even hinted; but the afternoon walk I had with his Grace, on the first day of his arrival, I did shadow it very delicately how much it was to be feared our poor Carry could not, that she dared not, betray her liege lord in an evening dress. Nothing more, upon my veracity! And Carry has this moment received the most beautiful green box, containing two of the most heavenly old lace shawls that you ever beheld. We divine it is to hide poor Carry's matrimonial blue mark! We know nothing. Will you imagine Carry is for not accepting it! Priority of birth does not imply superior wits, dear—no allusion to you. I have undertaken all. Arch looks, but nothing pointed. His Grace will understand the exquisite expression of feminine gratitude. It is so sweet to deal with true nobility. Carry has only to look as she always does. One sees Strike sitting on her. Her very pliability has rescued her from being utterly squashed long ere this! The man makes one vulgar. It would have been not the slightest use asking me to be a Christian had I wedded Strike. But think of the fairy presents! It has determined me not to be expelled by Mr. Forth—quite. Tell Silva he is not forgotten. But, my dear, between us alone, men are so selfish, that it is too evident they do not care for private conversations to turn upon a lady's husband: not to be risked, only now and then.

"I hear that the young ladies and the young gentlemen have been out riding a race. The poor little Bonner girl cannot ride, and she says to Carry that Rose wishes to break our brother's neck. The child hardly wishes that, but she is feelingless. If Evan could care for Miss Bonner, he might have B. C.! Oh, it is not so very long a shot, my dear. I am on the spot, remember. Old Mrs. Bonner is a most just-minded spirit. Juliana is a cripple, and her grandmother wishes to be sure that when she departs to her Lord the poor cripple may not be chased from this home of hers. Rose cannot calculate—Harry is in disgrace—there is really no knowing. This is how I have reckoned; L10,000 extra to Rose; perhaps L1000 or nothing to H.; all the rest of ready-money—a large sum—no use guessing—to Lady Jocelyn; and B. C. to little Bonner—it is worth L40,000 Then she sells, or stops—permanent resident. It might be so soon, for I can see worthy Mrs. Bonner to be breaking visibly. But young men will not see with wiser eyes than their own. Here is Evan risking his neck for an indifferent—there's some word for 'not soft.' In short, Rose is the cold-blooded novice, as I have always said, the most selfish of the creatures on two legs.

"Adieu! Would you have dreamed that Major Nightmare's gallantry to his wife would have called forth a gallantry so truly touching and delicate? Can you not see Providence there? Out of Evil—the Catholics again!

"Address. If Lord Lax—'s half-brother. If wrong in noddle. This I know you will attend to scrupulously. Ridiculous words are sometimes the most expressive. Once more, may Heaven bless you all! I thought of you in church last Sunday.

"I may tell you this: young Mr. Laxley is here. He—but it was Evan's utter madness was the cause, and I have not ventured a word to him. He compelled Evan to assert his rank, and Mr. Forth's face has been one concentrated sneer since THEN. He must know the origin of the Cogglesbys, or something. Now you will understand the importance. I cannot be more explicit. Only—the man must go.

"P.S. I have just ascertained that Lady Jocelyn is quite familiar with Andrew's origin!! She must think my poor Harriet an eccentric woman. Of course I have not pretended to rank here, merely gentry. It is gentry in reality, for had poor Papa been legitimized, he would have been a nobleman. You know that; and between the two we may certainly claim gentry. I twiddle your little good Andrew to assert it for us twenty times a day. Of all the dear little manageable men! It does you infinite credit that you respect him as you do. What would have become of me I do not know.

"P.S. I said two shawls—a black and a white. The black not so costly—very well. And so delicate of him to think of the mourning! But the white, my dear, must be family—must! Old English point. Exquisitely chaste. So different from that Brussels poor Andrew surprised you with. I know it cost money, but this is a question of taste. The Duke reconciles me to England and all my troubles! He is more like poor Papa than any one of the men I have yet seen. The perfect gentleman! I do praise myself for managing an invitation to our Carry. She has been a triumph."

Admire the concluding stroke. The Countess calls this letter a purely business communication. Commercial men might hardly think so; but perhaps ladies will perceive it. She rambles concentrically, if I may so expound her. Full of luxurious enjoyment of her position, her mind is active, and you see her at one moment marking a plot, the next, with a light exclamation, appeasing her conscience, proud that she has one; again she calls up rival forms of faith, that she may show the Protestant its little shortcomings, and that it is slightly in debt to her (like Providence) for her constancy, notwithstanding. The Protestant you see, does not confess, and she has to absolve herself, and must be doing it internally while she is directing outer matters. Hence her slap at King Henry VIII. In fact, there is much more business in this letter than I dare to indicate; but as it is both impertinent and unpopular to dive for any length of time beneath the surface (especially when there are few pearls to show for it), we will discontinue our examination.

The Countess, when she had dropped the letter in the bag, returned to her chamber, and deputed Dorothy Loring, whom she met on the stairs, to run and request Rose to lend her her album to beguile the afternoon with; and Dorothy dances to Rose, saying, "The Countess de Lispy-Lispy would be delighted to look at your album all the afternoon."

"Oh what a woman that is!" says Rose. "Countess de Lazy-Lazy, I think."

The Countess, had she been listening, would have cared little for accusations on that head. Idlesse was fashionable: exquisite languors were a sign of breeding; and she always had an idea that she looked more interesting at dinner after reclining on a couch the whole of the afternoon. The great Mel and his mate had given her robust health, and she was able to play the high-born invalid without damage to her constitution. Anything amused her; Rose's album even, and the compositions of W. H., E. H., D. F., and F. L. The initials F. L. were diminutive, and not unlike her own hand, she thought. They were appended to a piece of facetiousness that would not have disgraced the abilities of Mr. John Raikes; but we know that very stiff young gentlemen betray monkey-minds when sweet young ladies compel them to disport. On the whole, it was not a lazy afternoon that the Countess passed, and it was not against her wish that others should think it was.

XX

Break-Neck Leap

The August sun was in mid-sky, when a troop of ladies and cavaliers issued from the gates of Beckley Court, and winding through the hopgardens, emerged on the cultivated slopes bordering the downs. Foremost, on her grey cob, was Rose, having on her right her uncle Seymour, and on her left Ferdinand Laxley. Behind came Mrs. Evremonde, flanked by Drummond and Evan. Then followed Jenny Graine, supported by Harry and William Harvey. In the rear came an open carriage, in which Miss Carrington and the Countess de Saldar were borne, attended by Lady Jocelyn and Andrew Cogglesby on horseback. The expedition had for its object the selection of a run of ground for an amateur steeple-chase: the idea of which had sprung from Laxley's boasts of his horsemanship: and Rose, quick as fire, had backed herself, and Drummond and Evan, to beat him. The mention of the latter was quite enough for Laxley.

"If he follows me, let him take care of his neck," said that youth.

"Why, Ferdinand, he can beat you in anything!" exclaimed Rose, imprudently.

But the truth was, she was now more restless than ever. She was not distant with Evan, but she had a feverish manner, and seemed to thirst to make him show his qualities, and excel, and shine. Billiards, or jumping, or classical acquirements, it mattered not—Evan must come first. He had crossed the foils with Laxley, and disarmed him; for Mel his father had seen him trained for a military career. Rose made a noise about the encounter, and Laxley was eager for his opportunity, which he saw in the proposed mad gallop.

Now Mr. George Uplift, who usually rode in buckskins whether he was after the fox or fresh air, was out on this particular morning; and it happened that, as the cavalcade wound beneath the down, Mr. George trotted along the ridge. He was a fat-faced, rotund young squire—a bully where he might be, and an obedient creature enough where he must be—good-humoured when not interfered with; fond of the table, and brimful of all the jokes of the county, the accent of which just seasoned his speech. He had somehow plunged into a sort of half-engagement with Miss Carrington. At his age, and to ladies of Miss Carrington's age, men unhappily do not plunge head-foremost, or Miss Carrington would have had him long before. But he was at least in for it half a leg; and a desperate maiden, on the criminal side of thirty, may make much of that. Previous to the visit of the Countess de Saldar, Mr. George had been in the habit of trotting over to Beckley three or four times a week. Miss Carrington had a little money: Mr. George was heir to his uncle. Miss Carrington was lean and blue-eyed.

Mr. George was black-eyed and obese. By everybody, except Mr. George, the match was made: but that exception goes for little in the country, where half the population are talked into marriage, and gossips entirely devote themselves to continuing the species. Mr. George was certain that he had not been fighting shy of the fair Carrington of late, nor had he been unfaithful. He had only been in an extraordinary state of occupation. Messages for Lady Racial had to be delivered, and he had become her cavalier and escort suddenly. The young squire was bewildered; but as he was only one leg in love—if the sentiment may be thus spoken of figuratively—his vanity in his present office kept him from remorse or uneasiness.

He rode at an easy pace within sight of the home of his treasure, and his back turned to it. Presently there rose a cry from below. Mr. George looked about. The party of horsemen hallooed: Mr. George yoicked. Rose set her horse to gallop up; Seymour Jocelyn cried "fox," and gave the view; hearing which Mr. George shouted, and seemed inclined to surrender; but the fun seized him, and, standing up in his stirrups, he gathered his coat-tails in a bunch, and waggled them with a jolly laugh, which was taken up below, and the clamp of hoofs resounded on the turf as Mr. George led off, after once more, with a jocose twist in his seat, showing them the brush mockingly. Away went fox, and a mad chase began. Seymour acted as master of the hunt. Rose, Evan, Drummond, and Mrs. Evremonde and Dorothy, skirted to the right, all laughing, and full of excitement. Harry bellowed the direction from above. The ladies in the carriage, with Lady Jocelyn and Andrew, watched them till they flowed one and all over the shoulder of the down.

"And who may the poor hunted animal be?" inquired the Countess.

"George Uplift," said Lady Jocelyn, pulling out her watch. "I give him twenty minutes."

"Providence speed him!" breathed the Countess, with secret fervour.

"Oh, he hasn't a chance," said Lady Jocelyn. "The squire keeps wretched beasts."

"Is there not an attraction that will account for his hasty capture?" said the Countess, looking tenderly at Miss Carrington, who sat a little straighter, and the Countess, hating manifestations of stiff-backedness, could not forbear adding: "I am at war with my sympathies, which should be with the poor brute flying from his persecutors."

She was in a bitter state of trepidation, or she would have thought twice before she touched a nerve of the enamoured lady, as she knew she did in calling her swain a poor brute, and did again by pertinaciously pursuing:

"Does he then shun his captivity?"

"Touching a nerve" is one of those unforgivable small offences which, in our civilized state, produce the social vendettas and dramas that, with savage nations, spring from the spilling of blood. Instead of an eye for an eye, a tooth for a tooth, we demand a nerve for a nerve. "Thou hast touched me where I am tender thee, too, will I touch."

Miss Carrington had been alarmed and hurt at the strange evasion of Mr. George; nor could she see the fun of his mimicry of the fox and his flight away from instead of into her neighbourhood. She had also, or she now thought it, remarked that when Mr. George had been spoken of casually, the Countess had not looked a natural look. Perhaps it was her present inflamed fancy. At any rate the Countess was offensive now. She was positively vulgar, in consequence, to the mind of Miss Carrington, and Miss Carrington was drawn to think of a certain thing Ferdinand Laxley had said he had heard from the mouth of this lady's brother when ale was in him. Alas! how one seed of a piece of folly will lurk and sprout to confound us; though, like the cock in the eastern tale, we peck up zealously all but that one!

The carriage rolled over the turf, attended by Andrew, and Lady Jocelyn, and the hunt was seen; Mr. George some forty paces a-head; Seymour gaining on him, Rose next.

"Who's that breasting Rose?" said Lady Jocelyn, lifting her glass.

"My brother-in-law, Harrington," returned Andrew.

"He doesn't ride badly," said Lady Jocelyn. "A little too military. He must have been set up in England."

"Oh, Evan can do anything," said Andrew enthusiastically. "His father was a capital horseman, and taught him fencing, riding, and every accomplishment. You won't find such a young fellow, my lady—"

"The brother like him at all?" asked Lady Jocelyn, still eyeing the chase.

"Brother? He hasn't got a brother," said Andrew.

Lady Jocelyn continued: "I mean the present baronet."

She was occupied with her glass, and did not observe the flush that took hold of Andrew's ingenuous cheeks, and his hurried glance at and off the quiet eye of the Countess. Miss Carrington did observe it.

Mr. Andrew dashed his face under the palm of his hand, and murmured:

"Oh-yes! His brother-in-law isn't much like him—ha! ha!"

And then the poor little man rubbed his hands, unconscious of the indignant pity for his wretched abilities in the gaze of the Countess; and he must have been exposed—there was a fear that the ghost of Sir Abraham would have darkened this day, for Miss Carrington was about to speak, when Lady Jocelyn cried: "There's a purl! Somebody's down."

The Countess was unaware of the nature of a purl, but she could have sworn it to be a piece of Providence.

"Just by old Nat Hodges' farm, on Squire Copping's ground," cried Andrew, much relieved by the particular individual's misfortune. "Dear me, my lady! how old Tom and I used to jump the brook there, to be sure! and when you were no bigger than little Miss Loring—do you remember old Tom? We're all fools one time in our lives!"

"Who can it be?" said Lady Jocelyn, spying at the discomfited horseman. "I'm afraid it's poor Ferdinand."

They drove on to an eminence from which the plain was entirely laid open.

"I hope my brother will enjoy his ride this day," sighed the Countess. "It will be his limit of enjoyment for a lengthened period!"

She perceived that Mr. George's capture was inevitable, and her heart sank; for she was sure he would recognize her, and at the moment she misdoubted her powers. She dreamed of flight.

"You're not going to leave us?" said Lady Jocelyn. "My dear Countess, what will the future member do without you? We have your promise to stay till the election is over."

"Thanks for your extreme kind courtesy, Lady Jocelyn," murmured the Countess: "but my husband—the Count."

"The favour is yours," returned her ladyship. "And if the Count cannot come, you at least are at liberty?"

"You are most kind," said the Countess.

"Andrew and his wife I should not dare to separate for more than a week," said Lady Jocelyn. "He is the great British husband. The proprietor! 'My wife' is his unanswerable excuse."

"Yes," Andrew replied cheerily. "I don't like division between man and wife, I must say."

The Countess dared no longer instance the Count, her husband. She was heard to murmur that citizen feelings were not hers:

"You suggested Fallow field to Melville, did you not?" asked Lady Jocelyn.

"It was the merest suggestion," said the Countess, smiling.

"Then you must really stay to see us through it," said her ladyship. "Where are they now? They must be making straight for break-neck fence. They'll have him there. George hasn't pluck for that."

"Hasn't what?"

It was the Countess who requested to know the name of this other piece of Providence Mr. George Uplift was deficient in.

"Pluck-go," said her ladyship hastily, and telling the coachman to drive to a certain spot, trotted on with Andrew, saying to him: "I'm afraid we are thought vulgar by the Countess."

Andrew considered it best to reassure her gravely.

"The young man, her brother, is well-bred," said Lady Jocelyn, and Andrew was very ready to praise Evan.

Lady Jocelyn, herself in slimmer days a spirited horsewoman, had correctly estimated Mr. George's pluck. He was captured by Harry and Evan close on the leap, in the act of shaking his head at it; and many who inspected the leap would have deemed it a sign that wisdom weighted the head that would shake long at it; for it consisted of a post and rails, with a double ditch.

Seymour Jocelyn, Mrs. Evremonde, Drummond, Jenny Graine, and William Harvey, rode with Mr. George in quest of the carriage, and the captive was duly delivered over.

"But where's the brush?" said Lady Jocelyn, laughing, and introducing him to the Countess, who dropped her head, and with it her veil.

"Oh! they leave that on for my next run," said Mr. George, bowing civilly.

"You are going to run again?"

Miss Carrington severely asked this question; and Mr. George protested.

"Secure him, Louisa," said Lady Jocelyn. "See here: what's the matter with poor Dorothy?"

Dorothy came slowly trotting up to them along the green lane, and thus expressed her grief, between sobs:

"Isn't it a shame? Rose is such a tyrant. They're going to ride a race and a jump down in the field, and it's break-neck leap, and Rose won't allow me to stop and see it, though she knows I'm just as fond of Evan as she is; and if he's killed I declare it will be her fault; and it's all for her stupid, dirty old pocket handkerchief!"

"Break-neck fence!" said Lady Jocelyn; "that's rather mad."

"Do let's go and see it, darling Aunty Joey," pleaded the little maid. Lady Jocelyn rode on, saying to herself: "That girl has a great deal of devil in her." The lady's thoughts were of Rose.

"Black Lymport'd take the leap," said Mr. George, following her with the rest of the troop. "Who's that fellow on him?"

"His name's Harrington," quoth Drummond.

"Oh, Harrington!" Mr. George responded; but immediately laughed—"Harrington? "'Gad, if he takes the leap it'll be odd—another of the name. That's where old Mel had his spill."

"Who?" Drummond inquired.

"Old Mel Harrington—the Lymport wonder. Old Marquis Mel," said Mr. George. "Haven't ye heard of him?"

"What! the gorgeous tailor!" exclaimed Lady Jocelyn. "How I regret never meeting that magnificent snob! that efflorescence of sublime imposture! I've seen the Regent; but one's life doesn't seem complete without having seen his twin-brother. You must give us warning when you have him down at Croftlands again, Mr. George."

"'Gad, he'll have to come a long distance—poor old Mel!" said Mr. George; and was going on, when Seymour Jocelyn stroked his moustache to cry, "Look! Rosey's starting 'em, by Jove!"

The leap, which did not appear formidable from where they stood, was four fields distant from the point where Rose, with a handkerchief in her hand, was at that moment giving the signal to Laxley and Evan.

Miss Carrington and the Countess begged Lady Jocelyn to order a shout to be raised to arrest them, but her ladyship marked her good sense by saying: "Let them go, now they're about it"; for she saw that to make a fuss now matters had proceeded so far, was to be uncivil to the inevitable.

The start was given, and off they flew. Harry Jocelyn, behind them, was evidently caught by the demon, and clapped spurs to his horse to have his fling as well, for the fun of the thing; but Rose, farther down the field, rode from her post straight across him, to the imminent peril of a mutual overset; and the party on the height could see Harry fuming, and Rose coolly looking him down, and letting him understand what her will was; and her mother, and Drummond, and Seymour who beheld this, had a common sentiment of admiration for the gallant girl. But away went the rivals. Black Lymport was the favourite, though none of the men thought he would be put at the fence. The excitement became contagious. The Countess threw up her veil. Lady Jocelyn, and Seymour, and Drummond, galloped down the lane, and Mr. George was for accompanying them, till the line of Miss Carrington's back gave him her unmistakeable opinion of such a course of conduct, and he had to dally and fret by her side. Andrew's arm was tightly grasped by the Countess. The rivals were crossing the second field, Laxley a little a-head.

"He's holding in the black mare—that fellow!" said Mr. George. "'Gad, it looks like going at the fence. Fancy Harrington!"

They were now in the fourth field, a smooth shorn meadow. Laxley was two clear lengths in advance, but seemed riding, as Mr. George remarked, more for pace than to take the jump. The ladies kept plying random queries and suggestions: the Countess wishing to know whether they could not be stopped by a countryman before they encountered any danger. In the midst of their chatter, Mr. George rose in his stirrups, crying:

"Bravo, the black mare!"

"Has he done it?" said Andrew, wiping his poll.

"He? No, the mare!" shouted Mr. George, and bolted off, no longer to be restrained.

The Countess, doubly relieved, threw herself back in the carriage, and Andrew drew a breath, saying: "Evan has beat him—I saw that! The other's horse swerved right round."

"I fear," said Mrs. Evremonde, "Mr. Harrington has had a fall. Don't be alarmed—it may not be much."

"A fall!" exclaimed the Countess, equally divided between alarms of sisterly affection and a keen sense of the romance of the thing.

Miss Carrington ordered the carriage to be driven round. They had not gone far when they were met by Harry Jocelyn riding in hot haste, and he bellowed to the coachman to drive as hard as he could, and stop opposite Brook's farm.

The scene on the other side of the fence would have been a sweet one to the central figure in it had his eyes then been open. Surrounded by Lady Jocelyn, Drummond, Seymour, and the rest, Evan's dust-stained body was stretched along the road, and his head was lying in the lap of Rose, who, pale, heedless of anything spoken by those around her, and with her lips set and her eyes turning wildly from one to the other, held a gory handkerchief to his temple with one hand, and with the other felt for the motion of his heart.

But heroes don't die, you know.

XXI

Tribulations and Tactics of the Countess

"You have murdered my brother, Rose Jocelyn!"

"Don't say so now."

Such was the interchange between the two that loved the senseless youth, as he was being lifted into the carriage.

Lady Jocelyn sat upright in her saddle, giving directions about what was to be done with Evan and the mare, impartially.

"Stunned, and a good deal shaken, I suppose; Lymport's knees are terribly cut," she said to Drummond, who merely nodded. And Seymour remarked, "Fifty guineas knocked off her value!" One added, "Nothing worse, I should think"; and another, "A little damage inside, perhaps." Difficult to say whether they spoke of Evan or the brute.

No violent outcries; no reproaches cast on the cold-blooded coquette; no exclamations on the heroism of her brother! They could absolutely spare a thought for the animal! And Evan had risked his life for this, and might die unpitied. The Countess diversified her grief with a deadly bitterness against the heartless Jocelyns.

Oh, if Evan dies! will it punish Rose sufficiently?

Andrew expressed emotion, but not of a kind the Countess liked a relative to be seen exhibiting; for in emotion worthy Andrew betrayed to her his origin offensively.

"Go away and puke, if you must," she said, clipping poor Andrew's word about his "dear boy." She could not help speaking in that way—he was so vulgar. A word of sympathy from Lady Jocelyn might have saved her from the sourness into which her many conflicting passions were resolving; and might also have saved her ladyship from the rancour she had sown in the daughter of the great Mel by her selection of epithets to characterize him.

Will it punish Rose at all, if Evan dies?

Rose saw that she was looked at. How could the Countess tell that Rose envied her the joy of holding Evan in the carriage there? Rose, to judge by her face, was as calm as glass. Not so well seen through, however. Mrs. Evremonde rode beside her, whose fingers she caught, and twined her own with them tightly once for a fleeting instant. Mrs. Evremonde wanted no further confession of her state.

Then Rose said to her mother, "Mama, may I ride to have the doctor ready?"

Ordinarily, Rose would have clapped heel to horse the moment the thought came. She waited for the permission, and flew off at a gallop, waving back Laxley, who was for joining her.

"Franks will be a little rusty about the mare," the Countess heard Lady Jocelyn say; and Harry just then stooped his head to the carriage, and said, in his blunt fashion, "After all, it won't show much."

"We are not cattle!" exclaimed the frenzied Countess, within her bosom. Alas! it was almost a democratic outcry they made her guilty of; but she was driven past patience. And as a further provocation, Evan would open his eyes. She laid her handkerchief over them with loving delicacy, remembering in a flash that her own face had been all the while exposed to Mr. George Uplift; and then the terrors of his presence at Beckley Court came upon her, and the fact that she had not for the last ten minutes been the serene Countess de Saldar; and she quite hated Andrew, for vulgarity in others evoked vulgarity in her, which was the reason why she ranked vulgarity as the chief of the deadly sins. Her countenance for Harry and all the others save poor Andrew was soon the placid heaven-confiding sister's again; not before Lady Jocelyn had found cause to observe to Drummond:

"Your Countess doesn't ruffle well."

But a lady who is at war with two or three of the facts of Providence, and yet will have Providence for her ally, can hardly ruffle well. Do not imagine that the Countess's love for her brother was hollow. She was assured when she came up to the spot where he fell, that there was no danger; he had but dislocated his shoulder, and bruised his head a little. Hearing this, she rose out of her clamorous heart, and seized the opportunity for a small burst of melodrama. Unhappily, Lady Jocelyn, who gave the tone to the rest, was a Spartan in matters of this sort; and as she would have seen those dearest to her bear the luck of the field, she could see others. When the call for active help reached her, you beheld a different woman.

The demonstrativeness the Countess thirsted for was afforded her by Juley Bonner, and in a measure by her sister Caroline, who loved Evan passionately. The latter was in riding attire, about to mount to ride and meet them, accompanied by the Duke. Caroline had hastily tied up her hair; a rich golden brown lump of it hung round her cheek; her limpid eyes and anxiously-nerved brows impressed the Countess wonderfully as she ran down the steps and bent her fine well-filled bust forward to ask the first hurried question.

The Countess patted her shoulder. "Safe, dear," she said aloud, as one who would not make much of it. And in a whisper, "You look superb."

I must charge it to Caroline's beauty under the ducal radiance, that a stream of sweet feelings entering into the Countess made her forget to tell her sister that George Uplift was by. Caroline had not been abroad, and her skin was not olive-hued; she was a beauty, and a majestic figure, little altered since the day when the wooden marine marched her out of Lymport.

The Countess stepped from the carriage to go and cherish Juliana's petulant distress; for that unhealthy little body was stamping with impatience to have the story told to her, to burst into fits of pathos; and while Seymour and Harry assisted Evan to descend, trying to laugh off the pain he endured, Caroline stood by, soothing him with words and tender looks.

Lady Jocelyn passed him, and took his hand, saying, "Not killed this time!"

"At your ladyship's service to-morrow," he replied, and his hand was kindly squeezed.

"My darling Evan, you will not ride again?" Caroline cried, kissing him on the steps; and the Duke watched the operation, and the Countess observed the Duke.

That Providence should select her sweetest moments to deal her wounds, was cruel; but the Countess just then distinctly heard Mr. George Uplift ask Miss Carrington.

"Is that lady a Harrington?"

"You perceive a likeness?" was the answer.

Mr. George went "Whew!—tit-tit-tit!" with the profound expression of a very slow mind.

The scene was quickly over. There was barely an hour for the ladies to dress for dinner. Leaving Evan in the doctor's hand, and telling Caroline to dress in her room, the Countess met Rose, and gratified her vindictiveness, while she furthered her projects, by saying:

"Not till my brother is quite convalescent will it be adviseable that you should visit him. I am compelled to think of him entirely now. In his present state he is not fit to be, played with."

Rose, stedfastly eyeing her, seemed to swallow down something in her throat, and said:

"I will obey you, Countess. I hoped you would allow me to nurse him."

"Quiet above all things, Rose Jocelyn!" returned the Countess, with the suavity of a governess, who must be civil in her sourness. "If you would not complete this morning's achievement—stay away."

The Countess declined to see that Rose's lip quivered. She saw an unpleasantness in the bottom of her eyes; and now that her brother's decease was not even remotely to be apprehended, she herself determined to punish the cold, unimpressionable coquette of a girl. Before returning to Caroline, she had five minutes' conversation with. Juliana, which fully determined her to continue the campaign at Beckley Court, commence decisive movements, and not to retreat, though fifty George Uplofts menaced her. Consequently, having dismissed Conning on a message to Harry Jocelyn, to ask him for a list of the names of the new people they were to meet that day at dinner, she said to Caroline:

"My dear, I think it will be incumbent on us to depart very quickly."

Much to the Countess's chagrin and astonishment, Caroline replied:

"I shall hardly be sorry."

"Not sorry? Why, what now, dear one? Is it true, then, that a flagellated female kisses the rod? Are you so eager for a repetition of Strike?"

Caroline, with some hesitation, related to her more than the Countess had ventured to petition for in her prayers.

"Oh! how exceedingly generous!" the latter exclaimed. "How very refreshing to think that there are nobles in your England as romantic, as courteous, as delicate as our own foreign ones! But his Grace is quite an exceptional nobleman. Are you not touched, dearest Carry?"

Caroline pensively glanced at the reflection of her beautiful arm in the glass, and sighed, pushing back the hair from her temples.

"But, for mercy's sake!" resumed the Countess, in alarm at the sigh, "do not be too—too touched. Do, pray, preserve your wits. You weep! Caroline, Caroline! O my goodness; it is just five-and-twenty minutes to the first dinner-bell, and you are crying! For God's sake, think of your face! Are you going to be a Gorgon? And you show the marks twice as long as any other, you fair women. Squinnying like this! Caroline, for your Louisa's sake, do not!"

Hissing which, half angrily and half with entreaty, the Countess dropped on her knees. Caroline's fit of tears subsided. The eldest of the sisters, she was the kindest, the fairest, the weakest.

"Not," said the blandishing Countess, when Caroline's face was clearer, "not that my best of Carrys does not look delicious in her shower. Cry, with your hair down, and you would subdue any male creature on two legs. And that reminds me of that most audacious Marquis de Remilla. He saw a dirty drab of a fruit-girl crying in Lisbon streets one day, as he was riding in the carriage of the Duchesse de Col da Rosta, and her husband and duena, and he had a letter for her—the Duchesse. They loved! How deliver the letter? 'Save me!' he cried to the Duchesse, catching her hand, and pressing his heart, as if very sick. The Duchesse felt the paper—turned her hand over on her knee, and he withdrew his. What does my Carry think was the excuse he tendered the Duke? This—and this gives you some idea of the wonderful audacity of those dear Portuguese—that he—he must precipitate himself and marry any woman he saw weep, and be her slave for the term of his natural life, unless another woman's hand at the same moment restrained him! There!" and the Countess's eyes shone brightly.

"How excessively imbecile!" Caroline remarked, hitherto a passive listener to these Lusitanian contes.

It was the first sign she had yet given of her late intercourse with a positive Duke, and the Countess felt it, and drew back. No more anecdotes for Caroline, to whom she quietly said:

"You are very English, dear!"

"But now, the Duke—his Grace," she went on, "how did he inaugurate?"

"I spoke to him of Evan's position. God forgive me!—I said that was the cause of my looks being sad."

"You could have thought of nothing better," interposed the Countess. "Yes?"

"He said, if he might clear them he should be happy!

"In exquisite language, Carry, of course."

"No; just as others talk."

"Hum!" went the Countess, and issued again brightly from a cloud of reflection, with the remark: "It was to seem business-like—the commerciality of the English mind. To the point—I know. Well, you perceive, my sweetest, that Evan's interests are in your hands. You dare not quit the field. In one week, I fondly trust, he will be secure. What more did his Grace say? May we not be the repository of such delicious secresies?"

Caroline gave tremulous indications about the lips, and the Countess jumped to the bell and rang it, for they were too near dinner for the trace of a single tear to be permitted. The bell and the appearance of Conning effectually checked the flood.

While speaking to her sister, the Countess had hesitated to mention George Uplift's name, hoping that, as he had no dinner-suit, he would not stop to dinner that day, and would fall to the charge of Lady Racial once more. Conning, however, brought in a sheet of paper on which the names of the guests were written out by Harry, a daily piece of service he performed for the captivating dame, and George Uplift's name was in the list.

"We will do the rest, Conning-retire," she said, and then folding Caroline in her arms, murmured, the moment they were alone, "Will my Carry dress her hair plain to-day, for the love of her Louisa?"

"Goodness! what a request!" exclaimed Caroline, throwing back her head to see if her Louisa could be serious.

"Most inexplicable—is it not? Will she do it?"

"Flat, dear? It makes a fright of me."

"Possibly. May I beg it?"

"But why, dearest, why? If I only knew why!"

"For the love of your Louy."

"Plain along the temples?"

"And a knot behind."

"And a band along the forehead?"

"Gems, if they meet your favour."

"But my cheek-bones, Louisa?"

"They are not too prominent, Carry."

"Curls relieve them."

"The change will relieve the curls, dear one."

Caroline looked in the glass, at the Countess, as polished a reflector, and fell into a chair. Her hair was accustomed to roll across her shoulders in heavy curls. The Duke would find a change of the sort singular. She should not at all know herself with her hair done differently: and for a lovely woman to be transformed to a fright is hard to bear in solitude, or in imagination.

"Really!" she petitioned.

"Really—yes, or no?" added the Countess.

"So unaccountable a whim!" Caroline looked in the glass dolefully, and pulled up her thick locks from one cheek, letting them fall on the instant.

"She will?" breathed the Countess.

"I really cannot," said Caroline, with vehemence.

The Countess burst into laughter, replying: "My poor child! it is not my whim—it is your obligation. George Uplift dines here to-day. Now do you divine it? Disguise is imperative for you."

Mrs. Strike, gazing in her sister's face, answered slowly, "George? But how will you meet him?" she hurriedly asked.

"I have met him," rejoined the Countess, boldly. "I defy him to know me. I brazen him! You with your hair in my style are equally safe. You see there is no choice. Pooh! contemptible puppy!"

"But I never,"—Caroline was going to say she never could face him. "I will not dine. I will nurse Evan."

"You have faced him, my dear," said the Countess, "and you are to change your head-dress simply to throw him off his scent."

As she spoke the Countess tripped about, nodding her head like a girl. Triumph in the sense of her power over all she came in contact with, rather elated the lady.

Do you see why she worked her sister in this roundabout fashion? She would not tell her George Uplift was in the house till she was sure he intended to stay, for fear of frightening her. When the necessity became apparent, she put it under the pretext of a whim in order to see how far Caroline, whose weak compliance she could count on, and whose reticence concerning the Duke annoyed her, would submit to it to please her sister; and if she rebelled positively, why to be sure it was the Duke she dreaded to shock: and, therefore, the Duke had a peculiar hold on her: and, therefore, the Countess might reckon that she would do more than she pleased to confess to remain with the Duke, and was manageable in that quarter. All this she learnt without asking. I need not add, that Caroline sighingly did her bidding.

"We must all be victims in our turn, Carry," said the Countess. "Evan's prospects—it may be, Silva's restoration—depend upon your hair being dressed plain to-day. Reflect on that!"

Poor Caroline obeyed; but she was capable of reflecting only that her face was unnaturally lean and strange to her.

The sisters tended and arranged one another, taking care to push their mourning a month or two ahead and the Countess animadverted on the vulgar mind of Lady Jocelyn, who would allow a "gentleman to sit down at a gentlewoman's table, in full company, in pronounced undress": and Caroline, utterly miserable, would pretend that she wore a mask and kept grimacing as they do who are not accustomed to paint on the cheeks, till the Countess checked her by telling her she should ask her for that before the Duke.

After a visit to Evan, the sisters sailed together into the drawing-room.

"Uniformity is sometimes a gain," murmured the Countess, as they were parting in the middle of the room. She saw that their fine figures, and profiles, and resemblance in contrast, produced an effect. The Duke wore one of those calmly intent looks by which men show they are aware of change in the heavens they study, and are too devout worshippers to presume to disapprove. Mr. George was standing by Miss Carrington, and he also watched Mrs. Strike. To bewilder him yet more the Countess persisted in fixing her eyes upon his heterodox apparel, and Mr. George became conscious and uneasy. Miss Carrington had to address her question to him twice before he heard. Melville Jocelyn, Sir John Loring, Sir Franks, and Hamilton surrounded the Countess, and told her what they had decided on with regard to the election during the day; for Melville was warm in his assertion that they would not talk to the Countess five minutes without getting a hint worth having.

"Call to us that man who is habited like a groom," said the Countess, indicating Mr. George. "I presume he is in his right place up here?"

"Whew—take care, Countess—our best man. He's good for a dozen," said Hamilton.

Mr. George was brought over and introduced to the Countess de Saldar.

"So the oldest Tory in the county is a fox?" she said, in allusion to the hunt. Never did Caroline Strike admire her sister's fearful genius more than at that moment.

Mr. George ducked and rolled his hand over his chin, with "ah-um!" and the like, ended by a dry laugh.

"Are you our supporter, Mr. Uplift?"

"Tory interest, ma—um—my lady."

"And are you staunch and may be trusted?"

"'Pon my honour, I think I have that reputation."

"And you would not betray us if we give you any secrets? Say ''Pon my honour,' again. You launch it out so courageously."

The men laughed, though they could not see what the Countess was driving at. She had for two minutes spoken as she spoke when a girl, and George—entirely off his guard and unsuspicious—looked unenlightened. If he knew, there were hints enough for him in her words.

If he remained blind, they might pass as air. The appearance of the butler cut short his protestation as to his powers of secresy.

The Countess dismissed him.

"You will be taken into our confidence when we require you." And she resumed her foreign air in a most elaborate and overwhelming bow.

She was now perfectly satisfied that she was safe from Mr. George, and, as she thoroughly detested the youthful squire, she chose to propagate a laugh at him by saying with the utmost languor and clearness of voice, as they descended the stairs:

"After all, a very clever fox may be a very dull dog—don't you think?"

Gentlemen in front of her, and behind, heard it, and at Mr. George's expense her reputation rose.

Thus the genius of this born general prompted her to adopt the principle in tactics—boldly to strike when you are in the dark as to your enemy's movements.

XXII

In which the Daughters of the Great Mel Have to Digest Him at Dinner

You must know, if you would form an estimate of the Countess's heroic impudence, that a rumour was current in Lymport that the fair and well-developed Louisa Harrington, in her sixteenth year, did advisedly, and with the intention of rendering the term indefinite, entrust her guileless person to Mr. George Uplift's honourable charge. The rumour, unflavoured by absolute malignity, was such; and it went on to say, that the sublime Mel, alive to the honour of his family, followed the fugitives with a pistol, and with a horsewhip, that he might chastise the offender according to the degree of his offence. It was certain that he had not used the pistol: it was said that he had used the whip. The details of the interview between Mel and Mr. George were numerous, but at the same time various. Some declared that he put a pistol to Mr. George's ear, and under pressure of that persuader got him into the presence of a clergyman, when he turned sulky; and when the pistol was again produced, the ceremony would have been performed, had not the outraged Church cried out for help. Some vowed that Mr. George had referred all questions implying a difference between himself and Mel to their mutual fists for decision. At any rate, Mr. George turned up in Fallow field subsequently; the fair Louisa, unhurt and with a quiet mind, in Lymport; and this amount of truth the rumours can be reduced to—that Louisa and Mr. George had been acquainted. Rumour and gossip know how to build: they always have some solid foundation, however small. Upwards of twelve years had run since Louisa went to the wife of the brewer—a period quite long enough for Mr. George to forget any one in; and she was altogether a different creature; and, as it was true that Mr. George was a dull one, she was, after the test she had put him to, justified in hoping that Mel's progeny might pass unchallenged anywhere out of Lymport. So, with Mr. George facing her at table, the Countess sat down, determined to eat and be happy.

A man with the education and tastes of a young country squire is not likely to know much of the character of women; and of the marvellous power they have of throwing a veil of oblivion between themselves and what they don't want to remember, few men know much. Mr. George had thought, when he saw Mrs. Strike leaning to Evan, and heard she was a Harrington, that she was rather like the Lymport family; but the reappearance of Mrs. Strike, the attention of the Duke of Belfield to her, and the splendid tactics of the Countess, which had extinguished every thought in the thought of himself, drove Lymport out of his mind.

There were some dinner guests at the table-people of Fallow field, Beckley, and Bodley. The Countess had the diplomatist on one side, the Duke on the other. Caroline was under the charge of Sir Franks. The Countess, almost revelling in her position opposite Mr. George, was ambitious to lead the conversation, and commenced, smiling at Melville:

"We are to be spared politics to-day? I think politics and cookery do not assimilate."

"I'm afraid you won't teach the true Briton to agree with you," said Melville, shaking his head over the sums involved by this British propensity.

"No," said Seymour. "Election dinners are a part of the Constitution": and Andrew laughed: "They make Radicals pay as well as Tories, so it's pretty square."

The topic was taken up, flagged, fell, and was taken up again. And then Harry Jocelyn said:

"I say, have you worked the flags yet? The great Mel must have his flags."

The flags were in the hands of ladies, and ladies would look to the rosettes, he was told.

Then a lady of the name of Barrington laughed lightly, and said:

"Only, pray, my dear Harry, don't call your uncle the 'Great Mel' at the election."

"Oh! very well," quoth Harry: "why not?"

"You'll get him laughed at—that's all."

"Oh! well, then, I won't," said Harry, whose wits were attracted by the Countess's visage.

Mrs. Barrington turned to Seymour, her neighbour, and resumed:

"He really would be laughed at. There was a tailor—he was called the Great Mel—and he tried to stand for Fallow field once. I believe he had the support of Squire Uplift—George's uncle—and others. They must have done it for fun! Of course he did not get so far as the hustings;

but I believe he had flags, and principles, and all sorts of things worked ready. He certainly canvassed."

"A tailor—canvassed—for Parliament?" remarked an old Dowager, the mother of Squire Copping. "My what are we coming to next?"

"He deserved to get in," quoth Aunt Bel: "After having his principles worked ready, to eject the man was infamous."

Amazed at the mine she had sprung, the Countess sat through it, lamenting the misery of owning a notorious father. Happily Evan was absent, on his peaceful blessed bed!

Bowing over wine with the Duke, she tried another theme, while still, like a pertinacious cracker, the Great Mel kept banging up and down the table.

"We are to have a feast in the open air, I hear. What you call pic-nic."

The Duke believed there was a project of the sort.

"How exquisitely they do those things in Portugal! I suppose there would be no scandal in my telling something now. At least we are out of Court-jurisdiction."

"Scandal of the Court!" exclaimed his Grace, in mock horror.

"The option is yours to listen. The Queen, when young, was sweetly pretty; a divine complexion; and a habit of smiling on everybody. I presume that the young Habral, son of the first magistrate of Lisbon, was also smiled on. Most innocently, I would swear! But it operated on the wretched youth! He spent all his fortune in the purchase and decoration of a fairy villa, bordering on the Val das Rosas, where the Court enjoyed its rustic festivities, and one day a storm! all the ladies hurried their young mistress to the house where the young Habral had been awaiting her for ages. None so polished as he! Musicians started up, the floors were ready, and torches beneath them!—there was a feast of exquisite wines and viands sparkling. Quite enchantment. The girl-Queen was in ecstasies. She deigned a dance with the young Habral, and then all sat down to supper; and in the middle of it came the cry of Fire! The Queen shrieked; the flames were seen all around; and if the arms of the young Habral were opened to save her, or perish, could she cast a thought on Royalty, and refuse? The Queen was saved the villa was burnt; the young Habral was ruined, but, if I know a Portuguese, he was happy till he died, and well remunerated! For he had held a Queen to his heart! So that was a pic-nic!"

The Duke slightly inclined his head.

"Vrai Portughez derrendo," he said. "They tell a similar story in Spain, of one of the Queens—I forget her name. The difference between us and your Peninsular cavaliers is, that we would do as much for uncrowned ladies."

"Ah! your Grace!" The Countess swam in the pleasure of a nobleman's compliment.

"What's the story?" interposed Aunt Bel.

An outline of it was given her. Thank heaven, the table was now rid of the Great Mel. For how could he have any, the remotest relation with Queens and Peninsular pic-nics? You shall hear.

Lady Jocelyn happened to catch a word or two of the story.

"Why," said she, "that's English! Franks, you remember the ballet divertissement they improvised at the Bodley race-ball, when the magnificent footman fired a curtain and caught up Lady Racial, and carried her—"

"Heaven knows where!" cried Sir Franks. "I remember it perfectly. It was said that the magnificent footman did it on purpose to have that pleasure."

"Ay, of course," Hamilton took him up. "They talked of prosecuting the magnificent footman."

"Ay," followed Seymour, "and nobody could tell where the magnificent footman bolted. He vanished into thin air."

"Ay, of course," Melville struck in; "and the magic enveloped the lady for some time."

At this point Mr. George Uplift gave a horse-laugh. He jerked in his seat excitedly.

"Bodley race-ball!" he cried; and looking at Lady Jocelyn: "Was your ladyship there, then? Why—ha! ha! why, you have seen the Great Mel, then! That tremendous footman was old Mel himself!"

Lady Jocelyn struck both her hands on the table, and rested her large grey eyes, full of humorous surprise, on Mr. George.

There was a pause, and then the ladies and gentlemen laughed.

"Yes," Mr. George went on, "that was old Mel. I'll swear to him."

"And that's how it began?" murmured Lady Jocelyn.

Mr. George nodded at his plate discreetly.

"Well," said Lady Jocelyn, leaning back, and lifting her face upward in the discursive fulness of her fancy, "I feel I am not robbed. 'Il y a des miracles, et j'en ai vu'. One's life seems more perfect when one has seen what nature can do. The fellow was stupendous! I conceive him present.

Who'll fire a house for me? Is it my deficiency of attraction, or a total dearth of gallant snobs?"

The Countess was drowned. The muscles of her smiles were horribly stiff and painful. Caroline was getting pale. Could it be accident that thus resuscitated Mel, their father, and would not let the dead man die? Was not malice at the bottom of it? The Countess, though she hated Mr. George infinitely, was clear-headed enough to see that Providence alone was trying her. No glances were exchanged between him and Laxley, or Drummond.

Again Mel returned to his peace, and again he had to come forth.

"Who was this singular man you were speaking about just now?" Mrs. Evremonde asked.

Lady Jocelyn answered her: "The light of his age. The embodied protest against our social prejudice. Combine—say, Mirabeau and Alcibiades, and the result is the Lymport Tailor:—he measures your husband in the morning: in the evening he makes love to you, through a series of pantomimic transformations. He was a colossal Adonis, and I'm sorry he's dead!"

"But did the man get into society?" said Mrs. Evremonde. "How did he manage that?"

"Yes, indeed! and what sort of a society!" the dowager Copping interjected. "None but bachelor-tables, I can assure you. Oh! I remember him. They talked of fetching him to Dox Hall. I said, No, thank you, Tom; this isn't your Vauxhall."

"A sharp retort," said Lady Jocelyn, "a most conclusive rhyme; but you're mistaken. Many families were glad to see him, I hear. And he only consented to be treated like a footman when he dressed like one. The fellow had some capital points. He fought two or three duels, and behaved like a man. Franks wouldn't have him here, or I would have received him. I hear that, as a conteur, he was inimitable. In short, he was a robust Brummel, and the Regent of low life."

This should have been Mel's final epitaph.

Unhappily, Mrs. Melville would remark, in her mincing manner, that the idea of the admission of a tailor into society seemed very unnatural; and Aunt Bel confessed that her experience did not comprehend it.

"As to that," said Lady Jocelyn, "phenomena are unnatural. The rules of society are lightened by the exceptions. What I like in this Mel is, that though he was a snob, and an impostor, he could still make himself respected by his betters. He was honest, so far; he acknowledged his tastes, which were those of Franks, Melville, Seymour, and George—the tastes of a gentleman. I prefer him infinitely to your cowardly democrat, who barks for what he can't get, and is generally beastly. In fact, I'm not sure that I haven't a secret passion for the great tailor."

"After all, old Mel wasn't so bad," Mr. George Uplift chimed in.

"Granted a tailor—you didn't see a bit of it at table. I've known him taken for a lord. And when he once got hold of you, you couldn't give him up. The squire met him first in the coach, one winter. He took him for a Russian nobleman—didn't find out what he was for a month or so. Says Mel, 'Yes, I make clothes. You find the notion unpleasant; guess how disagreeable it is to me.' The old squire laughed, and was glad to have him at Croftlands as often as he chose to come. Old Mel and I used to spar sometimes; but he's gone, and I should like to shake his fist again."

Then Mr. George told the "Bath" story, and episodes in Mel's career as Marquis; and while he held the ear of the table, Rose, who had not spoken a word, and had scarcely eaten a morsel during dinner, studied the sisters with serious eyes. Only when she turned them from the Countess to Mrs. Strike, they were softened by a shadowy drooping of the eyelids, as if for some reason she deeply pitied that lady.

Next to Rose sat Drummond, with a face expressive of cynical enjoyment. He devoted uncommon attention to the Countess, whom he usually shunned and overlooked. He invited her to exchange bows over wine, in the fashion of that day, and the Countess went through the performance with finished grace and ease. Poor Andrew had all the time been brushing back his hair, and making strange deprecatory sounds in his throat, like a man who felt bound to assure everybody at table he was perfectly happy and comfortable.

"Material enough for a Sartoriad," said Drummond to Lady Jocelyn.

"Excellent. Pray write it forthwith, Drummond", replied her ladyship; and as they exchanged talk unintelligible to the Countess, this lady observed to the Duke:

"It is a relief to have buried that subject."

The Duke smiled, raising an eyebrow; but the persecuted Countess perceived she had been much too hasty when Drummond added,

"I'll make a journey to Lymport in a day or two, and master his history."

"Do," said her ladyship; and flourishing her hand, "'I sing the Prince of Snobs!'"

"Oh, if it's about old Mel, I'll sing you material enough," said Mr. George. "There! you talk of it's being unnatural, his dining out at respectable tables. Why, I believe—upon my honour, I believe it's a fact—he's supped and thrown dice with the Regent."

Lady Jocelyn clapped her hands. "A noble culmination, Drummond! The man's an Epic!"

"Well, I think old Mel was equal to it," Mr. George pursued. "He gave me pretty broad hints; and this is how it was, if it really happened, you know. Old Mel had a friend; some say he was more. Well, that was a fellow, a great gambler. I dare say you've heard of him—Burley Bennet—him that won Ryelands Park of one of the royal dukes—died worth upwards of L100,000; and old Mel swore he ought to have had it, and would if he hadn't somehow offended him. He left the money to Admiral Harrington, and he was a relation of Mel's."

"But are we then utterly mixed up with tailors?" exclaimed Mrs. Barrington.

"Well, those are the facts," said Mr. George.

The wine made the young squire talkative. It is my belief that his suspicions were not awake at that moment, and that, like any other young country squire, having got a subject he could talk on, he did not care to discontinue it. The Countess was past the effort to attempt to stop him. She had work enough to keep her smile in the right place.

Every dinner may be said to have its special topic, just as every age has its marked reputation. They are put up twice or thrice, and have to contend with minor lights, and to swallow them, and then they command the tongues of men and flow uninterruptedly. So it was with the great Mel upon this occasion. Curiosity was aroused about him. Aunt Bel agreed with Lady Jocelyn that she would have liked to know the mighty tailor. Mrs. Shorne but very imperceptibly protested against the notion, and from one to another it ran. His Grace of Belfield expressed positive approval of Mel as one of the old school.

"Si ce n'est pas le gentilhomme, au moins, c'est le gentilhomme manque," said Lady Jocelyn. "He is to be regretted, Duke. You are right. The stuff was in him, but the Fates were unkind. I stretch out my hand to the pauvre diable."

"I think one learns more from the mock magnifico than from anything else," observed his Grace.

"When the lion saw the donkey in his own royal skin, said Aunt Bel, "add the rhyme at your discretion—he was a wiser lion, that's all."

"And the ape that strives to copy one—he's an animal of judgement," said Lady Jocelyn. "We will be tolerant to the tailor, and the Countess must not set us down as a nation of shopkeepers: philosophically tolerant."

The Countess started, and ran a little broken "Oh!" affably out of her throat, dipped her lips to her tablenapkin, and resumed her smile.

"Yes," pursued her ladyship; "old Mel stamps the age gone by. The gallant adventurer tied to his shop! Alternate footman and marquis, out of intermediate tailor! Isn't there something fine in his buffoon imitation of the real thing? I feel already that old Mel belongs to me. Where is the great man buried? Where have they, set the funeral brass that holds his mighty ashes?"

Lady Jocelyn's humour was fully entered into by the men. The women smiled vacantly, and had a common thought that it was ill-bred of her to hold forth in that way at table, and unfeminine of any woman to speak continuously anywhere.

"Oh, come!" cried Mr. George, who saw his own subject snapped away from him by sheer cleverness; "old Mel wasn't only a buffoon, my lady, you know. Old Mel had his qualities. He was as much a 'no-nonsense' fellow, in his way, as a magistrate, or a minister."

"Or a king, or a constable," Aunt Bel helped his illustration.

"Or a prince, a poll-parrot, a Perigord-pie," added Drummond, whose gravity did not prevent Mr. George from seeing that he was laughed at.

"Well, then, now, listen to this," said Mr. George, leaning his two hands on the table resolutely. Dessert was laid, and, with a full glass beside him, and a pear to peel, he determined to be heard.

The Countess's eyes went mentally up to the vindictive heavens. She stole a glance at Caroline, and was alarmed at her excessive pallor. Providence had rescued Evan from this!

"Now, I know this to be true," Mr. George began. "When old Mel was alive, he and I had plenty of sparring, and that—but he's dead, and I'll do him justice. I spoke of Burley Bennet just now. Now, my lady, old Burley was, I think, Mel's half-brother, and he came, I know, somewhere out of Drury Lane-one of the courts near the theatre—I don't know much of London. However, old Mel wouldn't have that. Nothing less than being born in St. James's Square would content old Mel, and he must have a Marquis for his father. I needn't be more particular. Before ladies—ahem! But Burley was the shrewd hand of the two. Oh-h-h! such a card! He knew the way to get into company without false pretences. Well, I told you, he had lots more than L100,000—some said two—and he gave up Ryelands; never asked for it, though he won it. Consequence was, he commanded the services of somebody pretty high. And it was he got Admiral Harrington made a captain, posted, commodore, admiral, and K.C.B., all in seven years! In the Army it'd have been half the time, for the H.R.H. was stronger in that department. Now, I know old Burley promised Mel to leave him his money, and called the Admiral an ungrateful dog. He didn't give Mel much at a time—now and then a twenty-pounder or so—I saw the cheques. And old Mel expected the money, and looked over his daughters like a turkey-cock. Nobody good enough for them. Whacking handsome gals—three! used to be called the Three Graces of Lymport. And one day Burley comes and visits Mel, and sees the girls. And he puts his finger on the eldest, I can tell you. She was a spanker! She was the handsomest gal, I think, ever I saw. For the mother's a fine woman, and what with the mother, and what with old Mel—"

"We won't enter into the mysteries of origin," quoth Lady Jocelyn.

"Exactly, my lady. Oh, your servant, of course. Before ladies. A Burley Bennet, I said. Long and short was, he wanted to take her up to London. Says old Mel: 'London's a sad place.'—'Place to make money,' says Burley. 'That's not work for a young gal,' says Mel. Long and short was, Burley wanted to take her, and Mel wouldn't let her go." Mr. George lowered his tone, and mumbled, "Don't know how to explain it very well before ladies. What Burley wanted was—it wasn't quite honourable, you know, though there was a good deal of spangles on it, and whether a real H.R.H., or a Marquis, or a Viscount, I can't say, but—the offer was tempting to a tradesman. 'No,' says Mel; like a chap planting his flagstaff and sticking to it. I believe that to get her to go with him, Burley offered to make a will on the spot, and to leave every farthing of his money and property—upon my soul, I believe it to be true—to Mel and his family, if he'd let the gal go. 'No,' says Mel. I like the old bird! And Burley got in a rage, and said he'd leave every farthing to the sailor. Says Mel: 'I'm a poor tradesman; but I have and I always will have the feelings of a gentleman, and they're more to me than hard cash, and the honour of my daughter, sir, is dearer to me than my blood. Out of the house!' cries Mel. And away old Burley went, and left every penny to the sailor, Admiral Harrington, who never noticed 'em an inch. Now, there!"

All had listened to Mr. George attentively, and he had slurred the apologetic passages, and emphasized the propitiatory "before ladies" in a way to make himself well understood a generation back.

"Bravo, old Mel!" rang the voice of Lady Jocelyn, and a murmur ensued, in the midst of which Rose stood up and hurried round the table to Mrs. Strike, who was seen to rise from her chair; and as she did so, the ill-arranged locks fell from their unnatural restraint down over her shoulders; one great curl half forward to the bosom, and one behind her right ear. Her eyes were wide, her whole face, neck, and fingers, white as marble. The faintest tremor of a frown on her brows, and her shut lips, marked the continuation of some internal struggle, as if with her last conscious force she kept down a flood of tears and a wild outcry which it was death to hold. Sir Franks felt his arm touched, and looked up, and caught her, as Rose approached. The Duke and other gentlemen went to his aid, and as the beautiful woman was borne out white and still as a corpse, the Countess had this dagger plunged in her heart from the mouth of Mr. George, addressing Miss Carrington:

"I swear I didn't do it on purpose. She's Carry Harrington, old Mel's daughter, as sure as she's flesh and blood!"

XXIII

Treats of a Handkerchief

Running through Beckley Park, clear from the chalk, a little stream gave light and freshness to its pasturage. Near where it entered, a bathing-house of white marble had been built, under which the water flowed, and the dive could be taken to a paved depth, and you swam out over a pebbly bottom into sun-light, screened by the thick-weeded banks, loose-strife and willow-herb, and mint, nodding over you, and in the later season long-plumed yellow grasses. Here at sunrise the young men washed their limbs, and here since her return home English Rose loved to walk by night. She had often spoken of the little happy stream to Evan in Portugal, and when he came to Beckley Court, she arranged that he should sleep in a bed-room overlooking it. The view was sweet and pleasant to him, for all the babbling of the water was of Rose, and winding in and out, to East, to North, it wound to embowered hopes in the lover's mind, to tender dreams; and often at dawn, when dressing, his restless heart embarked on it, and sailed into havens, the phantom joys of which coloured his life for him all the day. But most he loved to look across it when the light fell. The palest solitary gleam along its course spoke to him rich promise. The faint blue beam of a star chained all his longings, charmed his sorrows to sleep. Rose like a fairy had breathed her spirit here, and it was a delight to the silly luxurious youth to lie down, and fix some image of a flower bending to the stream on his brain, and in the cradle of fancies that grew round it, slide down the tide of sleep.

From the image of a flower bending to the stream, like his own soul to the bosom of Rose, Evan built sweet fables. It was she that exalted him, that led him through glittering chapters of adventure. In his dream of deeds achieved for her sake, you may be sure the young man behaved worthily, though he was modest when she praised him, and his limbs trembled when the land whispered of his great reward to come. The longer he stayed at Beckley the more he lived in this world within world, and if now and then the harsh outer life smote him, a look or a word from Rose encompassed him again, and he became sensible only of a distant pain.

At first his hope sprang wildly to possess her, to believe, that after he had done deeds that would have sent ordinary men in the condition of shattered hulks to the hospital, she might be his. Then blow upon blow was struck, and he prayed to be near her till he died: no more. Then she, herself, struck him to the ground, and sitting in his chamber, sick and weary, on the evening of his mishap, Evan's sole desire was to obtain the handkerchief he had risked his neck for. To have that, and hold it to his heart, and feel it as a part of her, seemed much.

Over a length of the stream the red round harvest-moon was rising, and the weakened youth was this evening at the mercy of the charm that encircled him. The water curved, and dimpled, and flowed flat, and the whole body of it rushed into the spaces of sad splendour. The clustered trees stood like temples of darkness; their shadows lengthened supernaturally; and a pale gloom crept between them on the sward. He had been thinking for some time that Rose would knock at his door, and give him her voice, at least; but she did not come; and when he had gazed out on the stream till his eyes ached, he felt that he must go and walk by it. Those little flashes of the hurrying tide spoke to him of a secret rapture and of a joy-seeking impulse; the pouring onward of all the blood of life to one illumined heart, mournful from excess of love.

Pardon me, I beg. Enamoured young men have these notions. Ordinarily Evan had sufficient common sense and was as prosaic as mankind could wish him; but he has had a terrible fall in the morning, and a young woman rages in his brain. Better, indeed, and "more manly," were he to strike and raise huge bosses on his forehead, groan, and so have done with it. We must let him go his own way.

At the door he was met by the Countess. She came into the room without a word or a kiss, and when she did speak, the total absence of any euphuism gave token of repressed excitement yet more than her angry eyes and eager step. Evan had grown accustomed to her moods, and if one moment she was the halcyon, and another the petrel, it no longer disturbed him, seeing that he was a stranger to the influences by which she was affected. The Countess rated him severely for not seeking repose and inviting sympathy. She told him that the Jocelyns had one and all combined in an infamous plot to destroy the race of Harrington, and that Caroline had already succumbed to their assaults; that the Jocelyns would repent it, and sooner than they thought for; and that the only friend the Harringtons had in the house was Miss Bonner, whom Providence would liberally reward.

Then the Countess changed to a dramatic posture, and whispered aloud, "Hush: she is here. She is so anxious. Be generous, my brother, and let her see you!"

"She?" said Evan, faintly. "May she come, Louisa?" He hoped for Rose.

"I have consented to mask it," returned the Countess. "Oh, what do I not sacrifice for you!"

She turned from him, and to Evan's chagrin introduced Juliana Bonner.

"Five minutes, remember!" said the Countess. "I must not hear of more." And then Evan found himself alone with Miss Bonner, and very uneasy. This young lady had restless brilliant eyes, and a contraction about the forehead which gave one the idea of a creature suffering perpetual headache. She said nothing, and when their eyes met she dropped hers in a manner that made silence too expressive. Feeling which, Evan began:

"May I tell you that I think it is I who ought to be nursing you, not you me?"

Miss Bonner replied by lifting her eyes and dropping them as before, murmuring subsequently, "Would you do so?"

"Most certainly, if you did me the honour to select me."

The fingers of the young lady commenced twisting and intertwining on her lap. Suddenly she laughed:

"It would not do at all. You won't be dismissed from your present service till you're unfit for any other."

"What do you mean?" said Evan, thinking more of the unmusical laugh than of the words.

He received no explanation, and the irksome silence caused him to look through the window, as an escape for his mind, at least. The waters streamed on endlessly into the golden arms awaiting them. The low moon burnt through the foliage. In the distance, over a reach of the flood, one tall aspen shook against the lighted sky.

"Are you in pain?" Miss Bonner asked, and broke his reverie.

"No; I am going away, and perhaps I sigh involuntarily."

"You like these grounds?"

"I have never been so happy in any place."

"With those cruel young men about you?"

Evan now laughed. "We don't call young men cruel, Miss Bonner."

"But were they not? To take advantage of what Rose told them—it was base!"

She had said more than she intended, possibly, for she coloured under his inquiring look, and added: "I wish I could say the same as you of Beckley. Do you know, I am called Rose's thorn?"

"Not by Miss Jocelyn herself, certainly!"

"How eager you are to defend her. But am I not—tell me—do I not look like a thorn in company with her?"

"There is but the difference that ill health would make."

"Ill health? Oh, yes! And Rose is so much better born."

"To that, I am sure, she does not give a thought."

"Not Rose? Oh!"

An exclamation, properly lengthened, convinces the feelings more satisfactorily than much logic. Though Evan claimed only the handkerchief he had won, his heart sank at the sound. Miss Bonner watched him, and springing forward, said sharply:

"May I tell you something?"

"You may tell me what you please."

"Then, whether I offend you or not, you had better leave this."

"I am going," said Evan. "I am only waiting to introduce your tutor to you."

She kept her eyes on him, and in her voice as well there was a depth, as she returned:

"Mr. Laxley, Mr. Forth, and Harry, are going to Lymport to-morrow."

Evan was looking at a figure, whose shadow was thrown towards the house from the margin of the stream.

He stood up, and taking the hand of Miss Bonner, said:

"I thank you. I may, perhaps, start with them. At any rate, you have done me a great service, which I shall not forget."

The figure by the stream he knew to be that of Rose. He released Miss Bonner's trembling moist hand, and as he continued standing, she moved to the door, after once following the line of his eyes into the moonlight.

Outside the door a noise was audible. Andrew had come to sit with his dear boy, and the Countess had met and engaged and driven him to the other end of the passage, where he hung remonstrating with her.

"Why, Van," he said, as Evan came up to him, "I thought you were in a profound sleep. Louisa said—"

"Silly Andrew!" interposed the Countess, "do you not observe he is sleep-walking now?" and she left them with a light laugh to go to Juliana, whom she found in tears. The Countess was quite aware of the efficacy of a little bit of burlesque lying to cover her retreat from any petty exposure.

Evan soon got free from Andrew. He was under the dim stars, walking to the great fire in the East. The cool air refreshed him. He was simply going to ask for his own, before he went, and had no cause to fear what would be thought by any one. A handkerchief! A man might fairly win that, and carry it out of a very noble family, without having to blush for himself.

I cannot say whether he inherited his feeling for rank from Mel, his father, or that the Countess had succeeded in instilling it, but Evan never took Republican ground in opposition to those who insulted him, and never lashed his "manhood" to assert itself, nor compared the fineness of his instincts with the behaviour of titled gentlemen. Rather he seemed to admit the distinction between his birth and that of a gentleman, admitting it to his own soul, as it were, and struggled simply as men struggle against a destiny. The news Miss Bonner had given him sufficed to break a spell which could not have endured another week; and Andrew, besides, had told him of Caroline's illness. He walked to meet Rose, honestly intending to ask for his own, and wish her good-bye.

Rose saw him approach, and knew him in the distance. She was sitting on a lower branch of the aspen, that shot out almost from the root, and stretched over the intervolving rays of light on the tremulous water. She could not move to meet him. She was not the Rose whom we have hitherto known. Love may spring in the bosom of a young girl, like Helper in the evening sky, a grey speck in a field of grey, and not be seen or known, till surely as the circle advances the faint planet gathers fire, and, coming nearer earth, dilates, and will and must be seen and known. When Evan lay like a dead man on the ground, Rose turned upon herself as the author of his death, and then she felt this presence within her, and her heart all day had talked to her of it, and was throbbing now, and would not be quieted. She could only lift her eyes and give him her hand; she could not speak. She thought him cold, and he was; cold enough to think that she and her cousin were not unlike in their manner, though not deep enough to reflect that it was from the same cause.

She was the first to find her wits: but not before she spoke did she feel, and start to feel, how long had been the silence, and that her hand was still in his.

"Why did you come out, Evan? It was not right."

"I came to speak to you. I shall leave early to-morrow, and may not see you alone."

"You are going—?"

She checked her voice, and left the thrill of it wavering in him.

"Yes, Rose, I am going; I should have gone before."

"Evan!" she grasped his hand, and then timidly retained it. "You have not forgiven me? I see now. I did not think of any risk to you. I only wanted you to beat. I wanted you to be first and best. If you knew how I thank God for saving you! What my punishment would have been!"

Till her eyes were full she kept them on him, too deep in emotion to be conscious of it.

He could gaze on her tears coldly.

"I should be happy to take the leap any day for the prize you offered. I have come for that."

"For what, Evan?" But while she was speaking the colour mounted in her cheeks, and she went on rapidly:

"Did you think it unkind of me not to come to nurse you. I must tell you, to defend myself. It was the Countess, Evan. She is offended with me—very justly, I dare say. She would not let me come. What could I do? I had no claim to come."

Rose was not aware of the import of her speech. Evan, though he felt more in it, and had some secret nerves set tingling and dancing, was not to be moved from his demand.

"Do you intend to withhold it, Rose?"

"Withhold what, Evan? Anything that you wish for is yours."

"The handkerchief. Is not that mine?"

Rose faltered a word. Why did he ask for it? Because he asked for nothing else, and wanted no other thing save that.

Why did she hesitate? Because it was so poor a gift, and so unworthy of him.

And why did he insist? Because in honour she was bound to surrender it.

And why did she hesitate still? Let her answer.

"Oh, Evan! I would give you anything but that; and if you are going away, I should beg so much to keep it."

He must have been in a singular state not to see her heart in the refusal, as was she not to see his in the request. But Love is blindest just when the bandage is being removed from his forehead.

"Then you will not give it me, Rose? Do you think I shall go about boasting 'This is Miss Jocelyn's handkerchief, and I, poor as I am, have won it'?"

The taunt struck aslant in Rose's breast with a peculiar sting. She stood up.

"I will give it you, Evan."

Turning from him she drew it forth, and handed it to him hurriedly. It was warm. It was stained with his blood. He guessed where it had been nestling, and, now, as if by revelation, he saw that large sole star in the bosom of his darling, and was blinded by it and lost his senses.

"Rose! beloved!"

Like the flower of his nightly phantasy bending over the stream, he looked and saw in her sweet face the living wonders that encircled his image; she murmuring: "No, you must hate me."

"I love you, Rose, and dare to say it—and it's unpardonable. Can you forgive me?"

She raised her face to him.

"Forgive you for loving me?" she said.

Holy to them grew the stillness: the ripple suffused in golden moonlight: the dark edges of the leaves against superlative brightness. Not a chirp was heard, nor anything save the cool and endless carol of the happy waters, whose voices are the spirits of silence. Nature seemed consenting that their hands should be joined, their eyes intermingling. And when Evan, with a lover's craving, wished her lips to say what her eyes said so well, Rose drew his fingers up, and, with an arch smile and a blush, kissed them. The simple act set his heart thumping, and from the look of love, she saw an expression of pain pass through him. Her fealty—her guileless, fearless truth—which the kissing of his hand brought vividly before him, conjured its contrast as well in this that was hidden from her, or but half suspected. Did she know—know and love him still? He thought it might be: but that fell dead on her asking:

"Shall I speak to Mama to-night?"

A load of lead crushed him.

"Rose!" he said; but could get no farther.

Innocently, or with well-masked design, Rose branched off into little sweet words about his bruised shoulder, touching it softly, as if she knew the virtue that was in her touch, and accusing her selfish self as she caressed it:

"Dearest Evan! you must have been sure I thought no one like you. Why did you not tell me before? I can hardly believe it now! Do you know," she hurried on, "they think me cold and heartless,—am I? I must be, to have made you run such risk; but yet I'm sure I could not have survived you."

Dropping her voice, Rose quoted Ruth. As Evan listened, the words were like food from heaven poured into his spirit.

"To-morrow," he kept saying to himself, "to-morrow I will tell her all. Let her think well of me a few short hours."

But the passing minutes locked them closer; each had a new link—in a word, or a speechless breath, or a touch: and to break the marriage of their eyes there must be infinite baseness on one side, or on the other disloyalty to love.

The moon was a silver ball, high up through the aspen-leaves. Evan kissed the hand of Rose, and led her back to the house. He had appeased his conscience by restraining his wild desire to kiss her lips.

In the hall they parted. Rose whispered, "Till death!" giving him her hands.

XXIV

The Countess Makes Herself Felt

There is a peculiar reptile whose stroke is said to deprive men of motion. On the day after the great Mel had stalked the dinner-table of Beckley Court, several of the guests were sensible of the effect of this creature's mysterious touch, without knowing what it was that paralyzed them. Drummond Forth had fully planned to go to Lymport. He had special reasons for making investigations with regard to the great Mel. Harry, who was fond of Drummond, offered to accompany him, and Laxley, for the sake of a diversion, fell into the scheme. Mr. George Uplift was also to be of the party, and promised them fun. But when the time came to start, not one could be induced to move: Laxley was pressingly engaged by Rose: Harry showed the rope the Countess held him by; Mr. George made a singular face, and seriously advised Drummond to give up the project.

"Don't rub that woman the wrong way," he said, in a private colloquy they had. "By Jingo, she's a Tartar. She was as a gal, and she isn't changed, Lou Harrington. Fancy now: she knew me, and she faced me out, and made me think her a stranger! 'Gad, I'm glad I didn't speak to the others. Lord's sake, keep it quiet. Don't rouse that woman, now, if you want to keep a whole skin."

Drummond laughed at his extreme earnestness in cautioning him, and appeared to enjoy his dread of the Countess. Mr. George would not tell how he had been induced to change his mind. He repeated his advice with a very emphatic shrug of the shoulder.

"You seem afraid of her," said Drummond.

"I am. I ain't ashamed to confess it. She's a regular viper, my boy!" said Mr. George. "She and I once were pretty thick—least said soonest mended, you know. I offended her. Wasn't quite up to her mark—a tailor's daughter, you know. 'Gad, if she didn't set an Irish Dragoon Captain on me!—I went about in danger of my life. The fellow began to twist his damned black moustaches the moment he clapped eyes on me—bullied me till, upon my soul, I was almost ready to fight him! Oh, she was a little tripping Tartar of a bantam hen then. She's grown since she's been countessed, and does it peacocky. Now, I give you fair warning, you know. She's more than any man's match."

"I dare say I shall think the same when she has beaten me," quoth cynical Drummond, and immediately went and gave orders for his horse to be saddled, thinking that he would tread on the head of the viper.

But shortly before the hour of his departure, Mrs. Evremonde summoned him to her, and showed him a slip of paper, on which was written, in an uncouth small hand:

"Madam: a friend warns you that your husband is coming here. Deep interest in your welfare is the cause of an anonymous communication. The writer wishes only to warn you in time."

Mrs. Evremonde told Drummond that she had received it from one of the servants when leaving the breakfast-room. Beyond the fact that a man on horseback had handed it to a little boy, who had delivered it over to the footman, Drummond could learn nothing. Of course, all thought of the journey to Lymport was abandoned. If but to excogitate a motive for the origin of the document, Drummond was forced to remain; and now he had it, and now he lost it again; and as he was wandering about in his maze, the Countess met him with a "Good morning, Mr., Forth. Have I impeded your expedition by taking my friend Mr. Harry to cavalier me to-day?"

Drummond smilingly assured her that she had not in any way disarranged his projects, and passed with so absorbed a brow that the Countess could afford to turn her head and inspect him, without fear that he would surprise her in the act. Knocking the pearly edge of her fan on her teeth, she eyed him under her joined black lashes, and deliberately read his thoughts in the mere shape of his back and shoulders. She read him through and through, and was unconscious of the effective attitude she stood in for the space of two full minutes, and even then it required one of our unhappy sex to recall her. This was Harry Jocelyn.

"My friend," she said to him, with a melancholy smile, "my one friend here!"

Harry went through the form of kissing her hand, which he had been taught, and practised cunningly as the first step of the ladder.

"I say, you looked so handsome, standing as you did just now," he remarked; and she could see how far beneath her that effective attitude had precipitated the youth.

"Ah!" she sighed, walking on, with the step of majesty in exile.

"What the deuce is the matter with everybody to-day?" cried Harry. "I'm hanged if I can make it out. There's the Carrington, as you call her, I met her with such a pair of eyes, and old George looking as if he'd been licked, at her heels; and there's Drummond and his lady fair moping about the lawn, and my mother positively getting excited—there's a miracle! and Juley's sharpening her nails for somebody, and if Ferdinand don't look out, your brother'll be walking off with Rosey—that's my opinion."

"Indeed," said the Countess. "You really think so?"

"Well, they come it pretty strong together."

"And what constitutes the 'come it strong,' Mr. Harry?"

"Hold of hands; you know," the young gentleman indicated.

"Alas, then! must not we be more discreet?"

"Oh! but it's different. With young people one knows what that means."

"Deus!" exclaimed the Countess, tossing her head weariedly, and Harry perceived his slip, and down he went again.

What wonder that a youth in such training should consent to fetch and carry, to listen and relate, to play the spy and know no more of his office than that it gave him astonishing thrills of satisfaction, and now and then a secret sweet reward?

The Countess had sealed Miss Carrington's mouth by one of her most dexterous strokes. On leaving the dinner-table over-night, and seeing that Caroline's attack would preclude their instant retreat, the gallant Countess turned at bay. A word aside to Mr. George Uplift, and then the Countess took a chair by Miss Carrington. She did all the conversation, and supplied all the smiles to it, and when a lady has to do that she is justified in striking, and striking hard, for to abandon the pretence of sweetness is a gross insult from one woman to another.

The Countess then led circuitously, but with all the ease in the world, to the story of a Portuguese lady, of a marvellous beauty, and who was deeply enamoured of the Chevalier Miguel de Rasadio, and engaged to be married to him: but, alas for her! in the insolence of her happiness she wantonly made an enemy in the person of a most unoffending lady, and she repented it. While sketching the admirable Chevalier, the Countess drew a telling portrait of Mr. George Uplift, and gratified her humour and her wrath at once by strong truth to nature in the description and animated encomiums on the individual. The Portuguese lady, too, a little resembled Miss Carrington, in spite of her marvellous beauty. And it was odd that Miss Carrington should give a sudden start and a horrified glance at the Countess just when the Countess was pathetically relating the proceeding taken by the revengeful lady on the beautiful betrothed of the Chevalier Miguel de Rasadio: which proceeding was nothing other than to bring to the Chevalier's knowledge that his beauty had a defect concealed by her apparel, and that the specks in his fruit were not one, or two, but, Oh! And the dreadful sequel to the story the Countess could not tell: preferring ingeniously to throw a tragic veil over it. Miss Carrington went early to bed that night.

The courage that mounteth with occasion was eminently the attribute of the Countess de Saldar. After that dreadful dinner she (since the weaknesses of great generals should not be altogether ignored), did pray for flight and total obscurity, but Caroline could not be left in her hysteric state, and now that she really perceived that Evan was progressing and on the point of sealing his chance, the devoted lady resolved to hold her ground. Besides, there was the pic-nic. The Countess had one dress she had not yet appeared in, and it was for the picnic she kept it. That small motives are at the bottom of many illustrious actions is a modern discovery; but I shall not adopt the modern principle of magnifying the small motive till it overshadows my noble heroine. I remember that the small motive is only to be seen by being borne into the range of my vision by a powerful microscope; and if I do more than see—if I carry on my reflections by the aid of the glass, I arrive at conclusions that must be false. Men who dwarf human nature do this. The gods are juster. The Countess, though she wished to remain for the pic-nic, and felt warm in anticipation of the homage to her new dress, was still a gallant general and a devoted sister, and if she said to herself, "Come what may, I will stay for that pic-nic, and they shall not brow-beat me out of it," it is that trifling pleasures are noisiest about the heart of human nature: not that they govern us absolutely. There is mob-rule in minds as in communities, but the Countess had her appetites in excellent drill. This pic-nic surrendered, represented to her defeat in all its ignominy. The largest longest-headed of schemes ask occasionally for something substantial and immediate. So the Countess stipulated with Providence for the pic-nic. It was a point to be passed: "Thorough flood, thorough fire."

In vain poor Andrew Cogglesby, to whom the dinner had been torture, and who was beginning to see the position they stood in at Beckley, begged to be allowed to take them away, or to go alone. The Countess laughed him into submission. As a consequence of her audacious spirits she grew more charming and more natural, and the humour that she possessed, but which, like her other faculties, was usually subordinate to her plans, gave spontaneous bursts throughout the day, and delighted her courtiers. Nor did the men at all dislike the difference of her manner with them, and with the ladies. I may observe that a woman who shows a marked depression in the presence of her own sex will be thought very superior by ours; that is, supposing she is clever and agreeable. Manhood distinguishes what flatters it. A lady approaches. "We must be proper," says the Countess, and her hearty laugh dies with suddenness and is succeeded by the maturest gravity. And the Countess can look a profound merriment with perfect sedateness when there appears to be an equivoque in company. Finely secret are her glances, as if under every eye-lash there lurked the shade of a meaning. What she meant was not so clear. All this was going on, and Lady Jocelyn was simply amused, and sat as at a play.

"She seems to have stepped out of a book of French memoirs," said her ladyship. "La vie galante et devote—voila la Comtesse."

In contradistinction to the other ladies, she did not detest the Countess because she could not like her.

"Where's the harm in her?" she asked. "She doesn't damage the men, that I can see. And a person you can laugh at and with, is inexhaustible."

"And how long is she to stay here?" Mrs. Shorne inquired. Mrs. Melville remarking: "Her visit appears to be inexhaustible."

"I suppose she'll stay till the Election business is over," said Lady Jocelyn.

The Countess had just driven with Melville to Fallow field in Caroline's black lace shawl.

"Upwards of four weeks longer!" Mrs. Melville interjected.

Lady Jocelyn chuckled.

Miss Carrington was present. She had been formerly sharp in her condemnation of the Countess—her affectedness, her euphuism, and her vulgarity. Now she did not say a word, though she might have done it with impunity.

"I suppose, Emily, you see what Rose is about?" said Mrs. Melville. "I should not have thought it adviseable to have that young man here, myself. I think I let you know that."

"One young man's as good as another," responded her ladyship. "I've my doubts of the one that's much better. I fancy Rose is as good a judge by this time as you or I."

Mrs. Melville made an effort or two to open Lady Jocelyn's eyes, and then relapsed into the confident serenity inspired by evil prognostications.

"But there really does seem some infatuation about these people!" exclaimed Mrs. Shorne, turning to Miss Current. "Can you understand it? The Duke, my dear! Things seem to be going on in the house, that really—and so openly."

"That's one virtue," said Miss Current, with her imperturbable metallic voice, and face like a cold clear northern sky. "Things done in secret throw on the outsiders the onus of raising a scandal."

"You don't believe, then?" suggested Mrs. Shorne.

Miss Current replied: "I always wait for a thing to happen first."

"But haven't you seen, my dear?"

"I never see anything, my dear."

"Then you must be blind, my dear."

"On the contrary, that's how I keep my sight, my dear."

"I don't understand you," said Mrs. Shorne.

"It's a part of the science of optics, and requires study," said Miss Current.

Neither with the worldly nor the unworldly woman could the ladies do anything. But they were soon to have their triumph.

A delicious morning had followed the lovely night. The stream flowed under Evan's eyes, like something in a lower sphere, now. His passion took him up, as if a genie had lifted him into mid-air, and showed him the world on a palm of a hand; and yet, as he dressed by the window, little chinks in the garden wall, and nectarines under their shiny leaves, and the white walks of the garden, were stamped on his hot brain accurately and lastingly. Ruth upon the lips of Rose: that voice of living constancy made music to him everywhere. "Thy God shall be my God." He had heard it all through the night. He had not yet broken the tender charm sufficiently to think that he must tell her the sacrifice she would have to make. When partly he did, the first excuse he clutched at was, that he had not even kissed her on the forehead. Surely he had been splendidly chivalrous? Just as surely he would have brought on himself the scorn of the chivalrous or of the commonly balanced if he had been otherwise. The grandeur of this or of any of his proceedings, then, was forfeited, as it must needs be when we are in the false position: we can have no glory though martyred. The youth felt it, even to the seeing of why it was; and he resolved, in justice to the dear girl, that he would break loose from his fetters, as we call our weakness. Behold, Rose met him descending the stairs, and, taking his hand, sang, unabashed, by the tell-tale colour coming over her face, a stave of a little Portuguese air that they had both been fond of in Portugal; and he, listening to it, and looking in her eyes, saw that his feelings in—the old time had been hers. Instantly the old time gave him its breath, the present drew back.

Rose, now that she had given her heart out, had no idea of concealment. She would have denied nothing to her aunts: she was ready to confide it to her mother. Was she not proud of the man she loved? When Evan's hand touched hers she retained it, and smiled up at him frankly, as it were to make him glad in her gladness. If before others his eyes brought the blood to her cheeks, she would perhaps drop her eye-lids an instant, and then glance quickly level again to reassure him. And who would have thought that this boisterous, boyish creature had such depths of eye! Cold, did they call her? Let others think her cold. The tender knowledge of her—the throbbing secret they held in common sang at his heart. Rose made no confidante, but she attempted no mystery. Evan should have risen to the height of the noble girl. But the dearer and sweeter her bearing became, the more conscious he was of the dead weight he was dragging: in truth her behaviour stamped his false position to hard print the more he admired her for it, and he had shrinkings from the feminine part it imposed on him to play.

XXV

In which the Stream Flows Muddy and Clear

An Irish retriever-pup of the Shannon breed, Pat by name, was undergoing tuition on the sward close by the kennels, Rose's hunting-whip being passed through his collar to restrain erratic propensities. The particular point of instruction which now made poor Pat hang out his tongue, and agitate his crisp brown curls, was the performance of the "down-charge"; a ceremony demanding implicit obedience from the animal in the midst of volatile gambadoes, and a simulation of profound repose when his desire to be up and bounding was mighty. Pat's Irish eyes were watching Rose, as he lay with his head couched between his forepaws in the required attitude. He had but half learnt his lesson; and something in his half-humorous, half-melancholy look talked to Rose more eloquently than her friend Ferdinand at her elbow. Laxley was her assistant dog-breaker. Rose would not abandon her friends because she had accepted a lover. On the contrary, Rose was very kind to Ferdinand, and perhaps felt bound to be so to-day. To-day, also, her face was lighted; a readiness to colour, and an expression of deeper knowledge, which she now had, made the girl dangerous to friends. This was not Rose's fault but there is no doubt among the faculty that love is a contagious disease, and we ought not to come within miles of the creatures in whom it lodges.

Pat's tail kept hinting to his mistress that a change would afford him satisfaction. After a time she withdrew her wistful gaze from him, and listened entirely to Ferdinand: and it struck her that he spoke particularly well to-day, though she did not see so much in his eyes as in Pat's. The subject concerned his departure, and he asked Rose if she should be sorry. Rose, to make him sure of it, threw a music into her voice dangerous to friends. For she had given heart and soul to Evan, and had a sense, therefore, of being irredeemably in debt to her old associates, and wished to be doubly kind to them.

Pat took advantage of the diversion to stand up quietly and have a shake. He then began to kiss his mistress's hand, to show that all was right on both sides; and followed this with a playful pretence at a bite, that there might be no subsequent misunderstanding, and then a bark and a whine. As no attention was paid to this amount of plain-speaking, Pat made a bolt. He got no farther than the length of the whip, and all he gained was to bring on himself the terrible word of drill once more. But Pat had tasted liberty. Irish rebellion against constituted authority was exhibited. Pat would not: his ears tossed over his head, and he jumped to right and left, and looked the raggedest rapparee that ever his ancestry trotted after. Rose laughed at his fruitless efforts to get free; but Ferdinand meditatively appeared to catch a sentiment in them.

"Down-charge, Sir, will you? Ah, Pat! Pat! You'll have to obey me, my boy. Now, down-charge!"

While Rose addressed the language of reason to Pat, Ferdinand slipped in a soft word or two. Presently she saw him on one knee.

"Pat won't, and I will," said he.

"But Pat shall, and you had better not," said she. "Besides, my dear Ferdinand," she added, laughing, "you don't know how to do it."

"Do you want me to prostrate on all fours, Rose?"

"No. I hope not. Do get up, Ferdinand. You'll be seen from the windows."

Instead of quitting his posture, he caught her hand, and scared her with a declaration.

"Of all men, you to be on your knees! and to me, Ferdinand!" she cried, in discomfort.

"Why shouldn't I, Rose?" was this youth's answer.

He had got the idea that foreign cavalier manners would take with her; but it was not so easy to make his speech correspond with his posture, and he lost his opportunity, which was pretty. However, he spoke plain English. The interview ended by Rose releasing Pat from drill, and running off in a hurry. Where was Evan? She must have his consent to speak to her mother, and prevent a recurrence of these silly scenes.

Evan was with Caroline, his sister.

It was contrary to the double injunction of the Countess that Caroline should receive Evan during her absence, or that he should disturb the dear invalid with a visit. These two were not unlike both in organization and character, and they had not sat together long before they found each other out. Now, to further Evan's love-suit, the Countess had induced Caroline to continue yet awhile in the Purgatory Beckley Court had become to her; but Evan, in speaking of Rose, expressed a determination to leave her, and Caroline caught at it.

"Can you?—will you? Oh, dear Van! have you the courage? I—look at me—you know the home I go to, and—and I think of it here as a place to be happy in. What have our marriages done for us? Better that we had married simple stupid men who earn their bread, and would not have been ashamed of us! And, my dearest, it is not only that. None can tell what our temptations are. Louisa has strength, but I feel I have none; and though, dear, for your true interest, I would indeed sacrifice myself—I would, Van! I would!—it is not good for you to stay,—I know it is not. For you have Papa's sense of honour—and oh! if you should learn to despise me, my dear brother!"

She kissed him; her nerves were agitated by strong mental excitement. He attributed it to her recent attack of illness, but could not help asking, while he caressed her:

"What's that? Despise you?"

It may have been that Caroline felt then, that to speak of something was to forfeit something. A light glimmered across the dewy blue of her beautiful eyes. Desire to breathe it to him, and have his loving aid: the fear of forfeiting it, evil as it was to her, and at the bottom of all, that doubt we choose to encourage of the harm in a pleasant sin unaccomplished; these might be read in the rich dim gleam that swept like sunlight over sea-water between breaks of clouds.

"Dear Van! do you love her so much?"

Caroline knew too well that she was shutting her own theme with iron clasps when she once touched on Evan's.

Love her? Love Rose? It became an endless carol with Evan. Caroline sighed for him from her heart.

"You know—you understand me; don't you?" he said, after a breathless excursion of his fancy.

"I believe you love her, dear. I think I have never loved any one but my one brother."

His love for Rose he could pour out to Caroline; when it came to Rose's love for him his blood thickened, and his tongue felt guilty. He must speak to her, he said,—tell her all.

"Yes, tell her all," echoed Caroline. "Do, do tell her. Trust a woman utterly if she loves you, dear. Go to her instantly."

"Could you bear it?" said Evan. He began to think it was for the sake of his sisters that he had hesitated.

"Bear it? bear anything rather than perpetual imposture. What have I not borne? Tell her, and then, if she is cold to you, let us go. Let us go.

I shall be glad to. Ah, Van! I love you so." Caroline's voice deepened. "I love you so, my dear. You won't let your new love drive me out? Shall you always love me?"

Of that she might be sure, whatever happened.

"Should you love me, Van, if evil befel me?"

Thrice as well, he swore to her.

"But if I—if I, Van Oh! my life is intolerable! Supposing I should ever disgrace you in any way, and not turn out all you fancied me. I am very weak and unhappy."

Evan kissed her confidently, with a warm smile. He said a few words of the great faith he had in her: words that were bitter comfort to Caroline. This brother, who might save her, to him she dared not speak. Did she wish to be saved? She only knew that to wound Evan's sense of honour and the high and chivalrous veneration for her sex and pride in himself and those of his blood, would be wicked and unpardonable, and that no earthly pleasure could drown it. Thinking this, with her hands joined in pale dejection, Caroline sat silent, and Evan left her to lay bare his heart to Rose. On his way to find Rose he was stopped by the announcement of the arrival of Mr. Raikes, who thrust a bundle of notes into his hand, and after speaking loudly of "his curricle," retired on important business, as he said, with a mysterious air. "I'm beaten in many things, but not in the article Luck," he remarked; "you will hear of me, though hardly as a tutor in this academy."

Scanning the bundle of notes, without a reflection beyond the thought that money was in his hand; and wondering at the apparition of the curricle, Evan was joined by Harry Jocelyn, and Harry linked his arm in Evan's and plunged with extraordinary spontaneity and candour into the state of his money affairs. What the deuce he was to do for money he did not know. From the impressive manner in which he put it, it appeared to be one of Nature's great problems that the whole human race were bound to set their heads together to solve. A hundred pounds—Harry wanted no more, and he could not get it. His uncles? they were as poor as rats; and all the spare money they could club was going for Mel's Election expenses. A hundred and fifty was what Harry really wanted; but he could do with a hundred. Ferdinand, who had plenty, would not even lend him fifty. Ferdinand had dared to hint at a debt already unsettled, and he called himself a gentleman!

"You wouldn't speak of money-matters now, would you, Harrington?"

"I dislike the subject, I confess," said Evan.

"And so do I" Harry jumped at the perfect similarity between them. "You can't think how it bothers one to have to talk about it. You and I are tremendously alike."

Evan might naturally suppose that a subject Harry detested, he would not continue, but for a whole hour Harry turned it over and over with grim glances at Jewry.

"You see," he wound up, "I'm in a fix. I want to help that poor girl, and one or two things—"

"It's for that you want it?" cried Evan, brightening to him. "Accept it from me."

It is a thing familiar to the experience of money-borrowers, that your "last chance" is the man who is to accommodate you; but we are always astonished, nevertheless; and Harry was, when notes to the amount of the largest sum named by him were placed in his hand by one whom he looked upon as the last to lend.

"What a trump you are, Harrington!" was all he could say; and then he was for hurrying Evan into the house, to find pen and paper, and write down a memorandum of the loan: but Evan insisted upon sparing him the trouble, though Harry, with the admirable scruples of an inveterate borrower, begged hard to be allowed to bind himself legally to repay the money.

"'Pon my soul, Harrington, you make me remember I once doubted whether you were one of us—rather your own fault, you know!" said Harry. "Bury that, won't you?"

"'Till your doubts recur," Evan observed; and Harry burst out, "'Gad, if you weren't such a melancholy beggar, you'd be the jolliest fellow I know! There, go after Rosey. Dashed if I don't think you're ahead of Ferdinand, long chalks. Your style does for girls. I like women."

With a chuckle and a wink, Harry swung-off. Evan had now to reflect that he had just thrown away part of the price of his bondage to Tailordom; the mention of Rose filled his mind. Where was she? Both were seeking one another. Rose was in the cypress walk. He saw the star-like figure up the length of it, between the swelling tall dark pillars, and was hurrying to her, resolute not to let one minute of deception blacken further the soul that loved so true a soul. She saw him, and stood smiling, when the Countess issued, shadow-like, from a side path, and declared that she must claim her brother for a few instants. Would her sweet Rose pardon her? Rose bowed coolly. The hearts of the lovers were chilled, not that they perceived any malice in the Countess, but their keen instincts felt an evil fate.

The Countess had but to tell Evan that she had met the insolvent in apples, and recognized him under his change of fortune, and had no doubt that at least he would amuse the company. Then she asked her brother the superfluous question, whether he loved her, which Evan answered satisfactorily enough, as he thought; but practical ladies require proofs.

"Quick," said Evan, seeing Rose vanish, "what do you want? I'll do anything."

"Anything? Ah, but this will be disagreeable to you."

"Name it at once. I promise beforehand."

The Countess wanted Evan to ask Andrew to be the very best brother-in-law in the world, and win, unknown to himself, her cheerful thanks, by lending Evan to lend to her the sum of one hundred pounds, as she was in absolute distress for money.

"Really, Louisa, this is a thing you might ask him yourself," Evan remonstrated.

"It would not become me to do so, dear," said the Countess, demurely; and inasmuch as she had already drawn on Andrew in her own person pretty largely, her views of propriety were correct in this instance.

Evan had to consent before he could be released. He ran to the end of the walk through the portal, into the park. Rose was not to be seen. She had gone in to dress for dinner. The opportunity might recur, but would his courage come with it? His courage had sunk on a sudden; or it may have been that it was worst for this young man to ask for a loan of money, than to tell his beloved that he was basely born, vile, and unworthy, and had snared her into loving him; for when he and Andrew were together, money was not alluded to. Andrew, however, betrayed remarkable discomposure. He said plainly that he wanted to leave Beckley Court, and wondered why he didn't leave, and whether he was on his head or his feet, and how he had been such a fool as to come.

"Do you mean that for me?" said sensitive Evan.

"Oh, you! You're a young buck," returned Andrew, evasively. "We common-place business men-we 're out of our element; and there's poor Carry can't sit down to their dinners without an upset. I thank God I'm a Radical, Van; one man's the same as another to me, how he's born, as long as he's honest and agreeable. But a chap like that George Uplift to look down on anybody! "'Gad, I've a good mind to bring in a Bill for the Abolition of the Squirearchy."

Ultimately, Andrew somehow contrived to stick a hint or two about the terrible dinner in Evan's quivering flesh. He did it as delicately as possible, half begging pardon, and perspiring profusely. Evan grasped his hand, and thanked him. Caroline's illness was now explained to him.

"I'll take Caroline with me to-morrow," he said. "Louisa wishes to stay—there's a pic-nic. Will you look to her, and bring her with you?"

"My dear Van," replied Andrew, "stop with Louisa? Now, in confidence, it's as bad as a couple of wives; no disrespect to my excellent good Harry at home; but Louisa—I don't know how it is—but Louisa, you lose your head, you're in a whirl, you're an automaton, a teetotum! I haven't a notion of what I've been doing or saying since I came here. My belief is, I've been lying right and left. I shall be found out to a certainty: Oh! if she's made her mind up for the pic-nic, somebody must stop. I can only tell you, Van, it's one perpetual vapour-bath to me. There'll be room for two in my trousers when I get back. I shall have to get the tailor to take them in a full half."

Here occurred an opening for one of those acrid pleasantries which console us when there is horrid warfare within.

"You must give me the work," said Evan, partly pleased with his hated self for being able to jest on the subject, as a piece of preliminary self-conquest.

"Aha!" went Andrew, as if the joke were too good to be dwelt on; "Hem"; and by way of diverting from it cleverly and naturally, he remarked that the weather was fine. This made Evan allude to his letter written from Lymport, upon which Andrew said: "tush! pish! humbug! nonsense! won't hear a word. Don't know anything about it. Van, you're going to be a brewer. I say you are. You're afraid you can't? I tell you, sir, I've got a bet on it. You're not going to make me lose, are you—eh? I have, and a stiff bet, too. You must and shall, so there's an end. Only we can't make arrangements just yet, my boy. Old Tom—very good old fellow—but, you know—must get old Tom out of the way, first. Now go and dress for dinner. And Lord preserve us from the Great Mel to-day!" Andrew mumbled as he turned away.

Evan could not reach his chamber without being waylaid by the Countess. Had he remembered the sister who sacrificed so much for him? "There, there!" cried Evan, and her hand closed on the delicious golden whispers of bank-notes. And, "Oh, generous Andrew! dear good Evan!" were the exclamations of the gratified lady.

There remained nearly another hundred. Evan laid out the notes, and eyed them while dressing. They seemed to say to him, "We have you now." He was clutched by a beneficent or a most malignant magician. The former seemed due to him, considering the cloud on his fortunes. This enigma might mean, that by submitting to a temporary humiliation, for a trial of him—in fact, by his acknowledgement of the fact, loathed though it was,—he won a secret overlooker's esteem, gained a powerful ally. Here was the proof, he held the proof. He had read Arabian Tales and could believe in marvels; especially could he believe in the friendliness of a magical thing that astounded without hurting him.

He, sat down in his room at night and wrote a fairly manful letter to Rose; and it is to be said of the wretch he then saw himself, that he pardoned her for turning from so vile a pretender. He heard a step in the passage. It was Polly Wheedle. Polly had put her young mistress to bed, and was retiring to her own slumbers. He made her take the letter and promise to deliver it immediately. Would not to-morrow morning do, she asked, as Miss Rose was very sleepy. He seemed to hesitate—he was picturing how Rose looked when very sleepy. Why should he surrender this darling? And subtler question—why should he make her unhappy? Why disturb her at all in her sweet sleep?

"Well," said Evan. "To-morrow will do.—No, take it to-night, for God's sake!" he cried, as one who bursts the spell of an opiate. "Go at once." The temptation had almost overcome him.

Polly thought his proceedings queer. And what could the letter contain? A declaration, of course. She walked slowly along the passage, meditating on love, and remotely on its slave, Mr. Nicholas Frim. Nicholas had never written her a letter; but she was determined that he should, some day. She wondered what love-letters were like? Like valentines without the Cupids. Practical valentines, one might say. Not vapoury and wild, but hot and to the point. Delightful things! No harm in peeping at a love-letter, if you do it with the eye of a friend.

Polly spelt just a word when a door opened at her elbow. She dropped her candle and curtsied to the Countess's voice. The Countess desired her to enter, and all in a tremble Polly crept in. Her air of guilt made the Countess thrill. She had merely called her in to extract daily gossip. The corner of the letter sticking up under Polly's neck attracted her strangely, and beginning with the familiar, "Well, child," she talked of things interesting to Polly, and then exhibited the pic-nic dress. It was a lovely half-mourning; airy sorrows, gauzy griefs, you might imagine to constitute the wearer. White delicately striped, exquisitely trimmed, and of a stuff to make the feminine mouth water!

Could Polly refuse to try it on, when the flattering proposal met her ears? Blushing, shame-faced, adoring the lady who made her look adorable, Polly tried it on, and the Countess complimented her, and made a doll of her, and turned her this way and that way, and intoxicated her.

"A rich husband, Polly, child! and you are a lady ready made."

Infamous poison to poor Polly; but as the thunder destroys small insects, exalted schemers are to be excused for riding down their few thousands. Moreover, the Countess really looked upon domestics as being only half-souls.

Dressed in her own attire again, Polly felt in her pockets, and at her bosom, and sang out: "Oh, my—Oh, where! Oh!"

The letter was lost. The letter could not be found. The Countess grew extremely fatigued, and had to dismiss Polly, in spite of her eager petitions to be allowed to search under the carpets and inside the bed.

In the morning came Evan's great trial. There stood Rose. She turned to him, and her eyes were happy and unclouded.

"You are not changed?" he said.

"Changed? what could change me?"

The God of true hearts bless her! He could hardly believe it.

"You are the Rose I knew yesterday?"

"Yes, Evan. But you—you look as if you had not slept."

"You will not leave me this morning, before I go, Rose? Oh, my darling! this that you do for me is the work of an angel-nothing less! I have been a coward. And my beloved! to feel vile is agony to me—it makes me feel unworthy of the hand I press. Now all is clear between us. I go: I am forgiven."

Rose repeated his last words, and then added hurriedly:

"All is clear between us? Shall I speak to Mama this morning? Dear Evan! it will be right that I should."

For the moment he could not understand why, but supposing a scrupulous honesty in her, said: "Yes, tell Lady Jocelyn all."

"And then, Evan, you will never need to go."

They separated. The deep-toned sentence sang in Evan's heart. Rose and her mother were of one stamp. And Rose might speak for her mother. To take the hands of such a pair and be lifted out of the slough, he thought no shame: and all through the hours of the morning the image of two angels stooping to touch a leper, pressed on his brain like a reality, and went divinely through his blood.

Toward mid-day Rose beckoned to him, and led him out across the lawn into the park, and along the borders of the stream.

"Evan," she said, "shall I really speak to Mama?"

"You have not yet?" he answered.

"No. I have been with Juliana and with Drummond. Look at this, Evan." She showed a small black speck in the palm of her hand, which turned out, on your viewing it closely, to be a brand of the letter L. "Mama did that when I was a little girl, because I told lies. I never could distinguish between truth and falsehood; and Mama set that mark on me, and I have never told a lie since. She forgives anything but that. She will be our friend; she will never forsake us, Evan, if we do not deceive her. Oh, Evan! it never is of any use. But deceive her, and she cannot forgive you. It is not in her nature."

Evan paused before he replied: "You have only to tell her what I have told you. You know everything."

Rose gave him a flying look of pain: "Everything, Evan? What do I know?"

"Ah, Rose! do you compel me to repeat it?"

Bewildered, Rose thought: "Have I slept and forgotten it?"

He saw the persistent grieved interrogation of her eyebrows.

"Well!" she sighed resignedly: "I am yours; you know that, Evan."

But he was a lover, and quarrelled with her sigh.

"It may well make you sad now, Rose."

"Sad? no, that does not make me sad. No; but my hands are tied. I cannot defend you or justify myself; and induce Mama to stand by us. Oh, Evan! you love me! why can you not open your heart to me entirely, and trust me?"

"More?" cried Evan: "Can I trust you more?" He spoke of the letter: Rose caught his hand.

"I never had it, Evan. You wrote it last night? and all was written in it? I never saw it—but I know all."

Their eyes fronted. The gates of Rose's were wide open, and he saw no hurtful beasts or lurking snakes in the happy garden within, but Love, like a fixed star.

"Then you know why I must leave, Rose."

"Leave? Leave me? On the contrary, you must stay by me, and support me. Why, Evan, we have to fight a battle."

Much as he worshipped her, this intrepid directness of soul startled him-almost humbled him. And her eyes shone with a firm cheerful light, as she exclaimed: "It makes me so happy to think you were the first to mention this. You meant to be, and that's the same thing. I heard it this morning: you wrote it last night. It's you I love, Evan. Your birth, and what you were obliged to do—that's nothing. Of course I'm sorry for it, dear. But I'm more sorry for the pain I must have sometimes put you to. It happened through my mother's father being a merchant; and that side of the family the men and women are quite sordid and unendurable; and that's how it came that I spoke of disliking tradesmen. I little thought I should ever love one sprung from that class."

She turned to him tenderly.

"And in spite of what my birth is, you love me, Rose?"

"There's no spite in it, Evan. I do."

Hard for him, while his heart was melting to caress her, the thought that he had snared this bird of heaven in a net! Rose gave him no time for reflection, or the moony imagining of their raptures lovers love to dwell upon.

"You gave the letter to Polly, of course?"

"Yes."

"Oh, naughty Polly! I must punish you," Rose apostrophized her. "You might have divided us for ever. Well, we shall have to fight a battle, you understand that. Will you stand by me?"

Would he not risk his soul for her?

"Very well, Evan. Then—but don't be sensitive. Oh, how sensitive you are! I see it all now. This is what we shall have to do. We shall have to speak to Mama to-day—this morning. Drummond has told me he is going to speak to her, and we must be first. That's decided. I begged a couple of hours. You must not be offended with Drummond. He does it out of pure affection for us, and I can see he's right—or, at least, not quite wrong. He ought, I think, to know that he cannot change me. Very well, we shall win Mama by what we do. My mother has ten times my wits, and yet I manage her like a feather. I have only to be honest and straightforward. Then Mama will gain over Papa. Papa, of course, won't like it. He's quiet and easy, but he likes blood, but he also likes peace better; and I think he loves Rosey—as well as somebody—almost? Look, dear, there is our seat where we—where you would rob me of my handkerchief. I can't talk any more."

Rose had suddenly fallen from her prattle, soft and short-breathed.

"Then, dear," she went on, "we shall have to fight the family. Aunt Shorne will be terrible. My poor uncles! I pity them. But they will come round. They always have thought what I did was right, and why should they change their minds now? I shall tell them that at their time of life a change of any kind is very unwise and bad for them. Then there is Grandmama Bonner. She can hurt us really, if she pleases. Oh, my dear Evan! if you had only been a curate! Why isn't your name Parsley? Then my Grandmama the Countess of Elburne. Well, we have a Countess on our side, haven't we? And that reminds me, Evan, if we're to be happy and succeed, you must promise one thing: you will not tell the Countess, your sister. Don't confide this to her. Will you promise?"

Evan assured her he was not in the habit of pouring secrets into any bosom, the Countess's as little as another's.

"Very well, then, Evan, it's unpleasant while it lasts, but we shall gain the day. Uncle Melville will give you an appointment, and then?"

"Yes, Rose," he said, "I will do this, though I don't think you can know what I shall have to endure-not in confessing what I am, but in feeling that I have brought you to my level."

"Does it not raise me?" she cried.

He shook his head.

"But in reality, Evan—apart from mere appearances—in reality it does! it does!"

"Men will not think so, Rose, nor can I. Oh, my Rose! how different you make me. Up to this hour I have been so weak! torn two ways! You give me double strength."

Then these lovers talked of distant days—compared their feelings on this and that occasion with mutual wonder and delight. Then the old hours lived anew. And—did you really think that, Evan? And—Oh, Rose! was that your dream? And the meaning of that by-gone look: was it what they fancied? And such and such a tone of voice; would it bear the wished interpretation? Thus does Love avenge himself on the unsatisfactory Past and call out its essence.

Could Evan do less than adore her? She knew all, and she loved him! Since he was too shy to allude more than once to his letter, it was natural that he should not ask her how she came to know, and how much the "all" that she knew comprised. In his letter he had told all; the condition of his parents, and his own. Honestly, now, what with his dazzled state of mind, his deep inward happiness, and love's endless delusions, he abstained from touching the subject further. Honestly, therefore, as far as a lover can be honest.

So they toyed, and then Rose, setting her fingers loose, whispered: "Are you ready?" And Evan nodded; and Rose, to make him think light of the matter in hand, laughed: "Pluck not quite up yet?"

"Quite, my Rose!" said Evan, and they walked to the house, not quite knowing what they were going to do.

On the steps they met Drummond with Mrs. Evremonde. Little imagining how heart and heart the two had grown, and that Evan would understand him, Drummond called to Rose playfully: "Time's up."

"Is it?" Rose answered, and to Mrs. Evremonde

"Give Drummond a walk. Poor Drummond is going silly."

Evan looked into his eyes calmly as he passed.

"Where are you going, Rose?" said Mrs. Evremonde.

"Going to give my maid Polly a whipping for losing a letter she ought to have delivered to me last night," said Rose, in a loud voice, looking at Drummond. "And then going to Mama. Pleasure first—duty after. Isn't that the proverb, Drummond?"

She kissed her fingers rather scornfully to her old friend.

BOOK V

XXVI

Mrs. Mel Makes a Bed for Herself and Family

The last person thought of by her children at this period was Mrs. Mel: nor had she been thinking much of them till a letter from Mr. Goren arrived one day, which caused her to pass them seriously in review. Always an early bird, and with maxims of her own on the subject of rising and getting the worm, she was standing in a small perch in the corner of the shop, dictating accounts to Mrs. Fiske, who was copying hurriedly, that she might earn sweet intervals for gossip, when Dandy limped up and delivered the letter. Mrs. Fiske worked hard while her aunt was occupied in reading it, for a great deal of fresh talk follows the advent of the post, and may be reckoned on. Without looking up, however, she could tell presently that the letter had been read through. Such being the case, and no conversation coming of it, her curiosity was violent. Her aunt's face, too, was an index of something extraordinary. That inflexible woman, instead of alluding to the letter in any way, folded it up, and renewed her dictation. It became a contest between them which should show her human nature first. Mrs. Mel had to repress what she knew; Mrs. Fiske to control the passion for intelligence. The close neighbourhood of one anxious to receive, and one capable of giving, waxed too much for both.

"I think, Anne, you are stupid this morning," said Mrs. Mel.

"Well, I am, aunt," said Mrs. Fiske, pretending not to see which was the first to unbend, "I don't know what it is. The figures seem all dazzled like. I shall really be glad when Evan comes to take his proper place."

"Ah!" went Mrs. Mel, and Mrs. Fiske heard her muttering. Then she cried out: "Are Harriet and Caroline as great liars as Louisa?"

Mrs. Fiske grimaced. "That would be difficult, would it not, aunt?"

"And I have been telling everybody that my son is in town learning his business, when he's idling at a country house, and trying to play his father over again! Upon my word, what with liars and fools, if you go to sleep a minute you have a month's work on your back."

"What is it, aunt?" Mrs. Fiske feebly inquired.

"A gentleman, I suppose! He wouldn't take an order if it was offered. Upon my word, when tailors think of winning heiresses it's time we went back to Adam and Eve."

"Do you mean Evan, aunt?" interposed Mrs. Fiske, who probably did not see the turns in her aunt's mind.

"There—read for yourself," said Mrs. Mel, and left her with the letter.

Mrs. Fiske read that Mr. Goren had been astonished at Evan's non-appearance, and at his total silence; which he did not consider altogether gentlemanly behaviour, and certainly not such as his father would have practised. Mr. Goren regretted his absence the more as he would have found him useful in a remarkable invention he was about to patent, being a peculiar red cross upon shirts—a fortune to the patentee; but as Mr. Goren had no natural heirs of his body, he did not care for that. What affected him painfully was the news of Evan's doings at a noble house, Beckley Court, to wit, where, according to the report of a rich young gentleman friend, Mr. Raikes (for whose custom Mr. Goren was bound to thank Evan), the youth who should have been learning the science of Tailoring, had actually passed himself off as a lord, or the son of one, or something of the kind, and had got engaged to a wealthy heiress, and would, no doubt, marry her if not found out. Where the chances of detection were so numerous, Mr. Goren saw much to condemn in the idea of such a marriage. But "like father like son," said Mr. Goren. He thanked the Lord that an honest tradesman was not looked down upon in this country; and, in fact, gave Mrs. Mel a few quiet digs to waken her remorse in having missed the man that he was.

When Mrs. Fiske met her aunt again she returned her the letter, and simply remarked: "Louisa."

Mrs. Mel nodded. She understood the implication.

The General who had schemed so successfully to gain Evan time at Beckley Court in his own despite and against a hundred obstructions, had now another enemy in the field, and one who, if she could not undo her work, could punish her. By the afternoon coach, Mrs. Mel, accompanied by Dandy her squire, was journeying to Fallow field, bent upon things. The faithful squire was kept by her side rather as a security for others than for, his particular services. Dandy's arms were crossed, and his countenance was gloomy. He had been promised a holiday that afternoon to give his mistress, Sally, Kilne's cook, an airing, and Dandy knew in his soul that Sally, when she once made up her mind to an excursion, would go, and would not go alone, and that her very force of will endangered her constancy. He had begged humbly to be allowed to stay, but Mrs. Mel could not trust him. She ought to have told him so, perhaps. Explanations were not approved of by this well-intended despot, and however beneficial her resolves might turn out for all parties, it was natural that in the interim the children of her rule should revolt, and Dandy, picturing his Sally flaunting on the arm of some accursed low marine, haply, kicked against Mrs. Mel's sovereignty, though all that he did was to shoot out his fist from time to time, and grunt through his set teeth: "Iron!" to express the character of her awful rule.

Mrs. Mel alighted at the Dolphin, the landlady of which was a Mrs. Hawkshaw, a rival of Mrs. Sockley of the Green Dragon. She was welcomed by Mrs. Hawkshaw with considerable respect. The great Mel had sometimes slept at the Dolphin.

"Ah, that black!" she sighed, indicating Mrs. Mel's dress and the story it told.

"I can't give you his room, my dear Mrs. Harrington, wishing I could! I'm sorry to say it's occupied, for all I ought to be glad, I dare say, for he's an old gentleman who does you a good turn, if you study him. But there! I'd rather have had poor dear Mr. Harrington in my best bed than old or young—Princes or nobodies, I would—he was that grand and pleasant."

Mrs. Mel had her tea in Mrs. Hawkshaw's parlour, and was entertained about her husband up to the hour of supper, when a short step and a querulous voice were heard in the passage, and an old gentleman appeared before them.

"Who's to carry up my trunk, ma'am? No man here?"

Mrs. Hawkshaw bustled out and tried to lay her hand on a man. Failing to find the growth spontaneous, she returned and begged the old gentleman to wait a few moments and the trunk would be sent up.

"Parcel o' women!" was his reply. "Regularly bedevilled. Gets worse and worse. I'll carry it up myself."

With a wheezy effort he persuaded the trunk to stand on one end, and then looked at it. The exertion made him hot, which may account for the rage he burst into when Mrs. Hawkshaw began flutteringly to apologize.

"You're sure, ma'am, sure—what are you sure of? I'll tell you what I am sure of—eh? This keeping clear of men's a damned pretence. You don't impose upon me. Don't believe in your pothouse nunneries—not a bit. Just like you! when you are virtuous it's deuced inconvenient. Let one of the maids try? No. Don't believe in 'em."

Having thus relieved his spleen the old gentleman addressed himself to further efforts and waxed hotter. He managed to tilt the trunk over, and thus gained a length, and by this method of progression arrived at the foot of the stairs, where he halted, and wiped his face, blowing lustily.

Mrs. Mel had been watching him with calm scorn all the while. She saw him attempt most ridiculously to impel the trunk upwards by a similar process, and thought it time to interfere.

"Don't you see you must either take it on your shoulders, or have a help?"

The old gentleman sprang up from his peculiarly tight posture to blaze round at her. He had the words well-peppered on his mouth, but somehow he stopped, and was subsequently content to growl: "Where's the help in a parcel of petticoats?"

Mrs. Mel did not consider it necessary to give him an answer. She went up two or three steps, and took hold of one handle of the trunk, saying: "There; I think it can be managed this way," and she pointed for him to seize the other end with his hand.

He was now in that unpleasant state of prickly heat when testy old gentlemen could commit slaughter with ecstasy. Had it been the maid holding a candle who had dared to advise, he would have overturned her undoubtedly, and established a fresh instance of the impertinence, the uselessness and weakness of women. Mrs. Mel topped him by half a head, and in addition stood three steps above him; towering like a giantess. The extreme gravity of her large face dispersed all idea of an assault. The old gentleman showed signs of being horribly injured: nevertheless, he put his hand to the trunk; it was lifted, and the procession ascended the stairs in silence.

The landlady waited for Mrs. Mel to return, and then said:

"Really, Mrs. Harrington, you are clever. That lifting that trunk's as good as a lock and bolt on him. You've as good as made him a Dolphin—him that was one o' the oldest Green Dragons in Fallifield. My thanks to you most sincere."

Mrs. Mel sent out to hear where Dandy had got to after which, she said: "Who is the man?"

"I told you, Mrs. Harrington—the oldest Green Dragon. His name, you mean? Do you know, if I was to breathe it out, I believe he'd jump out of the window. He'd be off, that you might swear to. Oh, such a whimsical! not ill-meaning—quite the contrary. Study his whims, and you'll never want. There's Mrs. Sockley—she's took ill. He won't go there—that's how I've caught him, my dear—but he pays her medicine, and she looks to him the same. He hate a sick house: but he pity a sick woman. Now, if I can only please him, I can always look on him as half a Dolphin, to say the least; and perhaps to-morrow I'll tell you who he is, and what, but not to-night; for there's his supper to get over, and that, they say, can be as bad as the busting of one of his own vats. Awful!"

"What does he eat?" said Mrs. Mel.

"A pair o' chops. That seem simple, now, don't it? And yet they chops make my heart go pitty-pat."

"The commonest things are the worst done," said Mrs. Mel.

"It ain't that; but they must be done his particular way, do you see, Mrs. Harrington. Laid close on the fire, he say, so as to keep in the juice. But he ups and bounces in a minute at a speck o' black. So, one thing or the other, there you are: no blacks, no juices, I say."

"Toast the chops," said Mrs. Mel.

The landlady of the Dolphin accepted this new idea with much enlightenment, but ruefully declared that she was afraid to go against his precise instructions. Mrs. Mel then folded her hands, and sat in quiet reserve. She was one of those numerous women who always know themselves to be right. She was also one of those very few whom Providence favours by confounding dissentients. She was positive the chops would be ill-cooked: but what could she do? She was not in command here; so she waited serenely for the certain disasters to enthrone her. Not that the matter of the chops occupied her mind particularly: nor could she dream that the pair in question were destined to form a part of her history, and divert the channel of her fortunes. Her thoughts were about her own immediate work; and when the landlady rushed in with the chops under a cover, and said: "Look at 'em, dear Mrs. Harrington!" she had forgotten that she was again to be proved right by the turn of events.

"Oh, the chops!" she responded. "Send them while they are hot."

"Send 'em! Why you don't think I'd have risked their cooling? I have sent 'em; and what do he do but send 'em travelling back, and here they be; and what objections his is I might study till I was blind, and I shouldn't see 'em."

"No; I suppose not," said Mrs. Mel. "He won't eat 'em?"

"Won't eat anything: but his bed-room candle immediately. And whether his sheets are aired. And Mary says he sniffed at the chops; and that gal really did expect he'd fling them at her. I told you what he was. Oh, dear!"

The bell was heard ringing in the midst of the landlady's lamentations.

"Go to him yourself," said Mrs. Mel. "No Christian man should go to sleep without his supper."

"Ah! but he ain't a common Christian," returned Mrs. Hawkshaw.

The old gentleman was in a hurry to know when his bed-room candle was coming up, or whether they intended to give him one at all that night; if not, let them say so, as he liked plain-speaking. The moment Mrs. Hawkshaw touched upon the chops, he stopped her mouth.

"Go about your business, ma'am. You can't cook 'em. I never expected you could: I was a fool to try you. It requires at least ten years' instruction before a man can get a woman to cook his chop as he likes it."

"But what was your complaint, sir?" said Mrs. Hawkshaw, imploringly.

"That's right!" and he rubbed his hands, and brightened his eyes savagely. "That's the way. Opportunity for gossip! Thing's well done—down it goes: you know that. You can't have a word over it—eh? Thing's done fit to toss on a dungheap, aha! Then there's a cackle! My belief is, you do it on purpose. Can't be such rank idiots. You do it on purpose. All done for gossip!"

"Oh, sir, no!" The landlady half curtsied.

"Oh, ma'am, yes!" The old gentleman bobbed his head.

"No, indeed, sir!" The landlady shook hers.

"Damn it, ma'am, I swear you do."

Symptoms of wrath here accompanied the declaration; and, with a sigh and a very bitter feeling, Mrs. Hawkshaw allowed him to have the last word. Apparently this—which I must beg to call the lady's morsel—comforted his irascible system somewhat; for he remained in a state of composure eight minutes by the clock. And mark how little things hang together. Another word from the landlady, precipitating a retort from him, and a gesture or muttering from her; and from him a snapping outburst, and from her a sign that she held out still; in fact, had she chosen to battle for that last word, as in other cases she might have done, then would he have exploded, gone to bed in the dark, and insisted upon sleeping: the consequence of which would have been to change this history. Now while Mrs. Hawkshaw was upstairs, Mrs. Mel called the servant, who took her to the kitchen, where she saw a prime loin of mutton; off which she cut two chops with a cunning hand: and these she toasted at a gradual distance, putting a plate beneath them, and a tin behind, and hanging the chops so that they would turn without having to be pierced. The bell rang twice before she could say the chops were ready. The first time, the maid had to tell the old gentleman she was taking up his water. Her next excuse was, that she had dropped her candle. The chops ready—who was to take them?

"Really, Mrs. Harrington, you are so clever, you ought, if I might be so bold as say so; you ought to end it yourself," said the landlady. "I can't ask him to eat them: he was all but on the busting point when I left him."

"And that there candle did for him quite," said Mary, the maid.

"I'm afraid it's chops cooked for nothing," added the landlady.

Mrs. Mel saw them endangered. The maid held back: the landlady feared.

"We can but try," she said.

"Oh! I wish, mum, you'd face him, 'stead o' me," said Mary; "I do dread that old bear's den."

"Here, I will go," said Mrs. Mel. "Has he got his ale? Better draw it fresh, if he drinks any."

And upstairs she marched, the landlady remaining below to listen for the commencement of the disturbance. An utterance of something certainly followed Mrs. Mel's entrance into the old bear's den. Then silence. Then what might have been question and answer. Then—was Mrs. Mel assaulted? and which was knocked down? It really was a chair being moved to the table. The door opened.

"Yes, ma'am; do what you like," the landlady heard. Mrs. Mel descended, saying: "Send him up some fresh ale."

"And you have made him sit down obedient to those chops?" cried the landlady. "Well might poor dear Mr. Harrington—pleasant man as he was!—say, as he used to say, 'There's lovely women in the world, Mrs. Hawkshaw,' he'd say, 'and there's Duchesses,' he'd say, 'and there's they that can sing, and can dance, and some,' he says, 'that can cook.' But he'd look sly as he'd stoop his head and shake it. 'Roll 'em into one,' he says, 'and not any of your grand ladies can match my wife at home.'

And, indeed, Mrs. Harrington, he told me he thought so many a time in the great company he frequented."

Perfect peace reigning above, Mrs. Hawkshaw and Mrs. Mel sat down to supper below; and Mrs. Hawkshaw talked much of the great one gone. His relict did not care to converse about the dead, save in their practical aspect as ghosts; but she listened, and that passed the time. By-and-by, the old gentleman rang, and sent a civil message to know if the landlady had ship's rum in the house.

"Dear! here's another trouble," cried the poor woman. "No—none!"

"Say, yes," said Mrs. Mel, and called Dandy, and charged him to run down the street to the square, and ask for the house of Mr. Coxwell, the maltster, and beg of him, in her name, a bottle of his ship's rum.

"And don't you tumble down and break the bottle, Dandy. Accidents with spirit-bottles are not excused."

Dandy went on the errand, after an energetic grunt.

In due time he returned with the bottle, whole and sound, and Mr. Coxwell's compliments. Mrs. Mel examined the cork to see that no process of suction had been attempted, and then said:

"Carry it up to him, Dandy. Let him see there's a man in the house besides himself."

"Why, my dear," the landlady turned to her, "it seems natural to you to be mistress where you go. I don't at all mind, for ain't it my profit? But you do take us off our legs."

Then the landlady, warmed by gratitude, told her that the old gentleman was the great London brewer, who brewed there with his brother, and brewed for himself five miles out of Fallow field, half of which and a good part of the neighbourhood he owned, and his name was Mr. Tom Cogglesby.

"Oh!" said Mrs. Mel. "And his brother is Mr. Andrew."

"That's it," said the landlady. "And because he took it into his head to go and to choose for himself, and be married, no getting his brother, Mr. Tom, to speak to him. Why not, indeed? If there's to be no marrying, the sooner we lay down and give up, the better, I think. But that's his way. He do hate us women, Mrs. Harrington. I have heard he was crossed. Some say it was the lady of Beckley Court, who was a Beauty, when he was only a poor cobbler's son."

Mrs. Mel breathed nothing of her relationship to Mr. Tom, but continued from time to time to express solicitude about Dandy. They heard the door open, and old Tom laughing in a capital good temper, and then Dandy came down, evidently full of ship's rum.

"He's pumped me!" said Dandy, nodding heavily at his mistress.

Mrs. Mel took him up to his bed-room, and locked the door. On her way back she passed old Tom's chamber, and his chuckles were audible to her.

"They finished the rum," said Mrs. Hawkshaw.

"I shall rate him for that to-morrow," said Mrs. Mel. "Giving that poor beast liquor!"

"Rate Mr. Tom! Oh! Mrs. Harrington! Why, he'll snap your head off for a word."

Mrs. Mel replied that her head would require a great deal of snapping to come off.

During this conversation they had both heard a singular intermittent noise above. Mrs. Hawkshaw was the first to ask:

"What can it be? More trouble with him? He's in his bed-room now."

"Mad with drink, like Dandy, perhaps," said Mrs. Mel.

"Hark!" cried the landlady. "Oh!"

It seemed that Old Tom was bouncing about in an extraordinary manner. Now came a pause, as if he had sworn to take his rest: now the room shook and the windows rattled.

"One 'd think, really, his bed was a frying-pan, and him a live fish in it," said the landlady. "Oh—there, again! My goodness! have he got a flea?"

The thought was alarming. Mrs. Mel joined in:

"Or a —"

"Don't! don't, my dear!" she was cut short. "Oh! one o' them little things 'd be ruin to me. To think o' that! Hark at him! It must be. And what's to do? I've sent the maids to bed. We haven't a man. If I was to go and knock at his door, and ask?"

"Better try and get him to be quiet somehow."

"Ah! I dare say I shall make him fire out fifty times worse."

Mrs. Hawkshaw stipulated that Mrs. Mel should stand by her, and the two women went up-stairs and stood at Old Tom's door. There they could hear him fuming and muttering imprecations, and anon there was an interval of silence, and then the room was shaken, and the cursings recommenced.

"It must be a fight he's having with a flea," said the landlady. "Oh! pray heaven, it is a flea. For a flea, my dear-gentlemen may bring that theirselves; but a b——, that's a stationary, and born of a bed. Don't you hear? The other thing 'd give him a minute's rest; but a flea's hop-hop-off and on. And he sound like an old gentleman worried by a flea. What are you doing?"

Mrs. Mel had knocked at the door. The landlady waited breathlessly for the result. It appeared to have quieted Old Tom.

"What's the matter?" said Mrs. Mel, severely.

The landlady implored her to speak him fair, and reflect on the desperate things he might attempt.

"What's the matter? Can anything be done for you?"

Mr. Tom Cogglesby's reply comprised an insinuation so infamous regarding women when they have a solitary man in their power, that it cannot be placed on record.

"Is anything the matter with your bed?"

"Anything? Yes; anything is the matter, ma'am. Hope twenty live geese inside it's enough-eh? Bed, do you call it? It's the rack! It's damnation! Bed? Ha!"

After delivering this, he was heard stamping up and down the room.

"My very best bed!" whispered the landlady. "Would it please you, sir, to change—I can give you another?"

"I'm not a man of experiments, ma'am-'specially in strange houses."

"So very, very sorry!"

"What the deuce!" Old Tom came close to the door. "You whimpering! You put a man in a beast of a bed—you drive him half mad—and then begin to blubber! Go away."

"I am so sorry, sir!"

"If you don't go away, ma'am, I shall think your intentions are improper."

"Oh, my goodness!" cried poor Mrs. Hawkshaw. "What can one do with him?" Mrs. Mel put Mrs. Hawkshaw behind her.

"Are you dressed?" she called out.

In this way Mrs. Mel tackled Old Tom. He was told that should he consent to cover himself decently, she would come into his room and make his bed comfortable. And in a voice that dispersed armies of innuendoes, she bade him take his choice, either to rest quiet or do her bidding. Had Old Tom found his master at last, and in one of the hated sex? Breathlessly Mrs. Hawkshaw waited his answer, and she was an astonished woman when it came.

"Very well, ma'am. Wait a couple of minutes. Do as you like."

On their admission to the interior of the chamber, Old Tom was exhibited in his daily garb, sufficiently subdued to be civil and explain the cause of his discomfort. Lumps in his bed: he was bruised by them. He supposed he couldn't ask women to judge for themselves—they'd be shrieking—but he could assure them he was blue all down his back.

Mrs. Mel and Mrs. Hawkshaw turned the bed about, and punched it, and rolled it.

"Ha!" went Old Tom, "what's the good of that? That's just how I found it. Moment I got into bed geese began to put up their backs."

Mrs. Mel seldom indulged in a joke, and then only when it had a proverbial cast. On the present occasion, the truth struck her forcibly, and she said:

"One fool makes many, and so, no doubt, does one goose."

Accompanied by a smile the words would have seemed impudent; but spoken as a plain fact, and with a grave face, it set Old Tom blinking like a small boy ten minutes after the whip.

"Now," she pursued, speaking to him as to an old child, "look here. This is how you manage. Knead down in the middle of the bed. Then jump into the hollow. Lie there, and you needn't wake till morning."

Old Tom came to the side of the bed. He had prepared himself for a wretched night, an uproar, and eternal complaints against the house, its inhabitants, and its foundations; but a woman stood there who as much as told him that digging his fist into the flock and jumping into the hole—into that hole under his, eyes—was all that was wanted! that he had been making a noise for nothing, and because he had not the wit to hit on a simple contrivance! Then, too, his jest about the geese—this woman had put a stop to that! He inspected the hollow cynically. A man might instruct him on a point or two: Old Tom was not going to admit that a woman could.

"Oh, very well; thank you, ma'am; that's your idea. I'll try it. Good night."

"Good night," returned Mrs. Mel. "Don't forget to jump into the middle."

"Head foremost, ma'am?"

"As you weigh," said Mrs. Mel, and Old Tom trumped his lips, silenced if not beaten. Beaten, one might almost say, for nothing more was heard of him that night.

He presented himself to Mrs. Mel after breakfast next morning.

"Slept well, ma'am."

"Oh! then you did as I directed you," said Mrs. Mel.

"Those chops, too, very good. I got through 'em."

"Eating, like scratching, only wants a beginning," said Mrs. Mel.

"Ha! you've got your word, then, as well as everybody else. Where's your Dandy this morning, ma'am?"

"Locked up. You ought to be ashamed to give that poor beast liquor. He won't get fresh air to-day."

"Ha! May I ask you where you're going to-day, ma'am?"

"I am going to Beckley."

"So am I, ma'am. What d' ye say, if we join company. Care for insinuations?"

"I want a conveyance of some sort," returned Mrs. Mel.

"Object to a donkey, ma'am?"

"Not if he's strong and will go."

"Good," said Old Tom; and while he spoke a donkey-cart stopped in front of the Dolphin, and a well-dressed man touched his hat.

"Get out of that damned bad habit, will you?" growled Old Tom. "What do you mean by wearing out the brim o' your hat in that way? Help this woman in."

Mrs. Mel helped herself to a part of the seat.

"We are too much for the donkey," she said.

"Ha, that's right. What I have, ma'am, is good. I can't pretend to horses, but my donkey's the best. Are you going to cry about him?"

"No. When he's tired I shall either walk or harness you," said Mrs. Mel.

This was spoken half-way down the High Street of Fallow field. Old Tom looked full in her face, and bawled out:

"Deuce take it. Are you a woman?"

"I have borne three girls and one boy," said Mrs. Mel.

"What sort of a husband?"

"He is dead."

"Ha! that's an opening, but 'tain't an answer. I'm off to Beckley on a marriage business. I'm the son of a cobbler, so I go in a donkey-cart. No damned pretences for me. I'm going to marry off a young tailor to a gal he's been playing the lord to. If she cares for him she'll take him: if not, they're all the luckier, both of 'em."

"What's the tailor's name?" said Mrs. Mel.

"You are a woman," returned Old Tom. "Now, come, ma'am, don't you feel ashamed of being in a donkeycart?"

"I'm ashamed of men, sometimes," said Mrs. Mel; "never of animals."

"'Shamed o' me, perhaps."

"I don't know you."

"Ha! well! I'm a man with no pretences. Do you like 'em? How have you brought up your three girls and one boy? No pretences—eh?"

Mrs. Mel did not answer, and Old Tom jogged the reins and chuckled, and asked his donkey if he wanted to be a racer.

"Should you take me for a gentleman, ma'am?"

"I dare say you are, sir, at heart. Not from your manner of speech."

"I mean appearances, ma'am."

"I judge by the disposition."

"You do, ma'am? Then, deuce take it, if you are a woman, you're —" Old Tom had no time to conclude.

A great noise of wheels, and a horn blown, caused them both to turn their heads, and they beheld a curricle descending upon them vehemently, and a fashionably attired young gentleman straining with all his might at the reins. The next instant they were rolling on the bank. About twenty yards ahead the curricle was halted and turned about to see the extent of the mischief done.

"Pardon, a thousand times, my worthy couple," cried the sonorous Mr. Raikes. "What we have seen we swear not to divulge. Franco and Fred—your pledge!"

"We swear!" exclaimed this couple.

But suddenly the cheeks of Mr. John Raikes flushed. He alighted from the box, and rushing up to Old Tom, was shouting, "My bene—"

"Do you want my toe on your plate?" Old Tom stopped him with.

The mysterious words completely changed the aspect of Mr. John Raikes. He bowed obsequiously and made his friend Franco step down and assist in the task of reestablishing the donkey, who fortunately had received no damage.

XXVII

Exhibits Rose's Generalship; Evan's Performance on the Second Fiddle; and the Wretchedness of the Countess

We left Rose and Evan on their way to Lady Jocelyn. At the library-door Rose turned to him, and with her chin archly lifted sideways, said:

"I know what you feel; you feel foolish."

Now the sense of honour, and of the necessity of acting the part it imposes on him, may be very strong in a young man; but certainly, as a rule, the sense of ridicule is more poignant, and Evan was suffering horrid pangs. We none of us like to play second fiddle. To play second fiddle to a young woman is an abomination to us all. But to have to perform upon that instrument to the darling of our hearts—would we not rather die? nay, almost rather end the duet precipitately and with violence. Evan, when he passed Drummond into the house, and quietly returned his gaze, endured the first shock of this strange feeling. There could be no doubt that he was playing second fiddle to Rose. And what was he about to do? Oh, horror! to stand like a criminal, and say, or worse, have said for him, things to tip the ears with fire! To tell the young lady's mother that he had won her daughter's love, and meant—what did he mean? He knew not. Alas! he was second fiddle; he could only mean what she meant. Evan loved Rose deeply and completely, but noble manhood was strong in him. You may sneer at us, if you please, ladies. We have been educated in a theory, that when you lead off with the bow, the order of Nature is reversed, and it is no wonder therefore, that, having stript us of one attribute, our fine feathers moult, and the majestic cock-like march which distinguishes us degenerates. You unsex us, if I may dare to say so. Ceasing to be men, what are we? If we are to please you rightly, always allow us to play First.

Poor Evan did feel foolish. Whether Rose saw it in his walk, or had a loving feminine intuition of it, and was aware of the golden rule I have just laid down, we need not inquire. She hit the fact, and he could only stammer, and bid her open the door.

"No," she said, after a slight hesitation, "it will be better that I should speak to Mama alone, I see. Walk out on the lawn, dear, and wait for me. And if you meet Drummond, don't be angry with him. Drummond is very fond of me, and of course I shall teach him to be fond of you. He only thinks. . . what is not true, because he does not know you. I do thoroughly, and there, you see, I give you my hand."

Evan drew the dear hand humbly to his lips. Rose then nodded meaningly, and let her eyes dwell on him, and went in to her mother to open the battle.

Could it be that a flame had sprung up in those grey eyes latterly? Once they were like morning before sunrise. How soft and warm and tenderly transparent they could now be! Assuredly she loved him. And he, beloved by the noblest girl ever fashioned, why should he hang his head, and shrink at the thought of human faces, like a wretch doomed to the pillory? He visioned her last glance, and lightning emotions of pride and happiness flashed through his veins. The generous, brave heart! Yes, with her hand in his, he could stand at bay—meet any fate. Evan accepted Rose because he believed in her love, and judged it by the strength of his own; her sacrifice of her position he accepted, because in his soul he knew he should have done no less. He mounted to the level of her nobleness, and losing nothing of the beauty of what she did, it was not so strange to him.

Still there was the baleful reflection that he was second fiddle to his beloved. No harmony came of it in his mind. How could he take an initiative? He walked forth on the lawn, where a group had gathered under the shade of a maple, consisting of Drummond Forth, Mrs. Evremonde, Mrs. Shorne, Mr. George Uplift, Seymour Jocelyn, and Ferdinand Laxley. A little apart Juliana Bonner was walking with Miss Carrington. Juliana, when she saw him, left her companion, and passing him swiftly, said, "Follow me presently into the conservatory."

Evan strolled near the group, and bowed to Mrs. Shorne, whom he had not seen that morning.

The lady's acknowledgement of his salute was constrained, and but a shade on the side of recognition. They were silent till he was out of earshot. He noticed that his second approach produced the same effect. In the conservatory Juliana was awaiting him.

"It is not to give you roses I called you here, Mr. Harrington," she said.

"Not if I beg one?" he responded.

"Ah! but you do not want them from. . . It depends on the person."

"Pluck this," said Evan, pointing to a white rose.

She put her fingers to the stem.

"What folly!" she cried, and turned from it.

"Are you afraid that I shall compromise you?" asked Evan.

"You care for me too little for that."

"My dear Miss Bonner!"

"How long did you know Rose before you called her by her Christian name?"

Evan really could not remember, and was beginning to wonder what he had been called there for. The little lady had feverish eyes and fingers, and seemed to be burning to speak, but afraid.

"I thought you had gone," she dropped her voice, "without wishing me good-bye."

"I certainly should not do that, Miss Bonner."

"Formal!" she exclaimed, half to herself. "Miss Bonner thanks you. Do you think I wish you to stay? No friend of yours would wish it. You do not know the selfishness—brutal!—of these people of birth, as they call it."

"I have met with nothing but kindness here," said Evan.

"Then go while you can feel that," she answered; "for it cannot last another hour. Here is the rose." She broke it from the stem and handed it to him. "You may wear that, and they are not so likely to call you an adventurer, and names of that sort. I am hardly considered a lady by them."

An adventurer! The full meaning of the phrase struck Evan's senses when he was alone. Miss Bonner knew something of his condition, evidently. Perhaps it was generally known, and perhaps it was thought that he had come to win Rose for his worldly advantage! The idea was overwhelmingly new to him. Up started self-love in arms. He would renounce her.

It is no insignificant contest when love has to crush self-love utterly. At moments it can be done. Love has divine moments. There are times also when Love draws part of his being from self-love, and can find no support without it.

But how could he renounce her, when she came forth to him,—smiling, speaking freshly and lightly, and with the colour on her cheeks which showed that she had done her part? How could he retract a step?

"I have told Mama, Evan. That's over. She heard it first from me."

"And she?"

"Dear Evan, if you are going to be sensitive, I'll run away. You that fear no danger, and are the bravest man I ever knew! I think you are really trembling. She will speak to Papa, and then—and then, I suppose, they will both ask you whether you intend to give me up, or no. I'm afraid you'll do the former."

"Your mother—Lady Jocelyn listened to you, Rose? You told her all?"

"Every bit."

"And what does she think of me?"

"Thinks you very handsome and astonishing, and me very idiotic and natural, and that there is a great deal of bother in the world, and that my noble relatives will lay the blame of it on her. No, dear, not all that; but she talked very sensibly to me, and kindly. You know she is called a philosopher: nobody knows how deep-hearted she is, though. My mother is true as steel. I can't separate the kindness from the sense, or I would tell you all she said. When I say kindness, I don't mean any 'Oh, my child,' and tears, and kisses, and maundering, you know. You mustn't mind her thinking me a little fool. You want to know what she thinks of you. She said nothing to hurt you, Evan, and we have gained ground so far, and now we'll go and face our enemies. Uncle Mel expects to hear about your appointment, in a day or two, and—"

"Oh, Rose!" Evan burst out.

"What is it?"

"Why must I owe everything to you?"

"Why, dear? Why, because, if you do, it's very much better than your owing it to anybody else. Proud again?"

Not proud: only second fiddle.

"You know, dear Evan, when two people love, there is no such thing as owing between them."

"Rose, I have been thinking. It is not too late. I love you, God knows! I did in Portugal: I do now—more and more. But Oh, my bright angel!" he ended the sentence in his breast.

"Well? but—what?"

Evan sounded down the meaning of his "but." Stripped of the usual heroics, it was, "what will be thought of me?" not a small matter to any of us. He caught a distant glimpse of the little bit of bare selfishness, and shrank from it.

"Too late," cried Rose. "The battle has commenced now, and, Mr. Harrington, I will lean on your arm, and be led to my dear friends yonder. Do they think that I am going to put on a mask to please them? Not for anybody! What they are to know they may as well know at once."

She looked in Evan's face.

"Do you hesitate?"

He felt the contrast between his own and hers; between the niggard spirit of the beggarly receiver, and the high bloom of the exalted giver. Nevertheless, he loved her too well not to share much of her nature, and wedding it suddenly, he said:

"Rose; tell me, now. If you were to see the place where I was born, could you love me still?"

"Yes, Evan."

"If you were to hear me spoken of with contempt—"

"Who dares?" cried Rose. "Never to me!"

"Contempt of what I spring from, Rose. Names used. . . Names are used. . ."

"Tush!—names!" said Rose, reddening. "How cowardly that is! Have you finished? Oh, faint heart! I suppose I'm not a fair lady, or you wouldn't have won me. Now, come. Remember, Evan, I conceal nothing; and if anything makes you wretched here, do think how I love you."

In his own firm belief he had said everything to arrest her in her course, and been silenced by transcendent logic. She thought the same.

Rose made up to the conclave under the maple.

The voices hushed as they approached.

"Capital weather," said Rose. "Does Harry come back from London to-morrow—does anybody know?"

"Not aware," Laxley was heard to reply.

"I want to speak a word to you, Rose," said Mrs. Shorne.

"With the greatest pleasure, my dear aunt": and Rose walked after her.

"My dear Rose," Mrs. Shorne commenced, "your conduct requires that I should really talk to you most seriously. You are probably not aware of what you are doing: Nobody likes ease and natural familiarity more than I do. I am persuaded it is nothing but your innocence. You are young to the world's ways, and perhaps a little too headstrong, and vain."

"Conceited and wilful," added Rose.

"If you like the words better. But I must say—I do not wish to trouble your father—you know he cannot bear worry—but I must say, that if you do not listen to me, he must be spoken to."

"Why not Mama?"

"I should naturally select my brother first. No doubt you understand me."

"Any distant allusion to Mr. Harrington?"

"Pertness will not avail you, Rose."

"So you want me to do secretly what I am doing openly?"

"You must and shall remember you are a Jocelyn, Rose."

"Only half, my dear aunt!"

"And by birth a lady, Rose."

"And I ought to look under my eyes, and blush, and shrink, whenever I come near a gentleman, aunt!"

"Ah! my dear. No doubt you will do what is most telling. Since you have spoken of this Mr. Harrington, I must inform you that I have it on certain authority from two or three sources, that he is the son of a small shopkeeper at Lymport."

Mrs. Shorne watched the effect she had produced.

"Indeed, aunt?" cried Rose. "And do you know this to be true?"

"So when you talk of gentlemen, Rose, please be careful whom you include."

"I mustn't include poor Mr. Harrington? Then my Grandpapa Bonner is out of the list, and such numbers of good worthy men?"

Mrs. Shorne understood the hit at the defunct manufacturer. She said: "You must most distinctly give me your promise, while this young adventurer remains here—I think it will not be long—not to be compromising yourself further, as you now do. Or—indeed I must—I shall let your parents perceive that such conduct is ruin to a young girl in your position, and certainly you will be sent to Elburne House for the winter."

Rose lifted her hands, crying: "Ye Gods!—as Harry says. But I'm very much obliged to you, my dear aunt. Concerning Mr. Harrington, wonderfully obliged. Son of a small—! Is it a t-t-tailor, aunt?"

"It is—I have heard."

"And that is much worse. Cloth is viler than cotton! And don't they call these creatures sn-snips? Some word of that sort?"

"It makes little difference what they are called."

"Well, aunt, I sincerely thank you. As this subject seems to interest you, go and see Mama, now. She can tell you a great deal more: and, if you want her authority, come back to me."

Rose then left her aunt in a state of extreme indignation. It was a clever move to send Mrs. Shorne to Lady Jocelyn. They were antagonistic, and, rational as Lady Jocelyn was, and with her passions under control, she was unlikely to side with Mrs. Shorne.

Now Rose had fought against herself, and had, as she thought, conquered. In Portugal Evan's half insinuations had given her small suspicions, which the scene on board the Jocasta had half confirmed: and since she came to communicate with her own mind, she bore the attack of all that rose against him, bit by bit. She had not been too blind to see the unpleasantness of the fresh facts revealed to her. They did not change her; on the contrary, drew her to him faster—and she thought she had completely conquered whatever could rise against him. But when Juliana Bonner told her that day that Evan was not only the son of the thing, but the thing himself, and that his name could be seen any day in Lymport, and that he had come from the shop to Beckley, poor Rosey had a sick feeling that almost sank her. For a moment she looked back wildly to the doors of retreat. Her eyes had to feed on Evan, she had to taste some of the luxury of love, before she could gain composure, and then her arrogance towards those she called her enemies did not quite return.

"In that letter you told me all—all—all, Evan?"

"Yes, all-religiously."

"Oh, why did I miss it!"

"Would it give you pleasure?"

She feared to speak, being tender as a mother to his sensitiveness. The expressive action of her eyebrows sufficed. She could not bear concealment, or doubt, or a shadow of dishonesty; and he, gaining force of soul to join with hers, took her hands and related the contents of the letter fully. She was pale when he had finished. It was some time before she was able to get free from the trammels of prejudice, but when she did, she did without reserve, saying: "Evan, there is no man who would have done so much." These little exaltations and generosities bind lovers tightly. He accepted the credit she gave him, and at that we need not wonder. It helped him further to accept herself, otherwise could he—his name known to be on a shop-front—have aspired to her still? But, as an unexampled man, princely in soul, as he felt, why, he might kneel to Rose Jocelyn. So they listened to one another, and blinded the world by putting bandages on their eyes, after the fashion of little boys and girls.

Meantime the fair being who had brought these two from the ends of the social scale into this happy tangle, the beneficent Countess, was wretched. When you are in the enemy's country you are dependent on the activity and zeal of your spies and scouts, and the best of these—Polly Wheedle, to wit—had proved defective, recalcitrant even. And because a letter had been lost in her room! as the Countess exclaimed to herself, though Polly gave her no reasons. The Countess had, therefore, to rely chiefly upon personal observation, upon her intuitions, upon her sensations in the proximity of the people to whom she was opposed; and from these she gathered that she was, to use the word which seemed fitting to her, betrayed. Still to be sweet, still to smile and to amuse,—still to give her zealous attention to the business of the diplomatist's Election, still to go through her church-services devoutly, required heroism; she was equal to it, for she had remarkable courage; but it was hard to feel no longer at one with Providence. Had not Providence suggested Sir Abraham to her? killed him off at the right moment in aid of her? And now Providence had turned, and the assistance she had formerly received from that Power, and given thanks for so profusely, was the cause of her terror. It was absolutely as if she had been borrowing from a Jew, and were called upon to pay fifty-fold interest.

"Evan!" she writes in a gasp to Harriet. "We must pack up and depart. Abandon everything. He has disgraced us all, and ruined himself. Impossible that we can stay for the pic-nic. We are known, dear. Think of my position one day in this house! Particulars when I embrace you. I dare not trust a letter here. If Evan had confided in me! He is impenetrable. He will be low all his life, and I refuse any more to sully myself in attempting to lift him. For Silva's sake I must positively break the connection. Heaven knows what I have done for this boy, and will support me in the feeling that I have done enough. My conscience at least is safe."

Like many illustrious Generals, the Countess had, for the hour, lost heart. We find her, however, the next day, writing:

"Oh! Harriet! what trials for sisterly affection! Can I possibly—weather the gale, as the old L—— sailors used to say? It is dreadful. I fear I am by duty bound to stop on. Little Bonner thinks Evan quite a duke's son, has been speaking to her Grandmama, and to-day, this morning, the venerable old lady quite as much as gave me to understand that an union between our brother and her son's child would sweetly gratify her, and help her to go to her rest in peace. Can I chase that spark of comfort from one so truly pious? Dearest Juliana! I have anticipated Evan's feeling for her, and so she thinks his conduct cold. Indeed, I told her, point blank, he loved her. That, you know, is different from saying, dying of love, which would have been an untruth. But, Evan, of course! No getting him! Should Juliana ever reproach me, I can assure the child that any man is in love with any woman—which is really the case. It is, you dear humdrum! what the dictionary calls 'nascent.' I never liked the word, but it stands for a fact."

The Countess here exhibits the weakness of a self-educated intelligence. She does not comprehend the joys of scholarship in her employment of Latinisms. It will be pardoned to her by those who perceive the profound piece of feminine discernment which precedes it.

"I do think I shall now have courage to stay out the pic-nic," she continues. "I really do not think all is known. Very little can be known, or I am sure I could not feel as I do. It would burn me up. George Up—does not dare; and his most beautiful lady-love had far better not. Mr. Forth may repent his whispers. But, Oh! what Evan may do! Rose is almost detestable. Manners, my dear? Totally deficient!

"An ally has just come. Evan's good fortune is most miraculous. His low friend turns out to be a young Fortunatus; very original, sparkling, and in my hands to be made much of. I do think he will—for he is most zealous—he will counteract that hateful Mr. Forth, who may soon have work enough. Mr. Raikes (Evan's friend) met a mad captain in Fallow field! Dear Mr. Raikes is ready to say anything; not from love of falsehood, but because he is ready to think it. He has confessed to me that Evan told him! Louisa de Saldar has changed his opinion, and much impressed this eccentric young gentleman. Do you know any young girl who wants a fortune, and would be grateful?

"Dearest! I have decided on the pic-nic. Let your conscience be clear, and Providence cannot be against you. So I feel. Mr. Parsley spoke very beautifully to that purpose last Sunday in the morning service. A little too much through his nose, perhaps; but the poor young man's nose is a great organ, and we will not cast it in his teeth more than nature has done. I said so to my diplomatist, who was amused. If you are sparklingly vulgar with the English, you are aristocratic. Oh! what principle we women require in the thorny walk of life. I can show you a letter when we meet that will astonish humdrum. Not so diplomatic as the writer thought! Mrs. Melville (sweet woman!) must continue to practise civility; for a woman who is a wife, my dear, in verity she lives in a glass house, and let her fling no stones. 'Let him who is without sin.' How beautiful that Christian sentiment! I hope I shall be pardoned, but it always seems to me that what we have to endure is infinitely worse than any other suffering, for you find no comfort for the children of T——s in Scripture, nor any defence of their dreadful position.

Robbers, thieves, Magdalens! but, no! the unfortunate offspring of that class are not even mentioned: at least, in my most diligent perusal of the Scriptures, I never lighted upon any remote allusion; and we know the Jews did wear clothing. Outcasts, verily! And Evan could go, and write—but I have no patience with him. He is the blind tool of his mother, and anybody's puppet."

The letter concludes, with horrid emphasis:

"The Madre in Beckley! Has sent for Evan from a low public-house! I have intercepted the messenger. Evan closeted with Sir Franks. Andrew's horrible old brother with Lady Jocelyn. The whole house, from garret to kitchen, full of whispers!"

A prayer to Providence closes the communication.

XXVIII

Tom Cogglesey's Proposition

The appearance of a curricle and a donkey-cart within the gates of Beckley Court, produced a sensation among the men of the lower halls, and a couple of them rushed out, with the left calf considerably in advance, to defend the house from violation. Toward the curricle they directed what should have been a bow, but was a nod. Their joint attention was then given to the donkey-cart, in which old Tom Cogglesby sat alone, bunchy in figure, bunched in face, his shrewd grey eyes twinkling under the bush of his eyebrows.

"Oy, sir—you! my man!" exclaimed the tallest of the pair, resolutely. "This won't do. Don't you know driving this sort of conveyance slap along the gravel 'ere, up to the pillars, 's unparliamentary? Can't be allowed. Now, right about!"

This address, accompanied by a commanding elevation of the dexter hand, seemed to excite Mr. Raikes far more than Old Tom. He alighted from his perch in haste, and was running up to the stalwart figure, crying, "Fellow!" when, as you tell a dog to lie down, Old Tom called out, "Be quiet, Sir!" and Raikes halted with prompt military obedience.

The sight of the curricle acting satellite to the donkey-cart staggered the two footmen.

"Are you lords?" sang out Old Tom.

A burst of laughter from the friends of Mr. Raikes, in the curricle, helped to make the powdered gentlemen aware of a sarcasm, and one with no little dignity replied that they were not lords.

"Oh! Then come and hold my donkey."

Great irresolution was displayed at the injunction, but having consulted the face of Mr. Raikes, one fellow, evidently half overcome by what was put upon him, with the steps of Adam into exile, descended to the gravel, and laid his hand on the donkey's head.

"Hold hard!" cried Old Tom. "Whisper in his ear. He'll know your language."

"May I have the felicity of assisting you to terra firma?" interposed Mr. Raikes, with the bow of deferential familiarity.

"Done that once too often," returned Old Tom, jumping out. "There.

What's the fee? There's a crown for you that ain't afraid of a live donkey; and there's a sixpenny bit for you that are—to keep up your courage; and when he's dead you shall have his skin—to shave by."

"Excellent!" shouted Raikes.

"Thomas!" he addressed a footman, "hand in my card. Mr. John Feversham Raikes."

"And tell my lady, Tom Cogglesby's come," added the owner of that name.

We will follow Tom Cogglesby, as he chooses to be called.

Lady Jocelyn rose on his entering the library, and walking up to him, encountered him with a kindly full face.

"So I see you at last, Tom?" she said, without releasing his hand; and Old Tom mounted patches of red in his wrinkled cheeks, and blinked, and betrayed a singular antiquated bashfulness, which ended, after a mumble of "Yes, there he was, and he hoped her ladyship was well," by his seeking refuge in a chair, where he sat hard, and fixed his attention on the leg of a table.

"Well, Tom, do you find much change in me?" she was woman enough to continue.

He was obliged to look up.

"Can't say I do, my lady."

"Don't you see the grey hairs, Tom?"

"Better than a wig," rejoined he.

Was it true that her ladyship had behaved rather ill to Old Tom in her youth? Excellent women have been naughty girls, and young Beauties will have their train. It is also very possible that Old Tom had presumed upon trifles, and found it difficult to forgive her his own folly.

"Preferable to a wig? Well, I would rather see you with your natural thatch. You're bent, too. You look as if you had kept away from Beckley a little too long."

"Told you, my lady, I should come when your daughter was marriageable."

"Oho! that's it? I thought it was the Election!

"Election be — hem!—beg pardon, my lady."

"Swear, Tom, if it relieves you. I think it bad to check an oath or a sneeze."

"I'm come to see you on business, my lady, or I shouldn't have troubled you."

"Malice?"

"You'll see I don't bear any, my lady."

"Ah! if you had only sworn roundly twenty-five years ago, what a much younger man you would have been! and a brave capital old friend whom I should not have missed all that time."

"Come!" cried Old Tom, varying his eyes rapidly between her ladyship's face and the floor, "you acknowledge I had reason to."

"Mais, cela va sans dire."

"Cobblers' sons ain't scholars, my lady."

"And are not all in the habit of throwing their fathers in our teeth, I hope!"

Old Tom wriggled in his chair. "Well, my lady, I'm not going to make a fool of myself at my time o' life. Needn't be alarmed now. You've got the bell-rope handy and a husband on the premises."

Lady Jocelyn smiled, stood up, and went to him. "I like an honest fist," she said, taking his. "We're not going to be doubtful friends, and we won't snap and snarl. That's for people who're independent of wigs, Tom. I find, for my part, that a little grey on the top of any head cools the temper amazingly. I used to be rather hot once."

"You could be peppery, my lady."

"Now I'm cool, Tom, and so must you be; or, if you fight, it must be in my cause, as you did when you thrashed that saucy young carter. Do you remember?"

"If you'll sit ye down, my lady, I'll just tell you what I'm come for," said Old Tom, who plainly showed that he did remember, and was alarmingly softened by her ladyship's retention of the incident.

Lady Jocelyn returned to her place.

"You've got a marriageable daughter, my lady?"

"I suppose we may call her so," said Lady Jocelyn, with a composed glance at the ceiling.

"'Gaged to be married to any young chap?"

"You must put the question to her, Tom."

"Ha! I don't want to see her."

At this Lady Jocelyn looked slightly relieved. Old Tom continued.

"Happen to have got a little money—not so much as many a lord's got, I dare say; such as 'tis, there 'tis. Young fellow I know wants a wife, and he shall have best part of it. Will that suit ye, my lady?"

Lady Jocelyn folded her hands. "Certainly; I've no objection. What it has to do with me I can't perceive."

"Ahem!" went Old Tom. "It won't hurt your daughter to be married now, will it?"

"Oh! my daughter is the destined bride of your 'young fellow,'" said Lady Jocelyn. "Is that how it's to be?"

"She"—Old Tom cleared his throat "she won't marry a lord, my lady; but she—'hem—if she don't mind that—'ll have a deuced sight more hard cash than many lord's son 'd give her, and a young fellow for a husband, sound in wind and limb, good bone and muscle, speaks grammar and two or three languages, and—"

"Stop!" cried Lady Jocelyn. "I hope this is not a prize young man? If he belongs, at his age, to the unco quid, I refuse to take him for a son-in-law, and I think Rose will, too."

Old Tom burst out vehemently: "He's a damned good young fellow, though he isn't a lord."

"Well," said Lady Jocelyn, "I've no doubt you're in earnest, Tom. It's curious, for this morning Rose has come to me and given me the first chapter of a botheration, which she declares is to end in the common rash experiment. What is your 'young fellow's' name? Who is he? What is he?"

"Won't take my guarantee, my lady?"

"Rose—if she marries—must have a name, you know?"

Old Tom hit his knee. "Then there's a pill for ye to swallow, for he ain't the son of a lord."

"That's swallowed, Tom. What is he?"

"He's the son of a tradesman, then, my lady." And Old Tom watched her to note the effect he had produced.

"More 's the pity," was all she remarked.

"And he'll have his thousand a year to start with; and he's a tailor, my lady."

Her ladyship opened her eyes.

"Harrington's his name, my lady. Don't know whether you ever heard of it."

Lady Jocelyn flung herself back in her chair. "The queerest thing I ever met!" said she.

"Thousand a year to start with," Old Tom went on, "and if she marries—I mean if he marries her, I'll settle a thousand per ann. on the first baby-boy or gal."

"Hum! Is this gross collusion, Mr. Tom?" Lady Jocelyn inquired.

"What does that mean?"

"Have you spoken of this before to any one?"

"I haven't, my lady. Decided on it this morning. Hem! you got a son, too. He's fond of a young gal, or he ought to be. I'll settle him when I've settled the daughter."

"Harry is strongly attached to a dozen, I believe," said his mother. "Well, Tom, we'll think of it. I may as well tell you: Rose has just been here to inform me that this Mr. Harrington has turned her head, and that she has given her troth, and all that sort of thing. I believe such was not to be laid to my charge in my day."

"You were open enough, my lady," said Old Tom. "She's fond of the young fellow? She'll have a pill to swallow! poor young woman!"

Old Tom visibly chuckled. Lady Jocelyn had a momentary temptation to lead him out, but she did not like the subject well enough to play with it.

"Apparently Rose has swallowed it," she said.

"Goose, shears, cabbage, and all!" muttered Old Tom. "Got a stomach!—she knows he's a tailor, then? The young fellow told her? He hasn't been playing the lord to her?"

"As far as he's concerned, I think he has been tolerably honest, Tom, for a man and a lover."

"And told her he was born and bound a tailor?"

"Rose certainly heard it from him."

Slapping his knee, Old Tom cried: "Bravo!" For though one part of his nature was disappointed, and the best part of his plot disarranged, he liked Evan's proceeding and felt warm at what seemed to him Rose's scorn of rank.

"She must be a good gal, my lady. She couldn't have got it from t' other side. Got it from you. Not that you—"

"No," said Lady Jocelyn, apprehending him. "I'm afraid I have no Republican virtues. I'm afraid I should have rejected the pill. Don't be angry with me," for Old Tom looked sour again; "I like birth and position, and worldly advantages, and, notwithstanding Rose's pledge of the instrument she calls her heart, and in spite of your offer, I shall, I tell you honestly, counsel her to have nothing to do with—"

"Anything less than lords," Old Tom struck in. "Very well. Are you going to lock her up, my lady?"

"No. Nor shall I whip her with rods."

"Leave her free to her choice?"

"She will have my advice. That I shall give her. And I shall take care that before she makes a step she shall know exactly what it leads to. Her father, of course, will exercise his judgement." (Lady Jocelyn said this to uphold the honour of Sir Franks, knowing at the same time perfectly well that he would be wheedled by Rose.) "I confess I like this Mr. Harrington. But it's a great misfortune for him to have had a notorious father. A tailor should certainly avoid fame, and this young man will have to carry his father on his back. He'll never throw the great Mel off."

Tom Cogglesby listened, and was really astonished at her ladyship's calm reception of his proposal.

"Shameful of him! shameful!" he muttered perversely: for it would have made him desolate to have had to change his opinion of her ladyship after cherishing it, and consoling himself with it, five-and-twenty years. Fearing the approach of softness, he prepared to take his leave.

"Now—your servant, my lady. I stick to my word, mind: and if your people here are willing, I—I've got a candidate up for Fall'field—I'll knock him down, and you shall sneak in your Tory. Servant, my lady."

Old Tom rose to go. Lady Jocelyn took his hand cordially, though she could not help smiling at the humility of the cobbler's son in his manner of speaking of the Tory candidate.

"Won't you stop with us a few days?"

"I'd rather not, I thank ye."

"Won't you see Rose?"

"I won't. Not till she's married."

"Well, Tom, we're friends now?"

"Not aware I've ever done you any harm, my lady."

"Look me in the face."

The trial was hard for him. Though she had been five-and-twenty years a wife, she was still very handsome: but he was not going to be melted, and when the perverse old fellow obeyed her, it was with an aspect of resolute disgust that would have made any other woman indignant. Lady Jocelyn laughed.

"Why, Tom, your brother Andrew's here, and makes himself comfortable with us. We rode by Brook's farm the other day. Do you remember Copping's pond—how we dragged it that night? What days we had!"

Old Tom tugged once or twice at his imprisoned fist, while these youthful frolics of his too stupid self and the wild and beautiful Miss Bonner were being recalled.

"I remember!" he said savagely, and reaching the door hurled out: "And I remember the Bull-dogs, too! servant, my lady." With which he effected a retreat, to avoid a ringing laugh he heard in his ears.

Lady Jocelyn had not laughed. She had done no more than look and smile kindly on the old boy. It was at the Bull-dogs, a fall of water on the borders of the park, that Tom Cogglesby, then a hearty young man, had been guilty of his folly: had mistaken her frank friendliness for a return of his passion, and his stubborn vanity still attributed her rejection of his suit to the fact of his descent from a cobbler, or, as he put it, to her infernal worship of rank.

"Poor old Tom!" said her ladyship, when alone. "He's rough at the rind, but sound at the core." She had no idea of the long revenge Old Tom cherished, and had just shaped into a plot to be equal with her for the Bull-dogs.

XXIX

Prelude to an Engagement

Money was a strong point with the Elburne brood. The Jocelyns very properly respected blood; but being, as Harry, their youngest representative, termed them, poor as rats, they were justified in considering it a marketable stuff; and when they married they married for money. The Hon. Miss Jocelyn had espoused a manufacturer, who failed in his contract, and deserved his death. The diplomatist, Melville, had not stepped aside from the family traditions in his alliance with Miss Black, the daughter of a bold bankrupt, educated in affluence; and if he touched nothing but L5000 and some very pretty ringlets, that was not his fault. Sir Franks, too, mixed his pure stream with gold. As yet, however, the gold had done little more than shine on him; and, belonging to expectancy, it might be thought unsubstantial. Beckley Court was in the hands of Mrs. Bonner, who, with the highest sense of duty toward her only living child, was the last to appreciate Lady Jocelyn's entire absence of demonstrative affection, and severely reprobated her daughter's philosophic handling of certain serious subjects. Sir Franks, no doubt, came better off than the others; her ladyship brought him twenty thousand pounds, and Harry had ten in the past tense, and Rose ten in the future; but living, as he had done, a score of years anticipating the demise of an incurable invalid, he, though an excellent husband and father, could scarcely be taught to imagine that the Jocelyn object of his bargain was attained. He had the semblance of wealth, without the personal glow which absolute possession brings. It was his habit to call himself a poor man, and it was his dream that Rose should marry a rich one. Harry was hopeless. He had been his Grandmother's pet up to the years of adolescence: he was getting too old for any prospect of a military career he had no turn for diplomacy, no taste for any of the walks open to blood and birth, and was in headlong disgrace with the fountain of goodness at Beckley Court, where he was still kept in the tacit understanding that, should Juliana inherit the place, he must be at hand to marry her instantly, after the fashion of the Jocelyns. They were an injured family; for what they gave was good, and the commercial world had not behaved honourably to them. Now, Ferdinand Laxley was just the match for Rose. Born to a title and fine estate, he was evidently fond of her, and there had been a gentle hope in the bosom of Sir Franks that the family fatality would cease, and that Rose would marry both money and blood.

From this happy delusion poor Sir Franks was awakened to hear that his daughter had plighted herself to the son of a tradesman: that, as the climax to their evil fate, she who had some blood and some money of her own—the only Jocelyn who had ever united the two—was desirous of wasting herself on one who had neither. The idea was so utterly opposed to the principles Sir Franks had been trained in, that his intellect could not grasp it. He listened to his sister, Mrs. Shorne: he listened to his wife; he agreed with all they said, though what they said was widely diverse: he consented to see and speak to Evan, and he did so, and was much the most distressed. For Sir Franks liked many things in life, and hated one thing alone—which was "bother." A smooth world was his delight. Rose knew this, and her instruction to Evan was: "You cannot give me up—you will go, but you cannot give me up while I am faithful to you: tell him that." She knew that to impress this fact at once on the mind of Sir Franks would be a great gain; for in his detestation of bother he would soon grow reconciled to things monstrous: and hearing the same on both sides, the matter would assume an inevitable shape to him. Mr. Second Fiddle had no difficulty in declaring the eternity of his sentiments; but he toned them with a despair Rose did not contemplate, and added also his readiness to repair, in any way possible, the evil done. He spoke of his birth and position. Sir Franks, with a gentlemanly delicacy natural to all lovers of a smooth world, begged him to see the main and the insurmountable objection. Birth was to be desired, of course, and position, and so forth: but without money how can two young people marry? Evan's heart melted at this generous way of putting it. He said he saw it, he had no hope: he would go and be forgotten: and begged that for any annoyance his visit might have caused Sir Franks and Lady Jocelyn, they would pardon him. Sir Franks shook him by the hand, and the interview ended in a dialogue on the condition of the knees of Black Lymport, and on horseflesh in Portugal and Spain.

Following Evan, Rose went to her father and gave him a good hour's excitement, after which the worthy gentleman hurried for consolation to Lady Jocelyn, whom he found reading a book of French memoirs, in her usual attitude, with her feet stretched out and her head thrown back, as in a distant survey of the lively people screening her from a troubled world. Her ladyship read him a piquant story, and Sir Franks capped it with another from memory; whereupon her ladyship held him wrong in one turn of the story, and Sir Franks rose to get the volume to verify, and while he was turning over the leaves, Lady Jocelyn told him incidentally of old Tom Cogglesby's visit and proposal. Sir Franks found the passage, and that her ladyship was right, which it did not move her countenance to hear.

"Ah!" said he, finding it no use to pretend there was no bother in the world, "here's a pretty pickle! Rose says she will have that fellow."

"Hum!" replied her ladyship. "And if she keeps her mind a couple of years, it will be a wonder."

"Very bad for her this sort of thing—talked about," muttered Sir Franks. "Ferdinand was just the man."

"Well, yes; I suppose it's her mistake to think brains an absolute requisite," said Lady Jocelyn, opening her book again, and scanning down a column.

Sir Franks, being imitative, adopted a similar refuge, and the talk between them was varied by quotations and choice bits from the authors they had recourse to. Both leaned back in their chairs, and spoke with their eyes on their books.

"Julia's going to write to her mother," said he.

"Very filial and proper," said she.

"There'll be a horrible hubbub, you know, Emily."

"Most probably. I shall get the blame; 'cela se concoit'."

"Young Harrington goes the day after to-morrow. Thought it better not to pack him off in a hurry."

"And just before the pic-nic; no, certainly. I suppose it would look odd."

"How are we to get rid of the Countess?"

"Eh? This Bautru is amusing, Franks; but he's nothing to Vandy. 'Homme incomparable!' On the whole I find Menage rather dull. The Countess? what an accomplished liar that woman is! She seems to have stepped out of Tallemant's Gallery. Concerning the Countess, I suppose you had better apply to Melville."

"Where the deuce did this young Harrington get his breeding from?"

"He comes of a notable sire."

"Yes, but there's no sign of the snob in him."

"And I exonerate him from the charge of 'adventuring' after Rose. George Uplift tells me—I had him in just now—that the mother is a woman of mark and strong principle. She has probably corrected the too luxuriant nature of Mel in her offspring. That is to say in this one. 'Pour les autres, je ne dis pas'. Well, the young man will go; and if Rose chooses to become a monument of constancy, we can do nothing. I shall give my advice; but as she has not deceived me, and she is a reasonable being, I shan't interfere. Putting the case at the worst, they will not want money. I have no doubt Tom Cogglesby means what he says, and will do it. So there we will leave the matter till we hear from Elburne House."

Sir Franks groaned at the thought.

"How much does he offer to settle on them?" he asked.

"A thousand a year on the marriage, and the same amount to the first child. I daresay the end would be that they would get all."

Sir Franks nodded, and remained with one eye-brow pitiably elevated above the level of the other.

"Anything but a tailor!" he exclaimed presently, half to himself.

"There is a prejudice against that craft," her ladyship acquiesced. "Beranger—let me see—your favourite Frenchman, Franks, wasn't it his father?—no, his grandfather. 'Mon pauvre et humble grand-pyre,' I think, was a tailor. Hum! the degrees of the thing, I confess, don't affect me. One trade I imagine to be no worse than another."

"Ferdinand's allowance is about a thousand," said Sir Franks, meditatively.

"And won't be a farthing more till he comes to the title," added her ladyship.

"Well," resumed Sir Franks, "it's a horrible bother!"

His wife philosophically agreed with him, and the subject was dropped.

Lady Jocelyn felt with her husband, more than she chose to let him know, and Sir Franks could have burst into anathemas against fate and circumstances, more than his love of a smooth world permitted. He, however, was subdued by her calmness; and she, with ten times the weight of brain, was manoeuvred by the wonderful dash of General Rose Jocelyn. For her ladyship, thinking, "I shall get the blame of all this," rather sided insensibly with the offenders against those who condemned them jointly; and seeing that Rose had been scrupulously honest and straightforward in a very delicate matter, this lady was so constituted that she could not but applaud her daughter in her heart. A worldly woman would have acted, if she had not thought, differently; but her ladyship was not a worldly woman.

Evan's bearing and character had, during his residence at Beckley Court, become so thoroughly accepted as those of a gentleman, and one of their own rank, that, after an allusion to the origin of his breeding, not a word more was said by either of them on that topic. Besides, Rose had dignified him by her decided conduct.

By the time poor Sir Franks had read himself into tranquillity, Mrs. Shorne, who knew him well, and was determined that he should not enter upon his usual negociations with an unpleasantness: that is to say, to forget it, joined them in the library, bringing with her Sir John Loring and Hamilton Jocelyn. Her first measure was to compel Sir Franks to put down his book. Lady Jocelyn subsequently had to do the same.

"Well, what have you done, Franks?" said Mrs. Shorne.

"Done?" answered the poor gentleman. "What is there to be done? I've spoken to young Harrington."

"Spoken to him! He deserves horsewhipping! Have you not told him to quit the house instantly?"

Lady Jocelyn came to her husband's aid: "It wouldn't do, I think, to kick him out. In the first place, he hasn't deserved it."

"Not deserved it, Emily!—the commonest, low, vile, adventuring tradesman!"

"In the second place," pursued her ladyship, "it's not adviseable to do anything that will make Rose enter into the young woman's sublimities. It's better not to let a lunatic see that you think him stark mad, and the same holds with young women afflicted with the love-mania. The sound of sense, even if they can't understand it, flatters them so as to keep them within bounds. Otherwise you drive them into excesses best avoided."

"Really, Emily," said Mrs. Shorne, "you speak almost, one would say, as an advocate of such unions."

"You must know perfectly well that I entirely condemn them," replied her ladyship, who had once, and once only, delivered her opinion of the nuptials of Mr. and Mrs. Shorne.

In self-defence, and to show the total difference between the cases, Mrs. Shorne interjected: "An utterly penniless young adventurer!"

"Oh, no; there's money," remarked Sir Franks.

"Money is there?" quoth Hamilton, respectfully.

"And there's wit," added Sir John, "if he has half his sister's talent."

"Astonishing woman!" Hamilton chimed in; adding, with a shrug, "But, egad!"

"Well, we don't want him to resemble his sister," said Lady Jocelyn. "I acknowledge she's amusing."

"Amusing, Emily!" Mrs. Shorne never encountered her sister-in-law's calmness without indignation. "I could not rest in the house with such a person, knowing her what she is. A vile adventuress, as I firmly believe. What does she do all day with your mother? Depend upon it, you will repent her visit in more ways than one."

"A prophecy?" asked Lady Jocelyn, smiling.

On the grounds of common sense, on the grounds of propriety, and consideration of what was due to themselves, all agreed to condemn the notion of Rose casting herself away on Evan. Lady Jocelyn agreed with Mrs. Shorne; Sir Franks with his brother, and Sir John. But as to what they were to do, they were divided. Lady Jocelyn said she should not prevent Rose from writing to Evan, if she had the wish to do so.

"Folly must come out," said her ladyship. "It's a combustible material. I won't have her health injured. She shall go into the world more. She will be presented at Court, and if it's necessary to give her a dose or two to counteract her vanity, I don't object. This will wear off, or, 'si c'est veritablement une grande passion, eh bien' we must take what Providence sends us."

"And which we might have prevented if we had condescended to listen to the plainest worldly wisdom," added Mrs. Shorne.

"Yes," said Lady Jocelyn, equably, "you know, you and I, Julia, argue from two distinct points. Girls may be shut up, as you propose. I don't think nature intended to have them the obverse of men. I'm sure their mothers never designed that they should run away with footmen, riding-masters, chance curates, as they occasionally do, and wouldn't if they had points of comparison. My opinion is that Prospero was just saved by the Prince of Naples being wrecked on his island, from a shocking mis-alliance between his daughter and the son of Sycorax. I see it clearly. Poetry conceals the extreme probability, but from what I know of my sex, I should have no hesitation in turning prophet also, as to that."

What could Mrs. Shorne do with a mother who talked in this manner? Mrs. Melville, when she arrived to take part in the conference, which gradually swelled to a family one, was equally unable to make Lady Jocelyn perceive that her plan of bringing up Rose was, in the present result of it, other than unlucky.

Now the two Generals—Rose Jocelyn and the Countess de Saldar—had brought matters to this pass; and from the two tactical extremes:

the former by openness and dash; the latter by subtlety, and her own interpretations of the means extended to her by Providence. I will not be so bold as to state which of the two I think right. Good and evil work together in this world. If the Countess had not woven the tangle, and gained Evan time, Rose would never have seen his blood,—never have had her spirit hurried out of all shows and forms and habits of thought, up to the gates of existence, as it were, where she took him simply as God created him and her, and clave to him. Again, had Rose been secret, when this turn in her nature came, she would have forfeited the strange power she received from it, and which endowed her with decision to say what was in her heart, and stamp it lastingly there. The two Generals were quite antagonistic, but no two, in perfect ignorance of one another's proceedings, ever worked so harmoniously toward the main result. The Countess was the skilful engineer: Rose the General of cavalry. And it did really seem that, with Tom Cogglesby and his thousands in reserve, the victory was about to be gained. The male Jocelyns, an easy race, decided that, if the worst came to the worst, and Rose proved a wonder, there was money, which was something.

But social prejudice was about to claim its champion. Hitherto there had been no General on the opposite side. Love, aided by the Countess, had engaged an inert mass. The champion was discovered in the person of the provincial Don Juan, Mr. Harry Jocelyn. Harry had gone on a mysterious business of his own to London. He returned with a green box under his arm, which, five minutes after his arrival, was entrusted to Conning, in company with a genial present for herself, of a kind not perhaps so fit for exhibition; at least they both thought so, for it was given in the shades. Harry then went to pay his respects to his mother, who received him with her customary ironical tolerance. His father, to whom he was an incarnation of bother, likewise nodded to him and gave him a finger. Duty done, Harry looked round him for pleasure, and observed nothing but glum faces. Even the face of John Raikes was, heavy. He had been hovering about the Duke and Miss Current for an hour, hoping the Countess would come and give him a promised introduction. The Countess stirred not from above, and Jack drifted from group to group on the lawn, and grew conscious that wherever he went he brought silence with him. His isolation made him humble, and when Harry shook his hand, and said he remembered Fallow field and the fun there, Mr. Raikes thanked him.

Harry made his way to join his friend Ferdinand, and furnished him with the latest London news not likely to appear in the papers. Laxley was distant and unamused. From the fact, too, that Harry was known to be the Countess's slave, his presence produced the same effect in the different circles about the grounds, as did that of John Raikes. Harry began to yawn and wish very ardently for his sweet lady. She, however, had too fine an instinct to descend.

An hour before dinner, Juliana sent him a message that she desired to see him.

"Jove! I hope that girl's not going to be blowing hot again," sighed the conqueror.

He had nothing to fear from Juliana. The moment they were alone she asked him, "Have you heard of it?"

Harry shook his head and shrugged.

"They haven't told you? Rose has engaged herself to Mr. Harrington, a tradesman, a tailor!"

"Pooh! have you got hold of that story?" said Harry. "But I'm sorry for old Ferdy. He was fond of Rosey. Here's another bother!"

"You don't believe me, Harry?"

Harry was mentally debating whether, in this new posture of affairs, his friend Ferdinand would press his claim for certain moneys lent.

"Oh, I believe you," he said. "Harrington has the knack with you women. Why, you made eyes at him. It was a toss-up between you and Rosey once."

Juliana let this accusation pass.

"He is a tradesman. He has a shop in Lymport, I tell you, Harry, and his name on it. And he came here on purpose to catch Rose. And now he has caught her, he tells her. And his mother is now at one of the village inns, waiting to see him. Go to Mr. George Uplift; he knows the family. Yes, the Countess has turned your head, of course; but she has schemed, and schemed, and told such stories—God forgive her!"

The girl had to veil her eyes in a spasm of angry weeping.

"Oh, come! Juley!" murmured her killing cousin. Harry boasted an extraordinary weakness at the sight of feminine tears. "I say! Juley! you know if you begin crying I'm done for, and it isn't fair."

He dropped his arm on her waist to console her, and generously declared to her that he always had been, very fond of her. These scenes were not foreign to the youth. Her fits of crying, from which she would burst in a frenzy of contempt at him, had made Harry say stronger things; and the assurances of profound affection uttered in a most languid voice will sting the hearts of women.

Harry still went on with his declarations, heating them rapidly, so as to bring on himself the usual outburst and check. She was longer in coming to it this time, and he had a horrid fear, that instead of dismissing him fiercely, and so annulling his words, the strange little person was going to be soft and hold him to them. There were her tears, however, which she could not stop.

"Well, then, Juley, look. I do, upon my honour, yes—there, don't cry any more—I do love you."

Harry held his breath in awful suspense. Juliana quietly disengaged her waist, and looking at him, said, "Poor Harry! You need not lie any more to please me."

Such was Harry's astonishment, that he exclaimed,

"It isn't a lie! I say, I do love you." And for an instant he thought and hoped that he did love her.

"Well, then, Harry, I don't love you," said Juliana; which revealed to our friend that he had been mistaken in his own emotions. Nevertheless, his vanity was hurt when he saw she was sincere, and he listened to her, a moody being. This may account for his excessive wrath at Evan Harrington after Juliana had given him proofs of the truth of what she said.

But the Countess was Harrington's sister! The image of the Countess swam before him. Was it possible? Harry went about asking everybody he met. The initiated were discreet; those who had the whispers were open. A bare truth is not so convincing as one that discretion confirms. Harry found the detestable news perfectly true.

"Stop it by all means if you can," said his father.

"Yes, try a fall with Rose," said his mother.

"And I must sit down to dinner to-day with a confounded fellow, the son of a tailor, who's had the impudence to make love to my sister!" cried Harry. "I'm determined to kick him out of the house!—half."

"To what is the modification of your determination due?" Lady Jocelyn inquired, probably suspecting the sweet and gracious person who divided Harry's mind.

Her ladyship treated her children as she did mankind generally, from her intellectual eminence. Harry was compelled to fly from her cruel shafts. He found comfort with his Aunt Shorne, and she as much as told Harry that he was the head of the house, and must take up the matter summarily. It was expected of him. Now was the time for him to show his manhood.

Harry could think of but one way to do that.

"Yes, and if I do—all up with the old lady," he said, and had to explain that his Grandmama Bonner would never leave a penny to a fellow who had fought a duel.

"A duel!" said Mrs. Shorne. "No, there are other ways. Insist upon his renouncing her. And Rose—treat her with a high hand, as becomes you. Your mother is incorrigible, and as for your father, one knows him of old. This devolves upon you. Our family honour is in your hands, Harry."

Considering Harry's reputation, the family honour must have got low: Harry, of course, was not disposed to think so. He discovered a great deal of unused pride within him, for which he had hitherto not found an agreeable vent. He vowed to his aunt that he would not suffer the disgrace, and while still that blandishing olive-hued visage swam before his eyes, he pledged his word to Mrs. Shorne that he would come to an understanding with Harrington that night.

"Quietly," said she. "No scandal, pray."

"Oh, never mind how I do it," returned Harry, manfully. "How am I to do it, then?" he added, suddenly remembering his debt to Evan.

Mrs. Shorne instructed him how to do it quietly, and without fear of scandal. The miserable champion replied that it was very well for her to tell him to say this and that, but—and she thought him demented—he must, previous to addressing Harrington in those terms, have money.

"Money!" echoed the lady. "Money!"

"Yes, money!" he iterated doggedly, and she learnt that he had borrowed a sum of Harrington, and the amount of the sum.

It was a disastrous plight, for Mrs. Shorne was penniless.

She cited Ferdinand Laxley as a likely lender.

"Oh, I'm deep with him already," said Harry, in apparent dejection.

"How dreadful are these everlasting borrowings of yours!" exclaimed his aunt, unaware of a trifling incongruity in her sentiments. "You must speak to him without—pay him by-and-by. We must scrape the money together. I will write to your grandfather."

"Yes; speak to him! How can I when I owe him? I can't tell a fellow he's a blackguard when I owe him, and I can't speak any other way. I ain't a diplomatist. Dashed if I know what to do!"

"Juliana," murmured his aunt.

"Can't ask her, you know."

Mrs. Shorne combated the one prominent reason for the objection: but there were two. Harry believed that he had exhausted Juliana's treasury. Reproaching him further for his wastefulness, Mrs. Shorne promised him the money should be got, by hook or by crook, next day.

"And you will speak to this Mr. Harrington to-night, Harry? No allusion to the loan till you return it. Appeal to his sense of honour."

The dinner-bell assembled the inmates of the house. Evan was not among them. He had gone, as the Countess said aloud, on a diplomatic mission to Fallow field, with Andrew Cogglesby. The truth being that he had finally taken Andrew into his confidence concerning the letter, the annuity, and the bond. Upon which occasion Andrew had burst into a laugh, and said he could lay his hand on the writer of the letter.

"Trust Old Tom for plots, Van! He'll blow you up in a twinkling, the cunning old dog! He pretends to be hard—he's as soft as I am, if it wasn't for his crotchets. We'll hand him back the cash, and that's ended. And—eh? what a dear girl she is! Not that I'm astonished. My Harry might have married a lord—sit at top of any table in the land! And you're as good as any man.

That's my opinion. But I say she's a wonderful girl to see it."

Chattering thus, Andrew drove with the dear boy into Fallow field. Evan was still in his dream. To him the generous love and valiant openness of Rose, though they were matched in his own bosom, seemed scarcely human. Almost as noble to him were the gentlemanly plainspeaking of Sir Franks and Lady Jocelyn's kind commonsense. But the more he esteemed them, the more unbounded and miraculous appeared the prospect of his calling their daughter by the sacred name, and kneeling with her at their feet. Did the dear heavens have that in store for him? The horizon edges were dimly lighted.

Harry looked about under his eye-lids for Evan, trying at the same time to compose himself for the martyrdom he had to endure in sitting at table with the presumptuous fellow. The Countess signalled him to come within the presence. As he was crossing the room, Rose entered, and moved to meet him, with: "Ah, Harry! back again! Glad to see you."

Harry gave her a blunt nod, to which she was inattentive.

"What!" whispered the Countess, after he pressed the tips of her fingers. "Have you brought back the grocer?"

Now this was hard to stand. Harry could forgive her her birth, and pass it utterly by if she chose to fall in love with him; but to hear the grocer mentioned, when he knew of the tailor, was a little too much, and what Harry felt his ingenuous countenance was accustomed to exhibit. The Countess saw it. She turned her head from him to the diplomatist, and he had to remain like a sentinel at her feet. He did not want to be thanked for the green box: still he thought she might have favoured him with one of her much-embracing smiles:

In the evening, after wine, when he was warm, and had almost forgotten the insult to his family and himself, the Countess snubbed him. It was unwise on her part, but she had the ghastly thought that facts were oozing out, and were already half known. She was therefore sensitive tenfold to appearances; savage if one failed to keep up her lie to her, and was guilty of a shadow of difference of behaviour. The picnic over, our General would evacuate Beckley Court, and shake the dust off her shoes, and leave the harvest of what she had sown to Providence. Till then, respect, and the honours of war! So the Countess snubbed him, and he being full of wine, fell into the hands of Juliana, who had witnessed the little scene.

"She has made a fool of others as well as of you," said Juliana.

"How has she?" he inquired.

"Never mind. Do you want to make her humble and crouch to you?"

"I want to see Harrington," said Harry.

"He will not return to-night from Fallow field. He has gone there to get Mr. Andrew Cogglesby's brother to do something for him. You won't have such another chance of humbling them both—both! I told you his mother is at an inn here. The Countess has sent Mr. Harrington to Fallow field to be out of the way, and she has told her mother all sorts of falsehoods."

"How do you know all that?" quoth Harry. "By Jove, Juley! talk about plotters! No keeping anything from you, ever!"

"Never mind. The mother is here. She must be a vulgar woman. Oh! if you could manage, Harry, to get this woman to come—you could do it so easily! while they are at the pie-nic tomorrow. It would have the best effect on Rose. She would then understand! And the Countess!"

"I could send the old woman a message!" cried Harry, rushing into the scheme, inspired by Juliana's fiery eyes. "Send her a sort of message to say where we all were."

"Let her know that her son is here, in some way," Juley resumed.

"And, egad! what an explosion!" pursued Harry. "But, suppose—"

"No one shall know, if you leave it to me-if you do just as I tell you, Harry. You won't be treated as you were this evening after that, if you bring down her pride. And, Harry, I hear you want money—I can give you some."

"You're a perfect trump, Juley!" exclaimed her enthusiastic cousin.

"But, no; I can't take it. I must kiss you, though."

He put a kiss upon her cheek. Once his kisses had left a red waxen stamp; she was callous to these compliments now.

"Will you do what I advise you to-morrow?" she asked.

After a slight hesitation, during which the olive-hued visage flitted faintly in the distances of his brain, Harry said:

"It'll do Rose good, and make Harrington cut. Yes! I declare I will."

Then they parted. Juliana went to her bed-room, and flung herself upon the bed hysterically. As the tears came thick and fast, she jumped up to lock the door, for this outrageous habit of crying had made her contemptible in the eyes of Lady Jocelyn, and an object of pity to Rose. Some excellent and noble natures cannot tolerate disease, and are mystified by its ebullitions. It was very sad to see the slight thin frame grasped by those wan hands to contain the violence of the frenzy that possessed her! the pale, hapless face rigid above the torment in her bosom! She had prayed to be loved like other girls, and her readiness to give her heart in return had made her a by-word in the house. She went to the window and leaned out on the casement, looking towards Fallowfield over the downs, weeping bitterly, with a hard shut mouth. One brilliant star hung above the ridge, and danced on her tears.

"Will he forgive me?" she murmured. "Oh, my God! I wish we were dead together!"

Her weeping ceased, and she closed the window, and undressed as far away from the mirror as she could get; but its force was too much for her, and drew her to it. Some undefined hope had sprung in her suddenly. With nervous slow steps she approached the glass, and first brushing back the masses of black hair from her brow, looked as for some new revelation. Long and anxiously she perused her features: the wide bony forehead; the eyes deep-set and rounded with the scarlet of recent tears, the thin nose-sharp as the dead; the weak irritable mouth and sunken cheeks. She gazed like a spirit disconnected from what she saw. Presently a sort of forlorn negative was indicated by the motion of her head.

"I can pardon him," she said, and sighed. "How could he love such a face!"

XXX

The Battle of the Bull-Dogs. Part I

At the South-western extremity of the park, with a view extending over wide meadows and troubled mill waters, yellow barn-roofs and weather-gray old farm-walls, two grassy mounds threw their slopes to the margin of the stream. Here the bull-dogs held revel. The hollow between the slopes was crowned by a bending birch, which rose three-stemmed from the root, and hung a noiseless green shower over the basin of green it shadowed. Beneath it the interminable growl sounded pleasantly; softly shot the sparkle of the twisting water, and you might dream things half-fulfilled. Knots of fern were about, but the tops of the mounds were firm grass, evidently well rolled, and with an eye to airy feet. Olympus one eminence was called, Parnassus the other. Olympus a little overlooked Parnassus, but Parnassus was broader and altogether better adapted for the games of the Muses. Round the edges of both there was a well-trimmed bush of laurel, obscuring only the feet of the dancers from the observing gods. For on Olympus the elders reclined. Great efforts had occasionally been made to dispossess and unseat them, and their security depended mainly on a hump in the middle of the mound which defied the dance.

Watteau-like groups were already couched in the shade. There were ladies of all sorts: town-bred and country-bred: farmers' daughters and daughters of peers: for this pic-nic, as Lady Jocelyn, disgusting the Countess, would call it, was in reality a "fete champetre", given annually, to which the fair offspring of the superior tenants were invited the brothers and fathers coming to fetch them in the evening. It struck the eye of the Countess de Saldar that Olympus would be a fitting throne for her, and a point whence her shafts might fly without fear of a return. Like another illustrious General at Salamanca, she directed a detachment to take possession of the height. Courtly Sir John Loring ran up at once, and gave the diplomatist an opportunity to thank her flatteringly for gaining them two minutes to themselves. Sir John waved his handkerchief in triumph, welcoming them under an awning where carpets and cushions were spread, and whence the Countess could eye the field. She was dressed ravishingly; slightly in a foreign style, the bodice being peaked at the waist, as was then the Portuguese persuasion. The neck, too, was deliciously veiled with fine lace—and thoroughly veiled, for it was a feature the Countess did not care to expose to the vulgar daylight. Off her gentle shoulders, as it were some fringe of cloud blown by the breeze this sweet lady opened her bosom to, curled a lovely black lace scarf: not Caroline's. If she laughed, the tinge of mourning lent her laughter new charms. If she sighed, the exuberant array of her apparel bade the spectator be of good cheer. Was she witty, men surrendered reason and adored her. Only when she entered the majestic mood, and assumed the languors of greatness, and recited musky anecdotes of her intimacy with it, only then did mankind, as represented at Beckley Court, open an internal eye and reflect that it was wonderful in a tailor's daughter. And she felt that mankind did so reflect. Her instincts did not deceive her. She knew not how much was known; in the depths of her heart she kept low the fear that possibly all might be known; and succeeding in this, she said to herself that probably nothing was known after all. George Uplift, Miss Carrington, and Rose, were the three she abhorred. Partly to be out of their way, and to be out of the way of chance shots (for she had heard names of people coming that reminded her of Dubbins's, where, in past days, there had been on one awful occasion a terrific discovery made), the Countess selected Olympus for her station. It was her last day, and she determined to be happy. Doubtless, she was making a retreat, but have not illustrious Generals snatched victory from their pursuers? Fair, then, sweet, and full of grace, the Countess moved. As the restless shifting of colours to her motions was the constant interchange of her semisorrowful manner and ready archness. Sir John almost capered to please her, and the diplomatist in talking to her forgot his diplomacy and the craft of his tongue.

It was the last day also of Caroline and the Duke. The Countess clung to Caroline and the Duke more than to Evan and Rose. She could see the first couple walking under an avenue of limes, and near them that young man or monkey, Raikes, as if in ambush. Twice they passed him, and twice he doffed his hat and did homage.

"A most singular creature!" exclaimed the Countess. "It is my constant marvel where my brother discovered such a curiosity. Do notice him."

"That man? Raikes?" said the diplomatist. "Do you know he is our rival? Harry wanted an excuse for another bottle last night, and proposed the 'Member' for Fallowfield. Up got this Mr. Raikes and returned thanks."

"Yes?" the Countess negligently interjected in a way she had caught from Lady Jocelyn.

"Cogglesby's nominee, apparently."

"I know it all," said the Countess. "We need have no apprehension. He is docile. My brother-in-law's brother, you see, is most eccentric. We can manage him best through this Mr. Raikes, for a personal application would be ruin. He quite detests our family, and indeed all the aristocracy."

Melville's mouth pursed, and he looked very grave.

Sir John remarked: "He seems like a monkey just turned into a man."

"And doubtful about the tail," added the Countess.

The image was tolerably correct, but other causes were at the bottom of the air worn by John Raikes. The Countess had obtained an invitation for him, with instructions that he should come early, and he had followed them so implicitly that the curricle was flinging dust on the hedges between Fallow field and Beckley but an hour or two after the chariot of Apollo had mounted the heavens, and Mr. Raikes presented himself at the breakfast table. Fortunately for him the Countess was there. After the repast she introduced him to the Duke: and he bowed to the Duke, and the Duke bowed to him: and now, to instance the peculiar justness in the mind of Mr. Raikes, he, though he worshipped a coronet and would gladly have recalled the feudal times to a corrupt land, could not help thinking that his bow had beaten the Duke's and was better. He would rather not have thought so, for it upset his preconceptions and threatened a revolution in his ideas. For this reason he followed the Duke, and tried, if possible, to correct, or at least chasten the impressions he had of possessing a glaring advantage over the nobleman. The Duke's second notice of him was hardly a nod. "Well!" Mr. Raikes reflected, "if this is your Duke, why, egad! for figure and style my friend Harrington beats him hollow." And Raikes thought he knew who could conduct a conversation with superior dignity and neatness. The torchlight of a delusion was extinguished in him, but he did not wander long in that gloomy cavernous darkness of the disenchanted, as many of us do, and as Evan had done, when after a week at Beckley Court he began to examine of what stuff his brilliant father, the great Mel, was composed. On the contrary, as the light of the Duke dwindled, Raikes gained in lustre. "In fact," he said, "there's nothing but the title wanting." He was by this time on a level with the Duke in his elastic mind.

Olympus had been held in possession by the Countess about half an hour, when Lady Jocelyn mounted it, quite unconscious that she was scaling a fortified point. The Countess herself fired off the first gun at her.

"It has been so extremely delightful up alone here, Lady Jocelyn: to look at everybody below! I hope many will not intrude on us!"

"None but the dowagers who have breath to get up," replied her ladyship, panting. "By the way, Countess, you hardly belong to us yet. You dance?"

"Indeed, I do not."

"Oh, then you are in your right place. A dowager is a woman who doesn't dance: and her male attendant is—what is he? We will call him a fogy."

Lady Jocelyn directed a smile at Melville and Sir John, who both protested that it was an honour to be the Countess's fogy.

Rose now joined them, with Laxley morally dragged in her wake.

"Another dowager and fogy!" cried the Countess, musically. "Do you not dance, my child?"

"Not till the music strikes up," rejoined Rose. "I suppose we shall have to eat first."

"That is the Hamlet of the pic-nic play, I believe," said her mother.

"Of course you dance, don't you, Countess?" Rose inquired, for the sake of amiable conversation.

The Countess's head signified: "Oh, no! quite out of the question": she held up a little bit of her mournful draperies, adding: "Besides, you, dear child, know your company, and can select; I do not, and cannot do so. I understand we have a most varied assembly!"

Rose shut her eyes, and then looked at her mother. Lady Jocelyn's face was undisturbed; but while her eyes were still upon the Countess, she drew her head gently back, imperceptibly. If anything, she was admiring the lady; but Rose could be no placid philosophic spectator of what was to her a horrible assumption and hypocrisy. For the sake of him she loved, she had swallowed a nauseous cup bravely. The Countess was too much for her. She felt sick to think of being allied to this person. She had a shuddering desire to run into the ranks of the world, and hide her head from multitudinous hootings. With a pang of envy she saw her friend Jenny walking by the side of William Harvey, happy, untried, unoffending: full of hope, and without any bitter draughts to swallow!

Aunt Bel now came tripping up gaily.

"Take the alternative, 'douairiere or demoiselle'?" cried Lady Jocelyn. "We must have a sharp distinction, or Olympus will be mobbed."

"Entre les deux, s'il vous plait," responded Aunt Bel. "Rose, hurry down, and leaven the mass. I see ten girls in a bunch. It's shocking. Ferdinand, pray disperse yourself. Why is it, Emily, that we are always in excess at pic-nics? Is man dying out?"

"From what I can see," remarked Lady Jocelyn, "Harry will be lost to his species unless some one quickly relieves him. He's already half eaten up by the Conley girls. Countess, isn't it your duty to rescue him?"

The Countess bowed, and murmured to Sir John:

"A dismissal!"

"I fear my fascinations, Lady Jocelyn, may not compete with those fresh young persons."

"Ha! ha! 'fresh young persons,'" laughed Sir John for the ladies in question were romping boisterously with Mr. Harry.

The Countess inquired for the names and condition of the ladies, and was told that they sprang from Farmer Conley, a well-to-do son of the soil, who farmed about a couple of thousand acres between Fallow field and Beckley, and bore a good reputation at the county bank.

"But I do think," observed the Countess, "it must indeed be pernicious for any youth to associate with that class of woman. A deterioration of manners!"

Rose looked at her mother again. She thought "Those girls would scorn to marry a tradesman's son!"

The feeling grew in Rose that the Countess lowered and degraded her. Her mother's calm contemplation of the lady was more distressing than if she had expressed the contempt Rose was certain, according to her young ideas, Lady Jocelyn must hold.

Now the Countess had been considering that she would like to have a word or two with Mr. Harry, and kissing her fingers to the occupants of Olympus, and fixing her fancy on the diverse thoughts of the ladies and gentlemen, deduced from a rapturous or critical contemplation of her figure from behind, she descended the slope.

Was it going to be a happy day? The well-imagined opinions of the gentleman on her attire and style, made her lean to the affirmative; but Rose's demure behaviour, and something—something would come across her hopes. She had, as she now said to herself, stopped for the pic-nic, mainly to give Caroline a last opportunity of binding the Duke to visit the Cogglesby saloons in London. Let Caroline cleverly contrive this, as she might, without any compromise, and the stay at Beckley Court would be a great gain. Yes, Caroline was still with the Duke; they were talking earnestly. The Countess breathed a short appeal to Providence that Caroline might not prove a fool. Overnight she had said to Caroline: "Do not be so English. Can one not enjoy friendship with a nobleman without wounding one's conscience or breaking with the world? My dear, the Duke visiting you, you cow that infamous Strike of yours. He will be utterly obsequious! I am not telling you to pass the line. The contrary. But we continentals have our grievous reputation because we dare to meet as intellectual beings, and defy the imputation that ladies and gentlemen are no better than animals."

It sounded very lofty to Caroline, who, accepting its sincerity, replied:

"I cannot do things by halves. I cannot live a life of deceit. A life of misery—not deceit."

Whereupon, pitying her poor English nature, the Countess gave her advice, and this advice she now implored her familiars to instruct or compel Caroline to follow.

The Countess's garment was plucked at. She beheld little Dorothy Loring glancing up at her with the roguish timidity of her years.

"May I come with you?" asked the little maid, and went off into a prattle: "I spent that five shillings—I bought a shilling's worth of sweet stuff, and nine penn'orth of twine, and a shilling for small wax candles to light in my room when I'm going to bed, because I like plenty of light by the looking-glass always, and they do make the room so hot! My Jane declared she almost fainted, but I burnt them out! Then I only had very little left for a horse to mount my doll on; and I wasn't going to get a screw, so I went to Papa, and he gave me five shillings. And, oh, do you know, Rose can't bear me to be with you. Jealousy, I suppose, for you're very agreeable. And, do you know, your Mama is coming to-day? I've got a Papa and no Mama, and you've got a Mama and no Papa. Isn't it funny? But I don't think so much of it, as you're grown up. Oh, I'm quite sure she is coming, because I heard Harry telling Juley she was, and Juley said it would be so gratifying to you."

A bribe and a message relieved the Countess of Dorothy's attendance on her.

What did this mean? Were people so base as to be guilty of hideous plots in this house? Her mother coming! The Countess's blood turned deadly chill. Had it been her father she would not have feared, but her mother was so vilely plain of speech; she never opened her mouth save to deliver facts: which was to the Countess the sign of atrocious vulgarity.

But her mother had written to say she would wait for Evan in Fallow field! The Countess grasped at straws. Did Dorothy hear that? And if Harry and Juliana spoke of her mother, what did that mean? That she was hunted, and must stand at bay!

"Oh, Papa! Papa! why did you marry a Dawley?" she exclaimed, plunging to what was, in her idea, the root of the evil.

She had no time for outcries and lamentations. It dawned on her that this was to be a day of battle. Where was Harry? Still in the midst of the Conley throng, apparently pooh-poohing something, to judge by the twist of his mouth.

The Countess delicately signed for him to approach her. The extreme delicacy of the signal was at least an excuse for Harry to perceive nothing. It was renewed, and Harry burst into a fit of laughter at some fun of one of the Conley girls. The Countess passed on, and met Juliana pacing by herself near the lower gates of the park. She wished only to see how Juliana behaved. The girl looked perfectly trustful, as much so as when the Countess was pouring in her ears the tales of Evan's growing but bashful affection for her.

"He will soon be here," whispered the Countess. "Has he told you he will come by this entrance?"

"No," replied Juliana.

"You do not look well, sweet child."

"I was thinking that you did not, Countess?"

"Oh, indeed, yes! With reason, alas! All our visitors have by this time arrived, I presume?"

"They come all day."

The Countess hastened away from one who, when roused, could be almost as clever as herself, and again stood in meditation near the joyful Harry. This time she did not signal so discreetly. Harry could not but see it, and the Conley girls accused him of cruelty to the beautiful dame, which novel idea stung Harry with delight, and he held out to indulge in it a little longer. His back was half turned, and as he talked noisily, he could not observe the serene and resolute march of the Countess toward him. The youth gaped when he found his arm taken prisoner by the insertion of a small deliciously-gloved and perfumed hand through it. "I must claim you for a few moments," said the Countess, and took the startled Conley girls one and all in her beautiful smile of excuse.

"Why do you compromise me thus, sir?"

These astounding words were spoken out of the hearing of the Conley girls.

"Compromise you!" muttered Harry.

Masterly was the skill with which the Countess contrived to speak angrily and as an injured woman, while she wore an indifferent social countenance.

"I repeat, compromise me. No, Mr. Harry Jocelyn, you are not the jackanapes you try to make people think you: you understand me."

The Countess might accuse him, but Harry never had the ambition to make people think him that: his natural tendency was the reverse: and he objected to the application of the word jackanapes to himself, and was ready to contest the fact of people having that opinion at all. However, all he did was to repeat: "Compromise!"

"Is not open unkindness to me compromising me?"

"How?" asked Harry.

"Would you dare to do it to a strange lady? Would you have the impudence to attempt it with any woman here but me? No, I am innocent; it is my consolation; I have resisted you, but you by this cowardly behaviour place me—and my reputation, which is more—at your mercy. Noble behaviour, Mr. Harry Jocelyn! I shall remember my young English gentleman."

The view was totally new to Harry.

"I really had no idea of compromising you," he said. "Upon my honour, I can't see how I did it now!"

"Oblige me by walking less in the neighbourhood of those fat-faced glaring farm-girls," the Countess spoke under her breath; "and don't look as if you were being whipped. The art of it is evident—you are but carrying on the game.—Listen. If you permit yourself to exhibit an unkindness to me, you show to any man who is a judge, and to every woman, that there has been something between us. You know my innocence—yes! but you must punish me for having resisted you thus long."

Harry swore he never had such an idea, and was much too much of a man and a gentleman to behave in that way.—And yet it seemed wonderfully clever! And here was the Countess saying:

"Take your reward, Mr. Harry Jocelyn. You have succeeded; I am your humble slave. I come to you and sue for peace. To save my reputation I endanger myself. This is generous of you."

"Am I such a clever fellow?" thought the young gentleman. "Deuced lucky with women": he knew that: still a fellow must be wonderfully, miraculously, clever to be able to twist and spin about such a woman as this in that way. He did not object to conceive that he was the fellow to do it. Besides, here was the Countess de Saldar-worth five hundred of the Conley girls—almost at his feet!

Mollified, he said: "Now, didn't you begin it?"

"Evasion!" was the answer. "It would be such pleasure to you so see a proud woman weep! And if yesterday, persecuted as I am, with dreadful falsehoods abroad respecting me and mine, if yesterday I did seem cold to your great merits, is it generous of you to take this revenge?"

Harry began to scent the double meaning in her words. She gave him no time to grow cool over it. She leaned, half abandoned, on his arm. Arts feminine and irresistible encompassed him. It was a fatal mistake of Juliana's to enlist Harry Jocelyn against the Countess de Saldar. He engaged, still without any direct allusion to the real business, to move heaven and earth to undo all that he had done, and the Countess implied an engagement to do—what? more than she intended to fulfil.

Ten minutes later she was alone with Caroline.

"Tie yourself to the Duke at the dinner," she said, in the forcible phrase she could use when necessary. "Don't let them scheme to separate you. Never mind looks—do it!"

Caroline, however, had her reasons for desiring to maintain appearances. The Countess dashed at her hesitation.

"There is a plot to humiliate us in the most abominable way. The whole family have sworn to make us blush publicly. Publicly blush! They have written to Mama to come and speak out. Now will you attend to me, Caroline? You do not credit such atrocity? I know it to be true."

"I never can believe that Rose would do such a thing," said Caroline. "We can hardly have to endure more than has befallen us already."

Her speech was pensive, as of one who had matter of her own to ponder over. A swift illumination burst in the Countess's mind.

"No? Have you, dear, darling Carry? not that I intend that you should! but to-day the Duke would be such ineffable support to us. May I deem you have not been too cruel to-day? You dear silly English creature, 'Duck,' I used to call you when I was your little Louy. All is not yet lost, but I will save you from the ignominy if I can. I will!"

Caroline denied nothing—confirmed nothing, just as the Countess had stated nothing. Yet they understood one another perfectly. Women have a subtler language than ours: the veil pertains to them morally as bodily, and they see clearer through it.

The Countess had no time to lose. Wrath was in her heart. She did not lend all her thoughts to self-defence.

Without phrasing a word, or absolutely shaping a thought in her head, she slanted across the sun to Mr. Raikes, who had taken refreshment, and in obedience to his instinct, notwithstanding his enormous pretensions, had commenced a few preliminary antics.

"Dear Mr. Raikes!" she said, drawing him aside, "not before dinner!"

"I really can't contain the exuberant flow!" returned that gentleman. "My animal spirits always get the better of me," he added confidentially.

"Suppose you devote your animal spirits to my service for half an hour."

"Yours, Countess, from the 'os frontis' to the chine!" was the exuberant rejoinder.

The Countess made a wry mouth.

"Your curricle is in Beckley?"

"Behold!" said Jack. "Two juveniles, not half so blest as I, do from the seat regard the festive scene o'er yon park palings. They are there, even Franko and Fred. I'm afraid I promised to get them in at a later period of the day. Which sadly sore my conscience doth disturb! But what is to be done about the curricle, my Countess?"

"Mr. Raikes," said the Countess, smiling on him fixedly, "you are amusing; but in addressing me, you must be precise, and above all things accurate. I am not your Countess!"

He bowed profoundly. "Oh, that I might say my Queen!"

The Countess replied: "A conviction of your lunacy would prevent my taking offence, though I might wish you enclosed and guarded."

Without any further exclamations, Raikes acknowledged a superior.

"And, now, attend to me," said the Countess. "Listen:

You go yourself, or send your friends instantly to Fallow field. Bring with you that girl and her child. Stop: there is such a person. Tell her she is to be spoken to about the prospects of the poor infant. I leave that to your inventive genius. Evan wishes her here. Bring her, and should you see the mad captain who behaves so oddly, favour him with a ride. He says he dreams his wife is here, and he will not reveal his name! Suppose it should be my own beloved husband! I am quite anxious."

The Countess saw him go up to the palings and hold a communication with his friends Franko and Fred. One took the whip, and after mutual flourishes, drove away.

"Now!" mused the Countess, "if Captain Evremonde should come!" It would break up the pic-nic. Alas! the Countess had surrendered her humble hopes of a day's pleasure. But if her mother came as well, what a diversion that would be! If her mother came before the Captain, his arrival would cover the retreat; if the Captain preceded her, she would not be noticed. Suppose her mother refrained from coming? In that case it was a pity, but the Jocelyns had brought it on themselves.

This mapping out of consequences followed the Countess's deeds, and did not inspire them. Her passions sharpened her instincts, which produced her actions. The reflections ensued: as in nature, the consequences were all seen subsequently! Observe the difference between your male and female Generals.

On reflection, too, the Countess praised herself for having done all that could be done. She might have written to her mother: but her absence would have been remarked: her messenger might have been overhauled and, lastly, Mrs. Mel—"Gorgon of a mother!" the Countess cried out: for Mrs. Mel was like a Fate to her. She could remember only two occasions in her whole life when she had been able to manage her mother, and then by lying in such a way as to distress her conscience severely.

"If Mama has conceived this idea of coming, nothing will impede her. My prayers will infuriate her!" said the Countess, and she was sure that she had acted both rightly and with wisdom.

She put on her armour of smiles: she plunged into the thick of the enemy. Since they would not allow her to taste human happiness—she had asked but for the pic-nic! a small truce! since they denied her that, rather than let them triumph by seeing her wretched, she took into her bosom the joy of demons. She lured Mr. George Uplift away from Miss Carrington, and spoke to him strange hints of matrimonial disappointments, looking from time to time at that apprehensive lady, doating on her terrors. And Mr. George seconded her by his clouded face, for he was ashamed not to show that he did not know Louisa Harrington in the Countess de Saldar, and had not the courage to declare that he did. The Countess spoke familiarly, but without any hint of an ancient acquaintance between them. "What a post her husband's got!" thought Mr. George, not envying the Count. He was wrong: she was an admirable ally. All over the field the Countess went, watching for her mother, praying that if she did come, Providence might prevent her from coming while they were at dinner. How clearly Mrs. Shorne and Mrs. Melville saw her vulgarity now! By the new light of knowledge, how certain they were that they had seen her ungentle training in a dozen little instances.

"She is not well-bred, 'cela se voit'," said Lady Jocelyn.

"Bred! it's the stage! How could such a person be bred?" said Mrs. Shorne.

Accept in the Countess the heroine who is combating class-prejudices, and surely she is pre-eminently noteworthy. True, she fights only for her family, and is virtually the champion of the opposing institution misplaced. That does not matter: the Fates may have done it purposely: by conquering she establishes a principle. A Duke adores her sister, the daughter of the house her brother, and for herself she has many protestations in honour of her charms: nor are they empty ones. She can confound Mrs. Melville, if she pleases to, by exposing an adorer to lose a friend. Issuing out of Tailordom, she, a Countess, has done all this; and it were enough to make her glow, did not little evils, and angers, and spites, and alarms so frightfully beset her.

The sun of the pic-nic system is dinner. Hence philosophers may deduce that the pic-nic is a British invention. There is no doubt that we do not shine at the pic-nic until we reflect the face of dinner. To this, then, all who were not lovers began seriously to look forward, and the advance of an excellent county band, specially hired to play during the entertainment, gave many of the guests quite a new taste for sweet music; and indeed we all enjoy a thing infinitely more when we see its meaning.

About this time Evan entered the lower park-gates with Andrew. The first object he encountered was John Raikes in a state of great depression. He explained his case:

"Just look at my frill! Now, upon my honour, you know, I'm good-tempered; I pass their bucolic habits, but this is beyond bearing. I was near the palings there, and a fellow calls out, 'Hi! will you help the lady over?' Holloa! thinks I, an adventure! However, I advised him to take her round to the gates. The beast burst out laughing. 'Now, then,' says he, and I heard a scrambling at the pales, and up came the head of a dog. 'Oh! the dog first,' says I. 'Catch by the ears,' says he. I did so. 'Pull,' says he. ''Gad, pull indeed!', The beast gave a spring and came slap on my chest, with his dirty wet muzzle on my neck! I felt instantly it was the death of my frill, but gallant as you know me, I still asked for the lady. 'If you will please, or an it meet your favour, to extend your hand to me!' I confess I did think it rather odd, the idea of a lady coming in that way over the palings! but my curst love of adventure always blinds me. It always misleads my better sense, Harrington. Well, instead of a lady, I see a fellow—he may have been a lineal descendant of Cedric the Saxon. 'Where's the lady?' says I. 'Lady?' says he, and stares, and then laughs: 'Lady! why,' he jumps over, and points at his beast of a dog, 'don't you know a bitch when you see one?' I was in the most ferocious rage! If he hadn't been a big burly bully, down he'd have gone. 'Why didn't you say what it was?' I roared. 'Why,' says he, 'the word isn't considered polite!' I gave him a cut there. I said, 'I rejoice to be positively assured that you uphold the laws and forms of civilization, sir.' My belief is he didn't feel it."

"The thrust sinned in its shrewdness," remarked Evan, ending a laugh.

"Hem!" went Mr. Raikes, more contentedly: "after all, what are appearances to the man of wit and intellect? Dress, and women will approve you: but I assure you they much prefer the man of wit in his slouched hat and stockings down. I was introduced to the Duke this morning. It is a curious thing that the seduction of a Duchess has always been one of my dreams."

At this Andrew Cogglesby fell into a fit of laughter.

"Your servant," said Mr. Raikes, turning to him. And then he muttered "Extraordinary likeness! Good Heavens! Powers!"

From a state of depression, Mr. Raikes—changed into one of bewilderment. Evan paid no attention to him, and answered none of his hasty undertoned questions. Just then, as they were on the skirts of the company, the band struck up a lively tune, and quite unconsciously, the legs of Raikes, affected, it may be, by supernatural reminiscences, loosely hornpiped. It was but a moment: he remembered himself the next: but in that fatal moment eyes were on him. He never recovered his dignity in Beckley Court: he was fatally mercurial.

"What is the joke against this poor fellow?" asked Evan of Andrew.

"Never mind, Van. You'll roar. Old Tom again. We'll see by-and-by, after the champagne. He—this young Raikes-ha! ha!—but I can't tell you." And Andrew went away to Drummond, to whom he was more communicative. Then he went to Melville, and one or two others, and the eyes of many became concentrated on Raikes, and it was observed as a singular sign that he was constantly facing about, and flushing the fiercest red. Once he made an effort to get hold of Evan's arm and drag him away, as one who had an urgent confession to be delivered of, but Evan was talking to Lady Jocelyn, and other ladies, and quietly disengaged his arm without even turning to notice the face of his friend. Then the dinner was announced, and men saw the dinner. The Countess went to shake her brother's hand, and with a very gratulatory visage, said through her half-shut teeth.

"If Mama appears, rise up and go away with her, before she has time to speak a word." An instant after Evan found himself seated between Mrs. Evremonde and one of the Conley girls. The dinner had commenced. The first half of the Battle of the Bull-dogs was as peaceful as any ordinary pic-nic, and promised to the general company as calm a conclusion.

XXXI

The Battle of the Bull-Dogs. Part II

If it be a distinct point of wisdom to hug the hour that is, then does dinner amount to a highly intellectual invitation to man, for it furnishes the occasion; and Britons are the wisest of their race, for more than all others they take advantage of it. In this Nature is undoubtedly our guide, seeing that he who, while feasting his body allows to his soul a thought for the morrow, is in his digestion curst, and becomes a house of evil humours. Now, though the epicure may complain of the cold meats, a dazzling table, a buzzing company, blue sky, and a band of music, are incentives to the forgetfulness of troubles past and imminent, and produce a concentration of the faculties. They may not exactly prove that peace is established between yourself and those who object to your carving of the world, but they testify to an armistice.

Aided by these observations, you will understand how it was that the Countess de Saldar, afflicted and menaced, was inspired, on taking her seat, to give so graceful and stately a sweep to her dress that she was enabled to conceive woman and man alike to be secretly overcome by it. You will not refuse to credit the fact that Mr. Raikes threw care to the dogs, heavy as was that mysterious lump suddenly precipitated on his bosom; and you will think it not impossible that even the springers of the mine about to explode should lose their subterranean countenances. A generous abandonment to one idea prevailed. As for Evan, the first glass of champagne rushed into reckless nuptials with the music in his head, bringing Rose, warm almost as life, on his heart. Sublime are the visions of lovers! He knew he must leave her on the morrow; he feared he might never behold her again; and yet he tasted bliss, for it seemed within the contemplation of the Gods that he should dance with his darling before dark-haply waltz with her! Oh, heaven! he shuts his eyes, blinded. The band wheels off meltingly in a tune all cadences, and twirls, and risings and sinkings, and passionate outbursts trippingly consoled. Ah! how sweet to waltz through life with the right partner. And what a singular thing it is to look back on the day when we thought something like it! Never mind: there may be spheres where it is so managed—doubtless the planets have their Hanwell and Bedlam.

I confess that the hand here writing is not insensible to the effects of that first glass of champagne. The poetry of our Countess's achievements waxes rich in manifold colours: I see her by the light of her own pleas to Providence. I doubt almost if the hand be mine which dared to make a hero play second fiddle, and to his beloved. I have placed a bushel over his light, certainly. Poor boy! it was enough that he should have tailordom on his shoulders: I ought to have allowed him to conquer Nature, and so come out of his eclipse. This shall be said of him: that he can play second fiddle without looking foolish, which, for my part, I call a greater triumph than if he were performing the heroics we are more accustomed to. He has steady eyes, can gaze at the right level into the eyes of others, and commands a tongue which is neither struck dumb nor set in a flutter by any startling question. The best instances to be given that he does not lack merit are that the Jocelyns, whom he has offended by his birth, cannot change their treatment of him, and that the hostile women, whatever they may say, do not think Rose utterly insane. At any rate, Rose is satisfied, and her self-love makes her a keen critic. The moment Evan appeared, the sickness produced in her by the Countess passed, and she was ready to brave her situation. With no mock humility she permitted Mrs. Shorne to place her in a seat where glances could not be interchanged. She was quite composed, calmly prepared for conversation with any one. Indeed, her behaviour since the hour of general explanation had been so perfectly well-contained, that Mrs. Melville said to Lady Jocelyn:

"I am only thinking of the damage to her. It will pass over—this fancy. You can see she is not serious. It is mere spirit of opposition. She eats and drinks just like other girls. You can see that the fancy has not taken such very strong hold of her."

"I can't agree with you," replied her ladyship. "I would rather have her sit and sigh by the hour, and loathe roast beef. That would look nearer a cure."

"She has the notions of a silly country girl," said Mrs. Shorne.

"Exactly," Lady Jocelyn replied. "A season in London will give her balance."

So the guests were tolerably happy, or at least, with scarce an exception, open to the influences of champagne and music. Perhaps Juliana was the wretchedest creature present. She was about to smite on both cheeks him she loved, as well as the woman she despised and had been foiled by. Still she had the consolation that Rose, seeing the vulgar mother, might turn from Evan: a poor distant hope, meagre and shapeless like herself. Her most anxious thoughts concerned the means of getting money to lockup Harry's tongue. She could bear to meet the Countess's wrath, but not Evan's offended look. Hark to that Countess!

"Why do you denominate this a pic-nic, Lady Jocelyn? It is in verity a fete!"

"I suppose we ought to lie down 'A la Grecque' to come within the term," was the reply. "On the whole, I prefer plain English for such matters."

"But this is assuredly too sumptuous for a pic-nic, Lady Jocelyn. From what I can remember, pic-nic implies contribution from all the guests. It is true I left England a child!"

Mr. George Uplift could not withhold a sharp grimace: The Countess had throttled the inward monitor that tells us when we are lying, so grievously had she practised the habit in the service of her family.

"Yes," said Mrs. Melville, "I have heard of that fashion, and very stupid it is."

"Extremely vulgar," murmured Miss Carrington.

"Possibly," Lady Jocelyn observed; "but good fun. I have been to pic-nics, in my day. I invariably took cold pie and claret. I clashed with half-a-dozen, but all the harm we did was to upset the dictum that there can be too much of a good thing. I know for certain that the bottles were left empty."

"And this woman," thought the Countess, "this woman, with a soul so essentially vulgar, claims rank above me!" The reflection generated contempt of English society, in the first place, and then a passionate desire for self-assertion.

She was startled by a direct attack which aroused her momentarily lulled energies.

A lady, quite a stranger, a dry simpering lady, caught the Countess's benevolent passing gaze, and leaning forward, said: "I hope her ladyship bears her affliction as well as can be expected?"

In military parlance, the Countess was taken in flank. Another would have asked—What ladyship? To whom do you allude, may I beg to inquire? The Countess knew better. Rapid as light it shot through her that the relict of Sir Abraham was meant, and this she divined because she was aware that devilish malignity was watching to trip her.

A little conversation happening to buzz at the instant, the Countess merely turned her chin to an angle, agitated her brows very gently, and crowned the performance with a mournful smile. All that a woman must feel at the demise of so precious a thing as a husband, was therein eloquently expressed: and at the same time, if explanations ensued, there were numerous ladyships in the world, whom the Countess did not mind afflicting, should she be hard pressed.

"I knew him so well!" resumed the horrid woman, addressing anybody. "It was so sad! so unexpected! but he was so subject to affection of the throat. And I was so sorry I could not get down to him in time. I had not seen him since his marriage, when I was a girl!—and to meet one of his children!—But, my dear, in quinsey, I have heard that there is nothing on earth like a good hearty laugh."

Mr. Raikes hearing this, sucked down the flavour of a glass of champagne, and with a look of fierce jollity, interposed, as if specially charged by Providence to make plain to the persecuted Countess his mission and business there: "Then our vocation is at last revealed to us! Quinsey-doctor! I remember when a boy, wandering over the paternal mansion, and envying the life of a tinker, which my mother did not think a good omen in me. But the traps of a Quinsey-doctor are even lighter. Say twenty good jokes, and two or three of a practical kind. A man most enviable!"

"It appears," he remarked aloud to one of the Conley girls, "that quinsey is needed before a joke is properly appreciated."

"I like fun," said she, but had not apparently discovered it.

What did that odious woman mean by perpetually talking about Sir Abraham? The Countess intercepted a glance between her and the hated Juliana. She felt it was a malignant conspiracy: still the vacuous vulgar air of the woman told her that most probably she was but an instrument, not a confederate, and was only trying to push herself into acquaintance with the great: a proceeding scorned and abominated by the Countess, who longed to punish her for her insolent presumption. The bitterness of her situation stung her tenfold when she considered that she dared not.

Meantime the champagne became as regular in its flow as the Bull-dogs, and the monotonous bass of these latter sounded through the music, like life behind the murmur of pleasure, if you will. The Countess had a not unfeminine weakness for champagne, and old Mr. Bonner's cellar was well and choicely stocked. But was this enjoyment to the Countess?—this dreary station in the background! "May I emerge?" she as much as implored Providence.

The petition was infinitely tender. She thought she might, or it may be that nature was strong, and she could not restrain herself.

Taking wine with Sir John, she said:

"This bowing! Do you know how amusing it is deemed by us Portuguese? Why not embrace? as the dear Queen used to say to me."

"I am decidedly of Her Majesty's opinion," observed Sir John, with emphasis, and the Countess drew back into a mingled laugh and blush.

Her fiendish persecutor gave two or three nods. "And you know the Queen!" she said.

She had to repeat the remark: whereupon the Countess murmured, "Intimately."

"Ah, we have lost a staunch old Tory in Sir Abraham," said the lady, performing lamentation.

What did it mean? Could design lodge in that empty-looking head with its crisp curls, button nose, and diminishing simper? Was this picnic to be made as terrible to the Countess by her putative father as the dinner had been by the great Mel? The deep, hard, level look of Juliana met the Countess's smile from time to time, and like flimsy light horse before a solid array of infantry, the Countess fell back, only to be worried afresh by her perfectly unwitting tormentor.

"His last days?—without pain? Oh, I hope so!" came after a lapse of general talk.

"Aren't we getting a little funereal, Mrs. Perkins?" Lady Jocelyn asked, and then rallied her neighbours.

Miss Carrington looked at her vexedly, for the fiendish Perkins was checked, and the Countess in alarm, about to commit herself, was a pleasant sight to Miss Carrington.

"The worst of these indiscriminate meetings is that there is no conversation," whispered the Countess, thanking Providence for the relief.

Just then she saw Juliana bend her brows at another person. This was George Uplift, who shook his head, and indicated a shrewd-eyed, thin, middle-aged man, of a lawyer-like cast; and then Juliana nodded, and George Uplift touched his arm, and glanced hurriedly behind for champagne. The Countess's eyes dwelt on the timid young squire most affectionately. You never saw a fortress more unprepared for dread assault.

"Hem!" was heard, terrific. But the proper pause had evidently not yet come, and now to prevent it the Countess strained her energies and tasked her genius intensely. Have you an idea of the difficulty of keeping up the ball among a host of ill-assorted, stupid country people, who have no open topics, and can talk of nothing continuously but scandal of their neighbours, and who, moreover, feel they are not up to the people they are mixing with? Darting upon Seymour Jocelyn, the Countess asked touchingly for news of the partridges. It was like the unlocking of a machine. Seymour was not blythe in his reply, but he was loud and forcible; and when he came to the statistics—oh, then you would have admired the Countess!—for comparisons ensued, braces were enumerated, numbers given were contested, and the shooting of this one jeered at, and another's sure mark respectfully admitted. And how lay the coveys? And what about the damage done by last winter's floods? And was there good hope of the pheasants? Outside this latter the Countess hovered. Twice the awful "Hem!" was heard. She fought on. She kept them at it. If it flagged she wished to know this or that, and finally thought that, really, she should like herself to try one shot. The women had previously been left behind. This brought in the women. Lady Jocelyn proposed a female expedition for the morrow.

"I believe I used to be something of a shot, formerly," she said.

"You peppered old Tom once, my lady," remarked Andrew, and her ladyship laughed, and that foolish Andrew told the story, and the Countess, to revive her subject, had to say: "May I be enrolled to shoot?" though she detested and shrank from fire-arms.

"Here are two!" said the hearty presiding dame. "Ladies, apply immediately to have your names put down."

The possibility of an expedition of ladies now struck Seymour vividly, and said he: "I'll be secretary"; and began applying to the ladies for permission to put down their names. Many declined, with brevity, muttering, either aloud or to themselves, "unwomanly"; varied by "unladylike": some confessed cowardice; some a horror of the noise close to their ears; and there was the plea of nerves. But the names of half-a-dozen ladies were collected, and then followed much laughter, and musical hubbub, and delicate banter. So the ladies and gentlemen fell one and all into the partridge pit dug for them by the Countess: and that horrible "Hem!" equal in force and terror to the roar of artillery preceding the charge of ten thousand dragoons, was silenced—the pit appeared impassable. Did the Countess crow over her advantage? Mark her: the lady's face is entirely given up to partridges. "English sports are so much envied abroad," she says: but what she dreads is a reflection, for that leads off from the point. A portion of her mind she keeps to combat them in Lady Jocelyn and others who have the tendency: the rest she divides between internal-prayers for succour, and casting about for another popular subject to follow partridges. Now, mere talent, as critics say when they are lighting candles round a genius, mere talent would have hit upon pheasants as the natural sequitur, and then diverged to sports—a great theme, for it ensures a chorus of sneers at foreigners, and so on probably to a discussion of birds and beasts best adapted to enrapture the palate of man. Stories may succeed, but they are doubtful, and not to be trusted, coming after cookery. After an exciting subject which has made the general tongue to wag, and just enough heated the brain to cause it to cry out for spiced food—then start your story: taking care that it be mild; for one too marvellous stops the tide, the sense of climax being strongly implanted in all bosoms. So the Countess told an anecdote—one of Mel's. Mr. George Uplift was quite familiar with it, and knew of one passage that would have abashed him to relate "before ladies." The sylph-like ease with which the Countess floated over this foul abysm was miraculous. Mr. George screwed his eye-lids queerly, and closed his jaws with a report, completely beaten. The anecdote was of the character of an apologue, and pertained to game. This was, as it happened, a misfortune; for Mr. Raikes had felt himself left behind by the subject; and the stuff that was in this young man being naturally ebullient, he lay by to trip it, and take a lead. His remarks brought on him a shrewd cut from the Countess, which made matters worse; for a pun may also breed puns, as doth an anecdote. The Countess's stroke was so neat and perfect that it was something for the gentlemen to think over; and to punish her for giving way to her cleverness and to petty vexation, "Hem!" sounded once more, and then: "May I ask you if the present Baronet is in England?"

Now Lady Jocelyn perceived that some attack was directed against her guest. She allowed the Countess to answer:

"The eldest was drowned in the Lisbon waters"

And then said: "But who is it that persists in serving up the funeral baked meats to us?"

Mrs. Shorne spoke for her neighbour: "Mr. Farnley's cousin was the steward of Sir Abraham Harrington's estates."

The Countess held up her head boldly. There is a courageous exaltation of the nerves known to heroes and great generals in action when they feel sure that resources within themselves will spring up to the emergency, and that over simple mortals success is positive.

"I had a great respect for Sir Abraham," Mr. Farnley explained, "very great. I heard that this lady" (bowing to the Countess) "was his daughter."

Lady Jocelyn's face wore an angry look, and Mrs. Shorne gave her the shade of a shrug and an expression implying, "I didn't!"

Evan was talking to Miss Jenny Graine at the moment rather earnestly. With a rapid glance at him, to see that his ears were closed, the Countess breathed:

"Not the elder branch!—Cadet!"

The sort of noisy silence produced by half-a-dozen people respirating deeply and moving in their seats was heard. The Countess watched Mr. Farnley's mystified look, and whispered to Sir John: "Est-ce qu'il comprenne le Francais, lui?"

It was the final feather-like touch to her triumph. She saw safety and a clear escape, and much joyful gain, and the pleasure of relating her sufferings in days to come. This vista was before her when, harsh as an execution bell, telling her that she had vanquished man, but that Providence opposed her, "Mrs. Melchisedec Harrington!" was announced to Lady Jocelyn.

Perfect stillness reigned immediately, as if the pic-nic had heard its doom.

"Oh! I will go to her," said her ladyship, whose first thought was to spare the family. "Andrew, come and give me your arm."

But when she rose Mrs. Mel was no more than the length of an arm from her elbow.

In the midst of the horrible anguish she was enduring, the Countess could not help criticizing her mother's curtsey to Lady Jocelyn. Fine, but a shade too humble. Still it was fine; all might not yet be lost.

"Mama!" she softly exclaimed, and thanked heaven that she had not denied her parent.

Mrs. Mel did not notice her or any of her children. There was in her bosom a terrible determination to cast a devil out of the one she best loved. For this purpose, heedless of all pain to be given, or of impropriety, she had come to speak publicly, and disgrace and humiliate, that she might save him from the devils that had ruined his father.

"My lady," said the terrible woman, thanking her in reply to an invitation that she should be seated, "I have come for my son. I hear he has been playing the lord in your house, my lady. I humbly thank your ladyship for your kindness to him, but he is nothing more than a tailor's son, and is bound a tailor himself that his father may be called an honest man. I am come to take him away."

Mrs. Mel seemed to speak without much effort, though the pale flush of her cheeks showed that she felt what she was doing. Juliana was pale as death, watching Rose. Intensely bright with the gem-like light of her gallant spirit, Rose's eyes fixed on Evan. He met them. The words of Ruth passed through his heart. But the Countess, who had given Rose to Evan, and the Duke to Caroline, where was her supporter? The Duke was entertaining Caroline with no less dexterity, and Rose's eyes said to Evan: "Feel no shame that I do not feel!" but the Countess stood alone. It is ever thus with genius! to quote the numerous illustrious authors who have written of it.

What mattered it now that in the dead hush Lady Jocelyn should assure her mother that she had been misinformed, and that Mrs. Mel was presently quieted, and made to sit with others before the fruits and wines? All eyes were hateful—the very thought of Providence confused her brain. Almost reduced to imbecility, the Countess imagined, as a reality, that Sir Abraham had borne with her till her public announcement of relationship, and that then the outraged ghost would no longer be restrained, and had struck this blow.

The crushed pic-nic tried to get a little air, and made attempts at conversation. Mrs. Mel sat upon the company with the weight of all tailordom.

And now a messenger came for Harry. Everybody was so zealously employed in the struggle to appear comfortable under Mrs. Mel, that his departure was hardly observed. The general feeling for Evan and his sisters, by their superiors in rank, was one of kindly pity. Laxley, however, did not behave well. He put up his glass and scrutinized Mrs. Mel, and then examined Evan, and Rose thought that in his interchange of glances with any one there was a lurking revival of the scene gone by. She signalled with her eyebrows for Drummond to correct him, but Drummond had another occupation. Andrew made the diversion. He whispered to his neighbour, and the whisper went round, and the laugh; and Mr. Raikes grew extremely uneasy in his seat, and betrayed an extraordinary alarm. But he also was soon relieved. A messenger had come from Harry to Mrs. Evremonde, bearing a slip of paper. This the lady glanced at, and handed it to Drummond. A straggling pencil had traced these words:

"Just running by S.W. gates—saw the Captain coming in—couldn't stop to stop him—tremendous hurry—important. Harry J."

Drummond sent the paper to Lady Jocelyn. After her perusal of it a scout was despatched to the summit of Olympus, and his report proclaimed the advance in the direction of the Bull-dogs of a smart little figure of a man in white hat and white trousers, who kept flicking his legs with a cane.

Mrs. Evremonde rose and conferred with her ladyship an instant, and then Drummond took her arm quietly, and passed round Olympus to the East, and Lady Jocelyn broke up the sitting.

Juliana saw Rose go up to Evan, and make him introduce her to his mother. She turned lividly white, and went to a corner of the park by herself, and cried bitterly.

Lady Jocelyn, Sir Franks, and Sir John, remained by the tables, but before the guests were out of ear-shot, the individual signalled from Olympus presented himself.

"There are times when one can't see what else to do but to lie," said her ladyship to Sir Franks, "and when we do lie the only way is to lie intrepidly."

Turning from her perplexed husband, she exclaimed:

"Ah! Lawson?"

Captain Evremonde lifted his hat, declining an intimacy.

"Where is my wife, madam?"

"Have you just come from the Arctic Regions?"

"I have come for my wife, madam!"

His unsettled grey eyes wandered restlessly on Lady Jocelyn's face. The Countess standing near the Duke, felt some pity for the wife of that cropped-headed, tight-skinned lunatic at large, but deeper was the Countess's pity for Lady Jocelyn, in thinking of the account she would have to render on the Day of Judgement, when she heard her ladyship reply—

"Evelyn is not here."

Captain Evremonde bowed profoundly, trailing his broad white hat along the sward.

"Do me the favour to read this, madam," he said, and handed a letter to her.

Lady Jocelyn raised her brows as she gathered the contents of the letter.

"Ferdinand's handwriting!" she exclaimed.

"I accuse no one, madam,—I make no accusation. I have every respect for you, madam,—you have my esteem. I am sorry to intrude, madam, an intrusion is regretted. My wife runs away from her bed, madam, and I have the law, madam, the law is with the husband. No force!" He lashed his cane sharply against his white legs. "The law, madam. No brute force!" His cane made a furious whirl, cracking again on his legs, as he reiterated, "The law!"

"Does the law advise you to strike at a tangent all over the country in search for her?" inquired Lady Jocelyn.

Captain Evremonde became ten times more voluble and excited.

Mrs. Mel was heard by the Countess to say: "Her ladyship does not know how to treat madmen."

Nor did Sir Franks and Sir John. They began expostulating with him.

"A madman gets madder when you talk reason to him," said Mrs. Mel.

And now the Countess stepped forward to Lady Jocelyn, and hoped she would not be thought impertinent in offering her opinion as to how this frantic person should be treated. The case indeed looked urgent. Many gentlemen considered themselves bound to approach and be ready in case of need. Presently the Countess passed between Sir Franks and Sir John, and with her hand put up, as if she feared the furious cane, said:

"You will not strike me?"

"Strike a lady, madam?" The cane and hat were simultaneously lowered.

"Lady Jocelyn permits me to fetch for you a gentleman of the law. Or will you accompany me to him?"

In a moment, Captain Evremonde's manners were subdued and civilized, and in perfectly sane speech he thanked the Countess and offered her his arm. The Countess smilingly waved back Sir John, who motioned to attend on her, and away she went with the Captain, with all the glow of a woman who feels that she is heaping coals of fire on the heads of her enemies.

Was she not admired now?

"Upon my honour," said Lady Jocelyn, "they are a remarkable family," meaning the Harringtons.

What farther she thought she did not say, but she was a woman who looked to natural gifts more than the gifts of accidents; and Evan's chance stood high with her then. So the battle of the Bull-dogs was fought, and cruelly as the Countess had been assailed and wounded, she gained a victory; yea, though Demogorgon, aided by the vindictive ghost of Sir Abraham, took tangible shape in the ranks opposed to her. True, Lady Jocelyn, forgetting her own recent intrepidity, condemned her as a liar; but the fruits of the Countess's victory were plentiful. Drummond Forth, fearful perhaps of exciting unjust suspicions in the mind of Captain Evremonde, disappeared altogether. Harry was in a mess which threw him almost upon Evan's mercy, as will be related. And, lastly, Ferdinand Laxley, that insufferable young aristocrat, was thus spoken to by Lady Jocelyn.

"This letter addressed to Lawson, telling him that his wife is here, is in your handwriting, Ferdinand. I don't say you wrote it—I don't think you could have written it. But, to tell you the truth, I have an unpleasant impression about it, and I think we had better shake hands and not see each other for some time."

Laxley, after one denial of his guilt, disdained to repeat it. He met her ladyship's hand haughtily, and, bowing to Sir Franks, turned on his heel.

So, then, in glorious complete victory, the battle of the Bull-dogs ended!

Of the close of the pic-nic more remains to be told.

For the present I pause, in observance of those rules which demand that after an exhibition of consummate deeds, time be given to the spectator to digest what has passed before him.

BOOK VI

XXXII

In which Evan's Light Begins to Twinkle Again

The dowagers were now firmly planted on Olympus. Along the grass lay the warm strong colours of the evening sun, reddening the pine-stems and yellowing the idle aspen-leaves. For a moment it had hung in doubt whether the pic-nic could survive the two rude shocks it had received. Happily the youthful element was large, and when the band, refreshed by chicken and sherry, threw off half-a-dozen bars of one of those irresistible waltzes that first catch the ear, and then curl round the heart, till on a sudden they invade and will have the legs, a rush up Parnassus was seen, and there were shouts and laughter and commotion, as over other great fields of battle the corn will wave gaily and mark the reestablishment of nature's reign.

How fair the sight! Approach the twirling couples. They talk as they whirl. "Fancy the run-away tailor!" is the male's remark, and he expects to be admired for it, and is.

"That make-up Countess—his sister, you know—didn't you see her? she turned green," says Creation's second effort, almost occupying the place of a rib.

"Isn't there a run-away wife, too?"

"Now, you mustn't be naughty!"

They laugh and flatter one another. The power to give and take flattery to any amount is the rare treasure of youth.

Undoubtedly they are a poetical picture; but some poetical pictures talk dreary prose; so we will retire.

Now, while the dancers carried on their business, and distance lent them enchantment, Rose stood by Juliana, near an alder which hid them from the rest.

"I don't accuse you," she was saying; "but who could have done this but you? Ah, Juley! you will never get what you want if you plot for it. I thought once you cared for Evan. If he had loved you, would I not have done all that I could for you both? I pardon you with all my heart."

"Keep your pardon!" was the angry answer. "I have done more for you, Rose. He is an adventurer, and I have tried to open your eyes and make you respect your family. You may accuse me of what you like, I have my conscience."

"And the friendship of the Countess," added Rose.

Juliana's figure shook as if she had been stung.

"Go and be happy—don't stay here and taunt me," she said, with a ghastly look. "I suppose he can lie like his sister, and has told you all sorts of tales."

"Not a word—not a word!" cried Rose. "Do you think my lover could tell a lie?"

The superb assumption of the girl, and the true portrait of Evan's character which it flashed upon Juliana, were to the latter such intense pain, that she turned like one on the rack, exclaiming:

"You think so much of him? You are so proud of him? Then, yes! I love him too, ugly, beastly as I am to look at! Oh, I know what you think! I loved him from the first, and I knew all about him, and spared him pain. I did not wait for him to fall from a horse. I watched every chance of his being exposed. I let them imagine he cared for me. Drummond would have told what he knew long before—only he knew there would not be much harm in a tradesman's son marrying me. And I have played into your hands, and now you taunt me!"

Rose remembered her fretful unkindness to Evan on the subject of his birth, when her feelings toward him were less warm. Dwelling on that alone, she put her arms round Juliana's stiffening figure, and said: "I dare say I am much more selfish than you. Forgive me, dear."

Staring at her, Juliana replied, "Now you are acting."

"No," said Rose, with a little effort to fondle her; "I only feel that I love you better for loving him."

Generous as her words sounded, and were, Juliana intuitively struck to the root of them, which was comfortless. For how calm in its fortune, how strong in its love, must Rose's heart be, when she could speak in this unwonted way!

"Go, and leave me, pray," she said.

Rose kissed her burning cheek. "I will do as you wish, dear. Try and know me better, and be sister Juley as you used to be. I know I am thoughtless, and horribly vain and disagreeable sometimes. Do forgive me. I will love you truly."

Half melting, Juliana pressed her hand.

"We are friends?" said Rose. "Good-bye"; and her countenance lighted, and she moved away, so changed by her happiness! Juliana was jealous of a love strong as she deemed her own to overcome obstacles. She called to her: "Rose! Rose, you will not take advantage of what I have told you, and repeat it to any one?"

Instantly Rose turned with a glance of full contempt over her shoulder.

"To whom?" she asked.

"To any one."

"To him? He would not love me long if I did!"

Juliana burst into fresh tears, but Rose walked into the sunbeams and the circle of the music.

Mounting Olympus, she inquired whether Ferdinand was within hail, as they were pledged to dance the first dance together. A few hints were given, and then Rose learnt that Ferdinand had been dismissed.

"And where is he?" she cried with her accustomed impetuosity. "Mama!—of course you did not accuse him—but, Mama! could you possibly let him go with the suspicion that you thought him guilty of writing an anonymous letter?"

"Not at all," Lady Jocelyn replied. "Only the handwriting was so extremely like, and he was the only person who knew the address and the circumstances, and who could have a motive—though I don't quite see what it is—I thought it as well to part for a time."

"But that's sophistry!" said Rose. "You accuse or you exonerate. Nobody can be half guilty. If you do not hold him innocent you are unjust!" Lady Jocelyn rejoined: "Yes? It's singular what a stock of axioms young people have handy for their occasions."

Rose loudly announced that she would right this matter.

"I can't think where Rose gets her passion for hot water," said her mother, as Rose ran down the ledge.

Two or three young gentlemen tried to engage her for a dance. She gave them plenty of promises, and hurried on till she met Evan, and, almost out of breath, told him the shameful injustice that had been done to her friend.

"Mama is such an Epicurean! I really think she is worse than Papa. This disgraceful letter looks like Ferdinand's writing, and she tells him so; and, Evan! will you believe that instead of being certain it's impossible any gentleman could do such a thing, she tells Ferdinand she shall feel more comfortable if she doesn't see him for some time? Poor Ferdinand! He has had so much to bear!"

Too sure of his darling to be envious now of any man she pitied, Evan said, "I would forfeit my hand on his innocence!"

"And so would I," echoed Rose. "Come to him with me, dear. Or no," she added, with a little womanly discretion, "perhaps it would not be so well—you're not very much cast down by what happened at dinner?"

"My darling! I think of you."

"Of me, dear? Concealment is never of any service. What there is to be known people may as well know at once. They'll gossip for a month, and then forget it. Your mother is dreadfully outspoken, certainly; but she has better manners than many ladies—I mean people in a position: you understand me? But suppose, dear, this had happened, and I had said nothing to Mama, and then we had to confess? Ah, you'll find I'm wiser than you imagine, Mr. Evan."

"Haven't I submitted to somebody's lead?"

"Yes, but with a sort of 'under protest.' I saw it by the mouth. Not quite natural. You have been moody ever since—just a little. I suppose it's our manly pride. But I'm losing time. Will you promise me not to brood over that occurrence? Think of me. Think everything of me. I am yours; and, dearest, if I love you, need you care what anybody else thinks? We will soon change their opinion."

"I care so little," said Evan, somewhat untruthfully, "that till you return I shall go and sit with my mother."

"Oh, she has gone. She made her dear old antiquated curtsey to Mama and the company. 'If my son has not been guilty of deception, I will leave him to your good pleasure, my lady.' That's what she said. Mama likes her, I know. But I wish she didn't mouth her words so precisely: it reminds me of—" the Countess, Rose checked herself from saying. "Good-bye. Thank heaven! the worst has happened. Do you know what I should do if I were you, and felt at all distressed? I should keep repeating," Rose looked archly and deeply up under his eyelids, "'I am the son of a tradesman, and Rose loves me,' over and over, and then, if you feel ashamed, what is it of?"

She nodded adieu, laughing at her own idea of her great worth; an idea very firmly fixed in her fair bosom, notwithstanding. Mrs. Melville said of her, "I used to think she had pride." Lady Jocelyn answered, "So she has. The misfortune is that it has taken the wrong turning."

Evan watched the figure that was to him as that of an angel—no less! She spoke so frankly to them as she passed: or here and there went on with a light laugh. It seemed an act of graciousness that she should open her mouth to one! And, indeed, by virtue of a pride which raised her to the level of what she thought it well to do, Rose was veritably on higher ground than any present. She no longer envied her friend Jenny, who, emerging from the shades, allured by the waltz, dislinked herself from William's arm, and whispered exclamations of sorrow at the scene created by Mr. Harrington's mother. Rose patted her hand, and said: "Thank you, Jenny dear but don't be sorry. I'm glad. It prevents a number of private explanations."

"Still, dear!" Jenny suggested.

"Oh! of course, I should like to lay my whip across the shoulders of the person who arranged the conspiracy," said Rose. "And afterwards I don't mind returning thanks to him, or her, or them."

William cried out, "I'm always on your side, Rose."

"And I'll be Jenny's bridesmaid," rejoined Rose, stepping blithely away from them.

Evan debated whither to turn when Rose was lost to his eyes. He had no heart for dancing. Presently a servant approached, and said that Mr. Harry particularly desired to see him. From Harry's looks at table, Evan judged that the interview was not likely to be amicable. He asked the direction he was to take, and setting out with long strides, came in sight of Raikes, who walked in gloom, and was evidently labouring under one of his mountains of melancholy. He affected to be quite out of the world; but finding that Evan took the hint in his usual prosy manner, was reduced to call after him, and finally to run and catch him.

"Haven't you one single spark of curiosity?" he began.

"What about?" said Evan.

"Why, about my amazing luck! You haven't asked a question. A matter of course."

Evan complimented him by asking a question: saying that Jack's luck certainly was wonderful.

"Wonderful, you call it," said Jack, witheringly. "And what's more wonderful is, that I'd give up all for quiet quarters in the Green Dragon. I knew I was prophetic. I knew I should regret that peaceful hostelry. Diocletian, if you like. I beg you to listen. I can't walk so fast without danger."

"Well, speak out, man. What's the matter with you?" cried Evan, impatiently.

Jack shook his head: "I see a total absence of sympathy," he remarked. "I can't."

"Then stand out of the way."

Jack let him pass, exclaiming, with cold irony, "I will pay homage to a loftier Nine!"

Mr. Raikes could not in his soul imagine that Evan was really so little inquisitive concerning a business of such importance as the trouble that possessed him. He watched his friend striding off, incredulously, and then commenced running in pursuit.

"Harrington, I give in; I surrender; you reduce me to prose. Thy nine have conquered my nine!—pardon me, old fellow. I'm immensely upset. This is the first day in my life that I ever felt what indigestion is. Egad, I've got something to derange the best digestion going!

"Look here, Harrington. What happened to you today, I declare I think nothing of. You owe me your assistance, you do, indeed; for if it hadn't been for the fearful fascinations of your sister—that divine Countess—I should have been engaged to somebody by this time, and profited by the opportunity held out to me, and which is now gone. I'm disgraced. I'm known. And the worst of it is, I must face people. I daren't turn tail. Did you ever hear of such a dilemma?"

"Ay," quoth Evan, "what is it?"

Raikes turned pale. "Then you haven't heard of it?" "Not a word."

"Then it's all for me to tell. I called on Messrs. Grist. I dined at the Aurora afterwards. Depend upon it, Harrington, we're led by a star. I mean, fellows with anything in them are. I recognized our Fallow field host, and thinking to draw him out, I told our mutual histories. Next day I went to these Messrs. Grist. They proposed the membership for Fallow field, five hundred a year, and the loan of a curricle, on condition. It's singular, Harrington; before anybody knew of the condition I didn't care about it a bit. It seemed to me childish. Who would think of minding wearing a tin plate? But now!—the sufferings of Orestes—what are they to mine? He wasn't tied to his Furies. They did hover a little above him; but as for me, I'm scorched; and I mustn't say where: my mouth is locked; the social laws which forbid the employment of obsolete words arrest my exclamations of despair. What do you advise?"

Evan stared a moment at the wretched object, whose dream of meeting a beneficent old gentleman had brought him to be the sport of a cynical farceur. He had shivers on his own account, seeing something of himself magnified, and he loathed the fellow, only to feel more acutely what a stigma may be.

"It's a case I can't advise in," he said, as gently as he could. "I should be off the grounds in a hurry."

"And then I'm where I was before I met the horrid old brute!" Raikes moaned.

"I told him over a pint of port-and noble stuff is that Aurora port!—I told him—I amused him till he was on the point of bursting—I told him I was such a gentleman as the world hadn't seen—minus money. So he determined to launch me. He said I should lead the life of such a gentleman as the world had not yet seen—on that simple condition, which appeared to me childish, a senile whim; rather an indulgence of his."

Evan listened to the tribulations of his friend as he would to those of a doll—the sport of some experimental child. By this time he knew something of old Tom Cogglesby, and was not astonished that he should have chosen John Raikes to play one of his farces on. Jack turned off abruptly the moment he saw they were nearing human figures, but soon returned to Evan's side, as if for protection.

"Hoy! Harrington!" shouted Harry, beckoning to him. "Come, make haste! I'm in a deuce of a mess."

The two Wheedles—Susan and Polly—were standing in front of him, and after his call to Evan, he turned to continue some exhortation or appeal to the common sense of women, largely indulged in by young men when the mischief is done.

"Harrington, do speak to her. She looks upon you as a sort of parson. I can't make her believe I didn't send for her. Of course, she knows I'm fond of her. My dear fellow," he whispered, "I shall be ruined if my grandmother hears of it. Get her away, please. Promise anything."

Evan took her hand and asked for the child.

"Quite well, sir," faltered Susan.

"You should not have come here."

Susan stared, and commenced whimpering: "Didn't you wish it, sir?"

"Oh, she's always thinking of being made a lady of," cried Polly. "As if Mr. Harry was going to do that. It wants a gentleman to do that."

"The carriage came for me, sir, in the afternoon," said Susan, plaintively, "with your compliments, and would I come. I thought—"

"What carriage?" asked Evan.

Raikes, who was ogling Polly, interposed grandly, "Mine!"

"And you sent in my name for this girl to come here?" Evan turned wrathfully on him.

"My dear Harrington, when you hit you knock down. The wise require but one dose of experience. The Countess wished it, and I did dispatch."

"The Countess!" Harry exclaimed; "Jove! do you mean to say that the Countess—"

"De Saldar," added Jack. "In Britain none were worthy found."

Harry gave a long whistle.

"Leave at once," said Evan to Susan. "Whatever you may want send to me for. And when you think you can meet your parents, I will take you to them. Remember that is what you must do."

"Make her give up that stupidness of hers, about being made a lady of, Mr. Harrington," said the inveterate Polly.

Susan here fell a-weeping.

"I would go, sir," she said. "I'm sure I would obey you: but I can't. I can't go back to the inn. They're beginning to talk about me, because—because I can't—can't pay them, and I'm ashamed."

Evan looked at Harry.

"I forgot," the latter mumbled, but his face was crimson. He put his hands in his pockets. "Do you happen to have a note or so?" he asked.

Evan took him aside and gave him what he had; and this amount, without inspection or reserve, Harry offered to Susan. She dashed his hand impetuously from her sight.

"There, give it to me," said Polly. "Oh, Mr. Harry! what a young man you are!"

Whether from the rebuff, or the reproach, or old feelings reviving, Harry was moved to go forward, and lay his hand on Susan's shoulder and mutter something in her ear that softened her.

Polly thrust the notes into her bosom, and with a toss of her nose, as who should say, "Here's nonsense they're at again," tapped Susan on the other shoulder, and said imperiously: "Come, Miss!"

Hurrying out a dozen sentences in one, Harry ended by suddenly kissing Susan's cheek, and then Polly bore her away; and Harry, with great solemnity, said to Evan:

"'Pon my honour, I think I ought to! I declare I think I love that girl. What's one's family? Why shouldn't you button to the one that just suits you? That girl, when she's dressed, and in good trim, by Jove! nobody 'd know her from a born lady. And as for grammar, I'd soon teach her that."

Harry began to whistle: a sign in him that he was thinking his hardest.

"I confess to being considerably impressed by the maid Wheedle," said Raikes.

"Would you throw yourself away on her?" Evan inquired.

Apparently forgetting how he stood, Mr. Raikes replied:

"You ask, perhaps, a little too much of me. One owes consideration to one's position. In the world's eyes a matrimonial slip outweighs a peccadillo. No. To much the maid might wheedle me, but to Hymen! She's decidedly fresh and pert—the most delicious little fat lips and cocky nose; but cease we to dwell on her, or of us two, to! one will be undone."

Harry burst into a laugh: "Is this the T.P. for Fallow field?"

"M.P. I think you mean," quoth Raikes, serenely; but a curious glance being directed on him, and pursuing him pertinaciously, it was as if the pediment of the lofty monument he topped were smitten with violence. He stammered an excuse, and retreated somewhat as it is the fashion to do from the presence of royalty, followed by Harry's roar of laughter, in which Evan cruelly joined.

"Gracious powers!" exclaimed the victim of ambition, "I'm laughed at by the son of a tailor!" and he edged once more into the shade of trees.

It was a strange sight for Harry's relatives to see him arm-in-arm with the man he should have been kicking, challenging, denouncing, or whatever the code prescribes: to see him talking to this young man earnestly, clinging to him affectionately, and when he separated from him, heartily wringing his hand. Well might they think that there was something extraordinary in these Harringtons. Convicted of Tailordom, these Harringtons appeared to shine with double lustre. How was it? They were at a loss to say. They certainly could say that the Countess was egregiously affected and vulgar; but who could be altogether complacent and sincere that had to fight so hard a fight? In this struggle with society I see one of the instances where success is entirely to be honoured and remains a proof of merit. For however boldly antagonism may storm the ranks of society, it will certainly be repelled, whereas affinity cannot be resisted; and they who, against obstacles of birth, claim and keep their position among the educated and refined, have that affinity. It is, on the whole, rare, so that society is not often invaded. I think it will have to front Jack Cade again before another Old Mel and his progeny shall appear. You refuse to believe in Old Mel? You know not nature's cunning.

Mrs. Shorne, Mrs. Melville, Miss Carrington, and many of the guests who observed Evan moving from place to place, after the exposure, as they called it, were amazed at his audacity. There seemed such a quietly superb air about him. He would not look out of his element; and this, knowing what they knew, was his offence. He deserved some commendation for still holding up his head, but it was love and Rose who kept the fires of his heart alive.

The sun had sunk. The figures on the summit of Parnassus were seen bobbing in happy placidity against the twilight sky. The sun had sunk, and many of Mr. Raikes' best things were unspoken. Wandering about in his gloom, he heard a feminine voice:

"Yes, I will trust you."

"You will not repent it," was answered.

Recognizing the Duke, Mr. Raikes cleared his throat.

"A-hem, your Grace! This is how the days should pass. I think we should diurnally station a good London band on high, and play his Majesty to bed—the sun. My opinion is, it would improve the crops. I'm not, as yet, a landed proprietor—"

The Duke stepped aside with him, and Raikes addressed no one for the next twenty minutes. When he next came forth Parnassus was half deserted. It was known that old Mrs. Bonner had been taken with a dangerous attack, and under this third blow the pic-nic succumbed. Simultaneously with the messenger that brought the news to Lady Jocelyn, one approached Evan, and informed him that the Countess de Saldar urgently entreated him to come to the house without delay. He also wished to speak a few words to her, and stepped forward briskly. He had no prophetic intimations of the change this interview would bring upon him.

XXXIII

The Hero Takes His Rank in the Orchestra

The Countess was not in her dressing-room when Evan presented himself. She was in attendance on Mrs. Bonner, Conning said; and the primness of Conning was a thing to have been noticed by any one save a dreamy youth in love. Conning remained in the room, keeping distinctly aloof. Her duties absorbed her, but a presiding thought mechanically jerked back her head from time to time: being the mute form of, "Well, I never!" in Conning's rank of life and intellectual capacity. Evan remained quite still in a chair, and Conning was certainly a number of paces beyond suspicion, when the Countess appeared, and hurling at the maid one of those feminine looks which contain huge quartos of meaning, vented the cold query:

"Pray, why did you not come to me, as you were commanded?"

"I was not aware, my lady," Conning drew up to reply, and performed with her eyes a lofty rejection of the volume cast at her, and a threat of several for offensive operations, if need were.

The Countess spoke nearer to what she was implying "You know I object to this: it is not the first time."

"Would your ladyship please to say what your ladyship means?"

In return for this insolent challenge to throw off the mask, the Countess felt justified in punishing her by being explicit. "Your irregularities are not of yesterday," she said, kindly making use of a word of double signification still.

"Thank you, my lady." Conning accepted the word in its blackest meaning. "I am obliged to you. If your ladyship is to be believed, my character is not worth much. But I can make distinctions, my lady."

Something very like an altercation was continued in a sharp, brief undertone; and then Evan, waking up to the affairs of the hour, heard Conning say:

"I shall not ask your ladyship to give me a character."

The Countess answering with pathos: "It would, indeed, be to give you one."

He was astonished that the Countess should burst into tears when Conning had departed, and yet more so that his effort to console her should bring a bolt of wrath upon himself.

"Now, Evan, now see what you have done for us-do, and rejoice at it. The very menials insult us. You heard what that creature said? She can make distinctions. Oh! I could beat her. They know it: all the servants know it: I can see it in their faces. I feel it when I pass them. The insolent wretches treat us as impostors; and this Conning—to defy me! Oh! it comes of my devotion to you. I am properly chastized. I passed Rose's maid on the stairs, and her reverence was barely perceptible."

Evan murmured that he was very sorry, adding, foolishly: "Do you really care, Louisa, for what servants think and say?"

The Countess sighed deeply: "Oh! you are too thickskinned! Your mother from top to toe! It is too dreadful! What have I done to deserve it? Oh, Evan, Evan!"

Her head dropped in her lap. There was something ludicrous to Evan in this excess of grief on account of such a business; but he was tender-hearted and wrought upon to declare that, whether or not he was to blame for his mother's intrusion that afternoon, he was ready to do what he could to make up to the Countess for her sufferings: whereat the Countess sighed again: asked him what he possibly could do, and doubted his willingness to accede to the most trifling request.

"No; I do in verity believe that were I to desire you to do aught for your own good alone, you would demur, Van."

He assured her that she was mistaken.

"We shall see," she said.

"And if once or twice, I have run counter to you, Louisa—"

"Abominable language!" cried the Countess, stopping her ears like a child. "Do not excruciate me so. You laugh! My goodness! what will you come to!"

Evan checked his smile, and, taking her hand, said:

"I must tell you; that, on the whole, I see nothing to regret in what has happened to-day. You may notice a change in the manners of the servants and some of the country squiresses, but I find none in the bearing of the real ladies, the true gentlemen, to me."

"Because the change is too fine for you to perceive it," interposed the Countess.

"Rose, then, and her mother, and her father!" Evan cried impetuously.

"As for Lady Jocelyn!" the Countess shrugged:

"And Sir Franks!" her head shook: "and Rose, Rose is, simply self-willed; a 'she will' or 'she won't' sort of little person. No criterion! Henceforth the world is against us. We have to struggle with it: it does not rank us of it!"

"Your feeling on the point is so exaggerated, my dear Louisa", said Evan, "one can't bring reason to your ears. The tattle we shall hear we shall outlive. I care extremely for the good opinion of men, but I prefer my own; and I do not lose it because my father was in trade."

"And your own name, Evan Harrington, is on a shop," the Countess struck in, and watched him severely from under her brow, glad to mark that he could still blush.

"Oh, heaven!" she wailed to increase the effect, "on a shop! a brother of mine!"

"Yes, Louisa. It may not last. . . I did it—is it not better that a son should blush, than cast dishonour on his father's memory?"

"Ridiculous boy-notion!"

"Rose has pardoned it, Louisa—cannot you? I find that the naturally vulgar and narrow-headed people, and cowards who never forego mean advantages, are those only who would condemn me and my conduct in that."

"And you have joy in your fraction of the world left to you!" exclaimed his female-elder.

Changeing her manner to a winning softness, she said:

"Let me also belong to the very small party! You have been really romantic, and most generous and noble; only the shop smells! But, never mind, promise me you will not enter it."

"I hope not," said Evan.

"You do hope that you will not officiate? Oh, Evan the eternal contemplation of gentlemen's legs! think of that! Think of yourself sculptured in that attitude!" Innumerable little prickles and stings shot over Evan's skin.

"There—there, Louisa!" he said, impatiently; "spare your ridicule. We go to London to-morrow, and when there I expect to hear that I have an appointment, and that this engagement is over." He rose and walked up and down the room.

"I shall not be prepared to go to-morrow," remarked the Countess, drawing her figure up stiffly.

"Oh! well, if you can stay, Andrew will take charge of you, I dare say."

"No, my dear, Andrew will not—a nonentity cannot—you must."

"Impossible, Louisa," said Evan, as one who imagines he is uttering a thing of little consequence. "I promised Rose."

"You promised Rose that you would abdicate and retire? Sweet, loving girl!"

Evan made no answer.

"You will stay with me, Evan."

"I really can't," he said in his previous careless tone.

"Come and sit down," cried the Countess, imperiously.

"The first trifle is refused. It does not astonish me. I will honour you now by talking seriously to you. I have treated you hitherto as a child. Or, no—" she stopped her mouth; "it is enough if I tell you, dear, that poor Mrs. Bonner is dying, and that she desires my attendance on her to refresh her spirit with readings on the Prophecies, and Scriptural converse. No other soul in the house can so soothe her."

"Then, stay," said Evan.

"Unprotected in the midst of enemies! Truly!"

"I think, Louisa, if you can call Lady Jocelyn an enemy, you must read the Scriptures by a false light."

"The woman is an utter heathen!" interjected the Countess. "An infidel can be no friend. She is therefore the reverse. Her opinions embitter her mother's last days. But now you will consent to remain with me, dear Van!"

An implacable negative responded to the urgent appeal of her eyes.

"By the way," he said, for a diversion, "did you know of a girl stopping at an inn in Fallow field?"

"Know a barmaid?" the Countess's eyes and mouth were wide at the question.

"Did you send Raikes for her to-day?"

"Did Mr. Raikes—ah, Evan! that creature reminds me, you have no sense of contrast. For a Brazilian ape—he resembles, if he is not truly one—what contrast is he to an English gentleman! His proximity and acquaintance—rich as he may be—disfigure you. Study contrast!"

Evan had to remind her that she had not answered him: whereat she exclaimed: "One would really think you had never been abroad. Have you not evaded me, rather?"

The Countess commenced fanning her languid brows, and then pursued: "Now, my dear brother, I may conclude that you will acquiesce in my moderate wishes. You remain. My venerable friend cannot last three days. She is on the brink of a better world! I will confide to you that it is of the utmost importance we should be here, on the spot, until the sad termination! That is what I summoned you for. You are now at liberty. Ta-ta, as soon as you please."

She had baffled his little cross-examination with regard to Raikes, but on the other point he was firm. She would listen to nothing: she affected that her mandate had gone forth, and must be obeyed; tapped with her foot, fanned deliberately, and was a consummate queen, till he turned the handle of the door, when her complexion deadened, she started up, trembling, and tripping towards him, caught him by the arm, and said: "Stop! After all that I have sacrificed for you! As well try to raise the dead as a Dawley from the dust he grovels in! Why did I consent to visit this place? It was for you. I came, I heard that you had disgraced yourself in drunkenness at Fallow field, and I toiled to eclipse that, and I did. Young Jocelyn thought you were what you are I could spit the word at you! and I dazzled him to give you time to win this minx, who will spin you like a top if you get her. That Mr. Forth knew it as well, and that vile young Laxley. They are gone! Why are they gone? Because they thwarted me—they crossed your interests—I said they should go. George Uplift is going to-day. The house is left to us; and I believe firmly that Mrs. Bonner's will contains a memento of the effect of our frequent religious conversations. So you would leave now? I suspect nobody, but we are all human, and Wills would not have been tampered with for the first time. Besides, and the Countess's imagination warmed till she addressed her brother as a confederate, we shall then see to whom Beckley Court is bequeathed. Either way it may be yours. Yours! and you suffer their plots to drive you forth. Do you not perceive that Mama was brought here to-day on purpose to shame us and cast us out? We are surrounded by conspiracies, but if our faith is pure who can hurt us? If I had not that consolation—would that you had it, too!—would it be endurable to me to see those menials whispering and showing their forced respect? As it is, I am fortified to forgive them. I breathe another atmosphere. Oh, Evan! you did not attend to Mr. Parsley's beautiful last sermon. The Church should have been your vocation."

From vehemence the Countess had subsided to a mournful gentleness. She had been too excited to notice any changes in her brother's face during her speech, and when he turned from the door, and still eyeing her fixedly, led her to a chair, she fancied from his silence that she had subdued and convinced him. A delicious sense of her power, succeeded by a weary reflection that she had constantly to employ it, occupied her mind, and when presently she looked up from the shade of her hand, it was to agitate her head pitifully at her brother.

"All this you have done for me, Louisa," he said.

"Yes, Evan,—all!" she fell into his tone.

"And you are the cause of Laxley's going? Did you know anything of that anonymous letter?"

He was squeezing her hand-with grateful affection, as she was deluded to imagine.

"Perhaps, dear,—a little," her conceit prompted her to admit.

"Did you write it?"

He gazed intently into her eyes, and as the question shot like a javelin, she tried ineffectually to disengage her fingers; her delusion waned; she took fright, but it was too late; he had struck the truth out of her before she could speak. Her spirit writhed like a snake in his hold. Innumerable things she was ready to say, and strove to; the words would not form on her lips.

"I will be answered, Louisa."

The stern manner he had assumed gave her no hope of eluding him. With an inward gasp, and a sensation of nakedness altogether new to her, dismal, and alarming, she felt that she could not lie. Like a creature forsaken of her staunchest friend, she could have flung herself to the floor. The next instant her natural courage restored her. She jumped up and stood at bay.

"Yes. I did."

And now he was weak, and she was strong, and used her strength.

"I wrote it to save you. Yes. Call on your Creator, and be my judge, if you dare. Never, never will you meet a soul more utterly devoted to you, Evan. This Mr. Forth, this Laxley, I said, should go, because they were resolved to ruin you, and make you base. They are gone. The responsibility I take on myself. Nightly—during the remainder of my days—I will pray for pardon."

He raised his head to ask sombrely: "Is your handwriting like Laxley's?"

"It seems so," she answered, with a pitiful sneer for one who could arrest her exaltation to inquire about minutiae. "Right or wrong, it is done, and if you choose to be my judge, think whether your own conscience is clear. Why did you come here? Why did you stay? You have your free will,—do you deny that? Oh, I will take the entire blame, but you must not be a hypocrite, Van. You know you were aware. We had no confidences. I was obliged to treat you like a child; but for you to pretend to suppose that roses grow in your path—oh, that is paltry! You are a hypocrite or an imbecile, if that is your course."

Was he not something of the former? The luxurious mist in which he had been living, dispersed before his sister's bitter words, and, as she designed he should, he felt himself her accomplice. But, again, reason struggled to enlighten him; for surely he would never have done a thing so disproportionate to the end to be gamed! It was the unconnected action of his brain that thus advised him. No thoroughly-fashioned, clear-spirited man conceives wickedness impossible to him: but wickedness so largely mixed with folly, the best of us may reject as not among our temptations. Evan, since his love had dawned, had begun to talk with his own nature, and though he knew not yet how much it would stretch or contract, he knew that he was weak and could not perform moral wonders without severe struggles. The cynic may add, if he likes—or without potent liquors.

Could he be his sister's judge? It is dangerous for young men to be too good. They are so sweeping in their condemnations, so sublime in their conceptions of excellence, and the most finished Puritan cannot out-do their demands upon frail humanity. Evan's momentary self-examination saved him from this, and he told the Countess, with a sort of cold compassion, that he himself dared not blame her.

His tone was distinctly wanting in admiration of her, but she was somewhat over-wrought, and leaned her shoulder against him, and became immediately his affectionate, only too-zealous, sister; dearly to be loved, to be forgiven, to be prized: and on condition of inserting a special petition for pardon in her orisons, to live with a calm conscience, and to be allowed to have her own way with him during the rest of her days.

It was a happy union—a picture that the Countess was lured to admire in the glass.

Sad that so small a murmur should destroy it for ever!

"What?" cried the Countess, bursting from his arm.

"Go?" she emphasized with the hardness of determined unbelief, as if plucking the words, one by one, out of her reluctant ears. "Go to Lady Jocelyn, and tell her I wrote the letter?"

"You can do no less, I fear," said Evan, eyeing the floor and breathing a deep breath.

"Then I did hear you correctly? Oh, you must be mad-idiotic! There, pray go away, Evan. Come in the morning. You are too much for my nerves."

Evan rose, putting out his hand as if to take hers and plead with her. She rejected the first motion, and repeated her desire for him to leave her; saying, cheerfully—

"Good night, dear; I dare say we shan't meet till the morning."

"You can't let this injustice continue a single night, Louisa?" said he.

She was deep in the business of arrangeing a portion of her attire.

"Go-go; please," she responded.

Lingering, he said: "If I go, it will be straight to Lady Jocelyn."

She stamped angrily.

"Only go!" and then she found him gone, and she stooped lower to the glass, to mark if the recent agitation were observable under her eyes. There, looking at herself, her heart dropped heavily in her bosom. She ran to the door and hurried swiftly after Evan, pulling him back speechlessly.

"Where are you going, Evan?"

"To Lady Jocelyn."

The unhappy victim of her devotion stood panting.

"If you go, I—I take poison!" It was for him now to be struck; but he was suffering too strong an anguish to be susceptible to mock tragedy. The Countess paused to study him. She began to fear her brother. "I will!" she reiterated wildly, without moving him at all. And the quiet inflexibility of his face forbade the ultimate hope which lies in giving men a dose of hysterics when they are obstinate. She tried by taunts and angry vituperations to make him look fierce, if but an instant, to precipitate her into an exhibition she was so well prepared for.

"Evan! what! after all my love, my confidence in you—I need not have told you—to expose us! Brother? would you? Oh!"

"I will not let this last another hour," said Evan, firmly, at the same time seeking to caress her. She spurned his fruitless affection, feeling, nevertheless, how cruel was her fate; for, with any other save a brother, she had arts at her disposal to melt the manliest resolutions. The glass showed her that her face was pathetically pale; the tones of her voice were rich and harrowing. What did they avail with a brother? "Promise me," she cried eagerly, "promise me to stop here—on this spot-till I return."

The promise was extracted. The Countess went to fetch Caroline. Evan did not count the minutes. One thought was mounting in his brain-the scorn of Rose. He felt that he had lost her. Lost her when he had just won her! He felt it, without realizing it. The first blows of an immense grief are dull, and strike the heart through wool, as it were. The belief of the young in their sorrow has to be flogged into them, on the good old educational principle. Could he do less than this he was about to do? Rose had wedded her noble nature to him, and it was as much her spirit as his own that urged him thus to forfeit her, to be worthy of her by assuming unworthiness.

There he sat neither conning over his determination nor the cause for it, revolving Rose's words about Laxley, and nothing else. The words were so sweet and so bitter; every now and then the heavy smiting on his heart set it quivering and leaping, as the whip starts a jaded horse.

Meantime the Countess was participating in a witty conversation in the drawing-room with Sir John and the Duke, Miss Current, and others; and it was not till after she had displayed many graces, and, as one or two ladies presumed to consider, marked effrontery, that she rose and drew Caroline away with her. Returning to her dressing-room, she found that Evan had faithfully kept his engagement; he was on the exact spot where she had left him.

Caroline came to him swiftly, and put her hand to his forehead that she might the better peruse his features, saying, in her mellow caressing voice: "What is this, dear Van, that you will do? Why do you look so wretched?"

"Has not Louisa told you?"

"She has told me something, dear, but I don't know what it is. That you are going to expose us? What further exposure do we need? I'm sure, Van, my pride—what I had—is gone. I have none left!"

Evan kissed her brows warmly. An explanation, full of the Countess's passionate outcries of justification, necessity, and innocence in higher than fleshly eyes, was given, and then the three were silent.

"But, Van," Caroline commenced, deprecatingly, "my darling! of what use—now! Whether right or wrong, why should you, why should you, when the thing is done, dear?—think!"

"And you, too, would let another suffer under an unjust accusation?" said Evan.

"But, dearest, it is surely your duty to think of your family first. Have we not been afflicted enough? Why should you lay us under this fresh burden?"

"Because it's better to bear all now than a life of remorse," answered Evan.

"But this Mr. Laxley—I cannot pity him; he has behaved so insolently to you throughout! Let him suffer."

"Lady Jocelyn," said Evan, "has been unintentionally unjust to him, and after her kindness—apart from the right or wrong—I will not—I can't allow her to continue so."

"After her kindness!" echoed the Countess, who had been fuming at Caroline's weak expostulations. "Kindness! Have I not done ten times for these Jocelyns what they have done for us? O mio Deus! why, I have bestowed on them the membership for Fallow field: I have saved her from being a convicted liar this very day. Worse! for what would have been talked of the morals of the house, supposing the scandal. Oh! indeed I was tempted to bring that horrid mad Captain into the house face to face with his flighty doll of a wife, as I, perhaps, should have done, acting by the dictates of my conscience. I lied for Lady Jocelyn, and handed the man to a lawyer, who withdrew him. And this they owe to me! Kindness? They have given us bed and board, as the people say. I have repaid them for that."

"Pray be silent, Louisa," said Evan, getting up hastily, for the sick sensation Rose had experienced came over him. His sister's plots, her untruth, her coarseness, clung to him and seemed part of his blood. He now had a personal desire to cut himself loose from the wretched entanglement revealed to him, whatever it cost.

"Are you really, truly going?" Caroline exclaimed, for he was near the door.

"At a quarter to twelve at night!" sneered the Countess, still imagining that he, like herself, must be partly acting.

"But, Van, is it—dearest, think! is it manly for a brother to go and tell of his sister? And how would it look?"

Evan smiled. "Is it that that makes you unhappy? Louisa's name will not be mentioned—be sure of that."

Caroline was stooping forward to him. Her figure straightened: "Good Heaven, Evan! you are not going to take it on yourself? Rose!—she will hate you."

"God help me!" he cried internally.

"Oh, Evan, darling! consider, reflect!" She fell on her knees, catching his hand. "It is worse for us that you should suffer, dearest! Think of the dreadful meanness and baseness of what you will have to acknowledge."

"Yes!" sighed the youth, and his eyes, in his extreme pain, turned to the Countess reproachfully.

"Think, dear," Caroline hurried on, "he gains nothing for whom you do this—you lose all. It is not your deed. You will have to speak an untruth. Your ideas are wrong—wrong, I know they are. You will have to lie. But if you are silent, the little, little blame that may attach to us will pass away, and we shall be happy in seeing our brother happy."

"You are talking to Evan as if he had religion," said the Countess, with steady sedateness. And at that moment, from the sublimity of his pagan virtue, the young man groaned for some pure certain light to guide him: the question whether he was about to do right made him weak. He took Caroline's head between his two hands, and kissed her mouth. The act brought Rose to his senses insufferably, and she—his Goddess of truth and his sole guiding light-spurred him afresh.

"My family's dishonour is mine, Caroline. Say nothing more—don't think of me. I go to Lady Jocelyn tonight. To-morrow we leave, and there's the end. Louisa, if you have any new schemes for my welfare, I beg you to renounce them."

"Gratitude I never expected from a Dawley!" the Countess retorted.

"Oh, Louisa! he is going!" cried Caroline; "kneel to him with me: stop him: Rose loves him, and he is going to make her hate him."

"You can't talk reason to one who's mad," said the Countess, more like the Dawley she sprang from than it would have pleased her to know.

"My darling! My own Evan! it will kill me," Caroline exclaimed, and passionately imploring him, she looked so hopelessly beautiful, that Evan was agitated, and caressed her, while he said, softly: "Where our honour is not involved I would submit to your smallest wish."

"It involves my life—my destiny!" murmured Caroline.

Could he have known the double meaning in her words, and what a saving this sacrifice of his was to accomplish, he would not have turned to do it feeling abandoned of heaven and earth.

The Countess stood rigidly as he went forth. Caroline was on her knees, sobbing.

XXXIV

A Pagan Sacrifice

Three steps from the Countess's chamber door, the knot of Evan's resolution began to slacken. The clear light of his simple duty grew cloudy and complex. His pride would not let him think that he was shrinking, but cried out in him, "Will you be believed?" and whispered that few would believe him guilty of such an act. Yet, while something said that full surely Lady Jocelyn would not, a vague dread that Rose might, threw him back on the luxury of her love and faith in him. He found himself hoping that his statement would be laughed at. Then why make it?

No: that was too blind a hope. Many would take him at his word; all—all save Lady Jocelyn! Rose the first! Because he stood so high with her now he feared the fall. Ah, dazzling pinnacle! our darlings shoot us up on a wondrous juggler's pole, and we talk familiarly to the stars, and are so much above everybody, and try to walk like creatures with two legs, forgetting that we have but a pin's point to stand on up there. Probably the absence of natural motion inspires the prophecy that we must ultimately come down: our unused legs wax morbidly restless. Evan thought it good that Rose should lift her head to look at him; nevertheless, he knew that Rose would turn from him the moment he descended from his superior station. Nature is wise in her young children, though they wot not of it, and are always trying to rush away from her. They escape their wits sooner than their instincts.

But was not Rose involved in him, and part of him? Had he not sworn never to renounce her? What was this but a betrayal?

Go on, young man: fight your fight. The little imps pluck at you: the big giant assails you: the seductions of the soft-mouthed siren are not wanting. Slacken the knot an instant, and they will all have play. And the worst is, that you may be wrong, and they may be right! For is it, can it be proper for you to stain the silvery whiteness of your skin by plunging headlong into yonder pitch-bath? Consider the defilement! Contemplate your hideous aspect on issuing from that black baptism!

As to the honour of your family, Mr. Evan Harrington, pray, of what sort of metal consists the honour of a tailor's family?

One little impertinent imp ventured upon that question on his own account. The clever beast was torn back and strangled instantaneously by his experienced elders, but not before Evan's pride had answered him. Exalted by Love, he could dread to abase himself and strip off his glittering garments; lowered by the world, he fell back upon his innate worth.

Yes, he was called on to prove it; he was on his way to prove it. Surrendering his dearest and his best, casting aside his dreams, his desires, his aspirations, for this stern duty, he at least would know that he made himself doubly worthy of her who abandoned him, and the world would scorn him by reason of his absolute merit. Coming to this point, the knot of his resolve tightened again; he hugged it with the furious zeal of a martyr.

Religion, the lack of which in him the Countess deplored, would have guided him and silenced the internal strife. But do not despise a virtue purely Pagan. The young who can act readily up to the Christian light are happier, doubtless: but they are led, they are passive: I think they do not make such capital Christians subsequently. They are never in such danger, we know; but some in the flock are more than sheep. The heathen ideal it is not so very easy to attain, and those who mount from it to the Christian have, in my humble thought, a firmer footing.

So Evan fought his hard fight from the top of the stairs to the bottom. A Pagan, which means our poor unsupported flesh, is never certain of his victory. Now you will see him kneeling to his Gods, and anon drubbing them; or he makes them fight for him, and is complacent at the issue. Evan had ceased to pick his knot with one hand and pull it with the other: but not finding Lady Jocelyn below, and hearing that she had retired for the night, he mounted the stairs, and the strife recommenced from the bottom to the top. Strange to say, he was almost unaware of any struggle going on within him. The suggestion of the foolish little imp alone was loud in the heart of his consciousness; the rest hung more in his nerves than in his brain. He thought: "Well, I will speak it out to her in the morning"; and thought so sincerely, while an ominous sigh of relief at the reprieve rose from his over-burdened bosom.

Hardly had the weary deep breath taken flight, when the figure of Lady Jocelyn was seen advancing along the corridor, with a lamp in her hand. She trod heavily, in a kind of march, as her habit was; her large fully-open grey eyes looking straight ahead. She would have passed him, and he would have let her pass, but seeing the unusual pallor on her face, his love for this lady moved him to step forward and express a hope that she had no present cause for sorrow.

Hearing her mother's name, Lady Jocelyn was about to return a conventional answer. Recognizing Evan, she said:

"Ah! Mr. Harrington! Yes, I fear it's as bad as it can be. She can scarcely outlive the night."

Again he stood alone: his chance was gone. How could he speak to her in her affliction? Her calm sedate visage had the beauty of its youth, when lighted by the animation that attends meetings or farewells. In her bow to Evan, he beheld a lovely kindness more unique, if less precious, than anything he had ever seen on the face of Rose. Half exultingly, he reflected that no opportunity would be allowed him now to teach that noble head and truest of human hearts to turn from him: the clear-eyed morrow would come: the days of the future would be bright as other days!

Wrapped in the comfort of his cowardice, he started to see Lady Jocelyn advancing to him again.

"Mr. Harrington," she said, "Rose tells me you leave us early in the morning. I may as well shake your hand now. We part very good friends. I shall always be glad to hear of you."

Evan pressed her hand, and bowed. "I thank you, madam," was all he could answer.

"It will be better if you don't write to Rose."

Her tone was rather that of a request than an injunction.

"I have no right to do so, my lady."

"She considers that you have: I wish her to have, a fair trial."

His voice quavered. The philosophic lady thought it time to leave him.

"So good-bye. I can trust you without extracting a promise. If you ever have need of a friend, you know you are at liberty to write to me."

"You are tired, my lady?" He put this question more to dally with what he ought to be saying.

"Tolerably. Your sister, the Countess, relieves me in the night. I fancy my mother finds her the better nurse of the two."

Lady Jocelyn's face lighted in its gracious pleasant way, as she just inclined her head: but the mention of the Countess and her attendance on Mrs. Bonner had nerved Evan: the contrast of her hypocrisy and vile scheming with this most open, noble nature, acted like a new force within him. He begged Lady Jocelyn's permission to speak with her in private. Marking his fervid appearance, she looked at him seriously.

"Is it really important?"

"I cannot rest, madam, till it is spoken."

"I mean, it doesn't pertain to the delirium? We may sleep upon that."

He divined her sufficiently to answer: "It concerns a piece of injustice done by you, madam, and which I can help you to set right."

Lady Jocelyn stared somewhat. "Follow me into my dressing-room," she said, and led the way.

Escape was no longer possible. He was on the march to execution, and into the darkness of his brain danced John Raikes, with his grotesque tribulations. It was the harsh savour of reality that conjured up this flighty being, who probably never felt a sorrow or a duty. The farce Jack lived was all that Evan's tragic bitterness could revolve, and seemed to be the only light in his mind. You might have seen a smile on his mouth when he was ready to ask for a bolt from heaven to crush him.

"Now," said her ladyship, and he found that the four walls enclosed them, "what have I been doing?"

She did not bid him be seated. Her brevity influenced him to speak to the point.

"You have dismissed Mr. Laxley, my lady: he is innocent."

"How do you know that?"

"Because,"—a whirl of sensations beset the wretched youth, "because I am guilty."

His words had run ahead of his wits; and in answer to Lady Jocelyn's singular exclamation he could but simply repeat them.

Her head drew back; her face was slightly raised; she looked, as he had seen her sometimes look at the Countess, with a sort of speculative amazement.

"And why do you come to tell me?"

"For the reason that I cannot allow you to be unjust, madam."

"What on earth was your motive?"

Evan stood silent, flinching from her frank eyes.

"Well, well, well!" Her ladyship dropped into a chair, and thumped her knees.

There was lawyer's blood in Lady Jocelyn's veins she had the judicial mind. A confession was to her a confession. She tracked actions up to a motive; but one who came voluntarily to confess needed no sifting. She had the habit of treating things spoken as facts.

"You absolutely wrote that letter to Mrs. Evremonde's husband!"

Evan bowed, to avoid hearing his own lie.

"You discovered his address and wrote to him, and imitated Mr. Laxley's handwriting, to effect the purpose you may have had?"

Her credulity did require his confirmation of it, and he repeated: "It is my deed."

"Hum! And you sent that premonitory slip of paper to her?"

"To Mrs. Evremonde?"

"Somebody else was the author of that, perhaps?"

"It is all on me."

"In that case, Mr. Harrington, I can only say that it's quite right you should quit this house to-morrow morning."

Her ladyship commenced rocking in her chair, and then added: "May I ask, have you madness in your family? No? Because when one can't discern a motive, it's natural to ascribe certain acts to madness. Had Mrs. Evremonde offended you? or Ferdinand—but one only hears of such practices towards fortunate rivals, and now you have come to undo what you did! I must admit, that taking the monstrousness of the act and the inconsequence of your proceedings together, the whole affair becomes more incomprehensible to me than it was before. Would it be unpleasant to you to favour me with explanations?"

She saw the pain her question gave him, and, passing it, said:

"Of course you need not be told that Rose must hear of this?"

"Yes," said Evan, "she must hear it."

"You know what that's equivalent to? But, if you like, I will not speak to her till you, have left us."

"Instantly," cried Evan. "Now-to-night! I would not have her live a minute in a false estimate of me."

Had Lady Jocelyn's intellect been as penetrating as it was masculine, she would have taken him and turned him inside out in a very short time; for one who would bear to see his love look coldly on him rather than endure a minute's false estimate of his character, and who could yet stoop to concoct a vile plot, must either be mad or simulating the baseness for some reason or other. She perceived no motive for the latter, and she held him to be sound in the head, and what was spoken from the mouth she accepted. Perhaps, also, she saw in the complication thus offered an escape for Rose, and was the less inclined to elucidate it herself. But if her intellect was baffled, her heart was unerring. A man proved guilty of writing an anonymous letter would not have been allowed to stand long in her room. She would have shown him to the door of the house speedily; and Evan was aware in his soul that he had not fallen materially in her esteem. He had puzzled and confused her, and partly because she had the feeling that this young man was entirely trustworthy, and because she never relied on her feelings, she let his own words condemn him, and did not personally discard him. In fact, she was a veritable philosopher. She permitted her fellows to move the world on as they would, and had no other passions in the contemplation of the show than a cultured audience will usually exhibit.

"Strange,—most strange! I thought I was getting old!" she said, and eyed the culprit as judges generally are not wont to do. "It will be a shock to Rose. I must tell you that I can't regret it. I would not have employed force with her, but I should have given her as strong a taste of the world as it was in my power to give. Girls get their reason from society. But, come! if you think you can make your case out better to her, you shall speak to her first yourself."

"No, my lady," said Evan, softly.

"You would rather not?"

"I could not."

"But, I suppose, she'll want to speak to you when she knows it."

"I can take death from her hands, but I cannot slay myself."

The language was natural to his condition, though the note was pitched high. Lady Jocelyn hummed till the sound of it was over, and an idea striking her, she said:

"Ah, by the way, have you any tremendous moral notions?"

"I don't think I have, madam."

"People act on that mania sometimes, I believe. Do you think it an outrage on decency for a wife to run away from a mad husband whom they won't shut up, and take shelter with a friend? Is that the cause? Mr. Forth is an old friend of mine. I would trust my daughter with him in a desert, and stake my hand on his honour."

"Oh, Lady Jocelyn!" cried Evan. "Would to God you might ever have said that of me! Madam, I love you. I shall never see you again. I shall never meet one to treat me so generously. I leave you, blackened in character—you cannot think of me without contempt. I can never hope that this will change. But, for your kindness let me thank you."

And as speech is poor where emotion is extreme—and he knew his own to be especially so—he took her hand with petitioning eyes, and dropping on one knee, reverentially kissed it.

Lady Jocelyn was human enough to like to be appreciated. She was a veteran Pagan, and may have had the instinct that a peculiar virtue in this young one was the spring of his conduct. She stood up and said: "Don't forget that you have a friend here."

The poor youth had to turn his head from her.

"You wish that I should tell Rose what you have told me at once, Mr. Harrington?"

"Yes, my lady; I beg that you will do so."

"Well!"

And the queer look Lady Jocelyn had been wearing dimpled into absolute wonder. A stranger to Love's cunning, she marvelled why he should desire to witness the scorn Rose would feel for him.

"If she's not asleep, then, she shall hear it now," said her ladyship. "You understand that it will be mentioned to no other person."

"Except to Mr. Laxley, madam, to whom I shall offer the satisfaction he may require. But I will undertake that."

"Just as you think proper on that matter," remarked her philosophical ladyship, who held that man was a fighting animal, and must not have his nature repressed.

She lighted him part of the way, and then turned off to Rose's chamber.

Would Rose believe it of him? Love combated his dismal foreboding. Strangely, too, now that he had plunged into his pitch-bath, the guilt seemed to cling to him, and instead of hoping serenely, or fearing steadily, his spirit fell in a kind of abject supplication to Rose, and blindly trusted that she would still love even if she believed him base. In his weakness he fell so low as to pray that she might love that crawling reptile who could creep into a house and shrink from no vileness to win her.

XXXV

Rose Wounded

The light of morning was yet cold along the passages of the house when Polly Wheedle, hurrying to her young mistress, met her loosely dressed and with a troubled face.

"What 's the matter, Polly? I was coming to you."

"O, Miss Rose! and I was coming to you. Miss Bonner's gone back to her convulsions again. She's had them all night. Her hair won't last till thirty, if she keeps on giving way to temper, as I tell her: and I know that from a barber."

"Tush, you stupid Polly! Does she want to see me?"

"You needn't suspect that, Miss. But you quiet her best, and I thought I'd come to you. But, gracious!"

Rose pushed past her without vouchsafing any answer to the look in her face, and turned off to Juliana's chamber, where she was neither welcomed nor repelled. Juliana said she was perfectly well, and that Polly was foolishly officious: whereupon Rose ordered Polly out of the room, and said to Juliana, kindly: "You have not slept, dear, and I have not either. I am so unhappy."

Whether Rose intended by this communication to make Juliana eagerly attentive, and to distract her from her own affair, cannot be said, but something of the effect was produced.

"You care for him, too," cried Rose, impetuously. "Tell me, Juley: do you think him capable of any base action? Do you think he would do what any gentleman would be ashamed to own? Tell me."

Juliana looked at Rose intently, but did not reply.

Rose jumped up from the bed. "You hesitate, Juley? What? Could you think so?"

Young women after a common game are shrewd. Juliana may have seen that Rose was not steady on the plank she walked, and required support.

"I don't know," she said, turning her cheek to her pillow.

"What an answer!" Rose exclaimed. "Have you no opinion? What did you say yesterday? It's silent as the grave with me: but if you do care for him, you must think one thing or the other."

"I suppose not, then—no," said Juliana.

Repeating the languid words bitterly, Rose continued:

"What is it to love without having faith in him you love? You make my mind easier."

Juliana caught the implied taunt, and said, fretfully:

"I'm ill. You're so passionate. You don't tell me what it is. How can I answer you?"

"Never mind," said Rose, moving to the door, wondering why she had spoken at all: but when Juliana sprang forward, and caught her by the dress to stop her, and with a most unwonted outburst of affection, begged of her to tell her all, the wound in Rose's breast began to bleed, and she was glad to speak.

"Juley, do you-can you believe that he wrote that letter which poor Ferdinand was—accused of writing?"

Juliana appeared to muse, and then responded: "Why should he do such a thing?"

"O my goodness, what a girl!" Rose interjected.

"Well, then, to please you, Rose, of course I think he is too honourable."

"You do think so, Juley? But if he himself confessed it—what then? You would not believe him, would you?"

"Oh, then I can't say. Why should he condemn himself?"

"But you would know—you would know that he was a man to suffer death rather than be guilty of the smallest baseness. His birth—what is that!" Rose filliped her fingers: "But his acts—what he is himself you would be sure of, would you not? Dear Juley! Oh, for heaven's sake, speak out plainly to me."

A wily look had crept over Juliana's features.

"Certainly," she said, in a tone that belied it, and drawing Rose to her bosom, the groan she heard there was passing sweet to her.

"He has confessed it to Mama," sobbed Rose. "Why did he not come to me first? He has confessed it—the abominable thing has come out of his own mouth. He went to her last night. . ."

Juliana patted her shoulders regularly as they heaved. When words were intelligible between them, Juliana said:

"At least, dear, you must admit that he has redeemed it."

"Redeemed it? Could he do less?" Rose dried her eyes vehemently, as if the tears shamed her. "A man who could have let another suffer for his crime—I could never have lifted my head again. I think I would have cut off this hand that plighted itself to him! As it is, I hardly dare look at myself. But you don't think it, dear? You know it to be false! false! false!"

"Why should Mr. Harrington confess it?" said Juliana.

"Oh, don't speak his name!" cried Rose.

Her cousin smiled. "So many strange things happen," she said, and sighed.

"Don't sigh: I shall think you believe it!" cried Rose. An appearance of constrained repose was assumed. Rose glanced up, studied for an instant, and breathlessly uttered: "You do, you do believe it, Juley?"

For answer, Juliana hugged her with much warmth, and recommenced the patting.

"I dare say it's a mistake," she remarked. "He may have been jealous of Ferdinand. You know I have not seen the letter. I have only heard of it. In love, they say, you ought to excuse. . . And the want of religious education! His sister. . ."

Rose interrupted her with a sharp shudder. Might it not be possible that one who had the same blood as the Countess would stoop to a momentary vileness.

How changed was Rose from the haughty damsel of yesterday!

"Do you think my lover could tell a lie?" "He—would not love me long if I did!"

These phrases arose and rang in Juliana's ears while she pursued the task of comforting the broken spirit that now lay prone on the bed, and now impetuously paced the room. Rose had come thinking the moment Juliana's name was mentioned, that here was the one to fortify her faith in Evan: one who, because she loved, could not doubt him. She moaned in a terror of distrust, loathing her cousin: not asking herself why she needed support. And indeed she was too young for much clear self-questioning, and her blood was flowing too quickly for her brain to perceive more than one thing at a time.

"Does your mother believe it?" said Juliana, evading a direct assault.

"Mama? She never doubts what you speak," answered Rose, disconsolately.

"She does?"

"Yes."

Whereat Juliana looked most grave, and Rose felt that it was hard to breathe.

She had grown very cold and calm, and Juliana had to be expansive unprovoked.

"Believe nothing, dear, till you hear it from his own lips. If he can look in your face and say that he did it. . . well, then! But of course he cannot. It must be some wonderful piece of generosity to his rival."

"So I thought, Juley! so I thought," cried Rose, at the new light, and Juliana smiled contemptuously, and the light flickered and died, and all was darker than before in the bosom of Rose. She had borne so much that this new drop was poison.

"Of course it must be that, if it is anything," Juliana pursued. "You were made to be happy, Rose. And consider, if it is true, people of very low birth, till they have lived long with other people, and if they have no religion, are so very likely to do things. You do not judge them as you do real gentlemen, and one must not be too harsh—I only wish to prepare you for the worst."

A dim form of that very idea had passed through Rose, giving her small comfort.

"Let him tell you with his own lips that what he has told your mother is true, and then, and not till then, believe him," Juliana concluded, and they kissed kindly, and separated. Rose had suddenly lost her firm step, but no sooner was Juliana alone than she left the bed, and addressed her visage to the glass with brightening eyes, as one who saw the glimmer of young hope therein.

"She love him! Not if he told me so ten thousand times would I believe it! and before he has said a syllable she doubts him. Asking me in that frantic way! as if I couldn't see that she wanted me to help her to her faith in him, as she calls it. Not name his name? Mr. Harrington! I may call him Evan: some day!"

Half-uttered, half-mused, the unconscious exclamations issued from her, and for many a weary day since she had dreamed of love, and studied that which is said to attract the creature, she had not been so glowingly elated or looked so much farther in the glass than its pale reflection.

XXXVI

Before Breakfast

Cold through the night the dark-fringed stream had whispered under Evan's eyes, and the night breeze voiced "Fool, fool!" to him, not without a distant echo in his heart. By symbols and sensations he knew that Rose was lost to him. There was no moon: the water seemed aimless, passing on carelessly to oblivion. Now and then, the trees stirred and talked, or a noise was heard from the pastures. He had slain the life that lived in them, and the great glory they were to bring forth, and the end to which all things moved. Had less than the loss of Rose been involved, the young man might have found himself looking out on a world beneath notice, and have been sighing for one more worthy of his clouded excellence but the immense misery present to him in the contemplation of Rose's sad restrained contempt, saved him from the silly elation which is the last, and generally successful, struggle of human nature in those who can so far master it to commit a sacrifice. The loss of that brave high young soul-Rose, who had lifted him out of the mire with her own white hands: Rose, the image of all that he worshipped: Rose, so closely wedded to him that to be cut away from her was to fall like pallid clay from the soaring spirit: surely he was stunned and senseless when he went to utter the words to her mother! Now that he was awake, and could feel his self-inflicted pain, he marvelled at his rashness and foolishness, as perhaps numerous mangled warriors have done for a time, when the battle-field was cool, and they were weak, and the uproar of their jarred nerves has beset them, lying uncherished.

By degrees he grew aware of a little consolatory touch, like the point of a needle, in his consciousness. Laxley would certainly insult him! In that case he would not refuse to fight him. The darkness broke and revealed this happy prospect, and Evan held to it an hour, and could hardly reject it when better thoughts conquered. For would it not be sweet to make the strength of his arm respected? He took a stick, and ran his eye musingly along the length, trifling with it grimly. The great Mel had been his son's instructor in the chivalrous science of fence, and a maitre d'armes in Portugal had given him polish. In Mel's time duels with swords had been occasionally fought, and Evan looked on the sword as the weapon of combat. Face to face with his adversary—what then were birth or position? Action!—action! he sighed for it, as I have done since I came to know that his history must be morally developed. A glow of bitter pleasure exalted him when, after hot passages, and parryings and thrusts, he had disarmed Ferdinand Laxley, and bestowing on him his life, said: "Accept this worthy gift of the son of a tailor!" and he wiped his sword, haply bound up his wrist, and stalked off the ground, the vindicator of man's natural dignity. And then he turned upon himself with laughter, discovering a most wholesome power, barely to be suspected in him yet; but of all the children of glittering Mel and his solid mate, Evan was the best mixed compound of his parents.

He put the stick back in its corner and eyed his wrist, as if he had really just gone through the pretty scene he had just laughed at. It was nigh upon reality, for it suggested the employment of a handkerchief, and he went to a place and drew forth one that had the stain of his blood on it, and the name of Rose at one end. The beloved name was half-blotted by the dull-red mark, and at that sight a strange tenderness took hold of Evan. His passions became dead and of old date. This, then, would be his for ever! Love, for whom earth had been too small, crept exultingly into a nut-shell. He clasped the treasure on his breast, and saw a life beyond his parting with her.

Strengthened thus, he wrote by the morning light to Laxley. The letter was brief, and said simply that the act of which Laxley had been accused, Evan Harrington was responsible for. The latter expressed regret that Laxley should have fallen under a false charge, and, at the same time, indicated that if Laxley considered himself personally aggrieved, the writer was at his disposal.

A messenger had now to be found to convey it to the village-inn. Footmen were stirring about the house, and one meeting Evan close by his door, observed with demure grin, that he could not find the gentleman's nether-garments. The gentleman, it appeared, was Mr. John Raikes, who according to report, had been furnished with a bed at the house, because of a discovery, made at a late period over-night, that farther the gentleman could not go. Evan found him sleeping soundly. How much the poor youth wanted a friend! Fortune had given him instead a born buffoon; and it is perhaps the greatest evil of a position like Evan's, that, with cultured feelings, you are likely to meet with none to know you. Society does not mix well in money-pecking spheres. Here, however, was John Raikes, and Evan had to make the best of him.

"Eh?" yawned Jack, awakened; "I was dreaming I was Napoleon Bonaparte's right-hand man."

"I want you to be mine for half-an-hour," said Evan.

Without replying, the distinguished officer jumped out of bed at a bound, mounted a chair, and peered on tip-toe over the top, from which, with a glance of self-congratulation, he pulled the missing piece of apparel, sighed dejectedly as he descended, while he exclaimed:

"Safe! but no distinction can compensate a man for this state of intolerable suspicion of everybody. I assure you, Harrington, I wouldn't be Napoleon himself—and I have always been his peculiar admirer—to live and be afraid of my valet! I believe it will develop cancer sooner or later in me. I feel singular pains already. Last night, after crowning champagne with ale, which produced a sort of French Revolution in my interior—by the way, that must have made me dream of Napoleon last night, with my lower members in revolt against my head, I had to sit and cogitate for hours on a hiding-place for these-call them what you will. Depend upon it, Harrington, this world is no such funny affair as we fancy."

"Then it is true, that you could let a man play pranks on you," said Evan. "I took it for one of your jokes."

"Just as I can't believe that you're a tailor," returned Jack. "It's not a bit more extraordinary."

"But, Jack, if you cause yourself to be contemptible—"

"Contemptible!" cried Jack. "This is not the tone I like. Contemptible! why it's my eccentricity among my equals. If I dread the profane vulgar, that only proves that I'm above them. Odi, etc. Besides, Achilles had his weak point, and egad, it was when he faced about! By Jingo! I wish I'd had that idea yesterday. I should have behaved better."

Evan could see that the creature was beginning to rely desperately on his humour.

"Come," he said, "be a man to-day. Throw off your motley. When I met you that night so oddly, you had been acting like a worthy fellow, trying to earn your bread in the best way you could—"

"And precisely because I met you, of all men, I've been going round and round ever since," said Jack. "A clown or pantaloon would have given me balance. Say no more. You couldn't help it. We met because we were the two extremes."

Sighing, "What a jolly old inn!" Raikes rolled himself over in the sheets, and gave two or three snug jolts indicative of his determination to be comfortable while he could.

"Do you intend to carry on this folly, Jack?"

"Say, sacrifice," was the answer. "I feel it as much as you possibly could, Mr. Harrington. Hear the facts," Jack turned round again. "Why did I consent to this absurdity? Because of my ambition. That old fellow, whom I took to be a clerk of Messrs. Grist, said: 'You want to cut a figure in the world—you're armed now.' A sort of Fortunatus's joke. It was his way of launching me. But did he think I intended this for more than a lift? I his puppet? He, sir, was my tool! Well, I came. All my efforts were strained to shorten the period of penance. I had the best linen, and put on captivating manners. I should undoubtedly have won some girl of station, and cast off my engagement like an old suit, but just mark!—now mark how Fortune tricks us! After the pic-nic yesterday, the domestics of the house came to clear away, and the band being there, I stopped them and bade them tune up, and at the same time seizing the maid Wheedle, away we flew. We danced, we whirled, we twirled. Ale upon this! My head was lost. 'Why don't it last for ever?' says I. 'I wish it did,' says she. The naivete enraptured me. 'Oooo!' I cried, hugging her, and then, you know, there was no course open to a man of honour but to offer marriage and make a lady of her. I proposed: she accepted me, and here I am, eternally tied to this accurst insignia, if I'm to keep my promise! Isn't that a sacrifice, friend H.? There's no course open to me. The poor girl is madly in love. She called me a 'rattle!' As a gentleman, I cannot recede."

Evan got up and burst into damnable laughter at this burlesque of himself. Telling the fellow the service he required, and receiving a groaning assurance that the letter should, without loss of time, be delivered in proper style, the egoist, as Jack heartily thought him, fell behind his; knitted brows, and, after musing abstractedly, went forth to light upon his fate.

But a dread of meeting had seized both Rose and Evan. She had exhausted her first sincerity of unbelief in her interview with Juliana: and he had begun to consider what he could say to her. More than the three words "I did it," would not be possible; and if she made him repeat them, facing her truthful eyes, would he be man enough to strike her bared heart twice? And, ah! the sullen brute he must seem, standing before her dumb, hearing her sigh, seeing her wretched effort not to show how unwillingly her kind spirit despised him. The reason for the act—she would ask for that! Rose would not be so philosophic as her mother. She would grasp at every chance to excuse the deed. He cried out against his scheming sister in an agony, and while he did so, encountered Miss Carrington and Miss. Bonner in deep converse. Juliana pinched her arm, whereupon Miss Carrington said: "You look merry this morning, Mr. Harrington": for he was unawares smiling at the image of himself in the mirror of John Raikes. That smile, transformed to a chuckling grimace, travelled to Rose before they met.

Why did she not come to him?

A soft voice at his elbow made his blood stop. It was Caroline. She kissed him, answering his greeting: "Is it good morning?"

"Certainly," said he. "By the way, don't forget that the coach leaves early."

"My darling Evan! you make me so happy. For it was really a mistaken sense of honour. For what can at all excuse a falsehood, you know, Evan!"

Caroline took his arm, and led him into the sun, watching his face at times. Presently she said: "I want just to be assured that you thought more wisely than when you left us last night."

"More wisely?" Evan turned to her with a playful smile.

"My dear brother! you did not do what you said you would do?"

"Have you ever known me not to do what I said I would do?"

"Evan! Good heaven! you did it? Then how can you remain here an instant? Oh, no, no!—say no, darling!"

"Where is Louisa?" he inquired.

"She is in her room. She will never appear at breakfast, if she knows this."

"Perhaps more solitude would do her good," said Evan.

"Remember, if this should prove true, think how you punish her!"

On that point Evan had his own opinion.

"Well, I shall never have to punish you in this way, my love, he said fondly, and Caroline dropped her eyelids.

"Don't think that I am blaming her," he added, trying to feel as honestly as he spoke. "I was mad to come here. I see it all now. Let us keep to our place. We are all the same before God till we disgrace ourselves." Possibly with that sense of shame which some young people have who are not professors of sounding sentences, or affected by missionary zeal, when they venture to breathe the holy name, Evan blushed, and walked on humbly silent. Caroline murmured: "Yes, yes! oh, brother!" and her figure drew to him as if for protection. Pale, she looked up.

"Shall you always love me, Evan?"

"Whom else have I to love?"

"But always—always? Under any circumstances?"

"More and more, dear. I always have, and shall. I look to you now. I have no home but in your heart now."

She was agitated, and he spoke warmly to calm her.

The throb of deep emotion rang in her rich voice. "I will live any life to be worthy of your love, Evan," and she wept.

To him they were words and tears without a history.

Nothing further passed between them. Caroline went to the Countess: Evan waited for Rose. The sun was getting high. The face of the stream glowed like metal. Why did she not come? She believed him guilty from the mouth of another? If so, there was something less for him to lose. And now the sacrifice he had made did whisper a tale of mortal magnificence in his ears: feelings that were not his noblest stood up exalted. He waited till the warm meadow-breath floating past told that the day had settled into heat, and then he waited no more, but quietly walked into the house with the strength of one who has conquered more than human scorn.

XXXVII

The Retreat from Beckley

Never would the Countess believe that brother of hers, idiot as by nature he might be, and heir to unnumbered epithets, would so far forget what she had done for him, as to drag her through the mud for nothing: and so she told Caroline again and again, vehemently.

It was about ten minutes before the time for descending to the breakfast-table. She was dressed, and sat before the glass, smoothing her hair, and applying the contents of a pot of cold cream to her forehead between-whiles. With perfect sincerity she repeated that she could not believe it. She had only trusted Evan once since their visit to Beckley; and that this once he should, when treated as a man, turn traitor to their common interests, and prove himself an utter baby, was a piece of nonsense her great intelligence indignantly rejected.

"Then, if true," she answered Caroline's assurances finally, "if true, he is not his father's son!"

By which it may be seen that she had indeed taken refuge in the Castle of Negation against the whole army of facts.

"He is acting, Carry. He is acting the ideas of his ridiculous empty noddle!"

"No," said Caroline, mournfully, "he is not. I have never known Evan to lie."

"Then you must forget the whipping he once had from his mother—little dolt! little selfish pig! He obtains his reputation entirely from his abominable selfishness, and then stands tall, and asks us to admire him. He bursts with vanity. But if you lend your credence to it, Carry, how, in the name of goodness, are you to appear at the breakfast?

"I was going to ask you whether you would come," said Caroline, coldly.

"If I can get my hair to lie flat by any means at all, of course!" returned the Countess. "This dreadful horrid country pomade! Why did we not bring a larger stock of the Andalugian Regenerator? Upon my honour, my dear, you use a most enormous quantity; I must really tell you that."

Conning here entered to say that Mr. Evan had given orders for the boxes to be packed and everything got ready to depart by half-past eleven o'clock, when the fly would call for them and convey them to Fallow field in time to meet the coach for London.

The Countess turned her head round to Caroline like an astonished automaton.

"Given orders!" she interjected.

"I have very little to get ready," remarked Caroline.

"Be so good as to wait outside the door one instant," said the Countess to Conning, with particular urbanity.

Conning heard a great deal of vigorous whispering within, and when summoned to re-appear, a note was handed to her to convey to Mr. Harrington immediately. He was on the lawn; read it, and wrote back three hasty lines in pencil.

"Louisa. You have my commands to quit this house, at the hour named, this day. You will go with me. E. H."

Conning was again requested to wait outside the Countess's door. She was the bearer of another note. Evan read it likewise; tore it up, and said that there was no answer.

The Castle of Negation held out no longer. Ruthless battalions poured over the walls, blew up the Countess's propriety, made frightful ravages in her complexion. Down fell her hair.

"You cannot possibly go to breakfast," said Caroline.

"I must! I must!" cried the Countess. "Why, my dear, if he has done it-wretched creature! don't you perceive that, by withholding our presences, we become implicated with him?" And the Countess, from a burst of frenzy, put this practical question so shrewdly, that Caroline's wits succumbed to her.

"But he has not done it; he is acting!" she pursued, restraining her precious tears for higher purposes, as only true heroines can. "Thinks to frighten me into submission!"

"Do you not think Evan is right in wishing us to leave, after—after—" Caroline humbly suggested.

"Say, before my venerable friend has departed this life," the Countess took her up. "No, I do not. If he is a fool, I am not. No, Carry: I do not jump into ditches for nothing. I will have something tangible for all that I have endured. We are now tailors in this place, remember. If that stigma is affixed to us, let us at least be remunerated for it. Come."

Caroline's own hard struggle demanded all her strength yet she appeared to hesitate. "You will surely not disobey Evan, Louisa?"

"Disobey?" The Countess amazedly dislocated the syllables. "Why, the boy will be telling you next that he will not permit the Duke to visit you! Just your English order of mind, that cannot—brutes!—conceive of friendship between high-born men and beautiful women. Beautiful as you truly are, Carry, five years more will tell on you. But perhaps my dearest is in a hurry to return to her Maxwell? At least he thwacks well!"

Caroline's arm was taken. The Countess loved an occasional rhyme when a point was to be made, and went off nodding and tripping till the time for stateliness arrived, near the breakfast-room door. She indeed was acting. At the bottom of her heart there was a dismal rage of passions: hatred of those who would or might look tailor in her face: terrors concerning the possible re-visitation of the vengeful Sir Abraham: dread of Evan and the efforts to despise him: the shocks of many conflicting elements. Above it all her countenance was calmly, sadly sweet: even as you may behold some majestic lighthouse glimmering over the tumult of a midnight sea.

An unusual assemblage honoured the breakfast that morning. The news of Mrs. Bonner's health was more favourable. How delighted was the Countess to hear that! Mrs. Bonner was the only firm ground she stood on there, and after receiving and giving gentle salutes, she talked of Mrs. Bonner, and her night-watch by the sick bed, in a spirit of doleful hope. This passed off the moments till she could settle herself to study faces. Decidedly, every lady present looked glum, with the single exception of Miss Current. Evan was by Lady Jocelyn's side. Her ladyship spoke to him; but the Countess observed that no one else did. To herself, however, the gentlemen were as attentive as ever. Evan sat three chairs distant from her.

If the traitor expected his sister to share in his disgrace, by noticing him, he was in error. On the contrary, the Countess joined the conspiracy to exclude him, and would stop a mild laugh if perchance he looked up. Presently Rose entered. She said "Good morning" to one or two, and glided into a seat.

That Evan was under Lady Jocelyn's protection soon became generally apparent, and also that her ladyship was angry: an exhibition so rare with her that it was the more remarked. Rose could see that she was a culprit in her mother's eyes. She glanced from Evan to her. Lady Jocelyn's mouth shut hard. The girl's senses then perceived the something that was afloat at the table; she thought with a pang of horror: "Has Juliana told?" Juliana smiled on her; but the aspect of Mrs. Shorne, and of Miss

Carrington, spoke for their knowledge of that which must henceforth be the perpetual reproof to her headstrong youth.

"At what hour do you leave us?" said Lady Jocelyn to Evan.

"When I leave the table, my lady. The fly will call for my sisters at half-past eleven."

"There is no necessity for you to start in advance?"

"I am going over to see my mother."

Rose burned to speak to him now. Oh! why had she delayed! Why had she swerved from her good rule of open, instant explanations? But Evan's heart was stern to his love. Not only had she, by not coming, shown her doubt of him,—she had betrayed him!

Between the Countess, Melville, Sir John, and the Duke, an animated dialogue was going on, over which Miss Current played like a lively iris. They could not part with the Countess. Melville said he should be left stranded, and numerous pretty things were uttered by other gentlemen: by the women not a word. Glancing from certain of them lingeringly to her admirers, the Countess smiled her thanks, and then Andrew, pressed to remain, said he was willing and happy, and so forth; and it seemed that her admirers had prevailed over her reluctance, for the Countess ended her little protests with a vanquished bow. Then there was a gradual rising from table. Evan pressed Lady Jocelyn's hand, and turning from her bent his head to Sir Franks, who, without offering an exchange of cordialities, said, at arm's length: "Good-bye, sir." Melville also gave him that greeting stiffly. Harry was perceived to rush to the other end of the room, in quest of a fly apparently. Poor Caroline's heart ached for her brother, to see him standing there in the shadow of many faces. But he was not left to stand alone. Andrew quitted the circle of Sir John, Seymour Jocelyn, Mr. George Uplift, and others, and linked his arm to Evan's. Rose had gone. While Evan looked for her despairingly to say his last word and hear her voice once more, Sir Franks said to his wife:

"See that Rose keeps up-stairs."

"I want to speak to her," was her ladyship's answer, and she moved to the door.

Evan made way for her, bowing.

"You will be ready at half-past eleven, Louisa," he said, with calm distinctness, and passed from that purgatory.

Now honest Andrew attributed the treatment Evan met with to the exposure of yesterday. He was frantic with democratic disgust.

"Why the devil don't they serve me like that; eh? 'Cause I got a few coppers! There, Van! I'm a man of peace; but if you'll call any man of'em out I'll stand your second—'pon my soul, I will. They must be cowards, so there isn't much to fear. Confound the fellows, I tell 'em every day I'm the son of a cobbler, and egad, they grow civiller. What do they mean? Are cobblers ranked over tailors?"

"Perhaps that's it," said Evan.

"Hang your gentlemen!" Andrew cried.

"Let us have breakfast first," uttered a melancholy voice near them in the passage.

"Jack!" said Evan. "Where have you been?"

"I didn't know the breakfast-room," Jack returned, "and the fact is, my spirits are so down, I couldn't muster up courage to ask one of the footmen. I delivered your letter. Nothing hostile took place. I bowed fiercely to let him know what he might expect. That generally stops it. You see, I talk prose. I shall never talk anything else!"

Andrew recommenced his jests of yesterday with Jack. The latter bore them patiently, as one who had endured worse.

"She has rejected me!" he whispered to Evan. "Talk of the ingratitude of women! Ten minutes ago I met her. She perked her eyebrows at me!—tried to run away. 'Miss Wheedle': I said. 'If you please, I'd rather not,' says she. To cut it short, the sacrifice I made to her was the cause. It's all over the house. She gave the most excruciating hint. Those low-born females are so horribly indelicate. I stood confounded. Commending his new humour, Evan persuaded him to breakfast immediately, and hunger being one of Jack's solitary incitements to a sensible course of conduct, the disconsolate gentleman followed its dictates. "Go with him, Andrew," said Evan. "He is here as my friend, and may be made uncomfortable."

"Yes, yes,—ha! ha! I'll follow the poor chap," said Andrew. "But what is it all about? Louisa won't go, you know. Has the girl given you up because she saw your mother, Van? I thought it was all right. Why the deuce are you running away?"

"Because I've just seen that I ought never to have come, I suppose," Evan replied, controlling the wretched heaving of his chest.

"But Louisa won't go, Van."

"Understand, my dear Andrew, that I know it to be quite imperative. Be ready yourself with Caroline. Louisa will then make her choice. Pray help me in this. We must not stay a minute more than is necessary in this house."

"It's an awful duty," breathed Andrew, after a pause. "I see nothing but hot water at home. Why—but it's no use asking questions. My love to your mother. I say, Van,—now isn't Lady Jocelyn a trump?"

"God bless her!" said Evan. And the moisture in Andrew's eyes affected his own.

"She's the staunchest piece of woman-goods I ever—I know a hundred cases of her!"

"I know one, and that's enough," said Evan.

Not a sign of Rose! Can Love die without its dear farewell on which it feeds, away from the light, dying by bits? In Evan's heart Love seemed to die, and all the pangs of a death were there as he trod along the gravel and stepped beneath the gates of Beckley Court.

Meantime the gallant Countess was not in any way disposed to retreat on account of Evan's defection. The behaviour toward him at the breakfast-table proved to her that he had absolutely committed his egregious folly, and as no General can have concert with a fool, she cut him off from her affections resolutely. Her manifest disdain at his last speech, said as much to everybody present. Besides, the lady was in her element here, and compulsion is required to make us relinquish our element. Lady Jocelyn certainly had not expressly begged of her to remain: the Countess told Melville so, who said that if she required such an invitation she should have it, but that a guest to whom they were so much indebted, was bound to spare them these formalities.

"What am I to do?"

The Countess turned piteously to the diplomatist's wife.

She answered, retiringly: "Indeed I cannot say."

Upon this, the Countess accepted Melville's arm, and had some thoughts of punishing the woman.

They were seen parading the lawn. Mr. George Uplift chuckled singularly.

"Just the old style," he remarked, but corrected the inadvertence with a "hem!" committing himself more shamefully the instant after. "I'll wager she has the old Dip. down on his knee before she cuts."

"Bet can't be taken," observed Sir John Loring. "It requires a spy."

Harry, however, had heard the remark, and because he wished to speak to her, let us hope, and reproach her for certain things when she chose to be disengaged, he likewise sallied out, being forlorn as a youth whose sweet vanity is much hurt.

The Duke had paired off with Mrs. Strike. The lawn was fair in sunlight where they walked. The air was rich with harvest smells, and the scent of autumnal roses. Caroline was by nature luxurious and soft. The thought of that drilled figure to which she was returning in bondage, may have thrown into bright relief the polished and gracious nobleman who walked by her side, shadowing forth the chances of a splendid freedom. Two lovely tears fell from her eyes. The Duke watched them quietly.

"Do you know, they make me jealous?" he said.

Caroline answered him with a faint smile.

"Reassure me, my dear lady; you are not going with your brother this morning?"

"Your Grace, I have no choice!"

"May I speak to you as your warmest friend? From what I hear, it appears to be right that your brother should not stay. To the best of my ability I will provide for him: but I sincerely desire to disconnect you from those who are unworthy of you. Have you not promised to trust in me? Pray, let me be your guide."

Caroline replied to the heart of his words: "I dare not."

"What has changed you?"

"I am not changed, but awakened," said Caroline.

The Duke paced on in silence.

"Pardon me if I comprehend nothing of such a change," he resumed. "I asked you to sacrifice much; all that I could give in return I offered. Is it the world you fear?"

"What is the world to such as I am?"

"Can you consider it a duty to deliver yourself bound to that man again?"

"Heaven pardon me, my lord, I think of that too little!"

The Duke's next question: "Then what can it be?" stood in his eyes.

"Oh!" Caroline's touch quivered on his arm, "Do not suppose me frivolous, ungrateful, or—or cowardly. For myself you have offered more happiness than I could have hoped for. To be allied to one so generous, I could bear anything. Yesterday you had my word: give it me back to-day!"

Very curiously the Duke gazed on her, for there was evidence of internal torture across her forehead.

"I may at least beg to know the cause for this request?"

She quelled some throbbing in her bosom. "Yes."

He waited, and she said: "There is one—if I offended him, I could not live. If now I followed my wishes, he would lose his faith in the last creature that loves him. He is unhappy. I could bear what is called disgrace, my lord—I shudder to say it—I could sin against heaven; but I dare not do what would make him despise me."

She was trembling violently; yet the nobleman, in his surprise, could not forbear from asking who this person might be, whose influence on her righteous actions was so strong.

"It is my brother, my lord," she said.

Still more astonished, "Your brother!" the Duke exclaimed. "My dearest lady, I would not wound you; but is not this a delusion? We are so placed that we must speak plainly. Your brother I have reason to feel sure is quite unworthy of you."

"Unworthy? My brother Evan? Oh! he is noble, he is the best of men!"

"And how, between yesterday and to-day, has he changed you?"

"It is that yesterday I did not know him, and to-day I do."

Her brother, a common tradesman, a man guilty of forgery and the utmost baseness—all but kicked out of the house! The Duke was too delicate to press her further. Moreover, Caroline had emphasized the "yesterday" and "to-day," showing that the interval which had darkened Evan to everybody else, had illumined him to her. He employed some courtly eloquence, better unrecorded; but if her firm resolution perplexed him, it threw a strange halo round the youth from whom it sprang.

The hour was now eleven, and the Countess thought it full time to retire to her entrenchment in Mrs. Bonner's chamber. She had great things still to do: vast designs were in her hand awaiting the sanction of Providence. Alas! that little idle promenade was soon to be repented. She had joined her sister, thinking it safer to have her upstairs till they were quit of Evan. The Duke and the diplomatist loitering in the rear, these two fair women sailed across the lawn, conscious, doubtless, over all their sorrows and schemes, of the freight of beauty they carried.

What meant that gathering on the steps? It was fortuitous, like everything destined to confound us. There stood Lady Jocelyn with Andrew, fretting his pate. Harry leant against a pillar, Miss Carrington, Mrs. Shorne, and Mrs. Melville, supported by Mr. George Uplift, held watchfully by. Juliana, with Master Alec and Miss Dorothy, were in the background.

Why did our General see herself cut off from her stronghold, as by a hostile band? She saw it by that sombre light in Juliana's eyes, which had shown its ominous gleam whenever disasters were on the point of unfolding.

Turning to Caroline, she said: "Is there a back way?"

Too late! Andrew called.

"Come along, Louisa, Just time, and no more. Carry, are you packed?"

This in reality was the first note of the retreat from Beckley; and having blown it, the hideous little trumpeter burst into scarlet perspirations, mumbling to Lady Jocelyn: "Now, my lady, mind you stand by me."

The Countess walked straight up to him.

"Dear Andrew! this sun is too powerful for you. I beg you, withdraw into the shade of the house."

She was about to help him with all her gentleness.

"Yes, yes. All right," Louisa rejoined Andrew. "Come, go and pack. The fly 'll be here, you know—too late for the coach, if you don't mind, my lass. Ain't you packed yet?"

The horrible fascination of vulgarity impelled the wretched lady to answer: "Are we herrings?" And then she laughed, but without any accompaniment.

"I am now going to dear Mrs. Bonner," she said, with a tender glance at Lady Jocelyn.

"My mother is sleeping," her ladyship remarked.

"Come, Carry, my darling!" cried Andrew.

Caroline looked at her sister. The Countess divined Andrew's shameful trap.

"I was under an engagement to go and canvass this afternoon," she said.

"Why, my dear Louisa, we've settled that in here this morning," said Andrew. "Old Tom only stuck up a puppet to play with. We've knocked him over, and march in victorious—eh, my lady?"

"Oh!" exclaimed the Countess, "if Mr. Raikes shall indeed have listened to my inducements!"

"Deuce a bit of inducements!" returned Andrew. "The fellow's ashamed of himself-ha! ha! Now then, Louisa."

While they talked, Juliana had loosed Dorothy and Alec, and these imps were seen rehearsing a remarkable play, in which the damsel held forth a hand and the cavalier advanced and kissed it with a loud smack, being at the same time reproached for his lack of grace.

"You are so English!" cried Dorothy, with perfect languor, and a malicious twitter passed between two or three. Mr. George spluttered indiscreetly.

The Countess observed the performance. Not to convert the retreat into a total rout, she, with that dark flush which was her manner of blushing, took formal leave of Lady Jocelyn, who, in return, simply said: "Good-bye, Countess." Mrs. Strike's hand she kindly shook.

The few digs and slaps and thrusts at gloomy Harry and prim Miss Carrington and boorish Mr. George, wherewith the Countess, torn with wrath, thought it necessary to cover her retreat, need not be told. She struck the weak alone: Juliana she respected. Masterly tactics, for they showed her power, gratified her vengeance, and left her unassailed. On the road she had Andrew to tear to pieces. O delicious operation! And O shameful brother to reduce her to such joys! And, O Providence! may a poor desperate soul, betrayed through her devotion, unremunerated for her humiliation and absolute hard work, accuse thee? The Countess would have liked to. She felt it to be the instigation of the devil, and decided to remain on the safe side still.

Happily for Evan, she was not ready with her packing by half-past eleven. It was near twelve when he, pacing in front of the inn, observed Polly Wheedle, followed some yards in the rear by John Raikes, advancing towards him. Now Polly had been somewhat delayed by Jack's persecutions, and Evan declining to attend to the masked speech of her mission, which directed him to go at once down a certain lane in the neighbourhood of the park, some minutes were lost.

"Why, Mr. Harrington," said Polly, "it's Miss Rose: she's had leave from her Ma. Can you stop away, when it's quite proper?"

Evan hesitated. Before he could conquer the dark spirit, lo, Rose appeared, walking up the village street. Polly and her adorer fell back.

Timidly, unlike herself, Rose neared him.

"I have offended you, Evan. You would not come to me: I have come to you."

"I am glad to be able to say good-bye to you, Rose," was his pretty response.

Could she have touched his hand then, the blood of these lovers rushing to one channel must have made all clear. At least he could hardly have struck her true heart with his miserable lie. But that chance was lost they were in the street, where passions have no play.

"Tell me, Evan,—it is not true."

He, refining on his misery, thought, She would not ask it if she trusted me: and answered her: "You have heard it from your mother, Rose."

"But I will not believe it from any lips but yours, Evan. Oh, speak, speak!"

It pleased him to think: How could one who loved me believe it even then?

He said: "It can scarcely do good to make me repeat it, Rose."

And then, seeing her dear bosom heave quickly, he was tempted to fall on his knees to her with a wild outcry of love. The chance was lost. The inexorable street forbade it.

There they stood in silence, gasping at the barrier that divided them.

Suddenly a noise was heard. "Stop! stop!" cried the voice of John Raikes. "When a lady and gentleman are talking together, sir, do you lean your long ears over them—ha?"

Looking round, Evan beheld Laxley a step behind, and Jack rushing up to him, seizing his collar, and instantly undergoing ignominious prostration for his heroic defence of the privacy of lovers.

"Stand aside"; said Laxley, imperiously. "Rosey so you've come for me. Take my arm. You are under my protection."

Another forlorn "Is it true?" Rose cast toward Evan with her eyes. He wavered under them.

"Did you receive my letter?" he demanded of Laxley.

"I decline to hold converse with you," said Laxley, drawing Rose's hand on his arm.

"You will meet me to-day or to-morrow?"

"I am in the habit of selecting my own company."

Rose disengaged her hand. Evan grasped it. No word of farewell was uttered. Her mouth moved, but her eyes were hard shut, and nothing save her hand's strenuous pressure, equalling his own, told that their parting had been spoken, the link violently snapped.

Mr. John Raikes had been picked up and pulled away by Polly. She now rushed to Evan: "Good-bye, and God bless you, dear Mr. Harrington. I'll find means of letting you know how she is. And he shan't have her, mind!"

Rose was walking by Laxley's side, but not leaning on his arm. Evan blessed her for this. Ere she was out of sight the fly rolled down the street. She did not heed it, did not once turn her head. Ah, bitter unkindness!

When Love is hurt, it is self-love that requires the opiate. Conning gave it him in the form of a note in a handwriting not known to him. It said:

I do not believe it, and nothing will ever make me.

JULIANA

Evan could not forget these words. They coloured his farewell to Beckley: the dear old downs, the hopgardens, the long grey farms walled with clipped yew, the home of his lost love! He thought of them through weary nights when the ghostly image with the hard shut eyelids and the quivering lips would rise and sway irresolutely in air till a shape out of the darkness extinguished it. Pride is the God of Pagans. Juliana had honoured his God. The spirit of Juliana seemed to pass into the body of Rose, and suffer for him as that ghostly image visibly suffered.

XXXVIII

In which We Have to See in the Dark

So ends the fourth act of our comedy.

After all her heroism and extraordinary efforts, after, as she feared, offending Providence—after facing Tailordom—the Countess was rolled away in a dingy fly unrewarded even by a penny, for what she had gone through. For she possessed eminently the practical nature of her sex; and though she would have scorned, and would have declined to handle coin so base, its absence was upbraidingly mentioned in her spiritual outcries. Not a penny!

Nor was there, as in the miseries of retreat she affected indifferently to imagine, a Duke fished out of the ruins of her enterprise, to wash the mud off her garments and edge them with radiance. Caroline, it became clear to her, had been infected by Evan's folly. Caroline, she subsequently learnt, had likewise been a fool. Instead of marvelling at the genius that had done so much in spite of the pair of fools that were the right and left wing of her battle array, the simple-minded lady wept. She wanted success, not genius. Admiration she was ever ready to forfeit for success.

Nor did she say to the tailors of earth: "Weep, for I sought to emancipate you from opprobrium by making one of you a gentleman; I fought for a great principle and have failed." Heroic to the end, she herself shed all the tears; took all the sorrow.

Where was consolation? Would any Protestant clergyman administer comfort to her? Could he? might he do so? He might listen, and quote texts; but he would demand the harsh rude English for everything; and the Countess's confessional thoughts were all innuendoish, aerial; too delicate to live in our shameless tongue. Confession by implication, and absolution; she could know this to be what she wished for, and yet not think it. She could see a haven of peace in that picture of the little brown box with the sleekly reverend figure bending his ear to the kneeling Beauty outside, thrice ravishing as she half-lifts the veil of her sins and her visage!—yet she started alarmed to hear it whispered that the fair penitent was the Countess de Saldar; urgently she prayed that no disgraceful brother might ever drive her to that!

Never let it be a Catholic priest!—she almost fashioned her petition into words. Who was to save her? Alas! alas! in her dire distress—in her sense of miserable pennilessness, she clung to Mr. John Raikes, of the curricle, the mysteriously rich young gentleman; and on that picture, with Andrew roguishly contemplating it, and Evan, with feelings regarding his sister that he liked not to own, the curtain commiseratingly drops.

As in the course of a stream you come upon certain dips, where, but here and there, a sparkle or a gloom of the full flowing water is caught through deepening foliage, so the history that concerns us wanders out of day for a time, and we must violate the post and open written leaves to mark the turn it takes.

First we have a letter from Mr. Goren to Mrs. Mel, to inform her that her son has arrived and paid his respects to his future instructor in the branch of science practised by Mr. Goren.

"He has arrived at last," says the worthy tradesman. "His appearance in the shop will be highly gentlemanly, and when he looks a little more pleasing, and grows fond of it, nothing will be left to be desired. The ladies, his sisters, have not thought proper to call. I had hopes of the custom of Mr. Andrew Cogglesby. Of course you wish him to learn tailoring thoroughly?"

Mrs. Mel writes back, thanking Mr. Goren, and saying that "she had shown the letter to inquiring creditors, and that she does wish her son to learn his business from the root." This produces a second letter from Mr. Goren, which imparts to her that at the root of the tree, of tailoring the novitiate must sit no less than six hours a day with his legs crossed and doubled under him, cheerfully plying needle and thread; and that, without this probation, to undergo which the son resolutely objects, all hope of his climbing to the top of the lofty tree, and viewing mankind from an eminence, must be surrendered.

"If you do not insist, my dear Mrs. Harrington, I tell you candidly, your son may have a shop, but he will be no tailor."

Mrs. Mel understands her son and his state of mind well enough not to insist, and is resigned to the melancholy consequence.

Then Mr. Goren discovers an extraordinary resemblance between Evan and his father: remarking merely that the youth is not the gentleman his father was in a shop, while he admits, that had it been conjoined to business habits, he should have envied his departed friend.

He has soon something fresh to tell; and it is that young Mr. Harrington is treating him cavalierly. That he should penetrate the idea or appreciate the merits of Mr. Goren's Balance was hardly to be expected at present: the world did not, and Mr. Goren blamed no young man for his ignorance. Still a proper attendance was requisite. Mr. Goren thought it very singular that young Mr. Harrington should demand all the hours of the day for his own purposes, up to half-past four. He found it difficult to speak to him as a master, and begged that Mrs. Harrington would, as a mother.

The reply of Mrs. Mel is dashed with a trifle of cajolery. She has heard from her son, and seeing that her son takes all that time from his right studies, to earn money wherewith to pay debts of which Mr. Goren is cognizant, she trusts that their oldest friend will overlook it.

Mr. Goren rejoins that he considers that he need not have been excluded from young Mr. Harrington's confidence. Moreover, it is a grief to him that the young gentleman should refrain from accepting any of his suggestions as to the propriety of requesting some, at least, of his rich and titled acquaintance to confer on him the favour of their patronage. "Which they would not repent," adds Mr. Goren, "and might learn to be very much obliged to him for, in return for kindnesses extended to him."

Notwithstanding all my efforts, you see, the poor boy is thrust into the shop. There he is, without a doubt. He sleeps under Mr. Goren's roof: he (since one cannot be too positive in citing the punishment of such a Pagan) stands behind a counter: he (and, oh! choke, young loves, that have hovered around him! shrink from him in natural horror, gentle ladies!) handles the shears. It is not my fault. He would be a Pagan. If you can think him human enough still to care to know how he feels it, I must tell you that he feels it hardly-at all. After a big blow, a very little one scarcely counts. What are outward forms and social ignominies to him whose heart has been struck to the dust? His Gods have fought for him, and there he is! He deserves no pity.

But he does not ask it of you, the callous Pagan! Despise him, if you please, and rank with the Countess, who despises him most heartily. Dipping further into the secrets of the post, we discover a brisk correspondence between Juliana Bonner and Mrs. Strike.

"A thousand thanks to you, my dear Miss Bonner," writes the latter lady. "The unaffected interest you take in my brother touches me deeply. I know him to be worthy of your good opinion. Yes, I will open my heart to you, dearest Juliana; and it shall, as you wish, be quite secret between us. Not to a soul!

"He is quite alone. My sisters Harriet and Louisa will not see him, and I can only do so by stealth. His odd other little friend sometimes drives me out on Sundays, to a place where I meet him; and the Duke of Belfield kindly lends me his carriage. Oh, that we might never part! I am only happy with him!

"Ah, do not doubt him, Juliana, for anything he does! You say, that now the Duke has obtained for him the Secretaryship to my husband's Company, he should not thing, and you do not understand why. I will tell you. Our poor father died in debt, and Evan receives money which enables him by degrees to liquidate these debts, on condition that he consents to be what I dislike as much as you can. He bears it; you can have no idea of his pride! He is too proud to own to himself that it debases him—too proud to complain. It is a tangle—a net that drags him down to it but whatever he is outwardly, he is the noblest human being in the world to me, and but for him, oh, what should I be? Let me beg you to forgive it, if you can. My darling has no friends. Is his temper as sweet as ever? I can answer that. Yes, only he is silent, and looks—when you look into his eyes—colder, as men look when they will not bear much from other men.

"He has not mentioned her name. I am sure she has not written.

"Pity him, and pray for him."

Juliana then makes a communication, which draws forth the following:—

"Mistress of all the Beckley property-dearest, dearest Juliana! Oh! how sincerely I congratulate you! The black on the letter alarmed me so, I could hardly open it, my fingers trembled so; for I esteem you all at Beckley; but when I had opened and read it, I was recompensed. You say you are sorry for Rose. But surely what your Grandmama has done is quite right. It is just, in every sense. But why am I not to tell Evan? I am certain it would make him very happy, and happiness of any kind he needs so much! I will obey you, of course, but I cannot see why. Do you know, my dear child, you are extremely mysterious, and puzzle me. Evan takes a pleasure in speaking of you. You and Lady Jocelyn are his great themes. Why is he to be kept ignorant of your good fortune? The spitting of blood is bad. You must winter in a warm climate. I do think that London is far better for you in the late Autumn than Hampshire. May I ask my sister Harriet to invite you to reside with her for some weeks? Nothing, I know, would give her greater pleasure."

Juliana answers this—

"If you love me—I sometimes hope that you do—but the feeling of being loved is so strange to me that I can only believe it at times—but, Caroline—there, I have mustered up courage to call you by your Christian name at last—Oh, dear Caroline! if you do love me, do not tell Mr. Harrington. I go on my knees to you to beg you not to tell him a word. I have no reasons indeed not any; but I implore you again never even to hint that I am anything but the person he knew at Beckley.

"Rose has gone to Elburne House, where Ferdinand, her friend, is to meet her. She rides and sings the same, and keeps all her colour.

"She may not, as you imagine, have much sensibility. Perhaps not enough. I am afraid that Rose is turning into a very worldly woman!

"As to what you kindly say about inviting me to London, I should like it, and I am my own mistress. Do you know, I think I am older than your brother! I am twenty-three. Pray, when you write, tell me if he is older than that. But should I not be a dreadful burden to you? Sometimes I have to keep to my chamber whole days and days. When that happens now, I think of you entirely. See how I open my heart to you. You say that you do to me. I wish I could really think it."

A postscript begs Caroline "not to forget about the ages."

In this fashion the two ladies open their hearts, and contrive to read one another perfectly in their mutual hypocrisies.

Some letters bearing the signatures of Mr. John Raikes, and Miss Polly Wheedle, likewise pass. Polly inquires for detailed accounts of the health and doings of Mr. Harrington. Jack replies with full particulars of her own proceedings, and mild corrections of her grammar. It is to be noted that Polly grows much humbler to him on paper, which being instantly perceived by the mercurial one, his caressing condescension to her is very beautiful. She is taunted with Mr. Nicholas Frim, and answers, after the lapse of a week, that the aforesaid can be nothing to her, as he "went in a passion to church last Sunday and got married." It appears that they had quarrelled, "because I danced with you that night." To this Mr. Raikes rejoins in a style that would be signified by "ahem!" in language, and an arrangement of the shirt collar before the looking-glass, in action.

BOOK VII

XXXIX

In the Domain of Tailordom

There was peace in Mr. Goren's shop. Badgered Ministers, bankrupt merchants, diplomatists with a headache—any of our modern grandees under difficulties, might have envied that peace over which Mr. Goren presided: and he was an enviable man. He loved his craft, he believed that he had not succeeded the millions of antecedent tailors in vain; and, excepting that trifling coquetry with shirt-fronts, viz., the red crosses, which a shrewd rival had very soon eclipsed by representing nymphs triangularly posed, he devoted himself to his business from morning to night; as rigid in demanding respect from those beneath him, as he was profuse in lavishing it on his patrons. His public boast was, that he owed no man a farthing; his secret comfort, that he possessed two thousand pounds in the Funds. But Mr. Goren did not stop here. Behind these external characteristics he nursed a passion. Evan was astonished and pleased to find in him an enthusiastic fern-collector. Not that Mr. Harrington shared the passion, but the sight of these brown roots spread out, ticketed, on the stained paper, after supper, when the shutters were up and the house defended from the hostile outer world; the old man poring over them, and naming this and that spot where, during his solitary Saturday afternoon and Sunday excursions, he had lighted on the rare samples exhibited this contrast of the quiet evening with the sordid day humanized Mr. Goren to him. He began to see a spirit in the rigid tradesman not so utterly dissimilar to his own, and he fancied that he, too, had a taste for ferns. Round Beckley how they abounded!

He told Mr. Goren so, and Mr. Goren said:

"Some day we'll jog down there together, as the saying goes."

Mr. Goren spoke of it as an ordinary event, likely to happen in the days to come: not as an incident the mere mention of which, as being probable, stopped the breath and made the pulses leap.

For now Evan's education taught him to feel that he was at his lowest degree. Never now could Rose stoop to him. He carried the shop on his back. She saw the brand of it on his forehead. Well! and what was Rose to him, beyond a blissful memory, a star that he had once touched?

Self-love kept him strong by day, but in the darkness of night came his misery; wakening from tender dreams, he would find his heart sinking under a horrible pressure, and then the fair fresh face of Rose swam over him; the hours of Beckley were revived; with intolerable anguish he saw that she was blameless—that he alone was to blame. Yet worse was it when his closed eyelids refused to conjure up the sorrowful lovely nightmare, and he lay like one in a trance, entombed-wretched Pagan! feeling all that had been blindly; when the Past lay beside him like a corpse that he had slain.

These nightly torments helped him to brave what the morning brought. Insensibly also, as Time hardened his sufferings, Evan asked himself what the shame of his position consisted in. He grew stiff-necked. His Pagan virtues stood up one by one to support him. Andrew, courageously evading the interdict that forbade him to visit Evan, would meet him by appointment at City taverns, and flatly offered him a place in the Brewery. Evan declined it, on the pretext that, having received Old Tom's money for the year, he must at least work out that term according to the conditions. Andrew fumed and sneered at Tailordom. Evan said that there was peace in Mr. Goren's shop. His sharp senses discerned in Andrew's sneer a certain sincerity, and he revolted against it. Mr. John Raikes, too, burlesqued Society so well, that he had the satisfaction of laughing at his enemy occasionally. The latter gentleman was still a pensioner, flying about town with the Countess de Saldar, in deadly fear lest that fascinating lady should discover the seat of his fortune; happy, notwithstanding. In the mirror of Evan's little world, he beheld the great one from which he was banished.

Now the dusk of a winter's afternoon was closing over London, when a carriage drew up in front of Mr. Goren's shop, out of which, to Mr. Goren's chagrin, a lady stepped, with her veil down. The lady entered, and said that she wished to speak to Mr. Harrington. Mr. Goren made way for her to his pupil; and was amazed to see her fall into his arms, and hardly gratified to hear her say: "Pardon me, darling, for coming to you in this place."

Evan asked permission to occupy the parlour.

"My place," said Mr. Goren, with humble severity, over his spectacles, "is very poor. Such as it is, it is at the lady's service."

Alone with her, Evan was about to ease his own feelings by remarking to the effect that Mr. Goren was human like the rest of us, but Caroline cried, with unwonted vivacity:

"Yes, yes, I know; but I thought only of you. I have such news for you! You will and must pardon my coming—that's my first thought, sensitive darling that you are!" She kissed him fondly. "Juliana Bonner is in town, staying with us!"

"Is that your news?" asked Evan, pressing her against his breast.

"No, dear love—but still! You have no idea what her fortune—Mrs. Bonner has died and left her—but I mustn't tell you. Oh, my darling! how she admires you! She—she could recompense you; if you would! We will put that by, for the present. Dear! the Duke has begged you, through me, to accept—I think it's to be a sort of bailiff to his estates—I don't know rightly. It's a very honourable post, that gentlemen take: and the income you are to have, Evan, will be near a thousand a year. Now, what do I deserve for my news?"

She put up her mouth for another kiss, out of breath.

"True?" looked Evan's eyes.

"True!" she said, smiling, and feasting on his bewilderment.

After the bubbling in his brain had a little subsided, Evan breathed as a man on whom fresh air is blown. Were not these tidings of release? His ridiculous pride must nevertheless inquire whether Caroline had been begging this for him.

"No, dear—indeed!" Caroline asserted with more than natural vehemence. "It's something that you yourself have done that has pleased him. I don't know what. Only he says, he believes you are a man to be trusted with the keys of anything—and so you are. You are to call on him to-morrow. Will you?"

While Evan was replying, her face became white. She had heard the Major's voice in the shop. His military step advanced, and Caroline, exclaiming, "Don't let me see him!" bustled to a door. Evan nodded, and she slipped through. The next moment he was facing the stiff marine.

"Well, young man," the Major commenced, and, seating himself, added, "be seated. I want to talk to you seriously, sir. You didn't think fit to wait till I had done with the Directors today. You're devilishly out in your discipline, whatever you are at two and two. I suppose there's no fear of being intruded on here? None of your acquaintances likely to be introducing themselves to me?"

"There is not one that I would introduce to you," said Evan.

The Major nodded a brief recognition of the compliment, and then, throwing his back against the chair, fired out: "Come, sir, is this your doing?"

In military phrase, Evan now changed front. His first thought had been that the Major had come for his wife. He perceived that he himself was the special object of his visitation.

"I must ask you what you allude to," he answered.

"You are not at your office, but you will speak to me as if there was some distinction between us," said the Major. "My having married your sister does not reduce me to the ranks, I hope."

The Major drummed his knuckles on the table, after this impressive delivery.

"Hem!" he resumed. "Now, sir, understand, before you speak a word, that I can see through any number of infernal lies. I see that you're prepared for prevarication. By George! it shall come out of you, if I get it by main force. The Duke compelled me to give you that appointment in my Company. Now, sir, did you, or did you not, go to him and deliberately state to him that you believed the affairs of the Company to be in a bad condition—infamously handled, likely to involve his honour as a gentleman? I ask you, sir, did you do this, or did you not do it?"

Evan waited till the sharp rattle of the Major's close had quieted.

"If I am to answer the wording of your statement, I may say that I did not."

"Very good; very good; that will do. Are you aware that the Duke has sent in his resignation as a Director of our Company?"

"I hear of it first from you."

"Confound your familiarity!" cried the irritable officer, rising. "Am I always to be told that I married your sister? Address me, sir, as becomes your duty."

Evan heard the words "beggarly tailor" mumbled "out of the gutters," and "cursed connection." He stood in the attitude of attention, while the Major continued:

"Now, young man, listen to these facts. You came to me this day last week, and complained that you did not comprehend some of our transactions and affairs. I explained them to your damned stupidity. You went away. Three days after that, you had an interview with the Duke. Stop, sir! What the devil do you mean by daring to speak while I am speaking? You saw the Duke, I say. Now, what took place at that interview?"

The Major tried to tower over Evan powerfully, as he put this query. They were of a common height, and to do so, he had to rise on his toes, so that the effect was but momentary.

"I think I am not bound to reply," said Evan.

"Very well, sir; that will do." The Major's fingers were evidently itching for an absent rattan. "Confess it or not, you are dismissed from your post. Do you hear? You are kicked in the street. A beggarly tailor you were born, and a beggarly tailor you will die."

"I must beg you to stop, now," said Evan. "I told you that I was not bound to reply: but I will. If you will sit down, Major Strike, you shall hear what you wish to know."

This being presently complied with, though not before a glare of the Major's eyes had shown his doubt whether it might not be construed into insolence, Evan pursued:

"I came to you and informed you that I could not reconcile the cash-accounts of the Company, and that certain of the later proceedings appeared to me to jeopardize its prosperity. Your explanations did not satisfy me. I admit that you enjoined me to be silent. But the Duke, as a Director, had as strong a right to claim me as his servant, and when he questioned me as to the position of the Company, I told him what I thought, just as I had told you."

"You told him we were jobbers and swindlers, sir!"

"The Duke inquired of me whether I would, under the circumstances, while proceedings were going on which I did not approve of, take the responsibility of allowing my name to remain—"

"Ha! ha! ha!" the Major burst out. This was too good a joke. The name of a miserable young tailor! "Go on, sir, go on!" He swallowed his laughter like oil on his rage.

"I have said sufficient."

Jumping up, the Major swore by the Lord, that he had said sufficient.

"Now, look you here, young man." He squared his finger before Evan, eyeing him under a hard frown, "You have been playing your game again, as you did down at that place in Hampshire. I heard of it—deserved to be shot, by heaven! You think you have got hold of the Duke, and you throw me over. You imagine, I dare say, that I will allow my wife to be talked about to further your interests—you self-seeking young dog! As long as he lent the Company his name, I permitted a great many things. Do you think me a blind idiot, sir? But now she must learn to be satisfied with people who've got no titles, or carriages, and who can't give hundred guinea compliments. You're all of a piece-a set of. . ."

The Major paused, for half a word was on his mouth which had drawn lightning to Evan's eyes.

Not to be baffled, he added: "But look you, sir. I may be ruined. I dare say the Company will go to the dogs—every ass will follow a Duke. But, mark, this goes on no more. I will be no woman's tally. Mind, sir, I take excellent care that you don't traffic in your sister!"

The Major delivered this culminating remark with a well-timed deflection of his forefinger, and slightly turned aside when he had done.

You might have seen Evan's figure rocking, as he stood with his eyes steadily levelled on his sister's husband.

The Major, who, whatever he was, was physically no coward, did not fail to interpret the look, and challenge it.

Evan walked to the door, opened it, and said, between his teeth, "You must go at once."

"Eh, sir, eh? what's this?" exclaimed the warrior but the door was open, Mr. Goren was in the shop; the scandal of an assault in such a house, and the consequent possibility of his matrimonial alliance becoming bruited in the newspapers, held his arm after it had given an involuntary jerk. He marched through with becoming dignity, and marched out into the street; and if necks unelastic and heads erect may be taken as the sign of a proud soul and of nobility of mind, my artist has the Major for his model.

Evan displayed no such a presence. He returned to the little parlour, shut and locked the door to the shop, and forgetting that one was near, sat down, covered his eyes, and gave way to a fit of tearless sobbing. With one foot in the room Caroline hung watching him. A pain that she had never known wrung her nerves. His whole manhood seemed to be shaken, as if by regular pulsations of intensest misery. She stood in awe of the sight till her limbs failed her, and then staggering to him she fell on her knees, clasping his, passionately kissing them.

XL

In which the Countess Still Scents Game

Mr. Raikes and his friend Frank Remand, surnamed Franko, to suit the requirements of metre, in which they habitually conversed, were walking arm-in-arm along the drive in Society's Park on a fine frosty Sunday afternoon of midwinter. The quips and jokes of Franko were lively, and he looked into the carriages passing, as if he knew that a cheerful countenance is not without charms for their inmates. Raikes' face, on the contrary, was barren and bleak. Being of that nature that when a pun was made he must perforce outstrip it, he fell into Franko's humour from time to time, but albeit aware that what he uttered was good, and by comparison transcendent, he refused to enjoy it. Nor when Franko started from his arm to declaim a passage, did he do other than make limp efforts to unite himself to Franko again. A further sign of immense depression in him was that instead of the creative, it was the critical faculty he exercised, and rather than reply to Franko in his form of speech, he scanned occasional lines and objected to particular phrases. He had clearly exchanged the sanguine for the bilious temperament, and was fast stranding on the rocky shores of prose. Franko bore this very well, for he, like Raikes in happier days, claimed all the glances of lovely woman as his own, and on his right there flowed a stream of Beauties. At last he was compelled to observe: "This change is sudden: wherefore so downcast? With tigrine claw thou mangiest my speech, thy cheeks are like December's pippin, and thy tongue most sour!"

"Then of it make a farce!" said Raikes, for the making of farces was Franko's profession. "Wherefore so downcast! What a line! There! let's walk on. Let us the left foot forward stout advance. I care not for the herd."

"'Tis love!" cried Franko.

"Ay, an' it be!" Jack gloomily returned.

"For ever cruel is the sweet Saldar?"

Raikes winced at this name.

"A truce to banter, Franko!" he said sternly: but the subject was opened, and the wound.

"Love!" he pursued, mildly groaning. "Suppose you adored a fascinating woman, and she knew—positively knew—your manly weakness, and you saw her smiling upon everybody, and she told you to be happy, and egad, when you came to reflect, you found that after three months' suit you were nothing better than her errand-boy? A thing to boast of, is it not, quotha?"

"Love's yellow-fever, jealousy, methinks," Franko commenced in reply; but Raikes spat at the emphasized word.

"Jealousy!—who's jealous of clergymen and that crew? Not I, by Pluto! I carried five messages to one fellow with a coat-tail straight to his heels, last week. She thought I should drive my curricle—I couldn't afford an omnibus! I had to run. When I returned to her I was dirty. She made remarks!"

"Thy sufferings are severe—but such is woman!" said Franko. "'Gad, it's a good idea, though." He took out a note-book and pencilled down a point or two. Raikes watched the process sardonically.

"My tragedy is, then, thy farce!" he exclaimed. "Well, be it so! I believe I shall come to song-writing again myself shortly-beneath the shield of Catnach I'll a nation's ballads frame. I've spent my income in four months, and now I'm living on my curricle. I underlet it. It's like trade—it's as bad as poor old Harrington, by Jove! But that isn't the worst, Franko!" Jack dropped his voice: "I believe I'm furiously loved by a poor country wench."

"Morals!" was Franko's most encouraging reproof.

"Oh, I don't think I've even kissed her," rejoined Raikes, who doubted because his imagination was vivid. "It's my intellect that dazzles her. I've got letters—she calls me clever. By Jove! since I gave up driving I've had thoughts of rushing down to her and making her mine in spite of home, family, fortune, friends, name, position—everything! I have, indeed."

Franko looked naturally astonished at this amount of self-sacrifice. "The Countess?" he shrewdly suggested.

"I'd rather be my Polly's prince,
Than yon great lady's errand-boy!"

Raikes burst into song.

He stretched out his hand, as if to discard all the great ladies who were passing. By the strangest misfortune ever known, the direction taken by his fingers was toward a carriage wherein, beautifully smiling opposite an elaborately reverend gentleman of middle age, the Countess de Saldar was sitting. This great lady is not to be blamed for deeming that her errand-boy was pointing her out vulgarly on a public promenade. Ineffable disdain curled off her sweet olive visage. She turned her head.

"I'll go down to that girl to-night," said Raikes, with compressed passion. And then he hurried Franko along to the bridge, where, behold, the Countess alighted with the gentleman, and walked beside him into the gardens.

"Follow her," said Raikes, in agitation. "Do you see her? by yon long-tailed raven's side? Follow her, Franko! See if he kisses her hand-anything! and meet me here in half an hour. I'll have evidence!"

Franko did not altogether like the office, but Raikes' dinners, singular luck, and superiority in the encounter of puns, gave him the upper hand with his friend, and so Franko went.

Turning away from the last glimpse of his Countess, Raikes crossed the bridge, and had not strolled far beneath the bare branches of one of the long green walks, when he perceived a gentleman with two ladies leaning on him.

"Now, there," moralized this youth; "now, what do you say to that? Do you call that fair? He can't be happy, and it's not in nature for them to be satisfied. And yet, if I went up and attempted to please them all by taking one away, the probabilities are that he would knock me down. Such is life! We won't be made comfortable!"

Nevertheless, he passed them with indifference, for it was merely the principle he objected to; and, indeed, he was so wrapped in his own conceptions, that his name had to be called behind him twice before he recognized Evan Harrington, Mrs. Strike, and Miss Bonner. The arrangement he had previously thought good, was then spontaneously adopted. Mrs. Strike reposed her fair hand upon his arm, and Juliana, with a timid glance of pleasure, walked ahead in Evan's charge. Close neighbourhood between the couples was not kept. The genius of Mr. Raikes was wasted in manoeuvres to lead his beautiful companion into places where he could be seen with her, and envied. It was, perhaps, more flattering that she should betray a marked disposition to prefer solitude in his society. But this idea illumined him only near the moment of parting. Then he saw it; then he groaned in soul, and besought Evan to have one more promenade, saying, with characteristic cleverness in the masking of his real thoughts: "It gives us an appetite, you know."

In Evan's face and Juliana's there was not much sign that any protraction of their walk together would aid this beneficent process of nature. He took her hand gently, and when he quitted it, it dropped.

"The Rose, the Rose of Beckley Court!" Raikes sang aloud. "Why, this is a day of meetings. Behold John Thomas in the rear-a tower of plush and powder! Shall I rush-shall I pluck her from the aged stem?"

On the gravel-walk above them Rose passed with her aristocratic grandmother, muffled in furs. She marched deliberately, looking coldly before her. Evan's face was white, and Juliana, whose eyes were fixed on him, shuddered.

"I'm chilled," she murmured to Caroline. "Let us go." Caroline eyed Evan with a meaning sadness.

"We will hurry to our carriage," she said.

They were seen to make a little circuit so as not to approach Rose; after whom, thoughtless of his cruelty, Evan bent his steps slowly, halting when she reached her carriage. He believed—rather, he knew that she had seen him. There was a consciousness in the composed outlines of her face as she passed: the indifference was too perfect. Let her hate him if she pleased. It recompensed him that the air she wore should make her appearance more womanly; and that black dress and crape-bonnet, in some way, touched him to mournful thoughts of her that helped a partial forgetfulness of wounded self.

Rose had driven off. He was looking at the same spot, where Caroline's hand waved from her carriage. Juliana was not seen. Caroline requested her to nod to him once, but she would not. She leaned back hiding her eyes, and moving a petulant shoulder at Caroline's hand.

"Has he offended you, my child?"

Juliana answered harshly:

"No-no."

The wheels rolled on, and Caroline tried other subjects, knowing possibly that they would lead Juliana back to this of her own accord.

"You saw how she treated him?" the latter presently said, without moving her hand from before her eyes.

"Yes, dear. He forgives her, and will forget it."

"Oh!" she clenched her long thin hand, "I pray that I may not die before I have made her repent it. She shall!"

Juliana looked glitteringly in Caroline's face, and then fell a-weeping, and suffered herself to be folded and caressed. The storm was long subsiding.

"Dearest! you are better now?" said Caroline.

She whispered: "Yes."

"My brother has only to know you, dear—"

"Hush! That's past." Juliana stopped her; and, on a deep breath that threatened to break to sobs, she added in a sweeter voice than was common to her, "Ah, why—why did you tell him about the Beckley property?"

Caroline vainly strove to deny that she had told him. Juliana's head shook mournfully at her; and now Caroline knew what Juliana meant when she begged so earnestly that Evan should be kept ignorant of her change of fortune.

Some days after this the cold struck Juliana's chest, and she sickened. The three sisters held a sitting to consider what it was best to do with her. Caroline proposed to take her to Beckley without delay. Harriet was of opinion that the least they could do was to write to her relatives and make them instantly aware of her condition.

But the Countess said "No," to both. Her argument was, that Juliana being independent, they were by no means bound to "bundle" her, in her state, back to a place where she had been so shamefully maltreated: that here she would live, while there she would certainly die: that absence of excitement was her medicine, and that here she had it. Mrs. Andrew, feeling herself responsible as the young lady's hostess, did not acquiesce in the Countess's views till she had consulted Juliana; and then apologies for giving trouble were breathed on the one hand; sympathy, condolences, and professions of esteem, on the other. Juliana said, she was but slightly ill, would soon recover. Entreated not to leave them before she was thoroughly re-established, and to consent to be looked on as one of the family, she sighed, and said it was the utmost she could hope. Of course the ladies took this compliment to themselves, but Evan began to wax in importance. The Countess thought it nearly time to acknowledge him, and supported the idea by a citation of the doctrine, that to forgive is Christian. It happened, however, that Harriet, who had less art and more will than her sisters, was inflexible. She, living in a society but a few steps above Tailordom, however magnificent in expenditure and resources, abhorred it solemnly. From motives of prudence, as well as personal disgust, she continued firm in declining to receive her brother. She would not relent when the Countess pointed out a dim, a dazzling prospect, growing out of Evan's proximity to the heiress of Beckley Court; she was not to be moved when Caroline suggested that the specific for the frail invalid was Evan's presence. As to this, Juliana was sufficiently open, though, as she conceived, her art was extreme.

"Do you know why I stay to vex and trouble you?" she asked Caroline. "Well, then, it is that I may see your brother united to you all: and then I shall go, happy."

The pretext served also to make him the subject of many conversations. Twice a week a bunch of the best flowers that could be got were sorted and arranged by her, and sent namelessly to brighten Evan's chamber.

"I may do such a thing as this, you know, without incurring blame," she said.

The sight of a love so humble in its strength and affluence, sent Caroline to Evan on a fruitless errand. What availed it, that accused of giving lead to his pride in refusing the heiress, Evan should declare that he did not love her? He did not, Caroline admitted as possible, but he might. He might learn to love her, and therefore he was wrong in wounding her heart. She related flattering anecdotes. She drew tearful pictures of Juliana's love for him: and noticing how he seemed to prize his bouquet of flowers, said:

"Do you love them for themselves, or the hand that sent them?"

Evan blushed, for it had been a struggle for him to receive them, as he thought, from Rose in secret. The flowers lost their value; the song that had arisen out of them, "Thou livest in my memory," ceased. But they came still. How many degrees from love gratitude may be, I have not reckoned. I rather fear it lies on the opposite shore. From a youth to a girl, it may yet be very tender; the more so, because their ages commonly exclude such a sentiment, and nature seems willing to make a transition stage of it. Evan wrote to Juliana. Incidentally he expressed a wish to see her. Juliana was under doctor's interdict: but she was not to be prevented from going when Evan wished her to go. They met in the park, as before, and he talked to her five minutes through the carriage window.

"Was it worth the risk, my poor child?" said Caroline, pityingly.

Juliana cried: "Oh! I would give anything to live!"

A man might have thought that she made no direct answer.

"Don't you think I am patient? Don't you think I am very patient?" she asked Caroline, winningly, on their way home.

Caroline could scarcely forbear from smiling at the feverish anxiety she showed for a reply that should confirm her words and hopes.

"So we must all be!" she said, tend that common-place remark caused Juliana to exclaim: "Prisoners have lived in a dungeon, on bread and water, for years!"

Whereat Caroline kissed her so tenderly that Juliana tried to look surprised, and failing, her thin lips quivered; she breathed a soft "hush," and fell on Caroline's bosom.

She was transparent enough in one thing; but the flame which burned within her did not light her through.

Others, on other matters, were quite as transparent to her.

Caroline never knew that she had as much as told her the moral suicide Evan had committed at Beckley; so cunningly had she been probed at intervals with little casual questions; random interjections, that one who loved him could not fail to meet; petty doubts requiring elucidations. And the Countess, kind as her sentiments had grown toward the afflicted creature, was compelled to proclaim her densely stupid in material affairs. For the Countess had an itch of the simplest feminine curiosity to know whether the dear child had any notion of accomplishing a certain holy duty of the perishable on this earth, who might possess worldly goods; and no hints—not even plain speaking, would do. Juliana did not understand her at all.

The Countess exhibited a mourning-ring on her finger, Mrs. Bonner's bequest to her.

"How fervent is my gratitude to my excellent departed friend for this! A legacy, however trifling, embalms our dear lost ones in the memory!"

It was of no avail. Juliana continued densely stupid. Was she not worse? The Countess could not, "in decency," as she observed, reveal to her who had prompted Mrs. Bonner so to bequeath the Beckley estates as to "ensure sweet Juliana's future"; but ought not Juliana to divine it?—Juliana at least had hints sufficient.

Cold Spring winds were now blowing. Juliana had resided no less than two months with the Cogglesbys. She was entreated still to remain, and she did. From Lady Jocelyn she heard not a word of remonstrance; but from Miss Carrington and Mrs. Shorne she received admonishing letters. Finally, Mr. Harry Jocelyn presented himself. In London, and without any of that needful subsistence which a young gentleman feels the want of in London more than elsewhere, Harry began to have thoughts of his own, without any instigation from his aunts, about devoting himself to business. So he sent his card up to his cousin, and was graciously met in the drawing-room by the Countess, who ruffled him and smoothed him, and would possibly have distracted his soul from business had his circumstances been less straitened. Juliana was declared to be too unwell to see him that day. He called a second time, and enjoyed a similar greeting. His third visit procured him an audience alone with Juliana, when, at once, despite the warnings of his aunts, the frank fellow plunged, "medias res". Mrs. Bonner had left him totally dependent on his parents and his chances.

"A desperate state of things, isn't it, Juley? I think I shall go for a soldier—common, you know."

Instead of shrieking out against such a debasement of his worth and gentility, as was to be expected, Juliana said:

"That's what Mr. Harrington thought of doing."

"He! If he'd had the pluck he would."

"His duty forbade it, and he did not."

"Duty! a confounded tailor! What fools we were to have him at Beckley!"

"Has the Countess been unkind to you Harry?"

"I haven't seen her to-day, and don't want to. It's my little dear old Juley I came for."

"Dear Harry!" she thanked him with eyes and hands. "Come often, won't you?"

"Why, ain't you coming back to us, Juley?"

"Not yet. They are very kind to me here. How is Rose?"

"Oh, quite jolly. She and Ferdinand are thick again. Balls every night. She dances like the deuce. They want me to go; but I ain't the sort of figure for those places, and besides, I shan't dance till I can lead you out."

A spur of laughter at Harry's generous nod brought on Juliana's cough. Harry watched her little body shaken and her reddened eyes. Some real emotion—perhaps the fear which healthy young people experience at the sight of deadly disease—made Harry touch her arm with the softness of a child's touch.

"Don't be alarmed, Harry," she said. "It's nothing—only Winter. I'm determined to get well."

"That's right," quoth he, recovering. "I know you've got pluck, or you wouldn't have stood that operation."

"Let me see: when was that?" she asked slyly.

Harry coloured, for it related to a time when he had not behaved prettily to her.

"There, Juley, that's all forgotten. I was a fool-a scoundrel, if you like. I'm sorry for it now."

"Do you want money, Harry?"

"Oh, money!"

"Have you repaid Mr. Harrington yet?"

"There—no, I haven't. Bother it! that fellow's name's always on your tongue. I'll tell you what, Juley—but it's no use. He's a low, vulgar adventurer."

"Dear Harry," said Juliana, softly; "don't bring your aunts with you when you come to see me."

"Well, then I'll tell you, Juley. It's enough that he's a beastly tailor."

"Quite enough," she responded; "and he is neither a fool nor a scoundrel."

Harry's memory for his own speech was not quick. When Juliana's calm glance at him called it up, he jumped from his chair, crying: "Upon my honour, I'll tell you what, Juley! If I had money to pay him to-morrow, I'd insult him on the spot."

Juliana meditated, and said: "Then all your friends must wish you to continue poor."

This girl had once been on her knees to him. She had looked up to him with admiring love, and he had given her a crumb or so occasionally, thinking her something of a fool, and more of a pest; but now he could not say a word to her without being baffled in an elderly-sisterly tone exasperating him so far that he positively wished to marry her, and coming to the point, offered himself with downright sincerity, and was rejected. Harry left in a passion. Juliana confided the secret to Caroline, who suggested interested motives, which Juliana would not hear of.

"Ah," said the Countess, when Caroline mentioned the case to her, "of course the poor thing cherishes her first offer. She would believe a curate to be disinterested! But mind that Evan has due warning when she is to meet him. Mind that he is dressed becomingly."

Caroline asked why.

"Because, my dear, she is enamoured of his person. These little unhealthy creatures are always attracted by the person. She thinks it to be Evan's qualities. I know better: it is his person. Beckley Court may be lost by a shabby coat!"

The Countess had recovered from certain spiritual languors into which she had fallen after her retreat. Ultimate victory hung still in the balance. Oh! if Evan would only marry this little sufferer, who was so sure to die within a year! or, if she lived (for marriage has often been as a resurrection to some poor female invalids), there was Beckley Court, a splendid basis for future achievements. Reflecting in this fashion, the Countess pardoned her brother. Glowing hopes hung fresh lamps in her charitable breast. She stepped across the threshold of Tailordom, won Mr. Goren's heart by her condescension, and worked Evan into a sorrowful mood concerning the invalid. Was not Juliana his only active friend? In return, he said things which only required a little colouring to be very acceptable to her.

The game waxed exciting again. The enemy (the Jocelyn party) was alert, but powerless. The three sisters were almost wrought to perform a sacrifice far exceeding Evan's. They nearly decided to summon him to the house: but the matter being broached at table one evening, Major Strike objected to it so angrily that they abandoned it, with the satisfactory conclusion that if they did wrong it was the Major's fault.

Meantime Juliana had much on her conscience. She knew Evan to be innocent, and she allowed Rose to think him guilty. Could she bring her heart to join them? That was not in her power: but desiring to be lulled by a compromise, she devoted herself to make his relatives receive him; and on days of bitter winds she would drive out to meet him, answering all expostulations with—"I should not go if he were here."

The game waxed hot. It became a question whether Evan should be admitted to the house in spite of the Major. Juliana now made an extraordinary move. Having the Count with her in the carriage one day, she stopped in front of Mr. Goren's shop, and Evan had to come out. The Count returned home extremely mystified. Once more the unhappy Countess was obliged to draw bills on the fabulous; and as she had recommenced the system, which was not without its fascinations to her, Juliana, who had touched the spring, had the full benefit of it. The Countess had deceived her before—what of that? She spoke things sweet to hear. Who could be false that gave her heart food on which it lived?

One night Juliana returned from her drive alarmingly ill. She was watched through the night by Caroline and the Countess alternately. In the morning the sisters met.

"She has consented to let us send for a doctor," said Caroline.

"Her chief desire seems to be a lawyer," said the Countess.

"Yes, but the doctor must be sent for first."

"Yes, indeed! But it behoves us to previse that the doctor does not kill her before the lawyer comes."

Caroline looked at Louisa, and said: "Are you ignorant?"

"No—what?" cried the Countess eagerly.

"Evan has written to tell Lady Jocelyn the state of her health, and—"

"And that naturally has aggravated her malady!" The Countess cramped her long fingers. "The child heard it from him yesterday! Oh, I could swear at that brother!"

She dropped into a chair and sat rigid and square-jawed, a sculpture of unutterable rage.

In the afternoon Lady Jocelyn arrived. The doctor was there—the lawyer had gone. Without a word of protest Juliana accompanied her ladyship to Beckley Court. Here was a blow!

But Andrew was preparing one more mighty still. What if the Cogglesby Brewery proved a basis most unsound? Where must they fall then? Alas! on that point whence they sprang. If not to Perdition—Tailordom!

XLI

Reveals an Abominable Plot of the Brothers Cogglesby

A lively April day, with strong gusts from the Southwest, and long sweeping clouds, saluted the morning coach from London to Lymport. Thither Tailordom triumphant was bearing its victim at a rattling pace, to settle him, and seal him for ever out of the ranks of gentlemen: Society, meantime, howling exclusion to him in the background: "Out of our halls, degraded youth: The smiles of turbaned matrons: the sighs of delicate maids; genial wit, educated talk, refined scandal, vice in harness, dinners sentineled by stately plush: these, the flavour of life, are not for you, though you stole a taste of them, wretched impostor! Pay for it with years of remorse!"

The coach went rushing against the glorious high wind. It stirred his blood, freshened his cheeks, gave a bright tone of zest to his eyes, as he cast them on the young green country. Not banished from the breath of heaven, or from self-respect, or from the appetite for the rewards that are to follow duties done! Not banished from the help that is always reached to us when we have fairly taken the right road: and that for him is the road to Lymport. Let the kingdom of Gilt Gingerbread howl as it will! We are no longer children, but men: men who have bitten hard at experience, and know the value of a tooth: who have had our hearts bruised, and cover them with armour: who live not to feed, but look to food that we may live! What matters it that yonder high-spiced kingdom should excommunicate such as we are? We have rubbed off the gilt, and have assumed the command of our stomachs. We are men from this day!

Now, you would have thought Evan's companions, right and left of him, were the wretches under sentence, to judge from appearances. In contrast with his look of insolent pleasure, Andrew, the moment an eye was on him, exhibited the cleverest impersonation of the dumps ever seen: while Mr. Raikes was from head to foot nothing better than a moan made visible. Nevertheless, they both agreed to rally Evan, and bid him be of good cheer.

"Don't be down, Van; don't be down, my boy," said Andrew, rubbing his hands gloomily.

"I? do I look it?" Evan answered, laughing.

"Capital acting!" exclaimed Raikes. "Try and keep it up."

"Well, I hope you're acting too," said Evan.

Raikes let his chest fall like a collapsing bellows.

At the end of five minutes, he remarked: "I've been sitting on it the whole morning! There's violent inflammation, I'm persuaded. Another hour, and I jump slap from the summit of the coach!"

Evan turned to Andrew.

"Do you think he'll be let off?"

"Mr. Raikes? Can't say. You see, Van, it depends upon how Old Tom has taken his bad luck. Ahem! Perhaps he'll be all the stricter; and as a man of honour, Mr. Raikes, you see, can't very well—"

"By Jove! I wish I wasn't a man of honour!" Raikes interposed, heavily.

"You see, Van, Old Tom's circumstances'—Andrew ducked, to smother a sort of laughter—'are now such that he'd be glad of the money to let him off, no doubt; but Mr. Raikes has spent it, I can't lend it, and you haven't got it, and there we all are. At the end of the year he's free, and he—ha! ha! I'm not a bit the merrier for laughing, I can tell you."

Catching another glimpse of Evan's serious face, Andrew fell into louder laughter; checking it with doleful solemnity.

Up hill and down hill, and past little homesteads shining with yellow crocuses; across wide brown heaths, whose outlines raised in Evan's mind the night of his funeral walk, and tossed up old feelings dead as the whirling dust. At last Raikes called out:

"The towers of Fallow field; heigho!"

And Andrew said:

"Now then, Van: if Old Tom's anywhere, he's here. You get down at the Dragon, and don't you talk to me, but let me go in. It'll be just the hour he dines in the country. Isn't it a shame of him to make me face every man of the creditors—eh?"

Evan gave Andrew's hand an affectionate squeeze, at which Andrew had to gulp down something—reciprocal emotion, doubtless.

"Hark," said Raikes, as the horn of the guard was heard. "Once that sound used to set me caracoling before an abject multitude. I did wonders. All London looked on me! It had more effect on me than champagne. Now I hear it—the whole charm has vanished! I can't see a single old castle. Would you have thought it possible that a small circular bit of tin on a man's person could produce such changes in him?"

"You are a donkey to wear it," said Evan.

"I pledged my word as a gentleman, and thought it small, for the money!" said Raikes. "This is the first coach I ever travelled on, without making the old whip burst with laughing. I'm not myself. I'm haunted. I'm somebody else."

The three passengers having descended, a controversy commenced between Evan and Andrew as to which should pay. Evan had his money out; Andrew dashed it behind him; Evan remonstrated.

"Well, you mustn't pay for us two, Andrew. I would have let you do it once, but—"

"Stuff!" cried Andrew. "I ain't paying—it's the creditors of the estate, my boy!"

Evan looked so ingenuously surprised and hurt at his lack of principle, that Andrew chucked a sixpence at a small boy, saying,

"If you don't let me have my own way, Van, I'll shy my purse after it. What do you mean, sir, by treating me like a beggar?"

"Our friend Harrington can't humour us," quoth Raikes. "For myself, I candidly confess I prefer being paid for"; and he leaned contentedly against one of the posts of the inn till the filthy dispute was arranged to the satisfaction of the ignobler mind. There Andrew left them, and went to Mrs. Sockley, who, recovered from her illness, smiled her usual placid welcome to a guest.

"You know me, ma'am?"

"Oh, yes! The London Mr. Cogglesby!"

"Now, ma'am, look here. I've come for my brother. Don't be alarmed. No danger as yet. But, mind! if you attempt to conceal him from his lawful brother, I'll summon here the myrmidons of the law."

Mrs. Sockley showed a serious face.

"You know his habits, Mr. Cogglesby; and one doesn't go against any one of his whimsies, or there's consequences: but the house is open to you, sir. I don't wish to hide him."

Andrew accepted this intelligent evasion of Tom Cogglesby's orders as sufficient, and immediately proceeded upstairs. A door shut on the first landing. Andrew went to this door and knocked. No answer. He tried to open it, but found that he had been forestalled. After threatening to talk business through the key-hole, the door was unlocked, and Old Tom appeared.

"So! now you're dogging me into the country. Be off; make an appointment. Saturday's my holiday. You know that."

Andrew pushed through the doorway, and, by way of an emphatic reply and a silencing one, delivered a punch slap into Old Tom's belt.

"Confound you, Nan!" said Old Tom, grimacing, but friendly, as if his sympathies had been irresistibly assailed.

"It's done, Tom! I've done it. Won my bet, now," Andrew exclaimed. "The women-poor creatures! What a state they're in. I pity 'em."

Old Tom pursed his lips, and eyed his brother incredulously, but with curious eagerness.

"Oh, Lord! what a face I've had to wear!" Andrew continued, and while he sank into a chair and rubbed his handkerchief over his crisp hair, Old Tom let loose a convinced and exulting, "ha! ha!"

"Yes, you may laugh. I've had all the bother," said Andrew.

"Serve ye right—marrying such cattle," Old Tom snapped at him.

"They believe we're bankrupt—owe fifty thousand clear, Tom!"

"Ha! ha!"

"Brewery stock and household furniture to be sold by general auction, Friday week."

"Ha! ha!"

"Not a place for any of us to poke our heads into. I talked about 'pitiless storms' to my poor Harry—no shelter to be had unless we go down to Lymport, and stop with their brother in shop!"

Old Tom did enjoy this. He took a great gulp of air for a tremendous burst of laughter, and when this was expended and reflection came, his features screwed, as if the acidest of flavours had ravished his palate.

"Bravo, Nan! Didn't think you were man enough. Ha! ha! Nan—I say—eh? how did ye get on behind the curtains?"

The tale, to guess by Andrew's face, appeared to be too strongly infused with pathos for revelation.

"Will they go, Nan, eh? d' ye think they'll go?"

"Where else can they go, Tom? They must go there, or on the parish, you know."

"They'll all troop down to the young tailor—eh?"

"They can't sleep in the parks, Tom."

"No. They can't get into Buckingham Palace, neither—'cept as housemaids. "'Gad, they're howling like cats, I'd swear—nuisance to the neighbourhood—ha! ha!"

Old Tom's cruel laughter made Andrew feel for the unhappy ladies. He stuck his forehead, and leaned forward, saying: "I don't know—

'pon my honour, I don't know—can't think we've—quite done right to punish 'em so."

This acted like cold water on Old Tom's delight. He pitched it back in the shape of a doubt of what Andrew had told him. Whereupon Andrew defied him to face three miserable women on the verge of hysterics; and Old Tom, beginning to chuckle again, rejoined that it would bring them to their senses, and emancipate him.

"You may laugh, Mr. Tom," said Andrew; "but if poor Harry should find me out, deuce a bit more home for me."

Old Tom looked at him keenly, and rapped the table. "Swear you did it, Nan."

"You promise you'll keep the secret," said Andrew.

"Never make promises."

"Then there's a pretty life for me! I did it for that poor dear boy. You were only up to one of your jokes—I see that. Confound you, Old Tom, you've been making a fool of me."

The flattering charge was not rejected by Old Tom, who now had his brother to laugh at as well. Andrew affected to be indignant and desperate.

"If you'd had a heart, Tom, you'd have saved the poor fellow without any bother at all. What do you think? When I told him of our smash—ha! ha! it isn't such a bad joke-well, I went to him, hanging my head, and he offered to arrange our affairs—that is—"

"Damned meddlesome young dog!" cried Old Tom, quite in a rage.

"There—you're up in a twinkling," said Andrew. "Don't you see he believed it, you stupid Old Tom? Lord! to hear him say how sorry he was, and to see how glad he looked at the chance of serving us!"

"Serving us!" Tom sneered.

"Ha!" went Andrew. "Yes. There. You're a deuced deal prouder than fifty peers. You're an upside-down old despot!"

No sharper retort rising to Old Tom's lips, he permitted his brother's abuse of him to pass, declaring that bandying words was not his business, he not being a Parliament man.

"How about the Major, Nan? He coming down, too?"

"Major!" cried Andrew. "Lucky if he keeps his commission. Coming down? No. He's off to the Continent."

"Find plenty of scamps there to keep him company," added Tom. "So he's broke—eh? ha! ha!"

"Tom," said Andrew, seriously, "I'll tell you all about it, if you'll swear not to split on me, because it would really upset poor Harry so. She'd think me such a beastly hypocrite, I couldn't face her afterwards."

"Lose what pluck you have—eh?" Tom jerked out his hand, and bade his brother continue.

Compelled to trust in him without a promise, Andrew said: "Well, then, after we'd arranged it, I went back to Harry, and begged her to have poor Van at the house told her what I hoped you'd do for him about getting him into the Brewery. She's very kind, Tom, 'pon my honour she is. She was willing, only—"

"Only—eh?"

"Well, she was so afraid it'd hurt her sisters to see him there."

Old Tom saw he was in for excellent fun, and wouldn't spoil it for the world.

"Yes, Nan?"

"So I went to Caroline. She was easy enough; and she went to the Countess."

"Well, and she—?"

"She was willing, too, till Lady Jocelyn came and took Miss Bonner home to Beckley, and because Evan had written to my lady to fetch her, the Countess—she was angry. That was all. Because of that, you know. But yet she agreed. But when Miss Bonner had gone, it turned out that the Major was the obstacle. They were all willing enough to have Evan there, but the Major refused. I didn't hear him. I wasn't going to ask him. I mayn't be a match for three women, but man to man, eh, Tom? You'd back me there? So Harry said the Major 'd make Caroline miserable, if his wishes were disrespected. By George, I wish I'd know, then. Don't you think it odd, Tom, now? There's a Duke of Belfield the fellow had hooked into his Company; and—through Evan I heard—the Duke had his name struck off. After that, the Major swore at the Duke once or twice, and said Caroline wasn't to go out with him. Suddenly, he insists that she shall go. Days the poor thing kept crying! One day, he makes her go. She hasn't the spirit of my Harry or the Countess. By good luck, Van, who was hunting ferns for some friends of his, met them on Sunday in Richmond Park, and Van took her away from the Duke. But, Tom, think of Van seeing a fellow watching her wherever she went, and hearing the Duke's coachman tell that fellow he had orders to drive his master and a lady hard on to the sea that night. I don't believe it—it wasn't Caroline! But what do you think of our finding out that beast of a spy to be in the Major's pay?

We did. Van put a constable on his track; we found him out, and he confessed it. A fact, Tom! That decided me. If it was only to get rid of a brute, I determined I'd do it, and I did. Strike came to me to get my name for a bill that night. "'Gad, he looked blanker than his bill when he heard of us two bankrupt. I showed him one or two documents I'd got ready. Says he: 'Never mind; it'll only be a couple of hundred more in the schedule.' Stop, Tom! he's got some of our blood. I don't think he meant it. He is hard pushed. Well, I gave him a twentier, and he was off the next night. You'll soon see all about the Company in the papers."

At the conclusion of Andrew's recital, Old Tom thrummed and looked on the floor under a heavy frown. His mouth worked dubiously, and, from moment to moment, he plucked at his waistcoat and pulled it down, throwing back his head and glaring.

"I've knocked that fellow over once," he said. "Wish he hadn't got up again."

Andrew nodded.

"One good thing, Nan. He never boasted of our connection. Much obliged to him."

"Yes," said Andrew, who was gladly watching Old Tom's change of mood with a quiescent aspect.

"Um!—must keep it quiet from his poor old mother."

Andrew again affirmatived his senior's remarks. That his treatment of Old Tom was sound, he presently had proof of. The latter stood up, and after sniffing in an injured way for about a minute, launched out his right leg, and vociferated that he would like to have it in his power to kick all the villains out of the world: a modest demand Andrew at once chimed in with; adding that, were such a faculty extended to him, he would not object to lose the leg that could benefit mankind so infinitely, and consented to its following them. Then, Old Tom, who was of a practical turn, meditated, swung his foot, and gave one grim kick at the imaginary bundle of villains, discharged them headlong straight into space. Andrew, naturally imitative, and seeing that he had now to kick them flying, attempted to excel Old Tom in the vigour of his delivery. No wonder that the efforts of both were heating: they were engaged in the task of ridding the globe of the larger half of its inhabitants. Tom perceived Andrew's useless emulation, and with a sound translated by "yack," sent his leg out a long way. Not to be outdone, Andrew immediately, with a still louder "yack," committed himself to an effort so violent that the alternative between his leg coming off, or his being taken off his leg, was propounded by nature, and decided by the laws of gravity in a trice. Joyful grunts were emitted by Old Tom at the sight of Andrew prostrate, rubbing his pate. But Mrs. Sockley, to whom the noise of Andrew's fall had suggested awful fears of a fratricidal conflict upstairs, hurried forthwith to announce to them that the sovereign remedy for human ills, the promoter of concord, the healer of feuds, the central point of man's destiny in the flesh—Dinner, was awaiting them.

To the dinner they marched.

Of this great festival be it simply told that the supply was copious and of good quality—much too good and copious for a bankrupt host: that Evan and Mr. John Raikes were formally introduced to Old Tom before the repast commenced, and welcomed some three minutes after he had decided the flavour of his first glass; that Mr. Raikes in due time preferred his petition for release from a dreadful engagement, and furnished vast amusement to the company under Old Tom's hand, until, by chance, he quoted a scrap of Latin, at which the brothers Cogglesby, who would have faced peers and princes without being disconcerted, or performing mental genuflexions, shut their mouths and looked injured, unhappy, and in the presence of a superior: Mr. Raikes not being the man to spare them. Moreover, a surprise was afforded to Evan. Andrew stated to Old Tom that the hospitality of Main Street, Lymport,—was open to him. Strange to say, Old Tom accepted it on the spot, observing, "You're master of the house—can do what you like, if you're man enough," and adding that he thanked him, and would come in a day or two. The case of Mr. Raikes was still left uncertain, for as the bottle circulated, he exhibited such a faculty for apt, but to the brothers, totally incomprehensible quotation, that they fled from him without leaving him time to remember what special calamity was on his mind, or whether this earth was other than an abode conceived in great jollity for his life-long entertainment.

XLII

Juliana

The sick night-light burned steadily in Juliana's chamber. On a couch, beside her bed, Caroline lay sleeping, tired with a long watch. Two sentences had been passed on Juliana: one on her heart: one on her body: "Thou art not loved"; and, "Thou must die." The frail passion of her struggle against her destiny was over with her. Quiet as that quiet which Nature was taking her to, her body reposed. Calm as the solitary night-light before her open eyes, her spirit was wasting away. "If I am not loved, then let me die!" In such a sense she bowed to her fate.

At an hour like this, watching the round of light on the ceiling, with its narrowing inner rings, a sufferer from whom pain has fled looks back to the shores she is leaving, and would be well with them who walk there. It is false to imagine that schemers and workers in the dark are destitute of the saving gift of conscience. They have it, and it is perhaps made livelier in them than with easy people; and therefore, they are imperatively spurred to hoodwink it. Hence, their self-delusion is deep and endures. They march to their object, and gaining or losing it, the voice that calls to them is the voice of a blind creature, whom any answer, provided that the answer is ready, will silence. And at an hour like this, when finally they snatch their minute of sight on the threshold of black night, their souls may compare with yonder shining circle on the ceiling, which, as the light below gasps for air, contracts, and extends but to mingle with the darkness. They would be nobler, better, boundlessly good to all;—to those who have injured them to those whom they have injured. Alas! for any definite deed the limit of their circle is immoveable, and they must act within it. The trick they have played themselves imprisons them. Beyond it, they cease to be.

Lying in this utter stillness, Juliana thought of Rose; of her beloved by Evan. The fever that had left her blood, had left it stagnant, and her thoughts were quite emotionless. She looked faintly on a far picture. She saw Rose blooming with pleasures in Elburne House, sliding as a boat borne by the river's tide to sea, away from her living joy. The breast of Rose was lucid to her, and in that hour of insight she had clear knowledge of her cousin's heart; how it scoffed at its base love, and unwittingly betrayed the power on her still, by clinging to the world and what it would give her to fill the void; how externally the lake was untroubled, and a mirror to the passing day; and how within there pressed a flood against an iron dam. Evan, too, she saw. The Countess was right in her judgement of Juliana's love. Juliana looked very little to his qualities. She loved him when she thought him guilty, which made her conceive that her love was of a diviner cast than Rose was capable of. Guilt did not spoil his beauty to her; his gentleness and glowing manhood were unchanged; and when she knew him as he was, the revelation of his high nature simply confirmed her impression of his physical perfections. She had done him a wrong; at her death news would come to him, and it might be that he would bless her name. Because she sighed no longer for those dear lips and strong arms to close about her tremulous frame, it seemed to her that she had quite surrendered him. Generous to Evan, she would be just to Rose. Beneath her pillow she found pencil and paper, and with difficulty, scarce seeing her letters in the brown light, she began to trace lines of farewell to Rose. Her conscience dictated to her thus, "Tell Rose that she was too ready to accept his guilt; and that in this as in all things, she acted with the precipitation of her character. Tell her that you always trusted, and that now you know him innocent. Give her the proofs you have. Show that he did it to shield his intriguing sister. Tell her that you write this only to make her just to him. End with a prayer that Rose may be happy."

Ere Juliana had finished one sentence, she resigned the pencil. Was it not much, even at the gates of death, to be the instrument to send Rose into his arms? The picture swayed before her, helping her weakness. She found herself dreaming that he had kissed her once. Dorothy, she remembered, had danced up to her one day, to relate what the maids of the house said of the gentleman—(at whom, it is known, they look with the licence of cats toward kings); and Dorothy's fresh careless mouth had told how one observant maid, amorously minded, proclaimed of Evan, to a companion of her sex, that, "he was the only gentleman who gave you an idea of how he would look when he was kissing you." Juliana cherished that vision likewise. Young ladies are not supposed to do so, if menial maids are; but Juliana did cherish it, and it possessed her fancy. Bear in your recollection that she was not a healthy person. Diseased little heroines may be made attractive, and are now popular; but strip off the cleverly woven robe which is fashioned to cover them, and you will find them in certain matters bearing a resemblance to menial maids.

While the thoughts of his kiss lasted, she could do nothing; but lay with her two hands out on the bed, and her eyelids closed. Then waking, she took the pencil again. It would not move: her bloodless fingers fell from it.

"If they do not meet, and he never marries, I may claim him in the next world," she mused.

But conscience continued uneasy. She turned her wrist and trailed a letter from beneath the pillow. It was from Mrs. Shorne. Juliana knew the contents. She raised it unopened as high as her faltering hands permitted, and read like one whose shut eyes read syllables of fire on the darkness.

"Rose has at last definitely engaged herself to Ferdinand, you will be glad to hear, and we may now treat her as a woman."

Having absorbed these words, Juliana's hand found strength to write, with little difficulty, what she had to say to Rose. She conceived it to be neither sublime nor generous: not even good; merely her peculiar duty. When it was done, she gave a long, low sigh of relief.

Caroline whispered, "Dearest child, are you awake?"

"Yes," she answered.

"Sorrowful, dear?"

"Very quiet."

Caroline reached her hand over to her, and felt the paper. "What is this?"

"My good-bye to Rose. I want it folded now."

Caroline slipped from the couch to fulfil her wish. She enclosed the pencilled scrap of paper, sealed it, and asked, "Is that right?"

"Now unlock my desk," Juliana uttered, feebly. "Put it beside a letter addressed to a law-gentleman. Post both the morning I am gone."

Caroline promised to obey, and coming to Juliana to mark her looks, observed a faint pleased smile dying away, and had her hand gently squeezed. Juliana's conscience had preceded her contentedly to its last sleep; and she, beneath that round of light on the ceiling, drew on her counted breaths in peace till dawn.

XLIII

Rose

Have you seen a young audacious spirit smitten to the earth? It is a singular study; and, in the case of young women, a trap for inexperienced men. Rose, who had commanded and managed every one surrounding her since infancy, how humble had she now become!—how much more womanly in appearance, and more child-like at heart! She was as wax in Lady Elburne's hands. A hint of that veiled episode, the Beckley campaign, made Rose pliant, as if she had woven for herself a rod of scorpions. The high ground she had taken; the perfect trust in one; the scorn of any judgement, save her own; these had vanished from her. Rose, the tameless heroine who had once put her mother's philosophy in action, was the easiest filly that turbaned matron ever yet drove into the straight road of the world. It even surprised Lady Jocelyn to see how wonderfully she had been broken in by her grandmother. Her ladyship wrote to Drummond to tell him of it, and Drummond congratulated her, saying, however: "Changes of this sort don't come of conviction. Wait till you see her at home. I think they have been sticking pins into the sore part."

Drummond knew Rose well. In reality there was no change in her. She was only a suppliant to be spared from ridicule: spared from the application of the scourge she had woven for herself.

And, ah! to one who deigned to think warmly still of such a disgraced silly creature, with what gratitude she turned! He might well suppose love alone could pour that profusion of jewels at his feet.

Ferdinand, now Lord Laxley, understood the merits of his finger-nails better than the nature of young women; but he is not to be blamed for presuming that Rose had learnt to adore him. Else why did she like his company so much? He was not mistaken in thinking she looked up to him. She seemed to beg to be taken into his noble serenity. In truth she sighed to feel as he did, above everybody!—she that had fallen so low! Above everybody!—born above them, and therefore superior by grace divine! To this Rose Jocelyn had come—she envied the mind of Ferdinand.

He, you may be sure, was quite prepared to accept her homage. Rose he had always known to be just the girl for him; spirited, fresh, and with fine teeth; and once tied to you safe to be staunch. They walked together, rode together, danced together. Her soft humility touched him to eloquence. Say she was a little hypocrite, if you like, when the blood came to her cheeks under his eyes. Say she was a heartless minx for allowing it to be bruited that she and Ferdinand were betrothed. I can but tell you that her blushes were blushes of gratitude to one who could devote his time to such a disgraced silly creature, and that she, in her abject state, felt a secret pleasure in the protection Ferdinand's name appeared to extend over her, and was hardly willing to lose it.

So far Lady Elburne's tact and discipline had been highly successful. One morning, in May, Ferdinand, strolling with Rose down the garden made a positive appeal to her common sense and friendly feeling; by which she understood that he wanted her consent to his marriage with her.

Rose answered:

"Who would have me?"

Ferdinand spoke pretty well, and ultimately got possession of her hand. She let him keep it, thinking him noble for forgetting that another had pressed it before him.

Some minutes later the letters were delivered. One of them contained Juliana's dark-winged missive.

"Poor, poor Juley!" said Rose, dropping her head, after reading all that was on the crumpled leaf with an inflexible face. And then, talking on, long low sighs lifted her bosom at intervals. She gazed from time to time with a wistful conciliatory air on Ferdinand. Rushing to her chamber, the first cry her soul framed was:

"He did not kiss me!"

The young have a superstitious sense of something incontestably true in the final protestations of the dead. Evan guiltless! she could not quite take the meaning this revelation involved. That which had been dead was beginning to move within her; but blindly: and now it stirred and troubled; now sank. Guiltless all she had thought him! Oh! she knew she could not have been deceived. But why, why had he hidden his sacrifice from her?

"It is better for us both, of course," said Rose, speaking the world's wisdom, parrot-like, and bursting into tears the next minute. Guiltless, and gloriously guiltless! but nothing—nothing to her!

She tried to blame him. It would not do. She tried to think of that grovelling loathsome position painted to her by Lady Elburne's graphic hand. Evan dispersed the gloomy shades like sunshine. Then in a sort of terror she rejoiced to think she was partially engaged to Ferdinand, and found herself crying again with exultation, that he had not kissed her: for a kiss on her mouth was to Rose a pledge and a bond.

The struggle searched her through: bared her weakness, probed her strength; and she, seeing herself, suffered grievously in her self-love. Am I such a coward, inconstant, cold? she asked. Confirmatory answers coming, flung her back under the shield of Ferdinand if for a moment her soul stood up armed and defiant, it was Evan's hand she took.

To whom do I belong? was another terrible question. In her ideas, if Evan was not chargeable with that baseness which had sundered them he might claim her yet, if he would. If he did, what then? Must she go to him?

Impossible: she was in chains. Besides, what a din of laughter there would be to see her led away by him. Twisting her joined hands: weeping for her cousin, as she thought, Rose passed hours of torment over Juliana's legacy to her.

"Why did I doubt him?" she cried, jealous that any soul should have known and trusted him better. Jealous and I am afraid that the kindling of that one feature of love relighted the fire of her passion thus fervidly. To be outstripped in generosity was hateful to her. Rose, naturally, could not reflect that a young creature like herself, fighting against the world, as we call it, has all her faculties at the utmost stretch, and is often betrayed by failing nature when the will is still valiant.

And here she sat-in chains! "Yes! I am fit only to be the wife of an idle brainless man, with money and a title," she said, in extreme self-contempt. She caught a glimpse of her whole life in the horrid tomb of his embrace, and questions whether she could yield her hand to him—whether it was right in the eyes of heaven, rushed impetuously to console her, and defied anything in the shape of satisfactory affirmations. Nevertheless, the end of the struggle was, that she felt that she was bound to Ferdinand.

"But this I will do," said Rose, standing with heat-bright eyes and deep-coloured cheeks before the glass. "I will clear his character at Beckley. I will help him. I will be his friend. I will wipe out the injustice I did him." And this bride-elect of a lord absolutely added that she was unworthy to be the wife of a tailor!

"He! how unequalled he is! There is nothing he fears except shame. Oh! how sad it will be for him to find no woman in his class to understand him and be his helpmate!"

Over, this sad subject, of which we must presume her to be accurately cognizant, Rose brooded heavily. By mid-day she gave her Grandmother notice that she was going home to Juliana's funeral.

"Well, Rose, if you think it necessary to join the ceremony," said Lady Elburne. "Beckley is bad quarters for you, as you have learnt. There was never much love between you cousins."

"No, and I don't pretend to it," Rose answered. "I am sorry poor Juley's gone."

"She's better gone for many reasons—she appears to have been a little venomous toad," said Lady Elburne; and Rose, thinking of a snakelike death-bite working through her blood, rejoined: "Yes, she isn't to be pitied she's better off than most people."

So it was arranged that Rose should go. Ferdinand and her aunt, Mrs. Shorne, accompanied her. Mrs. Shorne gave them their opportunities, albeit they were all stowed together in a carriage, and Ferdinand seemed willing to profit by them; but Rose's hand was dead, and she sat by her future lord forming the vow on her lips that they should never be touched by him.

Arrived at Beckley, she, to her great delight, found Caroline there, waiting for the funeral. In a few minutes she got her alone, and after kisses, looked penetratingly into her lovely eyes, shook her head, and said: "Why were you false to me?"

"False?" echoed Caroline.

"You knew him. You knew why he did that. Why did you not save me?"

Caroline fell upon her neck, asking pardon. She spared her the recital of facts further than the broad avowal. Evan's present condition she plainly stated: and Rose, when the bitter pangs had ceased, made oath to her soul she would rescue him from it.

In addition to the task of clearing Evan's character, and rescuing him, Rose now conceived that her engagement to Ferdinand must stand ice-bound till Evan had given her back her troth. How could she obtain it from him? How could she take anything from one so noble and so poor! Happily there was no hurry; though before any bond was ratified, she decided conscientiously that it must be done.

You see that like a lithe snake she turns on herself, and must be tracked in and out. Not being a girl to solve the problem with tears, or outright perfidy, she had to ease her heart to the great shock little by little—sincere as far as she knew: as far as one who loves may be. The day of the funeral came and went. The Jocelyns were of their mother's opinion: that for many reasons Juliana was better out of the way. Mrs. Bonner's bequest had been a severe blow to Sir Franks. However, all was now well. The estate naturally lapsed to Lady Jocelyn. No one in the house dreamed of a will, signed with Juliana's name, attested, under due legal forms, being in existence. None of the members of the family imagined that at Beckley Court they were then residing on somebody else's ground.

Want of hospitable sentiments was not the cause that led to an intimation from Sir Franks to his wife, that Mrs. Strike must not be pressed to remain, and that Rose must not be permitted to have her own way in this. Knowing very well that Mrs. Shorne spoke through her husband's mouth, Lady Jocelyn still acquiesced, and Rose, who had pressed Caroline publicly to stay, had to be silent when the latter renewed her faint objections; so Caroline said she would leave on the morrow morning.

Juliana, with her fretfulness, her hand bounties, her petty egoisms, and sudden far-leaping generosities, and all the contradictory impulses of her malady, had now departed utterly. The joys of a landed proprietor mounted into the head of Sir Franks. He was up early the next morning, and he and Harry walked over a good bit of the ground before breakfast. Sir Franks meditated making it entail, and favoured Harry with a lecture on the duty of his shaping the course of his conduct at once after the model of the landed gentry generally.

"And you may think yourself lucky to come into that catalogue—the son of a younger son!" said Sir Franks, tapping Mr. Harry's shoulder. Harry also began to enjoy the look and smell of land. At the breakfast, which, though early, was well attended, Harry spoke of the adviseability of felling timber here, planting there, and so forth, after the model his father held up. Sir Franks nodded approval of his interest in the estate, but reserved his opinion on matters of detail.

"All I beg of you is," said Lady Jocelyn, "that you won't let us have turnips within the circuit of a mile"; which was obligingly promised.

The morning letters were delivered and opened with the customary calmness.

"Letter from old George," Harry sings out, and buzzes over a few lines. "Halloa!—Hum!" He was going to make a communication, but catching sight of Caroline, tossed the letter over to Ferdinand, who read it and tossed it back with the comment of a careless face.

"Read it, Rosey?" says Harry, smiling bluntly.

Rather to his surprise, Rose took the letter. Study her eyes if you wish to gauge the potency of one strong dose of ridicule on an ingenuous young heart. She read that Mr. George Uplift had met "our friend Mr. Snip" riding, by moonlight, on the road to Beckley. That great orbed night of their deep tender love flashed luminously through her frame, storming at the base epithet by which her lover was mentioned, flooding grandly over the ignominies cast on him by the world. She met the world, as it were, in a death-grapple; she matched the living heroic youth she felt him to be, with that dead wooden image of him which it thrust before her. Her heart stood up singing like a craven who sees the tide of victory setting toward him. But this passed beneath her eyelids. When her eyes were lifted, Ferdinand could have discovered nothing in them to complain of, had his suspicions been light to raise: nor could Mrs. Shorne perceive that there was the opening for a shrewd bodkin-thrust. Rose had got a mask at last: her colour, voice, expression, were perfectly at command. She knew it to be a cowardice to wear any mask: but she had been burnt, horribly burnt: how much so you may guess from the supple dissimulation of such a bold clear-visaged girl. She conquered the sneers of the world in her soul: but her sensitive skin was yet alive to the pangs of the scorching it had been subjected to when weak, helpless, and betrayed by Evan, she stood with no philosophic parent to cry fair play for her, among the skilful torturers of Elburne House.

Sir Franks had risen and walked to the window.

"News?" said Lady Jocelyn, wheeling round in her chair.

The one eyebrow up of the easy-going baronet signified trouble of mind. He finished his third perusal of a letter that appeared to be written in a remarkably plain legal hand, and looking as men do when their intelligences are just equal to the comprehension or expression of an oath, handed the letter to his wife, and observed that he should be found in the library. Nevertheless he waited first to mark its effect on Lady Jocelyn. At one part of the document her forehead wrinkled slightly.

"Doesn't sound like a joke!" he said.

She answered:

"No."

Sir Franks, apparently quite satisfied by her ready response, turned on his heel and left the room quickly.

An hour afterward it was rumoured and confirmed that Juliana Bonner had willed all the worldly property she held in her own right, comprising Beckley Court, to Mr. Evan Harrington, of Lymport, tailor. An abstract of the will was forwarded. The lawyer went on to say, that he had conformed to the desire of the testatrix in communicating the existence of the aforesaid will six days subsequent to her death, being the day after her funeral.

There had been railing and jeering at the Countess de Saldar, the clever outwitted exposed adventuress, at Elburne House and Beckley Court. What did the crowing cleverer aristocrats think of her now?

On Rose the blow fell bitterly. Was Evan also a foul schemer? Was he of a piece with his intriguing sister? His close kinship with the Countess had led her to think baseness possible to him when it was confessed by his own mouth once. She heard black names cast at him and the whole of the great Mel's brood, and incapable of quite disbelieving them merited, unable to challenge and rebut them, she dropped into her recent state of self-contempt: into her lately-instilled doubt whether it really was in Nature's power, unaided by family-portraits, coats-of-arms, ball-room practice, and at least one small phial of Essence of Society, to make a Gentleman.

XLIV

Contains a Warning to All Conspirators

This, if you have done me the favour to read it aright, has been a chronicle of desperate heroism on the part of almost all the principal personages represented. But not the Countess de Saldar, scaling the embattled fortress of Society; nor Rose, tossing its keys to her lover from the shining turret-tops; nor Evan, keeping bright the lamp of self-respect in his bosom against South wind and East; none excel friend Andrew Cogglesby, who, having fallen into Old Tom's plot to humiliate his wife and her sisters, simply for Evan's sake, and without any distinct notion of the terror, confusion, and universal upset he was bringing on his home, could yet, after a scared contemplation of the scene when he returned from his expedition to Fallow field, continue to wear his rueful mask; and persevere in treacherously outraging his lofty wife.

He did it to vindicate the ties of blood against accidents of position. Was he justified? I am sufficiently wise to ask my own sex alone.

On the other side, be it said (since in our modern days every hero must have his weak heel), that now he had gone this distance it was difficult to recede. It would be no laughing matter to tell his solemn Harriet that he had been playing her a little practical joke. His temptations to give it up were incessant and most agitating; but if to advance seemed terrific, there was, in stopping short, an awfulness so overwhelming that Andrew abandoned himself to the current, his real dismay adding to his acting powers.

The worst was, that the joke was no longer his: it was Old Tom's. He discovered that he was in Old Tom's hands completely. Andrew had thought that he would just frighten the women a bit, get them down to Lymport for a week or so, and then announce that matters were not so bad with the Brewery as he had feared; concluding the farce with a few domestic fireworks. Conceive his dismay when he entered the house, to find there a man in possession.

Andrew flew into such a rage that he committed an assault on the man. So ungovernable was his passion, that for some minutes Harriet's measured voice summoned him from over the banisters above, quite in vain. The miserable Englishman refused to be taught that his house had ceased to be his castle. It was something beyond a joke, this! The intruder, perfectly docile, seeing that by accurate calculation every shake he got involved a bottle of wine for him, and ultimate compensation probably to the amount of a couple of sovereigns, allowed himself to be lugged up stairs, in default of summary ejection on the point of Andrew's toe into the street. There he was faced to the lady of the house, who apologized to him, and requested her husband to state what had made him guilty of this indecent behaviour. The man showed his papers. They were quite in order. "At the suit of Messrs. Grist."

"My own lawyers!" cried Andrew, smacking his forehead; and Old Tom's devilry flashed on him at once. He sank into a chair.

"Why did you bring this person up here?" said Harriet, like a speaking statue.

"My dear!" Andrew answered, and spread out his hand, and waggled his head; "My—please!—I—I don't know. We all want exercise."

The man laughed, which was kindly of him, but offensive to Mrs. Cogglesby, who gave Andrew a glance which was full payment for his imbecile pleasantry, and promised more.

With a hospitable inquiry as to the condition of his appetite, and a request that he would be pleased to satisfy it to the full, the man was dismissed: whereat, as one delivered of noxious presences, the Countess rustled into sight. Not noticing Andrew, she lisped to Harriet: "Misfortunes are sometimes no curses! I bless the catarrh that has confined Silva to his chamber, and saved him from a bestial exhibition."

The two ladies then swept from the room, and left Andrew to perspire at leisure.

Fresh tribulations awaited him when he sat down to dinner. Andrew liked his dinner to be comfortable, good, and in plenty. This may not seem strange. The fact is stated that I may win for him the warm sympathies of the body of his countrymen. He was greeted by a piece of cold boiled neck of mutton and a solitary dish of steaming potatoes. The blank expanse of table-cloth returned his desolate stare.

"Why, what's the meaning of this?" Andrew brutally exclaimed, as he thumped the table.

The Countess gave a start, and rolled a look as of piteous supplication to spare a lady's nerves, addressed to a ferocious brigand. Harriet answered: "It means that I will have no butcher's bills."

"Butcher's bills! butcher's bills!" echoed Andrew; "why, you must have butcher's bills; why, confound! why, you'll have a bill for this, won't you, Harry? eh? of course!"

"There will be no more bills dating from yesterday," said his wife.

"What! this is paid for, then?"

"Yes, Mr. Cogglesby; and so will all household expenses be, while my pocket-money lasts."

Resting his eyes full on Harriet a minute, Andrew dropped them on the savourless white-rimmed chop, which looked as lonely in his plate as its parent dish on the table. The poor dear creature's pocket-money had paid for it! The thought, mingling with a rush of emotion, made his ideas spin. His imagination surged deliriously. He fancied himself at the Zoological Gardens, exchanging pathetic glances with a melancholy marmoset. Wonderfully like one the chop looked! There was no use in his trying to eat it. He seemed to be fixing his teeth in solid tears. He choked. Twice he took up knife and fork, put them down again, and plucking forth his handkerchief, blew a tremendous trumpet, that sent the Countess's eyes rolling to the ceiling, as if heaven were her sole refuge from such vulgarity.

"Damn that Old Tom!" he shouted at last, and pitched back in his chair.

"Mr. Cogglesby!" and "In the presence of ladies!" were the admonishing interjections of the sisters, at whom the little man frowned in turns.

"Do you wish us to quit the room, sir?" inquired his wife.

"God bless your soul, you little darling!" he apostrophized that stately person. "Here, come along with me, Harry. A wife's a wife, I say—hang it! Just outside the room—just a second! or up in a corner will do."

Mrs. Cogglesby was amazed to see him jump up and run round to her. She was prepared to defend her neck from his caress, and refused to go: but the words, "Something particular to tell you," awakened her curiosity, which urged her to compliance. She rose and went with him to the door.

"Well, sir; what is it?"

No doubt he was acting under a momentary weakness he was about to betray the plot and take his chance of forgiveness; but her towering port, her commanding aspect, restored his courage. (There may be a contrary view of the case.) He enclosed her briskly in a connubial hug, and remarked with mad ecstasy: "What a duck you are, Harry! What a likeness between you and your mother."

Mrs. Cogglesby disengaged herself imperiously. Had he called her aside for this gratuitous insult? Contrite, he saw his dreadful error.

"Harry! I declare!" was all he was allowed to say. Mrs. Cogglesby marched back to her chair, and recommenced the repast in majestic silence.

Andrew sighed; he attempted to do the same. He stuck his fork in the blanched whiskerage of his marmoset, and exclaimed: "I can't!"

He was unnoticed.

"You do not object to plain diet?" said Harriet to Louisa.

"Oh, no, in verity!" murmured the Countess. "However plain it be! Absence of appetite, dearest. You are aware I partook of luncheon at mid-day with the Honourable and Reverend Mr. Duffian. You must not look condemnation at your Louy for that. Luncheon is not conversion!"

Harriet observed that this might be true; but still, to her mind, it was a mistake to be too intimate with dangerous people. "And besides," she added, "Mr. Duffian is no longer 'the Reverend.' We deprive all renegades of their spiritual titles. His worldly ones let him keep."

Her superb disdain nettled the Countess.

"Dear Harriet!" she said, with less languor, "You are utterly and totally and entirely mistaken. I tell you so positively. Renegade! The application of such a word to such a man! Oh! and it is false, Harriet quite! Renegade means one who has gone over to the Turks, my dear. I am almost certain I saw it in Johnson's Dictionary, or an improvement upon Johnson, by a more learned author. But there is the fact, if Harriet can only bring her—shall I say stiff-necked prejudices to envisage it?"

Harriet granted her sister permission to apply the phrases she stood in need of, without impeaching her intimacy with the most learned among lexicographers.

"And is there no such thing as being too severe?" the Countess resumed. "What our enemies call unchristian!"

"Mr. Duffian has no cause to complain of us," said Harriet.

"Nor does he do so, dearest. Calumny may assail him; you may utterly denude him—"

"Adam!" interposed Andrew, distractedly listening. He did not disturb the Countess's flow.

"You may vilify and victimize Mr. Duffian, and strip him of the honours of his birth, but, like the Martyrs, he will still continue the perfect nobleman. Stoned, I assure you that Mr. Duffian would preserve his breeding. In character he is exquisite; a polish to defy misfortune."

"I suppose his table is good?" said Harriet, almost ruffled by the Countess's lecture.

"Plate," was remarked in the cold tone of supreme indifference.

"Hem! good wines?" Andrew asked, waking up a little and not wishing to be excluded altogether.

"All is of the very best," the Countess pursued her eulogy, not looking at him.

"Don't you think you could—eh, Harry?—manage a pint for me, my dear?" Andrew humbly petitioned. "This cold water—ha! ha! my stomach don't like cold bathing."

His wretched joke rebounded from the impenetrable armour of the ladies.

"The wine-cellar is locked," said his wife. "I have sealed up the key till an inventory can be taken by some agent of the creditors."

"What creditors?" roared Andrew.

"You can have some of the servants' beer," Mrs. Cogglesby appended.

Andrew studied her face to see whether she really was not hoisting him with his own petard. Perceiving that she was sincerely acting according to her sense of principle, he fumed, and departed to his privacy, unable to stand it any longer.

Then like a kite the Countess pounced upon his character. Would the Honourable and Reverend Mr. Duflian decline to participate in the sparest provender? Would he be guilty of the discourtesy of leaving table without a bow or an apology, even if reduced to extremest poverty? No, indeed! which showed that, under all circumstances, a gentleman was a gentleman. And, oh! how she pitied her poor Harriet—eternally tied to a most vulgar little man, without the gilding of wealth.

"And a fool in his business to boot, dear!"

"These comparisons do no good," said Harriet. "Andrew at least is not a renegade, and never shall be while I live. I will do my duty by him, however poor we are. And now, Louisa, putting my husband out of the question, what are your intentions? I don't understand bankruptcy, but I imagine they can do nothing to wife and children. My little ones must have a roof over their heads; and, besides, there is little Maxwell. You decline to go down to Lymport, of course."

"Decline!" cried the Countess, melodiously; "and do not you?"

"As far as I am concerned—yes. But I am not to think of myself."

The Countess meditated, and said: "Dear Mr. Duflian has offered me his hospitality. Renegades are not absolutely inhuman. They may be generous. I have no moral doubt that Mr. Duflian would, upon my representation—dare I venture?"

"Sleep in his house! break bread with him!" exclaimed Harriet. "What do you think I am made of? I would perish—go to the workhouse, rather!"

"I see you trooping there," said the Countess, intent on the vision.

"And have you accepted his invitation for yourself, Louisa?"

The Countess was never to be daunted by threatening aspects. She gave her affirmative with calmness and a deliberate smile.

"You are going to live with him?"

"Live with him! What expressions! My husband accompanies me."

Harriet drew up.

"I know nothing, Louisa, that could give me more pain."

The Countess patted Harriet's knee. "It succeeds to bankruptcy, assuredly. But would you have me drag Silva to the—the shop, Harriet, love? Alternatives!"

Mrs. Andrew got up and rang the bell to have the remains of their dinner removed. When this was done, she said,

"Louisa, I don't know whether I am justified: you told me to-day I might keep my jewels, trinkets, and lace, and such like. To me, I know they do not belong now: but I will dispose of them to procure you an asylum somewhere—they will fetch, I should think, L400,—to prevent your going to Mr. Duffian."

No exhibition of great-mindedness which the Countess could perceive, ever found her below it.

"Never, love, never!" she said.

"Then, will you go to Evan?"

"Evan? I hate him!" The olive-hued visage was dark. It brightened as she added, "At least as much as my religious sentiments permit me to. A boy who has thwarted me at every turn!—disgraced us! Indeed, I find it difficult to pardon you the supposition of such a possibility as your own consent to look on him ever again, Harriet."

"You have no children," said Mrs. Andrew.

The Countess mournfully admitted it.

"There lies your danger with Mr. Duffian, Louisa!"

"What! do you doubt my virtue?" asked the Countess.

"Pish! I fear something different. You understand me. Mr. Duflian's moral reputation is none of the best, perhaps."

"That was before he renegaded," said the Countess.

Harriet bluntly rejoined: "You will leave that house a Roman Catholic."

"Now you have spoken," said the Countess, pluming. "Now let me explain myself. My dear, I have fought worldly battles too long and too earnestly. I am rightly punished. I do but quote Herbert Duffian's own words: he is no flatterer though you say he has such soft fingers. I am now engaged in a spiritual contest. He is very wealthy! I have resolved to rescue back to our Church what can benefit the flock of which we form a portion, so exceedingly!"

At this revelation of the Countess's spiritual contest, Mrs. Andrew shook a worldly head.

"You have no chance with men there, Louisa."

"My Harriet complains of female weakness!"

"Yes. We are strong in our own element, Louisa. Don't be tempted out of it."

Sublime, the Countess rose:

"Element! am I to be confined to one? What but spiritual solaces could assist me to live, after the degradations I have had heaped on me? I renounce the world. I turn my sight to realms where caste is unknown. I feel no shame there of being a tailor's daughter. You see, I can bring my tongue to name the thing in its actuality. Once, that member would have blistered. Confess to me that, in spite of your children, you are tempted to howl at the idea of Lymport—"

The Countess paused, and like a lady about to fire off a gun, appeared to tighten her nerves, crying out rapidly:

"Shop! Shears! Geese! Cabbage! Snip! Nine to a man!"

Even as the silence after explosions of cannon, that which reigned in the room was deep and dreadful.

"See," the Countess continued, "you are horrified you shudder. I name all our titles, and if I wish to be red in my cheeks, I must rouge. It is, in verity, as if my senseless clay were pelted, as we heard of Evan at his first Lymport boys' school. You remember when he told us the story? He lisped a trifle then. 'I'm the thon of a thnip.' Oh! it was hell-fire to us, then; but now, what do I feel? Why, I avowed it to Herbert Duffian openly, and he said, that the misfortune of dear Papa's birth did not the less enable him to proclaim himself in conduct a nobleman's offspring—"

"Which he never was." Harriet broke the rhapsody in a monotonous low tone: the Countess was not compelled to hear:

"—and that a large outfitter—one of the very largest, was in reality a merchant, whose daughters have often wedded nobles of the land, and become ancestresses! Now, Harriet, do you see what a truly religious mind can do for us in the way of comfort? Oh! I bow in gratitude to Herbert Duffian. I will not rest till I have led him back to our fold, recovered from his error. He was our own preacher and pastor. He quitted us from conviction. He shall return to us from conviction."

The Countess quoted texts, which I respect, and will not repeat. She descanted further on spiritualism, and on the balm that it was to tailors and their offspring; to all outcasts from Society.

Overpowered by her, Harriet thus summed up her opinions: "You were always self-willed, Louisa."

"Say, full of sacrifice, if you would be just," added the Countess; "and the victim of basest ingratitude."

"Well, you are in a dangerous path, Louisa."

Harriet had the last word, which usually the Countess was not disposed to accord; but now she knew herself strengthened to do so, and was content to smile pityingly on her sister.

Full upon them in this frame of mind, arrived Caroline's great news from Beckley.

It was then that the Countess's conduct proved a memorable refutation of cynical philosophy: she rejoiced in the good fortune of him who had offended her! Though he was not crushed and annihilated (as he deserved to be) by the wrong he had done, the great-hearted woman pardoned him!

Her first remark was: "Let him thank me for it or not, I will lose no moment in hastening to load him with my congratulations."

Pleasantly she joked Andrew, and defended him from Harriet now.

"So we are not all bankrupts, you see, dear brother-in-law."

Andrew had become so demoralized by his own plot, that in every turn of events he scented a similar piece of human ingenuity. Harriet was angry with his disbelief, or say, the grudging credit he gave to the glorious news. Notwithstanding her calmness, the thoughts of Lymport had sickened her soul, and it was only for the sake of her children, and from a sense of the dishonesty of spending a farthing of the money belonging, as she conceived, to the creditors, that she had consented to go.

"I see your motive, Mr. Cogglesby," she observed. "Your measures are disconcerted. I will remain here till my brother gives me shelter."

"Oh, that'll do, my love; that's all I want," said Andrew, sincerely.

"Both of you, fools!" the Countess interjected. "Know you Evan so little? He will receive us anywhere: his arms are open to his kindred: but to his heart the road is through humiliation, and it is to his heart we seek admittance."

"What do you mean?" Harriet inquired.

"Just this," the Countess answered in bold English and her eyes were lively, her figure elastic: "We must all of us go down to the old shop and shake his hand there—every man Jack of us!—I'm only quoting the sailors, Harriet—and that's the way to win him."

She snapped her fingers, laughing. Harriet stared at her, and so did Andrew, though for a different reason. She seemed to be transformed. Seeing him inclined to gape, she ran up to him, caught up his chin between her ten fingers, and kissed him on both cheeks, saying:

"You needn't come, if you're too proud, you know, little man!"

And to Harriet's look of disgust, the cause for which she divined with her native rapidity, she said: "What does it matter? They will talk, but they can't look down on us now. Why, this is my doing!"

She came tripping to her tall sister, to ask plaintively "Mayn't I be glad?" and bobbed a curtsey.

Harriet desired Andrew to leave them. Flushed and indignant she then faced the Countess.

"So unnecessary!" she began. "What can excuse your indiscretion, Louisa?"

The Countess smiled to hear her talking to her younger sister once more. She shrugged.

"Oh, if you will keep up the fiction, do. Andrew knows—he isn't an idiot—and to him we can make light of it now. What does anybody's birth matter, who's well off!"

It was impossible for Harriet to take that view. The shop, if not the thing, might still have been concealed from her husband, she thought.

"It mattered to me when I was well off," she said, sternly.

"Yes; and to me when I was; but we've had a fall and a lesson since that, my dear. Half the aristocracy of England spring from shops!—Shall I measure you?"

Harriet never felt such a desire to inflict a slap upon mortal cheek. She marched away from her in a tiff. On the other hand, Andrew was half fascinated by the Countess's sudden re-assumption of girlhood, and returned—silly fellow! to have another look at her. She had ceased, on reflection, to be altogether so vivacious: her stronger second nature had somewhat resumed its empire: still she was fresh, and could at times be roguishly affectionate and she patted him, and petted him, and made much of him; slightly railed at him for his uxoriousness and domestic subjection, and proffered him her fingers to try the taste of. The truth must be told: Mr. Duflian not being handy, she in her renewed earthly happiness wanted to see her charms in a woman's natural mirror: namely, the face of man: if of man on his knees, all the better and though a little man is not much of a man, and a sister's husband is, or should be, hardly one at all, still some sort of a reflector he must be. Two or three jests adapted to Andrew's palate achieved his momentary captivation.

He said: "'Gad, I never kissed you in my life, Louy."

And she, with a flavour of delicate Irish brogue, "Why don't ye catch opportunity by the tail, then?"

Perfect innocence, I assure you, on both sides.

But mark how stupidity betrays. Andrew failed to understand her, and act on the hint immediately. Had he done so, the affair would have been over without a witness. As it happened, delay permitted Harriet to assist at the ceremony.

"It wasn't your mouth, Louy," said Andrew.

"Oh, my mouth!—that I keep for, my chosen," was answered.

"'Gad, you make a fellow almost wish—" Andrew's fingers worked over his poll, and then the spectre of righteous wrath flashed on him—naughty little man that he was! He knew himself naughty, for it was the only time since his marriage that he had ever been sorry to see his wife. This is a comedy, and I must not preach lessons of life here: but I am obliged to remark that the husband must be proof, the sister-in-law perfect, where arrangements exist that keep them under one roof. She may be so like his wife! Or, from the knowledge she has of his circumstances, she may talk to him almost as his wife. He may forget that she is not his wife! And then again, the small beginnings, which are in reality the mighty barriers, are so easily slid over. But what is the use of telling this to a pure generation? My constant error is in supposing that I write for the wicked people who begat us.

Note, however, the difference between the woman and the man! Shame confessed Andrew's naughtiness; he sniggered pitiably: whereas the Countess jumped up, and pointing at him, asked her sister what she thought of that. Her next sentence, coolly delivered, related to some millinery matter. If this was not innocence, what is?

Nevertheless, I must here state that the scene related, innocent as it was, and, as one would naturally imagine, of puny consequence, if any, did no less a thing than, subsequently, to precipitate the Protestant Countess de Saldar into the bosom of the Roman Catholic Church. A little bit of play!

It seems barely just. But if, as I have heard, a lady has trod on a pebble and broken her nose, tremendous results like these warn us to be careful how we walk. As for play, it was never intended that we should play with flesh and blood.

And, oh, be charitable, matrons of Britain! See here, Andrew Cogglesby, who loved his wife as his very soul, and who almost disliked her sister; in ten minutes the latter had set his head spinning! The whole of the day he went about the house meditating frantically on the possibility of his Harriet demanding a divorce.

She was not the sort of woman to do that. But one thing she resolved to do; and it was, to go to Lymport with Louisa, and having once got her out of her dwelling-place, never to allow her to enter it, wherever it might be, in the light of a resident again. Whether anything but the menace of a participation in her conjugal possessions could have despatched her to that hateful place, I doubt. She went: she would not let Andrew be out of her sight. Growing haughtier toward him at every step, she advanced to the strange old shop. EVAN HARRINGTON over the door! There the Countess, having meantime returned to her state of womanhood, shared her shudders. They entered, and passed in to Mrs. Mel, leaving their footman, apparently, in the rear. Evan was not visible. A man in the shop, with a yard measure negligently adorning his shoulders, said that Mr. Harrington was in the habit of quitting the shop at five.

"Deuced good habit, too," said Andrew.

"Why, sir," observed another, stepping forward, "as you truly say—yes. But—ah! Mr. Andrew Cogglesby? Pleasure of meeting you once in Fallow field! Remember Mr. Perkins?—the lawyer, not the maltster. Will you do me the favour to step out with me?"

Andrew followed him into the street.

"Are you aware of our young friend's good fortune?" said Lawyer Perkins. "Yes. Ah! Well!—Would you believe that any sane person in his condition, now—nonsense apart—could bring his mind wilfully to continue a beggar? No. Um! Well; Mr. Cogglesby, I may tell you that I hold here in my hands a document by which Mr. Evan Harrington transfers the whole of the property bequeathed to him to Lady Jocelyn, and that I have his orders to execute it instantly, and deliver it over to her ladyship, after the will is settled, probate, and so forth: I presume there will be an arrangement about his father's debts. Now what do you think of that?"

"Think, sir,—think!" cried Andrew, cocking his head at him like an indignant bird, "I think he's a damned young idiot to do so, and you're a confounded old rascal to help him."

Leaving Mr. Perkins to digest his judgement, which he had solicited, Andrew bounced back into the shop.

XLV

In which the Shop Becomes the Centre of Attraction

Under the first lustre of a May-night, Evan was galloping over the moon-shadowed downs toward Beckley. At the ridge commanding the woods, the park, and the stream, his horse stopped, as if from habit, snorted, and puffed its sides, while he gazed steadily across the long lighted vale. Soon he began to wind down the glaring chalk-track, and reached grass levels. Here he broke into a round pace, till, gaining the first straggling cottages of the village, he knocked the head of his whip against the garden-gate of one, and a man came out, who saluted him, and held the reins.

"Animal does work, sir," said the man.

Evan gave directions for it to be looked to, and went on to the doorway, where he was met by a young woman. She uttered a respectful greeting, and begged him to enter.

The door closed, he flung himself into a chair, and said:

"Well, Susan, how is the child?"

"Oh! he's always well, Mr. Harrington; he don't know the tricks o' trouble yet."

"Will Polly be here soon?"

"At a quarter after nine, she said, sir."

Evan bade her sit down. After examining her features quietly, he said:

"I'm glad to see you here, Susan. You don't regret that you followed my advice?"

"No, sir; now it's over, I don't. Mother's kind enough, and father doesn't mention anything. She's a-bed with bile—father's out."

"But what? There's something on your mind."

"I shall cry, if I begin, Mr. Harrington."

"See how far you can get without."

"Oh! Sir, then," said Susan, on a sharp rise of her bosom, "it ain't my fault. I wouldn't cause trouble to Mr. Harry, or any friend of yours; but, sir, father have got hold of his letters to me, and he says, there's a promise in 'em—least, one of 'em; and it's as good as law, he says—he heard it in a public-house; and he's gone over to Fall'field to a law-gentleman there." Susan was compelled to give way to some sobs. "It ain't for me—father does it, sir," she pleaded. "I tried to stop him, knowing how it'd vex you, Mr. Harrington; but he's heady about points, though a quiet man ordinary; and he says he don't expect—and I know now no gentleman 'd marry such as me—I ain't such a stupid gaper at words as I used to be; but father says it's for the child's sake, and he does it to have him provided for. Please, don't ye be angry with me, sir."

Susan's half-controlled spasms here got the better of her.

While Evan was awaiting the return of her calmer senses, the latch was lifted, and Polly appeared.

"At it again!" was her sneering comment, after a short survey of her apron-screened sister; and then she bobbed to Evan.

"It's whimper, whimper, and squeak, squeak, half their lives with some girls. After that they go wondering they can't see to thread a needle! The neighbours, I suppose. I should like to lift the top off some o' their houses. I hope I haven't kept you, sir."

"No, Polly," said Evan; "but you must be charitable, or I shall think you want a lesson yourself. Mr. Raikes tells me you want to see me. What is it? You seem to be correspondents."

Polly replied: "Oh, no, Mr. Harrington: only accidental ones—when something particular's to be said. And he dances-like on the paper, so that you can't help laughing. Isn't he a very eccentric gentleman, sir?"

"Very," said Evan. "I've no time to lose, Polly."

"Here, you must go," the latter called to her sister. "Now pack at once, Sue. Do rout out, and do leave off thinking you've got a candle at your eyes, for Goodness' sake!"

Susan was too well accustomed to Polly's usage to complain. She murmured a gentle "Good night, sir," and retired. Whereupon Polly exclaimed: "Bless her poor dear soft heart! It's us hard ones that get on best in the world. I'm treated better than her, Mr. Harrington, and I know I ain't worth half of her. It goes nigh to make one religious, only to see how exactly like Scripture is the way Beckley treats her, whose only sin is her being so soft as to believe in a man! Oh, dear! Mr. Harrington! I wish I had good news for you."

In spite of all his self-control, Evan breathed quickly and looked eagerly.

"Speak it out, Polly."

"Oh, dear! I must, I suppose," Polly answered. "Mr. Laxley's become a lord now, Mr. Harrington."

Evan tasted in his soul the sweets of contrast. "Well?"

"And my Miss Rose—she—"

"What?"

Moved by the keen hunger of his eyes, Polly hesitated. Her face betrayed a sudden change of mind.

"Wants to see you, sir," she said, resolutely.

"To see me?"

Evan stood up, so pale that Polly was frightened.

"Where is she? Where can I meet her?"

"Please don't take it so, Mr. Harrington."

Evan commanded her to tell him what her mistress had said.

Now up to this point Polly had spoken truth. She was positive her mistress did want to see him. Polly, also, with a maiden's tender guile, desired to bring them together for once, though it were for the last time, and for no good on earth. She had been about to confide to him her young mistress's position toward Lord Laxley, when his sharp interrogation stopped her. Shrinking from absolute invention, she remarked that of course she could not exactly remember Miss Rose's words; which seemed indeed too much to expect of her.

"She will see me to-night?" said Evan.

"I don't know about to-night," Polly replied.

"Go to her instantly. Tell her I am ready. I will be at the West park-gates. This is why you wrote, Polly? Why did you lose time? Don't delay, my good girl! Come!"

Evan had opened the door. He would not allow Polly an instant for expostulation; but drew her out, saying, "You will attend to the gates yourself. Or come and tell me the day, if she appoints another."

Polly made a final effort to escape from the pit she was being pushed into.

"Mr. Harrington! it wasn't to tell you this I wrote.

Miss Rose is engaged, sir."

"I understand," said Evan, hoarsely, scarcely feeling it, as is the case with men who are shot through the heart.

Ten minutes later he was on horseback by the Fallow field gates, with the tidings shrieking through his frame. The night was still, and stiller in the pauses of the nightingales. He sat there, neither thinking of them nor reproached in his manhood for the tears that rolled down his cheeks. Presently his horse's ears pricked, and the animal gave a low neigh. Evan's eyes fixed harder on the length of gravel leading to the house. There was no sign, no figure. Out from the smooth grass of the lane a couple of horsemen issued, and came straight to the gates. He heard nothing till one spoke. It was a familiar voice.

"By Jove, Ferdy, here is the fellow, and we've been all the way to Lymport!"

Evan started from his trance.

"It's you, Harrington?"

"Yes, Harry."

"Sir!" exclaimed that youth, evidently flushed with wine, "what the devil do you mean by addressing me by my Christian name?"

Laxley pushed his horse's head in front of Harry. In a manner apparently somewhat improved by his new dignity, he said: "We have ridden to Lymport to speak to you, sir. Favour me by moving a little ahead of the lodge."

Evan bowed, and moved beside him a short way down the lane, Harry following.

"The purport of my visit, sir," Laxley began, "was to make known to you that Miss Jocelyn has done me the honour to accept me as her husband. I learn from her that during the term of your residence in the house, you contrived to extract from her a promise to which she attaches certain scruples. She pleases to consider herself bound to you till you release her. My object is to demand that you will do so immediately."

There was no reply.

"Should you refuse to make this reparation for the harm you have done to her and her family," Laxley pursued, "I must let you know that there are means of compelling you to it, and that those means will be employed."

Harry, fuming at these postured sentences, burst out:

"What do you talk to the fellow in that way for? A fellow who makes a fool of my cousin, and then wants to get us to buy off my sister! What's he spying after here? The place is ours till we troop. I tell you there's only one way of dealing with him, and if you don't do it, I will."

Laxley pulled his reins with a jerk that brought him to the rear.

"Miss Jocelyn has commissioned you to make this demand on me in her name?" said Evan.

"I make it in my own right," returned—Laxley. "I demand a prompt reply."

"My lord, you shall have it. Miss Jocelyn is not bound to me by any engagement. Should she entertain scruples which I may have it in my power to obliterate, I shall not hesitate to do so—but only to her. What has passed between us I hold sacred."

"Hark at that!" shouted Harry. "The damned tradesman means money! You ass, Ferdinand! What did we go to Lymport for? Not to bandy words. Here! I've got my own quarrel with you, Harrington. You've been setting that girl's father on me. Can you deny that?"

It was enough for Harry that Evan did not deny it. The calm disdain which he read on Evan's face acted on his fury, and digging his heels into his horse's flanks he rushed full at him and dealt him a sharp flick with his whip. Evan's beast reared.

"Accept my conditions, sir, or afford me satisfaction," cried Laxley.

"You do me great honour, my lord; but I have told you I cannot," said Evan, curbing his horse.

At that moment Rose came among them. Evan raised his hat, as did Laxley. Harry, a little behind the others, performed a laborious mock salute, and then ordered her back to the house. A quick altercation ensued; the end being that Harry managed to give his sister the context of the previous conversation.

"Now go back, Rose," said Laxley. "I have particular business with Mr. Harrington."

"I came to see him," said Rose, in a clear voice.

Laxley reddened angrily.

"Then tell him at once you want to be rid of him," her brother called to her.

Rose looked at Evan. Could he not see that she had no word in her soul for him of that kind? Yes: but love is not always to be touched to tenderness even at the sight of love.

"Rose," he said, "I hear from Lord Laxley, that you fancy yourself not at liberty; and that you require me to disengage you."

He paused. Did he expect her to say there that she wished nothing of the sort? Her stedfast eyes spoke as much: but misery is wanton, and will pull all down to it. Even Harry was checked by his tone, and Laxley sat silent. The fact that something more than a tailor was speaking seemed to impress them.

"Since I have to say it, Rose, I hold you in no way bound to me. The presumption is forced upon me. May you have all the happiness I pray God to give you.

Gentlemen, good night!"

He bowed and was gone. How keenly she could have retorted on that false prayer for her happiness! Her limbs were nerveless, her tongue speechless. He had thrown her off—there was no barrier now between herself and Ferdinand. Why did Ferdinand speak to her with that air of gentle authority, bidding her return to the house? She was incapable of seeing, what the young lord acutely felt, that he had stooped very much in helping to bring about such a scene. She had no idea of having trifled with him and her own heart, when she talked feebly of her bondage to another, as one who would be warmer to him were she free. Swiftly she compared the two that loved her, and shivered as if she had been tossed to the embrace of a block of ice.

"You are cold, Rose," said Laxley, bending to lay his hand on her shoulder.

"Pray, never touch me," she answered, and walked on hastily to the house.

Entering it, she remembered that Evan had dwelt there. A sense of desolation came over her. She turned to Ferdinand remorsefully, saying: "Dear Ferdinand!" and allowed herself to be touched and taken close to him. When she reached her bed-room, she had time to reflect that he had kissed her on the lips, and then she fell down and shed such tears as had never been drawn from her before.

Next day she rose with an undivided mind. Belonging henceforth to Ferdinand, it was necessary that she should invest him immediately with transcendent qualities. The absence of character in him rendered this easy. What she had done for Evan, she did for him. But now, as if the Fates had been lying in watch to entrap her and chain her, that they might have her at their mercy, her dreams of Evan's high nature—hitherto dreams only—were to be realized. With the purposeless waywardness of her sex, Pony Wheedle, while dressing her young mistress, and though quite aware that the parting had been spoken, must needs relate her sister's story and Evan's share in it. Rose praised him like one forever aloof from him. Nay, she could secretly congratulate herself on not being deceived. Upon that came a letter from Caroline:

"Do not misjudge my brother. He knew Juliana's love for him and rejected it. You will soon have proofs of his disinterestedness. Then do not forget that he works to support us all. I write this with no hope save to make you just to him. That is the utmost he will ever anticipate."

It gave no beating of the heart to Rose to hear good of Evan now: but an increased serenity of confidence in the accuracy of her judgement of persons.

The arrival of Lawyer Perkins supplied the key to Caroline's communication. No one was less astonished than Rose at the news that Evan renounced the estate. She smiled at Harry's contrite stupefaction, and her father's incapacity of belief in conduct so singular, caused her to lift her head and look down on her parent.

"Shows he knows nothing of the world, poor young fellow!" said Sir Franks.

"Nothing more clearly," observed Lady Jocelyn. "I presume I shall cease to be blamed for having had him here?"

"Upon my honour, he must have the soul of a gentleman!" said the baronet. "There's nothing he can expect in return, you know!"

"One would think, Papa, you had always been dealing with tradesmen!" remarked Rose, to whom her father now accorded the treatment due to a sensible girl.

Laxley was present at the family consultation. What was his opinion? Rose manifested a slight anxiety to hear it.

"What those sort of fellows do never surprises me," he said, with a semi-yawn.

Rose felt fire on her cheeks.

"It's only what the young man is bound to do," said Mrs. Shorne.

"His duty, aunt? I hope we may all do it!" Rose interjected.

"Championing him again?"

Rose quietly turned her face, too sure of her cold appreciation of him to retort. But yesterday night a word from him might have made her his; and here she sat advocating the nobility of his nature with the zeal of a barrister in full swing of practice. Remember, however, that a kiss separates them: and how many millions of leagues that counts for in love, in a pure girl's thought, I leave you to guess.

Now, in what way was Evan to be thanked? how was he to be treated? Sir Franks proposed to go down to him in person, accompanied by Harry. Lady Jocelyn acquiesced. But Rose said to her mother:

"Will not you wound his sensitiveness by going to him there?"

"Possibly," said her ladyship. "Shall we write and ask him to come to us?"

"No, Mama. Could we ask him to make a journey to receive our thanks?"

"Not till we have solid ones to offer, perhaps."

"He will not let us help him, Mama, unless we have all given him our hands."

"Probably not. There's always a fund of nonsense in those who are capable of great things, I observe. It shall be a family expedition, if you like."

"What!" exclaimed Mrs. Shorne. "Do you mean that you intend to allow Rose to make one of the party? Franks! is that your idea?"

Sir Franks looked at his wife.

"What harm?" Lady Jocelyn asked; for Rose's absence of conscious guile in appealing to her reason had subjugated that great faculty.

"Simply a sense of propriety, Emily," said Mrs. Shorne, with a glance at Ferdinand.

"You have no objection, I suppose!" Lady Jocelyn addressed him.

"Ferdinand will join us," said Rose.

"Thank you, Rose, I'd rather not," he replied. "I thought we had done with the fellow for good last night."

"Last night?" quoth Lady Jocelyn.

No one spoke. The interrogation was renewed. Was it Rose's swift instinct which directed her the shortest way to gain her point? or that she was glad to announce that her degrading engagement was at an end? She said:

"Ferdinand and Mr. Harrington came to an understanding last night, in my presence."

That, strange as it struck on their ears, appeared to be quite sufficient to all, albeit the necessity for it was not so very clear. The carriage was ordered forthwith; Lady Jocelyn went to dress; Rose drew Ferdinand away into the garden. Then, with all her powers, she entreated him to join her.

"Thank you, Rose," he said; "I have no taste for the genus."

"For my sake, I beg it, Ferdinand."

"It's really too much to ask of me, Rose."

"If you care for me, you will."

"'Pon my honour, quite impossible!"

"You refuse, Ferdinand?"

"My London tailor 'd find me out, and never forgive me."

This pleasantry stopped her soft looks. Why she wished him to be with her, she could not have said. For a thousand reasons: which implies no distinct one something prophetically pressing in her blood.

XLVI

A Lovers' Parting

Now, to suppose oneself the fashioner of such a chain of events as this which brought the whole of the Harrington family in tender unity together once more, would have elated an ordinary mind. But to the Countess de Saldar, it was simply an occasion for reflecting that she had misunderstood—and could most sincerely forgive—Providence. She admitted to herself that it was not entirely her work; for she never would have had their place of meeting to be the Shop. Seeing, however, that her end was gained, she was entitled to the credit of it, and could pardon the means adopted. Her brother lord of Beckley Court, and all of them assembled in the old 193, Main Street, Lymport! What matter for proud humility! Providence had answered her numerous petitions, but in its own way. Stipulating that she must swallow this pill, Providence consented to serve her. She swallowed it with her wonted courage. In half an hour subsequent to her arrival at Lymport, she laid siege to the heart of Old Tom Cogglesby, whom she found installed in the parlour, comfortably sipping at a tumbler of rum-and-water. Old Tom was astonished to meet such an agreeable unpretentious woman, who talked of tailors and lords with equal ease, appeared to comprehend a man's habits instinctively, and could amuse him while she ministered to them.

"Can you cook, ma'am?" asked Old Tom.

"All but that," said the Countess, with a smile of sweet meaning.

"Ha! then you won't suit me as well as your mother."

"Take care you do not excite my emulation," she returned, graciously, albeit disgusted at his tone.

To Harriet, Old Tom had merely nodded. There he sat, in the arm-chair, sucking the liquor, with the glimpse of a sour chuckle on his cheeks. Now and then, during the evening, he rubbed his hands sharply, but spoke little. The unbending Harriet did not conceal her disdain of him. When he ventured to allude to the bankruptcy, she cut him short.

"Pray, excuse me—I am unacquainted with affairs of business—I cannot even understand my husband."

"Lord bless my soul!" Old Tom exclaimed, rolling his eyes.

Caroline had informed her sisters up-stairs that their mother was ignorant of Evan's change of fortune, and that Evan desired her to continue so for the present. Caroline appeared to be pained by the subject, and was glad when Louisa sounded his mysterious behaviour by saying:

"Evan has a native love of concealment—he must be humoured."

At the supper, Mr. Raikes made his bow. He was modest and reserved. It was known that this young gentleman acted as shopman there. With a tenderness for his position worthy of all respect, the Countess spared his feelings by totally ignoring his presence; whereat he, unaccustomed to such great-minded treatment, retired to bed, a hater of his kind. Harriet and Caroline went next. The Countess said she would wait up for Evan, but hearing that his hours of return were about the chimes of matins, she cried exultingly: "Darling Papa all over!" and departed likewise. Mrs. Mel, when she had mixed Old Tom's third glass, wished the brothers good night, and they were left to exchange what sentiments they thought proper for the occasion. The Countess had certainly, disappointed Old Tom's farce, in a measure; and he expressed himself puzzled by her. "You ain't the only one," said his brother. Andrew, with some effort, held his tongue concerning the news of Evan—his fortune and his folly, till he could talk to the youth in person.

All took their seats at the early breakfast next morning.

"Has Evan not come—home yet?" was the Countess's first question.

Mrs. Mel replied, "No."

"Do you know where he has gone, dear Mama?"

"He chooses his own way."

"And you fear that it leads somewhere?" added the Countess.

"I fear that it leads to knocking up the horse he rides."

"The horse, Mama! He is out on a horse all night! But don't you see, dear old pet! his morals, at least, are safe on horseback."

"The horse has to be paid for, Louisa," said her mother, sternly; and then, for she had a lesson to read to the guests of her son, "Ready money doesn't come by joking. What will the creditors think? If he intends to be honest in earnest, he must give up four-feet mouths."

"Fourteen-feet, ma'am, you mean," said Old Tom, counting the heads at table.

"Bravo, Mama!" cried the Countess, and as she was sitting near her mother, she must show how prettily she kissed, by pouting out her playful lips to her parent. "Do be economical always! And mind! for the sake of the wretched animals, I will intercede for you to be his inspector of stables."

This, with a glance of intelligence at her sisters.

"Well, Mr. Raikes," said Andrew, "you keep good hours, at all events—eh?"

"Up with the lark," said Old Tom. "Ha! 'fraid he won't be so early when he gets rid of his present habits—eh?"

"Nec dierum numerum, ut nos, sed noctium computant," said Mr. Raikes, and both the brothers sniffed like dogs that have put their noses to a hot coal, and the Countess, who was less insensible to the aristocracy of the dead languages than are women generally, gave him the recognition that is occasionally afforded the family tutor.

About the hour of ten Evan arrived. He was subjected to the hottest embrace he had ever yet received from his sister Louisa.

"Darling!" she called him before them all. "Oh! how I suffer for this ignominy I see you compelled for a moment to endure. But it is but for a moment. They must vacate; and you will soon be out of this horrid hole."

"Where he just said he was glad to give us a welcome," muttered Old Tom.

Evan heard him, and laughed. The Countess laughed too.

"No, we will not be impatient. We are poor insignificant people!" she said; and turning to her mother, added: "And yet I doubt not you think the smallest of our landed gentry equal to great continental seigneurs. I do not say the contrary."

"You will fill Evan's head with nonsense till you make him knock up a horse a week, and never go to his natural bed," said Mrs. Mel, angrily. "Look at him! Is a face like that fit for business?"

"Certainly, certainly not!" said the Countess.

"Well, Mother, the horse is dismissed,—you won't have to complain any more," said Evan, touching her hand. "Another history commences from to-day."

The Countess watched him admiringly. Such powers of acting she could not have ascribed to him.

"Another history, indeed!" she said. "By the way, Van, love! was it out of Glamorganshire—were we Tudors, according to Papa? or only Powys chieftains? It's of no moment, but it helps one in conversation."

"Not half so much as good ale, though!" was Old Tom's comment.

The Countess did not perceive its fitness, till Evan burst into a laugh, and then she said:

"Oh! we shall never be ashamed of the Brewery. Do not fear that, Mr. Cogglesby."

Old Tom saw his farce reviving, and encouraged the Countess to patronize him. She did so to an extent that called on her Mrs. Mel's reprobation, which was so cutting and pertinent, that Harriet was compelled to defend her sister, remarking that perhaps her mother would soon learn that Louisa was justified in not permitting herself and family to be classed too low. At this Andrew, coming from a private interview with Evan, threw up his hands and eyes as one who foretold astonishment but counselled humility. What with the effort of those who knew a little to imply a great deal; of those who knew all to betray nothing; and of those who were kept in ignorance to strain a fact out of the conflicting innuendos the general mystification waxed apace, and was at its height, when a name struck on Evan's ear that went through his blood like a touch of the torpedo.

He had been called into the parlour to assist at a consultation over the Brewery affairs. Raikes opened the door, and announced, "Sir Franks and Lady Jocelyn."

Them he could meet, though it was hard for his pride to pardon their visit to him there. But when his eyes discerned Rose behind them, the passions of his lower nature stood up armed. What could she have come for but to humiliate, or play with him?

A very few words enabled the Countess to guess the cause for this visit. Of course, it was to beg time! But they thanked Evan. For something generous, no doubt.

Sir Franks took him aside, and returning remarked to his wife that she perhaps would have greater influence with him. All this while Rose sat talking to Mrs. Andrew Cogglesby, Mrs. Strike, and Evan's mother. She saw by his face the offence she had committed, and acted on by one of her impulses, said: "Mama, I think if I were to speak to Mr. Harrington—"

Ere her mother could make light of the suggestion, Old Tom had jumped up, and bowed out his arm.

"Allow me to conduct ye to the drawing room, upstairs, young lady. He'll follow, safe enough!"

Rose had not stipulated for that. Nevertheless, seeing no cloud on her mother's face, or her father's, she gave Old Tom her hand, and awaited a movement from Evan. It was too late to object to it on either side. Old Tom had caught the tide at the right instant. Much as if a grim old genie had planted them together, the lovers found themselves alone.

"Evan, you forgive me?" she began, looking up at him timidly.

"With all my heart, Rose," he answered, with great cheerfulness.

"No. I know your heart better. Oh, Evan! you must be sure that we respect you too much to wound you. We came to thank you for your generosity. Do you refuse to accept anything from us? How can we take this that you thrust on us, unless in some way—"

"Say no more," he interposed. "You see me here. You know me as I am, now."

"Yes, yes!" the tears stood in her eyes. "Why did I come, you would ask? That is what you cannot forgive! I see now how useless it was. Evan! why did you betray me?"

"Betray you, Rose?"

"You said that you loved me once."

She was weeping, and all his spirit melted, and his love cried out: "I said 'till death,' and till death it will be, Rose."

"Then why, why did you betray me, Evan? I know it all. But if you blackened yourself to me, was it not because you loved something better than me? And now you think me false! Which of us two has been false? It's silly to talk of these things now too late! But be just. I wish that we may be friends. Can we, unless you bend a little?"

The tears streamed down her cheeks, and in her lovely humility he saw the baseness of that pride of his which had hitherto held him up.

"Now that you are in this house where I was born and am to live, can you regret what has come between us, Rose?"

Her lips quivered in pain.

"Can I do anything else but regret it all my life, Evan?"

How was it possible for him to keep his strength?

"Rose!" he spoke with a passion that made her shrink, "are you bound to this man?" and to the drooping of her eyes, "No. Impossible, for you do not love him. Break it. Break the engagement you cannot fulfil. Break it and belong to me. It sounds ill for me to say that in such a place. But Rose, I will leave it. I will accept any assistance that your father—that any man will give me. Beloved—noble girl! I see my falseness to you, though I little thought it at the time—fool that I was! Be my help, my guide-as the soul of my body! Be mine!"

“Oh, Evan!” she clasped her hands in terror at the change in him, that was hurrying her she knew not whither, and trembling, held them supplicatingly.

“Yes, Rose: you have taught me what love can be. You cannot marry that man.”

“But, my honour, Evan! No. I do not love him; for I can love but one. He has my pledge. Can I break it?”

The stress on the question choked him, just as his heart sprang to her.

“Can you face the world with me, Rose?”

“Oh, Evan! is there an escape for me? Think Decide!—No—no! there is not. My mother, I know, looks on it so. Why did she trust me to be with you here, but that she thinks me engaged to him, and has such faith in me? Oh, help me!—be my guide. Think whether you would trust me hereafter! I should despise myself.”

“Not if you marry him!” said Evan, bitterly. And then thinking as men will think when they look on the figure of a fair girl marching serenely to a sacrifice, the horrors of which they insist that she ought to know: half-hating her for her calmness—adoring her for her innocence: he said: “It rests with you, Rose. The world will approve you, and if your conscience does, why—farewell, and may heaven be your help.”

She murmured, “Farewell.”

Did she expect more to be said by him? What did she want or hope for now? And yet a light of hunger grew in her eyes, brighter and brighter, as it were on a wave of yearning.

“Take my hand once,” she faltered.

Her hand and her whole shape he took, and she with closed eyes let him strain her to his breast.

Their swoon was broken by the opening of the door, where Old Tom Cogglesby and Lady Jocelyn appeared.

“’Gad! he seems to have got his recompense—eh, my lady?” cried Old Tom. However satisfactorily they might have explained the case, it certainly did seem so.

Lady Jocelyn looked not absolutely displeased. Old Tom was chuckling at her elbow. The two principal actors remained dumb.

“I suppose, if we leave young people to settle a thing, this is how they do it,” her ladyship remarked.

“’Gad, and they do it well!” cried Old Tom.

Rose, with a deep blush on her cheeks, stepped from Evan to her mother. Not in effrontery, but earnestly, and as the only way of escaping from the position, she said: "I have succeeded, Mama. He will take what I offer."

"And what's that, now?" Old Tom inquired.

Rose turned to Evan. He bent and kissed her hand.

"Call it 'recompense' for the nonce," said Lady Jocelyn. "Do you still hold to your original proposition, Tom?"

"Every penny, my lady. I like the young fellow, and she's a jolly little lass—if she means it:—she's a woman."

"True," said Lady Jocelyn. "Considering that fact, you will oblige me by keeping the matter quiet."

"Does she want to try whether the tailor's a gentleman still, my lady-eh?"

"No. I fancy she will have to see whether a certain nobleman may be one."

The Countess now joined them. Sir Franks had informed her of her brother's last fine performance. After a short, uneasy pause, she said, glancing at Evan:—

"You know his romantic nature. I can assure you he was sincere; and even if you could not accept, at least—"

"But we have accepted, Countess," said Rose.

"The estate!"

"The estate, Countess. And what is more, to increase the effect of his generosity, he has consented to take a recompense."

"Indeed!" exclaimed the Countess, directing a stony look at her brother.

"May I presume to ask what recompense?"

Rose shook her head. "Such a very poor one, Countess! He has no idea of relative value."

The Countess's great mind was just then running hot on estates, and thousands, or she would not have played goose to them, you may be sure. She believed that Evan had been wheedled by Rose into the acceptance of a small sum of money, in return for his egregious gift.

With an internal groan, the outward aspect of which she had vast difficulty in masking, she said: "You are right—he has no head. Easily cajoled!"

Old Tom sat down in a chair, and laughed outright. Lady Jocelyn, in pity for the poor lady, who always amused her, thought it time to put an end to the scene.

"I hope your brother will come to us in about a week," she said. "May I expect the favour of your company as well?"

The Countess felt her dignity to be far superior as she responded: "Lady Jocelyn, when next I enjoy the gratification of a visit to your hospitable mansion, I must know that I am not at a disadvantage. I cannot consent to be twice pulled down to my brother's level."

Evan's heart was too full of its dim young happiness to speak, or care for words. The cold elegance of the Countess's curtsey to Lady Jocelyn: her ladyship's kindly pressure of his hand: Rose's stedfast look into his eyes: Old Tom's smothered exclamation that he was not such a fool as he seemed: all passed dream-like, and when he was left to the fury of the Countess, he did not ask her to spare him, nor did he defend himself. She bade adieu to him and their mutual relationship that very day. But her star had not forsaken her yet. Chancing to peep into the shop, to intrust a commission to Mr. John Raikes, who was there doing penance for his career as a gentleman, she heard Old Tom and Andrew laughing, utterly unlike bankrupts.

"Who'd have thought the women such fools! and the Countess, too!"

This was Andrew's voice. He chuckled as one emancipated. The Countess had a short interview with him (before she took her departure to join her husband, under the roof of the Honourable Herbert Duffian), and Andrew chuckled no more.

XLVII

A Year Later

The Countess de Saldar de Sancorvo to Her Sister Caroline

Rome

"Let the post-mark be my reply to your letter received through the Consulate, and most courteously delivered with the Consul's compliments. We shall yet have an ambassador at Rome—mark your Louisa's words. Yes, dearest! I am here, body and spirit! I have at last found a haven, a refuge, and let those who condemn me compare the peace of their spirits with mine. You think that you have quite conquered the dreadfulness of our origin. My love, I smile at you! I know it to be impossible for the Protestant heresy to offer a shade of consolation. Earthly-born, it rather encourages earthly distinctions. It is the sweet sovereign Pontiff alone who gathers all in his arms, not excepting tailors. Here, if they could know it, is their blessed comfort!

"Thank Harriet for her message. She need say nothing. By refusing me her hospitality, when she must have known that the house was as free of creditors as any foreigner under the rank of Count is of soap, she drove me to Mr. Duflian. Oh! how I rejoice at her exceeding unkindness! How warmly I forgive her the unsisterly—to say the least—vindictiveness of her unaccountable conduct! Her sufferings will one day be terrible. Good little Andrew supplies her place to me. Why do you refuse his easily afforded bounty? No one need know of it. I tell you candidly, I take double, and the small good punch of a body is only too delighted. But then, I can be discreet.

"Oh! the gentlemanliness of these infinitely maligned Jesuits! They remind me immensely of Sir Charles Grandison, and those frontispiece pictures to the novels we read when girls—I mean in manners and the ideas they impose—not in dress or length of leg, of course. The same winning softness; the same irresistible ascendancy over the female mind! They require virtue for two, I assure you, and so I told Silva, who laughed.

"But the charms of confession, my dear! I will talk of Evan first. I have totally forgiven him. Attache to the Naples embassy, sounds tol-lol. In such a position I can rejoice to see him, for it permits me to acknowledge him. I am not sure that, spiritually, Rose will be his most fitting helpmate. However, it is done, and I did it, and there is no more to be said. The behaviour of Lord Laxley in refusing to surrender a young lady who declared that her heart was with another, exceeds all I could have supposed. One of the noble peers among his ancestors must have been a pig! Oh! the Roman nobility! Grace, refinement, intrigue, perfect comprehension of your ideas, wishes—the meanest trifles! Here you have every worldly charm, and all crowned by Religion! This is my true delight. I feel at last that whatsoever I do, I cannot go far wrong while I am within hail of my gentle priest. I never could feel so before.

"The idea of Mr. Parsley proposing for the beautiful widow Strike! It was indecent to do so so soon—widowed under such circumstances! But I dare say he was as disinterested as a Protestant curate ever can be. Beauty is a good dowry to bring a poor, lean, worldly curate of your Church, and he knows that. Your bishops and arches are quite susceptible to beautiful petitioners, and we know here how your livings and benefices are dispensed. What do you intend to do? Come to me; come to the bosom of the old and the only true Church, and I engage to marry you to a Roman prince the very next morning or two. That is, if you have no ideas about prosecuting a certain enterprise which I should not abandon. In that case, stay. As Duchess of B., Mr. Duffian says you would be cordially welcome to his Holiness, who may see women. That absurd report is all nonsense. We do not kiss his toe, certainly, but we have privileges equally enviable. Herbert is all charm. I confess he is a little wearisome with his old ruins, and his Dante, the poet. He is quite of my opinion, that Evan will never wash out the trade stain on him until he comes over to the Church of Rome. I adjure you, Caroline, to lay this clearly before our dear brother. In fact, while he continues a Protestant, to me he is a tailor. But here Rose is the impediment. I know her to be just one of those little dogged minds that are incapable of receiving new impressions. Was it not evident in the way she stuck to Evan after I had once brought them together? I am not at all astonished that Mr. Raikes should have married her maid. It is a case of natural selection. But it is amusing to think of him carrying on the old business in 193, and with credit! I suppose his parents are to be pitied; but what better is the creature fit for? Mama displeases me in consenting to act as housekeeper to old Grumpus. I do not object to the fact, for it is prospective; but she should have insisted on another place of resort than

Fallow field. I do not agree with you in thinking her right in refusing a second marriage. Her age does not shelter her from scandal in your Protestant communities.

"I am every day expecting Harry Jocelyn to turn up.

He was rightly sent away, for to think of the folly Evan put into his empty head! No; he shall have another wife, and Protestantism shall be his forsaken mistress!

"See how your Louy has given up the world and its vanities! You expected me to creep up to you contrite and whimpering? On the contrary, I never felt prouder. And I am not going to live a lazy life, I can assure you. The Church hath need of me! If only for the peace it hath given me on one point, I am eternally bound to serve it.

"Postscript: I am persuaded of this; that it is utterly impossible for a man to be a true gentleman who is not of the true Church. What it is I cannot say; but it is as a convert that I appreciate my husband. Love is made to me, dear, for Catholics are human. The other day it was a question whether a lady or a gentleman should be compromised. It required the grossest fib. The gentleman did not hesitate. And why? His priest was handy. Fancy Lord Laxley in such a case. I shudder. This shows that your religion precludes any possibility of the being the real gentleman, and whatever Evan may think of himself, or Rose think of him, I Know The Thing."

A Note About the Author

George Meredith (1828–1909) was an English author and poet active during the Victorian era. Holding radical liberal beliefs, Meredith first worked in the legal field, seeking justice and reading law. However, he soon abandoned the field when he discovered his true passion for journalism and poetry. After leaving this profession behind, Meredith partnered with a man named Edward Gryffdh Peacock, founding and publishing a private literary magazine. Meredith published poetry collections, novels, and essays, earning him the acclaim of a respected author. Praised for his integrity, intelligence, and literary skill, Meredith was nominated for seven Nobel Prizes and was appointed to the order of Merit by King Edward the Seventh in 1905.

A Note from the Publisher

Spanning many genres, from non-fiction essays to literature classics to children's books and lyric poetry, Mint Edition books showcase the master works of our time in a modern new package. The text is freshly typeset, is clean and easy to read, and features a new note about the author in each volume. Many books also include exclusive new introductory material. Every book boasts a striking new cover, which makes it as appropriate for collecting as it is for gift giving. Mint Edition books are only printed when a reader orders them, so natural resources are not wasted. We're proud that our books are never manufactured in excess and exist only in the exact quantity they need to be read and enjoyed.

Printed in the USA
CPSIA information can be obtained
at www.ICGtesting.com
JSHW022203140824
68134JS00018B/826